The Countess von Rudolstadt

The Countess von Rudolstadt

George Sand

Translated by Gretchen van Slyke

PENN

University of Pennsylvania Press
Philadelphia

Published by
University of Pennsylvania Press
Philadelphia, Pennsylvania 19104-4112

10 9 8 7 6 5 4 3 2 1

A Cataloging-in-Publication record is available from the Library of Congress

ISBN: 978-0-8122-2014-8

Introduction

While this is not the first English translation of George Sand's *La Comtesse de Rudolstadt*, it is the first in over a hundred years,[1] and I feel that it is high time to make Sand's great novel about love and revolution once again available to readers for whom the original French might prove daunting.

George Sand (1804–76) began working on *La Comtesse de Rudolstadt*, one of her most ambitious, engaging novels, when she was some twelve years into her long and productive career as a novelist. A hefty tome even by nineteenth-century standards, *La Comtesse de Rudolstadt* is merely the last part (but one that stands alone remarkably well, as readers will see) of Sand's monumental novel entitled *Consuelo*. This work started out as a short story about the formative years of a fictional Venetian street singer, the daughter of a Spanish Gypsy, whom the great maestro Porpora discovered and trained for the opera. Sand modeled her eighteenth-century heroine in part on the opera singer Pauline Garcia Viardot, who made her Parisian début at age eighteen in October 1839 and promptly excited Sand's admiration because of her voice, her musicianship, and the rare qualities of her person. In June 1842, Sand wrote to Viardot, whom the author had now taken on like another daughter, "You are the priestess of the ideal, and it is your mission to cast it far and wide."[2] Fed by Sand's rich imagination and bold aspirations for social reform, the little sketch swelled into a sinuous novel of initiation drawing on such diverse models as Ann Radcliffe's Gothic tales and Goethe's *Wilhelm Meister*.[3]

In the first part of the long novel, Consuelo suffers betrayal at the hands of the childhood love to whom she was betrothed and suddenly leaves Venice for the depths of Bohemia, where the Hussite wars of religion had raged in the fifteenth century and still resonated in the hearts and minds of many of its people. It is there that Consuelo takes refuge among an aristocratic family and that Albert, the last descendant of the proud Rudolstadt line, falls in love with her. Despite her admiration and affection for Albert, she cannot wholeheartedly return his love, nor does she want to sacrifice her brilliant operatic career to marriage. Finally, when Albert is near death from some mysterious wasting disease, she agrees, out of a sense of compassion, but not without feelings of sorrow and dread, to become his wife. At the end of *Consuelo*, Albert dies, and *La Comtesse de Rudolstadt* follows the life of the young widow after her return to the stage in Vienna and Berlin, two great capitals of musical culture and political might in mid-eighteenth-century Europe. Now entirely free to pursue her career, she sinks deep into depression, tormented by the thought that her inability to love Albert contributed to his death and wondering how to reconcile the demands of her profession, of her heart, and of her conscience.

Consuelo's peregrinations manifest a quest undertaken on a number of levels: as a singer, as a woman, and as an unwilling subject of alienation and oppression. The worlds through which Consuelo moves are bewilderingly complex, where authoritarian rulers like Frederick the Great mingle with Enlightenment philosophers, sorcerers, charlatans, where secret societies are conspiring to change the world. The old order of political absolutism and female subjugation is beginning to crack, and Consuelo will undergo various ordeals and grueling initiations into radically redefined notions of social organization, including the place of women in marriage, the family, and the nation. While many of these promises remain unfulfilled in the course of Consuelo's life, they never cease to act as beacons of hope for the heroine of the novel, and for the author as well. Written some fifty years after the French Revolution, Sand's novel taps into many of the deep philosophical and religious currents that contributed to that staggering social upheaval, all the while aiming to channel their potential for the revolutions that will continue to work toward the realization of these ideals.

This time and these places are no gratuitous choices on the author's part. Sand was clearly fascinated by the eighteenth century, which she characterizes as "this enormous logogriph, this brilliant nebula, where so much cowardliness contrasts with such grandeur, so much knowledge with such ignorance, so much barbarism with such civilization, so much enlightenment with such errors, so much seriousness with such intoxication, so much unbelief with such faith, so much learned pedantry with such frivolous mockery, so much superstition with such proud reason. . . . A terrifying laboratory where so many heterogeneous forms were thrown into the crucible that their monstrous ebullition belched forth a torrent of smoke through which we are still marching, enveloped in darkness and confusion." In another use of this laboratory metaphor, Sand presents eighteenth-century Europe as "teeming with secret societies, underground laboratories where a great revolution, whose crater will be Germany and France, is being prepared." Drawing up a long catalogue of secret societies whose historical existence bears no doubt, Sand goes on to invent an even more secret society that will go by the name of the Invisibles and function as the missing link to the Illuminati of Bavaria. To Pierre Leroux, a socialist philosopher and one of many friends who provided her with documentation about various secret societies and underground political associations, she justified this leap by grumbling that imagination alone could fill out the little that could actually be learned about them. Sand was convinced, moreover, that their "heresies," as she called them, constituted "humanity's occult history," a matter merely adumbrated in official history and requiring in-depth work.[4]

Feeding her contemporaries' fascination as well as her own for such arcane conspiracies, her text abounds with stories about the terrifying works and shadowy origins of these mysterious characters. Sand's Invisibles are finally revealed as a covert army of philosophers and reformers who risk proscription, poverty, imprisonment, and death to pursue their goals. A supersecret society that remains carefully concealed from other secret societies, such as the Freemasons and Rosicrucians, the Invisibles stealthily work to achieve control of the latter and to use them as a "nursery out of which [to] choose the strong seedlings destined for transplantation in the sacred forest." In other words, for the nonviolent mission of regenerating society through a radical religious and philosophical understanding of the ideals that would become the watchwords of the French Revolution.

What is the source of the Invisibles' doctrine? They explain to Consuelo that their beliefs are a set of religious and political ideals that the Roman Catholic Church time and time again has condemned as heresy and endeavored to eradicate—tidings of evangelical equality that were revealed to the apostles of early Christianity and passed on down through history by the likes of John Wyclif in England, Jan Hus in Bohemia, and Martin Luther in Germany, and that would again erupt as the spirit of revolution in late eighteenth-century France. In the words of one of Consuelo's initiators, "*Liberty, fraternity, equality*: this is the mysterious, deep formula of the work of the Invisibles." While these words may seem hollow and trite to twenty-first-century readers who see them as little more than a decorative inscription on French monuments, in France of the 1840s they either harked back to the bloody miscarriage of the Revolution of 1789 or beckoned to its still unfulfilled promise; and in Consuelo's Europe these words were considered so new, dangerous, and untenable that they could be revealed only to the highest initiates of the Invisibles and only after lengthy and careful preparation.

One of Sand's inspirations for the Invisibles was the polemic written by the Jesuit Abbé Augustin Barruel, *Mémoires pour servir à l'histoire du jacobinisme*, first published in 1797. Barruel argued that the French Revolution was the result of a conspiracy planned and executed by various secret societies in accordance with their desires to destroy monarchies as well as the Roman Catholic Church.

When he reported in tones of abomination that the Freemasons' secret consisted in the words *liberté, égalité, fraternité*, Sand seized upon this detail with great enthusiasm. When Barruel blamed the Freemasons and the Illuminati of Bavaria for the French Revolution and traced the coming cataclysm back through the history of heresy, Sand would essentially repeat the same gesture, only replacing Barruel's shudders of horror with bounding enthusiasm. Indeed, her Invisibles, coming from a long line of predecessors, would pass on to the Illuminati of Bavaria "something like an electric current of sublime enthusiasm, ardent faith and terrible fanaticism," which they would in turn communicate to the French Revolution.

For Sand, and for the Invisibles as well, the word "heresy" carried an entirely positive meaning, and during her initiation Consuelo will hear these words out of the spokesman for the Invisibles: "At bottom, all heretics (I use this word with respect) agree on the main point, which is to destroy intellectual and material tyranny or at least to protest it." It must also be noted that *Consuelo* and *La Comtesse de Rudolstadt* show a particular fascination with the Taborites as well as all the Hussite factions in fifteenth-century Bohemia. This is so because Sand saw their protests in the name of equality and their war cry "The chalice for the people!" as an early formulation of the ideals of the French Revolution. As she explains in a companion volume distilling her research on the Hussites,[5] their bid for religious freedom from the Roman Catholic Church and political freedom from the Holy Roman Empire illustrates yet another chapter in the long struggle between the people's aspirations to evangelical equality, on the one hand, and the powerful hierarchies of church and state, on the other:

> Official religion, the established Church, has always followed the same system; the secret religion, the one still seeking to establish itself, this ideal society of equality, which begins with the sermons of Jesus, goes through centuries of Catholicism under the name of heresy, and leads here to the French Revolution, then takes a new shape and is subject to debate, for lack of anything better, in chartist societies[6] and hotbeds of communism,—this religion too is always the same, no matter what form it has taken, no matter under what name it has veiled itself, no matter what persecution it has endured. . . . Heresy in the past, socialism today, this is the shriek of the starving entrails and desolate hearts that call for true knowledge, the voice of the spirit, the religious, philosophical and social solution to the monstrous problem suspended over our heads for so many centuries. This is what heresy is, and nothing else: an idea essentially Christian in its principle, evangelical in its successive revelations, revolutionary in its endeavors and demands; and not a sterile quarrel over words, an overweening interpretation of the sacred texts, a suggestion of the Satanic spirit, a need for vengeance, adventure and vanity, as it has pleased the Roman church to define it in its indictments and denunciations. (38–40; my translation)

This militant faith and philosophy of history, which could be viewed as an early version of liberation theology, was inspired in good part by Pierre Leroux; and during the years that Sand spent writing *Consuelo* and *La Comtesse de Rudolstadt*, her letters bear frequent witness to the ways in which Leroux's thought transformed her life, bringing her out of despair and providing a system of belief far more satisfying to her than her childhood Catholicism. With regard to Leroux she wrote to a young poet in February 1843:

> as it is the only philosophy that is as clear as day and speaks to the heart like the Gospels, I plunged into it and was transformed. I found in it the calm, the strength, the faith, the hope and the patient, persevering love of humanity, the childhood treasures of which I had dreamed in Catholicism, but which had been destroyed by the examination of Catholicism, by the inadequacy of the obsolete cult, by the doubt and affliction that devour, in our times, those who haven't been besotted or warped by egotism and well-being. . . . In short, it is a whole religion both ancient and modern, and one needs to steep oneself in it, to incubate it tenderly.[7]

Pierre Leroux (1797–1871), a typesetter by profession, was part of the underground republican movement known as the Carbonari at the end of the Bourbon Restoration. After brief association with the Saint-Simonian sect in the early 1830s, he went on to form his own theories of community while continuing to play an influential role as a literary critic and philosopher. His major works, none of them translated into English, are *De l'Égalité* (1838), *La Réfutation de l'éclectisme* (1839) and *De l'Humanité* (1840), in addition to the popular *Encyclopédie nouvelle* (1838–41), which he coedited with Jean Reynaud. George Sand met Leroux in 1835, dedicated to him her 1839 novel *Spiridion*, and drew on his inspiration while composing *Consuelo* and *La Comtesse de Rudolstadt*, with significant parts of the latter work (especially chapters 31, 32, 38, 41, and 43) acting as introductions to various aspects of Leroux's thought. From February 1842 through February 1844, *Consuelo* and *La Comtesse de Rudolstadt* were published as installments in *La Revue Indépendante*, which Sand had recently founded with Leroux and Louis Viardot (Pauline Viardot's husband) for the diffusion of reformist ideas.

Despite Leroux's influence in France in the 1830s and 1840s, it has been customary among historians for well over a century to dismiss him as a woolly-minded aberration, largely because of his highly abstract and nebulous lucubrations. It should therefore give us pause that Heinrich Heine considered him one of the greatest philosophers of France, while another of Leroux's contemporaries, none other than Honoré de Balzac, portrayed him in his *Illusions perdues* as a profound philosopher and bold theoretician, always great, even in his errors. In order to give social reformers such as Leroux their due, some recent scholarship has endeavored to view them in their intellectual context—Paris in the 1840s—where mystical, socialist, republican, and feminist feeling came together in various strains of romantic socialism, so very different in mood, method, and aim from the so-called scientific socialism of the post-Marx era.[8] Although Romantic socialism failed to effect the broad reforms that it envisaged for mid-nineteenth-century society, it did make remarkable contributions to the political and literary discourse of the time.

Romantic socialism was not primarily an attack on private property or even capitalism, but a varied set of responses to the philosophy of the Enlightenment, to the 1789 Revolution, especially the bloody violence that soon engulfed its lofty promise, and to rapid socioeconomic change in the postrevolutionary period. Focusing on the moral and spiritual dimension of human existence, Romantic socialism challenged the principles of individualism upon which the liberal order of politics and economics was founded and lamented the isolation of the beings that this philosophy abandoned to the social struggle for survival. Leroux, along with many other Romantic socialists, judged that this concentration upon reason, individual rights, and economic competition had managed to destroy any real sense of community.

On the other hand, Leroux condemned socialist theories that would override the individual and make the community the sole repository of rights and privileges. Eager to avoid both errors, Leroux defined individuals in terms of what they had in common with their fellows rather than by the differences that set them apart, thereby upholding the individual while neutralizing the basic tenets of individualism. Leroux also insisted on redefining mankind in terms that he found more accurate than those of the rationalist tradition. Man was not just sensation and reason, but also sentiment: these three being as indivisibly united as the Trinity. Appealing to the powers of sensation, sentiment, and reason, Leroux aimed to convert his fellows to what he called the religion of Humanity, a new faith that he presented as a return to the spirit of primitive Christianity, as it was before its betrayal and perversion by the Roman Catholic hierarchy. Although Leroux drew on a wide variety of religious and philosophical traditions, his ideal social structure owed a great deal to early Christian communities, which he took as living demonstrations of the true meaning of *liberté, egalité, fraternité*. All the while inveighing against the power structure of the Roman Catholic Church, he endeavored to revitalize Christian spirituality so as to give society a sense of community and to put economic and political relationships on a footing of love and solidarity.

Through the religion of Humanity, Leroux hoped not only to remedy the exploitation of the workers and the politically powerless but to put an end to oppression of women as well. Whereas the Revolution of 1789 had refused to grant women the political rights of men, and Napoléon's *Code Civil* (1804) kept married women in a permanent state of tutelage under their husbands, Leroux proposed granting women the right to vote in 1851 and argued that marriage could only be based on equality and a mutual sense of responsibility between the spouses. Defining femininity in traditional albeit positive terms, Leroux saw women primarily in their relations to others, as mothers, sisters, partners, and lovers, ready and willing to love, nurture, and sacrifice themselves. Women's qualities were therefore key to the sense of community, cooperation, and solidarity that Leroux and others sought to develop in society. "Romantic socialists turned this definition of woman's nature into a source of power and a reason for her exaltation. It was woman's very relational quality that fit her for the future to which romantic socialists aspired. Woman was seen as less individualized and therefore less self-serving and egoistic than man; she was thus both the appropriate symbol for, and the ideal citizen of, the new social world that they imagined."[9]

The version of the biblical creation myth that Leroux presents in *De l'Humanité* provides insight into his views on the complementarity of the sexes. First of all, Leroux maintains that the creation story in Genesis does not concern an individual named Adam, but a symbol representing all humanity, a reflection of the androgynous nature of God. Likewise, the story about Eve's creation does not mean that she was drawn out of Adam's rib. Its proper interpretation signifies instead the separation into two discrete parts of the original androgyne that once contained Adam and Eve together in one body. When Adam and Eve were driven out of the Garden of Eden, psychological division followed upon physical separation. The knowledge that Adam and Eve gained after their fall from grace was disconnection from the androgyne's other half, isolation within individual identity, and loss of community—in other words, death; and as in Plato's *Symposium*, the two halves of the androgyne long for reunion, which in Leroux's mind will restore humanity's happiness and bring about a harmonious recognition of women's rights.

On the eve of her initiation into the Invisibles, Consuelo is stunned to learn that the father-confessor assigned to her is in fact a woman. In this century of patriarchal authority, Consuelo had naturally assumed that men alone would be admitted to this secret society,[10] but she learns that a woman not only stands among them but also enjoys membership in the Invisibles' supreme council, remedying the oversights and failures of discernment on the part of her male fellows and enjoying the prestige of a sibyl and Delphic oracle among the entire group. Indeed, the Invisibles declare themselves to be firm believers in the God-given equality of the sexes, all the while recognizing that the prevailing social and educational condition of women curtails full and immediate application of that precept. As they explain to Consuelo, "we profess the divine equality of men and women. Yet we are forced to recognize that the education of women, their social situation and habits, have had unfortunate results for your sex, to wit, a dangerous flightiness and whimsical instincts; and for this reason we cannot fully put the precept of equality into practice. There are only a few women that we can trust, and some secrets we will impart to you alone." Consuelo's father-confessor had initially disguised her sex under a mask, cap, wig, and even a fake beard, the ultimate token of patriarchy, but when she decides to whip them off, she is revealed as a strong and wise *mater dolorosa*, whom the text compares to both Niobe and the Virgin Mary—a fine example of "intelligence without the beard."

Sand, who was less critical of women than of the roles that they were made to play in the society of her day, uses this striking expression in a letter to Félicité de Lamennais, a priest of socialist leanings whom she much admired, who had recently rebuked women for their vanity and stupidity, especially those who dared aspire to be like men. Only apparently conceding to his views, she replies in a staunchly progressive tone, "That's the truth, master: but teach us to be so no longer, and the way to do that is perhaps not by telling us that the fault stems from our nature, but by showing us that it is due to the way that your sex has ruled over us up until now. And if we managed to make God love us as much as he does you men, he might just give us, in spite of you all, intelligence without the beard; and then you in turn would find yourselves in a pretty fix."[11]

Not only is Consuelo's assigned confessor among the Invisibles a woman, she also happens to be the mother of Albert von Rudolstadt, the moribund genius whom Consuelo had reluctantly agreed to marry a few years before. Identifying herself as Wanda z Prachalitz, she is a descendant of Jan Zizka, the indomitable leader of the Taborites in fifteenth-century Bohemia, and carries on their heretical, egalitarian spirit. Despite her position as Consuelo's mother-in-law, Wanda will renounce the prerogatives generally associated with this role and give highly unorthodox advice to the younger woman, who finds herself in a fierce predicament that needs to be sorted out before her initiation into the Invisibles. Consuelo has just learned that Albert von Rudolstadt is not in fact dead, and meanwhile she has fallen passionately in love with a mysterious stranger among the Invisibles. Must the erstwhile widow return to her husband out of a spirit of duty or trample her wedding vows and follow her heart? Wanda is eager to help Consuelo avoid her own experience of marriage, a loveless match that she contracted for the noblest of reasons, and which finally led to her being buried alive, in all senses of the word. For that reason Wanda asks Consuelo to give the Invisibles, and to her in particular, the right to dissolve or confirm her marriage to Albert. "Extraordinary legislators and secret architects of a new society," as Wanda calls them, the Invisibles aspire to discern right and true love from false and hollow attachment, to adjudicate between bad human laws and God's providential designs and to give the world a new ethic.

After making Consuelo confess her physical aversion to Albert as well as her desire for the stranger, Wanda maintains that sexual passions and instincts are given by God and therefore to be heeded. If Consuelo, in these circumstances, were to sacrifice her feelings for the stranger in order to live with her husband, their marriage would be little more than sworn prostitution; she would be committing a monstrous form of suicide, shamefully deceiving her spouse and putting at risk any children conceived of their union. Wanda asserts that the law of marriage is mutual desire and shared aspirations; where there is no such reciprocity, there is no equality; and where there is no equality, there is no real union. Far from requiring that Consuelo sacrifice her love for the stranger, God in fact denies her the right to contemplate such self-immolation. Yet the protection of love requires no divorce, for it is finally revealed that Consuelo's stranger is none other than Albert himself, come back from the grave like his mother. In any event, Wanda's notion of marriage was clearly revolutionary in Consuelo's century, and in Sand's century as well, where dowries continued to preside over nuptials and daughters were passed willy-nilly from the authority of their fathers to that of their husbands.

Sand knew firsthand the public and private hardships of nineteenth-century marriage. While immersed in the composition of *Consuelo* and *La Comtesse de Rudolstadt*, Sand received a letter from Mlle Leroyer de Chantepie, an unmarried forty-something writer from provincial France, asking her advice about the wisdom of seeking love and happiness in marriage. Approaching the age of forty herself and having meditated at length upon the situation of women in a society where marriage or a nun's celibacy were nearly their only respectable options, Sand replied that despite her convictions that love, fidelity, and motherhood were the "most necessary, important and sacred acts in a woman's life," no woman should enter into the contract of marriage as it was then defined by Napoléon's *Code Civil*:

I find society given over to the most dreadful chaos, and, amidst all the iniquities that I see consecrated by society, I consider, first and foremost, that the relations of men with women have been established in a manner that is unjust and absurd. I cannot therefore advise anyone to undertake a marriage sanctioned by a civil code that consecrates the woman's dependence, inferiority and social nullity. I've spent ten years thinking about it, and, after having wondered why all the loves in this world, whether they be legitimated or not by society, were all more or less unhappy, no matter the qualities and virtues of the souls so associated, I've become convinced of the radical impossibility of this perfect happiness, love's ideal, in conditions of inequality, inferiority and dependence of one sex with regard to the other. . . . A woman, giving herself to a man, is necessarily either chained or guilty.[12]

Judging that a total transformation of the world was necessary, but recognizing that radical change could not happen overnight, Sand did not renounce her hopes for women's happiness but deferred them to the brighter future set forth by Pierre Leroux, one that she felt sure to enjoy in a later life. In the meantime, what were women to do? Sand felt that they had no choice but to go on with life, even love and motherhood, doing their duty to the best of their abilities, bearing in mind the inevitability of suffering and humiliation in the here and now and consoling themselves with the thought of women's happiness in some time to come. And the path that she recommended to Mlle Leroyer de Chantepie is the one that the author herself had taken some years before, as she forcefully recounts to the painter Eugène Delacroix in August 1843: "In short, I no longer exist, as I've told you. A good three years ago I died, having willfully committed suicide to prevent myself from dying and prolonging the ridiculous throes of death. My ideal is no longer in my life here and now. It is in another world, another century, in another humanity, where I am sure to wake up after the salutary repose of death."[13]

Given the condition of women in nineteenth-century French society—provided with few and limited educational opportunities, lacking most civil rights and all political rights, subjected to the rule of their husbands in their lives and any property they might possess—Sand considered all women heretics, at least potentially, and was proud to add them to the long list of purveyors of the secret doctrine that she hailed as a promise of revolution throughout the ages. This is surely one of the main reasons why in the course of *Consuelo* and *La Comtesse de Rudolstadt* she frequently addresses her readers with the exclusively feminine form *lectrices*. In the previously cited companion piece that she wrote about the Hussite leader Jan Zizka, Sand further explains her concentration upon her female readers:

Women, when I remember that it's for you that I'm writing, I feel my heart more at ease; for I have never doubted that, despite your vices and failings, your notable laziness, your absurd coquetry and childish frivolity, there is in you something pure, enthusiastic, candid, great and generous, which men have lost or do not yet possess. You are beautiful children. Feeble heads, wretched educations, next to no forethought, empty memories, inert reasoning ability. It's not your fault! While your minds have remained idle, God has allowed your hearts to develop more freely than those of men and let you keep the sacred fire of love, the treasures of devotion, the tender charms of romantic insouciance and blind unselfishness. This is why, poor women, noble beings, whom it has not been within man's power to degrade, this is why the history of heresy must be of interest to you and touch you in a particular way; for you are the daughters of heresy, you are all heretics; you all protest in your hearts, you all protest in vain. Like the voice of the *protestant* Church of every century, your voice is stifled by the decree of the official Church of *society*. You are all by nature and necessity the disciples of Saint John, of Saint Francis, of the other great apostles of the ideal. You are all *poor* in the manner of the eternal disciples of evangelical poverty; for, according to the laws of marriage and the family, you own nothing; and it's to this absence of power and action in temporal interests that you owe this idealist tendency, this power of sentiment, these impulses of abnegation that make your souls the last sanctuary of truth, the last altars for sacrifice.[14]

If women have half-baked or unformed minds, Sand will attempt to reach them through their hearts and souls, seeing sentiment as an effective way into their intellect. This, moreover, is the way through which Consuelo's religious and political development is achieved in *Consuelo* and *La Comtesse de Rudolstadt*, and Sand often described her own education as a result of the same method. Thus, the character of Consuelo, modeled in part on Pauline Viardot, mirrors as well what Sand sees as the course of her own development, and the author clearly intends to encourage her readers to let their feelings guide them down similar paths. Writing novels is her own modest contribution toward changing the world, as she explains in a letter toward the end of 1842:

I may spend my entire life searching for the truth, without ever knowing how to formulate a single aspect of it. To each his own task. I do what I can. Born a writer of novels, I write novels—which means that I seek by virtue of a certain art to rouse emotion, to churn and shake things up, even to rattle the hearts of my contemporaries who are capable of emotion and need to be shaken up. Those who aren't capable of emotion say that I'm stirring up poison because I'm putting a bit of gall in the wine of their insolent drunkenness. . . . But I've roused emotion, and emotion prompts thought and investigation. That's all I wanted. To inspire doubt about the lie that is believed, to raise a hue and cry about a truth that is forgotten—that's enough for me, and my mission is no greater than that.[15]

As in *The Magic Flute*, the initiation in *La Comtesse de Rudolstadt* is immediately followed by a wedding. Yet these obvious points of comparison between Emanuel Schikaneder's libretto for *The Magic Flute* and Sand's novel mask profound differences. Whereas Tamino's ordeal in the opera takes place in a context structured upon the dichotomy of masculine versus feminine, good versus evil, *La Comtesse de Rudolstadt* rejects that view and celebrates instead the reunion of the androgyne, "the soul in two persons" consecrated by the wedding of Consuelo and Albert. At the conclusion of the opera, Tamino is granted the hand of his beloved Pamina as a reward for having withstood the rigors of his ordeal. At the end of *La Comtesse de Rudolstadt*, Consuelo is no reward for the hero. She is instead a heroine in her own right; having emerged victorious from her ordeals, she reaches a level of spiritual development attained by few men, and she wholeheartedly gives herself to Albert as his wife and partner. Thanks to Wanda's inspired intervention, the wedding of Consuelo and Albert among the Invisibles becomes an entirely different thing from unions contracted in the world. The bride and groom come together in mutual joy and shared passion, and their marriage is an expression of freely chosen love. Before God and the Invisibles, they vow to remain together throughout eternity, yet their covenant is to remain unwritten and therefore beyond the jurisdiction of any earthly authority, priest or magistrate. Sand's novel may well be the first woman-centered novel of initiation in European literature, and it is no accident that this revolutionary work was authored by "a highly literate woman, a consummate storyteller, fully cognizant of the novelistic, religious, and philosophical traditions which she was following as well as subverting."[16]

Another significant difference between the two works is this: whereas *The Magic Flute* ends on the blissful note of love triumphant, *La Comtesse de Rudolstadt* swings back into the stuff of life, with its burdens and disappointments. After her wedding Consuelo continues her singing career all over Europe while she and Albert secretly devote themselves to pursuing the work of the Invisibles. In Vienna around 1760, Consuelo loses her voice and disappears from the stage. At the same time, Albert is thrown into prison, endures a long, hopeless trial, and is finally expelled from Austria as a dangerous madman. After the Invisibles are finally dispersed and their organization destroyed, the couple enter upon a life of poverty, suffering, and persecution, and Albert's mind becomes unhinged. Despite all this, they do not lose their faith, and their love keeps its bright promise. Yet, with information about them becoming ever more fragmentary and unreliable, their story has no ending. Rather, the narrator refuses to provide one, invoking instead an E. T. A. Hoffmann novel with many different imagined endings, like a beautiful river branching out in the sands of a delta and vanishing into a thousand whimsical rivulets. The best of endings, this narrator maintains, are those that the readers undertake for themselves, in the narrator's stead.

The last glimpse of Consuelo and Albert in the novel is offered by a young disciple of the Bavarian Illuminati who, along with the sect's founder, has gone searching for Albert in the hopes of learning more about the new society that the Invisibles had been devising for the world. They come upon Consuelo, her husband, and three of their children wandering through the mountains of Bohemia, praying with the peasants and making music around the ruins of Albert's ancestral home. Albert is now insane and tenderly looked after by his wife and children, for they recognize that madness, treated with the proper respect and care, is "an exceptional faculty of the most poetically divine sort." By playing ancient folk ballads and sacred hymns of the Hussites for the Bohemian peasants, Albert imparts to them visions of the past and prophecies for the future, God's providential designs for humanity. For him, time and death are mere illusions, and the distinctions among past, present, and future vain niceties; God is eternal and so are those who partake of his essence. Assuming the mythic dimensions of Orpheus, Albert finally sends the Bavarian Illuminati off to France, which he predicts will soon become the present-day Tabor once so dear to the Hussites, the new light of the nations with the advent of the Revolution.

Now forty, perhaps fifty years old, and the mother of five children, Consuelo is still strong and lithe as a young maiden. While the Illuminati first take her for a fiery and adventurous queen of the Gypsies, they soon see her as the sister-soul guiding Albert through the storms of life, acting as a rampart of love between him and a hostile world. The family lives, as Consuelo explains to them, by sharing the humble ways of the peasants, bringing art and enthusiasm to these innately poetic souls and receiving their gifts of hospitality in turn. This way of life, Consuelo continues, fulfills the duties of the artist. It anticipates as well the God-given ideal for society, in which everything that is not based upon egalitarian exchange must disappear. Consuelo, too, winds up taking on mythical dimensions. Her husband proclaims her Heaven's consolation to all those in distress, the peace of the Lord promised to men of good will; and in a ballad for which she composed the music and Albert the lyrics, Consuelo becomes the incarnation of the Gentle Goddess of Poverty, humanity's "fertile mother, robust nurse and militant church," who nurtures all ages of the world with poetry, love, and the secrets of God.

Consuelo and Albert simultaneously look back to the War of the Hussites while casting an eye forward to the French Revolution, preparing its advent as well as apprehending its violent turn. Likewise, George Sand peers into the past in order to nourish her aspirations for future revolutions. The words that she uses to characterize the hopes and dreams of Consuelo, Albert, and all their companions in the Invisibles apply to her as well: "They believed themselves on the eve of an evangelical republic, like the disciples of Jesus eagerly awaiting the kingdom of God on earth, like the Bohemian Taborites who thought paradise close at hand, like the French Convention that years later felt it would soon win over the entire planet." While none of these groups attained the ideal shimmering before their eyes, it is clear to Sand that the efforts of all have made important contributions to humanity's progress: "Yet, without such mad confidence, where would the great sacrifices be; without great madness, where the great achievements? Without the utopia of the divine dreamer Jesus, where would the notion of human brotherhood be? . . . Without the noble chimeras of the eighteenth century, would we have conquered the rudiments of equality?" For all these ardent conspirators, life is a voyage through time and eternity, an ever unfolding process in which nothing ever lives in vain, nothing ever dies, nothing is ever lost, and history will be a wave of revolts and revolutions washing over the earth until the divine ideal is finally realized here below.

A Note to the Reader

Sand's text has occasional footnotes, which are reproduced as they appear there. I have added some explanatory comments on names and places; these appear at the end of the book, grouped by chapter.

Chapter I

The Italian Opera in Berlin, built during the first years of the reign of Frederick the Great, was then one of the most beautiful auditoriums in all Europe. There was no charge for admission, as the king paid for the show. Yet tickets were required because the boxes had all been permanently assigned: here the princes and princesses of the royal family, there the diplomats, then the traveling celebrities and the members of the Academy, elsewhere the generals; finally, everywhere the king's family, the king's household, the king's employees, the king's protégés; and no one had grounds for complaint, since it was the king's theater and the king's players. For the fine inhabitants of the fine city of Berlin there remained a few spots in the orchestra, occupied for the most part by the military, as every regiment had the right to send a certain number of men per company. Instead of the joyous, impressionable, and quick-witted populace of Paris, the artists looked out upon an orchestra thronged with *six-foot heroes*, as Voltaire used to call them. With their high-crowned caps, and most of them with their wives hoisted up on their shoulders, this rather brutish fellowship reeked of tobacco and schnapps, understood absolutely nothing, and looked goggle-eyed at everything. Out of respect for their orders, they neither clapped nor whistled, yet made lots of noise with their perpetual jostling.

Behind these gentlemen there were invariably two rows of boxes from which no one could see or hear a single thing. Yet, for reasons of propriety, the occupants of these boxes were forced to attend on a regular basis the performances that His Majesty so generously provided them. His Majesty never missed a show. This was a way of keeping a military eye on his numerous family and the restless anthill of his courtiers. Here he followed the example of his father, Big Willy, who had made the royal family and court spend every winter evening in front of third-rate German actors in a hall of poorly joined planks. Bored to death and chilled to the bone, there they sat without batting an eye while rain dripped down on them and the king snoozed. Frederick had suffered from this domestic tyranny; he had cursed it and endured it; and no sooner had he in turn become master than he promptly reestablished the same system, along with several other much more despotic and cruel customs, whose excellence he had come to recognize now that he was the only one in his kingdom not to suffer from them any longer.

Yet no one dared complain. The building was superb and luxuriously appointed, the artists remarkable, and the king, almost always standing in the orchestra near the footlights, his opera glass trained on the stage, gave an example of indefatigable enthusiasm for the arts.

Everyone knows how Voltaire, recently installed in Berlin, praised the splendors of the court of this *Solomon of the North*. Scorned by Louis XV, neglected by his patroness Mme de Pompadour, persecuted by the vulgar Jesuits, hooted down at the Théâtre-Français, he got fed up one day and came in search of honors, a salary, a chamberlain's title, a grand sash, and an intimate friendship with a philosopher-king, which, in his estimation, was more flattering than all the rest. Like an overgrown child, the great Voltaire was pouting at France and thought that he had really found a way to get the goat of his ungrateful compatriots. He was therefore a bit drunk on his new glory when he wrote to his friends that Berlin was as fine as Versailles, that *Phaëton* was the most beautiful opera ever, and that the prima donna had the most beautiful voice in all Europe.

Yet, at the time when we resume our tale (so as not to weary our dear readers, we'll let them know that nearly a year has passed since Consuelo's last adventures), winter in all its rigor had settled down on Berlin, the great king had shown his true colors a bit, and Voltaire was starting to feel singularly disillusioned about Prussia. Seated in his box between d'Argens and La Mettrie, he no longer pretended to love music, for which he had no more feeling than for true poetry. His bowels were bothering him, and he was mournfully remembering those thankless audiences in Parisian theaters, whose resistance had been such a bitter pill for him, whose applause had tasted so sweet, whose contact, in a word, had put him in such terrible turmoil that he had sworn not to expose himself to that again, even though he could think of nothing else and endlessly toiled for them.

Yet that evening the performance was excellent. It was carnival; the entire royal family, even the margraves who had married into the depths of the German provinces, had assembled in Berlin. *Titus* by Metastasio and Hasse was on the program, and the two leading members of the Italian company, Porporino and Porporina, had the starring roles.

With a slight effort of memory our dear readers will recall that these two were not husband and wife, as their stage names would seem to suggest. The first was Signor Uberti, an excellent contralto, and the second was the Zingarella Consuelo, with her admirable voice, both students of Professor Porpora, who had allowed them, according to the Italian custom of the time, to take their teacher's glorious name.

One must admit that in Prussia Signora Porporina did not sing with all the spirit of which she had felt capable in better days. While her colleague's clear contralto, sheltered by a secure livelihood, a habit of uncontested success and a fixed fee of fifteen thousand pounds for two months of work, resonated without fail under the vaulted ceiling of the Berlin Opera, the poor Zingarella, perhaps of a more romantic mind, certainly more disinterested and less accustomed to the icy North and the chilly reception of Prussian corporals, did not feel any electricity and sang with that conscientious, perfect method that kept her safe from criticism but failed to arouse any enthusiasm. There is a close reciprocal relationship between the enthusiasm of the dramatic artist and that of the audience, and there was no enthusiasm in Berlin during the glorious reign of Frederick the Great. Regularity, obedience, and what was called reason in the eighteenth century and especially at Frederick's court were the only virtues that could blossom in that atmosphere weighed and measured by the king's hand. In any assembly over which he presided, one breathed in and out only as much as the king deigned to allow. In that whole crowded auditorium there was but one spectator free to give way to his impressions, and that was the king. He himself was the entire audience, and even though he was a good musician and loved music, all his faculties and tastes were subordinated to such an icy logic that the royal opera glass fixed on every gesture and seemingly every inflection of the diva's voice, instead of stimulating her, made her feel totally paralyzed.

It was moreover fortunate for her to be subjected to this harrowing fascination. The tiniest dose of inspiration, the slightest burst of unexpected passion would probably have scandalized the king and his court, whereas intricate, arduous passages executed with the purity of an irreproachable instrument thrilled the king, the court, and Voltaire. As every one knows, Voltaire said, "Italian music is far superior to French music because it has more ornaments, and *triumphing over difficulty is something at least*." That sums up Voltaire's aesthetics. He could have said like a certain witty contemporary when someone asked if he liked music: it doesn't exactly bother me.

Everything was going well, and the opera was drawing to a close without mishap. The king was very pleased, and every now and then he turned around to nod in approval at his choirmaster. He was even preparing to applaud Porporina at the end of her cavatina, as he was kind enough to do in person and always judiciously. Just then, by some inexplicable whim, Porporina, in the middle of a brilliant trill that had never given her any trouble, stopped short, stared with a haggard eye into a corner of the auditorium, clasped her hands, exclaimed, "*Oh my God!*" and fell down flat in a faint on the stage. Porporino hastened to get her up; she had to be carried offstage; and the auditorium began to buzz with questions, remarks, and observations. During this commotion that muffled his curt, imperious tone, the king bellowed to the tenor still on stage, "Well, what's going on? What's the meaning of this? Conciolini, go have a look, and make it snappy!"

Conciolini returned a few seconds later. Respectfully bowing over the footlights near which the king was still standing, leaning on an elbow, he said, "Your Majesty, it's as though Signora Porporina were dead. It is feared that she'll be unable to finish the opera."

"Nonsense!" said the king shrugging his shoulders. "Get her a glass of water and some smelling salts, and let's wind this up as soon we can."

Conciolini, who had no desire to provoke the king and suffer a public broadside of temper, scurried back into the wings like a rat, and the king began a lively chat with the head of the orchestra and the musicians. Those in the audience who found the king's mood far more interesting than poor Porporina made extraordinary efforts, but all in vain, to hear what the monarch was saying.

Baron von Poelnitz, the king's great chamberlain and theater director, promptly appeared and gave Frederick an account of the situation. In Frederick's realm nothing happened with the solemnity imposed by an independent, powerful people. . . . The king's place was everywhere; the performance was his, and for him. No one was surprised to see him take the starring role in this unexpected interlude.

"Now let's see, Baron," said he in a voice loud enough to be heard by a portion of the orchestra, "won't this soon be over? It's ridiculous! Don't you have a doctor in the wings? You've always got to have a doctor at the theater."

"Sire, the doctor is with her. He doesn't dare bleed her for fear of aggravating her weakness and making it impossible for her to carry on. Yet he'll be forced to do so if she doesn't come out of her swoon."

"So it's serious! She's not faking?"

"Sire, this strikes me as very serious."

"In that case, drop the curtain, and let's get going. Better yet, let's have Porporino come sing us something for our trouble so that we don't end on a catastrophe."

Porporino obeyed and sang two pieces admirably well. The king clapped his hands, the audience imitated him, and the show was over. A minute later, while the court and townspeople were leaving, the king was up on stage, having Poelnitz show him the way to Porporina's dressing room.

When an actress is taken ill on stage, audiences are not always as compassionate as they ought to be. However much *dilettantes* may adore an idol, their pleasure is generally so egotistical that they are much more annoyed to forfeit some part of it due to an interrupted performance than they are affected by the victim's sufferings and anguish. A few *sensitive* ladies, as people then used to say, deplored the evening's catastrophe in the following terms.

"Poor little thing! She probably got *a frog* in her throat just as she was about to start on the trill, and for fear of getting it wrong, she preferred to have a spell."

"As for me, I'm willing to believe that she wasn't faking," said an even more sensitive lady. "You don't fall like a heap of bricks unless you're truly ill."

"Oh, who knows, my dear?" replied the first lady. "Great actresses fall as they wish, and they don't worry about hurting themselves a bit. It has such an effect on the audience!"

"What the devil was going on with Porporina this evening, for her to make such a scene?" La Mettrie asked the Marquis d'Argens in another part of the vestibule from which an elegant crowd was exiting. "Do you suppose her lover beat her?"

"Don't talk that way about a charming, virtuous girl," replied the marquis. "She hasn't got a lover, and if she ever does, she'll never deserve such outrage, unless he's the vilest of men."

"Oh! I beg your pardon, Marquis. I forgot that I was addressing the valiant champion and defender of all theater girls, past, present, and future! By the way, how is Mlle Cochois?"

At that same moment Princess Amalia, the king's sister and abbess of Quedlinburg, was saying to her usual confidante, the beautiful Countess von Kleist, while they were being driven back to the palace, "My dear child, did you notice how upset my brother got this evening?"

"No, Madame," replied Mme de Maupertuis, the princess's head governess, an excellent person, very simple and very absentminded, "I didn't notice."

"Well, I'm not talking to you," the princess retorted in the brusque, determined tone that made her seem so much like Frederick on occasion. "Do you notice anything? Notice the stars just now. I've got something to say to von Kleist that I don't want you to hear."

Mme de Maupertuis conscientiously closed her ears. The princess leaned over toward Mme von Kleist, seated across from her, and said, "Say what you will; it seems to me that the king, maybe for the first time in fifteen or twenty years, since the time that I've been old enough to observe and understand, is in love."

"Your Royal Highness said as much last year with regard to Signora Barberini. Yet the king had never dreamed of it."

"Never dreamed of it! You're wrong, my child. He had dreamed of it so much that when young Chancellor Cocceï made her his wife, my brother suffered three days long the worst repressed rage of his entire life."

"Your Highness is well aware that His Majesty cannot bear misalliances."

"Oh, yes, that's what it's called when people marry for love. A misalliance! Oh, what a grand word! Devoid of meaning, like all the words that rule the world and tyrannize every single soul."

The princess heaved a great sigh. Then, as was her custom, she slipped into another mood. Now ironic and impatient, she said to her head governess, "Maupertuis, you're eavesdropping! You're not looking at the stars, and those were my orders. It's no good being the wife of such a great scholar if you're going to listen to the twaddle of two silly women like von Kleist and me! Yes, I'm telling you," she said, turning back to her favorite, "the king had a vague fancy for that Barberini girl. I know from reliable sources that he often went for tea with Jordan and Chazols in her rooms after the show. She even attended a few midnight suppers at Sans-Souci, which was unheard of in Potsdam before she came along. Do you want to hear more? She stayed there, she had her own rooms for weeks, maybe for months on end. You see that I know quite well what's going on and that my brother's airs of mystery don't fool me."

"Since Your Royal Highness is so well informed, she knows that, for reasons . . . of State which it is not my place to guess, the king has occasionally wanted to make people think that he was less austere than generally assumed, even though at bottom. . . ."

"Even though at bottom my brother hasn't ever loved a woman, not even his own wife. That's what they say, and that's how things look, right? Well, I don't believe in his virtue, even less his coldness. Frederick has always been a hypocrite, you see. But he won't convince me that Signora Barberini stayed in his palace just to pretend to be his mistress. She's as pretty as an angel, devilishly smart, well-educated, and speaks I don't know how many languages."

"She's very virtuous and adores her husband."

"And her husband adores her, all the more because their marriage is a horrible misalliance, right, von Kleist? Come now, you don't want to answer me? I suspect, noble widow, that you are contemplating a misalliance with some poor page or skinny bachelor of science."

"And Your Highness would also like to see an unseemly love affair between the king and some girl from the Opera?"

"Oh! With Porporina the thing would be more plausible and the distance less alarming. I imagine that in the theater, as at court, there is a hierarchy, for that bias is the whim and malady of the human race. A singer must have a much higher opinion of herself than a dancer. Besides, people say that Porporina is more intelligent, better educated, more gracious, that she knows even more languages than Barberini. Speaking languages he doesn't know is my brother's little quirk. And then there's music, which he also pretends to love, even though he has no notion of it, you see? Yet another point of contact with our prima donna. Finally, she too goes to Potsdam in the summer; she has Barberini's old rooms in the new Sans-Souci, she sings in the king's little concerts....Isn't this enough for my conjecture to be true?"

"Your Highness vainly flatters herself to discover some weakness in the life of our great prince. All this is too conspicuous, too solemn for it to be a matter of love."

"No, not love; Frederick doesn't know what love is. But a certain attraction, a little intrigue. That's what everybody's whispering, and there's no denying it."

"No one believes it, Madame. They say that the king, to relieve his boredom, does his best to enjoy an actress's chatter and pretty trills. But after fifteen minutes he says, as though he were speaking to one of his secretaries, 'That's enough for today; if I want more tomorrow, I'll let you know.'"

"What a cad! If that's how he courted Mme de Cocceï, I'm not surprised that she couldn't put up with him. Does Porporina return the favor? What are people saying?"

"They say that she is perfectly modest, proper, timid, and sad."

"Well, that's the best way to please the king. Maybe she's very clever. If only she were! If only we could trust her!"

"Don't put your trust in anyone, Madame, I beg you, not even Mme de Maupertuis, who is sleeping so soundly."

"Let her snore. Awake or asleep, she's always the same old dolt. . . . Be that as it may, von Kleist, I want to get to know this Porporina and see if one can get anything out of her. I sorely regret having refused to have her in when the king proposed bringing her over one morning to make music. You know I was biased against her. . . ."

"For no good reason, I'm sure. It was altogether impossible. . . ."

"Well, now it's in the hands of God. I've been so racked with grief and horror for the last year that less important worries have vanished. I want to see the girl. Who knows if she won't succeed in winning from the king what we've been begging for in vain? That's what I've been thinking for the last few days, and since the only thing I think about is you know what, when I saw Frederick worried and upset about her this evening, I became firmer in the opinion that therein lay our salvation."

"Beware, Your Highness. . . . The danger is great."

"That's what you always say. I'm more wary and circumspect than you are. Well, we'll have to mull it over. Wake up, dear governess, we've arrived."

Chapter II

While the beautiful young abbess[1] was making these observations, the king swept into Porporina's dressing room without knocking. She had just begun to regain consciousness.

"Well, Mademoiselle," he said in a tone without much sympathy or even courtesy, "how are you feeling? Do you often suffer such spells? In your profession, that would be a serious inconvenience. Has something irked you? Are you so ill that you cannot answer me? Then you'll answer for her, Doctor. Is she seriously ill?"

"Indeed, Sire," replied the doctor. "Her pulse is scarcely perceptible, her circulation is greatly perturbed, and her basic functions seem suspended. Her skin is cold as ice."

"True," said the king, taking the girl's hand. "Her eyes are vacant, and her lips pale. Give her some of Dr. von Hoffmann's drops, damn it! I thought it was all a sham, and I was wrong. The girl is terribly ill. She's not unruly or flighty, right, Signor Porporino? Did anybody upset her tonight? Nobody's ever had any reason to complain about her, right?"

"Sire, she's not an actress, but an angel," replied Porporino.

"Nothing less, eh? Are you in love with her?"

"No, Sire, I have infinite respect for her; she's like a sister to me."

"Thanks to the two of you, to God as well who doesn't send actors straight to hell any longer, my theater is turning into a real academy of virtue! Look, she's coming around a bit. Porporina, you know who I am, don't you?"

"No, sir," she said, gazing with alarm at the king who was slapping her wrists.

"Perhaps she's had a seizure," said the king. "Have you ever noticed any signs of epilepsy?"

"Oh! Sire, impossible! What a dreadful thought," exclaimed Porporino, wounded by the king's boorish way of talking about such a fine person.

1. Frederick gave abbeys, canonries, and bishoprics to his favorites, military officers, and Protestant relatives. As Princess Amalia refused to marry, Frederick endowed her with the abbey of Quedlinburg, a royal benefice that provided an income of 100,000 pounds and the title which she bore after the fashion of Catholic canonesses.

"Hold on, don't bleed her," said the king, pushing away the doctor and his scalpel. "I don't like to see innocent blood spilled nonchalantly off the battlefield. You doctors aren't soldiers, but assassins. Leave her be, and give her some air. Porporino, don't let him bleed her. See here, that can kill a person! These doctors have some nerve. I'm turning her over to you. Take her home in your carriage, Poelnitz! She's your responsibility now. The greatest diva we've ever had, and we won't find another one like her right now, maybe never. By the way, what are you singing for me tomorrow, Conciolini?"

Chatting about some other matter, the king accompanied the tenor down the theater's stairs and went to supper with Voltaire, La Mettrie, d'Argens, Algarotti, and General Quintus Icilius.

Frederick was tough, violent, and profoundly selfish. He was also generous and kind, even tender and affectionate when the spirit moved him. There is no paradox here. Everyone knows the simultaneously terrifying and seductive character of that man of many faces, a complex constitution full of contrasts, like all strong natures, especially when they've been invested with absolute power and tried by turbulent times.

Over supper, amidst jokes and small talk that was by turns bitter, elegant, brutish and subtle, among these dear friends whom he failed to find endearing and these admirable wits whom he did not admire much at all, Frederick suddenly turned introspective. He looked preoccupied for a moment or two, then got up and said to his guests, "Carry on, I'm listening."

He went into the next room, took his cap and sword, gestured to a page to follow, and descended into the subterranean passages and mysterious stairways of his ancient palace. His guests, meanwhile, thinking that he was still within earshot, measured their words and dared not say a single thing that ought not fall on the king's ears. Besides, they were all so wary of each other (and for good reason) that anywhere at all within the borders of Prussia they always felt Frederick's terrifying, malicious spirit hovering overhead.

La Mettrie, a doctor whom the king rarely consulted and a reader to whom the king rarely listened, was the only one who knew no fear, nor did he inspire any. Considered altogether inoffensive, he had discovered a way to make himself invulnerable to harm. He did and said so many impertinent, outrageous, and silly things right under the royal nose that it was impossible to suspect him of anything more, and there was no enemy or spy who could ascribe to this impudent wag a wrong that he had not already openly, audaciously proclaimed before the king's eyes. He seemed to take literally the egalitarian philosophy that the king affected in private with the seven or eight people whom he honored with his familiarity. At that time, about ten years into his reign, Frederick, who was still a young man, had not entirely thrown off the informal affability of the crown prince, of the bold philosopher of Rheinsberg. Those who knew the man were careful not to trust him. Voltaire, the most pampered of all and the latest arrival, was starting to get worried, having caught a few glimpses of the tyrant's face beneath the mask of the good prince, of Dionysius of Syracuse lurking behind Marcus Aurelius. Yet La Mettrie, out of incredible naïveté, deep design, or bold indifference, gave the king the cavalier treatment that he purportedly desired. He removed his cravat, his wig, even his shoes in the king's rooms, lounged on the sofas, spoke his mind, openly contradicted the king, made offhand remarks about the vanity of this world's pomp, the throne, the altar, and all the other *preconceived ideas* against which present-day *reason* had done battle. In short, he acted like a true cynic, and his behavior gave so many grounds for disgrace or dismissal that it was a miracle to see him still standing when so many others had been knocked down and smashed for mere peccadillos. For people like Frederick, prone to suspicion and quick to take offense, an insidious word relayed by his spies, a semblance of hypocrisy, or a slight doubt create more of an impression than a thousand reckless stunts. Frederick, who considered La Mettrie insane, was often so astonished by the man that he would stop short, petrified with surprise, and say to himself, "The impudence of this animal is truly a scandal," then add this aside, "But the man is sincere, and he's not playing a double game with me. There's no way he could abuse me more in secret than he does right to my face. Yet all the rest of them, who do nothing but fawn at my feet, what don't they say and do when my back is turned and they stand back up? So La Mettrie must be the most honest man I've got, and I must tolerate him all the more because he's intolerable."

Thus, their routine was set. La Mettrie, who could no longer ruffle the king, even managed to make him chortle over capers that would have been judged revolting on the part of anyone else. From the very start Voltaire had launched into a system of adulation that he found impossible to sustain, and now even he was growing weary and strangely sick of it. La Mettrie, meanwhile, went on amusing himself. He was as much at ease with Frederick as with anybody else, and he felt no need to curse and overthrow an idol to whom he had neither sacrificed nor promised a single thing. For that reason Frederick, who was also growing weary of Voltaire, heartily enjoyed La Mettrie's company and could scarcely do without him since La Mettrie was the only one who did not merely pretend to enjoy Frederick's.

The Marquis d'Argens, a chamberlain with a stipend of six thousand francs (Voltaire, as first chamberlain, was paid twenty thousand francs), was a light philosopher, a facile, superficial writer, a true Frenchman of his time, kind, scatterbrained, libertine, sentimental, at one and the same time stout-hearted, effeminate, witty, generous, and derisive; a man neither young nor old, romantic as a swain, skeptical as a graybeard. Having spent his entire youth with actresses, deceiving and deceived in turn, but always madly in love with the latest one, he wound up contracting a secret marriage with Mlle Cochois, the star of the Comédie-Française in Berlin, a most ugly and most intelligent person, to whom he enjoyed giving an education. Frederick was still unaware of their clandestine union, and d'Argens carefully concealed it from those who could betray him. Voltaire, however, was in on the secret. D'Argens sincerely loved the king, but he was no more loved than anyone else. Frederick did not believe in anyone's affection, and poor d'Argens was now the accessory, now the butt of his cruelest jokes.

The colonel whom Frederick had decorated with the pompous sobriquet of Quintus Icilius was, as everyone knows, a man of French ancestry named Guichard. He was an energetic soldier, a clever tactician, also a great pillager, like all the men of his sort, and a courtier in the fullest sense of the term.

We shall say nothing about Algarotti, so as not to weary the reader with a whole gallery of historical characters. It will suffice to relate the worries of Frederick's guests while he was elsewhere. Finding no relief from the secret discomfort that oppressed them, they felt even more uneasy, unable to say a single word without glancing at the half-open door through which the king had passed, behind which he was perhaps keeping an eye on them.

La Mettrie was the sole exception. Observing that the table service had been neglected in the king's absence, he blurted out, "Gracious, how rude of the master of the house to leave us like this without servants or champagne, and I'm going to go see if he's there to bring him my complaint."

He got up and, without fear of indiscretion, went into the king's bedroom, then came back exclaiming, "Nobody there! How amusing! He may well have mounted up and gone for a torch-lit drill to stimulate his digestion. What an odd one he is!"

"You're the odd one!" replied Quintus Icilius, who could not stomach La Mettrie's strange ways.

"So the king has gone out?" asked Voltaire, beginning to breathe more easily.

"Yes, the king has gone out," said Baron von Poelnitz, entering the room. "I just ran across him in a back courtyard with a single page as escort. He was going totally incognito in his drab cloak. That's why I didn't know who he was."

This freshly arrived third chamberlain requires a word of explanation. Otherwise, the reader will never understand why someone other than La Mettrie dared talk about the king so unceremoniously. Poelnitz, whose age, stipend, and functions were equally problematic, was the Prussian baron, the Regency rake who, in his youth, had played such a brilliant role at the court of the Palatine princess, the Duke of Orleans' mother; a wild gambler whose debts the Prussian king no longer wished to reimburse, a great adventurer, a cynical libertine, very much a spy, a bit of a crook, a cheeky courtier who was fed, chained, scorned, ridiculed, and paid only a pittance by his master, who nevertheless could not do without him, for an absolute monarch always needs to have at hand a man who is capable of the worst things, who finds therein a compensation for his humiliations and the justification of his existence. At this time Poelnitz was also the director of His Majesty's theaters, a sort of supreme steward of the king's trivial pleasures. People already called him old Poelnitz, and that was still the case thirty years later. He was the eternal courtier and had been a page to the previous king. In his person he joined the elegant vices of the Regency, the cynical vulgarity of Big Willy's smoking dens, and the impertinent stiffness of Frederick the Great's witty, militaristic reign. As Frederick considered him in a chronic state of disgrace, Poelnitz worried little about losing favor. Besides, since he always acted as an agent *provocateur*, he truly had no fear that anyone could do him harm around the master who employed him.

"Good God! my dear Baron," exclaimed La Mettrie, "you should have followed the king and come back to tell us his adventures. Then, upon his return, we would have made him mad as hell saying that we'd seen everything without so much as leaving the table."

"Even better!" laughed Poelnitz, "We'd only tell him tomorrow, giving the sorcerer all the credit."

"What sorcerer?" asked Voltaire.

"The famous Count de Saint-Germain, who arrived here this morning."

"Truly? I'm very curious to know if he's a charlatan or a madman."

"There's the rub," said La Mettrie. "He plays his cards so close to his chest that nobody can decide."

"I say, that's not so crazy!" added Algarotti.

"Tell me about Frederick," said La Mettrie. "I'd like to whet his curiosity with a good anecdote so that he'll treat us to a supper of Saint-Germain and his antediluvian adventures. How amusing! Now let's see, where can our dear monarch be at this hour? Surely you know, Baron! You're too curious not to have followed him, or too clever not to have guessed."

"So you want me to tell you?" asked Poelnitz.

"I do hope," said Quintus, turning purple with indignation, "that you won't answer La Mettrie's strange questions. If His Majesty. . . ."

"Oh, my dear friend," said La Mettrie, "from ten in the evening until two in the morning no king is present here. Frederick established the rule once and for all, and it's the only rule I know: There are no kings at supper. Don't you see that this poor king gets bored? And you, bad servant and bad friend that you are, you're not eager to help him forget the burden of his greatness during the sweet hours of the night? Come, Poelnitz, dear Baron, tell us! Where is the king just now?"

"I don't wish to know," said Quintus, standing up and leaving the table.

"As you wish," said Poelnitz. "Let those who don't want to hear plug their ears."

"I'm opening mine," said La Mettrie.

"Here, here! Me, too!" chortled Algarotti.

"Gentlemen," said Poelnitz, "His Majesty is at Signora Porporina's place."

"And you really think we'll believe that one?" La Mettrie howled, adding a Latin phrase that I cannot translate because I don't know the tongue.

Quintus Icilius paled and left the room. Algarotti recited an Italian sonnet that I don't much understand either. Voltaire improvised four lines of verse comparing Frederick to Julius Caesar, at which point the three learned men exchanged smiles. Then Poelnitz continued with a solemn look, "I give you my word of honor that the king is at Porporina's."

"Couldn't you give us something else?" asked d'Argens, who found all this basically unpleasant, as he was not a man to betray others in order to augment his own credit.

Poelnitz replied, unperturbed, "Blast it, marquis, when the king tells us that you're at Mlle Cochois's place, we're not the least bit scandalized. So why are you scandalized about his being at Mlle Porporina's place?"

"On the contrary, you should feel edified," Algarotti chimed in. "And if it's true, I'll go proclaim it at Rome."

"And His Holiness, who likes to poke a bit of fun, will have the loveliest things to say," Voltaire added.

"At what will His Holiness be poking fun?" inquired the king, suddenly at the door of the dining room.

"At Frederick the Great's love affair with Porporina of Venice," La Mettrie brazenly replied.

The king paled, shot a terrifying look at his guests, who all paled more or less, except for La Mettrie. "What do you expect?" he calmly went on. "At the Opera this evening Monsieur de Saint-Germain predicted that when Saturn passed between Regulus and Virgo, His Majesty, followed by a page. . . ."

"Indeed, who is this Count de Saint-Germain?" asked the king, calm as could be. He took a seat and held out his glass so that La Mettrie would replenish his champagne.

They talked about the Count de Saint-Germain, and the storm was diverted without explosion. The initial impact of the remarks he had overheard—the impertinence of Poelnitz, who had betrayed him, and the audacity of La Mettrie, who had dared tell him so—had transported the king with rage. Yet, while La Mettrie was saying a word or two, Frederick remembered telling Poelnitz, at the first opportunity, to gossip about a certain topic and get the others going. So he repossessed himself with the supreme ease and freedom of mind that he enjoyed to the highest degree. There was no further mention of his nocturnal outing, as if no one had noticed a thing. Had it occurred to him, La Mettrie would have dared return to the charge. Yet his frivolous mind followed Frederick down the new path the king was blazing. In this way Frederick often managed to keep even La Mettrie under control. He treated him like a child ready to smash a mirror or jump out a window, to whom one showed a new toy to distract and divert him from his whim. Everybody had something to say and a good anecdote about the famous Count de Saint-Germain. Poelnitz claimed to have seen him in France twenty years earlier. "And when I saw him this morning," he added, "he looked as though it had been only yesterday. I remember one evening in France when, hearing mention of the passion of Our Lord Jesus Christ, he burst out in the most amusing and incredibly earnest fashion, 'But I'd told him that he'd wind up being killed by those nasty Jews. I even told him more or less everything that would happen to him, but he wouldn't listen. His zeal was such that he scorned every danger. That's why I'll never get over his tragic death. Just thinking about it brings tears to my eyes.' At that point the wretched little count began to weep, and he nearly made the rest of us weep, too."

"I'm not surprised to hear that about you," said the king. "After all, you're such a good Christian."

Three or four times already Poelnitz had, within the course of a day, changed religion to apply for various benefices or positions with which the king had led him on, as practical jokes.

"People tell that story everywhere," d'Argens said to the baron, "and it's nothing but a silly yarn. I've heard much better ones. To my mind, what makes this Count de Saint-Germain a person of interest and note is the quantity of observations, altogether new and ingenious, with which he explains events that have remained profound enigmas in history. No matter the topic or time period on which he is questioned, everyone finds it amazing, or so I'm told, that he either knows so much or comes up with so many plausible, interesting insights that are apt to shed a new light on the greatest mysteries."

"If he says plausible things," Algarotti remarked, "he must be a man of prodigious learning and extraordinary memory."

"Better than that!" said the king. "Scholarship alone cannot explain history. The man must have a powerful mind and profound knowledge of the human heart. Yet it remains to be seen if that fine constitution has been perverted by the desire to play a bizarre role, claiming to enjoy eternal life and the remembrance of things that preceded his life as a human. Or it may be that his brain, after long study and deep meditation, has become deranged and subject to monomania."

"I can at least vouch for our man's good faith and modesty," said Poelnitz. "It's not easy to get him to talk about the marvelous things he believes to have witnessed. He knows that people have called him a dreamer and a charlatan, and it's had quite an effect on him. That's why he won't discuss his supernatural power anymore."

"So, Sire, aren't you dying to hear and see the man?" asked La Mettrie. "I certainly am."

"Why so eager?" replied the king. "Seeing a madman is anything but jolly."

"If he's mad, right, but what if he isn't?"

"Are you listening, gentlemen?" asked the king. "This man, the epitome of unbelief and atheism, is falling for the supernatural and already believes in the eternal life of Saint-Germain! But that shouldn't come as any surprise, since everybody knows that La Mettrie is terrified of death, thunder, and ghosts."

"Fear of ghosts, that's a weakness, I confess," said La Mettrie. "As for fear of thunder and everything that is capable of killing us, I maintain that it's reasonable and wise. What the devil should we be afraid of, I ask you, if not of the very things that jeopardize our lives?"

"Long live Panurge!" said Voltaire.

"Back to Saint-Germain," La Mettrie continued, "Master Pantagruel should invite him to sup with us tomorrow."

"Certainly not," said the king. "You're crazy enough as it is, my poor fellow. If that man were to set foot in my house, the superstitious minds that here abound would instantly dream up a hundred ludicrous tales, and they'd soon make the rounds of the whole continent of Europe. Oh, reason! my dear Voltaire, may we soon see the reign of reason! That's the prayer that ought to be on our lips night and morning."

"Reason, reason!" spouted La Mettrie. "Reason is fine and good when it helps excuse and justify my passions, vices, or appetites. . . . Call them what you will! But when it becomes a bother, I demand the freedom to throw it out the door! What the hell, I want no part of any reason that forces me to act brave when I'm frightened, put on a stoical face when I'm suffering, look meek when

I'm fuming with rage. . . . Enough of it! That's not my kind of reason! It's a monster, a chimera dreamed up by those dotty old Greeks and Romans that you all admire, God knows why. May the reign of such reason never come! I don't like absolute power of any kind, and if somebody tried to force me not to believe in God, whose existence I happily and wholeheartedly reject, I believe that I'd go straight to the confessional, just for the sake of contradiction."

"Oh! You're capable of anything, as we all well know," said d'Argens, "even believing that Saint-Germain has a philosopher's stone."

"And why not? That would be so nice, and I could really use one!"

"Ah!" exclaimed Poelnitz, shaking pockets so empty that they refused to jingle while shooting a meaningful glance at the king, "may the reign of the philosopher's stone come as soon as possible! That's the prayer that night and morning. . . ."

"Right," interrupted Frederick, who always turned a deaf ear to such insinuations. "So this Saint-Germain also believes in the secret of making gold? That you hadn't mentioned!"

"Now then, let me invite him, on your behalf, to supper tomorrow night," said La Mettrie, "for I'm of the opinion that a bit of his secret wouldn't do you any harm either, Sire Gargantua! Both as king and reformer, you've got huge needs and a gigantic stomach."

"Pipe down, Panurge," Frederick replied. "Here's my verdict on Saint-Germain. He's an impudent impostor that I plan to put under strict surveillance, for we all know that someone with that fine secret takes more money out of a country than he leaves behind. Now then, gentlemen, have you already forgotten Cagliostro, the great necromancer, whom I wisely expelled from Berlin no more than six months ago?"

"And who made off with a hundred crowns of mine," said La Mettrie. "May the devil give him a dose of his own medicine!"

"And who would have done the same to Poelnitz, if he'd had a hundred crowns," d'Argens chimed in.

"You had him expelled," La Mettrie said to Frederick, "and he played a fine trick on you, no less."

"What trick?"

"Oh! so you don't know? Well, well, I've got a treat of a story for you."

"Brevity is the soul of wit," observed the king.

"Mine is brief. On the day Your Pantagruelian Majesty ordered the sublime Cagliostro to pack up his alembics, specters, and demons, it is common knowledge that he, in person, in his own carriage, at the stroke of noon, passed through all the city gates at one and the same time. Oh! more than twenty thousand people have attested to the fact. The guards posted at every gate all saw him, with the same hat, wig, carriage, baggage, horses, and you'll never rid them of the idea that there were five or six Cagliostros afoot that day."

Everyone had a good laugh, except for Frederick. The progress of reason, his dear reason, was something that he took very seriously. Superstition, which inspired Voltaire with such wit and glee, caused him merely scorn and indignation.

"That's the common man for you," he exclaimed, shrugging his shoulders. "Ah! Voltaire, that's the common man, and while you're alive and waving your torch with its splendid flame over the world! You've been exiled, persecuted, and embattled in every way, and Cagliostro only has to show his face, and everybody falls under his spell! They all but carry him in triumph."

"Are you aware," asked La Mettrie, "that your greatest ladies here at court believe in Cagliostro quite as much as the women in the street? Let me tell you that it was one of the finest beauties at your court who told me that remarkable tale."

"Mme von Kleist, I'll wager!" said the king.

"*It is thou who hast named her!*" recited La Mettrie.

"And now he's using informal address with the king," grumbled Quintus Icilius, having returned a few seconds earlier.

"That Kleist woman is insane," Frederick continued. "The most intrepid visionary, the most fanatic about horoscopes and spells. . . . She needs a good lesson and had better watch out! She addles the brains of all the ladies, and it's even said that she drove her husband mad, that he was sacrificing black billy goats to Satan so as to discover hidden treasure beneath our Brandenburg sands."

"But such things are the very height of fashion and refinement at your court, my dear old Pantagruel," said La Mettrie. "Why on earth do you want women to submit to your grumpy goddess of Reason? Women are on this earth to amuse themselves and us, too. By God, when they stop being silly, we men will be real fools! Mme von Kleist is charming with all her tales about sorcerers. She regales *Soror Amalia* with them. . . ."

"What does he mean by this *Soror Amalia*?" asked the king, taken aback.

"Well, your noble and charming sister, the abbess of Quedlinburg, who, as everyone knows, wholeheartedly believes in magic. . . . "

"Hush up, Panurge!" thundered the king, beating his snuffbox on the table.

Chapter III

There was a moment of silence as the bells slowly tolled the midnight hour.[1] Ordinarily, when a cloud came over his dear Trajan's face, Voltaire knew how to get the conversation rolling again and erase the bad feeling washing over the other guests. Yet that particular evening Voltaire, gloomy and out of sorts, was feeling the insidious attack of that Prussian spleen that promptly seized all the happy mortals summoned to contemplate Frederick in his glory. Just that morning La Mettrie had repeated to him Frederick's lethal quip, which turned the feigned friendship between the two great men into very real aversion.[2] So Voltaire kept quiet. "Indeed," he thought to himself, "let him throw away La Mettrie's peel when he so desires, let him glower and suffer, and let supper be over. I'm having a bout of colic, and all these compliments won't stop me from feeling it."

So Frederick had to give in and regain his philosophical composure all by himself.

"Since we're on the topic of Cagliostro," he said, "and the hour for ghost stories has just tolled, I'll tell you mine, and you'll decide what ought to be believed about sorcerers and their skills. My story is very true, and I learned it from the very person to whom it happened last summer. What happened at the theater tonight brings it back to mind, and perhaps there's a link between that and the story you're about to hear."

"Will it be a bit scary?" asked La Mettrie.

"Perhaps!" replied the king.

"In that case, I'm shutting the door behind me. I can't stand having a door open when people are talking about ghosts and the supernatural."

La Mettrie closed the door, and the king began his tale.

"Cagliostro, as you all know, had a knack for showing credulous folks

1. The Opera started and finished earlier than it did in our day. Frederick began supper at ten o'clock.

2. "I'm still keeping him because I need him. Come next year he won't be of any further use to me, and I'll get rid of him. *I squeeze the orange, then throw away the peel.*" This remark was known to be a raw wound for Voltaire's pride.

blackboards, rather magic mirrors, in which he would make absent individuals come into view. He claimed to be able to catch them unawares at the very moment and to reveal their most secret pursuits and deeds. Jealous wives went to him to learn about the infidelities of their husbands or lovers. There are even some lovers and husbands who have had from him strange revelations about the behavior of certain ladies, and I've heard that the magic mirror has betrayed some secret iniquities. One evening, in any case, the Italian singers at the Opera got together and offered him a lovely supper with good music in exchange for seeing a few of his tricks. He agreed and set up an appointment with Porporino, Conciolini, Signora Astrua, and Signora Porporina at his place in order to show them all the heaven or hell that they wished to see. The Barberinis even went along. Signora Giovanna Barberini asked to see the late doge of Venice, and as Cagliostro very properly raises the dead, she saw him, took a terrible fright, and was all in a state when she stepped out of the little dark room where the sorcerer had put her alone together with the ghost. I strongly suspect that the Barberini woman, who likes to poke a bit of fun, as Voltaire says, was pretending to be terrified to make fools of our Italian histrions, who by trade are not very brave and flatly refused to subject themselves to the same ordeal. Signora Porporina, with that sedate look you know, told Cagliostro that she would believe in his skill if he were to show her a person who was in her thoughts just then; there was no need for her to name that person since he, Cagliostro, was a sorcerer and was supposed to read her soul like a book. 'What you're asking of me is no trivial matter,' replied Cagliostro, 'and yet I believe that I can satisfy you as long as you swear by all that is most solemn and most terrible not to say a single word to the person that I'll show you, nor to make the slightest motion, gesture, or noise during the apparition.' Porporina pledged her word and very determinedly entered the little dark room. It is useful to remind you, gentlemen, that this young person has one of the most rigorous, soundest minds you can encounter; she is educated, reasons well about all matters, and I have cause to believe that she is impervious to any false and narrow ideas. She stayed in the viewing room long enough to amaze and worry her colleagues. Yet no one made a sound. When she came out, her face was exceedingly pale and, it is said, covered with tears. Yet she immediately said to them, 'Friends, if Cagliostro is a sorcerer, he's a sorcerer who lies; don't believe a single thing he shows you.' She refused to explain herself further. But after Conciolini, at one of my concerts a few days later, told me about that supernatural evening, I vowed to question Porporina and did just that the first time she came to sing at Sans-Souci. It wasn't easy to get her to talk.

"Here's what she finally told me: 'Without a doubt, Cagliostro has an extraordinary ability to create apparitions that are so like reality that even the coolest heads cannot fail to be moved. Yet he is no sorcerer, and he claimed to read my mind only because he surely knew a few particulars about my life. But his knowledge was incomplete, and I would not advise you, Sire (this is still Porporina talking, observed the king) to hire him as your minister of police, for he would make serious blunders. So, when I asked him to show me the absent person that I desired to see, I had in mind Professor Porpora, my music teacher, who is now in Vienna; and instead of him I saw appear in the magic room a very dear friend whom I lost this year.' "

"Good heavens!" d'Argens blurted out. "That's far trickier than producing a live one!"

"Wait, gentlemen," continued the king. "Cagliostro, ill-informed, had no idea that the person he had shown was dead; for, when the ghost had disappeared, he asked Signora Porporina if she was satisfied by what she had just seen. 'First of all, sir,' she said, 'I would like to understand what that was. Kindly explain it to me.' 'That is beyond my power,' he replied. 'Be content with knowing that your friend is calm and making himself useful.' Hearing that, she said, 'Alas, sir, you've unwittingly done me great harm. You've shown me a person that I never dreamed of seeing again, and now you claim that he is alive, whereas I closed his eyes six months ago!' That, gentlemen," Frederick continued, "shows you how sorcerers delude themselves while attempting to delude others, and how their schemes are foiled by something their secret police missed. Up to a certain point they penetrate the mysteries of families and intimate feelings. Given that all the stories in this world are more or less alike, and that those with an inclination for the supernatural don't generally take a close look at things, these sorcerers guess right twenty times out of thirty, but a third of the time they miss the mark. No one pays any attention to that, whereas everybody makes a great fuss when they get it right. It's absolutely the same thing with horoscopes and their predictions of a humdrum series of events that must of course happen to everybody, such as voyages, illnesses, the loss of a friend or relative, an inheritance, a meeting, an interesting letter, and other commonplaces of human life. Yet just imagine the catastrophes and domestic woes to which the false revelations of a Cagliostro expose weak, impassioned minds! A husband who takes his word for it and kills his innocent wife, a mother who goes mad with grief because she thinks that she has seen her absent son die, and a thousand other disasters caused by this purported divinatory skill of magicians! It's all infamous, and you must agree that I was right to expel from my realm this Cagliostro with all his great guesses and wonderful news about people dead and buried."

"That's all fine and good," said La Mettrie, "but it fails to explain to me how *Your Majesty's Porporina* saw the dead man upright. For, in short, if she has the qualities of mind affirmed by *Your Majesty*, this goes against *Your Majesty's* argument. True, the sorcerer made a mistake when he pulled a dead man out of his bag of tricks, instead of the live one that had been requested. But it's only all the more certain that he disposes of death and life; and, in that respect, he knows more than *Your Majesty*, who, with all due respect to *Your Majesty*, has had many men killed at war without ever being able to resurrect a single one."

"So we believe in the devil, my dear *subject*," said the king, laughing at the comic glances that La Mettrie shot in Quintus Icilius's direction at each emphatic utterance of the royal title.

"Why wouldn't we believe in Satan? Everybody heaps calumny on the poor old fellow, and he's so witty," La Mettrie retorted.

"Off to the stake with the Manichean!" said Voltaire, putting a candle near the young doctor's wig.

"Well, my sublime Fritz," he continued, "I've handed you a troublesome argument. Either the charming Porporina is silly and gullible, and she saw her dead man, or she's philosophical, and didn't see a thing. Yet she was frightened, which she admits, right?"

"She wasn't frightened," said the king. "She was grief-stricken, as you would be seeing a portrait that looks exactly like a person you have loved and knowing too well that you'll never see him again. But if all must be said, I'm inclined to think that she became frightened after the fact and did not emerge from the ordeal with her inner strength as sound as it once was. Since then she has been subject to attacks of black melancholy, which are always proof of weakness or disorder within us. I'm sure that her mind is still suffering from shock, even though she denies it. There are always consequences when one plays with lies. In my opinion, the sort of attack she had this evening is a result of that whole experience, and I would wager that her troubled brain harbors some dread of the magic power ascribed to Saint-Germain. I've been told that she does nothing but weep since returning home."

"Ah! that I can't believe, dear Majesty," said La Mettrie. "You've been to see her; therefore, she weeps no more."

"You're very curious, aren't you, Panurge, to learn the reason for my visit. You, too, d'Argens, despite your silence and airs of indifference, and the same may go for you, dear Voltaire."

"How could one fail to be curious about each and every thing that Frederick the Great sees fit to do?" replied Voltaire, who made an effort to oblige, seeing that the king was talking. "Perhaps certain men don't have the right to conceal anything when the least of their words is a precept, the least of their actions an example."

"My dear friend, you want to swell my head. Who wouldn't be proud to be praised by Voltaire? You were nevertheless making fun of me for the quarter hour that I was away. Yet you can't possibly think that in fifteen minutes I would have had the time to get as far as the Opera, where Porporina lives, recite her a long madrigal, and return on foot, for I was on foot."

"Bah! Sire, the Opera is very close by, and you win a battle in less time than that."

"Wrong, that requires much more time," replied the king in a rather chilly tone. "Just ask Quintus Icilius. As for the marquis, who has such intimate knowledge of actresses and their virtue, he'll tell you that it takes more than a quarter of an hour to conquer them."

"Well, well, Sire, that depends."

"Yes, that depends, but I hope for your own sake that Mlle Cochois gave you more trouble than that. The fact is, gentlemen, I did not see Signora Porporina tonight. I merely went to talk to her maid and find out how she was doing."

"You, Sire?" exclaimed La Mettrie.

"I wanted to take her myself a little flask I suddenly remembered having such good effects on those stomach spasms that would occasionally make me pass out. Well, you're speechless? Are you all flabbergasted? You want to praise my fatherly, kingly kindness, and you don't dare, for deep in your hearts you find me perfectly ludicrous."

"Indeed, Sire, if you've fallen in love like a mere mortal, I don't find it bad," said La Mettrie. "And I don't see that it's a matter for either praise or ridicule."

"Well, my good Panurge, I'm not at all in love, since one must speak one's mind. True, I'm a mere mortal, but I'm not the king of France, and the gallant ways that suit a great monarch like Louis XV would be most inappropriate for a modest margrave of Brandenburg like me. I've got other fish to fry to keep my poor little shop humming along, and there's no leisure for naps in the groves of Cytherea."

"In that case, I utterly fail to understand your concern for this little opera singer," said La Mettrie. "Unless it's the product of a raging fit of melomania, I simply give up."

"That being so, my friends, I'll have you know that I'm not Porporina's lover, nor am I in love with her. Yet I'm very attached to her because, in an incident too long to relate to you just now, she saved my life without knowing who I was. A bizarre adventure, which I'll relate to you another time. It's too late this evening, and Voltaire is falling asleep. Be content knowing that if I am here, and not in hell, where zeal wanted to send me, I owe it to that girl. Now you can understand that I, knowing her to be dangerously ill, might go see if she hadn't died and bring her a little flask of Dr. Stahl's remedy without wanting you for that reason to take me for the likes of a Richelieu or a Lauzun. Well, gentlemen, goodnight to you. I've been in my boots for the last eighteen hours, and in six hours I'll have to put them back on. I pray God to keep you under his holy, noble protection, as one says at the end of a letter."

. . . .

When the great clock of the palace struck twelve, the young and worldly Abbess of Quedlinburg had just slipped into her pink satin bed. While arranging her mistress's slippers on her ermine rug, the head chambermaid suddenly shuddered and uttered a shriek. Someone had just knocked on the door of the princess's bedroom.

"Well, have you gone mad?" asked the beautiful Amalia, half opening her bed curtains. "What's making you start and sigh like that?"

"Your Royal Highness didn't hear that knock?"

"There was a knock at the door? Then go see what it is."

"Oh! Madame, who alive would dare knock at Your Highness's door knowing that she's in bed?"

"No living person would dare? Is that what you're saying? In that case, it's a dead one. In the meantime, go open the door. Now there's another knock. Go on, you're making me impatient."

The chambermaid, more dead than alive, dragged herself to the door and quavered, "Who's there?"

"It's me, Mme von Kleist," replied a familiar voice. "If the princess is not yet asleep, tell her that I've got something important to tell her."

"Quick, quick! Let her in," exclaimed the princess, "and leave us alone."

As soon as the abbess and her favorite were alone, Mme von Kleist sat down on the foot of the bed and said, "Your Royal Highness was not mistaken. The king is madly in love with Porporina, and he is not yet her lover. That surely gives the girl, for the time being, unlimited influence over his mind."

"How did you come to learn this in the last hour?"

"While undressing for bed, I got my chambermaid chattering, and she told me that one of her sisters is Porporina's maid. So I start asking her questions, worming things out of her, and bit by bit I learn that this maid had just got back from visiting her sister at Porporina's place and that just as she was leaving, so was the king."

"Are you quite sure of this?"

"My maid saw the king as clearly as I'm seeing you now. He spoke to her, taking her for her sister, who was off in another room looking after her mistress who was either ill or pretending to be ill. The king asked about Porporina with extraordinary concern. He stamped his foot and looked thoroughly distressed when he was told that Porporina was still weeping. He didn't ask to see her, *for fear of bothering her*, he said. He gave her a very precious little flask for her mistress. Then he left, urging her to tell Porporina in the morning that he had come by at eleven in the evening."

"Here's an adventure, I hope!" exclaimed the princess, "and I dare not believe my ears. Does your maid really know what the king looks like?"

"Who doesn't know a king who is always out on horseback? Besides, a page had been sent as a scout five minutes earlier to see if the fair lady was alone. Meanwhile the king, wrapped and muffled, was waiting down in the street, all in disguise, as is his habit."

"So, disguise, anxiety, and especially respect. It's love, or I don't know what I'm talking about, von Kleist. And, despite the cold and the dark, you came to tell me right away. Ah! my poor child, how very kind!"

"Despite the ghosts, too! Do you know that for the last few nights there's been a new terror afoot in the castle? My footman was trembling like an idiot while escorting me down the halls."

"What's going on? The woman in white again?"

"Yes, *the Sweeper*."

"This time, we're not the ones playing that trick, my poor von Kleist! Our ghosts are far away. May God bring them back to us!"

"At first I thought the king was playing the ghost, since he now has reasons for wanting to chase nosy footmen out of his way. But I'm truly amazed to see that the witches' sabbath doesn't take place near his rooms nor along the way he takes to go see Porporina. The spirits are congregating around Your Highness. Now that I don't have anything to do with these doings, I must confess that I find them a bit frightening."

"What are you saying, child! How could you believe in ghosts, you who know them so well?"

"There's the rub! I've heard that ghosts sorely resent impostors. They thirst for revenge and hunt down the offenders."

"In that case, they'd really be taking their time, for they've left us in peace for over a year now. Go on, don't worry about such nonsense. As for these lost souls, we know precisely what to believe. Surely it's just some page or junior officer who comes by night to woo the prettiest of my chambermaids. That's why my old chambermaid, whom nobody bothers to woo any longer, was stricken with terror when she heard your knock. She almost refused to open the door. But why are we talking about that? Von Kleist, we've found out the king's secret, and we must take full advantage. But how are we going to do it?"

"We have to win over Porporina and be quick about it before his favor makes her vain and mistrustful."

"We must spare nothing, showering her with presents, promises, and compliments. Tomorrow you'll pay her a visit and ask her to send me some music, for example, original pieces by Porpora. She must have lots of unpublished manuscripts by Italian masters. You'll promise her in return manuscripts by Sebastian Bach, of which I have several. We'll begin by exchanging things. Then I'll ask her to come give me lessons. As soon as I've got her with me, I'll take it upon myself to seduce her, to put her under my control."

"I'll go tomorrow, Madame."

"Good night, von Kleist. Here, come give me a kiss, my one and only friend. Off to bed with you now, and if you catch a glimpse of the Sweeper out in the hall, take a good, long look and see if she's not wearing spurs under her dress."

Chapter IV

The next day, as Porporina was emerging from a distressing night's sleep and feeling quite overwhelmed, she found on her bed two objects that her chambermaid had just placed there, a little rock-crystal flask bearing a gold clasp engraved with the letter F under a royal crown as well as a sealed scroll. When Porporina asked about them, the maid told her that the king had come in person the night before to deliver the flask. Porporina was touched to hear about his visit, so respectful, so delicately naïve. "What a strange man!" she thought to herself, wondering how to reconcile such kindness in the private realm with such severity and despotism in public life. She slipped into a daydream, gradually forgetting about the king and turning her thoughts inward. When confused memories of the previous evening came back to her, she once again began to weep.

"What's this, Mademoiselle?" asked the maid, who was a kind-hearted chatterbox, "are you going to start sobbing again, as you did last night falling asleep? It broke our hearts, and the king, who was listening through the door, shook his head a few times like a man in pain. Yet many people would envy your lot, Mademoiselle. The king doesn't court every woman. I even hear that he doesn't court anybody at all. And, for sure, here he is in love with you!"

"In love! What are you saying there, you poor wretch?" Porporina exclaimed with a shudder. "Never again say such an absurd, indecent thing! The king in love with me, God in heaven!"

"Well, Mademoiselle, but what if he were?"

"God help me! But that's not the case, and it never will be. What is this scroll, Catherine?"

"A servant delivered it early this morning."

"Whose servant?"

"A hired servant. At first he wouldn't tell me who sent him, but he wound up admitting that he worked for a certain Count de Saint-Germain, who arrived here only yesterday."

"And why did you ask him so many questions?"

"Because I wanted to know, Mademoiselle!"

"How naïve! Now go."

As soon as Porporina was alone, she opened the scroll and found a parchment covered with bizarre, indecipherable characters. Although she had heard much talk about the Count de Saint-Germain, she was not acquainted with him. She turned the manuscript every which way. Completely baffled by it and bewildered as to why a person with whom she had never had anything to do would send her such a riddle, she concluded, along with many others, that he was insane. Yet, while examining the scroll she found a loose scrap of paper with these words, "Princess Amalia of Prussia takes great interest in divination and astrology. Deliver this parchment to her, and you can rest assured of her protection and favors." There was no signature, the handwriting was unknown to her, and the scroll bore no address. Porporina was amazed that the Count de Saint-Germain, in order to reach Princess Amalia, would turn to her, as she had never approached Her Highness. Thinking that the scroll had been delivered to her by mistake, she was about to roll it up and send it back. But when she picked up the sheet of rough white paper in which it was wrapped, she saw music printed on the inside face. This awakened a memory. It took her only a second to look for a certain symbol in a corner of the sheet, recognize it as one that she herself had scratched there with a pencil eighteen months before, and verify that this page of music was part of the complete score that she had given as an identifier. This memento from an absent, unhappy friend stirred up such tender feelings that she forgot her own sorrows. Yet she still did not know what to do with the arcane missive, nor why she had been charged with delivering it to the Prussian princess. Was it really to ensure her that lady's favor and protection? Porporina had neither desire nor need of that. Was it in order to set up a connection between the princess and the prisoner that would help save or succor the latter?

The young woman hesitated, remembering the proverb, "When in doubt, don't." Then she thought that there are good and bad proverbs, some for prudent egotism, others for courageous self-sacrifice. She stood up and said to herself, "*When in doubt, do*, when the only person you're putting in jeopardy is yourself and you can hope to serve your friend and fellow creature."

Still very weak and shattered by the crisis of the previous evening, she had nearly finished dressing in a somewhat leisurely fashion. While doing up her beautiful black hair, she wondered how to get the mysterious parchment promptly and safely to the princess. At that very moment there arrived a splendidly trimmed footman wanting to know if she was alone, if she could receive a visit from a nameless lady who wished to have a few words with her. The young singer often cursed the subjection in which artists of that time lived vis-à-vis people in high places. She was tempted to reply, in order to dismiss the importune lady, that she was with the male singers of the opera. While that was a way of shocking certain prudish ladies and driving them away, it was also guaranteed to attract others even faster, she told herself. Thus, she resigned herself to the visit, and Mme von Kleist entered a moment later.

The very polished great lady had resolved to use her charm and make the singer forget all matters of rank, but she was ill at ease. On the one hand, she had heard that the girl was very proud; on the other, Mme von Kleist, feeling most curious on her own account, was eager to make Porporina talk and reveal the very depths of her mind. For that reason, although the lovely lady was kind and harmless, there was just then something fake and forced in her whole countenance that struck Porporina. Curiosity is so close to treachery that it can make the most beautiful faces ugly.

Porporina recognized Mme von Kleist as the person whom she saw in Princess Amalia's box every evening at the opera. Knowing that Mme von Kleist was very fond of necromancy, her first impulse was to seize upon this pretext and request an interview with her mistress. Yet, as she dared not trust a person who was reputed to be a little eccentric and also something of a schemer, Porporina resolved to see what her game was and began scrutinizing her guest with the quiet, penetrating eye of someone on the defensive, therefore superior to attacks of restless curiosity.

At last the ice was broken, and when Mme von Kleist conveyed the princess's request for music, Porporina, masking her pleasure a bit at this happy juncture, ran to fetch several unpublished scores. Feeling a sudden burst of inspiration, she exclaimed, "Ah! What a joy, Madame, to lay all my little treasures at the feet of Her Highness, and I'd be so happy if she were to allow me to do so in person."

"Truly, my lovely child," asked Mme von Kleist, "you wish to speak to Her Royal Highness?"

"Yes, Madame," replied Porporina. "I'd throw myself at her feet and beg a favor that she would surely not refuse me, for I understand that she's a great musician and no doubt the patroness of many artists. People also say that she is as kind as she is beautiful. Were she to hear me out, I hope that she would help me get His Majesty to call my music teacher, the great Porpora, back to Berlin. The king had agreed that Porpora should come to Berlin. Upon his arrival at the border, he was turned away on the pretext of some faulty paperwork in his passport and virtually banished. Since then, despite His Majesty's assurances and promises, I haven't been able to get this interminable affair settled. I no longer dare importune the king with a request in which he can take only little interest, that always slips his mind, I'm sure. Yet, if the princess deigned say a word to the administrators in charge of expediting this business, I would have the joy of finally being reunited with my adoptive father, my one and only protector in the world."

"What you're saying amazes me no end," exclaimed Mme von Kleist. "What! the lovely Porporina, who I thought held the king in her sway, has to ask someone else's help for something that seems so simple? In this case, His Majesty must fear in your adoptive father, as you call him, a guardian too severe or an adviser too adverse to his interests."

"Try as I may, Madame, your meaning escapes me," replied Porporina with a seriousness that disconcerted Mme von Kleist.

"Apparently I'm wrong about the extreme benevolence and boundless admiration that the king professes for the greatest diva in the universe."

"It is not seemly for such a lady as Mme von Kleist to mock a poor, harmless artist without pretensions."

"Do you think I'm mocking you? Who could dream of mocking such an angel? Now then, I'm sure you'll win over the princess, who is a most impulsive person. She's already so fond of your talent. Once she sees you up close, she'll be just as fond of your person."

"On the contrary, Madame, I had been told that Her Royal Highness was always very hard on me, that she didn't like my homely face and highly disapproved of my singing method."

"Who on earth could tell you such lies?"

"The king told those lies!" replied the girl a bit mischievously.

"It was a trap, a test of your sweet, modest disposition," Mme von Kleist continued.

"As a mere mortal I have no right to lie to you like a very cunning great king, and this I want to prove by taking you and your musical scores straight off to see the princess."

"And you think she'll be glad to see me?"

"Will you trust me?"

"But if you're wrong, Madame, who'll be disgraced?"

"I alone, and you'll have my permission to tell one and all that while I boast about enjoying the princess's affection, she has for me neither respect nor regard."

"After you, Madame," said Porporina, ringing for her muff and mantelet. "I'm dressed very simply. Then again, I wasn't expecting you."

"You look charming as you are, and you'll find our dear princess in even more informal attire. Come, let's go."

Porporina put the mysterious scroll in her pocket, loaded Mme von Kleist's carriage with musical scores, and resolutely followed, telling herself, "For a man who risked his life for me, I can certainly risk wasting my time waiting around for a little princess."

For five minutes she sat in a dressing room while the abbess and her confidante exchanged the following words in the next room.

"Madame, I've brought her to you, she's in there."

"So soon? Oh, admirable ambassadress! How should I receive her? What is she like?"

"Reserved, prudent or simpleminded, highly secretive or admirably stupid."

"Oh, we'll soon find out!" exclaimed the princess, who was practiced in divining motives and doubting appearances. Her eyes flashed with excitement. "Show her in!"

During this short wait in the dressing room, Porporina had surveyed with surprise the strangest collection of paraphernalia that ever decorated a beautiful princess's inner sanctum: globes, compasses, astrolabes, astrological charts, jars filled with nameless mixtures, skulls—in short, a sorcerer's workshop. "My friend is not wrong," she thought to herself, "and the secrets of the king's sister are public knowledge. I don't even think that she tries to hide them. Otherwise, I wouldn't have been allowed to set eyes on all these bizarre objects. Come now, there's no reason to be afraid."

The abbess of Quedlinburg was then about twenty-eight or thirty years old. She had been pretty as an angel, and this was still the case in the evening by candlelight and viewed from afar, but seeing her close up, in full daylight, Porporina was surprised to find her withered and blotchy. Her blue eyes, once the most beautiful in the world and now red-rimmed as though she had just been crying, had a sickly glint as well as a deep transparence that did not inspire trust. Her family and the whole court had adored her, and for a long time she had been the most affable, lively, benevolent, and gracious princess ever portrayed in those novels about people of rank in the old patrician literature. Over the last few years, however, her character had deteriorated as well as her beauty. She had fits of bad, even violent temper that made her resemble Frederick at his worst. Without trying to take him as her model, and even secretly excoriating him, she seemed invincibly driven to take on every fault that she blamed in him. Thus, she risked becoming an imperious, absolute mistress as well as a narrow-minded, condescending woman of learning with a skeptical, bitter frame of mind. And yet, under these dreadful defects that were fatally spreading through her every day, one could still see signs of an innate kindness, a judicious mind, a courageous soul, and a passionate heart. So what was happening in the soul of that poor princess? She was being devoured by a terrible sorrow, and she had to smother it in her breast, suffering stoically beneath a cheerful mask in front of a curious, malevolent, or indifferent world. As a result of this continual disguise and self-constraint, she had managed to develop within herself two quite different beings, one that she dared reveal to almost no one, and one that she flaunted with a sort of hatred and despair. People noticed that her conversation had taken a lively, brilliant turn, but that nervous, forced gaiety pained the eye, and its icy, almost frightening effects seemed inexplicable. By turns childishly sentimental and harshly cruel, she astonished others as well as herself. Floods of tears extinguished the fires of her wrath; then, a sudden burst of ferocious irony or unholy disdain would break her out of the salutary depressions that she could neither harbor in her soul nor disclose on her countenance.

The first thing that Porporina noticed upon meeting the princess was that sort of duality within her. She had two aspects, two faces: one tender, the other threatening; and two voices, one sweet and harmonious that seemed God's gift to an angel, the other harsh and rasping that seemed to spew out of some fiend's burning breast. Amazed by such a bizarre creature, torn between fear and compassion, our heroine wondered whether it was a good or a bad genie that was going to invade and dominate her.

As for the princess, she found Porporina far more daunting than she had imagined. She had been hoping that the singer, stripped of her theater costumes and that makeup that, no matter what people may say, uglifies women in the extreme, would justify the things that Mme von Kleist had said to reassure her, that she was more ugly than beautiful. Yet her olive complexion, so smooth and without a single blemish, her dark eyes so strong and sweet, her frank mouth, her supple figure with its easy, natural carriage—the whole effect of a good, forthright creature brimming with composure or at least the inner strength that comes from integrity and true wisdom forced upon restless Amalia a sort of respect and even shame, as though she sensed in Porporina a soul of unassailable loyalty.

The princess endeavored to conceal her uneasiness. Taking note of this, Porporina was amazed, as one can believe, to see that such a great princess felt intimidated in her presence. So, in order to revive the conversation that was flagging at every moment, Porporina began opening one of her scores in which she had slipped the cabalistic letter, making sure that this huge sheet of parchment with its huge characters caught the princess's eye. Once the effect had been achieved, she made as though to remove it, as though she were surprised to find it there, but the abbess snatched it up and exclaimed, "What's this, Mademoiselle? In the name of Heaven, where did you get this?"

"If I must confess," replied Porporina in meaningful tone, "it's an astrological exercise. I was meaning to present it to Her Highness when she wished to ask me about a subject that is not altogether foreign to me."

The princess fastened her ardent gaze on Porporina, looked back at the magic characters, and dashed to a window. She studied the mysterious parchment for a second, then shrieked and sank, as though she were suffocating, into the arms of Mme von Kleist who, seeing her stagger, had raced toward her.

"Out, Mademoiselle," the queen's favorite hastily ordered. "Go back to the dressing room, don't say a word, don't call anybody, not a single, solitary person! Do you hear?"

"No, no, I don't want her to leave . . . ," choked the princess. "Here, I want her here, near me. Ah! my child," she exclaimed as soon as Porporina come close, "what a service you've rendered me!"

And convulsively seizing Porporina in her skinny, white arms, the princess clasped her to her heart and covered her cheeks with jerky, pointed kisses that left the poor child feeling bruised in body and soul.

"Obviously this country makes people insane," she thought to herself. "Several times I've thought I was going mad, and now I see that people of the highest rank are far worse off than I. There is madness in the air."

At last the princess removed her arms from Porporina's neck, then wrapped them around Mme von Kleist's, all the while shrieking, crying, and repeating in her strangest voice, "Saved! Saved! He is saved! My friends, my dear friends, Trenck has escaped from the fortress of Glatz; he's off and running, still running!"

And the poor princess fell into a fit of convulsive laughter, interspersed with sobs that were painful to the eyes and ears.

"Oh! Madame, for the love of God, contain your joy!" pleaded Mme von Kleist. "Beware that anyone hear you!"

Picking up the so-called cabala, which was nothing more than a coded letter from the Baron von Trenck, she helped the princess go on reading, a task interrupted thousands of times by bursts of feverish, almost frenetic joy.

Chapter V

"Seducing, by means that my *incomparable friend* provided me, the junior officers of the garrison, making a pact with a prisoner who shares my fondness for liberty, delivering a good punch to one guard, a swift kick to another, and a fine stroke of my sword to a third, making an amazing leap down to the base of the ramparts, while giving a shove to my friend who couldn't make up his mind fast enough and dislocated his foot in his fall, picking him up, throwing him over my shoulders, running in this fashion for a quarter of an hour, crossing the Neiss in a pea-soup fog and water up to my waist, taking off again in a run once I got to the other side, walking all night long, a dreadful night . . . getting lost, trudging through the snow round and round a mountain without knowing where we were, then hearing the bells of Glatz toll out the hour of four in the morning! that is to say, having wasted my time and energy only to find myself in the shadow of the city walls at dawn . . . , reviving my courage, entering a peasant's abode, putting my pistol to his throat and stealing two horses, then galloping off God knows where; conquering my liberty by means of a thousand tricks, terrors, pains, and struggles; finally finding myself penniless, practically naked, almost starving in a foreign land in brutal cold; but feeling free after having been condemned to a dreadful, perpetual captivity; thinking about an *adorable friend*, telling myself that this news will fill her with joy, making a thousand bold, delightful plans to come closer to her; this is being happier than Frederick of Prussia; this is being the happiest of men, the elect of Providence."

This was, in short, young Frederick von Trenck's letter to Princess Amalia, and the ease with which Mme von Kleist read it to her mistress proved to Porporina, who was both surprised and touched, that this method of correspondence was very familiar to them. There was a postscript that read, "The person who will give you this letter is as much to be trusted as the others were not. You can, in short, confide in her without reservation and give her all your messages for me, with the Count de Saint-Germain serving as our conduit, but it is necessary that the aforesaid count, who does not enjoy my complete trust, never hear your name. He must believe that I'm smitten with Porporina, even though that is not at all the case and my feelings for her have never gone beyond pure, untroubled friendship. So, let no cloud darken the lovely brow of the *goddess whom I adore*. I live for her alone and would sooner die than betray her."

While Mme von Kleist was deciphering the postscript aloud and dwelling on every word, Princess Amalia was scrutinizing Porporina's face for any sign of pain, humiliation, or resentment. Totally reassured by her angelic serenity, she once again began smothering the singer with kisses and exclaimed, "And to think I harbored suspicions about you, poor child! You don't know how jealous I was, how much I hated and cursed you! I wanted to think you ugly and a poor actress just because I feared thinking you too beautiful and good. This is on account of my brother who was afraid that I would take up with you. All the while pretending that he wanted to bring you to my concerts, he carefully led me to understand that you had been Trenck's mistress in Vienna, his idol, knowing full well that this was the way to keep me forever at a distance from you. And I believed it, while you've been risking life and limb to bring me this happy news! So you don't love the king? Oh, how right you are! Of all the men in the world, he's the most perverse, the most cruel."

"Oh! Madame, Madame!" cried Mme von Kleist, terrified by the princess's abandon and delirious volubility in front of Porporina. "To what dangers you'd be exposing yourself just now if she weren't an angel of courage and self-sacrifice!"

"That's true. . . . What a state I'm in! I must have lost my head. Shut the doors tight, von Kleist, and first check to see if anyone in the anterooms overheard me. As for her," the princess added, pointing to Porporina, "take a look and tell me if it's possible to doubt such a face. No, no! I'm not as careless as I look. Dear Porporina, don't think I'm opening my heart to you inadvertently, nor that I'll come to regret it in a calmer moment. You see, my child, I've got an infallible instinct, an eye that has never led me astray. It runs in the family, and my brother, the king who prides himself on the very same thing, can't hold a candle to me. No, you won't betray me, I see it, I know it! You wouldn't want to betray a woman devoured by an unhappy love, a woman who has suffered things no one can ever imagine."

"Oh! Madame, never!" said Porporina, kneeling down near her, as if to take God as her witness. "Neither you, nor Herr von Trenck, who saved my life, nor anyone in the world, for that matter!"

"He saved your life? Ah! I'm sure that he has saved many others! He is so brave, so good, so handsome! Don't you find him very handsome? Then again, you must not have looked at him too much. Otherwise, you'd be in love with him, and you aren't, isn't that true? You'll tell me how you met him, how he saved your life, but not now. I just couldn't listen. I have to talk, my heart is brimming over. For such a long time it's been drying up in my breast! I want to talk, then talk some more. Let me be, Kleist. I must vent my joy, or I'll burst. Just close the doors, keep watch, protect me, look after me. Have pity on me, my poor friends, for I am very happy!"

Thereupon the princess burst into tears.

"You know, I found him attractive from the first day I laid eyes on him," she said a few seconds later in a voice choked with sobs, but prey to such agitation that nothing could calm her. "He was eighteen, beautiful as an angel, and so knowledgeable, so frank, so brave! I was supposed to marry the king of Sweden. Oh yes! And my sister Ulrika was vexed to tears that I should become queen while she remained unmarried! 'My dear sister,' I told her, 'we can work this out. The great men who govern Sweden want a Catholic queen; I don't wish to abjure my religion. They want a nice little queen, very idle, very calm, very aloof from any political doings; if I were queen, I'd want to rule. I'm going to make all this clear to the ambassadors, and you'll see that tomorrow they'll write to their prince saying that you're right for Sweden and not I.' I did as I said, and my sister is the Queen of Sweden. Since that day I've been acting a part every day of my life. Ah! Porporina, you think you're an actress? No, you don't know what it's like acting a part one's whole life long, morning, noon, evening, and often at night. For everything that has breath around here does nothing but spy on us, trying to read our minds and betray us. I was forced to make a great show of grief and resentment when my sister, thanks to me, stole the throne of Sweden out from under my nose. I was forced to pretend that I detested Trenck and found him ridiculous, to make fun of him, and what else! All the while I was his adoring mistress, choking with drunken joy then as I am now! Ah! more than now, alas! But Trenck wasn't as strong and wary as I was. He wasn't born a prince, he didn't have my talent for lying and dissembling. The king discovered everything. As kings do, he lied and pretended to see nothing. But he persecuted Trenck, and this beautiful page, the king's favorite, became the object of his hatred and wrath. The king rained down on him humiliation and harsh treatment, kept him under arrest seven days out of eight. But on the eighth Trenck was in my arms, for nothing frightens or disheartens him. How can one not adore such courage? Well, the king entrusted him with a foreign mission. After he had brought the affair to a fine and speedy resolution, my brother was so vile as to accuse him of having handed over to his cousin Trenck the Pandur, who serves under Maria Theresa, the designs of our fortresses as well as military secrets. This was the way not only to get him away from me by locking him up forever but also to disgrace him and make him die of grief, despair, and rage in some horrible dungeon. See if I can honor and bless my brother. He's a great man, or so people say. But I'm telling you, he's a monster! Ah! Beware of loving him, girl. He'll snap you in two, like a twig. But you must pretend, you see, always pretend! In the atmosphere where we live, you have to breathe in secret. I pretend to worship my brother. I'm his beloved sister, as everyone knows, or thinks. . . . He attends to my every desire. He gathers cherries himself from the espaliers at Sans-Souci; he deprives himself, he who loves this one thing alone on this earth, in order to send them to me, and before handing them over to the page who will bring me the basket, he counts the cherries just to make sure that the page won't eat any on the way. What dainty care! What artlessness worthy of Henry IV of France and King René! Yet he makes my lover perish in an underground dungeon and tries to disgrace him in my eyes to punish me for loving him! What a big heart! What a good brother! And what love we have for each other!"

While she was talking, the princess went pale. Her voice grew weaker and weaker, then died. With her eyes bulging in a blank stare, she remained motionless, mute, and livid, having lost consciousness. Porporina, frightened, helped Mme von Kleist unlace her corset and carry her to bed, where she recovered her spirits a bit and went on muttering unintelligible things.

"This will pass, thank Heaven," said Mme von Kleist. "When she's in control of herself again, I'll call her maids. As for you, dear child, it is absolutely imperative that you go to the music room and sing for the walls, rather the ears of the anteroom. For without fail the king will learn of your visit, and it must not seem that you and the princess were occupied with anything other than music. The princess will be indisposed, which will help conceal her joy. She must not seem to know a thing about Trenck's escape, and the same goes for you. The king certainly knows about it by now. He'll be in a foul mood, entertaining horrible suspicions about every living soul. Be careful, very careful. If he finds out that you're the one who delivered this letter to the princess, we're both lost. In this country women, just as well as men, are sent to the fortress. And they are deliberately forgotten, just the same as men; they die there, just the same as men. Now that you've been warned, adieu. Go sing, then leave without fuss or mystery. We won't see you again for at least a week, in order to divert any suspicions. You may count on the princess's gratitude. She is magnificent and knows how to compensate dedication. . . ."

"Alas, Madame!" Porporina said in a sad voice, "you think that you have to use threats and promises with me? I'm sorry you think so!"

Worn out from all the violent emotions she had just shared, and still feeling ill from her own shock the evening before, Porporina nonetheless sat down at the harpsichord and began to sing. Behind her there opened a door so silently that it escaped her notice. All of a sudden she saw in an adjacent mirror the king standing right beside her. She started and wanted to get up, but the king, pressing the ends of his bony fingers down on her shoulder, forced her to sit and continue. She obeyed most reluctantly, uneasily. Never had she felt less inclined to sing, never had she found Frederick's presence more chilling, more contrary to musical inspiration.

"Sung to perfection," said the king after her piece. While singing she had been terrified to see him tiptoe up behind the half-open door of his sister's bedroom to eavesdrop. "Yet I'm sorry to say that this beautiful voice is not at its best this morning. You should have rested, instead of yielding to the odd whimsy of Princess Amalia, who summons you in order not to listen to you."

"Her Royal Highness was suddenly taken ill," she replied, frightened by the king's somber, worried look, "and I was ordered to keep on singing to distract her a bit."

"I assure you that it's a waste of energy. She's not listening to you one whit," said the king curtly. "She's in there whispering with Mme von Kleist, as though nothing at all had happened. Since that's the case, we can certainly whisper together here, without worrying about the two of them. The illness doesn't look serious to me. I think that in this category your sex goes very quickly from one extreme to the other. Last night everyone thought you were dead. Whoever would have thought that you'd be here this morning looking after my sister and entertaining her? Now, would you please tell me what on earth you're doing here all of a sudden?"

Porporina, stunned by the question, prayed for inspiration.

"Sire," she replied, striving for confidence, "I scarcely know the answer to that myself. This morning I was asked to give her this score. I thought I ought to bring it here myself and was meaning to leave my music in the anteroom and go right back home. Mme von Kleist caught sight of me. She mentioned my name to Her Highness, who was apparently curious to see me up close. I was forced to go in. Her Highness asked me about the style of several pieces of music. Then, when she felt ill, she ordered me to perform this piece for her while she was taking to her bed. And now, if I may go to the rehearsal . . ."

"It's not yet time," said the king. "I don't know why you're burning to run along when I want to chat with you."

"I always fear being out of place in the presence of Your Majesty."

"You have no common sense, my dear."

"All the more reason, Sire!"

"You shall stay," he said, forcing her to sit back down at the piano and remaining on his feet facing her.

Then he added, fixing on her a gaze half-paternal, half-inquisitorial, "Is it true, everything you've just told me?"

Porporina overcame her horror of lying. She had often told herself that she would be sincere with the terrifying man on her own account but tell a lie if it were ever a question of his victims' welfare. Now she was suddenly facing that moment of crisis in which the master's kindliness could turn to fury, which she would have gladly suffered rather than to stoop to dissimulation. Yet Trenck's fate and that of the princess depended on her wits and presence of mind. Calling the skill of the actress to her aid, she smiled knowingly and withstood the king's eagle eye, which looked more like a vulture's just then.

"Well," asked the king, "why don't you answer me?"

"Why does Your Majesty wish to frighten me by pretending to doubt what I've just said?"

"You don't seem at all frightened. On the contrary, I find your gaze quite bold this morning."

"Sire, one only fears what one hates. Why do you want me to fear you?"

Frederick bristled with armor like a crocodile so as not to be moved by this reply, the most flirtatious he had thus far obtained from Porporina. As was his habit, he immediately changed the subject, which is a great art, more difficult than one would think.

"Why did you faint on stage yesterday evening?"

"Sire, that's the least of Your Majesty's worries and my own secret."

"So what did you have for breakfast this morning to be taking such a perky tone with me?"

"I took a breath from a certain flask that filled me with confidence as to the kindness and justice of the one who brought it to me."

"Ah! so you took that for a declaration?" said Frederick icily, with cynical contempt.

"Thank God, no!" she replied, with a very sincere shudder of fear.

"Why do you say *Thank God*?"

"Because I know that Your Majesty only makes declarations of war, even to the ladies."

"You're neither the Czarina nor Maria Theresa. What kind of war can I have with you?"

"The kind a lion has with a gnat."

"And what gnat has been biting you, for you to cite such a fable? The gnat killed the lion, harassed him to death."

"It was no doubt a poor lion, irascible and therefore weak. So I couldn't have been thinking of that fable."

"But the gnat was grimly determined and had a nasty sting. Perhaps the fable suits you well!"

"Does Your Majesty think so?"

"Yes."

"Sire, are you lying?"

Frederick seized her wrist and convulsively squeezed it to make a bruise. There was anger and love in this bizarre gesture. Porporina's face did not change. The king looked at her red, swollen hand and added, "You've got courage!"

"No, Sire, but I don't pretend to lack courage, like everyone in your entourage."

"What do you mean?"

"That one often plays dead so as not to be killed. If I were you, I wouldn't like people to be so terrified of me."

"Who are you in love with?" asked the king, once again changing the subject.

"With no one, Sire."

"That being the case, why do you have attacks of nerves?"

"That doesn't concern the destiny of Prussia, and consequently the king doesn't care to know the answer to that question."

"So you think that it is the king speaking to you right now?"

"That would be impossible to forget."

"Yet that's what you must resolve to do. Never will the king speak to you; it's not the king's life you saved, Mademoiselle."

"But I haven't seen Baron von Kreutz again around here."

"If that's a reproach, it wouldn't be fair. It wasn't the king who went to inquire about your health yesterday, but Captain Kreutz."

"The distinction is too subtle for me, Captain."

"Well, try and learn. Here, when I put my cap on like that, a little to the left, I'll be the captain; when it tips to the right, I'll be the king; and according to who I am, you'll be Consuelo or Signorina Porporina."

"I see, Sire. Well, that I can't do. Your Majesty is free to be two, or three, or a hundred different people. I only know how to be one."

"You're lying! You wouldn't talk to me on stage in front of your fellow performers as you're doing right now."

"Sire, don't be too sure!"

"Well, you're certainly full of the devil today."

"That's because Your Majesty's cap is neither to the right nor the left, and I don't know to whom I'm speaking."

Overwhelmed by the attraction he felt to Porporina, especially at that moment, the king lifted his hand to his cap in a playful, genial way and tipped it so far down over his left ear that his terrifying face looked comical. He was doing his best to act like a mere mortal and a king on vacation, but all of a sudden he remembered that his purpose in coming here was not to take his mind off his worries, but to fathom the secrets of the Abbess of Quedlinburg. He peevishly whipped the cap off his head and dropped his smile. Furrowing his brow, he got up and said to the girl, "Stay here, I'll be back for you."

And he went into the bedroom of the princess, who trembled awaiting his visit. Mme von Kleist, having seen the king chatting with Porporina, had not dared leave her mistress's side. She had made futile attempts to hear their conversation, but not having been able to catch a single word because of the dimension of the rooms, she was more dead than alive.

As for Porporina, she shuddered at the thought of what was going to happen. Usually solemn and respectfully sincere with the king, she had just coerced herself to distract him, by means of coquetries somewhat contrived, from the dangerous interrogation he was starting to put her through. She had hoped to divert him altogether from torturing his poor sister. Frederick, however, was not a man to depart from his plan, and the poor creature's efforts failed in front of the despot's single-mindedness. She commended Princess Amalia to God, for she understood that the king was forcing her to stay there in order to compare her explanations with those being prepared in the next room. The great care with which he closed the door behind him on his way in there only confirmed her in this opinion. So she spent an uncomfortable quarter of an hour waiting, agitated with a bit of fever, frightened by the scheme in which she found herself involved, and unhappy with the role she was being made to play. With horror she recalled the insinuations that were beginning to come at her from all directions regarding the king's possible love for her and the sort of agitation that he himself had just betrayed in that respect with his strange behavior.

Chapter VI

Yet, my God! the cunning of the most terrifying Dominican who ever served as a great inquisitor, what chance does it stand against three women when love, fear, and friendship inspire them all to the same end? Frederick tried everything, but nothing worked, neither friendly endearments, nor provocative irony, nor surprise questions, nor feigned indifference, nor indirect threats. Mme von Kleist and Amalia explained Consuelo's presence in the princess's suite in absolutely the same terms that Consuelo had so felicitously improvised. This explanation was the most natural, the most plausible. Putting everything down to chance is the best way. Chance says nothing and issues no contradictions.

Worn out fighting, the king gave up, or changed tactics, for he suddenly exclaimed, "And Porporina, whom I'm forgetting in all this! Dear little sister, since you're feeling better, have her step in. Her chatter will entertain us."

"I feel like a nap," replied the princess, fearing a trap.

"Well then, wish her good day and dismiss her yourself."

With these words, the king got to the door ahead of Mme von Kleist, opened it himself, and called in Porporina.

But instead of sending her away, he on the spot began a dissertation on German and Italian music. Once that subject had been exhausted, he suddenly exclaimed, "Ah! Signora Porporina, here's a bit of news I was forgetting to tell you, something that will certainly please you: your friend, Baron von Trenck, is no longer in prison."

"Which Baron von Trenck, Sire?" she asked with cunning ingenuousness. "I know two of them, and they're both in prison."

"Oh! Trenck the Pandur will perish in Spielberg. It's the Prussian Trenck who has escaped."

"Well, Sire," replied Porporina, "as for me, I'm grateful to you. That was a fair and generous act on Your Majesty's part."

"Much obliged for the compliment, Mademoiselle. What do you think, my dear sister?"

"What are you talking about?" asked the princess. "I was half asleep and didn't hear you, brother."

"I'm talking about your protégé, the handsome Trenck, who has gone over the walls at Glatz."

"Ah! Good for him," said the princess with great composure.

"Bad for him," the king said curtly. "His case was coming up for study, and perhaps he could have cleared himself of the charges against him. His escape amounts to a confession of his crimes."

"If that's so, I forsake him," said Amalia still impassive.

"Mademoiselle Porporina will persist in defending him, I'm sure," Frederick continued. "I can see it in her eyes."

"I can't believe that he's a traitor," she said.

"Especially when the traitor is so handsome? Do you know, sister, that Mademoiselle Porporina is very close to Baron von Trenck?"

"May that do her a lot of good," Amalia said in a chilly voice. "If the man is disgraced, I nevertheless advise her to forget him. Now I wish you good day, Mademoiselle, for I feel very tired. Please come back in a few days to help me read that score. It looks quite beautiful."

"You're fond of music again?" asked the king. "I thought you had forsaken it altogether."

"I want to try and get back to it, and I hope, brother, that you'll agree to come help me. People say that you've made great progress, and now you'll give me lessons."

"We'll both take lessons from the signora. I'll bring her over."

"Fine. That will be delightful."

Mme von Kleist escorted Porporina back to the anteroom. Soon she was all alone in long hallways, knowing none too well how to get out of the palace and scarcely remembering how she had come in.

As the king's household was managed with the strictest economy, to say the least, one did not run across many footmen in the castle. Not finding a single one to give her any directions, Porporina began wandering aimlessly through the vast, dreary manor.

Preoccupied by what had just transpired, shattered with exhaustion, her stomach empty since the night before, Porporina felt very light-headed, but, as sometimes happens in such a case, a sickly excitement nevertheless sustained her physical strength. She walked haphazardly, faster than her normal pace. Pursued by her own thoughts, a source of strange torment since the evening before, she completely forgot where she was, lost her way, passed through hallways and courtyards, retraced her steps, climbed up and down stairs, crossed several people without thinking of asking them where to go, and finally found herself, as if on the far side of a dream, at the entrance of a huge hall filled with a motley collection of strange objects. On the threshold a solemn, polite figure gave her a very courteous greeting and invited her in.

Porporina recognized the very learned academician Stoss, the conservator of the castle's library and curio collection. Several times he had brought her precious manuscripts of Protestant music from the early Reformation, treasures of calligraphy with which he had enriched the royal holdings, so that she could read through them. When he learned that she was seeking a way out of the palace, he immediately offered to see her home. Yet he so earnestly begged her to take a look at the precious collection entrusted to his care, in which he took such legitimate pride, that she could not refuse a tour leaning on his arm. Easily entertained like all those with artistic constitutions, she was soon more interested than she had thought herself disposed to be. She became totally absorbed by an object to which the most worthy professor particularly insisted on drawing her attention.

"This drum which doesn't seem at all special at first glance, whose authenticity I even suspect, is nonetheless very famous," he said. "This much is sure. The membrane of this instrument of war is human skin, as you yourself can see by the trace of the pectoral bulge. This trophy, which His Majesty carried off from Prague in the glorious war that he has just concluded, is allegedly made from the skin of *Jan Zizka of the Chalice*, the famous head of the great Hussite revolt of the fifteenth century. It is said that he bequeathed this sacred hide to his fellow soldiers, promising them that *where it would be, there too would be victory*. The Bohemians say that the sound of this dreadful drum made their enemies take to their heels, that it conjured up the ghosts of their leaders who had died fighting for the holy cause and a thousand other marvels. . . . Yet, apart from the fact that such superstitions deserve only contempt in this splendid century of reason in which we are fortunate to live, Monsieur Lenfant, Her Majesty the Queen Mother's preacher and the author of a commendable history of the Hussites, asserts that Jan Zizka was buried with his skin on, that consequently. . . . You seem to be growing pale, Mademoiselle. . . . Are you ill, or does the sight of this bizarre object disgust you? This Zizka was a great scoundrel as well as a most ferocious rebel. . . ."

"That may be, Monsieur," replied Porporina, "but I have lived in Bohemia, and I've heard it said that he was a very great man. His memory is still as alive there as Louis XIV's in France, and he's considered the savior of his country."

"Alas! A country very poorly saved," said Herr Stoss with a smile. "However much I might beat the resonant breast of Bohemia's liberator, I wouldn't even conjure up his shamefully captive shade in the palace of the man who conquered his descendants."

While uttering these words in a pedantic tone, the commendable Herr Stoss ran his fingers over the membrane, which made a dull, sinister sound like that of drums when they are muffled in mourning and pounded in funeral marches. But this profane entertainment on the part of the learned conservator was suddenly cut short by a piercing shriek out of Porporina, who threw herself into his arms and hid her face in the crook of his shoulder, like a child terrified by some odd or dreadful thing.

The solemn Herr Stoss looked around for the cause of this sudden terror and saw, standing on the threshold, a person whose aspect engendered only disdain in him. He was going to wave him away, but by the time Porporina, still clinging to him, had left him free to move, the person was gone.

"Truly, Mademoiselle," he said, leading her to a chair into which she slumped, trembling and overwhelmed, "I do not understand what has come over you. I didn't see anything to cause such an upset."

"You didn't see anything, nobody at all?" Porporina's voice was faint, her mien distraught. "There, on the threshold. . . . You didn't see a man just standing there, looking at me with terrifying eyes?"

"I saw perfectly well a man who often wanders through the castle, who might like to make himself look terrifying, as you say so well. Yet I have to say that he doesn't intimidate me much, and I'm not taken in by him."

"You saw him? Ah! Monsieur, so he was really there? I wasn't just dreaming? My God, my God, what does this mean?"

"This means that, by virtue of the special protection of a lovable and august princess who, I believe, is entertained by his follies more than she lends credence to them, he has entered the castle on his way to see her Royal Highness."

"But who is he? What is his name?"

"You don't know? Why then are you afraid?"

"In the name of Heaven, Monsieur, just tell me who he is!"

"Well, Trismegistus, Princess Amalia's sorcerer! One of those charlatans who ply the trade of predicting the future, revealing hidden treasures, making gold, and a thousand other parlor tricks that were all the fashion here before the glorious reign of Frederick the Great. You've certainly heard, Signora, that the abbess of Quedlinburg is still fond. . . ."

"Yes, yes, Monsieur, I know she studies the Kaballah, out of curiosity no doubt. . . ."

"Oh, certainly! How could one think that a princess, who is so enlightened, so learned, would take a serious interest in such nonsense?"

"In short, Monsieur, you know the man!"

"Oh, I've known him for quite a while. For the last four years or so he has been appearing here at least once every six to eight months. Since he's very peaceable and doesn't dabble in intrigue, His Majesty, having no wish to deprive his dear sister of any innocent pastimes, tolerates his presence in the city and even his unrestricted access to the palace. He doesn't abuse the privilege and only practices his so-called science here with Her Highness. Herr von Golowkin is his protector and answers for him. That's all I can tell you. But why do you take such a lively interest in this, Mademoiselle?"

"Rest assured, Monsieur, it doesn't interest me in the least. And since I don't want you to take me for a madwoman, I must tell you that this man seemed to bear—an illusion no doubt—a striking resemblance to a person who was once dear to me, and who still is; for, isn't it true, Monsieur, that death doesn't sever the bonds of affection?"

"A noble sentiment, Mademoiselle, and most worthy of a person of your merit. But you've had quite a shock, and I see that you can hardly stand on your feet. Allow me to see you home."

Once home, Porporina took to her bed for several days, tormented by a fever and an extraordinary nervous commotion. Then there was a letter from Mme von Kleist inviting her to come make music in her rooms at eight in the evening. This was merely a pretext for furtively getting Porporina into the palace. Having made their way through secret passages to the princess's suite, they found her charmingly attired, even though the rooms were scarcely lit, and all her servants had been dismissed for the evening, as she claimed to be indisposed. She gave the singer a most affectionate welcome. Taking her arm like an old friend, she led Porporina to a pretty little round room lit with fifty candles, where a dainty, tastefully elegant supper had been served. French *rococo* style had not yet invaded the Prussian court. At that time, moreover, Prussian aristocrats displayed sovereign contempt for the reigning king of France and confined themselves to imitating the traditions of the century of Louis XIV, for whom Frederick, secretly eager to ape the great king, professed boundless admiration. Yet Princess Amalia was dressed in the latest fashion. Though more chastely adorned than Mme de Pompadour was wont to be, she was no less splendid. Mme von Kleist had also put on her loveliest finery. And yet there were but three place settings and not a single servant.

"You're flabbergasted by our little feast," laughed the princess. "Well, you'll be even more so when you hear that the three of us shall sup and serve each other, as Mme von Kleist and I have already prepared everything ourselves. We set the table and lit the candles, and I've never had such fun. For the first time in my life I dressed and did my hair all by myself, and, to my mind at least, I've never looked better. In short, we're going to entertain ourselves *incognito*! The king is at Potsdam for the night, the queen at Charlottenburg, my sisters with the queen mother at Montbijou, my brothers, I don't know where, so we're alone in the castle. I'm supposed to be ill, and I'm taking advantage of this night of freedom to feel myself live a little and celebrate with the two of you (the only people in the world whom I can trust) my dear Trenck's escape. So we're going to toast his health with champagne, and if one of us gets tipsy, the others will keep the secret. Ah! This splendid, jolly feast will outshine Frederick's fine philosophical suppers!"

They sat down, and the princess showed herself in a whole new light to Porporina. She was kind, congenial, unaffected, lively, beautiful as an angel, in a word, adorable that evening, as she had been in her salad days. She seemed to swim in happiness, a pure, generous, unselfish happiness. Her lover was fleeing far away from her, she did not know if she would ever see him again, but he was free, his sufferings were over, and this radiant lover was pouring blessings upon fate.

"Ah, how fine I feel between the two of you!" she said to her confidantes, who formed with her the loveliest trio that refined coquetry has ever hidden away from the eyes of men. "I feel as free as Trenck right now; I feel as benevolent as he has always been, as I believed I would never be again! The fortress of Glatz was always pressing my soul. At night it weighed on my breast like a nightmare. I was cold in my feather bed, thinking that the man I loved was shivering on damp flagstones in a dark dungeon. I was no longer alive and couldn't enjoy a single thing. Ah! dear Porporina, just imagine how horrible it feels to tell yourself: It's because of me that he's suffering all this! It's my fatal love that has buried him alive!

"That thought turned every morsel of food to gall, just like the Harpies' breath.

"Pour me some champagne, Porporina. I've never liked it, and for two years I've drunk only water. Well, now it tastes like ambrosia. The candlelight is lovely, the flowers smell sweet, the delicacies are exquisite, and most of all, you are beautiful as two angels, you and von Kleist! Oh! yes, I see, I hear, I breathe; I'm alive again, no longer the statue, the cadaver that I was. Here, raise a toast with me, first to Trenck's health, then to the friend who escaped with him; next, to the fine guards who let him escape and, finally, to my brother Frederick who couldn't prevent it. No, no bitter thought will trouble this festival day. Now I don't feel bitterness toward anyone. I think I love the king. Now then, to the king's health, Porporina! Long live the king!"

Her good-natured ways and the perfect equality that she made reign among the three enhanced the well-being that the joy of this poor princess communicated to her two lovely guests. She got up, changed the plates when it was her turn, carved, and served her companions with a childlike, moving pleasure.

"Ah! While I wasn't born for the life of equality, love at least has made me understand it," she said, "and my wretched situation has shown me the idiocy of these antiquated notions of rank and birth. My sisters aren't like me. My sister von Anspach would rather lose her head than drop the first curtsey to anyone not wearing a crown, and my sister von Bayreuth, who plays the philosopher and freethinker with Monsieur Voltaire, would rip out the eyes of any duchess who dared have a train even an inch longer than hers. It's because they've never loved, you see! They'll spend their whole lives inside that vacuum pump they call the dignity of their rank. Like mummies, they'll die embalmed in their majesty. They won't have known my bitter sorrows, but neither will they have had, at any time in their lives of etiquette and fancy balls, a quarter hour of abandon, pleasure, and trust like the one I'm savoring just now! My little dears, you must make this the perfect feast and speak to me tonight as though I weren't a princess. I want to be Amalia for you; no more 'Your Highness,' just Amalia. Ah, you look reluctant, von Kleist! The court has spoiled you, my child. You've taken in that unhealthy air, despite yourself. But you, dear Porporina, even though you're an actress, you seem a child of nature. You'll yield to my innocent desire."

"Yes, my dear Amalia, with all my heart I will, as a favor to you," laughed Porporina.

"Heavens!" exclaimed the princess. "If you only knew how it makes me feel to hear someone speaking to me like that, calling me *Amalia*! Amalia! Oh, *he* had such a way of saying my name, he did! I found it was the most beautiful name on earth, the sweetest name a woman ever bore whenever he'd say it."

Little by little the princess's soul became so enraptured that she forgot herself and turned all her attention to her friends, and this experiment in equality made her feel so grand, happy, and good that she instinctively sloughed off the acrimonious self that passion and suffering had developed in her. No longer talking only about herself, no longer giving herself a little pat on the back for being so lovable and simple, she asked Mme von Kleist about her family, situation, and sentiments, which she had neglected to do since being absorbed in her own sorrows. She also wanted to know about the life of the artist, the excitement of the theater, and Porporina's thoughts and feelings. Inspiring trust, enjoying it as well, she took infinite pleasure reading in the souls of others and finally seeing, in these beings different from her up to this point, beings of the same essence, as worthy in God's eyes, as well endowed by nature, as important on the face of the earth as she was, all qualities with regard to which she had long been convinced to take priority over others.

It was especially Porporina whose ingenuous replies and sympathetic expansiveness filled her with respect mingled with sweet surprise.

"You seem like an angel to me," the princess told her. "You, a theater girl! You speak and think more nobly than any crowned head of my acquaintance. I feel a respect for you that goes to the point of infatuation. You must accord me all your respect, lovely Porporina. You must open your heart to me and tell me your life, the circumstances of your birth, your upbringing, your loves, your sorrows, even your faults, if you've committed any. Of course, they can only be noble faults, like the one I keep not on my conscience but in the sanctuary of my heart. It is eleven o'clock, we've got the whole night before us, our little *orgy* is winding down since now we're only talking, and I see that the second bottle of champagne would be too much. Will you tell me your story as I'm asking you to do? I have a feeling that learning your heart and seeing a life where everything will be new and unfamiliar to me is going to teach me more about our real duties in this world than my own meditations have ever succeeded in doing. I feel able to listen and follow you as I've never been able to listen to anything alien to my passion. Will you gratify my wish?"

"I would gladly do so, Madame . . . ," Porporina replied.

"Who are you talking to? Where did that 'Madame' come from?" the princess merrily cut in.

"I say, my dear Amalia, that I'd be pleased to," Porporina continued, "if in my life there weren't a great, almost dreadful secret on which everything hinges, a secret that no need to pour out my feelings nor any impulse of the heart allows me to reveal."

"Well, my dear child, your secret is known to me! I kept quiet about it at the start of our supper out of discretion. Now I feel no compunction about putting my affection for you above such considerations."

"What! You know my secret!" exclaimed Porporina, petrified with surprise. "Oh, Madame, I beg your pardon! I think that's impossible."

"A penalty for that *Madame*. You're still treating me like a princess."

"Pardon me, Amalia . . . , but you can't know my secret, not unless you're really in league with Cagliostro, as some people say."

"After hearing about your adventure with Cagliostro some time ago, I was dying to know all the details. But this evening my motivation is not curiosity, but affection, as I said in all sincerity. So, to encourage you, I'll tell you that since this morning I know that Signora Consuelo Porporina could legitimately take, if she so desired, the title of Countess von Rudolstadt."

"In the name of Heaven, Madame . . . Amalia . . . Who on earth could have told you that?"

"My dear Rudolstadt, don't you know that my sister, the Margravine von Bayreuth, is here?"

"I'm aware of that."

"And that Supperville, her doctor, came with her?"

"I see. Monsieur Supperville failed to keep his word, his promise. He's blabbed!"

"Don't worry. He's only blabbed to me, and under the seal of secrecy. Besides, I don't see why you're so afraid of people finding out something that only does you such honor and can no longer do anyone harm. The Rudolstadt family has all died out except for an ancient canoness who'll soon join her brothers in the grave. True, in Saxony there are some Rudolstadt princes who are your close relatives, second cousins, and very proud of their name. Yet, if my brother is willing to support you, you'll bear the name and they won't dare protest . . . unless you go on preferring your name of Porporina, which is just as glorious and much sweeter to the ear."

"That is indeed my intention, no matter what happens," replied the singer. "Yet I'd really like to know how Monsieur Supperville came to tell all this. . . . When I've learned that, and when my conscience is no longer bound by an oath, I promise to tell you, Madame . . . Amalia, every single thing about that sad, strange wedding."

"Here's how it happened," said the princess. "One of my maids was ill, so I asked Supperville, who I had heard was here at the castle with my sister, to come by to see her. Supperville is an intelligent man whom I got to know when he was in residence here. He didn't ever like my brother, which put me at ease to chat with him. We just happened to start talking about music and opera and therefore about you. I said such fine things about you that he, whether trying to please me or speaking out of conviction, went even further and praised you to the skies. I liked listening to him and remarked as well a keen desire on his part to make me sense in you a romantic life worthy of interest and a magnanimity surpassing all my fine suppositions. I pressed him a good deal, I have to tell you, and he needed a good deal of coaxing, I must say in his defense. Finally, after making me promise not to betray him, he told me about your wedding at the deathbed of Count von Rudolstadt and your generous renunciation of all the rights and privileges that had become yours. You see, my child, without compunction you can tell me the rest if you are not duty bound to keep it from me."

"That being the case," said Porporina after a moment of silence and keen emotion, "although this tale will certainly reawaken terribly painful memories in me, especially since I've been here in Berlin, I'll trustfully reply to Your Majesty's . . . I mean, my dear Amalia's expressions of interest."

Chapter VII

"I was born somewhere or other in Spain, and I don't know exactly when, but I must be twenty-three or twenty-four. I don't know my father's name, and as for that of my mother's father, I'm quite sure that she had the same uncertainty about her own parents. In Venice she was known as the Zingara, and I the Zingarella. My mother gave me Maria del Consuelo as my patron saint, in other words, Our Lady of Consolation. My early years were rambling and wretched, my mother and I traveling on foot all over the world and living off our songs. I have a vague memory about our receiving hospitality at a castle in the Bohemian forest where a handsome adolescent named Albert, the lord's son, showered me with care and affection and gave my mother a guitar. The castle was the Castle of the Giants, of which I would one day refuse to be the lady. The young lord was Count Albert von Rudolstadt, whose wife I was to become.

"At the age of ten I started singing in the streets. One day when I was doing my little song on the Piazza San Marco in Venice in front of a café, Professor Porpora, who happened to be there, was struck by the accuracy of my voice and the natural method that my mother had passed on to me. He called me over, asked me questions, followed me back to my hovel, gave my mother some help, and promised her that he'd get me into the *scuola dei mendicanti*, one of those free music schools you find all over Italy. All the eminent singers, men and women, come out of these schools because they're run by the best music teachers. There I made rapid progress, and Professor Porpora grew fond of me. Before long that made me the butt of my fellow students' jealousy and mean tricks. Their unfair resentment and contempt for my rags gave me early on the habits of patience, reserve, and resignation.

"I don't remember when I first saw him, but it is certain that by the age of seven or eight I already loved a young man, or rather a boy, an abandoned orphan. Like me, he studied music thanks to patronage and charity; like me, he lived on the streets. Our friendship or love—for it was the same thing—was a chaste, delightful sentiment. The hours that weren't devoted to study we spent together, innocently wandering around. My mother, after having vainly opposed our feelings, sanctioned them by the promise she made us contract on her deathbed; namely, we would get married as soon as our work put us in a position to raise a family.

"By the time I was eighteen or nineteen my singing was fairly advanced. Count Zustiniani, a Venetian nobleman and the owner of the Teatro San Samuele, heard me singing in church and hired me as the female lead to replace Corilla, a lovely, robust virtuoso whose lover he had been and who was unfaithful to him. This same Zustiniani was also the patron of my fiancé, Anzoleto, who was hired with me to sing the male leads. Our débuts were heralded by the most brilliant auspices. He had a magnificent voice, an extraordinary natural facility, a seductive appearance. All the beautiful ladies took him under their wing. But he was lazy. His professor hadn't been as clever and zealous as mine. His success was less brilliant. At first he was sad, then spiteful, and finally jealous, and that's how I lost his love."

"Can that be," asked Princess Amalia, "for such a reason? Was he really so vile?"

"Alas! No, Madame, but he was vain and artistic. He managed to gain the patronage of Corilla, the disgraced and furious diva, who stole his heart away from me and soon had him wound and rip apart my own. One evening, Professor Porpora, who had always opposed our feelings since he maintains that no woman can become a great artist unless her heart remains a stranger to all passion and commitment, made me discover Anzoleto's betrayal. The next evening Count Zustiniani declared his love for me. I was far from expecting this and felt deeply offended. Anzoleto pretended to be jealous, to believe that I had been defiled. . . . He wanted to break things off with me. I fled into the night and went to see my professor, a man of quick inspiration who had got me used to quick execution. He gave me some letters, a small sum of money, and a travel itinerary. Then he put me in a gondola, accompanied me to the mainland, and at dawn I was off to Bohemia all by myself."

"Bohemia?" asked Mme von Kleist, wide-eyed with amazement at Porporina's courage and virtue.

"Yes, Madame. In our lingo of itinerant artists we often talk about *roaming through Bohemia*, which means launching into a perilous life of poverty, toil, and often shame, the life of the Zingari, whom the French also call Bohemians. As for me, I wasn't heading for that symbolic Bohemia to which I like so many others seemed destined by my fate, but toward the troubled, chivalrous land of the Czechs, the homeland of Hus and Zizka, the Bohemian Forest, and finally the Castle of the Giants where I was generously welcomed by the Rudolstadt family."

"But why were you going to them?" asked the princess, who was listening attentively. "Did they remember seeing you as a child?"

"Not in the least. I had forgotten about it myself. It was only much later and by accident, that Count Albert remembered, then helped me remember that little adventure; but in Germany, Professor Porpora had become a close acquaintance of the venerable Christian von Rudolstadt, the head of the family. Young Baroness Amalia, his niece, was asking for a governess, meaning a young lady-companion who would pretend to teach her music and relieve her boredom amid the austere, dreary life that one led at Riesenburg.[1] Her good, noble family welcomed me like a friend, almost a relative. Despite my good intentions, I didn't teach my pretty, capricious student a single thing, and. . . ."

"And Count Albert fell in love with you, as was bound to happen?"

"Alas! Madame, I can't speak lightly of such a solemn, painful thing. Count Albert, whom people took for a madman, who conjoined a sublime soul and an inspired spirit with such strange oddities and an altogether inexplicable disorder of the imagination. . . ."

"I've already heard that from Supperville, who didn't believe it nor try to explain it to me either. People said the young man had supernatural powers, the gift of prophecy, second sight, the ability to make himself invisible. . . . His family told the most extraordinary tales about him. . . . But all this stuff is impossible, and I hope you don't lend it any credence."

"Spare me, Madame, the pain and perplexity of taking a position on matters that go beyond my ken. I saw inconceivable things, and at certain moments Count Albert seemed to me superhuman. At other moments I only saw in him a poor wretch deprived of the light of reason by the very excess of his virtue. Yet at no time did I ever see him as an ordinary human. Delirious or calm, inspired or dejected, he was always the best, the fairest, either the most sagely enlightened or the most poetically fanatic of men. In a word, I cannot think of him or say his name without a shudder of respect, keen emotion, and a sort of horror, for I am the involuntary though not altogether innocent cause of his death."

"Now, now, dear Countess, dry your lovely eyes, take courage, and tell me more. I'm listening to you without irony or profane levity, I swear."

"In the beginning it was impossible for me to guess that he loved me. He never spoke to me, he didn't even seem to see me. I think he first took notice that I was at the castle when he heard me singing. I have to tell you that he was a fine musician and played the violin as no one in the world suspects it can be played. Yet I believe that I'm the only one at Riesenburg who ever heard him, for

1. The Castle of the Giants, in German.

his family never knew about that incomparable talent of his. So his love for me was born of a burst of enthusiasm and musical affinity. His cousin, Baroness Amalia, his fiancée of two years whom he didn't love, came to resent me, even though she didn't love him either. She let me know it in ways that were frank more so than mean; for along with her failings, she had a certain magnanimity. She was weary of Albert's coldness, the dreary castle, and one fine morning she left, kidnapping, as it were, her father, Baron Frederick, who was Count Christian's brother. Baron Frederick was an excellent man with a narrow, lazy mind and a simple heart, a slave to his daughter and a great fan of hunting."

"You haven't said a word about Count Albert's *invisibility*, when he would disappear for fifteen or twenty days at a time, then suddenly reappear, believing or pretending to believe that he hadn't left the house, unwilling or unable to say what he had been doing while everyone had been searching all over for him."

"Since Monsieur Supperville has already told you about this apparently supernatural phenomenon, I'll explain it to you. I'm the only one who can, for this was always a secret between Albert and me. Near the Castle of the Giants is a mountain called Schreckenstein,[2] and hidden away inside are a cave and several mysterious chambers, an ancient subterranean construction going back to the time of the Hussites. Albert, all the while reading a series of very daring philosophical opinions and with a religious enthusiasm carried to the point of mysticism, had remained in his heart a Hussite or, more exactly, a Taborite. As a descendant of King George Podiebrad on his mother's side, he had retained and developed the patriotic independence and evangelical equality with which the sermons of John Hus and the victories of Jan Zizka had, as it were, inoculated the Bohemians. . . ."

"How she talks about history and philosophy!" exclaimed the princess, casting an eye at Mme von Kleist. "Who would ever have tried to tell me that a theater girl would understand these things as I do, having spent my life poring over them in books? Wasn't I telling you, von Kleist, that among these beings that court opinion relegates to the lowest ranks of society there were minds equal if not superior to those formed in the highest ranks with such care and at such expense!"

"Alas, Madame!" continued Porporina, "I am very ignorant, and I hadn't read a thing before I arrived at Riesenburg. But there I heard so much talk about these matters, and I was forced to think so much in order to understand what was happening in Albert's mind that I wound up acquiring some notion of them."

2. The rock of horror.

"Yes, but you've gone mystical and a bit mad yourself, my child! Go ahead and admire the military campaigns of Jan Zizka and the republican spirit of Bohemia. On that score, my ideas may be just as democratic as yours, for love has revealed to me, too, a truth that contradicts what my pedants had taught me about peoples' rights and individual merit. Yet I don't share your admiration for Taborite fanaticism and their mania for Christian equality. It's absurd, unrealizable, and it leads to ferocious excesses. It's fine with me if they overthrow kings, and . . . I might give them a hand if necessary! Fine too if they set up republics like those in Sparta, Athens, Rome, or old Venice! I can accept that. But I don't like your bloodthirsty, filthy Taborites any better than the Waldensians of blazing memory, the odious Anabaptists of Munster and the Picards of ancient Germany."

"I heard Count Albert say that these are not all exactly the same thing," Consuelo modestly replied. "But I wouldn't dare discuss with Your Highness subjects that she has studied. Here in Berlin you've got historians and scholars who have dealt with these weighty matters, and you're a better judge than I of their wisdom and fairness. Yet, even with the good fortune of having a whole academy to teach me things, I doubt that my sympathies would change. But I'll go on with my tale."

"Yes, I interrupted you with pedantries, and I ask your forgiveness. Count Albert, who was infatuated with his forefathers' exploits (this is quite conceivable and quite excusable), who was also enamored of you, which is more natural and even more legitimate, wouldn't accept that you were not deemed his equal before God and man? He was quite right, but that was no reason to desert his father's house and leave his whole family in distress."

"That's the point I wanted to make," replied Consuelo. "For a long time he had been going off to the Hussite cave at Schreckenstein to dream and meditate, and he liked these subterranean dwellings all the more because only he and a poor, crazy peasant who followed him on his walks knew about them. He got into the habit of retreating there every time a domestic sorrow or violent emotion made him lose control of himself. He could feel his spells coming on, and to hide his delirium from his dismayed relatives, he would make his way to Schreckenstein through an underground passage that he had discovered, the entrance being a cistern in a flower-bed near his rooms. Once in his cave, he would forget the hours, the days, the weeks. Looked after by Zdenko, this peasant who was a poet and visionary, whose fanaticism was somewhat like his, Albert wouldn't dream of seeing the light of day again and returning home until the spell began to subside; and unfortunately his spells were growing each time longer and more intense. Finally, he was once gone so long that they thought he was dead, and I undertook to find his retreat. I succeeded but not without considerable trouble and danger. One night I had seen Zdenko stealthily creeping out of that cistern in the garden, and that's where I started down. Not knowing my way through these unfathomable depths, I nearly lost my life. At last I found Albert, managed to dissipate the dismal torpor in which he was immersed, brought him back to his relatives, and made him promise never to go back to that fateful cave without me. He gave in, but predicted that this would be a death sentence for him. That prediction was only too true."

"But how? On the contrary, you were bringing him back to life."

"No, Madame, not unless I managed to love him and never to be a cause of pain for him."

"What! You didn't love him? You went down into a hole, you risked your life going down into the bowels of the earth. . . ."

"Where crazy Zdenko, not understanding my intentions and eager to protect his master like a faithful, stupid dog, nearly killed me. A torrent nearly swallowed me up. Albert didn't recognize me at first and nearly made me share his madness, for fear and strong emotion make hallucinations contagious. . . . Finally, he lapsed into another spell of delirium while leading me back into the caves and came close to shutting me in and abandoning me there. . . . And to all that I exposed myself without loving Albert."

"So you had made a vow to Maria del Consuelo to save him?"

"Something like that, indeed," said Consuelo with a sad smile. "An act of tender pity for his family, of deep affection for him, perhaps romantic attraction, certainly sincere friendship, but not love, at least nothing like that blind, drunken, sweet love I had felt for that thankless Anzoleto, which I think wore my heart out prematurely! . . . What can I say, Madame? After that terrifying expedition I was delirious and at death's door. Albert, who is as great a doctor as he is a musician, saved me. My slow convalescence and his assiduous care put us on a close footing, like a sister and brother. He completely returned to his senses. His father gave me his blessing and cherished me like a daughter. His hunchbacked old aunt, Canoness Wenceslawa, an angel of tenderness and a patrician brimming with prejudices, would even have resigned herself to accepting me. Albert beseeched me to love him. Count Christian went so far as to plead his son's case. I was touched as well as frightened. I loved Albert as one loves virtue, truth, and ideal beauty; yet I was still afraid of him and abhorred the thought of becoming a countess, of contracting a marriage that would stir up the local gentry against him and his family, that would prompt accusations of sordid designs and vile intrigue against me. And then, must I confess it? This may be my only crime! . . . I missed my career, my freedom, my old teacher, my life as an artist, and that thrilling arena of the theater where I had momentarily appeared, blazing forth and disappearing like a meteor; that ardent stage where my love had been shattered, my grief consummated, that I thought I could always curse and scorn, yet where every night in my dreams people were either clapping or hooting me down. . . .

"This must seem to you strange and contemptible. Yet, when one has been reared for the theater, when one has worked her whole life long to join these battles and take these victories, when the first contests have been won, the thought of never going back is as frightening as would be to you, Madame and dear Amalia, the idea of not being a princess any longer except on stage, as I am now twice a week. . . ."

"Wrong, you're spouting nonsense, dear friend! If I could turn from a princess into an artist, I'd marry Trenck and be happy! You didn't want to turn from an artist into a princess to marry Rudolstadt. It's clear you didn't love him! But that's not your fault. . . . Love is not subject to command."

"Madame, that's an aphorism I'd very much like to be able to believe; it would put my conscience at rest. But I've spent my life trying to resolve this problem, and I'm not there yet."

"Let's see," said the princess. "This is a solemn matter, and as an abbess, I have to try and adjudicate cases of conscience. You doubt that we're free to love or not to love? So you think that love is a matter of choice and reason?"

"That's how it ought to be. A noble heart should be ruled not by what the world calls reason, which is nothing but folly and lies, but by that noble discernment that is merely the love of beauty and truth. You're proof of that, Madame, and I'm condemned by your example. Born to occupy a throne, you've sacrificed false grandeur to true passion, to the possession of a heart worthy of your own. I was born to be a queen, too (on stage), but I lacked the courage and generosity to make a joyful sacrifice of all that glittering, deceptive glory for the sake of the serene life and sublime affection being offered me. I was ready to do so out of a sense of devotion, but not without sorrow and dread; and Albert, who saw how anxious I was, didn't want me to agree to marry him as a sacrifice. He was asking me for enthusiasm, shared joys, a heart free of all regret. It wouldn't have been right to try and deceive him. Besides, is it possible to deceive anyone about such things? So I requested more time, which was granted me. I promised to do what I could to love him as he loved me. I was sincere, but it was terrifying to feel that I wanted my conscience not to force me into making this formidable commitment."

"What a strange girl you are! You still loved the *other one*, I'd wager!"

"Oh, my God! I truly believed that I didn't, but one morning while waiting for

Albert on the mountain to take a walk with him, I hear a voice down in the ravine; I recognize a piece that I had once studied with Anzoleto; above all I recognize that penetrating voice I had loved so dearly, and that Venetian accent so sweet to my memory; I lean over and see a man on horseback. It was he, Madame, Anzoleto!"

"Good God! What was he doing in Bohemia?"

"I've since learned that he had broken his contract and was fleeing Venice and Count Zustiniani's wrath. Soon weary of the quarrelsome, despotic love of Corilla, with whom he had performed again at the Teatro San Samuele to much applause, he had won the favors of a certain Clorinda, a second soprano and my old schoolmate, whom Zustiniani had made his mistress. As a man of the world, in other words, a frivolous libertine, the count took vengeance by taking back Corilla without dismissing Clorinda. In the middle of this double intrigue, Anzoleto became the butt of his rival's jokes, which he resented. Resentment turned to rage, and one fine summer night he delivered a tremendous kick to the gondola in which Zustiniani was enjoying the cool with Corilla. The gondola capsized, and they got off with a lukewarm bath. The waters of Venice are not deep everywhere. Yet Anzoleto, who felt sure that this joke would mean a little trip to the Prison of Lead, took flight. Headed for Prague, he passed by the Castle of the Giants.

"He continued on his way, and I caught up with Albert for a pilgrimage to the Schreckenstein cave that he wanted to see again with me. Gloomy and upset, I experienced the most painful emotions in that cave. The lugubrious place, the bones out of which Albert had fashioned an altar near the mysterious spring, the admirable, heartrending sounds of his violin, vague terrors, the shadows, the superstitious notions that came back to him in this place, from which I no longer had the strength to protect him. . . ."

"Say it all! He thought he was Jan Zizka. He claimed to have eternal life, the remembrance of centuries past. In short, he had the same delusions as the Count de Saint-Germain?"

"Well, yes, Madame, since you already know this, and his firm belief in that regard made such an impression on me that, instead of curing him of these notions, I almost came to share them."

"Could it be that, despite your brave heart, your head is weak and suggestible?"

"I cannot pretend to be a free thinker. Where would I have come by that? The only serious education I've had was given to me by Albert. How could I not fall under his influence and come to share his illusions? There were so many and such lofty truths in his soul that I couldn't distinguish fact from fallacy. In that cave I felt my mind coming unhinged. What terrified me the most was that I didn't find Zdenko there, as I had expected him to be. He hadn't been seen for several months. Because Zdenko had persisted in his rage against me, Albert had sent him away, expelled him from his presence, no doubt after some violent argument, for he seemed remorseful. Perhaps he thought that Zdenko had gone away and killed himself. In any case, he talked about him in puzzling terms and with a mysterious reserve that made me shudder. I imagined (God forgive me!) that in a fit of frenzy Albert, unable to make the poor wretch give up his murderous intentions toward me, had murdered him himself."

"And why did Zdenko hate you so?"

"That was a result of his madness. He had dreamed, he said, that I killed his master, then danced on his grave. Oh, Madame! That sinister prediction came true! My love killed Albert, and a week later I made my début here in Berlin in the merriest comic opera. True, I was forced to do so and felt sick at heart. Even so, Albert's somber fate had been fulfilled, in accordance with Zdenko's terrifying prognostic."

"My word, your story is so diabolical that I'm starting to lose my place as well as my wits. But go on. That will all be explained no doubt?"

"No, Madame. I never got an explanation for the fantastic world that Albert and Zdenko carried in their souls. Like me, you'll just have to make do with seeing what happened."

"Come on! At least, Rudolstadt hadn't killed his poor buffoon?"

"Zdenko wasn't a buffoon for him, but a companion in misery, a friend, a devoted servant. Albert mourned him, but, thank God, it had never crossed his mind to sacrifice his friend to his love for me. Yet I, foolish and guilty, felt sure that the deed had been done. There was a freshly turned grave in the cave. I went into a cold sweat when Albert, who was accusing himself of I-don't-know-what crime, told me that it contained what had been most dear to him before we had known each other. There was no doubt in my mind that this was Zdenko's tomb, and I ran out of the cave screaming like a madwoman and weeping like a baby."

"And with good reason," said Mme von Kleist. "I'd have been scared to death. A lover like your Albert wouldn't have suited me in the least. My worthy husband believed in the devil and made sacrifices to him. It's because of him that I'm such a coward. If I hadn't made up my mind to divorce him, he'd have driven me mad."

"It's clear that he nearly succeeded," said Princess Amalia. "I think you divorced a bit too late. But don't interrupt our Countess von Rudolstadt."

"When I got back to the castle with Albert, who followed me without giving a thought to clearing himself of my suspicions, can you guess who was there, Madame?"

"Anzoleto!"

"Having introduced himself as my brother, he was waiting for me. I don't know how he had learned en route that I lived there and was going to marry Albert; for people in the area were saying so before anything had been settled. Whether out of spite, a vestige of love, or a love of trouble, he had come back with the sudden intention of stopping the wedding and whisking me away from the count. He tried everything: entreaties, tears, enticements, and threats. I looked unshakable, but deep in my fainting heart I was upset and no longer felt in control. Thanks to the lie that had got him into the castle, and which I dared not refute, even though I had never mentioned to Albert this nonexistent brother, he spent the whole day at the castle. That evening the old count had us sing Venetian airs, and these songs of my adoptive land reawakened all my memories of childhood, of my pure love, beautiful dreams, and past happiness. I felt that I still loved . . . and that it wasn't the one I was supposed to love, wanted to love and had promised to love. In a whisper, Anzoleto begged me to allow him a visit to my room that night, threatening to come, despite my objections, at his own risk and especially at mine. I had only ever been a sister to him, so he put the best possible face on his intentions. He submitted to my decree and was leaving at daybreak, but he wanted to bid me farewell. I thought he intended to create a fuss in the castle, a scandal; that there would be some terrible scene with Albert and I would be sullied. I made a desperate resolution and carried it out. At midnight I packed a few necessities, wrote Albert a note, and took the little money I had (and, in parenthesis, forgetting the half of it). I left my room, jumped on Anzoleto's hired horse, paid his guide to help me get away, crossed the drawbridge, and reached the next town. This was my first time on a horse. I galloped four leagues, then sent the guide on his way. Pretending that I was going to wait for Anzoleto on the road to Prague, I gave the man false instructions about where my so-called brother was to meet me. I headed toward Vienna and at the break of day found myself alone, on foot, without resources, in an unknown country and marching as fast as I could to escape from these two loves that to my mind were equally deadly. Yet I must say that after a few hours the phantom of perfidious Anzoleto left my soul, never to return, whereas the pure image of my noble Albert followed me, like a shield and a promise for the future, through the dangers and toils of my voyage."

"And why were you going to Vienna, instead of back to Venice?"

"Professor Porpora had just arrived in Vienna, brought there by our ambassador, who wanted to restore his depleted fortune as well as his former glory which had paled and drooped before the successes of more felicitous innovators. I was lucky to make the acquaintance of an excellent boy, already a musician full of promise. On his travels through the Bohemian forest he had heard about me and decided to seek me out to ask that I recommend him to Porpora. We hiked back to Vienna together, often very tired, always merry, always friends and brothers. I grew all the more attached to him for two reasons: he didn't dream of courting me, nor did it ever cross my mind that he might dream of it. I dressed as a boy and played the role so well that I was the cause of all kinds of amusing misapprehensions. Yet there was one that was nearly fatal to both of us. I'll keep silent about the others so that this tale doesn't go on too long, and I'll only mention this one because I know that it will interest Your Highness much more than all the rest of my story."

Chapter VIII

"I guess you're going to talk to me about *him*," said the princess, pushing aside the candles to see the storyteller better and setting her elbows on the table.

"While Haydn and I were traveling down the banks of the Moldau, on the Bavarian border we were kidnapped by army recruiters working for your brother the king and delighted by the cheery prospect of becoming fife and drum in the glorious armies of His Majesty!"

"You, a drummer boy?" the princess burst out laughing. "Ah! If von Kleist had caught sight of you like that, I bet you would have swept her off her feet. My brother would have made you his page, and God knows what a swath you would have cut through the hearts of our lovely ladies. But what's this about Haydn? The name is familiar to me. I received some music from this Haydn a little while back, and it's good stuff. He's not the boy you're talking about?"

"I beg your pardon, Madame. Haydn is a boy of about twenty who looks about fifteen. He was my traveling companion, a true and faithful friend as well. At the edge of a little wood where our kidnappers stopped for lunch, we bolted. They followed. We ran like hares and were fortunate to catch up with a traveling coach in which the noble, handsome Frederick von Trenck and an erstwhile conquering hero, Count Hoditz von Roswald, were riding."

"You mean the husband of my aunt, the Margravine von Kulmbach?" exclaimed the princess. "There's another love-match for you, von Kleist! In her whole life, moreover, that's the only wise and honest thing my portly aunt ever did. So, what is he like, this Count Hoditz?"

Consuelo was about to undertake a full portrait of the lord of Roswald, but the princess interrupted with a thousand questions about Trenck, what he was wearing that day, down to every last detail. And when Consuelo told her how Trenck had flown to her defense, how he had almost taken a bullet, how finally he had chased off the marauders and freed a poor deserter whom they found bound hand and foot in their little cart, she had to start all over again, explaining every little thing and relating the most trivial of words. The princess's joy and emotion reached a zenith when she heard that once Trenck and Count Hoditz had taken the two young travelers into their coach, the baron paid no attention to Consuelo and kept gazing at a portrait hidden in his bosom, sighing and talking to the count about a mysterious love for a highly placed person, the joy and despair of his life.

When Consuelo was finally allowed to go on, she told how Count Hoditz, having divined her sex at Passau, had tried to take a bit too much advantage of the protection he had granted her, after which she ran away with Haydn to continue her humble, adventurous voyage on a boat going down the Danube.

Finally, she told how she with her shepherd's pipe and Haydn with his violin had been making peasants dance and playing for their supper when one evening, still disguised as Signor Bertoni, itinerant musician and zingaro by trade, she arrived at a nice little priory.

"The hospitaler of this priory," Consuelo continued, "was a passionate music-lover as well as an intelligent man with an excellent heart. He was very friendly to us, especially to me, and even wanted to adopt me, promising me a nice benefice if I would only take minor orders. I was growing weary of the male sex. I didn't like the tonsure any better than the drum, but a bizarre event made me stay on a bit with that kind host. A woman traveling by express coach went into labor at the priory gate and gave birth to a little girl that she abandoned the next morning, and I persuaded the fine canon to adopt the baby in my place. She was named Angela, after her father Anzoleto, and Madame Corilla, her mother, went off to Vienna to solicit a contract at the imperial theater. She got it, at my exclusion. Prince von Kaunitz presented her to Empress Maria Theresa as a respectable widow, and I was rejected, as someone accused and vehemently suspected of being in love with Joseph Haydn, who was taking lessons from Porpora and living in the same building as we did."

Consuelo detailed her interview with the great empress. Princess Amalia was very curious to hear about that extraordinary woman, whose virtue was considered most dubious in Berlin, where it was said that Prince von Kaunitz, Doctor Van Swieten, and the poet Metastasio were all her lovers.

Finally Consuelo recounted her reconciliation with Corilla in connection with Angela and her début in the leading roles at the imperial theater, thanks to that strange girl's twinges of conscience and burst of generosity. Then she turned to her sweet, noble friendship with Baron von Trenck at the Venetian ambassador's house and reported in minute detail that while saying their goodbyes they had agreed upon a way of communicating with each other if the persecution on the part of the Prussian king were to make it necessary. She talked about the musical score whose pages would serve both as the envelope and signature of the letters that he would send her, if need be, for his beloved Amalia and also explained how she had been recently enlightened by one of these sheets as to importance of the cabalistic text she had delivered to the princess.

These elucidations, of course, took more time than the rest of her story. Finally, after having recounted how she had left Vienna with Porpora and met Frederick the Great, wearing the uniform of a lowly officer and bearing the name of Baron von Kreutz, at the fabulous castle of Count Hoditz in Moravia, she was forced to mention the tremendous favor she had done the king without knowing who he was.

"This I'm curious to hear," said Mme von Kleist. "Herr von Poelnitz, who loves to prattle, confided to me that His Majesty recently told guests over supper that his feelings for the lovely Porporina were caused by something more serious than a simple passing fancy."

"Yet what I did was very simple," replied Mme von Rudolstadt. "I used my influence over a miserable fanatic to prevent him from assassinating the king. Karl, the wretched Bohemian giant that Baron von Trenck had rescued from the recruiters along with me, had become one of Count Hoditz's servants. He had just recognized the king and wanted to take vengeance on him for his wife and child, who had both died of poverty and grief after he'd been kidnapped for the second time. Fortunately, he hadn't forgotten that I had helped save him and given his wife a hand. He let himself be talked into giving up his gun. The king, concealed in a nearby lodge, overheard everything, as he has since told me. Afraid that his would-be assassin might suffer some relapse of rage, he decided to leave by a road other than the one where Karl had planned to ambush him. The king was traveling alone on horseback with Herr von Buddenbrock, so it's very likely that a good shot like Karl would not have missed his target. That very morning I had seen him hit the pigeon on a pole three times at the festivities that Count Hoditz had arranged for us."

"God knows," said the princess, with a dreamy look, "what changes that misfortune would have brought about in the politics of Europe and the fate of individuals! Now, my dear Rudolstadt, I think I know very well the rest of your story up until Count Albert's death. In Prague you met up with his uncle the baron, who took you back to the Castle of the Giants to see him die of some wasting disease only seconds after having married you. So you hadn't been able to make up your mind to love him?"

"Alas, Madame! I loved him too late, and I've been very cruelly punished for all my hesitations and love of the theater. Forced by Professor Porpora to make my début in Vienna, deceived by him about Albert's condition—he did away with the last letters of Albert, who I thought cured of his fatal love for me—I let myself get carried away by the glamour of the stage and wound up, while awaiting my contract in Berlin, performing in Vienna with a sort of rapture."

"And with glory!" the princess added. "That we know."

"Wretched, fatal glory," Consuelo went on. "What Your Highness doesn't know is that Albert made a secret trip to Vienna and saw me perform. Following me around like a mysterious shadow, he overheard me confess to Joseph Haydn in the wings of the theater that I couldn't give up singing without a dreadful sense of regret. Yet I loved Albert! I had recognized, I swear to God, that giving him up was even more impossible than giving up my vocation, and I had written to tell him this; but Porpora, who called our love a chimera, madness, had intercepted my letter and burned it. When I returned to the castle, Albert was wasting away before my very eyes. I gave him my troth and could not give him back life.

"I saw him lying in state, dressed like a lord of old, beautiful in the arms of death, his brow serene like that of an angel of forgiveness. but I couldn't accompany him to his final resting place. I left him on a candle-lit bier in the Castle of the Giants, under the watch of that poor, mad prophet, Zdenko, who shook my hand, laughing and rejoicing in his friend's tranquil sleep. He, at least, more pious and faithful than I, placed him in the tomb of his forefathers, not realizing that Albert would never rise from that bed of repose! And I left, dragged away by Porpora, a devoted but ferocious friend, with a fatherly but inflexible heart, who was shrieking in my ears even beside my husband's coffin, 'Next Saturday is your début in the *Virtuosi ridicoli*!'"

"The strange vicissitude, indeed, of an artist's life!" said the princess, wiping away a tear, for Porporina was sobbing at the end of her story. "But you haven't said a word, dear Consuelo, about your finest deed, and that's the thing that Supperville related to me admiringly. To spare the old canoness and abide by your romantic indifference to money and position, you gave up your title, your dower, and your name; you asked Supperville and Porpora, the only witnesses to this hasty wedding, to keep everything secret; and you came here, poor as before, a Zingarella as always. . . ."

"And an artist for ever!" Consuelo replied, "meaning independent, virginal and dead to all feelings of love, finally just what Porpora had ceaselessly portrayed to me as the ideal for a priestess of the Muses! He has won, my terrifying master! And now I'm right where he wanted me to be! I don't find that I'm any happier or better for it. Without loving, without feeling able to love any more, I no longer feel the flame of inspiration, the thrill of the theater. This icy climate and the atmosphere at court have thrown me into dreary despond. Porpora's absence, the sort of isolation I feel, and, if I may be so bold, Madame, the king's desire to extend my engagement here against my will. . . ."

"I should have guessed as much! Poor child, people think you're proud of the king's predilection for you, but you're his prisoner and his slave, like me, like his whole family, like his favorites, his soldiers, his pages, his little dogs. Oh, the prestige of kings, the halo of great princes, what a sullen face you show to those whose life is drained to supply your radiant beams! But, dear Consuelo, you still have lots of things to tell me which interest me as well. I expect you, sincere as you are, to tell me exactly on what terms you are with my brother, and I'll call forth your sincerity with my own. Believing that you were his mistress, and flattering myself that you could wheedle out of him a pardon for Trenck, I sought you out to place our cause in your hands. Now that we don't need you for that, thank Heaven, and I'm delighted to love you for yourself, I think that you can tell me everything without compromising yourself, all the more because my brother doesn't seem to have made much headway with you."

"Your way of saying that makes me shudder, Madame," said Consuelo, growing pale. "For a week now people with solemn looks have been whispering around me about this so-called inclination of *our king and master* for his sad, trembling subject. Up to that point I had never seen as a possibility between us anything more than lively conversation, obliging on his part, deferential on mine. He showed me friendship and excessive gratitude for such a simple gesture at Roswald. Yet there's a huge gulf between that and love, and I certainly hope he hasn't bridged it in his mind."

"I think the opposite. He's abrupt, teasing, and familiar with you. He talks to you as if you were a little boy and pats you on the head as he would one of his greyhounds. For the last few days he's been claiming to his friends that he's less enamored of you than of anyone else. All this proves that he's starting to fall in love. I know him well, and I'm telling you that in a short while you'll have to make a decision. What will you do? If you resist, you're done for. If you surrender, you're in even bigger trouble. What will you do, should the occasion arise?"

"I'll neither resist nor surrender, Madame. Like his recruits, I'll desert."

"That's not easy, and I don't much like the idea, for I'm growing uncommonly attached to you, and I think I'd rather send the recruiters back out after you than see you go. Come on, we'll find a way. This is a serious matter, requiring careful thought. Tell me everything that has happened since Count Albert died."

"A few bizarre and inexplicable events in the middle of a monotonous, gloomy life. I'll give you the bare facts, and perhaps Your Highness can help me understand them."

"I'll try, as long as you call me Amalia, as you were doing a little while ago.

It's not midnight, and I don't want to be Your Highness before broad daylight tomorrow."

So Porporina went on with her story.

"I already told Mme von Kleist, when she first paid me a visit, that on our way from Bohemia I was separated from Porpora at the Prussian border. Even now I still don't know if there was something wrong with his passport, or if the king had anticipated our arrival with one of those prodigiously fast orders forbidding Porpora's entry into his realm. That was my first thought, reprehensible perhaps, for I remembered the brusque levity and rebellious sincerity with which Porpora had defended Trenck's honor and blamed the king's harsh treatment of the man. We were having supper at Count Hoditz's castle in Moravia, and the king, passing himself off as Baron von Kreutz, had just told us about Trenck's alleged treachery and his imprisonment at Glatz. . . ."

"You don't say!" exclaimed the princess. "So Trenck is the reason why the king is displeased with Professor Porpora?"

"The king never mentioned it to me again, and I was afraid to bring it back up. But it is certain that, despite all my pleas and His Majesty's promises, Porpora has never been called back."

"And never will be," said Amalia. "The king forgets nothing and never forgives frank words when they hurt his pride. The Solomon of the North hates and persecutes anyone who doubts the infallibility of his judgments, especially when his decree is just a crude sham, an odious pretext for getting rid of an enemy. So, go ahead and grieve, my child. You'll never see Porpora in Berlin."

"Despite my sadness at his absence, I no longer wish to see him here, Madame, and I won't do anything more to try and get the king to pardon him. This morning I had a letter from my teacher telling me that the Imperial Theater of Vienna has accepted one of his operas. After a thousand setbacks he has finally achieved his goal, and the casting is about to begin. Now I'd rather think about joining him there than getting him here, but I'm very much afraid that I'm no freer to leave than I was free not to come."

"What do you mean by that?"

"At the border, when I saw Porpora being forced into his carriage and made to turn back, I wanted to go with him and give up my engagement in Berlin. I was so outraged about the brutality and obvious bad faith of such a reception that I would have paid the penalty with the sweat of my brow rather than going one step farther into a country ruled so despotically. Yet at the first sign I gave of my intentions, the policeman ordered me to get into another express coach that was brought out and hitched up in a flash. Finding myself surrounded by soldiers who were very determined to use force if necessary, I kissed Porpora with tears in my eyes and decided to allow myself to be driven to Berlin where I arrived at midnight, overwhelmed with exhaustion and distress. I was deposited in a pretty little house nearby the palace and not far from the Opera. It belonged to the king and was set up in such a way that I'd be absolutely alone. There were servants at my disposal, with supper ready and waiting. I learned that Herr von Poelnitz had received orders to arrange everything for my arrival. I had scarcely got settled when Baron von Kreutz asked if I could receive a visit. I had him immediately shown in as I was eager to complain about Porpora's treatment and ask for amends. For that reason I pretended not to know that Baron von Kreutz was Frederick II. This was plausible since Karl, the deserter, had told me without naming names that he had planned to assassinate a senior Prussian officer, and Count Hoditz hadn't told me who that really was until after the king had left Roswald. He entered the room looking pleasant and affable, different from the way I'd seen him in disguise. Under a false name and in a foreign land, he had been a bit ill at ease. It seemed to me that in Berlin he had slipped back into all the majesty of his role, that is, the sheltering kindness and generous amiability with which he can so skillfully adorn his omnipotence on occasion. He came forward offering me his hand and asking if I remembered seeing him somewhere. 'Indeed, Baron,' I replied, 'and I remember that you offered and promised me your services in Berlin if I ever happened to need them.' Then I gave him a lively account of my experiences at the border and asked if he couldn't transmit to the king a request that amends be made for the outrage inflicted upon an illustrious professor and the coercion exercised upon my person. 'Amends!' replied the king with a mischievous smile. 'Nothing less? Monsieur Porpora wishes to challenge the King of Prussia to a duel! Perhaps Mlle Porporina will require that the king approach her on bended knee!'

"This mockery made me even angrier. 'Your Majesty may add irony to injury,' I replied, 'but I'd rather have to bless the king than to fear him.'

"The king gave my arm a bit of a rough shake. 'Ah ha! you too are trying to outfox me!' he said fixing his penetrating eyes on mine. 'I thought you were simple and straightforward. But you knew exactly who I was at Roswald, right?' 'No, Sire,' I replied, 'I didn't know you, and would to heaven that I had never known you!' 'I can't say the same myself,' he said in a sweet tone of voice. 'Had it not been for you, I might have remained in some ditch on the grounds of Roswald. Success on the battlefield is no shield against an assassin's bullet, and I'll never forget that if I still hold Prussia's destiny in my hands, I owe it to a fine little soul who is the enemy of cowardly plots. For that reason, my dear Porporina, your bad temper won't make me ungrateful. Calm down please, and tell me all your complaints, for I haven't understood much thus far.'

"Either the king was pretending to know nothing about it, or maybe his police truly thought there was some procedural problem with my teacher's papers. In any case, he listened to my tale very attentively. Then, like a judge who doesn't want to pronounce a verdict without due consideration, he said, 'I'll look into all this and get back to you with a proper account of the matter. I'd be most surprised if, for no reason, my men had picked a quarrel with someone whose papers were in order. There must be some misunderstanding. I'll find out, rest assured, and if somebody went beyond his mandate, he'll be punished.'

"'Sire, that's not what I'm asking. I'm asking you to call Porpora back here to Berlin.' 'And that's what I'm promising you,' he replied. 'Now, stop looking so glum, and tell me how you penetrated the mystery of my disguise.'

"Then I began talking freely with the king, and I found him so kind, so amiable and his words so seductive that I forgot all my biases against him and just admired that judicious, brilliant mind, that easy benevolence that I had never found in Maria Theresa; in short, that delicacy of feeling expressed on every topic he broached in our conversation.

'Listen,' he said, picking up his cap on his way out, 'Here's a piece of friendly advice on your arrival here. Don't tell a single soul about the good turn you did me, and don't mention my visit tonight either. Although my eagerness to thank you only speaks highly for both of us, it would create a very false impression about the relations of intellect and affection I want to have with you. People would think you eager to curry, as they say in courtly circles, the master's favor. Some would be suspicious of you; others would be jealous. At the very least, you'd find yourself surrounded by a swarm of supplicants wanting to make you a conduit for their silly requests, and as you would probably have the good sense not to want to play this role, you'd be exposed to their obsessions or their enmity.' 'I promise Your Majesty that I'll do as ordered,' I replied. 'I haven't given you any orders, Consuelo, but I'm counting on your wisdom and rectitude. When I first set eyes on you, I saw a beautiful soul and a just mind; and it's because I wanted to make you the true pearl of my department of fine arts that I ordered from the depths of Silesia that immediately upon your arrival at the border you should be supplied with a carriage at my expense and driven to Berlin. It's not my fault if they made it a sort of prison on wheels and separated you from your protector. While you're waiting for him to be rendered to you, I'll take his place if you find me worthy of the same confidence and affection.'"

"I have to admit, *my dear Amalia*, that I was deeply moved by these fatherly words and delicate feelings. Perhaps there was also a touch of pride. Tears came to my eyes when the king gave me his hand in parting. I nearly kissed it, as was probably my duty. Yet, since I'm in the middle of a confession, I must say that just then I was gripped with terror and nearly paralyzed by the chill of suspicion. I felt that the king was making a fuss over me and flattering my pride to prevent me from telling others about that scene at Roswald, which could produce, in certain minds, an impression contrary to his interests. I also felt that he was afraid of looking like a fool for having shown me kindness and gratitude. Then, in a flash I thought of Prussia with its terrifying military regime, which Baron Trenck had described to me in such minute detail—the recruiters' ferocity, Karl's misfortunes, noble Trenck's imprisonment, which I attributed to the poor deserter's freedom; the screams of a soldier whom I saw being thrashed one morning while crossing a village; and the whole despotic system that makes the great Frederick's strength and glory. I could no longer feel any personal hatred for him. Yet I was already seeing him again as the absolute master, the natural enemy of those hearts that fail to understand the need for inhuman laws, that will never know how to penetrate the arcane mysteries of empires."

Chapter IX

"Since that day," Porporina went on, "the king hasn't paid me any more visits at home. He has, however, summoned me to Sans-Souci a few times, where I've even stayed several days in a row with my colleagues Porporino and Conciolini; and here at the palace, to play the harpsichord at his little concerts, accompanying Herr Graun or Benda on the violin, Herr Quantz on the flute, or even the king himself."

"Which is much less pleasant than accompanying the others," said the Prussian princess, "for I know from experience that whenever my dear brother hits a wrong note or loses the rhythm, he blames the people he's playing with and picks a quarrel."

"That's true," said Porporina. "And his clever teacher, Herr Quantz, hasn't always been safe from his petty injustices. Yet, when His Majesty lets himself go like that, he soon makes amends with marks of deference and delicate praise that are balm to wounded pride. With a fond word or just a whoop of admiration, he gets even artists, who are the touchiest people in the world, to forgive his harsh treatment and tantrums."

"But you, with everything you knew about him as well as your modest rectitude, you could allow yourself to be charmed by this basilisk?"

"I'll confess, Madame, I've quite often fallen under his sway without realizing it. These little tricks have never been part of my trade, I never fail to fall for them, and it's only later, when I'm thinking things through, that I see them for what they are. Also, I've often seen the king on stage and even sometimes in my dressing room after the performance. He's always been fatherly with me. But I've been alone with him just two or three times in the gardens at Sans-Souci, and only then, I must confess, after keeping my eye on the time of his walks and deliberately putting myself in his path. Then he would hail me or courteously approach, and I'd seize the occasion by the forelock to bring up Porpora and renew my request. Each time I'd get the same promises, but never any results. Later on I changed tactics and asked permission to go back to Vienna, but the king would listen to my pleas with fond reproach or icy silence, but most often with rather marked displeasure. My last try got me no further than the others; and even after the king had snapped, 'Leave, Mademoiselle, you are free,' I received neither the wages owed me, nor a passport, nor permission to travel. That's how things stand now, and I see nothing but flight as a resort if my position here becomes unbearable. Alas, Madame, though I was often hurt by Maria Theresa's lack of taste for music, it never occurred to me then that a music-loving king could be a far worse problem than an empress with a tin ear.

"That's the gist of my relations with His Majesty. Never have I had any reason to fear or even suspect this whim of loving me that Your Highness wants to ascribe to him. Yet I've sometimes taken pride in thinking that the king felt some sort of affection for me, thanks to my modest musical talent and the romantic episode in which I had the good fortune to save his life. He's often said as much to me, and with such grace, an air of such sincere abandon; and he's seemed to take such good-natured pleasure in our conversations that I've grown accustomed, perhaps unwittingly and certainly quite in spite of myself, to feeling some sort of affection for him too. That word may be odd and no doubt out of place in my mouth, but the fond respect and timid trust that this royal basilisk, as you call him, inspires in me with his presence, gaze, voice, and sweet words are as strange as they are sincere. We are not to hold anything back here, and it's agreed that I won't stand on ceremony. Well, I declare that I'm afraid of the king, almost horrified when he is out of sight, and I'm breathing the rarefied air of his empire; but when I see him, I'm under the spell and ready to give him all the proof of devotion that a shy but dutiful daughter can give an inflexible but kindly father."

"You're making me shudder," exclaimed the princess. "Good God, what if you gave him the upper hand or let him cajole you into betraying our cause!"

"Oh, Madame! Have no fear! That will never happen! When it's a matter of my friends or simply people other than myself, I challenge the king and even craftier sorts, if there be, to make me fall into a trap."

"That I believe. You are working on me, with your air of sincerity, the same spell that Frederick works on you. Now, don't get all excited; I'm not making any comparisons. Go on with your story and tell me about Cagliostro. I've heard tell that while doing his magic he showed you a dead man who was Count Albert, I suppose?"

"I'm prepared to satisfy you, noble Amalia, but if I decide to tell you yet another painful adventure, one that I'd like to be able to forget, I have the right, by our agreement, to ask you a few questions."

"I'm prepared to answer."

"Well, Madame, do you believe that the dead can leave the grave? Or, at least, that a reflection of their form, animated by the semblance of life, can be conjured up by a magician and take such hold of our imagination that it appears before our eyes and unsettles our minds?"

"That's a very complicated question, and all I can say is that I don't believe in anything impossible, no more in magic than in the resurrection of the dead. As for our poor, mad imagination, it's capable of anything."

"Your Highness doesn't believe in magic, and yet. . . . But I'm no doubt being indiscreet?"

"Out with it, 'And yet I'm a devotee of magic,' as everyone knows. Well, my child, let me explain that bizarre inconsistency to you at the proper time and place. Given that the magical formulas sent by the sorcerer Saint-Germain boiled down to a letter to me from Trenck, you can already sense that this so-called necromancy is apt to serve as a pretext for many things. But it would take a long time to reveal to you everything that magic hides from the eyes of ordinary folks, court espionage, and tyrannical laws. Just be patient, for I've resolved to initiate you into all my secrets. You're a worthier candidate than my dear von Kleist, with her timid, superstitious mind. Yes, such as you see, this tender heart, this angel of kindness has no common sense. She believes in the devil, sorcerers, ghosts, and omens, just as if she weren't intimately acquainted with all the mysteries of the philosopher's stone. She's like those alchemists in times past who would patiently, knowingly set about creating monsters, then shudder with horror at what they had wrought and wind up enslaved to some genie having emerged from their alembic."

"Perhaps I'd be no braver than Mme von Kleist," Porporina continued, "and I confess that I've had quite a sample of Cagliostro's power, if not of his infallibility. Just imagine, after having promised to make me see the person I had in mind, whose name he claimed to read in my eyes, he showed me someone else. What is more, he showed me this person as someone alive, all the while seeming to have no idea that he was dead. Yet, despite this double error, he resurrected before my eyes the husband I lost, which will never cease to be a painful, terrifying puzzle for me."

"He showed you some phantom or other, and your imagination did all the rest."

"It wasn't a matter of my imagination, let me assure you. I was expecting to see, behind a veil or reflected in a mirror, some portrait of Professor Porpora, for over supper I had mentioned his name several times, and while I was moaning about his absence, it hadn't escaped me that Cagliostro was paying close attention to my words. To make things easier for him, I decided on Porpora as the subject of the apparition and was resolutely waiting to see him, not taking things seriously up to that point. In short, if there was ever a moment in my life when I wasn't thinking about Count von Rudolstadt, it was just then. On the threshold of his magic laboratory Cagliostro asked if I would let him cover my eyes and lead me by the hand. Knowing him to be a gentleman, I didn't hesitate to accept his offer, on the sole condition that he not leave me alone for a second.

"'I was just about to ask you,' he said, 'not to leave my side or drop my hand, no matter what happens, no matter what feelings come over you.' I gave him my word, but a simple assertion wouldn't satisfy him. He made me solemnly swear not to make a single move or sound, in short, to remain mute and impassive during the apparition. Then he put on his glove, and after covering my head with a black velvet hood that went all the way down to my shoulders, he had me walk for five minutes or so, during which time I didn't hear any doors opening or closing. The hood prevented me from noticing any change of air, so I didn't know if we had left the laboratory, and in order to confuse my sense of direction, he led me this way and that. Finally, he stopped and removed the hood so deftly that I didn't even feel it come off. I knew that I was free to use my eyes again only because it was easier to breathe, but the darkness was so deep that eyes didn't do me any good. Yet, little by little I began to see a chink of light, at first flickering and feeble, then clear and bright in front of me. At first it seemed quite far away, and when it was fully lit, very close by. It was, I think, the effect of a light more or less intense shining behind a transparency. Cagliostro had me go right up to the chink, which came through the wall, and I saw on the other side of it a strangely decorated room with lots of candles systematically arranged. In its furnishings and layout it had all the characteristics of a magician's den. But I gave it just a passing glance, for my attention was absorbed by a person sitting at a table. He was alone, with his face hidden in his hands, as though immersed in meditation. I couldn't make out his features, and his size was disguised by an outfit the likes of which I have never seen. As far as I could see, it was a white satin robe or cloak lined with purple that fastened in front with bejeweled clasps of gold. These were covered in hieroglyphics among which I could discern a rose, a cross, a triangle, a skull, and several rich cordons of various colors. One thing alone was clear to me: This person was not Porpora. A few minutes later this mysterious character whom I had begun to take for a statue slowly moved his hands, and I distinctly saw Count Albert's face, not as I had seen it the last time, covered by the shadow of death, but lively in its pallor and brimming with soul in its serenity, in short, such as I had seen him in his finest hours of calm and confidence. I was on the verge of uttering a cry and breaking, with an involuntary movement, the plate of glass that separated me from him, but Cagliostro violently squeezed my hand, which reminded me of my oath and filled me with some vague terror. Just then, moreover, at the back of the room where my eyes were fixed on Albert, there opened a door, and several individuals, all unknown to me, all attired more or less like him, marched in with drawn swords. After having performed several odd movements, as though in a pantomime, each in turn took a solemn tone and addressed him in incomprehensible words. He stood up, marched toward them, and replied in words equally obscure and incomprehensible to me, even though I now know German as well as my mother tongue. This dialogue was like those one hears in dreams, and the eerie scene and supernatural apparition were so dreamlike that I tried to move just to make sure I wasn't really sleeping. Cagliostro, however, forced me to remain still, and Albert's voice rang so true in my ears that it was impossible for me to doubt the reality of what I was seeing. Finally, just when I was so carried away by the desire to speak to him that my oath was about to slip my mind, the black hood dropped back down over my head. I violently ripped it off, but the crystal star had vanished, and everything was dark. 'If you move so much as a muscle,' Cagliostro muttered in a quavering voice, 'neither one of us shall ever see the light of day again.' I had the strength to follow him and zigzag back and forth once again through long, empty spaces I didn't recognize. Finally, when the hood came off once and for all, I found myself back in his dimly lit laboratory, just as it had been at the beginning of this adventure. Cagliostro was very pale and still shaking, for on our way back I had felt that his arm was convulsed with tremors and that he was hurrying me along, as though he were prey to a great fright. His first words to me were bitter rebuke for my *breach of faith* and the *horrible dangers* to which I had exposed him by trying to violate my oaths. 'I should have remembered,' he said in a sharp, furious tone, 'that no woman feels bound by her word of honor, that one must beware of giving into their vain, reckless curiosity.'

"Up until that moment I hadn't dreamed of sharing my guide's terror. I had been so stunned by the idea of finding Albert once again alive that I hadn't stopped to wonder if this were humanly possible. I had even forgotten that death had forever taken this dear, precious friend away from me. The magician's keen emotion finally reminded me that this was all most extraordinary and that I had just seen a phantom. Yet my mind was beating back the impossible, and Cagliostro's harsh rebuke brought over me a sickly exasperation that saved me from weakness. My reply to him was brisk: 'You're pretending to take your own lies seriously, and that's a terribly cruel game. Oh yes, you're playing with the most sacred things, with death itself.' He hotly retorted, but with a commanding look, 'You faithless, feeble soul! You believe in death like the common herd, and yet you had a great master who told you a hundred times: *No one dies, noth-*

ing dies, there is no death. You accuse me of lying, yet you don't seem to realize that the only lie here is the very word of death in your impious mouth.' This strange reply, I confess, completely bewildered me and momentarily overwhelmed all my defenses. How could the man know so well my relations with Albert, even the mysteries of the doctrine? Did he share Albert's faith, or was he using it as a weapon to sway my imagination?

"I felt abashed and dismayed. But soon I told myself that I could not accept this crass interpretation of Albert's beliefs, that God alone, not this impostor Cagliostro, could conjure up death or reawaken life. Convinced at last that I had been the dupe of some inexplicable illusion, whose mystery I might fathom one day, I stood up and gave the sorcerer a chilly compliment on his know-how. With a touch of irony I asked him to explain the bizarre things that the ghostly figures were saying among themselves. On that matter it was impossible to give me satisfaction, he replied, and I would have to be content with having seen *that person* calm and *usefully employed*. 'It would be vain to ask,' he added, 'what he thinks and does in life. I don't even know his name. When he entered your mind and you asked to see him, there took place between the two of you a mysterious communication that my power was able to make effective to the point of bringing him before you. My knowledge goes no further.' 'Your knowledge,' I told him, 'doesn't even go that far; for I was thinking about Professor Porpora, and that's not the one your power conjured up.' 'I know nothing about that,' he said, with frightening seriousness, 'and I don't want to know. I saw nothing, neither in your thoughts, nor in the magic tableau. My mind couldn't bear such spectacles, and I need to maintain all my lucidity to work my power. Yet the laws of science are infallible, and you must have thought, perhaps without even knowing it, about somebody else, since Porpora isn't the one you saw.' "

"That is the madman's fine way of talking!" said the princess, shrugging her shoulders. "Each in his own way, but they all manage, by means of a certain specious reasoning that could be called the logic of insanity, never to run out of things to say and to addle our brains with their grand words."

"He certainly addled mine," Consuelo continued. "I just couldn't analyze things any longer. Albert's apparition, whether it was real or not, made me grieve even more that I had lost him forever, and I burst into tears. 'Consuelo,' said the magician in a solemn voice, giving me his hand on the way out (and you can be sure that his calling me by my real name, which nobody here knows, was a further reason for amazement), 'you have great faults for which amends must be made, and I hope that you'll do everything to regain your peace of mind.' I didn't have the strength to reply. In vain I tried to hide my tears from my colleagues who had been impatiently waiting for me in the nearby parlor. I was even more impatient to go home, and once I was alone and had given free rein to my grief, I spent the whole night lost in thoughts and commentary about the scenes of this fateful evening. The more I tried to understand it, the more I got lost in a maze of uncertainties, and I must admit that my suppositions were often madder and more morbid than would have been blind faith in the oracles of magic. Worn out by this fruitless labor, I resolved to suspend judgment until things became clear. Yet in the aftermath I've remained impressionable, subject to vapors, sick in spirit, and deeply sad. I haven't felt my friend's loss more keenly than I already had, but my feelings of remorse, which he had soothed with his generous forgiveness, have come to torture me relentlessly. Utterly free to exercise my profession as an artist, I've become quickly bored with the frivolous intoxication of success, and then, in this country where people's minds seem as dreary as the climate. . . ."

"And as despotism," added the abbess.

"In this country where I myself feel dreary and cold, I soon realized that I wouldn't make the progress that I had dreamed about. . . ."

"So what progress do you want to make? We've never heard anyone whose talents come close to yours, and I don't believe that there is a more perfect singer anywhere in the universe. This is not one of Frederick's compliments. I'm just saying what I think."

"Even if Your Highness were right, which I don't know," said Consuelo with a smile, "for, aside from Romanina and Tesi, I've scarcely heard anyone except for myself, I think there is always much to be attempted and something to be found that goes beyond everything achieved thus far. Well then, the ideal I once had, perhaps I could have pursued it in a life of action, struggle, bold undertaking, shared sympathies, in a word, enthusiasm. But the cold regularity prevailing here, the military order reaching even into the wings of the theater, the calm, continual good will of an audience that thinks about its business while lending us an ear, the king's weighty patronage that guarantees us success decreed in advance, the lack of competition and innovation in the troupe and repertoire, above all, the idea of indefinite captivity; this whole bourgeois way of life that we lead in Prussia, with its cool industriousness, dismal glory and inevitable greed, has stripped me of the hope, even the desire for improvement. There are days when I feel so sluggish, so utterly bereft of that touchy pride that feeds an artist's conscience that I'd pay someone to boo at me, just to wake me up. But alas, whether I miss my entrance or burn out before the end of my task, there's always the same applause. It gives me no pleasure when I don't deserve it. And it pains me when by accident I do something to deserve it, because then it is very officially reckoned, as carefully measured by etiquette as usual, and yet I feel that something more spontaneous should be my due! You must find all this childish, my noble Amalia, but you wanted to see deep into the soul of an actress, and I'm hiding nothing from you."

"You explain it all so naturally that I understand as though I were feeling it myself. As a favor to you, I can certainly hiss and boo when I see that you're sluggish, reserving the right to throw you a crown of roses once I've waked you up!"

"Alas, kind princess, the king wouldn't allow either one. The king doesn't want anyone to offend the members of his troupe, for he knows that jeers are soon followed by infatuation. So, despite your generous intentions, there is no remedy for my tedium. Plus, with every passing day I more and more regret having chosen an existence so false, so devoid of feeling rather than a life of love and devotion. Especially since that adventure with Cagliostro, a black melancholy has seized the depths of my soul. Every single night I dream about Albert and see him irritated with me, or indifferent and preoccupied, speaking some incomprehensible tongue and engrossed in meditations that have nothing to do with our love, such as he was in that magic scene. I wake up drenched in cold sweat and begin to weep thinking that, in the new existence into which death has led him, his aching, dismayed soul may be suffering the effects of my disdain and ingratitude. In short, I killed him, and that's a fact. And there's no man on this earth, even having made a pact with all the forces of heaven and hell, who can bring him back to me. So there's no way for me to make amends for anything in the useless, lonely life I'm dragging out, and my only desire is to see it end soon."

Chapter X

"Haven't you struck up any new friendships here?" asked Princess Amalia. "Among the many intelligent, talented people that my brother brags about having attracted from all the corners of the earth, isn't there anyone worthy of esteem?"

"Of course, Madame. Had I not felt inclined to solitude and seclusion, I could have found kindly souls. Mlle Cochois. . . ."

"The Marquise d'Argens, you mean?"

"Is that what she's called?"

"You're right to be discreet. So, she's a fine person?"

"Extremely, and basically very kind, even though she's somewhat vain about the marquis' lessons and attentions and tends to look down on her fellow performers."

"She would be deeply humiliated if she knew who you are. The Rudolstadt name is one of the most distinguished in all Saxony, and that of d'Argens is only minor nobility from Provence or Languedoc. And what about Mme de Cocceï, what is she like? Are you acquainted with her?"

"Since Mlle Barberini got married, she has stopped dancing at the Opera and lives in the country most of the time, which means I've haven't had many opportunities to see her. Of all the women at the theater she was the one with whom I felt the greatest affinity, and she and her husband often invited me to come for a visit at their estate. The king, however, let me know that he very much disliked the idea, and I was forced to give it up, without ever knowing why."

"I'll tell you why. The king courted Mlle Barberini, who preferred the Lord Chancellor's son, and the king is afraid that she'll be a bad example to you. But isn't there any man you're close to?"

"I'm very fond of Franz Benda, His Majesty's first violin. There are parallels between his destiny and mine. In his youth he led the life of a zingaro, as I did as a child. Like me, he has very little relish for the splendors of this world and prefers freedom to money. He's often told me that he fled the Saxon court to share the errant destiny of artists on the road, with all its joys and sorrows.

Society doesn't know that there are fine virtuosos out there on the streets and highways. An old blind Jew taught Benda what he knows while they were going up hill and down dale. His name was Lœbel, and Benda only speaks of him with admiration, even though he died on a pile of straw, perhaps even in a ditch. Before taking up the violin, Franz Benda had a superb voice and sang for a living. In Dresden, he got so bored and depressed that he lost his voice. With the fresh air and freedom of the vagabond life he found another talent, and his genius took off once again. It was this itinerant conservatory that trained the magnificent virtuoso whose collaboration is welcomed by His Majesty for his chamber music. Georg Benda, his youngest brother, is also an eccentric genius, epicurean one minute and misanthropic the next. His quirks make him difficult sometimes, but he's never boring. I think this one will never manage to *settle down* like his other brothers, who have now all resigned themselves to the golden chains of the king's predilection for music. But Georg, either because he's the youngest or just can't be tamed, always talks about running away. His boredom here is so wholehearted that it's a pleasure to share it with him."

"Aren't you hoping that this will result in your sharing something more tender? It wouldn't be the first time that love has been born of boredom."

"I'm without fear or hope in that regard," replied Consuelo, "for something tells me that it won't ever happen. As I've said, dear Amalia, there's something strange going on in me. Ever since Albert died, I love him, I think about him alone, I cannot love anyone but him. This may be the first time that love has ever been born of death, and yet that's what is happening to me. I cannot console myself for having denied happiness to someone who deserved it, and this stubborn remorse has become an obsession, a sort of passion, perhaps madness!"

"It looks a bit that way," said the princess. "At least, some kind of illness. . . . And yet one that I understand well and am also experiencing, for I love someone far away whom I may never see again. That's about the same thing as being in love with a dead man, isn't it? But tell me, my brother Prince Heinrich, isn't he a pleasant gentleman?"

"Yes, indeed."

"A great lover of beauty, the soul of an artist, a hero on the battlefield, a nice, striking face that stops short of being beautiful, a proud, independent mind, an enemy of despotism, the unruly, threatening slave of my brother the tyrant; in short, surely the best of the family. I've heard he's quite smitten with you. Hasn't he told you that?"

"I took it as a joke."

"And you don't want to take it seriously?"

"No, Madame."

"You're very difficult, my dear. What's wrong with him?"

"One big flaw, or at least one insurmountable obstacle stands in the way of my loving him. He's a prince."

"Thanks for the compliment, my sweet! So he had nothing to do with your fainting spell during the performance a few days ago? I've heard that the king was so jealous of the way Heinrich was looking at you that he had him put under arrest as the curtain was going up and that this sorrow made you ill."

"I had absolutely no idea that the prince had been put under arrest, and I'm quite sure that it wasn't because of me. The cause of my spell was something else altogether. Just imagine, Madame, in the middle of the piece I was singing somewhat mechanically, as is too often the case here, my eyes drift toward the front-row boxes near the stage. All of a sudden I catch sight of a pale figure standing at the back of Herr Golowkin's box and leaning ever so slightly forward as if to see me better. It was Albert, Madame. I swear to God, I saw him, recognized him. Perhaps it was an illusion, but it's impossible to have one more terrifying, more complete than that."

"You poor child! You're having visions, for sure."

"Oh, that's not all! Last week, after giving you the letter from Herr von Trenck, I got lost in the palace and ran into Herr Stoss at the entrance to the curio collection. I stopped to chat with him, and there I saw Albert again. This time he looked as threatening as he had looked indifferent the evening before at the theater, as he always looks in my dreams, wrathful or contemptuous."

"Did Herr Stoss see him, too?"

"Very clearly, and he said that it was a certain Trismegistus, whom Your Highness enjoys consulting in his quality as a necromancer."

"Good heavens!" exclaimed Mme von Kleist, going pale. "I just knew he was a real sorcerer! It's always terrified me to lay eyes on him. Despite that handsome face and noble mien, there's something diabolical in his physiognomy, and I'm sure that he, like Proteus, can change his appearance as he likes in order to frighten people. On top of that, he's surly and insubordinate like everyone of that ilk. Once when he was charting my horoscope, he rebuked me point-blank for having divorced Herr von Kleist because he was ruined. It was a terrible crime, he said. I tried to defend myself, and when he became a bit overbearing with me, I began to lose my temper. At that point he got vehement and predicted that I'd get married again, that my second husband would die by my fault, even more wretchedly than the first, but that I'd be well punished by private remorse and public reproach. As he was saying those words, he looked so dreadful that I took him for Herr von Kleist come back from the dead and went screaming into the rooms of Her Royal Highness."

"Yes, an amusing scene that was," said the princess who every now and then reverted, as though against her will, to her dry, bitter tone. "I laughed like mad."

"There was no reason for that!" Consuelo said artlessly. "But who on earth is this Trismegistus? And since Your Highness doesn't believe in sorcerers. . . ."

"I promised to tell you all about sorcery some day. Don't be in such hurry. For the time being, just know that the seer Trismegistus is a man for whom I have great respect, who will be most useful to the three of us, to many others as well!"

"I'd really like to see him again," said Consuelo. "Even though the thought makes me tremble, I'd like to assess in cold blood whether he looks as much like Count von Rudolstadt as I had imagined."

"If he looks like the count? Is that what you just said? Well, that brings to mind something I would have forgotten, and it may just give us a terribly trite explanation for this whole great mystery. Hold on, let me think. . . . Now I've got it. Listen, my poor child, and learn to beware of everything that seems supernatural. It's Trismegistus that Cagliostro showed you; for Trismegistus is involved with Cagliostro, and last year they were both here at the same time. It's Trismegistus that you saw in Count Golowkin's box at the theater; for Trismegistus stays in his house, and they both take an interest in chemistry or alchemy. Finally, it's Trismegistus that you saw in the castle the day after; for that was the day, and shortly after I dismissed you, that I saw Trismegistus, and in parenthesis, he gave me lots of details about Trenck's escape."

"For the purpose of bragging that he'd had a hand in it and getting Your Highness to reimburse him for sums that he certainly didn't spend on that," said Mme von Kleist. "Your Highness may think what she wishes, but I'm not afraid to say that the man is a crook."

"Which doesn't prevent him from being a great sorcerer! Isn't that right, von Kleist? How do you manage to have such respect for his skill and such contempt for his person?"

"Well, Madame, it all fits together just fine. People are awed by sorcerers, but they also detest them. It's exactly the same thing with the devil."

"And yet people want to see the devil and can't do without sorcerers? That's your logic, my fine von Kleist!"

"But, Madame," said Consuelo, eagerly listening to this bizarre discussion, "how do you know that he looks like Count von Rudolstadt?"

"I forgot to tell you. It's something I learned by simple accident. This morning when Supperville was telling me the story about you and Count Albert, everything he said about that strange character made me curious about his looks. Was he handsome? Did his physiognomy match his extraordinary imagination?

Supperville took a moment to think, then said, 'Well, Madame, it won't be hard to give you a good idea of that; for you have among your *toys* an eccentric who would bear a terrifying resemblance to poor old Rudolstadt if he were gaunter, more ashen-faced, and wore his hair differently. I'm talking about your sorcerer Trismegistus.' That's what it all boils down to, my charming widow, and it's no more mysterious than Cagliostro, Trismegistus, Saint-Germain, and company."

"You've just taken a huge weight off my chest and pulled a black veil off my head!" said Porporina. "I feel that I'm being reborn to life, waking out of some painful sleep! I can't thank you enough for this explanation! So I'm not crazy, I don't have visions, and I won't be afraid of myself any longer! . . . And yet, just see what the human heart is," she added after a moment of introspection. "I think I regret not feeling weak and afraid any longer. In my folly I had almost convinced myself that Albert really wasn't dead, that one day, after his terrifying apparitions had made me atone for all the hurt I caused him, he would come back to me serene and indulgent. Now I'm very sure about these deplorable certainties: Albert is sleeping in the tomb of his ancestors, he will not leave that place, nor will death release its prey!"

"You were able to doubt that? Well, that goes to show that there is some pleasure in madness. As for me, I had no hope that Trenck would get out of his Silesian dungeon; yet it was possible, and now it is so!"

"If I were to tell you, lovely Amalia, all the conjectures going round and round in my poor head, you'd see that they were unlikely, but not all impossible. For example, a spell of lethargy. . . . Albert was prone to it. . . . But it's just too painful to recall these mad suppositions, now that the man I took for Albert is a crook."

"Trismegistus isn't what one thinks. . . . But he's certainly not Count von Rudolstadt, for I've known him for several years, and during all this time, ostensibly at least, he's been a seer. Besides, he doesn't look as much like Count von Rudolstadt as you think. Supperville is too skilled a doctor to bury a man in a state of lethargy, nor does he believe in ghosts, and he ascertained differences that you couldn't see because you were upset."

"Oh, how I'd like to see this Trismegistus again!" said Consuelo with a preoccupied look.

"You may not be seeing him for quite a while," was the princess's chilly reply. "He left for Warsaw the very day you saw him here in the palace. He never stays more than three days in Berlin. But he'll certainly be back in a year."

"Ah, if he were Albert!" said Consuelo, deep in her musings.

The princess shrugged her shoulders.

"Fate has obviously decreed that I shall have nothing but crackpots for friends. This one takes my sorcerer for her late husband Canon von Kleist, and the other one for her late husband Count von Rudolstadt. Lucky for me, I've got a good head on my shoulders; otherwise, I might take him for Trenck, and God knows what would happen. Trismegistus must be a poor sorcerer not to take advantage of all these misapprehensions! Now, now, my lovely Porporina, don't look at me with such fear and dismay. Get hold of yourself. If Count Albert, instead of being dead, had awakened out of his lethargy, don't you think that people would have heard about such an interesting turn of events? Haven't you kept in touch with his family, and wouldn't they have told you about this?"

"I've lost all contact with them," replied Consuelo. "The Canoness Wenceslawa wrote me twice in the course of a year to give me two bits of sad news; the death of her older brother Christian, my husband's father, who didn't recover the memory of his misfortune before the end of his long, painful life; and that of her other brother Baron Frederick, who died hunting after he fell down a ravine on that fateful Mount Schreckenstein. I made polite replies without daring to offer my sad consolations in person. I had the impression from her letters that her heart was torn between kindness and condescension. She called me *dear child, generous friend*, but showed no sign of any desire for tender ministrations on my part."

"So you think that Albert, back from the dead, is leading a calm, secret life inside the Castle of the Giants without so much as sending you a note and without anyone outside suspecting a single thing?"

"No, Madame, I don't think so, since that would be altogether impossible, and I'm crazy to want to have any doubts," replied Consuelo, hiding her tear-streaked face in her hands.

As the night went on, the princess seemed to slip back into her usual bad disposition. Her flippant banter about matters so close to Consuelo's heart hurt her dreadfully.

"Now, don't be so glum," Amalia abruptly ordered. "What a fine party! You've told us stories that would make a devil's blood run cold. Von Kleist is white as a ghost and can't stop shaking. She's scared to death, I think! As for me, who wanted to be happy and have some fun, it hurts me to see you suffering, my poor child!"

The princess said these last words in a kind tone of voice. Lifting her head, Consuelo saw a tear of sympathy running down her cheek, while her lips were still contracted in an ironic smile. She kissed the hand that the abbess held out to her and inwardly pitied her for being unable to be humane four hours in a row.

"No matter how mysterious your Castle of the Giants, how fierce the canoness's pride, how close-lipped the servants, you can be sure that anything that happens there is no safer from publicity than anywhere else. They did their best to keep the lid on Count Albert's bizarre ways, but soon the whole province knew about them, and they had long been the gossip of the little court of Bayreuth when Supperville was called to treat your poor husband. There is now in that family another secret that they've no doubt been hiding just as carefully, but without preserving it any better from society's malice. I'm talking about the young Baroness Amalia running away with a handsome adventurer shortly after her cousin's death."

"I didn't know about that for quite a while myself. I'd even go so far as to say that some things do remain secret in this world, for one still doesn't know the name and station of the man who carried off the young baroness nor where he took her."

"Indeed, that's what Supperville told me. Well now, old Bohemia is a land of mysterious adventures, but that's no reason for Count Albert . . ."

"In name of heaven, Madame, let's not talk about that anymore. I beg your pardon for having worn you out with that long story, and when Your Highness wishes me to leave. . . ."

"Two in the morning!" exclaimed Mme von Kleist, shuddering at the lugubrious bells of the palace clock.

"In that case, my dear friends, we must go our separate ways," said the princess, getting up, "for my sister von Anspach is going to come wake me as early as seven with all kinds of stories about the wild oats her dear margrave is sowing. He recently got back from Paris and is madly in love with Mlle Clairon. My lovely Porporina, while we are the queens in name, you who reign on stage are in fact the queens of the world, and you've got the better lot. When it strikes your fancy, you can just snatch any crowned head away from us, and I wouldn't be surprised if one of these days Mlle Hippolyte Clairon, who is an intelligent girl, became the Margravine von Anspach, in competition with my sister, who is an idiot. Now, get me a fur cloak, von Kleist, and I'll escort the two of you down the hall."

"And Your Highness will return all by herself?" asked Mme von Kleist, who looked very worried.

"All by myself," Amalia replied, "and without any fear of the devil and goblins, who have nonetheless been holding plenary court in the castle for the last few nights, or so people say. Come along, Consuelo! We're going to watch Mme von Kleist fly into a fine fright as she goes down the hall."

The princess grabbed a candleholder and took the lead, dragging Mme von Kleist, who was in fact quite nervous. Consuelo followed. She too was a bit unnerved, without knowing why.

"I assure you, Madame, this is the fatal hour," said Mme von Kleist. "It's reckless to venture through this part of the castle right now. What would it cost you to let us wait half an hour more? At two thirty it's all over."

"No, no," replied Amalia. "It wouldn't bother me to run into her and see how she is."

"What are you talking about?" asked Consuelo, speeding up to ask Mme von Kleist.

"You mean you don't know?" asked the princess. "A woman in white goes round sweeping the palace stairs and halls when a member of the royal family is about to die, and she's been back for the last few nights. It seems to be here that she's been performing her antics, which means I'm the one in danger. That's why you see me so calm. My sister-in-law, the Queen of Prussia (the most feeble head ever to wear a crown!) can't sleep because of it, people tell me, and spends all her nights at Charlottenburg. Yet, as she has infinite respect for the Sweeper, as does the queen mother, who is equally bereft of reason in this regard, these fine ladies have forbidden anyone to watch for the ghost or to trouble her in any of her noble tasks. So the castle gets a good sweep, and by Lucifer himself, which doesn't prevent it from being really filthy, as you can see."

Just then a huge cat streaked out of the shadowy depths of the hallway and ran yowling and purring up to Mme von Kleist. She let out a piercing shriek and tried to make a dash for the princess's rooms. The princess, however, kept a firm grip on her, all the while making the air resound with her hoarse, rasping bursts of laughter, even more lugubrious than the wintry wind whistling through the vast palace. Consuelo shivered with cold, perhaps also fear, for the contortions on Mme von Kleist's face seemed to bear witness to true danger, and the princess's forced merriment and swagger did not vouch for a sincere sense of security on her part.

"I admire Your Royal Highness's unbelief," said Mme von Kleist in a quavering, slightly spiteful voice. "If like me she had seen and heard the woman in white the night before her august king and father died. . . ."

"Alas," replied Amalia in a satanic tone, "as I'm sure she's not here now to herald the death of my august brother, I'm delighted that she's coming for me. The she-devil knows that my happiness requires one death or the other."

"Oh, Madame! this is no time to say such things!" said Mme von Kleist, her teeth so tightly clenched that she could scarcely get her words out. "In the name of heaven, stop a second and listen! Doesn't that make you shudder?"

The princess stopped with a derisive air. Once her silk skirts, heavy and stiff as cardboard, had stopped rustling, our three heroines, who had almost reached the huge stairwell at the end of the hall, clearly heard the dry, uneven slap of a broom coming up the stone stairs step by step, sounding like a servant rushing through a chore.

The princess hesitated a second, then said in a determined voice, "As there's nothing supernatural about *that*, I want to know if it's a footman walking in his sleep or a page out for mischief. Pull down your veil, Porporina. You mustn't be seen with me. As for you, von Kleist, go ahead and faint, if that amuses you. I'm warning you, you're on your own. Come on, brave Rudolstadt, you who have faced worse things. Follow me if you love me."

Amalia marched confidently toward the stairs. Consuelo followed, not being allowed to hold the candlestick for the princess. Mme von Kleist, no less terrified to be left alone than to move forward, trailed behind, hanging on to Porporina's mantlet.

The infernal broom was no longer audible. The princess arrived at the banister and leaned over it with her candleholder in order to see further on down. Perhaps she was less calm than she wished to appear or saw some terrifying object. In any case, her hand slipped, and the vermeil candleholder along with its candle and indented crystal collaret went crashing down into the resounding depths of the spiral staircase. At that point, Mme von Kleist lost her head. Without a single thought to the princess or Consuelo, she took to her heels back through the dark and sought refuge at her mistress's door. The princess, meanwhile, torn between feelings of insuperable fear and shameful defeat, began a slow retreat with Consuelo, then gradually quickened her pace; for she could hear other footsteps behind her, and they weren't those of Consuelo, who was marching along beside her perhaps with a bit more resolve, yet without any swagger. With every passing second these strange footsteps were closer on their heels, echoing in the dark like those of an old woman clattering over tiles in high-heeled slippers, and the broom went on thudding against the wall, now on the right, now on the left. The short way back seemed long indeed to Consuelo. If there is something that can overwhelm the courage of truly resolute, sound minds, it is danger that can be neither anticipated nor understood. She had no use for bravado and didn't turn her head even once. The princess later maintained that she had to no avail turned around for a look in the darkness, and this could be neither confirmed nor denied. Consuelo only remembered that the princess did not slow down or say a single word to her during this forced retreat and that she rushed into her apartment and was so eager to shut the door that she nearly slammed it in Consuelo's face. Yet Amalia would not admit to her weakness. She soon regained her composure and began to mock Mme von Kleist, nearly in convulsions, and to rebuke her for being so cowardly and impolite. Consuelo's compassionate nature was pained by the favorite's violent state, and she managed to revive some pity in the princess's heart. Amalia deigned to see that Mme von Kleist, lying in a faint on the sofa, her face sunk in the cushions, was incapable of listening. By the time the poor thing, still weeping tears of fright, had pulled herself together, it was after three. Now tired of not being a princess, Amalia no longer cared to undress herself and see to her own needs. Perhaps she had also been struck by some sinister foreboding. She therefore decided to keep Mme von Kleist until morning.

"By then we will have found some way to gloss things over just in case my brother hears about this," said the princess. "As for you, Porporina, your being here would be much harder to explain, and I'd hate for anyone to see you leaving my rooms. So you've got to go right now all by yourself, for people are up and around terribly early in this dreadful joint. Come now, von Kleist, calm down. You're staying here with me. If you can make any sense at all, tell us what entrance you used and where you left your footman so that he can see Porporina home."

Fear makes people so profoundly selfish that Mme von Kleist, delighted not to have to face the terrors of the hallway once again and quite indifferent to any anxiety that Consuelo might be feeling about making her way alone, recovered all her wits and explained exactly where to go and what signal to use to meet up with her trusty servant in the lonely, sheltered spot outside the palace where he had been ordered to wait for his mistress.

Provided with these instructions and very sure not to get lost in the palace this time, Consuelo paid her respects to the princess, who took no pleasure in the idea of escorting her down the hall. The girl set out alone, feeling her way, and reached the forbidding staircase without hindrance. Guided by the light of a lantern burning on a lower level, she went down without any unpleasant encounters, even without fear. Armed with her will this time, she felt that she was fulfilling a duty toward the unfortunate Amalia, and in such circumstances Consuelo was always strong and courageous. At long last she let herself out of the palace by means of a mysterious little door for which Mme von Kleist had given her a key and found herself in a corner of a back courtyard. Once she was altogether beyond the palace, she followed the outside wall looking for the footman. As soon as she gave the signal, a shadow moved away from the wall and came straight toward her. A man wrapped in a huge cloak bowed and respectfully offered her his arm in silence.

Chapter XI

Consuelo remembered that Mme von Kleist, in order to make her many secret visits to Princess Amalia even more secret, often came to the castle on foot in the evening, leaning on the arm of her servant, with a black bonnet on her head and a dark cloak over the rest of her. No one there took any notice of her in this disguise, and she could pass as one of those women in distress who covertly beg and receive a bit of help from the generosity of princes. Yet, despite all the precautions taken by the princess and her confidante, their efforts were something of a stage secret. The king took no offense as it is better to leave some little scandals alone rather than noisily trying to put them down. He knew full well that the two ladies were more interested in Trenck than in magic. Even though his condemnation of both subjects was nearly equal, he closed his eyes and felt inwardly grateful that his sister's airs of mystery shielded him from responsibility in certain eyes. Playing the fool was fine with him, as he didn't want to give the impression that he approved of his sister's love affair and follies. That meant that the unfortunate Trenck had become the target of Frederick's severity, and even then it had been necessary to accuse him of imaginary crimes so that people wouldn't guess the real reasons for his disgrace.

When Mme von Kleist's servant offered Porporina his arm, she assumed that he was lending himself to her incognito as he did for his mistress. For that reason she did not hesitate to accept his services and let him help her over the icy cobblestones. Yet she had scarcely taken three steps when the man casually inquired, "Well, my lovely Countess, in what kind of a mood did you leave your whimsical Amalia?"

Despite the cold and the north wind, Consuelo felt blood rush to her cheeks. To all appearances, the servant had taken her for his mistress and betrayed a revolting intimacy with her. Porporina, seized with disgust, withdrew her arm and curtly replied, "You've made a mistake."

"I'm not in the habit of making mistakes," said the cloaked man, totally unruffled. "People may not be aware that the divine Porporina is the Countess von Rudolstadt, but the Count de Saint-Germain knows better."

"So who are you?" asked Consuelo, dumbfounded. "Aren't you one of Mme von Kleist's servants?"

"I belong to no one but myself and serve only the truth," said the stranger. "I've just said my name, but I see that it is unknown to Mme von Rudolstadt."

"You are the Count de Saint-Germain in person?"

"Who else could give you the name that no one knows as your own? Now, Countess, twice you've tried to take a step without my help, and both times you've nearly fallen. Please take my arm again. I know very well the way to your place, and I consider it a duty and an honor to get you home safe and sound."

"How kind of you, Count," replied Consuelo, too curious to refuse the offer made by this intriguing, bizarre man. "Now will you kindly explain why you call me by that name?"

"Because I want to earn your trust right away by proving that I am worthy of it. For a long time I've known about your marriage to Albert. I've kept it an inviolable secret and shall continue to do so for as long as you wish."

"I see that Monsieur Supperville has hardly respected my wishes in that regard," said Consuelo, jumping to conclusions about the count's source of information.

"Don't accuse poor Supperville. He didn't say a word, except to Princess Amalia, to pay her homage. He's not the one who told me."

"So who did?"

"Count Albert von Rudolstadt himself. Yes, I know you're going to say that he died during the final moments of the religious ceremony of your wedding. But I'll reply that there is no death, that no one, that nothing dies, that it is still possible to communicate with the departed, as the vulgar herd likes to say, when one knows their language and their life secrets."

"Since you know so much, Monsieur, you may also be aware that I am not easily persuaded by such assertions. I find them very painful, for they always bring to mind a misfortune that I know to be beyond remedy, despite the deceitful promises of magic."

"You're right to be wary of magicians and impostors. I know that Cagliostro frightened you with an apparition that was at least untimely. He surrendered to the vainglory of demonstrating his power without giving a thought to the state of your soul or the sublime nature of his mission. Yet Cagliostro is no impostor, far from it! But he's vain, which is why he's often deserved being called a charlatan."

"The same has been said about you, Count; and yet, as people generally add that you're a man of superior qualities, I'll be so bold as to tell you frankly what prejudices are working against the respect I have for you."

"Such noble words suit Consuelo, and I'm grateful for this appeal to my honesty," he calmly replied. "I'll prove myself worthy of it and speak to you without mystery. But here we are at your door, and the cold as well as the advanced hour forbid me to keep you out here any longer. If you want to learn matters of the utmost importance, on which your future depends, please allow me to speak to you freely."

"If you wish to come see me during the day, you'll find me home at the hour of your choosing."

"I must speak to you tomorrow. And tomorrow you'll have a visit from Frederick, whom I have no desire to see since I have no respect for him."

"Which Frederick do you mean, Count?"

"Oh, I'm not talking about our friend Frederick von Trenck, whom we managed to spring from his clutches, but the nasty little king of Prussia who is courting you. Now, tomorrow there's to be a grand masked ball at the Opera. Be there. No matter how you're disguised, I'll recognize you and see to it that you recognize me. In that crowd we can be safely alone together. Otherwise, my dealings with you would heap great misfortunes on sacred heads. So, until tomorrow, Countess."

With these words the Count de Saint-Germain made a deep bow and disappeared, leaving Consuelo petrified with amazement on her doorstep.

"In this kingdom of reason there is obviously a permanent conspiracy against reason," Consuelo muttered to herself as she was falling asleep. "No sooner do I escape one threat to my reason than another one looms up. Princess Amalia explained away the last mysteries and put my mind at rest, but at the same instant we meet or at least hear the ghostly sweeper knocking about this castle of doubt, this fortress of unbelief no differently than she would have done two centuries ago. I rid myself of the terrible fright that Cagliostro gave me, and now here's another magician who seems to know even more about my business. I can understand why these seers take note of every little thing about kings and influential or famous people, but why on earth should a poor girl like me, humble and discreet, find it impossible to keep anything secret from their investigations? This has me baffled and bewildered in spite of myself. Now then, let's take the princess's advice and assume that the future will explain this prodigy as well, and in the meantime, refrain from judgment. But it might be even more extraordinary if the king really were to pay me a visit tomorrow, as Saint-Germain predicted! It would be only the third time. Is this Saint-Germain his confidant? It is said that one must particularly beware of those who speak ill of the master. I'll try not to forget it."

The next day, at the stroke of one, a carriage without livery or coat of arms entered the courtyard of the house where Consuelo was living. The king, who just two hours before had let her know that she was to await his visit alone, marched in with his cap over his left ear, a smile on his lips, and a little basket in his hand.

"Here's Captain Kreutz bearing fruit from his garden," announced the king. "Evil-minded folks will say it's from Sans-Souci and meant for the king's dessert. But the king, thank God, isn't giving a thought to us, and this humble baron has come to spend an hour or two with his little friend."

This pleasant greeting, instead of putting Consuelo at ease, left her feeling strangely unsettled. Ever since she had begun conspiring against him by listening to Princess Amalia's secrets, it had been impossible for her to brave the royal inquisitor with unflinching frankness. From that point on she ought to have humored the king, maybe even flattered him and resorted to clever coquetries in order to divert his suspicions. Consuelo felt that this role did not suit her, that she would do a poor job of it, especially if it were true that Frederick had a *taste* for her, as one said at court, for fear of belittling the king's majesty by suggesting that he might feel *love* for an actress. Anxious and disconcerted, Consuelo awkwardly thanked the king for his excessive kindness. His physiognomy immediately changed, now as glum as it had been radiant.

"What's wrong?" he snapped, furrowing his brow. "Are you in a bad mood? Or ill? Why are you calling me *sire*? Am I interrupting some flirtation?"

"No, Sire," replied the girl, with a serenely frank look. "There's neither love nor flirtation in my life."

"That's good! Even so, what would I care? Yet I'd insist that you confess as much."

"Confess! Surely the captain meant to say 'confide'?"

"Explain the difference."

"The captain knows the difference."

"As you wish, but splitting hairs is no answer. If you were in love, I'd want to know."

"I don't understand why."

"You don't understand at all? Look me straight in the face. You've got a very vague look about you today."

"Captain, I think you're trying to ape the king. I hear that when he's interrogating a suspect, he stares him right in the eye. Believe me, he's the only one who can do that. Even so, if he came to my place to try that on me, I'd ask him to go back to work."

"Right. You'd just say, 'Get lost, Sire.' "

"Why not? The king belongs on his horse or his throne. If he dropped in on a whim, I'd be entitled not to put up with any surliness."

"Agreed. But I still don't have an answer to my question. You don't want to confide in me about your next love affair?"

"There is no next love affair for me. I've often told you that, Baron."

"Yes, but you were laughing, because that was the way I asked you the question. But if I'm now speaking seriously?"

"My answer is the same."

"Do you know that you're an odd person?"

"How so?"

"Because you're the only actress who is not taken up with some fine passion or love affair."

"You take a dim view of actresses, Captain."

"Not so! I've known some who were very well-behaved, but they were aiming to marry money. You, on the other hand, nobody knows what you've got in mind."

"My mind is on singing this evening."

"So you just live from day to day?"

"Nowadays."

"So it's not always been the case?"

"No, sir."

"You've been in love?"

"Yes, sir."

"Seriously?"

"Yes, sir."

"And for a long time?"

"Yes, sir."

"And what happened to him?"

"He's dead!"

"But you've found consolation?"

"No."

"Oh! You'll surely find consolation one day?"

"I'm afraid not."

"That's strange. So you don't want to marry?"

"Never."

"And you'll never love again?"

"Never."

"Not even a friend?"

"Not even a friend as fine ladies understand the term."

"Nonsense! If you went to Paris, and King Louis XV, that gallant chevalier. . . ."

"I don't like kings, Captain, and I detest gallant kings."

"Ah, I see! Their pages are more to your liking. A handsome gentleman like Trenck, for example!"

"I've never given a thought to his looks."

"Yet you've remained in touch with him!"

"If so, only for reasons of pure, honest friendship."

"So you admit that you're still in touch?"

"I didn't say that," replied Consuelo, fearing that this one bit of information might compromise the princess.

"So you deny it?"

"If it were the case, I wouldn't have any reason to deny it. But why is Captain Kreutz asking me all these questions? How can all this be interesting to him?"

"It's apparently interesting to the king," Frederick shot back, removing his cap and slamming it down on the head of an ancient white marble bust of Polyhymnia on the console.

"If the king were to honor me with a visit at home," said Consuelo, rising above her mounting terror, "I would assume that he wanted to hear some music, and I'd sit down at my harpsichord to sing him the aria from *Ariadne Abandoned*. . . ."

"The king doesn't like niceties. When the king is conducting an interrogation, he wants clear, simple answers. What did you go do at the palace last night? You can see that the king has the right to come lord it over you at your house, since you go to his house at all hours without his permission."

Consuelo quaked from head to toe. Fortunately, in all kinds of danger, she maintained a presence of mind that had always saved her as though by miracle. She remembered that Frederick often told lies to get at the truth and was known to drag confessions out of people mainly by catching them off guard. She kept up her defenses, put a smile on her pale face and replied, "That's a strange accusation, and I don't know what one can say to fanciful questions."

"Now you've found your tongue again," the king continued. "It's plain to see you're lying! Didn't you go to the palace last night? Answer *yes* or *no*!"

"Well then, no!" she said with courage, preferring the shame of being caught in a lie to trying to clear herself by the cowardly surrender of someone else's secret.

"You didn't leave the palace at three this morning, all alone?"

"No," said Consuelo. Having noticed a faint shadow of irresolution cross his face, she felt her strength returning. Now she had the upper hand in the king's little game of catching the other off guard.

"That's three times you've dared say no!" fumed king, his eyes blazing.

"And I'll dare make it four, if Your Majesty requires," replied Consuelo, determined to stand firm through the storm.

"Oh, I know that a woman will hold to a lie under torture the same way the early Christian martyrs held to what they believed to be the truth. Who on earth can flatter himself on getting a straight answer out of a woman? Listen here, Mademoiselle, up till now I've had respect for you, for I considered you a solitary exception to the vices of your sex, neither scheming nor treacherous nor brazen. Your character inspired in me a trust that went as far as affection. . . ."

"And now, Sire. . . ."

"Don't interrupt. Now I've formed my opinion, and you'll feel the effects. But listen carefully. If you are so unfortunate as to have meddled in some little palace intrigues, opening your ears to certain untoward secrets and doing certain dangerous favors, I won't be fooled for long, let there be no illusions about that; and you'll be driven out of here as shamefully as you were received with distinction and kindness."

"Sire," said Consuelo unabashed, "as it is my dearest and most abiding wish to leave Prussia, I'm grateful to be ordered out, whatever the pretext for my dismissal or the harshness of your rebuke."

"Ah! So that's how you take it!" Frederick roared, beside himself with rage. "How dare you speak to me that way!"

He raised his walking stick as though he meant to strike Consuelo, but the air of serene contempt with which she awaited this outrage made him come to his senses. He threw the stick across the room and entreated her, "Look here, forget any rights you may have to Captain Kreutz's gratitude, and speak to the king with proper respect. Push me too far, and I may punish you like an unruly child."

"Sire, I know that children are thrashed in your august family, and I've heard that Your Majesty once tried to avoid such treatment by running away. A zingara like me will find that easier than Crown Prince Frederick. If Your Majesty doesn't let me go within twenty-four hours, I'll personally put his mind at ease about my schemes by slipping out of Prussia without a passport. It's fine with me if I have to take off on foot and jump moats like deserters and smugglers."

"You're crazy!" said Frederick, shrugging his shoulders and striding across the room to hide his exasperation and remorse. "You'll get out of here, all right—nothing could please me more—but there'll be no scandal and no rush. I won't have you leaving me like this, displeased with me, with yourself as well. Where the devil did you get that sassy tongue? And what the devil is making me go so easy on you?"

"No doubt some quite unnecessary scruple of generosity. Your Majesty feels obliged to me because of a favor that I would have done for the least of his subjects with the same zeal. May Your Majesty consider his debt repaid a thousand times over and let me go as soon as possible. My freedom will be reward enough, and that's all I ask."

"What's this? There's still more? Will nothing make you change your tune?" asked the king, stunned by the girl's brazen single-mindedness. "This is not courage, but hatred!"

"And if it were," replied Consuelo, "would Your Majesty care one whit?"

"Good heavens! What do you mean, you wretched little girl?" asked the king, sounding earnestly pained. "You don't understand what you're saying, poor child. It takes a perverse soul to be insensitive to the hatred of its own kind."

"Does Frederick the Great consider Porporina a being of his own kind?"

"Intelligence and virtue alone raise certain individuals above others. You're a singer of genius. Your conscience ought to tell you if you're a worthy person. . . . But it's saying just the opposite right now, for your soul is brimming with bitterness and resentment."

"And if that were so, wouldn't the great Frederick have to take some of the blame for kindling these evil passions in a habitually peaceful, generous soul?"

"Come now, are you angry?" asked Frederick, reaching for the girl's hand. But he stopped himself, held back by that awkwardness that a streak of contempt and distaste for women had developed in him.

Consuelo had exaggerated her spite so as to drive back into the king's heart some tender feelings that were about to explode in the heat of the moment. Once she saw how bashful he was and realized that he was waiting for her to make a move, she lost all fear. Hers was an odd fate, for the only woman who could hold Frederick in her sway with some emotion resembling love was perhaps the only woman in his entire kingdom who loathed the idea of encouraging these feelings. True, Consuelo's pride and revulsion may have been the main reason why the king felt drawn to her. The despot found her rebellious soul as tempting as the conquest of a new province. Without realizing it or wanting to make such frivolous exploits a point of honor, he felt admiration and instinctive affinity for a hardy nature that he, in some respects, considered akin to his own.

"Now then," said he, suddenly shoving into his vest pocket the hand that he had advanced toward Consuelo, "stop telling me that I don't mind being hated, for you might make me think it's true, and I'd find that odious!"

"Yet you want to be feared."

"No, I want to be respected."

"So it's by means of a good flogging that your corporals inspire your soldiers with respect for your name."

"What's this? What are you talking about? What business is this of yours?"

"I'm giving *clear, simple* answers to Your Majesty's questions."

"You think I owe you an apology for a moment of temper provoked by your folly?"

"On the contrary! If you could break over my head the stick that rules Prussia, I'd beg Your Majesty to pick it back up."

"Nonsense! Given that this walking stick was a present from Voltaire, if I were to caress your shoulders with it a bit, you might become even wittier and mischievous. Look here, I'm very fond of this stick, but it's clear to me that you require amends."

With these words the king picked up his stick and tried to snap it in two. Even when he put it over his knee, the stick bent but would not break.

"You see," said the king, throwing it into the fire, "this stick is not, as you maintain, the symbol of my power. It's that of faithful Prussia, bending to my will without ever being broken. You'll do well to do the same, Porporina."

"And what is Your Majesty's will with regard to me? What a fine matter for exercising authority and troubling a great man's serenity!"

"It is my will that you give up the idea of leaving Berlin. Does that offend you?"

Frederick's keen, almost passionate look sufficiently explained the kind of amends he had in mind. Terror washed over Consuelo once again. She played dumb and said, "I'll never resign myself to that. It's too clear that I'd pay dearly the honor of amusing Your Majesty every now and then with my trills. Everyone here is subject to suspicion. The most insignificant, obscure creatures aren't safe from accusation, and I can't live this way."

"You're unhappy with your pay," the king continued. "It will be increased."

"No, Sire. My pay is satisfactory. I'm not greedy, as Your Majesty knows."

"True. It's only fair to say that you don't love money. One doesn't know, moreover, what you love!"

"Freedom, Sire."

"Who is interfering with your freedom? You're trying to pick a fight with me for no good reason. You just want to leave. That much is clear."

"Yes, Sire."

"Yes? Your mind is made up?"

"Yes, Sire."

"To hell with you then!"

The king grabbed his cap and his stick, untouched by the fire since it had rolled on the andirons, turned his back, and marched toward the door. As he was about to open it, he looked back at Consuelo with such an ingenuously sad face, so stricken with paternal grief, so different, in a word, from the monarch's terrifying brow or the skeptical philosopher's bitter smile that the poor child's heart filled with remorse. Having grown so inured to domestic storms like this with Porpora, she forgot that Frederick had fierce, personal feelings for her that had never entered the chaste, generous, and fervent soul of her adoptive father. She turned away to hide a furtive tear, but the king was sharp-eyed as a lynx. He retraced his steps and raised his stick again, but so tenderly this time, as if he were about to play with a child of his loins. "You detestable creature!" he said in a sweet, loving voice, "you don't have an ounce of affection for me!"

"You're very wrong, Baron," she replied, fascinated by this half comedy which was so cleverly making amends for the Frederick's real fit of brutal anger. "My fondness for Captain Kreutz equals my aversion to the King of Prussia."

"That's because you do not, cannot understand the King of Prussia," said Frederick. "So let's not talk about him. One day, after you've lived in this land long enough to understand its character and needs, you'll be fairer to the man who is doing his best to rule it properly. In the meantime, be a bit nicer to this poor baron who is so thoroughly bored with the court and courtiers, who came here for a few moments of peace and happiness with a pure soul and candid spirit. I was free for only an hour, and you've done nothing but quarrel with me the whole time. As long as you're a better hostess, I'll come back another time and bring along my greyhound Mopsule to amuse you. You behave yourself, and I'll give you a pretty white greyhound she's nursing right now. You'll have to take such good care of it! Ah, I almost forgot! Here's some poetry I've written, stanzas about music. You can set them to a melody, and my sister Amalia will enjoy singing them."

After several false starts, lots of gracious chatter, and frivolous cajoleries for the object of his benevolence, the king took a leisurely leave. He could prattle on when he wanted to, even though he was usually pithy, brisk, and very sensible. No one's conversation had more so-called substance, and nothing was rarer in that period than his serious, solid tone in small talk. Yet with Consuelo he had aimed to be pleasant and easy-going, and he succeeded well enough in seeming that way that she was occasionally filled with naïve wonderment. Once he had gone, she regretted as usual not having succeeded in giving him a distaste for her and the whim of these dangerous visits as well. The king, for his part, went away half annoyed with himself. He loved Consuelo in his own fashion and would have liked really to inspire her with the affection and admiration feigned by his false, witty friends. He might have given a lot, he who scarcely liked to give, to know once in his life the pleasure of being loved sincerely, without ulterior motives. Yet he realized that this was not easy to reconcile with the authority he did not want to relinquish. Like a glutted cat playing with a mouse ready to bolt, he could not decide whether he wanted to tame her or twist her neck. "She's going too far, and this will come to a bad end," he thought to himself, climbing into his carriage. "If she keeps on being so difficult, I'll have to see that she commit some offense and send her to a fortress for a while. That regime ought to take the edge off that proud courage. Yet I'd prefer to dazzle the girl and hold her in my sway as I do so many others. With a bit more time and patience, I'm sure to get the better of her. What a pesky, intriguing little chore this is! Let's just see! For sure, she mustn't leave right now, for then she'd go around bragging that she got away with telling me off. No, no! She leaves me nice and docile, or else broken. . . ." At which point the king, who had many other things to think about, as one can believe, opened a book so as not to waste five minutes on idle daydreams; and by the time he stepped out of his carriage, he could not quite remember what had been on his mind climbing in.

Porporina, quivering with worry, gave a bit more thought to the dangers of her situation. She upbraided herself for yielding and tacitly agreeing to give up the idea of leaving, but these meditations were interrupted by the delivery of money and letters from Mme von Kleist which Consuelo was to pass along to Saint-Germain, who would get them to Trenck. In addition to this responsibility, Consuelo might also have to play the role of the fugitive's mistress in order to cover up Princess Amalia's secret. She found herself involved in a nasty, dangerous situation, all the more because she did not really trust the mysterious agents with whom she had been put in contact and who seemed to want to meddle in her own secrets as well. She got busy with her disguise for the ball at the Opera, where she was to meet Saint-Germain, all the while thinking with resigned terror that she was on the brink of an abyss.

Chapter XII

As soon as the opera was over, the auditorium was leveled, lit up, and decorated according to custom, and the great masked ball known in Berlin as the *redoute* got under way at the stroke of midnight. It was quite a mixed crowd, for blue-blooded princes and perhaps even princesses found themselves mingled with all the local actors and actresses. Porporina slipped in alone disguised as a nun, her neck and shoulders hidden by the wimple, her body enveloped in the folds of the habit. She felt the need to make herself unrecognizable to circumvent any comments about her rendezvous with Saint-Germain. She was also eager to test the perspicacity of the man who had vaunted his ability to identify her no matter what her disguise. So all alone, and without even telling her maid, she had arranged this simple, easy costume. She arrived at the ball wrapped in a long fur-lined cloak that only came off once she was in the midst of the throng. Before she had even made her way around the ballroom, something worrisome caught her eye. Not just once but several times a masked figure that was about Consuelo's size, ostensibly of her sex, and dressed in the exact same habit danced up to her and joked about their identities.

"Dear sister," said this nun, "which one of us, I'd like to know, is the other's shade? And since you look lighter and airier than I, let me touch your hand to see if you're my twin or my ghost."

Consuelo repelled these attacks and tried to get to her dressing room to change her costume or some part of it so as to prevent confusion. She was afraid that if the Count de Saint-Germain, despite all her precautions, had had some revelation about her disguise, he might speak to her double and fill that one's ears with the secrets he had announced to her the evening before. But she was in no position to carry out that plan. Already a Capuchin monk had begun following her, then willy-nilly seized her arm.

"You won't escape me, sister," he said in a low voice. "I'm your father confessor, and I'm going to tell you your sins. You're Princess Amalia."

"And you're a novice, brother," said Consuelo, disguising her voice as one usually does at masked balls. "You don't know your penitents at all well."

"Oh, it's no good trying to change your voice, sister. I don't know if that is the habit of your order, but you're the Abbess of Quedlinburg. That you can admit to me, your brother Heinrich."

As the prince had often spoken to her, Consuelo recognized his strikingly guttural voice. To make sure that her double was in fact the princess, she said no once again, at which point the prince added, "I saw your costume at the tailor's. Since there are no secrets for princes, I found yours out. Come on, let's not waste time in idle chatter. You can't mean to tease me, dear sister, and I'm not following you just to be a pest. I've got some serious things to tell you. Come on over here."

Consuelo, who had made up her mind to show him her face rather than to learn family secrets by taking advantage of his mistake, let the prince lead her away. Yet once they were alone in a box and he began talking, she reluctantly pricked up her ears and felt entitled to hear him out.

"Beware of going too fast with Porporina," said the prince to his supposed sister. "It's not that I doubt her discretion or noble heart. The most important people in the *order* vouch for her; and even at the risk of your ragging me again about my feelings for her, I'll repeat that I share your sympathy for this lovely person. But neither they nor I think that you should take any chances with her before we're sure of her frame of mind. An undertaking that seizes upon a fiery imagination such as yours or a mind as righteously indignant as mine can at first terrify a shy girl who has probably never had anything to do with philosophy or politics. The reasons that moved you are not those that will make an impression on a woman from such a different sphere. Let Trismegistus or Saint-Germain take care of this initiation."

"But hasn't Trismegistus already left?" asked Consuelo, too fine an actress not to be able to imitate Princess Amalia's hoarse, unsteady voice.

"You ought to know that better than I, since he deals only with you. I don't know the man. But Saint-Germain strikes me as the cleverest, the most extraordinarily adept practitioner of the science that interests us. He's undertaken to win over the beautiful singer and keep her out of danger."

"Is she really in danger?" asked Consuelo.

"She will be if she goes on refusing the amorous attentions of the *Marquis*."

"What marquis?" asked Consuelo, dumbfounded.

"Your mind is wandering, sister! I'm talking about Fritz, the *grand lama*."

"Ah yes, the Margrave von Brandenburg!" said Consuelo, who finally understood that he meant the king. "So you're really sure that he's got his mind on that slip of a girl?"

"I won't go so far as to say that he's in love with her, but he's jealous. And then, sister dear, you've got to see how you're putting that poor little thing in jeopardy by making her your confidante. . . . Now, now, I know nothing about that, and I don't want to know a thing. But, in the name of heaven, be careful, and don't let *our friends* suspect that you have motives other than a love of liberty. We've decided to adopt your Countess von Rudolstadt. Once she's initiated and bound by oaths, promises, and threats, you'll be safe with her. But until then, I beg you, refrain from seeing her and telling her your concerns or ours. . . . And you can start by leaving this ball. It's hardly suitable for you to be here, and the *grand lama* will surely find out. Give me your arm, and I'll escort you to the door, but no further. I'm supposed to be under arrest at Potsdam, and the palace walls have eyes that can see through an iron mask."

Just then there was a knock at the door. As the prince did not open up, more knocks followed.

"What an impudent rascal to insist on entering a box where there's a lady present!" said the prince, showing his bearded mask at the little window in the door.

But there he saw a red domino with a ghastly pale face who made a strange gesture and said, "*It's raining.*"

This news seemed to make a great impression on the prince.

"Should I leave or stay?" he asked the red domino.

"You must go look for a nun just like this one out in the crowd," the domino replied, while the prince eagerly showed him in. "I'll take care of the lady," he added, gesturing toward Consuelo.

After they had exchanged a few whispers, the prince left without saying a word more to Porporina.

"Why did you take exactly the same disguise as the princess?" asked the domino, sitting down at the far end of the box. "That exposes her, yourself as well, to fatal errors. There I don't see your usual prudence or devotion to others."

"If my costume is just like someone else's, that is news to me," replied Consuelo warily.

"I thought it was a carnival prank that the two of you had arranged. Since that's not the case, Countess, and it's merely a coincidence, let's talk about you and abandon the princess to her fate."

"But it seems to me, Monsieur, that if someone's in danger, those who talk about devotion to others shouldn't stand idly by."

"The person who just left will look after that august madcap. You're no doubt aware that the matter concerns him more than it does us, since he too is courting you."

"You're wrong, Monsieur. I don't know him any better than I do you.

Moreover, you're talking neither like a friend nor a jester. Let me get back to the ball."

"First let me have the portfolio you were asked to give me."

"Certainly not. I don't have anything for anyone."

"Good for you. That's the way to talk. But with me there's no need for that. I'm the Count de Saint-Germain."

"I don't know that."

"Even if I were to take off my mask, you wouldn't recognize me. The only time you saw my face was that night in the dark. But here are my credentials."

The red domino gave Consuelo a sheet of music with a sign that she could not fail to recognize. She handed him the portfolio, not without trembling, and took care to add, "Mark my words. Nobody gave me any message for you. I alone am sending these letters and bills of exchange to the person you know."

"So you're Baron von Trenck's mistress?"

Frightened by the grievous lie that this question required of her, Consuelo kept still.

"Answer me, Madame," said the red domino. "The baron doesn't hide from us that he receives help and consolation from a person who loves him. So you're the baron's friend?"

"I am," was Consuelo's staunch reply. "And I'm equally amazed and offended by your questions. Can't I be the baron's friend without exposing myself to such coarse language and foul suspicions?"

"The situation is too serious for you to dwell on words. Listen carefully. You're charging me with a mission that jeopardizes my reputation and puts me in all kinds of personal danger. There may be some political conspiracy underneath all this, and that's not something in which I wish to get involved. I gave my word to Trenck's friends to help him out with a love affair. Let me make myself clear. I didn't promise to help out with a *friendship*. The word is too vague, and I find it unsettling. I know that you're incapable of telling a lie. If you positively declare that von Trenck is your lover and let me tell Albert von Rudolstadt. . . ."

"Good heavens! Don't torture me like this, Monsieur. Albert is dead!"

"That's what people say, I know. Yet he is forever alive for you and me."

"True enough, if you mean that in a religious or symbolic sense. Yet materially. . . ."

"Let's not argue. There's still a veil over your spirit, but it will be lifted. The crucial thing for me right now is knowing what you are to Trenck. If he's your lover, I'll deliver this portfolio on which his life may depend, for he is utterly without resources. If you refuse to say, I refuse to be your go-between."

"Well," said Consuelo with a painful effort, "he is my lover. Here's the portfolio and see that he gets it quickly."

"That's enough," said Saint-Germain, taking the portfolio. "Now, you brave, noble girl, let me tell you that I admire and respect you. This was only a test of your sense of dedication and self-sacrifice. Come now, I know everything! I know full well that you're lying out of generosity and that you've been faithful as a saint to your husband. I know that Princess Amalia, all the while making use of my services, doesn't trust me and that working to free herself from the *grand lama*'s tyranny doesn't stop her from acting like a princess and a tight-lipped one at that. That's her role, and she's not ashamed to expose you, a poor vagabond (as polite society likes to say) to eternal sorrow; yes, the greatest sorrow of all! that of standing in the way of your husband's brilliant resurrection and throwing his present existence into a limbo of doubt and despair. But fortunately there is always a chain of invisible hands stretching between your soul and Albert's, one working on this earth by light of day and the other laboring in an unknown world, in the shadow of mystery, far removed from the gaze of vulgar humans."

Despite her determination to keep up her guard against the specious perorations of so-called prophets, Consuelo was moved by this bizarre language.

"Please explain yourself, Count," she said, doing her best to sound cool and collected. "I'm well aware that Albert's role has not come to an end on this earth, that death's chilly breath has not destroyed his soul. Yet any connection between us is shrouded by a veil that may be lifted only when I myself die; that is, if God lets us enjoy a vague recollection of our previous lives. This is a mystery, and no one can abet the celestial influence that brings together in a new life those who loved each other in a past life. What notions are you trying to put into my head when you say that certain sympathies are watching over me and working toward that end?"

"I could only speak of myself and say that having known Albert from time immemorial, when I served under his orders in the war of the Hussites against Sigismund as well as later, during the Thirty Years' War, when he was. . . ."

"I know that you claim to remember all your previous lives, like Albert with his sick, disastrous persuasion. Would to God that I had never doubted his sincerity on that score! Yet this belief was so closely tied to a state of delirious frenzy in him that I never believed that this extraordinary, perhaps inadmissible power was real. So spare me the trouble of hearing about your weird conversations with Albert on the subject. I know that lots of people moved by idle curiosity would love to be in my place right now. They'd give you an encouraging smile and pretend to believe the fabulous stories that you reportedly tell so well. But I don't know how to play a role when I don't have to, and I'd be incapable of enjoying what they call your daydreams. They would remind me too much of Albert's, which terrified and tormented me. Please keep your stories for those who can share them. On no account would I want to deceive you by pretending to lend them any credence. Even if they didn't arouse any harrowing memories in me, I wouldn't want to make fun of you. So kindly answer my questions without trying to lead my mind astray with vague words and double meanings. To encourage your frankness I'll tell you that I already know that you've got particular and mysterious designs on me. You're supposed to initiate me into some forbidding secret, and people of high rank are counting on you to teach me the elements of some occult science."

"People of high rank sometimes say the strangest things, Countess," the count replied imperturbably. "Thank you for your honesty with me, and I'll refrain from touching on matters that you wouldn't understand, perhaps because you have no wish to understand them. Let me just say that there is indeed an occult science on which I pride myself, in which I am seconded by minds more enlightened than mine. Yet there's nothing supernatural about it since it is purely and simply the science of the human heart or, if you prefer, thorough knowledge of human life in its deepest motives and most secret deeds. And to prove to you that I'm not merely boasting, I'll tell you—only with your permission, of course—exactly what has been going on in your own heart since you've been separated from Count von Rudolstadt."

"Go ahead," replied Consuelo, "for there's no way for you to deceive me about that."

"Well, for the first time in your life you're in love, totally, truly in love. And the man you love, for whom you're shedding tears of repentance, since you didn't love him a year ago, the man whose absence gives you such bitter grief, whose disappearance has made your present life so drab and your future so dreary—it is not Baron von Trenck, for whom you've never felt more than friendship based on gratitude and serene affinity; nor Joseph Haydn, who is just your little brother in the fellowship of Apollo; nor King Frederick, who terrifies and intrigues you at one and the same time; nor the handsome Anzoleto, whom you can no longer respect. The man you love is the one you saw laid out on his deathbed, arrayed with the pomp that noble families in their pride put even in the tomb, on the shroud of the departed: Albert von Rudolstadt."

Consuelo was momentarily stunned to hear this revelation of her innermost feelings out of the mouth of a man she did not know. But then she thought to herself that the previous evening she had told her whole life to Princess Amalia and bared her heart. She also recalled the many hints that Prince Heinrich had just dropped about the princess's ties to a mysterious association in which the Count de Saint-Germain played a leading role. So she ceased to be amazed and ingenuously avowed that it was not much to his credit to know of matters that she had recently confided to a friend with a loose tongue.

"You mean the Abbess of Quedlinburg?" asked Saint-Germain. "Well, will you take my word of honor?"

"I have no right to call it into question," Porporina replied.

"So I give you my word of honor," said the count, "that the princess hasn't said a word to me about you, since I've never had the privilege of talking to her or her confidante Mme von Kleist."

"Yet you have dealings with her, at least indirectly?"

"Which consist in delivering Trenck's letters to her and receiving her letters to him from third parties. You can see that her trust in me doesn't go very far since she thinks that I'm not aware of the interest she takes in our fugitive. Anyway, there's nothing perfidious about the princess. She's merely crazy, like all oppressed people with a tyrannical bent. The servants of truth have placed a lot of hope in her and taken her under their wing. God willing, she won't make them regret it!"

"You misjudge an interesting, unhappy princess, Count, and perhaps you don't know her business well. As for me, I know nothing. . . ."

"It's no good lying, Consuelo. You just had a midnight supper with her, and I can tell you all about it."

The Count de Saint-Germain proceeded to report the minutest details of her supper the night before, from what the princess and Mme von Kleist had said to the finery they had worn, the menu, their meeting with the *sweeper*, etc. Then he went on to recount the king's visit to our heroine that morning, the words they had exchanged, his walking stick raised up over Consuelo, his threats, his remorse—every single thing down to their slightest gestures and the looks on their faces—as if he had been there himself. He ended by saying, "How very wrong of you, you naïve, generous child, to let yourself fall for these returns of affection and kindness that the king knows how to show on occasion. You'll come to regret it. The royal tiger will make you feel his claws unless you accept stronger, more honorable protection, something truly paternal and all-powerful that won't be limited to the narrow confines of the marquisate of Brandenburg, something that will hover over you on the whole face of the earth, even into the wilderness of the New World."

"As far as I know, God alone exercises such protection and offers it even to insignificant creatures like me," said Consuelo. "If I'm facing danger here, it's in God that I trust. I'd be suspicious of any other solicitude whose means and motives were unknown to me."

"It doesn't suit great souls to be suspicious," replied the count, "and it's because Mme von Rudolstadt is a great soul that she is entitled to protection from God's true servants. That is the only motive for this offer. As for the means, they are immense and as different in their power and morality from those of princes as God's purposes in their sublimity are different from those of the despots and little lords of this world. If you love and trust divine justice alone, you must see how it works through those good, intelligent people who are the ministers of God's will here below and the executors of his supreme Law. Righting wrongs, protecting the weak, repressing tyranny, encouraging and rewarding virtue, disseminating the principles of morality, preserving honor's sacred trust, such is the eternal mission of a glorious, venerable phalanx that has been carrying on under various names and forms since the dawn of history. Look at the crude, antihuman laws that rule the nations, mankind's prejudices and errors, the monstrous traces of barbarism all over the globe! In a world so poorly managed by ignorant masses and treacherous governments, how can any virtue bloom or truth come forward? Yet it happens, and one sees spotless lilies, flowers without blemish, souls like yours and Albert's rise up in splendor out of the mire. But do you think that they could keep their sweet perfume, shield themselves from the foul bites of snakes and lizards and withstand the storm without being sustained and preserved by propitious forces, helping hands? Do you think that Albert, that sublime man, a stranger to all vulgar turpitude, so far above humanity that he looked mad to the eyes of the profane, drew all his greatness and faith out of himself alone? Do you think he was an isolated phenomenon in the universe, that he never restored his strength in a circle of sympathy and hope? And you yourself, do you think that you would be what you are if the breath of God hadn't passed from Albert to you? But now that you are separated from him, thrown into a sphere unworthy of you, exposed to all kinds of danger and temptation; you, a theater girl, the confidante of a lovesick princess and the putative mistress of a king worn out by debauchery and chilled by egotism, do you hope to keep the immaculate purity of your pristine innocence if the mysterious wings of the archangels don't spread over you like a celestial shield? Watch out, Consuelo! It's not in yourself, at least not in yourself alone, that you'll find the strength you need. The very prudence on which you pride yourself will be easily undone by the wiles of the evil spirit lurking in the shadows around your virginal bed. Learn to respect the saintly militia, the invisible army of faith that already forms a rampart around you. They ask of you neither commitments nor services. They merely command that you be meek and trusting when you feel the unexpected effects of the salutary adoption. I've told you enough. Now it's up to you to think long and hard about what I've said. When the time comes and wondrous things start happening around you, remember that everything is possible for a community of believers working together, free and equal. Indeed, there are no limits to what they can do to reward merit. If you were to prove yourself worthy of winning from them a sublime prize, know that they could even resurrect Albert and give him back to you."

After this speech ringing with tones of enthusiastic conviction, the red domino stood up. Without waiting for Consuelo's reply, he bowed and left the box where she remained for a few instants, motionless, as though lost in strange reveries.

Chapter XIII

When at last Consuelo left the box, her only thought was to go home. In the corridors she was accosted by two masked figures, one of whom whispered to her, "Beware of the Count de Saint-Germain."

Consuelo thought she recognized the voice of Uberti Porporino, her fellow performer. Grabbing the sleeve of his domino, she asked, "Who is this Count de Saint-Germain? I don't know him."

But the other masked figure seized her free hand and said, "Beware of adventures and adventurers." As he did not even try to disguise his voice, Consuelo immediately recognized young Benda, the melancholy violinist.

And they hurried on, as though wanting to avoid her questions.

After all the trouble she had taken to come up with a good disguise, Consuelo was amazed to see how easily people recognized her. Accordingly, she hastened to leave. Yet it soon came to her attention that she was being observed and followed by another masked figure. Because of his size and bearing she thought it was Poelnitz, the director of the royal theaters and the king's chamberlain. As soon as he opened his mouth, she was sure of it, despite all his efforts to alter his voice and pronunciation. She made no reply to his idle chatter since it was clear that he wanted to loosen her tongue. She finally got rid of him and crossed the room, hoping to throw him off in case he tried to follow her again. There was a crowd, and it was not easy to reach the exit. At that point she turned around to make sure that no one was watching her and was rather surprised to see Poelnitz in a corner having what looked like a confidential chat with the red domino she thought to be the Count de Saint-Germain. Unaware that Poelnitz had met him in France, she feared that she had been betrayed by the *adventurer* and returned home devoured by anxiety, not so much for herself as for the princess, whose secret she had reluctantly divulged to a very dubious character.

The next morning she woke to find a crown of white roses suspended over her head. It was hanging from the crucifix that had belonged to her mother, which was never far from Consuelo. At the same time she noticed that the cypress branch that had trimmed the crucifix ever since a certain triumphant evening in Vienna when a nameless hand had thrown it on stage was missing. She searched for it high and low, to no avail. It seemed that someone had deliberately replaced that gloomy trophy with this fresh, lovely crown. Her chambermaid could not say how or when the substitution had been made. She claimed not to have left the house nor let anyone in the previous evening. While turning down her mistress's bed, she had not noticed whether the crown was already there. In short, she was so ingenuously amazed that it was hard to doubt her sincerity. The girl had a most disinterested soul, of which Consuelo had ample proof, and the only fault that Consuelo knew her to possess was a tremendous itch to talk and tell her mistress all manner of nonsense. Had she known anything at all, she never would have passed up the chance to wear Consuelo out with a long tale and the most tiresome details. She went on interminably about how mysterious and gallant it was for someone to have given her mistress this crown. Soon Consuelo was so bored that she told her maid not to worry about it any longer and sent her away. Alone again, she examined the crown with the utmost care. The flowers were fresh as could be, and their perfume summery sweet despite the season. Consuelo heaved a bitter sigh, thinking that such lovely roses in midwinter could scarcely have come from elsewhere than the conservatories of the royal residences and that her maid was perhaps right to attribute this homage to the king. "Yet he didn't know how much my cypress meant to me," she thought to herself. "So why would he have it taken away? No matter, a curse on the hand of whosoever is responsible for this profanation!" In her chagrin she pitched the crown across the room, at which point a little strip of parchment fell away. She picked it up and read the following message traced by an unknown hand, "Every noble act deserves a reward, and the only reward worthy of great souls is the homage of sympathetic souls. Let the cypress be gone from your bedside, generous sister, and may these flowers wreathe your brow, if only for an instant. They are the tiara of your betrothal, the pledge of your eternal union with virtue and the assurance of your admission to the communion of believers."

Consuelo, flabbergasted, pored long and hard over every letter, her imagination trying in vain to discover some vague resemblance with Count Albert's handwriting. Despite her suspicions about the sort of initiation to which certain parties seemed to be beckoning her, despite the repulsion she felt for the promises of magic, then so widespread in Germany and every part of Europe touched by the Enlightenment, despite the warnings from her friends about keeping up her defenses, the last words of the red domino as well as the expressions in this anonymous note fired her imagination with that lovely curiosity that could sooner be called poetic expectation. Without much understanding why, she obeyed the cordial command of these unknown friends, placed the crown on her tousled head and fixed her eyes on a mirror as though she expected to see a beloved ghost appear at her back.

The short, sharp ring of a bell startled Consuelo and roused her out of her daydream. She was informed that Herr von Buddenbrock had something to say to her on the spot. These last three words were enunciated with all the arrogance that the king's aide-de-camp put in his words and manners when out of his master's sight.

"Mademoiselle," he said when she joined him in the parlor, "you're following me to the palace at once. Hurry up, no one keeps the king waiting."

"I'm not going to see the king in slippers and a bathrobe," Porporina replied.

"I'll give you five minutes to make yourself decent," said Buddenbrock, pulling out his watch and waving her off to her bedroom.

Consuelo was frightened, yet determined to take upon herself all the dangers and disasters that could engulf the princess and Baron von Trenck. She got dressed in less than the appointed time and reappeared apparently calm before the king's aide-de-camp. Buddenbrock had thought that the king seemed put out while ordering him to bring in the delinquent. At that moment the king's anger became his own, without his knowing what it was about. But seeing how unruffled Consuelo looked, he remembered that the king had a great weakness for the girl. He told himself that she might just win the upcoming battle and bear a grudge against him for mistreating her. He saw fit to lower his tone, thinking that there would always be time to crush her once her disgrace had been consummated.

With a clumsy, stilted attempt at courtesy he offered her his hand and helped her into the carriage he had brought, sat down cap in hand opposite her, put on a subtle, discerning face and said, "Well, Mademoiselle, what a magnificent winter morning!"

"Indeed it is, Baron," Consuelo mockingly replied. "Magnificent weather for a little drive outside the walls."

With these words Consuelo was thinking with stoic cheer that she might just be spending the rest of this magnificent day on the road to some fortress. Yet Buddenbrock, who could not understand the serenity of heroic resignation, thought that she was threatening to have him disgraced and imprisoned if she got the upper hand in the stormy ordeal facing her. He blanched, tried to be pleasant, failed and sank back, bothered and bewildered, anxiously wondering what he had done to offend Porporina.

After being deposited in a small room, Consuelo had time to admire its rose-colored furniture, faded, sprinkled with snuff, frayed by the little dogs that were always sprawling on it—filthy, in other words. The king was not there yet, but she could hear his voice in the next room, and it was a dreadful voice when he was angry. "I tell you, I'll make an example of these scoundrels and purge Prussia of this vermin that's been eating away at her for too long a time," he exclaimed, making his boots creak, as if he were wildly pacing round the room.

"And Your Majesty will render a great service to reason and the kingdom of Prussia," another vòice replied. "But that's no reason why a woman. . . ."

"Oh yes it is, my dear Voltaire. Don't you know that the worst schemes, the most infernal plots are hatched in those little brains?"

"A woman, Sire, a woman!"

"Will you never stop repeating yourself? You love women, Voltaire! You suffered through the reign of a petticoat, and you don't know that they've got to be handled like soldiers or slaves when they meddle in serious matters?"

"But how can Your Majesty believe that there is anything serious in this whole business? It's tranquillizers and shower therapy that should be used with miracle workers and alchemists."

"You don't know what you're talking about, Voltaire! What if I were to tell you that La Mettrie, the poor wretch, has been poisoned?"

"As can happen to anyone who eats more than his stomach can take. Indigestion is a form of poisoning."

"I'm telling you, it wasn't just his gluttony that killed him. He was served eagle pâté and told it was pheasant."

"Prussian eagle is very deadly, I know, but it strikes with lightning, not poison."

"Now, now! Spare me metaphors. I'd bet a hundred to one he was poisoned. La Mettrie fell for all their nonsense, poor devil, and to anyone who wanted to listen he'd say in a manner half serious, half joking that they'd made him see ghosts and demons. He had been so incredulous, so flip, and they addled his wits. Once a friend to Trenck, he turned his back on him, and they punished him in their own way. Well, I'll punish them in turn, I will! And they won't forget it! As for those who mean to hide behind these vile hoaxes to weave their plots and thwart the vigilance of the law. . . ."

At that point the king shut the door that had been left slightly ajar, and Consuelo heard nothing more. She had to agonize for fifteen long minutes before Frederick finally marched in, looking dreadfully old and ugly in his wrath. Without saying a word to her or giving her so much as a glance, he carefully closed all the doors, and when he turned to her, there was something so diabolical about him that for a second she thought he meant to strangle her. She knew that in his fits of rage he reverted, as though despite himself, to his father's savage instincts, that he thought nothing of kicking the shins of his public officials black and blue when he was displeased with their conduct. La Mettrie would laugh at these cowardly acts of cruelty, asserting that they were excellent exercises for gout, from which the king prematurely suffered. Yet La Mettrie would no longer make the king laugh nor laugh at his expense. Two days earlier the man—young, nimble, plump, and fresh-faced—had dropped dead after gorging himself at table, and some dark fancy made the king relish the suspicion that either the hateful Jesuits or the scheming sorcerers then in fashion had engineered his death. Without admitting as much to himself, Frederick too was in the grip of that vague, childish terror that the occult sciences inspired all over Germany.

"Listen up, you!" he said, looking daggers at Consuelo. "You've been unmasked, you are lost, there's only one way for you to save your hide, and that's confessing everything at this very instant, without beating around the bush or holding anything back." As Consuelo was about to say something, he pointed at the floor and shouted, "On your knees, you miserable creature, on your knees! You can't confess such things standing up. Your forehead should already be in the dust. Down on your knees, I tell you, or I won't listen to a word."

"Since I have absolutely nothing to say to you, you don't have to listen," said Consuelo icily. "And you'll never get me down on my knees."

For a second the king considered knocking the crazy girl to the floor and trampling her underfoot. Consuelo unintentionally glanced at Frederick's hands and saw them convulsively reaching in her direction. His nails seemed to be getting longer and longer, arching out like the claws of a cat about to leap on its prey. But the royal claws immediately drew back. Although Frederick could be petty and mean, he was too noble-minded not to admire courage in others. He masked his feelings with a disdainful smile.

"You poor child," he said with a pitiful look, "they've managed to make a fanatic out of you. But listen! Every second counts. You can still redeem your life. In five minutes it'll be too late. I'm giving you the five minutes. Use them well. Make up your mind to reveal everything, or prepare to die."

"I'm all prepared right now," replied Consuelo, indignant that he was making an idle threat to frighten her.

"Be quiet and think hard." The king sat down at his desk and opened a book with an affectation of calm that betrayed a hint of painful, deep emotion.

Consuelo, all the while remembering Herr von Buddenbrock's grotesque imitation of the king when, with watch in hand, he too had given her five minutes to get dressed, decided to do as prescribed and use that time to draw up a plan of action. The thing most to be avoided, she felt, was the clever, probing interrogation that the king would throw around her like a net. Who could dream of confounding such a criminal judge? She risked falling into one of his traps, thinking that she was saving the princess while consummating her ruin. So she nobly resolved not to try and justify herself, not even to ask about the accusations lodged against her. She would instead exasperate the judge by her cheek until he wound up pronouncing his verdict without reason or justice, *ab irato*. Ten minutes later the king had not lifted his eyes from his book. Maybe he wanted to give her time to change her mind, maybe he was absorbed in his reading.

"Have you come to a decision?" he asked, finally putting down the book. He crossed his legs, keeping one elbow on the table.

"There is nothing for me to decide," replied Consuelo. "I am under the rule of injustice and violence. My only option is to endure the consequences."

"Are you accusing me of being violent and unjust?"

"If not you, then the absolute power you wield. It corrupts your soul and leads your judgment astray."

"Bravo. Now you're passing judgment on me, forgetting that you've only got seconds to redeem yourself from death."

"You have no right to dispose of my life; I'm not your subject. If you violate human rights, so much the worse. As for me, I'd rather die than live another day under your laws."

"You genuinely hate me!" said the king, seeming to understand what she was up to and foiling her plan by arming himself with cool contempt. "I see that you've been well trained, and this role of the Spartan virgin that you play so well exposes your accomplices and reveals their hand more than you think. But you don't know much about human rights and the law of nations. Every sovereign has the right to put to death anyone who comes into his territory to conspire against him."

"What! You think I'm conspiring against you?" Consuelo exclaimed, carried away by the conscience of the truth. Too indignant to try and exonerate herself, she shrugged her shoulders and turned her back as if she meant to leave, scarcely knowing what she was doing.

"Where are you going?" asked the king, struck by her air of irresistible candor.

"To prison, to the scaffold, wherever you like, provided that I be spared hearing that absurd accusation."

"You're really quite angry," the king snorted sardonically. "You want me to tell you why? You came here determined to drape yourself in the virtue of ancient Rome, and now you see that I'm amused by your performance. There's no greater mortification, especially for an actress, than falling flat in a role."

Consuelo did not say a word. She just crossed her arms and stared at the king with an assurance that nearly disconcerted him. To dodge her mounting anger, he had to break the silence and resume his devastating derision, still hoping that he could so irk the accused that she would drop her guard and attempt to defend herself.

"Oh yes," he said, as in reply to the silent language of that proud physiognomy, "I'm well aware that you've been led to believe that I was in love with you, that you think that you can defy me and get away with it. This whole thing would be very funny were it not for the involvement of certain people who mean a bit more to me than you do. You were so vain about playing a fine scene that it went to your head. Yet you should know that minor confidants are always sacrificed by those who use them. They're not the ones I intend to go after. They're so close to me that the only way that I can punish them is by riding roughshod over you right in front of their faces. It's up to you now. Are you going to undergo all this pain for people who have betrayed you and blamed everything on your indiscreet, ambitious zeal?"

"Sire," said Consuelo, "I don't know what you mean, but the way you're talking about confidants and those who use them makes me tremble for you."

"Meaning what?"

"Meaning that you would make me think that while you were a tyrant's prime victim, you would have turned Major Katte over to your father's inquisition."

The king went pale as death. It is common knowledge that after having tried to run away to England in his youth he had witnessed his confidant's head being cut off on his father's orders. Locked up in prison, he had been marched to a window and forced to watch his friend's blood running over the scaffold. That horrible scene, in which he was as innocent as possible, made a dreadful impression on him. Yet it is the fate of princes to follow the example of despotism even when they have been subjected to its cruelest effects. Suffering turned Frederick gloomy, and after a wretched youth in chains, he ascended to the throne imbued with the principles and prejudices of absolute power. There was no bloodier reproach than the one Consuelo pretended to aim at the king so as to remind him of his past woes and make him aware of his present injustice. He was wounded to the quick, which had no more salutary effect on his hardened soul than had Officer Katte's execution so many years before. He got up and said in a strange voice, "That's enough, you may go now."

He rang and, for the few seconds before his servants arrived, reopened his book and pretended to dive back into his reading. But his hand twitched nervously and made the page that he was trying to turn rustle.

A footman came in, the king gestured to him, and Consuelo was taken to another room. One of the king's little greyhounds had been keeping an eye on

Consuelo, wagging her tail and prancing about at her feet in order to get a nice pat, and when she left the room, the dog tried to follow her out. The king, who felt fatherly love for these little beasts alone, had to call Mopsule back as she went trotting through the door on the heels of the condemned woman. The king cherished the idea, strange but perhaps not unfounded, that his dogs could instinctively divine the feelings of those who approached him. He was suspicious of the people who always made them growl and felt sure that he could trust the ones the dogs fancied. Despite his inner turmoil Frederick had noticed Mopsule's pronounced affection for Porporina. When the greyhound came back to him, her head cast down in sadness, he pounded on the table and said to himself, "And yet the girl means me no harm!"

"Your Majesty called?" asked Buddenbrock appearing at another door.

"No!" replied the king, indignant about the courtier's eagerness to seize his prey. "Out! I'll ring for you later."

Hurt to be treated like a footman, Buddenbrock withdrew. While the king took a few seconds to meditate, Consuelo was kept under watch in the Gobelins room. At last the bell rang, and the mortified aide-de-camp promptly raced back to his master. Now the king looked mellow and talkative.

"Buddenbrock, what an admirable girl she is!" he exclaimed. "In Rome she would have deserved a triumphal procession, a chariot with four teams of horses and crowns of oak leaves! Get a post chaise hitched up, drive her out of town yourself, and put her under good escort to Spandau where she'll be locked up and treated as a prisoner of the State, and not according to the mildest regime. You understand?"

"Yes, Sire."

"Just a minute! Get into the carriage with her to go through town and give her a scare. It will be good to make her think that she'll be handed over to the executioner and flogged at all the crossroads as was done during my father's reign. While you're telling her all these tales, bear in mind that you're not to touch a single hair on her head, and you'll put on a glove before giving her your hand. Away with you now, and while you're admiring her stoic sacrifice, see how one ought to behave towards those who honor you with their trust. It won't do you any harm."

Chapter XIV

Consuelo was driven home in the same carriage that had taken her to the palace. Two sentries were posted at every door of her apartment inside the building. In his habitual imitation of the master's rigid punctuality, Herr von Buddenbrock gave her, *watch in hand*, an hour to do her packing and warned that her bags would be searched at the fortress where she was going to live. In her bedroom Consuelo found all her possessions in picturesque disarray. During her conference with the king, the secret police had come on orders to force every lock and seize all her papers. Consuelo, who had no manuscripts aside from music, felt sad thinking that she might have seen the last of her precious, dear composers, her only treasure. She had far fewer regrets about a few pieces of jewelry that various dignitaries in Vienna and Berlin had given her in return for her evenings of song. On the pretext that there might be seditious emblems or rings with secret compartments for poison among them, the whole lot had been taken. The king never knew a thing about it, and Consuelo never saw them again. The men who did Frederick's dirty work shamelessly indulged in such honest speculation. They were paid a pittance and knew that the king preferred to close his eyes to their plundering rather than to raise their salaries.

Consuelo first looked for her crucifix, and seeing that they had not thought to grab it, no doubt because it was not worth much, she whipped it off the wall into her pocket. The withered crown of roses was lying on the floor. She picked it up and was alarmed to see that the parchment strip with its mysterious encouragements was gone. That was the only thing that could be used against Consuelo to prove her involvement in an alleged conspiracy. But this feeble clue could give rise to how many interpretations! While her eyes were anxiously sweeping the room, she put her hand in her pocket and found it there, where she had automatically stuffed it when Buddenbrock had come for her an hour before.

With her mind at rest on that point, and sure in the knowledge that nothing in her papers could compromise anyone at all, Consuelo got busy packing what she needed. She did not hide from herself that she could be away for a very long time. There was no one to give her a hand as her maid had been arrested for questioning. Standing among the heaps of clothing that had been torn out of the wardrobes and strewn all over the furniture, she felt upset and a bit disoriented as well. All of a sudden something whistled through the air and dropped into the center of her room. It was a little note stuck through with a fat nail.

The words were few and to the point. "Do you want to escape? Show yourself at the window. In three minutes you'll be in safety."

Consuelo's first impulse was to dash to the window. Halfway there she stopped, for it occurred to her that running away would amount to an admission of guilt, and that, in a case such as hers, never fails to raise the question of accomplices. "Oh, Princess Amalia," she said to herself, "if it's true that you've betrayed me, I won't do the same to you! I'll repay my debt to Trenck. He saved my life; if need be, I'll sacrifice it for him."

Revived by that valiant notion, she fixed her mind on packing and was ready to go by the time Buddenbrock came for her. He seemed even meaner and more hypocritical than usual. Servile and haughty at the same time, Buddenbrock was jealous of his master's affections, like those old dogs that bite all the family friends. Still smarting from the lesson the king had meted out to him while prescribing the victim's torture, he was more than willing to take it out on her.

"I'm greatly distressed, Mademoiselle, to have been given such harsh orders. It's been a very long time since Berlin has seen the like. . . . Indeed, not since the time of King Frederick Wilhelm, the august father of His Majesty now on the throne. It was a cruel example of the severity of our laws and the dreadful power of our princes. I'll remember it my whole life long."

"What example do you mean?" asked Consuelo, starting to think that her life was in jeopardy.

"Nothing in particular," replied Buddenbrock. "I was referring to the entire reign of Frederick Wilhelm, which from one end to the other was an example of rigor never to be forgotten. Back then neither age nor sex mattered when there was a serious crime to be punished. I remember a very pretty, well-bred, and lovely young lady who occasionally received a visit from a certain distinguished person against the king's wishes. She was handed over to the executioner, flogged, and driven out of town."

"I know that story," said Consuelo, torn between terror and indignation. "The young lady was pure and virtuous. Her only crime was making music with His Majesty now on the throne, as you say, and then the crown prince. Has this same Frederick really suffered so little from the catastrophes he's brought down on others that he now wants to horrify me with threats of some equal infamy?"

"I don't think so, Signora. His Majesty does only great and righteous things. It's up to you to know if your innocence will shield you from his wrath. I'd like to think so. Yet a little while ago the king seemed perhaps angrier than I've ever seen him. He exclaimed that he'd been wrong to want to rule with indulgence, that never would a woman have been so bold while his father was alive. His Majesty uttered a few other words that make me fear that he's got some degrading punishment in mind for you, which one I don't know. . . . I don't want to try and guess. My role in this is very painful. I was ordered to take you straight to Spandau, and if we were to learn at the city gate that the king had given other orders, I would hasten to withdraw, as it would be beneath the dignity of my position to watch. . . ."

Seeing that the desired effect had been produced, that poor Consuelo was about to faint, Herr von Buddenbrock stopped. At that instant, she came close to repenting her devotion to others and could not help calling in her heart upon her unknown protectors. Yet, while staring at Buddenbrock with a haggard eye, she detected signs of a liar's hesitation on his face and began to feel less alarmed. All the same, her heart was pounding hard enough to rupture her rib cage when a policeman appeared at the city gate to have a word with Buddenbrock. Meanwhile, one of the grenadiers riding alongside the carriage approached the opposite door and hurriedly whispered, "Don't worry, Signora, there would be a lot of blood shed before anyone puts a hand on you."

Consuelo was in such a state that she could not make out the features of that unknown friend who promptly withdrew. The carriage went galloping off toward the fortress. An hour later Porporina was incarcerated at Spandau Castle according to all the usual formalities, or rather the few formalities required by absolute power.

The citadel, which was then considered impregnable, sits in the middle of the lake formed by the confluence of the Havel and the Spree. The day had turned dark and foggy, and Consuelo, having consummated her sacrifice, experienced that listless exhaustion that follows acts of energy and enthusiasm. Without so much as a glance at her surroundings, she was led to the dreary abode assigned to her. It was scarcely midday, yet she felt so drained that she threw herself down on the bed fully clothed and fell fast asleep. Her fatigue was accompanied by that delicious sense of security that is the fruit of a good conscience. Even though the bed was very hard and narrow, she enjoyed the best sleep. Consuelo had only been half asleep for a while when the citadel clock tolled midnight. A musician's ears are so sensitive that the bells roused her altogether. Sitting up in bed, she understood that she was in prison and that she would have to spend her first night there doing nothing but thinking since she had slept all day long. The prospect of such insomnia in idle darkness was far from pleasant, and she told herself that she had no choice but to resign herself to the fact and start getting used to it right away. Amazed not to feel cold, she was at least glad not to be suffering that bodily discomfort that paralyzes the mind. Outside the wind howled mournfully, the rain beat down on the panes, and through her narrow window Consuelo could see nothing but a dense network of iron bars against the murky depths of a cloudy, starless night.

The poor captive spent the first hour of this new and unfamiliar torture for her in a very lucid mode, her thoughts imbued with logic, reason, and philosophy. Yet bit by bit the effort wore her down, and the night started to feel gloomy. Her positive reflections became vague, weird reveries. Assailed by fantastic images, painful memories, and frightening anxieties, she found herself in a state that was neither waking nor sleeping, where all her thoughts took form and seemed to float through the darkness of her cell. Sometimes in her mind she was on stage singing an entire role that exhausted her, that gripped her memory obsessively, without her being able to get rid of it; sometimes she saw herself in the clutches of an executioner who was flogging her, tearing her bare shoulders to shreds, in front of a stupid, curious mob while the king threw her wrathful looks from high in his balcony and Anzoleto snickered in a corner. At last she fell into a kind of torpor where the only thing before her eyes was Albert's ghost lying in his tomb and vainly struggling to get up and come to her aid. Then that image vanished, and she thought she was sleeping on the ground in the Schreckenstein cave while the sublime, heartrending strains of Albert's violin sang an eloquent, plaintive prayer farther on back. Consuelo was in fact half asleep, and the sound of the instrument caressed her ear and calmed her soul. Even though the music was faint and far away, it went on so steadily, with such distinct modulations that she, without feeling any surprise, thought it was real. It seemed to her that this fantastic concert went on for over an hour, then began imperceptibly fading away. Consuelo had fallen back asleep, and it was dawn when she opened her eyes.

Consuelo's first concern was to examine her room. The day before she had not even given it a glance since her inner life had so totally absorbed her sense of physical existence. The cell in which she found herself was totally bare, but clean and well heated by a brick stove that was lit from outside and provided no light within. Yet it maintained a very tolerable temperature. Although a single arched window was the only source of light, the room was not too dark. The walls were white-washed and rather low.

There were three knocks, and the jailer bellowed through the door, "Prisoner number three, get up and dressed. Your cell will be visited in fifteen minutes."

Consuelo hastened to obey and tidy up her bed before the jailer returned. He brought her bread and water for the day, looking very respectful. With the starchy bearing of a butler in a fine house, he set the frugal prison fare down on the table as neatly and carefully as if he were serving an exquisite meal.

Consuelo studied the elderly man, finding nothing repulsive at first sight in his fine, kindly physiognomy. He had been designated as the women's attendant on account of his high morals, good manners, and unfailing discretion. Schwartz was his name, he said.

"I live down below," he said. "If you become ill, just call out your window."

"Don't you have a wife?" asked Consuelo.

"Indeed I do," he replied. "And if you absolutely require her care, she'll be at your service. Yet she's forbidden to communicate with the lady prisoners except in case of illness, and that's up to the doctor. I also have a son who'll share with me the honor of serving you. . . ."

"I have no need of so many servants. If it's all right with you, Herr Schwartz, I'll just deal with you or your wife."

"I know that my age and appearance reassure the ladies. Yet my son is no more to be feared than I am. He's an excellent boy, very pious, sweet, and firm."

The jailer pronounced the last word in a clear, meaningful way that the prisoner understood very well.

"Herr Schwartz," she said, "you'll have no need to be firm with me. I'm here almost of my own accord, and I have no intention to try and escape. As long as I'm treated decently, as one seems disposed to do, there'll be no complaints from me about the prison regime, whatever its rigors."

With these words Consuelo, who had eaten nothing for twenty-four hours and suffered pangs of hunger all night long, broke the dark bread and began gobbling it down.

Then she noticed that her resignation had made an impression on the old man, who looked both amazed and disgruntled.

"Your Ladyship doesn't find this coarse fare repugnant?" he asked, somewhat abashed.

"I won't hide from you that in the interests of my health I'd eventually like something more substantial. Yet if this is all that's available, I can make do."

"But weren't you used to living and eating well?"

"Of course."

"Well then," asked Schwartz with an insinuating look, "why don't you have yourself served proper food here, at your own expense?"

"Is that allowed?"

"Certainly!" exclaimed Schwartz, his eyes sparkling at the prospect of working out one of his little deals with her. He had feared that she was either too poor or too temperate to assure him this extra income. "If your Ladyship took care to conceal a bit of money on her person upon arriving here. . . . I'm not forbidden to provide her with the food she likes. My wife is a very good cook, and we have a very nice silver service."

"How very kind of you," said Consuelo, more disgusted than gratified to discover how greedy Schwartz was. "But the question is knowing if I indeed have any money. I was searched when I got here. I know that I was left a crucifix that means a lot to me, but I didn't notice if they took my purse."

"Your Ladyship didn't notice?"

"No. Does that surprise you?"

"But Your Ladyship no doubt knows what was in her purse?"

"Very nearly," said Consuelo, checking out her pockets, which she found completely empty. "Herr Schwartz," she announced with good cheer, "they cleaned me out, from what I can see. That means that I'll just have to content myself with the usual regime. So you mustn't get your hopes up."

"Well, Madame," replied Schwartz, visibly straining himself, "I'm going to give you proof that my family is honest and that you're dealing with people worthy of respect. Your purse is in my pocket, and here it is!" He flashed the purse in front of her eyes, then imperturbably put it back in his waistcoat pocket.

"May it bring you profit!" said Consuelo, stunned by his cheek.

"Hold on!" Schwartz continued, no less greedy than meticulous. "My wife is the one who searched you. She is under orders not to let the women prisoners keep any money, lest they try and corrupt their jailers. Yet when the jailers are incorruptible, that's a useless precaution. For that reason she didn't consider herself duty bound to turn your money over to the commanding officer. Yet, since one must in conscience obey the letter of the law, your purse cannot be returned directly to your care."

"So keep it, since that's your pleasure!" exclaimed Consuelo.

"Indeed, I'm going to keep it, and you'll wind up thanking me. I am the trustee of your funds, and I'll use them, as you see fit, to satisfy your needs. You'll have meals to your liking, a well-tended stove, even a better bed and all the linens you want. Every day I'll draw up a bill and pay myself out of your purse for that amount."

"Well done!" said Consuelo. "I see that one can bargain with the powers on high, and I have all due respect for the honesty of Herr Schwartz. And when this modest sum runs out, you'll help me replenish my purse?"

"I beg your Ladyship not to put it that way! That would be a breach of duty, to which I'll never stoop. But there'll be no problem, for Your Ladyship will let me know with whom she deposits her funds, in Berlin or elsewhere, and I'll settle up with him on a regular basis. My orders don't forbid that."

"Very good. You've found the fix for that regulation which is most inconsistent, since it allows you to treat us well, yet deprives us of the means to make you decide to do it. When my gold ducats are all gone, I'll see about arranging to have you paid. You can start by bringing me some chocolate. For dinner I'll have a chicken and vegetables. During the day you'll get me some books and at night provide me with light."

"Your Ladyship will have her chocolate in five minutes. Dinner will be no trouble at all, and I'll add a good soup, some little delicacies that please the ladies, plus coffee, which always helps against the humidity of this residence. As for the books and lamps, there's no way. I'd be fired immediately, and my conscience won't allow me to disobey orders."

"But aren't fancy food and delicacies prohibited as well?"

"No. Humane treatment for the ladies, particularly your Ladyship, is allowed in all matters relating to health and well-being."

"But boredom is just as detrimental to one's health!"

"Your Ladyship is mistaken. Eating well and resting the mind always fatten them up here. I could cite you a lady who arrived here just as slim as you are. Twenty years later she left weighing at least one hundred and eighty pounds."

"Thank you very much, Herr Schwartz. I have no desire to get so dreadfully fat, and I hope that you won't refuse me books and light."

"I humbly beg your Ladyship's pardon, but I won't commit any infractions against duty. Besides, Your Ladyship won't be bored, for she'll have her harpsichord and music here."

"Truly? Do I owe this consolation to you, Herr Schwartz?"

"No, Signora, those are His Majesty's orders. I also have instructions from the commanding officer to let these objects in and have them brought to your room."

Consuelo, delighted to be able to make music, did not think of asking for anything more. While Herr Schwarz arranged the rickety bed, the two straw-bottomed chairs, and the little pine table that were all her furniture, she merrily sipped her chocolate.

"Your Ladyship will need a chest of drawers," he said with that sweet look of people willing to lavish us with kindness and attention in exchange for our money. "And then a better bed, a carpet, a desk, an armchair, a washstand. . . ."

"I'll take the chest of drawers and the washstand," replied Consuelo, wanting to spare her resources. "There's no need for anything else. I'm not delicate, and please bring me only the things I've requested."

With a look of surprise bordering on contempt, Herr Schwartz wordlessly shook his head. When he got back to his most worthy wife, he said, "It's not mean, but it's poor. We won't make a lot off this one."

"What do you want it to spend?" asked Frau Schwartz, shrugging her shoulders. "This one's no great lady, but an actress, from what I hear."

"An actress!" Schwartz exclaimed. "Well, I'm delighted for our son Gottlieb."

"Shame on you!" said his wife with a scowl. "You want her to turn him into a circus performer?"

"You don't understand, wife. He's going to be a pastor. I'll never change my mind about that. He's done the necessary studies, and he's made of the right stuff. Yet he'll have to preach, and as he hasn't shown any signs of great eloquence so far, the actress will give him speech lessons."

"Not a bad idea, as long as she doesn't want to deduct her fees from our bills!"

"Don't you worry about that! She's utterly witless," replied Schwartz, sniggering and rubbing his hands together.

Chapter XV

The harpsichord, the same one that Consuelo had been renting at her own expense in Berlin, arrived during the day. She was delighted not to have to risk getting acquainted with a new instrument, perhaps less pleasing and reliable. While issuing orders that the harpsichord be sent to the prison, the king, who always tended to the tiniest details, asked whether it belonged to the prima donna. Learning that it was rented, he notified the owner, a violin maker, to say that he would guarantee the instrument's return, while the prisoner remained responsible for the rent; whereupon the violin maker pointed out that he had no recourse against a person in prison, especially if she were to die there. Herr von Poelnitz, who had been put in charge of this important negotiation, retorted with a laugh, "My dear man, you don't want to wrangle with the king over such a trifle. Besides, it won't get you anywhere. Your harpsichord is under arrest and will be locked up this very day at Spandau."

Porporina's manuscripts and scores arrived as well. While she was amazed at such amenity in her prison regime, the fortress commander came to explain that she would be continuing as the female lead singer at the royal theater.

"Such is His Majesty's will," he said. "Each time your name is put on the program at the Opera, a carriage under escort will convey you to the theater at the appointed hour and return you to bed at the fortress directly after the performance. These journeys to and fro will be conducted with clockwork precision and all due respect to you. I hope, Mademoiselle, that you won't attempt an escape, thereby forcing us to augment the rigors of your captivity. In accordance with the king's orders, you've been given a heated room and permission to walk on the rampart you see there whenever you wish. In short, we are responsible not only for your person but for your health and voice as well. The only rub is that you're to remain in solitary confinement, without communication of any sort with anyone inside these walls or out. As there are just a few ladies here and one jailer serves the whole wing, you'll be spared the unpleasantness of being tended by boors. Herr Schwartz's honest face and good manners ought to ease your mind in that respect. So, a little boredom will be your only hardship. Given your age and the brilliant situation you enjoyed. . . ."

"Don't worry, Herr Commandant," said Consuelo with a touch of pride. "I'm never bored as long as I can keep busy. Just one favor, please. May I have some writing materials and light for making music in the evenings?"

"That's altogether impossible. I'm desperately sorry to turn down the sole request of such a courageous person. Yet in compensation I can authorize you to sing whenever you wish, day or night. Yours is the only inhabited room in this isolated tower. True, the jailer lives below. Yet Herr Schwartz is too well bred to complain about hearing such a lovely voice, and I'm personally sorry to be out of earshot."

This dialogue, with Herr Schwartz looking on, ended in many deep bows, after which the elderly officer took his leave. Judging from the singer's composure, he felt sure that she had been sent to Spandau for some breach of theatrical discipline and for a few weeks at the very most. Consuelo herself did not know the reason for her arrest, whether it was for suspicion of complicity in a political conspiracy, for the simple crime of doing Frederick von Trenck a good turn, or merely for being Princess Amalia's discreet confidante.

For two or three days our captive felt more restless, disheartened, and bored than she wanted to admit to herself. The long nights, still fourteen hours in that wintry season, were particularly unpleasant while she clung to the hope that Herr Schwartz would deliver her from the dark with a supply of light, pens, and ink. But she soon learned that the obsequious Schwartz was endowed with inflexible tenacity. He was not evil, nor was he sadistic, like most of his kind. He was even pious and devout in his way, believing that he was serving God and saving his soul as long as he fulfilled every professional duty that could not be shirked. True, these reserved sins were few in number, generally situations where he stood a greater chance of putting his job in danger than making a dime on the prisoners. "What a simpleton," he said to his wife about Consuelo, "thinking that I'd risk getting myself fired just to earn a few *groschen* a day on candles!"

"You be careful now. No more dinners, not even a single one, when her money runs out," ordered Frau Schwartz, the Egeria of his greedy inspirations.

"Don't worry. She's got savings, she told me, and they're deposited with Porporino, another singer at the theater."

"That's a bad debt!" his wife went on. "Take another look at our Prussian law code and you'll see an article with regard to actors, which absolves any debtor from all claims on their behalf. Watch out that her depositary doesn't invoke the law and hold back the money when you show him your accounts."

"I'll just have her salary attached, since prison hasn't broken her engagement with the theater."

"And who says she's going to be paid? The king knows the law better than anyone, and if he sees fit to invoke it. . . ."

"You think of everything, wife!" said Herr Schwartz. "I'll be on my guard. No money? No hot meals, no heat, just regulation furnishings. Everything strictly by the book."

That is how Herr and Frau Schwartz discussed Consuelo and her fate. As for the prisoner, once it had become clear that the honest jailer was incorruptible in the matter of candles, she made the best of it and arranged her days so as not to suffer too much from the long nights. She stopped singing when it was light, saving that activity for the evening hours. She even tried to refrain from thinking about music and entertaining herself with musical reminiscences or inspirations until after dark. She devoted mornings and afternoons to meditations on her present plight, memories of the past and dreams about the future. That way she soon succeeded in splitting her life into two parts, one altogether philosophical and the other altogether musical; and she recognized that with painstaking care and perseverance a person can to some degree make the capricious, balky charger of fantasy, the odd muse of imagination function on a regular basis and subject them to her will. By living soberly, despite Herr Schwartz's prescriptions and insinuations, and getting lots of exercise, even without pleasure, on the rampart, she managed to feel very calm at day's end and made pleasant use of those dark hours that prisoners, forcing sleep to escape boredom, fill with phantoms and fidgeting. Allotting herself just six hours in bed, she was soon sure of peaceful slumber every night, without excess sleep one night ever compromising the next night's repose.

By the end of a week she was already so thoroughly used to her prison that it felt as if she had never lived otherwise. Her evenings, so forbidding at first, were now her favorite time; and the darkness, far from scaring her as she had expected, revealed treasures of musical conception that she had been carrying around inside, never finding a chance to put them to use and formulate their elements because of her bustling singing career. When she felt that improvising and singing from memory would fill her evenings, she let herself devote a few hours of daylight to noting her inspirations and studying her composers even more carefully than she had been able to do in a whirlwind of emotion or under the eye of an impatient, systematic professor. At first, she wrote music by taking a pin and pricking little holes between the lines, then by using little splinters of wood from her furniture that she blackened against the stove when it was good and hot. As both methods took a lot of time and her supply of ruled paper was very limited, she saw that it would be better to exercise her robust memory more and to file away there the many compositions that each evening brought forth. After getting them all down, she learned with practice to skip from one unwritten piece to another without mixing them up.

Yet, as her room was very warm, thanks to the extra fuel that Herr Schwartz added at no cost to the usual allotment, and the rampart where she walked was always raked by an icy wind, she inevitably went hoarse for a few days, which deprived her of the pleasure of going to sing in Berlin. On the very day that Herr von Pœlnitz, with the king's consent, had aimed to bring her back before an audience, the prison doctor, under orders to see her twice a week and report on her health, wrote to the baron that she had lost her voice. Her outing was thus delayed, and without the slightest twinge of disappointment on her part. She had no desire to breathe the air of freedom until prison had become such a familiar routine that she could return without regret.

For that reason she did not nurse her cold with all the love and care that a singer usually lavishes on her precious throat. Refusing to give up her walks on the ramparts, she had a slight fever for several nights and experienced a little phenomenon familiar to us all. Anyone with fever undergoes illusions that are more or less unpleasant. Some imagine that the angle formed by the walls of the apartment is closing in on them, getting tighter and tighter, finally squeezing and crushing their heads; then, little by little the angle opens up, setting them free and returning to its original position; then it starts tightening up again, and the whole cycle of distress and relief goes round and round again. Others take their bed for a wave that sweeps them up high as the canopy, then throws them down, then sweeps them up all over again, doggedly tossing them about. When the narrator of this true story is feverish, he has the bizarre illusion of a huge black shadow spreading out horizontally over a brilliant surface with him in its middle. The dark spot swimming over the imaginary ground never stops contracting and expanding. It dilates until it entirely covers the brilliant surface, then immediately shrinks down to a tenuous thread, after which the same process starts up over and over again. The dreamer would find nothing unpleasant about this vision, were it not for a sickly feeling rather difficult to explain that he himself is this obscure reflection of an unknown object restlessly floating over sands burnt by the rays of an invisible sun, and to such an extent that when the imaginary shadow contracts, he feels himself getting small and thin as the silhouette of a hair and when it expands, he feels the substance of his being distending in space like a mountain's shadow reaching over a valley. Yet there is neither mountain nor valley in this dream. There is nothing but the image of an opaque body performing in a sunny reflection the same exercise as a cat's black pupil in its transparent iris, and this waking hallucination turns into one of the strangest tortures.

We could cite several cases: one person sees the ceiling come crashing down at every instant when he has a fever; another thinks that he has turned into a globe floating through space; and two others take the space between their beds and the wall for the edge of an abyss, one falling off to the left and the other to the right. But each reader could furnish his observations and the phenomena of his own experience, which would not advance the question nor explain better than we can why every individual, over the course of a whole life or at least for a long period of years, has his own particular dream every night, why every attack of fever produces the same hallucination and the same anguish. This is a matter of physiology; and we think that a doctor might find a few signs that relate not to the source of the obvious problem, revealed by other symptoms no less obvious, but to the seat of a hidden problem deriving from a weakness in the patient's constitution and that it is dangerous to provoke by certain reagents.

Yet this is beyond my scope, and I beg the reader's pardon for having dared broach the topic.

As for our heroine, the hallucination brought on by her fever was naturally of a musical sort and involved her hearing. Slipping back into the dreamy state, awake or half-awake, through which her mind had drifted during her first night in prison, she imagined hearing Albert's violin with its plaintive wail and eloquent phrases, sometimes loud and clear as though the strings were resonating in her cell, sometimes faint as though the music were coming from the edge of the earth. There was something strangely distressing about the rise and fall of the imaginary sounds. When Consuelo thought that the vibration was drawing nearer, she felt terrified; when it appeared to reach its climax, an explosion of sound would hit her like a bolt of lightning. Then the volume would taper off, but without affording her much relief, for it was such an ever greater strain to try and hear the music fading away into the distance that she would soon fall into a faint and seem to lose all sense of hearing. Yet, the incessant return of the harmonious blast sent a thrill through her, made her shudder with terror and burn with unbearable heat as if the vigorous stroke of the ghostly bow had set the air on fire and unleashed a hurricane around her.

Chapter XVI

Yet Consuelo was not alarmed by her condition and changed almost nothing in her regimen, which meant that she was soon back on her feet. Her evenings were once again filled with song and followed by nights of deep, peaceful sleep.

One morning, the twelfth of her captivity, she had a note from Herr von Poelnitz with the news that she would be going out the following evening. "I've received permission from the king," he wrote, "to come fetch you myself in one of his carriages. If you give me your word not to fly out a window, I even hope to spare you the escort and let you reappear at the theater without those gloomy trappings. Rest assured that you have no friend more devoted than I, who deplore the rigorous, perhaps unjust treatment you are undergoing."

Porporina was somewhat surprised by the baron's sudden affection and delicate kindness. Up until then, in his many dealings as theater administrator with the prima donna, Herr von Poelnitz had been quite chilly and curt. The old rake was not fond of virtuous women, and several times he had even mocked her decorum and reserve right to her face. It was well known at court that the elderly chamberlain was the king's stool pigeon, but Consuelo was not privy to court secrets, nor was she aware that one could ply this loathsome trade without forfeiting the privileges of apparent social respectability. Yet a vague instinct of repulsion told Consuelo that Poelnitz was more to blame than anyone else for her plight. So she watched her tongue when late the next afternoon she found herself alone with him in a carriage speeding to Berlin.

"Well, my poor recluse," he said, "that's one devilishly tight spot they've got you in! Those stiff old guards are simply ferocious! On the pretext that I didn't have permission, they wouldn't let me into the citadel. It's no fault of yours, but for fifteen minutes I've been freezing out here waiting for you. Here, wrap up in this fur I brought along to save your voice, and tell me a bit about your adventures. What the devil happened at the last carnival ball? Everybody's wondering, and nobody has a clue. Several strange characters who to my mind weren't doing any harm seem to have vanished into thin air. The Count de Saint-Germain, one of your friends, I believe; plus, a certain Trismegistus, whom you may know as well, who was reportedly holed up at Herr von Golowkin's place; for people say you're on the best of terms with all these children of the devil. . . ."

"Have they been arrested?" asked Consuelo.

"Either that, or they've fled. Both versions are going round town."

"If they don't know any better than I the reason for their persecution, they'd have been wiser to sit tight and wait for time to do them justice."

"Or for the new moon which may change the king's mood. That's still the surest bet, and I advise you to sing well tonight. That'll have more effect on him than fine words. How the devil could you ever be so clumsy as to get yourself packed off to Spandau, my pretty friend? You stand accused of mere trifles, and for that the king wouldn't ever have uttered a condemnation so discourteous to a woman. You must have acted high and mighty with him, cap down over your ear and hand on the hilt on your sword, like the mad little thing that you are. So what's your crime? Come on, tell me. I bet I can fix things up for you. Take my advice, and instead of going back to that damp old mousetrap of Spandau, you'll sleep tonight in your pretty little apartment in Berlin. Come on, tell me everything. I've heard you shared an elegant supper in the palace with Princess Amalia and amused yourself in the middle of the night playing ghost and fooling around with a broom in the hallways to scare the wits out of the queen's maids of honor. Several apparently had miscarriages, and the babies born to the most virtuous of them will have little broom-shaped birthmarks on their noses. I've also heard that Madame von Kleist's *planetary* told your fortune and that Saint-Germain revealed to you the mysteries of the politics of Philip the Fair. The king just wants a good chuckle with his sister over these follies. Are you foolish enough to think otherwise? Besides, the king has such a childish weakness for the abbess. As for seers, he only wants to know if they take money for the nonsense they utter, in which case they are asked to leave the country, and that's that. So you see that you're deluding yourself about the importance of your role, and had you been willing to answer a few trivial questions, you wouldn't have spent such a dreary carnival as a political prisoner."

Consuelo let the old courtier babble on without interruption, and when he urged her to say something, she persisted in saying that she had no idea what he was talking about. Sensing a trap beneath that amiable frivolity, she held safely back.

Then Poelnitz changed tactics and said in a serious tone, "Good! You're suspicious of me, which I don't hold against you. On the contrary, I set great store by prudence. This being the case, I'll go ahead and speak openly. You're clearly trustworthy, and our secret is in good hands. I want you to know, Signora

Porporina, that I am more your friend than you think, for I'm one of yours. I've thrown in my lot with Prince Heinrich's camp."

"So Prince Heinrich has a camp?" asked Porporina, curious to learn in what plot she was involved.

"Don't pretend ignorance," the baron went on. "They're suffering a lot of persecution just now, but the cause is far from desperate. The *grand lama* or *Monsieur le marquis*, as you wish, isn't all that steady on his throne, and it wouldn't be impossible to topple him. Prussia is a fine old warhorse, but it mustn't be ridden too hard."

"So you're conspiring, Baron? Never would I have suspected that!"

"Who isn't these days? The little tyrant is surrounded by ostensibly devoted servants who have sworn to bring him down."

"How very careless of you, Baron, to confide in me this way."

"If I do so, it's with the authorization of the prince and princess."

"What princess?"

"You know which one. I don't think the others are conspiring! Except maybe the Margravine von Bayreuth, whose nose is out of joint about her paltry position, and she's been furious with the king ever since he took her to task for her secret dealings with Cardinal Fleury. That's already an old affair, but there's no end to a woman's spite, and Margravine *Guillemette* is no ordinary mind.[1] How does she strike you?"

"I've never had the privilege of hearing a single word out of her."

"But you've seen her in the Abbess of Quedlinburg's rooms!"

"I've been just once to see Princess Amalia, and the only other member of the royal family whom I saw there was the king."

"Never mind. Prince Heinrich told me to tell you. . . ."

"Truly, Baron?" asked Consuelo in a scornful tone.

"You'll see that I'm not joking. He'll have you know that things have not gone wrong for him, as they want to make you believe. None of his confidants has betrayed him. Saint-Germain is already in France working on an alliance between our conspiracy and the one that will very soon have Charles Edward back on the throne. The only one under arrest is Trismegistus, but the prince will arrange his escape. In the meantime, he knows that Trismegistus will keep his mouth shut. As for you, the prince begs you not to let yourself be intimidated by the *marquis'* threats and, above all, not to trust those who would pretend to be on your side to make you talk. That's the reason for the little test I gave you a moment ago, which you passed with flying colors, and I'll tell our hero, our

1. Sophie Wilhelmine, who signed her letters to Voltaire with the name *Soeur Guillemette.*

brave prince and future king, that you are one of the staunchest champions of his cause!"

Consuelo marveled at Herr von Poelnitz's aplomb and could not choke back a laugh. When the baron, stung by her contempt, inquired about the reason for her untoward burst of hilarity, she could only say, "You are admirable, sublime, Baron!"

In spite of herself, Consuelo once again started to laugh. She would have laughed while being thrashed with a stick, like Monsieur Jourdain's Nicole.

"When this attack of nerves is over," said Poelnitz, unperturbed, "perhaps you'll be so kind as to explain to me your intentions. Do you wish to betray the prince? Do you really think it was the princess who delivered you up to the king's wrath? Do you consider yourself freed from your oaths? Watch out, Mademoiselle! You may soon be sorry. Before long we'll turn Silesia over to Maria Theresa, who still has certain designs in mind. From that point on she'll be our powerful ally. Russia and France will surely reach out to Prince Heinrich; Madame de Pompadour hasn't forgotten how Frederick snubbed her. A strong coalition and a few years of war can easily topple this proud sovereign who is moreover hanging only by a thread. . . . With the new monarch's love you can expect great wealth. At the very least, the Elector of Saxony will lose the Polish throne, and Prince Heinrich will go reign in Warsaw, and so. . . ."

"So, according to you, Baron, there's a conspiracy to make Europe wallow in fire and blood all over again, and all for the pleasure of Prince Heinrich? And to satisfy his ambition, the prince would stoop so low as to betray his country into foreign hands? I have a hard time believing that such despicable things are possible. If that's unfortunately the truth, I'm deeply ashamed to pass as your accomplice. Let's put an end to this comedy, I beg you. For fifteen minutes you've been doing your clever best to make me confess imaginary crimes. I've heard you out to learn on what pretext I'm being kept in prison. I still don't know what I've done to deserve being pursued by such vile, relentless hatred. If you wish to tell me, I'll try and prove my innocence. Until then I can only say this: I'm amazed by all the fine things you're telling me, and I have no sympathy for such projects."

"If that's really all you know, Mademoiselle," said Poelnitz, greatly mortified, "I'm stunned that the prince would be so careless as to tell me to speak plainly to you, before making sure that you were a party to all his projects."

"I repeat, Baron, I know absolutely nothing about the prince's projects, but I'm very sure of this one thing. He never told you to say a single word to me about them. Please forgive me for flatly contradicting you, but I don't believe it. While I respect your age, I cannot help despising the hideous role you're playing with me just now."

"I'm scarcely wounded by the absurd suspicions of a woman's mind," he replied, finding it impossible to back away from his lies. "One day you'll do me justice. Persecution is upsetting, and prison necessarily inspires gloomy thoughts, so it comes as no surprise that you've suddenly lost your discernment and insight. In conspiracies one must always expect such vagaries, especially from the ladies, for which you have my pity and forgiveness. Besides, it may be that in all this you're nothing more than Trenck's devoted friend and an august princess's confidante. . . . These secrets are of such a delicate nature that I don't want to go into them with you. Prince Heinrich himself closes his eyes to them, even though he knows that his sister joined the conspiracy only because she hoped that Trenck would be rehabilitated and might marry her."

"I don't know anything about that either, Baron. And if you were truly devoted to an august princess, I don't think you'd be telling me such strange things about her."

When the racket of wheels on cobblestones put an end to this conversation, the baron, at wit's end, was greatly relieved. They were entering the city. Two sentries who did not mean to let Consuelo out of their sight escorted her to her dressing room and through the wings. She received a rather chilly welcome from the other members of the troupe. They loved her, but none of them felt the courage to protest by any outward signs the disgrace decreed by the king. They were sad, stiff, and seemingly stricken by the fear of contamination. Preferring to attribute this behavior not to cowardice but compassion, Consuelo read on their drawn faces that she was going to spend a long time in captivity. She did her best to show them that she was undaunted and stepped out onto the stage with pluck and self-assurance.

At that moment something rather odd happened in the auditorium. As Porporina's arrest had created a great stir, as every person in attendance was devoted to the king out of conviction or position, they all stuffed their hands into their pockets to resist applauding the disgraced singer out of desire or habit. Every eye was on the monarch who was sweeping an investigatory gaze over the crowd, seeming to impose utter silence on them. All of a sudden a crown of flowers came flying out of nowhere and landed at Porporina's feet. At one and the same time several voices said loudly enough to be heard in various parts of the auditorium, "*It's the king! The king's pardon*!" This remarkable assertion flew from mouth to mouth with the speed of lightning. Convinced that they were doing their duty as well as obliging the king, the audience began clapping, and a storm of applause, such as no one ever remembered hearing in Berlin, burst forth from every seat in the house. For several minutes Porporina, speechless and overwhelmed by such a bold protest, was unable to begin her role. Dumbfounded, the king turned around and gave the audience a dreadful look that was taken as a sign of support and encouragement. Buddenbrock himself, who was not sitting far from the king, asked young Benda what was going on. After being told that the crown came from the king, he began applauding with a miffed look that was truly comical. Porporina thought she was dreaming; the king was pinching himself to see if he were well awake.

Whatever the cause and aim of this triumphant ovation, Consuelo felt its salutary effects. She outdid herself and excited the same wild applause throughout the whole first act. During the first intermission, however, the misunderstanding had bit by bit dissipated, and only the humblest members of the audience, too far removed from the whispers of courtiers to learn the error of their ways, stubbornly went on showing their favor. Finally, at the second intermission, everyone knew from various speeches in the corridors and foyer that the king seemed most displeased with the audience's unreasonable attitude. It was said that Porporina, with unheard-of audacity, had formed a cabal and that anyone known to have participated in that little fiasco would surely regret it. During the third act, despite Porporina's marvelous singing, the auditorium fell into such a deep hush after each of her parts that one could have heard the flutter of a fly's wing. Meanwhile her fellow performers reaped all the fruits of this backlash.

Porporina had been promptly disillusioned about her triumph.

"My poor friend," said Conciolini handing her the crown in the wings after the first scene, "I pity you for having such dangerous friends. They'll seal your doom."

During the intermission Porporino came to her dressing room and whispered, "I had told you to watch out for Saint-Germain, but it was too late. There are traitors in every camp. Don't be any less faithful to friendship and docile to your conscience. You are defended by a stronger arm than the one oppressing you."

"What do you mean?" exclaimed Porporina. "Are you one of those. . . ."

"I mean that God will defend you," replied Porporino, who seemed afraid of being overheard and pointed to one of the partitions between the dressing rooms. They were ten feet tall but stopped considerably short of the ceiling, which meant that one could easily hear what was going on in the next cubicle.

"I foresaw that you would need money, and I've brought you some," he said in an even lower voice, handing her a purse.

"Thank you," said Consuelo. "If the jailer, who charges me high prices for supplies, comes after you with a bill, refuse to pay. This ought to keep him happy for a long time. He's a real usurer."

"That's enough," said Porporino, a good and loyal man. "I've got to go now.

If it looked as though we were sharing secrets, things would only be the worse for you."

He slipped away, and Consuelo received a visit from Mme de Cocceï (Signora Barberini), who bravely showed her lots of interest and affection. The Marquise d'Argens (Mlle Cochois) joined them, looking a bit starchy and talking like a queen on an errand of mercy. Consuelo was nonetheless grateful for her gesture and begged her not to jeopardize her husband's fine position by staying much longer.

The king asked Poelnitz, "Well, did you question her? Did you find a way to make her talk?"

"No more than if she'd been a statue," replied the baron.

"Did you make her understand that I'd pardon everything if she'd just tell me what she knows about the *sweeper* and what Saint-Germain said to her?"

"She couldn't care less."

"Did you frighten her about the duration of her captivity?"

"Not yet. Your Majesty had told me to go gently on her."

"So put a scare in her on the way back."

"I'll try, but it won't do any good."

"What is she? A saint, a martyr?"

"She's a fanatic, a woman possessed, maybe the devil in petticoats."

"In that case, she's in real trouble! I wash my hands of the girl. The season of Italian opera will be over in the next few days. See to it that they manage to finish up without her, and don't let me hear another word about her until next year."

"A whole year! Your Majesty will never stick to that!"

"Better than your head sticks to your shoulders, Poelnitz!"

Chapter XVII

Although Poelnitz had enough grudges against Porporina to seize this chance for revenge, he did nothing. He was a consummate coward and could only get nasty with those who threw themselves on his mercy. The slightest suggestion that he had overstepped his bounds made him cringe, and he seemed to feel instinctive respect for anyone who saw through his schemes. He had even been seen to turn away from those who pampered his vices to follow, his tail between his legs, others who trampled him underfoot. Was this because he knew his own weakness or cherished a memory of lost dignity? One would like to believe that in the most corrupt souls there is still a vestige of better instincts that have been stifled or subsist only as pain and remorse. It is a fact that for a long time Poelnitz had stuck close to Prince Heinrich, pretending to sympathize with his sorrows, often urging him to complain about his mistreatment at the hands of the king and giving him an example of how to do it; then he would go repeat the prince's words back to the king, even making them more venomous so as to magnify Frederick's wrath. Poelnitz had practiced this vile trade for reasons of pleasure; for, at bottom, he did not hate the prince. He did not hate anyone aside from the king, who went on redoubling his disgrace without wanting to line his pockets. Poelnitz loved guile for its own sake. Deception was a flattering triumph in his eyes. Stabbing the king in the back and getting others to do the same gave him real pleasure. And when he relayed these curses to Frederick, all the while priding himself on having provoked them, he inwardly enjoyed being able to pull the same trick on his master by concealing the joy he had felt jeering at the king, betraying him, revealing his foibles, follies, and vices to his enemies. Thus, both sides were his dupes, and that life of intrigue in which he stirred up hatred without exactly serving the hatred of any particular person was for him full of secret delights.

Prince Heinrich meanwhile wound up noticing that each time he let his sour feelings show in front of the obliging baron, a few hours later the king would be more angry and insulting with him than usual. If he complained to Poelnitz about being under arrest for twenty-four hours, he would find his sentence doubled the next day. Finally this prince, as frank as he was brave, as trusting as Frederick was suspicious, opened his eyes to the baron's wretched character. Rather than dealing with Poelnitz gingerly, he flew into a rage and let him have it. From that point on, the baron kowtowed to the prince and made no more mischief for him. Deep in his heart he even seemed to love the man, inasmuch as his heart was able to love. Tender feelings washed over Poelnitz as he extolled Prince Heinrich and his qualities. These marks of respect looked so sincere that people were amazed by the incomprehensible quirks of such a man.

The truth is that Poelnitz found the king's brother a thousand times more generous and tolerant than the king himself and would have preferred Heinrich as his master. Like the king, he had a sense or vague hunch about some sort of mysterious plot involving the prince. Yearning to be the one pulling the strings, he was eager to know if it stood a good enough chance of success for him to join in. So it was with the intention of clarifying things for his own sake that he had tried to deceive Consuelo. Had she revealed the little that she knew, he would not have tattled to the king, not unless Frederick had paid him handsomely. Yet Frederick was too thrifty to have great scoundrels at his orders.

Poelnitz had pried a few pieces of the puzzle out of the Count de Saint-Germain by saying with such conviction such dreadful things about the king that this clever adventurer had let his guard down a bit too far. Let it be said in passing that Saint-Germain had a streak of enthusiasm and folly; while he was phony and even jesuitical in many respects, there lay beneath all that a fanatical conviction that stood in remarkable contrast to these qualities and made him do many thoughtless things.

On the way back to the fortress, Poelnitz, a bit blasé about people's contempt for him and having already nearly forgotten Consuelo's sneers, was quite candid with her. Without any coaxing he confessed that he knew nothing, that everything he had said about the prince's dealings with foreign powers was just idle talk based on the strange conduct and secret relations of the prince and his sister with various suspicious characters.

"These comments do no honor to your Lordship's loyalty," said Consuelo. "Perhaps it would be better not to boast about them."

"These comments didn't originate with me," Poelnitz replied imperturbably. "They were hatched in the brain of our king and master, a sick and gloomy brain, if ever there was one, when seized with suspicion. And treating guesswork like facts is such a time-hallowed method among courtiers and diplomats that you're a total prig to be scandalized. Besides, I learned this from kings. They taught me what I know, and all my vices come from the two Prussian kings, father and son, whom I've been honored to serve. Telling a lie to get at the truth! Frederick has never done anything else, and he's considered a great man. It's all the rage now! Yet I'm called a scoundrel because I follow the error of his ways. It's so unfair!"

Poelnitz pestered Consuelo as much as he could to learn what was going on with her, the prince, the abbess, Trenck, the adventurers Saint-Germain and Trismegistus, as well as a great number of very important people, or so he said, who were mixed up in an inexplicable intrigue. He naïvely confessed that he would not hesitate to throw in his lot if there were something to it. To Consuelo it was clear that he was at last being frank with her. Yet there was no merit in her stubborn denials because she truly knew nothing.

After watching the gates of the fortress swing shut on Consuelo and her supposed secret, he wondered how to proceed with her. In the end, hoping that she would open up if he managed to get her back to Berlin, he resolved to exonerate her in the eyes of the king. Yet, no sooner had he broached the topic the next day than the king cut him off.

"Did she reveal anything?"

"Nothing, Sire."

"In that case, don't bother me. I've forbidden you to talk to me about her."

"Sire, she doesn't know a thing."

"Too bad for her! Don't ever let me hear you say her name again."

The tone of this decree precluded any rejoinder. Frederick indeed suffered when Porporina crossed his mind. He would feel a little tiny stab of pain deep in his heart and conscience as when a finger brushes over a thorn buried in the flesh. To avoid that discomfort he decided to dismiss its cause from his mind once and for all, which was no trouble at all. Less than a week later, thanks to his robust royal temperament and servile entourage, he no longer remembered that Consuelo had ever existed. Yet the unfortunate creature was at Spandau. The theater season was over, and her harpsichord had been taken away. The king had shown her this kindness the evening when the audience, with the best of intentions, had applauded her in front of his face. Prince Heinrich was under arrest indefinitely. The Abbess of Quedlinburg was seriously ill, as the king had been so cruel as to make her think that Trenck had been recaptured and dropped back down into the depths of some dungeon. Trismegistus and Saint-Germain had truly vanished, and the sweeper was no longer haunting the palace. The omen of her appearance had apparently been more or less fulfilled. Drained by several precocious infirmities, the king's youngest brother had passed away.

In addition to these domestic woes, Voltaire and the king had had their final falling out. Nearly all the biographers have maintained that Voltaire came out of this wretched squabble honorably. A closer look at the evidence shows that both parties disgraced themselves and that Frederick's role may have been the less petty of the two. More cold-blooded, implacable and selfish than Voltaire, Frederick knew neither envy nor hatred, and these burning little passions deprived Voltaire of the pride and dignity that Frederick could at least impersonate. Among the bitter little squabbles that gradually brought on the explosion, there was one in which the name of Consuelo was never uttered. Even so, it aggravated the sentence of deliberate oblivion weighing upon her. One evening d'Argens was reading the Parisian gazettes to Frederick, with Voltaire present. There were reports about the adventures of Mlle Clairon, interrupted right in the middle of her part by a poorly seated man who had yelled at her, "Speak up"; ordered to apologize to the audience for having regally replied, "And you pipe down"; finally packed off to the Bastille for having gone on with her role with equal amounts of pride and determination. The stage would not, however, be deprived of Mlle Clairon, the newspapers added. For the duration of her imprisonment, which they hoped and opined would be brief, she would be brought from the Bastille under escort to play Phèdre or Chimène, then taken back to her cell to sleep.

Voltaire was very close to Hippolyte Clairon, who had done a great deal to make his plays a success. This event made his blood boil. Forgetting that something similar and even more serious was happening right before his very eyes, he interrupted d'Argens at every word exclaiming, "Shame, shame on France! What an oaf! Heckling an actress like Mlle Clairon in such a stupid, vulgar way! The audience is nothing but a bunch of boors! The louts, the barbarians want an apology out of a woman, and a charming one at that! The Bastille! God almighty! Are you sure you've got it right, marquis? A woman sent to the Bastille in this day and age? And for a delightful repartee, witty, tasteful, and fitting? And this in France?"

"No doubt," said the king, "Clairon was playing Electra or Semiramis, and the audience, who didn't want to miss a single word, should find favor in the eyes of Monsieur de Voltaire."

At some other moment the king's remark would have been flattering. Yet Voltaire was struck by the king's ironic tone, which suddenly made him see what a blunder he had just committed. With a witty word or two he could easily have smoothed things over, but he was not in the mood. The king's spite rekindled his own, and he fired back, "No, Sire, even if Mlle Clairon had utterly ruined one of my roles, I shall never understand how the police anywhere in this world could be so brutal as to drag off and incarcerate as a political prisoner beauty, genius, and vulnerability."

This retort, along with a hundred others, and above all the cruel quips and cynical jests reported to the king by Poelnitz and others of his ilk, led to the famous breakup and provided Voltaire with the zestiest grievances, the most hilarious curses and cutting reproaches. Consuelo was only more thoroughly *forgotten* at Spandau, whereas Mlle Clairon at the end of her third day at the Bastille went free, triumphant and adored. Deprived of her harpsichord, the poor child summoned up all her courage to go on singing in the evenings and writing music. She rose to the occasion and soon noticed that her voice and exquisitely fine sense of pitch were benefiting from this dry, difficult exercise. The fear of singing a wrong note made her much more cautious. She listened even harder to herself, which required extraordinary efforts of memory and attention. Her manner gained breadth, substance, and refinement. Her compositions took on a simpler character, and in her prison she wrote airs of remarkable beauty and sublime sorrow. Yet it was not long before she understood how much losing the harpsichord jeopardized her physical and mental well-being. She felt a relentless need to keep busy and could not find relief from the stirring, stormy work of composition and performance in more restful sessions of reading and study. Little by little she felt her blood flushed with fever, her mind overcome with despair. Her temperament, energetic, happy, and tenderly expansive, was not made for physical and emotional isolation. A few weeks of this cruel regime might have spelled her death, had Providence not sent her a friend where she certainly did not expect to find one.

Chapter XVIII

On the floor below the cell assigned to our recluse there was a big, smoky room. The only light that ever touched the gloomy depths of the thick arched ceiling came from a fire in a huge hearth always filled with iron kettles boiling and grumbling at every possible pitch. Within these walls the Schwartz family would spend the whole day and conduct their clever culinary operations. While the wife mathematically combined the greatest number of dinners possible with the fewest ingredients imaginable, the husband sat at a table black with ink and oil. By the light of a lamp burning night and day in this somber sanctuary he artistically composed the most daunting bills stuffed with the most fabulous details. The skimpy meals were for the goodly number of prisoners that the officious jailer had managed to list as his boarders; the bills were to be submitted to their bankers or their family, but without being checked over by those who were experiencing this sumptuous fare. While the speculating couple fervently pursued their business, two more peaceable characters lived in silence under the hood of the fireplace, perfect strangers to the pleasures and profits of this operation. The first was a big orange cat, skinny and balding, who did nothing but lick his paws and roll in the ashes. The second was a young man, rather a boy, an even uglier specimen, who spent his immobile, contemplative life perusing an old book greasier than his mother's kettles and spinning endless dreams that resembled moronic bliss more than the meditations of a thinking being. The boy had baptized the cat with the name Beezelbub, no doubt in antithesis to the one he had received from his parents Herr and Frau Schwartz, to wit, the holy, sacred name of Gottlieb.

Up to the age of fifteen, Gottlieb, who was destined for the clergy, had worked hard and made swift progress in Protestant liturgy. For the last four years, however, he had been inert and sickly, never far from the fire, without any desire to move around or see the sun, unable to go on with his schooling. A sudden, chaotic growing spurt had reduced him to this languor and indolence. His long, skinny legs could scarcely hold up his enormously tall, almost disjointed frame. His arms were so weak and his hands so clumsy that he could not touch anything without breaking it. For that reason his tight-fisted mother had forbidden him to use his hands, and he was only too willing to obey. His bloated, beardless face and high, bare forehead rather made one think of a soft pear. His features were as irregular as the proportions of his body. He was so walleyed that he looked completely deranged, and his thick lips spread in a foolish grin. With his formless nose and pasty complexion, his flat ears planted far too low as well as his insipid face with its dreary crown of sparse stiff hairs, he resembled a poorly peeled turnip more so than any Christian. Such, at least, was his fine mother's poetic analogy.

Despite the disgrace that nature had lavished upon this poor creature, despite the shame and chagrin that Frau Schwartz felt whenever she set eyes on him, Gottlieb, an only child, an inoffensive and resigned invalid, was nonetheless the sole pride and joy of the authors of his days. Back when he had been less ugly, they had cherished the hope that he might turn out to be a handsome young lad. They had rejoiced in his studious boyhood and brilliant future. Despite the precarious condition to which they saw him reduced, they hoped that he would regain strength, intelligence, and good looks once his interminable growing phase was over. Needless to say, a mother's love makes the best of everything and is content with very little. Frau Schwartz, even though she was sharp and sarcastic with him, adored her hideous little Gottlieb. Had he not been ever present to her eye *like a statue of salt* (her own expression) in a corner of the hearth, she would have lost the courage to water down her sauces and pad her bills. Old Schwartz, who like many men put more pride than tenderness in his fatherly feelings, went on extorting and robbing his prisoners in the hope that one day Gottlieb would be a minister and famous preacher. Given that the child had been so articulate before his illness set in, Schwartz was obsessed with this idea. Yet for the last four years at least Gottlieb had not said one thing that made sense, and if he managed to string two or three words together, they were only meant for the ears of his cat Beezelbub. In short, Gottlieb had been pronounced a moron by the doctors, and his parents alone believed that he could be cured.

Yet one day Gottlieb, suddenly emerging from his apathy, let his parents know that he wanted to learn a trade to relieve his boredom and put his dreary years of languor to use. Even though manual labor was hardly worthy of a future minister of the Reformed Church, they gave into this harmless whim. His mind was so set on finding repose that they had no choice but to let him go study the art of shoemaking with a cobbler. His father would have preferred that his son choose a more elegant profession, but it was to no avail that they paraded every line of work in front of him. He stubbornly clung to Saint Crispin's trade and even claimed to feel the call of Providence. As this desire became an obsession with him, as the simple fear that his plans might be thwarted threw him into deep melancholy, they let him spend a month in a master cobbler's workshop. One fine morning he returned home with all the necessary tools and materials. Taking his accustomed place under the hood of his beloved fireplace, he declared that he had learned enough and had no more need of lessons. That was hardly credible. Yet his parents, hoping that he had grown disgusted with shoemaking and might go back to studying theology, welcomed him home without reproach or sarcasm. Then began a new era in Gottlieb's life, one entirely filled and enchanted by the imaginary making of a pair of shoes. For three or four hours a day he would pick up his last and awl and work on a shoe that no one ever wore because it was never finished. Recut, stretched, hammered, and sewn day after day, it took every possible shape except that of a shoe, which did not prevent the peaceable artisan from pursuing his work with pleasure, concentration, leisure, patience, and self-satisfaction, above and beyond the barbs of any criticism. At first his parents were a bit frightened by this monomania. Then they got used to it as to everything else, and the interminable shoe, which Gottlieb only put down for his book of sermons and prayers, was counted as just another infirmity. Nothing more was required of him aside from occasionally accompanying his father through hallways and courtyards for a breath of air. Yet, these walks greatly distressed Herr Schwartz because the children of the other jailers and citadel employees were always chasing after Gottlieb, imitating his lackadaisical, clumsy gait and shrieking in every key, "Shoes! Shoes! Cobbler, make us some shoes!"

Gottlieb took their heckling well, smiling at the nasty crew with angelic serenity, even stopping to reply, "Shoes? Of course, with all my heart. Come by so that I can take your measurements. Which one of you wants shoes?"

But Herr Schwartz would always drag him away so that he would not compromise himself with such riffraff, and the *cobbler* seemed neither angry nor anxious for having been torn away from his eager clients.

Early in her captivity, Herr Schwartz had humbly requested that Consuelo speak with Gottlieb to try and reawaken the memory and taste for eloquence with which he had seemed to be endowed as a child. All the while acknowledging his heir's sickly state and apathy, Herr Schwartz, faithful to the law of nature that La Fontaine expressed so well,

"Our little ones are more dainty and bonny,
More comely and pretty than all their peers,"

had not given a very faithful description of poor Gottlieb's charms. Otherwise, Consuelo might not have refused, as she had, to receive in her cell a lad of nineteen described to her as "a fine strapping fellow five feet eight inches tall, who would have made every recruiter in the land drool had it not been for a slight weakness in his arms and legs that, unfortunately for his health and fortunately for his independence, made him unfit for a military career." The captive thought that the company of a *child* of that age and size was hardly proper in her situation, and she flatly refused to see him; a discourtesy for which Frau Schwartz made her pay every day by thinning her broth with a pint of water.

In order to walk on the esplanade where she was allowed out for some air every day, Consuelo had to go down through the Schwartzes' nauseating dwelling, all with the permission and escort of her jailer. He did not need any coaxing, since *indefatigable complaisance* (in everything regarding services authorized by his orders) was itemized on his bills at a very stiff price. So it happened one day that while Consuelo was crossing the kitchen, one door of which opened out onto the esplanade, Gottlieb caught her eye. This face of an aborted baby on the body of a misshapen giant first struck her with disgust, then compassion. She spoke to him, benevolently asked him some questions and did her best to make him open up. Yet his mind seemed paralyzed by illness or excessive timidity, for he never followed her out onto the rampart except when forced by his parents and only replied to her in monosyllables. So she began to fear that her attentions were merely adding to the distress she supposed he felt. After having told his father that Gottlieb did not show the slightest disposition for oratory, she refrained from talking to him, even looking at him.

Although Frau Schwartz frisked Consuelo again the evening after she had seen her comrade Porporino and the Berlin audience for the last time, the singer managed to outwit this female Cerberus. The hour was late, the kitchen was dark, and Frau Schwartz was not happy to have been roused out of her first sleep. With Gottlieb fast asleep in a room, rather a cubbyhole that looked out into the culinary workshop, and Herr Schwartz having gone ahead upstairs to open the double iron door of her cell, Consuelo drew up close to the smoldering hearth and pretended to stroke Beelzebub. She was trying to find a way to keep her money out of the clutches of the *frisker* so as not to be at her absolute mercy any longer. While Frau Schwartz was lighting her lamp and putting on her glasses, Consuelo noticed at the back of the fireplace, which was Gottlieb's accustomed place, a recess in the wall at the height of her arm, and in this mysterious nook the poor moron's book of sermons and the never-finished shoe. This was his library and workshop. This hole blackened with soot and smoke held all of Gottlieb's treasures, all of his delights. With a quick, nimble hand she deposited her purse there, then patiently submitted herself to the old Fate, who importuned her at length, running her greasy, crooked fingers over every fold of her dress, surprised and furious not to find a single thing. As Consuelo did not attach much importance after all to pulling off this little scheme, she remained cool and collected. For this reason the jailer's wife was finally convinced that she was not concealing anything. As soon as the examination was over, she grabbed her purse and held it tight under her pelisse. Back in her cell she tried to find a good hiding place since she knew full well that during her walks every day they went over everything there with a fine-tooth comb. She found nothing better than to sew her little fortune into a belt and keep it on her person at all times, given that Frau Schwartz had no right to search her except after a trip outside the prison.

Yet the first sum of money that Frau Schwartz had seized from the prisoner the day of her arrival had run out a long time ago, thanks to Herr Schwartz's ingeniously concocted bills. After having made rather meager new expenditures and drawn up a rather fat new bill according to his prudent, profitable custom, he was too cowardly to talk business and ask for money from a person condemned not to have any. Having been informed by Consuelo on day one that her savings had been entrusted to Porporino, Schwartz, without so much as a word to her, went to Berlin and presented his bill to that faithful trustee. Forewarned by Consuelo, Porporino refused to pay up before the bill had been approved by the consumer herself and sent the creditor back to his friend, who had money, he knew, as he had just given her some.

Schwartz came back pale and desperate, screaming that he would go bankrupt and considering himself robbed, even though the first hundred ducats seized from the prisoner would have paid four times over all the charges she had run up in two months. Frau Schwartz endured this alleged injury with the philosophy that comes from greater strength of mind and perseverance.

"We've no doubt been sacked like victims in a forest," she replied. "But did you ever expect to make much off that prisoner? I warned you about this. An actress? They have no savings. And for her trustee, an actor? They have no honor! Well, we're out two hundred ducats, but we'll make it up with the other customers, who are good ones. This'll teach you not to offer your services recklessly to just anybody. I'm not sorry, Schwartz, that you've had this little lesson. Now, as for that little snip who doesn't even have the courtesy to come back with a gold Frederick in her pocket to pay the frisker for her trouble, who seems to consider Gottlieb a poor idiot because he doesn't flirt with her, I'm going to have the pleasure of putting her on a regime of dry, even moldy bread. What a rotter!"

Grumbling and shrugging her shoulders, Frau Schwartz went back to her business. Finding herself under the hood of the fireplace near Gottlieb, she asked while skimming her pots, "What have you got to say about this, you little slyboots?"

These words were said merely for the sake of talking for she knew that Gottlieb listened as well as his cat Beelzebub.

"My shoe is coming along, mother!" replied Gottlieb with a demented smile. "Soon I'll be starting a new pair!"

"Indeed!" said the old woman pitifully nodding her head. "So every day you make a pair? Keep it up, son. . . . That will earn you a good living! My God, my God!" she added, placing the covers back on her kettles. She sounded resigned to her sorrow, as if maternal indulgence had inspired tender feelings in this thoroughly petrified heart.

When her dinner failed to appear that day, Consuelo guessed what had happened, even though she found it hard to believe that a hundred ducats had been spent so fast on such meager fare. She had already drawn up a plan with regard to Herr and Frau Schwartz. She still had not received a single penny from the King of Prussia and greatly feared that old promises would be her only pay (Voltaire was leaving with the same wages). If she were held captive much longer, and if Schwartz did not change his terms, she knew that the little sums she had earned by delighting the ears of a few individuals less stingy but less rich would not go far. She wanted to force him to scale down his fees, and for two or three days she contented herself with the bread and water he brought her without seeming to notice the change in her regime. Her stove began to be as neglected as all the rest, and Consuelo endured the cold without complaint. Fortunately the intolerably severe weather was past. It was April, a season less springlike in Prussia than in France, but the temperatures were turning milder.

Before entering into negotiations with her greedy tyrant she thought it best to find a safe place for her money; for she had to expect an arbitrary search and seizure as soon as she admitted to having resources. Even though necessity cannot turn us into geniuses, it does make us see things clearly. Consuelo had no tools for hollowing out wood or lifting stones. Yet the next day while she was studying every nook and cranny of her cell with the minute patience that prisoners alone possess, she wound up discovering a brick that seemed not to fit into the wall as tightly as the others. By dint of scratching around the edges with her nails, she removed the mortar and saw that it was not, as elsewhere, cement, but some crumbly substance that she took for dry bits of bread. She managed to pull the brick out and found a little space, probably devised by some prisoner or other, back between this loose piece and the well-pointed masonry that formed the thick wall. All her doubts vanished when her fingers, searching around in this little cubbyhole, encountered several objects, veritable treasures for any prisoner: a package of pencils, a penknife, a flint stone, tinder, and several rolls of those skinny, coiled tapers that we call *cave rats*. Since there was no humidity in the wall, everything was in tip-top shape. Besides, these items could have been put there just a few days before the cell became hers. To them she added her purse as well as her little filigree crucifix on which Herr Schwartz had often fixed a covetous eye, remarking how much Gottlieb would like that *little trinket.* Then she put the brick back, cementing it in place with bits of her noonday bread. So that this mortar would be the same color as the rest, she darkened the crumbs by rubbing them on the floor. Now that there was no need to worry for a while about how to take care of her needs or how to spend her evenings, she steadfastly awaited the Schwartzes's visit and felt as proud and happy as if she had discovered a new world.

Schwartz meanwhile soon got tired of not finding any way to make money. Though his business might be small, a little was better than nothing, he would tell himself, and he was the first to break the silence by asking his *prisoner no. 3* if she had no more orders to place with him. Then Consuelo decided to say not that she had money but that every week she regularly received a sum by means impossible to discover.

"Yet if you were to figure it out, that would prevent me from spending anything," she said. "It's up to you to decide if you prefer strict obedience to your orders or honest profit."

After considerable strife, after futile searches of Consuelo's clothes, mattress, floor, and furniture over the course of several days, Schwartz began to think that some high-placed prison official was himself making it possible for her to communicate with the outside world. Corruption was everywhere in the prison hierarchy, and the underlings found it profitable not to check up on their more powerful colleagues.

"Let's just take what God sends our way!" said Schwartz with a sigh.

And he resigned himself to settling his accounts with Proporina on a weekly basis. She did not make a fuss about the first bill, but from then on arranged not to pay for anything more than twice its value. Even though Frau Schwartz found this very stingy, it did not prevent her from receiving her salary and more or less earning it.

Chapter XIX

It won't seem at all miraculous to those who are fond of reading stories about prisoners that this simple hiding place nonetheless escaped the jailers' eager scrutiny. Consuelo's little secret was not discovered. After her walk she inspected her treasures and found them intact. As soon as it was dark, her first thought was to push her mattress in front of the window, light her little candle, and start writing. We'll let her speak for herself. For a long time after her death Consuelo's manuscript remained in the hands of Canon***, but now it is in our possession. We are translating it from Italian.

The Diary of Consuelo
called Porporina
Prisoner at Spandau, April 175*

April 2nd .—Music is the only thing I've ever written, and though I'm at ease speaking several languages, I don't know whether I'm capable of expressing myself correctly in any one of them. I never thought that I'd have to paint whatever might occupy my heart and life in a language other than that of the divine art I profess. Words and sentences seemed so cold in comparison with what I was able to express in song! I could count the letters, rather notes I've dashed off, and haphazardly, in the three or four most critical points in my life. So this is the first time I've ever felt the need to retrace with words what I'm feeling, what's happening to me. It's even a great pleasure to give it a try. Illustrious, revered Porpora, dear, sweet Haydn, excellent and worthy Canon***, you who are my only friends, and perhaps you too, noble, hapless Baron von Trenck, my thoughts turn to you while I'm writing; it's to you that I'm telling my setbacks and trials. I feel that I'm talking to you, that I'm with you, that in my dreary solitude I'm escaping death's nothingness by initiating you into the mystery of my life. Perhaps I'll die here of boredom and misery, even though my physical strength and mental fortitude don't seem to have suffered many ill effects so far. Yet I don't know what evils the future holds in store for me, and if I succumb, at least you'll have a trace of me and a depiction of my death throes. It will be a legacy to whatever prisoner has this cell after me and finds the hiding place in the wall where I myself found the paper and pencils I'm using to write to you. Oh, now I thank my mother, who never knew how to write, for having seen to it that I learned how! Yes, writing is a great comfort in prison. My sad song could not get through these thick walls to your ears. The words that I'm writing will reach you some day. . . . And who knows if I won't soon find a way of sending them to you. I've always put my trust in Providence.

April 3rd.—My entries will be brief, without lengthy meditations. This small supply of paper, flimsy as silk, won't last forever, and it's possible that my captivity will. I'll say a few words to you every night before going to sleep. I don't want to waste my candle either. I cannot write during the day as I'd risk getting caught. I won't tell you why I was sent here. I don't know why, and if I tried to guess at the reason with you, I might compromise certain people who nonetheless told me nothing. Nor will I complain about the authors of my misfortune. If I were to give way to reproaches and resentment, I think I'd lose the strength sustaining me. Here I only want to think about those I love, also the one I loved.

Every evening I sing for two hours, and I think I'm making progress. What good will that do me? The vaults of my dungeon reply without hearing me. . . . But God hears me, and when I've composed a canticle and sing it to him with the fervor of my soul, I feel a celestial calm and fall asleep almost happy. It seems to me that I'm receiving a heavenly reply, that while I'm sleeping a mysterious voice is singing me another canticle more beautiful than mine, which I try to remember the next day and sing in turn. Now that I've got pencils and still a bit of ruled paper, I'm going to write down my compositions. Perhaps one day you'll try them out, my dear friends, and I won't be altogether dead.

April 4th.—This morning the robin came to my room and stayed for over a quarter of an hour. For two weeks I've been inviting him to do me this honor, and today at last he made up his mind. He lives in some old ivy that has dragged itself up as far as my window, which my jailers have spared since it greens up their door a few feet below. For a long time the pretty little bird had been watching me with a curious, wary eye. Attracted by the bread that I've been rolling up to look like little worms and wriggling at him, teasing him with the lure of living prey, he would flit over near the bars of my window as if carried by a gust of wind. As soon as he saw that he'd been tricked, he would give me a dirty look, squawk out something sounding like an insult, and fly away. And then these hideous iron bars, so close together and so black, through which we've made acquaintance look so much like a cage that he was horrified by them. Yet today, as I wasn't thinking about him any longer, he decided to fly through the bars into my room and, without giving a thought to me, I'm also quite sure, perched on a crosspiece of a chair. Not wanting to scare him away, I didn't move a muscle, and he began glancing around in amazement, just like an explorer discovering a new land and making his observations so that he could describe these wondrous things to his friends. He was astonished by me most of all. As long as I kept still, he seemed to find me very funny. With his big round eyes and beak up in the air like a little snub nose, his physiognomy is silly and saucy in the wittiest way. I finally coughed a bit to get a conversation going, and he took off all alarmed. But in his haste he couldn't find the window. He flew up to the ceiling and went madly round and round for a minute, then finally calmed down, seeing that I was not about to give chase. Exhausted more by his fright than his flight, he swooped down on the stove and seemed most pleasantly surprised by the heat, for this bird is very sensitive to the cold. He flitted around the room a bit more, then with secret pleasure returned to the stove several times to warm up his sweet little feet. He made so bold as to go peck at my little worms of bread lying on the table. After giving them a scornful shake and strewing them about, he was no doubt overcome with hunger and wound up swallowing one, which he didn't find too bad. Just then Herr Schwartz (my jailer) came in, and the dear little visitor found the window to make his escape. But I'm hoping he'll return, for all day long he has scarcely gone away, never stopped looking at me, as though he were promising to come back and letting me know that he no longer has such a poor opinion of me and my bread.

How I've gone on and on about a robin. I didn't think I was such a child. Does prison turn people into idiots? Or is there some mystery of sympathy and affection among all breathing things under the firmament? My harpsichord has been here for a few days now. I've been able to work, study, compose, sing. . . . So far none of that has moved me as much as the visit of this little bird, this being! Yes, he's a being, and that's why I felt my heart beat when I saw him close by. Yet my jailer is also a being, a being of my own kind. His wife, his son whom I see several times a day, the sentry who spends his days and nights marching back and forth on the rampart, never taking his eyes off me, they are better organized beings, natural friends, brothers and sisters before God. Yet the sight of them gives me much more pain than pleasure. For me, this jailer is a grate in the door of my cell, his wife a padlock, her son a stone embedded in the wall. In the soldier watching over me I see only a gun aimed in my direction. To my mind there's nothing human about them, nothing alive. They're machines, instruments of torture and death. Were it not for my fear of impiety, I would hate them. . . . Oh, my dear robin! You I love! There's no denying the feeling. Whoever can explain this kind of love!

April 5th.—Another event. Here's the note I received this morning. The handwriting was hard to read, and the slip of paper filthy.

"Sister, the spirit visits you, so you are a saint, I was very sure of it. I am your friend and servant. Dispose of me as you wish, and order all that you will of your brother."

Who is this friend, this improvised brother? I'll never guess. While opening my window to say hello to the robin this morning, I found this on the sill. Could he have brought it to me? I'm tempted to think that he is the one who wrote these words. In any case, he knows me, the dear little being, and he's beginning to love me. He practically never goes near the Schwartzes' kitchen. A smell of hot grease spews forth from their little kitchen window and wafts upstairs, which is not the least annoyance of my abode. But I no longer want to go elsewhere since my little bird is making this place his home. He's too refined to become familiar with this soup-slinging turnkey, his nasty wife, and their ugly offspring.[1] I'm clearly the one who enjoys his trust and affection. Today he came into my room again and gobbled up breakfast. When I took a walk at noon on the esplanade, he came down out of his ivy and flitted around my head, squawking all the while as if to tease me and make sure that I saw him. Ugly Gottlieb was at his door, watching me with his wild eyes and sniggering. He is always with a dreadful orange cat who fixes my robin with a gaze even more horrible than his master's. It makes me shudder. I hate that cat almost as much as Frau Schwartz with her prying fingers.

April 6th.—Another note this morning! This is becoming bizarre. The same crooked, pointy handwriting, a slovenly scrawl; the same rough wrapping paper as well. My Lindor is no hidalgo, but he's tender-hearted and full of enthusiasm: "Dear sister, soul chosen by God and marked by his finger, you are wary of me. You won't speak to me. Don't you have any orders for me? Is there nothing I can do for you? My life is yours. Give your brother his orders." I look at the sentry, a lout of a soldier who knits stockings while marching to and fro, shouldering his gun. He gazes back, looking as though he'd be more inclined to send me a bullet instead of a little love note. Wherever I turn my eyes, I see nothing but enormous gray walls bristling with nettles, bordered by a moat which is bordered by yet more fortifications. I don't know what they're called nor what purpose they serve, but they prevent me from seeing the water. At the top of this outer fortification I can see another sentry's cap plus the tip of his gun and hear him ferociously bellowing at every boat that approaches the citadel, "Steer

1. In an earlier paragraph Consuelo gave a few details about the Schwartz family. We have eliminated from her manuscript everything that would be a repetition for the reader.

clear!" If only I could see these boats, a little running water, and a bit of the countryside! I can only hear the slap of oars, every now and then a fisherman's song and far off in the distance, when the wind is blowing from that direction, the seething, swirling eddies formed by the confluence of the two rivers at a certain distance from the prison. But where are these mysterious notes and this fine devotion that I find so perplexing coming from? Maybe my robin knows, but the cunning little creature won't say.

April 7th.—While I was walking on my rampart and looking with all my eyes, I noticed a narrow little slit in the side of the tower where I live. It's about ten feet up from my window and almost entirely hidden by the topmost shoots of the ivy. With that little slit of a window no one can be living there, I thought with a shudder. Still I wanted to know for sure, so I tried to get Gottlieb out on the rampart by flattering his obsession, rather his unhappy passion, for making shoes. I asked him if he could make me a pair of slippers. For the first time he came up to me of his own accord and spoke without embarrassment. But his way of talking is as odd as his face, and I'm starting to think that he's no moron but a madman. "Shoes for you?" he asked. "No, I would not dare. It is written, *I am not worthy to unfasten the laces of his shoes.*"

I saw his mother standing just outside the door and ready to come join the conversation, which meant that there was no time to try and understand why he was being so humble or reverent. I hurriedly asked him if anyone lived on the floor above me, even though I was scarcely hoping for a sensible reply.

"Nobody lives there," was Gottlieb's very judicious reply. "It's not possible for anyone to live there. There's only a staircase going up to the platform."

"And the platform stands alone? It's not connected to anything?"

"Why are you asking me that, since you already know the answer?"

"No, I don't know, nor do I much care to know. I'm only trying to get you talking, Gottlieb, to see if you're as quick-witted as they say."

"My wits are very, very quick," said poor Gottlieb in a sad, solemn tone that did not square with his comic words.

"In that case, tell me," I asked (for time was precious), "how this courtyard is put together."

"Ask the robin," he replied with a strange smile. "He knows. He flies and goes everywhere. I don't know anything since I don't go anywhere."

"What? Not even to the top of the tower where you live? You don't know what's behind this wall?"

"Maybe I've been there, but I didn't take any notice. I hardly ever look at anything or anybody."

"Yet you look at the robin. You see him, you know him."

"Oh, him. That's different. One knows the angels well. That's no reason to look at walls."

"That's very deep what you've just said, Gottlieb. Could you explain it to me?"

"Ask the robin. I'm telling you, he knows everything. He can go everywhere, but he only ever visits his own kind. That's why he goes to your room."

"Thanks very much, Gottlieb. You take me for a bird."

"The robin is not a bird."

"So what is he?"

"An angel, as you know."

"In that case, I'm one too?"

"You said it."

"How gallant of you!"

"*Gallant!*" Gottlieb gave me a stunned look. "What does *gallant* mean?"

"You don't know the word?"

"No."

"How do you know that the robin comes to my room?"

"I saw him. Besides, he told me."

"So he talks to you?"

"Sometimes," sighed Gottlieb. "Very rarely. But yesterday he told me, 'No! I'll never go into your hell of a kitchen. Angels have no business with evil spirits.'"

"Would you be an evil spirit, Gottlieb?"

"Oh! No, not me, but. . . ."

Then, with an air of mystery, Gottlieb put a finger to his fat lips.

"Who then?"

He didn't say a word, but stealthily pointed at his cat, as if he were afraid that the cat might notice.

"Is that why you've given him such an ugly name? Beelzebub, right?"

"Hush! That's his name, and he knows it well. He's had that name since the beginning of the world, but he won't always have it."

"No doubt, once he's dead."

"He won't die, that one! He can't die, and that really annoys him because he doesn't know that one day he'll be forgiven."

Then we were interrupted by Frau Schwartz, amazed to see Gottlieb talking freely with me at last. She was overjoyed and asked if I were pleased with him.

"Most pleased, I assure you. Gottlieb is very interesting, and now it will be a pleasure getting him to open up."

"Ah! Fraulein, that will be a great help to us. The poor child doesn't have anyone to talk to, and with us he seems determined to keep his teeth clenched. You're a real character and stubborn to boot, aren't you, my poor Gottlieb? Here you are chatting away with this young lady you hardly know, while with your parents. . . ."

At that moment Gottlieb turned on his heel and disappeared into the kitchen, without even appearing to have heard his mother's voice.

"That's what he always does!" Frau Schwartz exclaimed. "When his father or I say something to him, twenty-nine times out of thirty you'd swear he'd gone deaf. But what was he saying, Fraulein? What the devil could he go on and on about for such a long time?"

"I confess that I didn't understand very well," I replied. "First, one would have to know what is on his mind. Leave me alone for a chat with him every now and then, and once I've figured it out, I'll tell you what's going on."

"But he's not demented, he is, Fraulein?"

"I don't think so," I said. May God forgive me that huge lie!

My first impulse was to spare the poor woman's illusion. She's truly a miserable witch, but she's also a mother and fortunate not to see that her son is crazy. This is still very strange. It must be that Gottlieb, who so naïvely showed me his peculiarities, is silently crazy with his parents. While thinking about this, I imagined that I might be able to get out of this poor simpleton some information about my fellow prisoners and just happen to learn who is writing me these anonymous notes. So I want to befriend him, all the more because his sympathies seem to me subject to those of the robin, who definitely honors me with his! There is poetry in the poor child's sick head! The little bird is an angel, the cat an evil spirit who will be forgiven! What is all this? These German minds, even the most deranged, have a wealth of imagination that I admire.

Frau Schwartz, at any rate, is very pleased that I was so kind, and we're on fine terms for the time being. Gottlieb's nonsense will entertain me. Poor creature! I've only begun to know him for a day now, and he doesn't inspire feelings of aversion in me any longer. A madman is probably not bad in this country, where intelligent, very reasonable people are so far from being good!

April 8th—A third note at my window.

"Dear sister, the platform stands alone, but the stairs leading up to it connect with another building, at the far end of which is an apartment occupied by a lady prisoner like you. Her name is a mystery, but the robin will tell you if you ask. By the way, this is what you wanted to learn from poor Gottlieb, what he wasn't able to tell you."

So who is this friend who knows, sees, and hears everything I do, everything I say? I'm perplexed. So he's invisible? This is all so marvelous that I'm seriously amused. It seems to me, as it did in my childhood, that I'm living in a fairy tale, that my robin is going to start talking all of a sudden. Yet, if it is true that the only thing lacking in this charming little imp is the ability to speak, it's only too certain that this lack is absolute or that I can't understand his language. He's completely used to me now. He comes to my room, leaves, and comes back again, he feels at home. I move and walk around, he flits away, but no farther than an arm's length and comes right back. If he really loved bread, he'd love me more, for I can't fool myself about why he's become attached to me. He's hungry. It's also a bit because he needs and likes to warm up on my stove. If I manage to catch a fly (there are still so few of them!), I'm sure he'll come take it from my fingers. He already takes a good, long look at the bits I offer him. If they were more tempting, he'd put aside all ceremony. Now I remember hearing Albert say that the only thing required for taming the most timid animals, as long as they had a spark of intelligence, was a few hours of steadfast patience. Once he met a zingara, a so-called witch, who never spent a day in the same spot of the woods without a few birds coming to light on her. It was said that she had magical powers, and she maintained that the birds revealed mysteries to her, as they did to Apollonius of Tyana, whom I also heard about from Albert. He said her whole secret was the patience with which she had studied the little creatures' instincts as well as a certain affinity of character that often shows up between beings of our own kind and those of another species. In Venice people raise a lot of birds; they have a passion for it, which I now understand. It's because that beautiful city, separated from the mainland, is something like a prison. They outdo themselves training nightingales. There the pigeons, protected by a special law and almost venerated by the population, are free to live on the old buildings, and they're so at home in the streets and squares that you've got to watch your step if you don't want to trample them underfoot. The seagulls in the harbor light on the sailors' arms. There are also renowned bird-tamers in Venice. As a child I was very close to a boy from a humble family who plied this trade. After an hour with the wildest of birds, he'd hand it back to you tame as could be. It's fun trying the same things on my robin, and now he's cozier and cozier with me with every passing minute. When I'm outside, he follows me around, calling to me. When I go to my window, he hurries over to me. Does he love me? Is he able to love me? I feel that I love him. He, on the other hand, knows me and isn't afraid of me, and that's all it is. The same way a baby in a cradle loves its wet nurse, no doubt. A baby! What tender feelings that must inspire! Alas, it seems to me that we only feel passionate love for those who can scarcely love us in return! Ingratitude and devotion or, at the least, indifference and passion, these are the eternal bride and groom in life. Anzoleto, you didn't love me. . . . And you, Albert, whom I loved so much, I let you die. . . . So here I am reduced to loving a robin! How can I complain that I don't deserve my lot? Are you thinking, my friends, that I'd dare joke about such a thing? No. Maybe solitude has addled my wits; my heart, deprived of affection, feeds on itself, and this paper is drenched with my tears.

I had promised myself not to waste any of this precious paper, and here I go covering it with childish drivel. It's a great comfort to me, and I can't help it. It's been raining all day long. I haven't seen Gottlieb; I haven't taken a walk. I've been busy with the robin all this time, and this puerile little business has wound up making me strangely sad. When the fickle, mischievous bird pecked at the pane to take leave of me, I gave in to him. I opened the window out of respect for that sacred liberty that men don't fear stealing from their own kind. Yet I felt hurt by that brief desertion, as if the creature owed me something for so much love and care. I really think I'm losing my mind, and it won't be long before I understand Gottlieb's ramblings perfectly.

April 9th.—What have I learned? Rather, what do I think I've learned? For I still don't know anything, although my imagination is working tremendously hard.

First of all, I've found out who is writing these mysterious notes. It's the last person I would have imagined. But that's not what is filling me with wonder right now. Never mind, I'll tell you everything that has happened today.

As soon as it was morning, I opened my little window. The single pane of glass is sufficiently big and clear, thanks to all my wiping, so that I don't lose a single ray of the scarce light that reaches me, for which I have to vie with the ugly grate. Even the ivy threatens to invade and plunge me into darkness, but I don't yet dare tear off a single leaf. This ivy is alive; it's free in its own way. What? Thwart it? Mutilate it? Yet I'll have to resolve to do that. The ivy feels the influence of April; it's growing fast, reaching out and taking hold everywhere. Its roots are fastened in the rock, but up it goes, looking for air and sun. The poor old human mind does just the same. Now I can understand how in ages past there were sacred plants . . . sacred animals. . . . The robin came right away and lit on my shoulder without further ado; then, as is his habit, he began looking all around and getting into everything. Poor creature! There's so little here to amuse him! Yet he is free, he can live in the fields, and he prefers this prison, his old ivy and my dreary cell. Maybe he loves me? No. He feels nice and warm in my room, and he's developing a taste for my bits of bread. Now it scares me that I've done such a good job taming him. What if he went into the Schwartzes' kitchen and fell prey to that nasty cat! My tender care for him would be the cause of that dreadful death. . . . Torn apart, devoured by a ferocious beast! And what do we do, poor, weak humans with our candid, defenseless hearts, aside from being tortured and destroyed by pitiless creatures who kill us slowly, making us feel their claws and cruel fangs!

The sun came up clear, and my cell was almost the color of a rose, like my old room at the *Corte Minelli* when the Venetian sun . . . but I mustn't think about that sun; never again will it rise over my head. May you, my dear friends, greet in my stead lovely Italy, the *vast skies*, and *il firmamento lucido* . . . that I'll surely never see again.

I asked to go out. Permission was granted, even though it was earlier than usual. And this is what I call going out! A platform some thirty feet long, bordered by a swamp and boxed in between high walls! Yet the place is not without beauty. At least I think so now that I've contemplated its every aspect. At night its very dreariness makes it beautiful. I'm sure that here there are many innocents like me and much worse off, in dungeons that they never leave, into which no ray of sun ever penetrates, that even the moon, that friend of desolate hearts, never visits. Ah, I'd be wrong to grumble. My God! If I had some dominion over this earth, I'd want to make people happy!...

Gottlieb scurried over to me, hobbling and smiling as broadly as he could with his petrified mouth. Nobody bothered him, he was left alone with me, and all of a sudden, what a miracle! he began talking almost like a rational being.

"I didn't write to you last night," he said, "and you didn't find any note at your window. That's because I didn't see you yesterday, and you didn't give me any orders."

"What are you saying! Gottlieb, are you the one who's been writing to me?"

"Who else could have done so? You hadn't guessed it was me? But I won't uselessly write you letters any longer, now that you don't mind talking to me. I don't mean to be a bother to you, I just want to be of service."

"Kind Gottlieb, so you have compassion for me? You take an interest in me?"

"Yes, because I recognized you as a spirit of light!"

"I'm nothing more than you are, Gottlieb. You're mistaken."

"I don't make mistakes. Don't I hear you sing?"

"You love music?"

"I love yours. It's in accord with God, with my heart."

"I can see that you've got a pious heart and a pure soul, Gottlieb."

"I'm striving to make them so. The angels will help me, and I'll triumph over the spirit of darkness that has burdened my poor body but without succeeding in taking my soul."

Little by little Gottlieb was carried away by enthusiasm. Even so, his poetic symbols remained noble and true. Finally, what can I say? This moron, this madman waxed truly eloquent about God's goodness, humanity's woes, the justice that Providence will bring forth with its rewards, evangelical virtues, the duties of the true believer, even about the arts, music, and poetry. I still haven't been able to grasp from what religion he's drawn all his ideas and this fervent zeal, for he seemed to me neither Catholic or Protestant, and even though he said several times that he believed in the one, true religion, the only thing I learned was that he, unbeknownst to his parents, belongs to a particular sect. Which one? I'm too ignorant to guess. Little by little I'll study the mystery of this soul singularly strong and beautiful, singularly ailing and afflicted. For, in short, poor Gottlieb is crazy, like Zdenko in his poetry . . . like Albert, too, in his sublime virtue! . . . After Gottlieb had gone on passionately for a while, enthusiasm got the better of him, and his madness reappeared. Then, in a childish manner I found distressing, he began babbling about the angel robin and the demon cat, also about his mother who has made a pact with the cat and the evil spirit dwelling in him, and finally about his father, who was turned to stone by a glance from the poor old tomcat Beelzebub. I managed to calm him down by distracting him from his gloomy fantasies, and I questioned him about the other prisoners. I no longer had any personal interest in learning these details because the notes, instead of being tossed down to my window from the top of the tower, as I once supposed, were hoisted up from below by Gottlieb, before dawn, by means of I-don't-know-what apparatus, no doubt something very simple. But Gottlieb, obeying my intentions with singular docility, had already looked into what I had seemed curious to know the day before. He told me that the prisoner in the building just behind mine was young and beautiful, that he had caught a glimpse of her. I wasn't paying much attention to his words when all of a sudden he said her name, which gave me a start. The captive's name is *Amalia*.

Amalia! What a sea of anxieties, what a world of memories the name arouses in me! I've known two Amalias, and they both hurled my destiny into the abyss with their secrets. Is this one the Prussian princess or the young Baroness von Rudolstadt? Neither one, no doubt. Gottlieb, who has no curiosity on his own part, who seems unable to take a step or ask a single question unless I push him forward like an automaton, could only tell me that her first name is Amalia. He has seen the captive but in his usual way, meaning through a cloud. She must be young and beautiful; Frau Schwartz says so. But Gottlieb admits that he's no authority on this score. Catching sight of her at her window, he only sensed that she was not *a good spirit, an angel.* Her family name is kept secret. She's rich and runs up bills with the Schwartzes. But she's in solitary confinement like me. She never goes out. She's often ill. That's all I've been able to extract from him. To learn more, Gottlieb only has to open his ears to his parents' chatter since they don't watch their tongues around him. He's promised to listen and tell me how long this Amalia has been here. As for her full name, the

Schwartzes don't seem to know what it is. Could this be the case if it were the Abbess of Quedlinburg? Could the king have thrown his sister in prison? Princesses wind up in prison like everybody else, and more so. The young Baroness von Rudolstadt. . . . What would she be doing here? What reason would he have had to deprive her of her liberty? Hold on! Now I'm falling prey to the curiosity of a recluse. Likewise, my elaborations on nothing more than a first name are the work of an idle, unhealthy imagination. Never mind. Until I learn the identity of this companion in misfortune whose name I find so moving, there'll be a mountain weighing on my heart.

May 1st.—For several days I've been unable to write. Various things have happened, and I'll quickly fill you in.

First, I haven't been well. Every now and then since my arrival here I've had bouts of brain fever that feel like minor episodes of the major attack I suffered at the Castle of the Giants after going underground in search of Albert. I have cruel attacks of insomnia interspersed with dreams where I don't know whether I'm waking or sleeping. In these moments it always seems to me that I hear that terrifying violin playing its old Bohemian tunes, hymns, and battle songs. This is so painful, yet when the fantasy starts to take hold, I can't help pricking up my ears and avidly taking in the feeble sounds that seem to waft my way on a far breeze. Sometimes I imagine the violin playing as it glides over the still waters round the citadel; at other times the sound comes slipping down the walls or up out of a dungeon's airhole. It has shattered my head as well as my heart. And yet when night comes, instead of thinking about entertaining myself by writing, I throw myself into bed and try my best to fall back into that half sleep that brings me my musical dream, rather my half dream, for there is something real at the bottom of it. A bona fide violin is surely resonating in some prisoner's room, but what is it playing, and how? It's too far away for me to hear anything but bits and pieces of sound. My sick mind is inventing the rest, I'm sure of it. This is my destiny henceforth: I can neither doubt that Albert is dead nor accept his death as a grievous fact. It's apparently my nature to go on hoping despite everything and not to submit to the cruelty of fate.

Three nights ago, having finally fallen into a deep sleep, I was awakened by a slight noise in my room. I opened my eyes. The night was very dark, and I couldn't make out a single thing. Yet I distinctly heard someone walking near my bed, albeit carefully. I thought it was Frau Schwartz taking the trouble to come check on me, and I spoke to her; the only reply was a deep sigh, and someone tiptoed out; I heard the door shut and the bolt slip into place; prostrate as I was, I fell back asleep without giving it much thought. The next day I had such a dim, muddled recollection that I wondered if it hadn't been a dream. That evening I had a final bout of fever worse than the others. Yet I much preferred the fever to my fretful insomnia and disjointed dreams. I had a deep sleep with lots of dreams but no sound of the lugubrious violin, and whenever I woke up, the difference between sleeping and waking was very clear to me. Once I heard the strong, regular breathing of a person sleeping not far from me. I even thought I could make out someone in my armchair. I wasn't frightened in the least. Frau Schwartz had brought me some herbal tea at midnight; I assumed she was still there. I waited for a while, not wanting to wake her. When I thought she was waking up of her own accord, I thanked her for looking after me and asked the time. At that point the person left, and I heard what sounded like a stifled sob, so heartrending, so terrifying that my brow beads with sweat whenever I remember it. I can't say why it made such an impression on me. I had the notion that they thought me very ill, perhaps dying, and were offering me a modicum of pity. Yet I didn't feel bad enough to consider myself in danger. Besides, I didn't care one way or another about dying a death that gave me so little pain or sensation, in the midst of a life that inspired so few regrets. As soon as Frau Schwartz returned at seven in the morning, since I had not gone back to sleep but spent the night's remaining hours in a state of perfect lucidity, I had a very clear memory of that strange visit. I asked the jailer's wife for an explanation, but she shook her head and said she didn't know what I was talking about. She had not come back after midnight, and since she had under her pillow all the keys to the cells entrusted to her care, I had certainly had a dream or a vision. Yet I was so far from having been delirious that around noon I felt well enough to want a breath of air. I went down on the esplanade, accompanied yet again by my robin, who seemed to congratulate me on the return of my strength. The weather was very pleasant. It's starting to get warm here, and balmy gusts of fresh air with faint scents of grasses blow in from the countryside, which lifts the heart, like it or not. Gottlieb ran up. He looked very different, and much uglier than usual. Yet there is an expression of angelic goodness and even lively intelligence in the chaos of that physiognomy when it lights up. His huge eyes were so red-rimmed and bloodshot that I asked if they hurt.

"They indeed hurt," he said, "because I've been crying a lot."

"What is making you so sad, my poor Gottlieb?"

"At midnight my mother came down from the cell and said to my father, 'Number 3 is very ill tonight. It's running a real fever. We've got to send for the doctor. I don't care to have that one die on us.' My mother thought I was asleep, but I hadn't wanted to nod off before knowing what she would say. I was well aware that you had a fever, but when I heard that it was dangerous, I couldn't help crying myself to sleep. And I must have gone on crying all night long because when I woke up this morning, my eyes were on fire and my pillow drenched with tears."

Poor Gottlieb's attachment touched me deeply, and I thanked him by squeezing that huge black paw of his that reeks of leather and cobbler's wax from miles away. Then it occurred to me that Gottlieb, in his simpleminded zeal, could have paid me that highly improper nocturnal visit. I asked if he hadn't got out of bed and come put an ear to my door. He assured me that he hadn't budged, and now I'm convinced of it. His sleeping nook must be in just the right place so that from my room I can hear him breathing and moaning through some fissure in the wall, maybe the hiding place where I keep my money and my diary. Who knows if that little cranny doesn't communicate by some invisible flue with the one in the kitchen hearth where Gottlieb also keeps his treasures, his book and cobbler's tools? This way at least I have a very special bond with Gottlieb, since both of us, like rats or bats, have a wretched little hole-in-the-wall nest where all our treasures are tucked away in the dark. I was going to hazard a question or two on that score when I saw someone leave the Schwartzes' place and march out on the esplanade, a person I hadn't seen here before. I was incredibly frightened by the sight, even though I still wasn't quite sure that it was he.

"Who's that?" I whispered to Gottlieb.

"It's nothing good," he whispered back. "He's the new adjutant. Just see how Beelzebub is arching his back and rubbing against his legs! I say, they're certainly well acquainted!"

"But what's his name?"

Gottlieb was about to answer when the adjutant gave him a kindly smile, pointed toward the kitchen, and said softly, "Young man, you're wanted inside. Your father is calling."

This was merely a pretext to be alone with me, and once Gottlieb was gone, I found myself face to face with . . . guess who, my dear Beppo? That nice, ferocious recruiter with whom we had such an untimely encounter two years ago in the Bohemian Forest, Herr Mayer in person. After that experience I'd know him anywhere. Except for being even plumper now, he's the same man, with that pleasant, easy manner, shifty look, treacherous affability, and the eternal *brrmmm, brrmmm* of his mouth as though he were always practising a trumpet piece. He had switched from supplying the army with musicians to finding them cannon fodder. Now, as a reward for his loyal, honorable services, he's a fortress officer, rather a military jailer, a job that suits him quite as well, after all, as being an ambulatory jailer, a charge he fulfilled with such grace.

"Mademoiselle," he said to me in French, "your humble servant! What a sweet little platform for your walks! There's air, space, a lovely view! Congratulations! It looks like you've *got it easy* in prison! On top of that, the weather's splendid, and it's truly a pleasure to be at Spandau with such beautiful sunshine, *brrmmm! brrmmm!*"

This insolent banter so disgusted me that I made no reply. Undaunted, he went on in Italian, "I beg your pardon for speaking to you in a language that you may not understand. I was forgetting that you're Italian, an Italian singer, right? A superb voice, I hear. As for me, I'm excessively fond of music. So I feel inclined to make your life just as pleasant as my orders allow. But where the deuce have I had the pleasure of seeing you before? I know your face; I swear, I know it perfectly!"

"At the theater in Berlin, no doubt, where I was singing this winter."

"No! I was in Silesia, second adjutant at Glatz. Fortunately that demon Trenck had his little escapade while I was out touring . . . on a mission, I mean, on the Saxon border. Otherwise, I wouldn't have had a promotion and I wouldn't be here, where things are pretty good, what with Berlin so close by; for it's such a dreary life, Signora, that of a fortress officer. You can't imagine how boring it is being so far away from a city, in some remote little backwater, for a passionate music-lover like me. . . . But where the devil have I had the pleasure of meeting you?"

"I don't remember ever having had the honor, Signore."

"I must have seen you on stage somewhere, in Italy, in Vienna. . . . Have you done a lot of traveling? How many theaters have you performed in?"

As I made no reply, he went on in his cheeky, nonchalant way. "Never mind! It'll come back to me. What was I saying? Oh yes, do you get bored, too?"

"No, Signore."

"But aren't you in solitary confinement? You're the one called Porporina, right?"

"Yes, Signore."

"Right! Prisoner no. 3. So, you don't desire a little entertainment, some company?"

"Not in the least, Signore," I promptly replied, thinking he was going to offer me his own.

"As you please. What a pity. There's another prisoner here, very well bred . . . a charming woman indeed, who would have been delighted to meet you, I'm sure."

"May I ask her name, Signore?"

"Amalia."

"Amalia what?"

"Amalia . . . *brrmmm! brrmmm!* Well, I don't have a clue! You're certainly curious, from what I can see. That's the malady of prisons."

Now I was sorry to have rebuffed Herr Mayer's advances; for after having despaired of meeting this mysterious Amalia and renounced the desire, I once again felt drawn to her out of commiseration. I also wished to clarify my suspicions. So I tried to be a little nicer to that repulsive Mayer, and soon he offered to put me in contact with prisoner no. 2, which is how he refers to this Amalia.

"If this breach of my arrest orders does not jeopardize your position, Signore, and if I can be of service to this lady who is said to be suffering from sadness and boredom. . . ."

"*Brrmmm! brrmmm!* So you follow the letter of the law, do you? Still such a good little girl. It's that fussy old Schwartz who must have put this fear of orders in you. Orders! Aren't they just a bugaboo? Orders are good for doorkeepers and assistant wardens, but we officers (while pronouncing this last word, Mayer puffed up like a man still unaccustomed to such an honorable title) close our eyes to innocent infractions. So would the king, were he in our shoes. Now, Signora, when you want something or other, just turn to me and no one else, and I promise you won't be needlessly bothered or browbeaten. Naturally indulgent and humane, I am. God made me that way. And then I love music. . . . If you wish to sing for me every now and then, in the evening, for instance, I'll come here and listen to you, and that way you'll have me wrapped around your little finger."

"I'll do my best to avoid imposing on your kindness, Signor Mayer."

"Mayer!" the adjutant exclaimed, abruptly cutting short the *brrmmm, brrmmm* that was still fluttering over his black, chapped lips. "Why do you call me Mayer? My name is not Mayer. Where in hell did you dig that one up?"

"How absentminded of me, Adjutant," I replied. "I beg your pardon. . . . Once I had a singing teacher by that name, and I spent the morning thinking about him."

"A singing teacher? That's not me. There are lots of Mayers in Germany. My name is Nanteuil. My family was originally from France."

"Well, Adjutant, how shall I announce myself to this lady? She doesn't know me and may refuse my visit, just as I nearly refused to make her acquaintance a little while ago. Solitude makes people so unsociable."

"Oh, whoever she is, the lovely lady will be delighted to have someone to talk to, take my word for it. Do you want to write her a note?"

"But I don't have anything to write with."

"That's impossible. Are you completely broke?"

"Even if I had money, Herr Schwartz is incorruptible. Besides, I don't know how to corrupt."

"Well then, this evening I'll take you to no. 2 myself . . . that is, after you've sung for me a bit."

Alarmed by the notion that perhaps Herr Mayer, or Monsieur Nanteuil as he now preferred to be known, meant to worm his way into my room, I was about to refuse when he clarified his intentions. Either he hadn't dreamed of paying me a visit, or he had read the feelings of horror and revulsion on my face.

"I'll listen from the platform that looks out over the little tower where you live," he said. "Voices rise, and I'll hear just fine. Then I'll have a woman open the doors and take you over. I won't see you. It wouldn't do, in fact, if it looked as if I myself were encouraging you to disobey orders, even though, after all, *brrmmm . . . brrmmm . . .* in such a fix there's a very simple solution. . . . You just grab your pistol, blow prisoner no. 3's head off and say you caught her right in the middle of an escape attempt. Ha, ha! Pretty funny, don't you think? You've always got to be cheerful in prison. Your most humble servant, Signora Porporina, till this evening."

I was at a loss to explain the wretched man's kindness and consideration. Also, despite myself, I was dreadfully afraid of him. I could not believe that a soul so narrow and base had such love for music that he would do this for the sole pleasure of listening to me sing. I assumed that the prisoner in question was none other than the Prussian princess, that by order of the king an interview had been set up for the purpose of spying on us and intercepting the state secrets that she was thought to have confided in me. So I awaited the meeting with equal parts of dread and desire, for I have absolutely no idea what truth there may be to the alleged conspiracy in which I'm accused of having a hand.

Nevertheless, considering it my duty to brave any and every danger to give moral support to a companion in misfortune, whoever she may be, I began singing at the appointed hour for the adjutant's tin ears. I sang very poorly, hardly inspired by the audience, still a bit feverish, and also quite convinced that he was listening only as a matter of form or perhaps not at all. When the clock struck eleven, I was seized with a rather childish terror. I imagined that Herr Mayer had secret orders to get rid of me, that he was really going to kill me just as soon as I set foot outside my cell, as he had jokingly predicted. When my door swung open, I was shaking all over. An old woman, very dirty and very ugly (much more so even than Frau Schwartz), motioned that I should follow, and she led the way up a steep, narrow stairway cut into the wall. When we reached the top, I found myself on the platform of the tower, some thirty feet above the esplanade where I walk during the day, and eighty or a hundred feet above the moat that stretches quite a long ways on this side of the fortress. The dreadful old crone guiding me told me to wait there a second and disappeared I knew not where. My worries had scattered, and I felt such a sense of well-being out in the fresh, pure air, with a magnificent moon, and up so high that my eyes could sweep at last over a vast horizon that I didn't fret about being left alone. The huge still waters into which the citadel plunges its black, motionless shadows, the trees and fields that I vaguely made out on the faraway shore, the immense sky, and even the bats freely flitting through the dark, my God! how grand and majestic all this seemed to me, after two months of contemplating slabs of wall and counting the rare stars that cross the narrow belt of sky that can be seen from my cell! But I didn't have time to enjoy it for long. Hearing footsteps, I turned around, and all my dreadful fears returned when I found myself face to face with Herr Mayer.

"Signora," he said, "I'm desperately sorry to have to say that you cannot see prisoner no. 2, at least for the time being. A very flighty person, in my view. Yesterday she was eager as could be for some company, but when I suggested yours just now, here's what she said. 'Prisoner no. 3? The one who sings in the tower, that I hear every evening? Oh, I know her voice well, and there's no need to tell me her name. I'm infinitely obliged to you for wanting to provide me a companion, but I'd rather never see another living soul than suffer the sight of that miserable creature. She's the cause of all my troubles, and I pray that she'll pay for them as dearly as I'm paying for the reckless affection I had for her!' That's the lady's opinion of you, Signora. It remains to be seen if you deserve it or not. That's a matter, as they say, for the tribunal of your conscience. As for me, it's none of my business, and I'm ready to take you back when you see fit."

"Right away, sir," I said, extremely mortified to stand accused of treachery in front of a wretch of his sort. In the depths of my heart I was also feeling a great deal of bitterness against whichever of the two Amalias who was showing me such injustice or ungratefulness.

"There's no need to rush," the new adjutant replied. "You seem to enjoy gazing at the moon. Take your time. It doesn't cost anything, nor does it do anyone harm."

I foolishly availed myself of another moment of the rascal's condescension. I couldn't tear myself away just like that from the lovely sight of which I might be deprived forever after. Moreover, despite myself, Mayer struck me as a miserable lackey too honored to await my orders. Taking advantage of my scorn, he made so bold as to try and make conversation.

"Do you know, Signora, that you sing devilishly well? I've never heard better in Italy, where I nonetheless frequented the best theaters and inspected the finest artists. Where did you make your début? How long have you been touring the country? Have you done a lot of traveling?"

And as I pretended not to hear his questions, he went on undeterred, "Do you occasionally travel on foot, dressed like a man?"

The question gave me a start, and I quickly said no. But he added, "Come on! You don't want to admit it, but I don't forget a single thing, and now I remember an amusing adventure that you can't have forgotten either."

"I don't know what you're talking about, Monsieur," I replied, leaving the battlements of the tower to go back to my cell.

"Hold on a second!" said Mayer. "I've got your key in my pocket, and you can't go back like that unless I take you. So, lovely child, allow me a word or two."

"Not a single word more, Monsieur. I want to go back to my room, and I'm sorry I ever left it."

"Well, well, don't you put on fine airs! As if one didn't know a little something about your adventures! So you thought I was stupid enough not to recognize you tramping through the Bohemian Forest with a little dark-haired fellow who wasn't too bad looking. What kind of a fool do you take me for? I wanted to grab the lad for the army of the Prussian king, but the lass would not have been for him. That's for sure! Even though people say he took a liking to you, and that it's for trying to brag about it that you wound up here! So there we are! Fortune has its whims, and there's no use grumbling. You've taken quite a tumble, but listen to me, don't act proud and just take what comes your way. I'm only a minor fortress officer, but here I'm more powerful than a king that nobody knows or fears because his commands come from too high up and too far away to be obeyed. As you can see, I've got the power to evade orders and make things easier for you here. Don't be ungrateful, and you'll see that an adjutant's protection at Spandau is as good as a king's in Berlin. Do you understand? Don't run away, scream, or do anything foolish. That would only make for scandal without doing a bit of good; I'll say what I like, and nobody will believe you. Come on, I don't mean to scare you. I'm naturally sweet and compassionate. But think it over; and when I see you again, remember that your fate is in my hands; I can toss you into a dungeon or provide you with all kinds of entertainment, starve you to death without any questions being asked or let you escape without anyone suspecting me. Think it over, I tell you, I'll give you some time. . . ." And as I made no reply, aghast that I had no way to shield myself from the outrage of such pretensions and the cruel humiliation of hearing them said aloud, the odious man added, no doubt thinking that I was hesitating, "And why not make up your mind right now? Do you need twenty-four hours to see the only reasonable decision, to reply to the love of a gentleman, still young, and rich enough to set you up abroad in a prettier dwelling than this hideous fortress?"

With these words the vile recruiter drew near, apparently intending, in his clumsy, impudent way, to bar my passage and take my hands. I ran toward the battlements of the tower, very determined to throw myself into the moat rather than to let myself be defiled by the most trivial caress. But just then a strange sight struck my eyes, and I hurriedly drew the adjutant's attention to that object so as to divert it from me. This was my salvation, but alas! it nearly cost the life of someone who may be worthier than I!

On the high rampart that stands on the other side of the moat, opposite the esplanade, a seemingly gigantic figure was running or rather flitting along the parapet with prodigious speed and skill. There is a tower at each end of the rampart, and when the phantom reached that point, it sprang up on the tower roof, which was at the same height as the balustrade, scampered like a cat up this steep cone and seemed to vanish into thin air.

"What the devil is that?" shouted the adjutant, forgetting his role as a ladies' man for the worries of a jailer. "I'll be damned, a prisoner on the lam! And the sentry's asleep, by the flesh of God! Sentry!" he cried in a stentorian voice, "on your guard! Sound the alarm! Sound the alarm!" And running toward a notch in the battlements where an alarm bell was hanging, he began clanging it with a vigor worthy of such a remarkable professor of infernal music. I've never heard anything gloomier than this bell shattering the noble stillness of the night with its ferocious clamor. It was the savage cry of violence and brutality troubling the harmony of free-breathing wave and wind. In one instant the whole prison was in turmoil. I heard the ominous racket of sentries grabbing their guns, snapping back the firing pins and randomly taking aim at the first thing that came into view. A red glare washed over the esplanade, eclipsing the lovely azurean-blue rays of moonlight; it was Herr Schwartz lighting a lantern. Signals rang back and forth from one rampart to another, followed by plaintive, weaker echoes. The alarm cannon soon added its terrifying, solemn note to this demonic symphony. Heavy steps resounded on the flagstones. I couldn't see a thing, but I heard every sound, and my heart was gripped with terror. Mayer had raced off, but I didn't dream of rejoicing about being rid of him. I bitterly reproached myself for having pointed out to him, without understanding what was going on, the escape of some poor prisoner. Frozen with terror, I awaited the end of the adventure, shuddering at every shot, anxiously listening for the screams of the wounded fugitive that would announce his disaster.

This went on for over an hour and, thank heaven, the fugitive was neither seen nor wounded. Just to make sure, I had joined the Schwartzes on the esplanade. They were so worried and upset themselves that it didn't occur to them to wonder at seeing me outside of my cell in the middle of the night. It may also be that they had been in league with Mayer about letting me out that night. After running around like a madman and making sure that none of his captives was missing, Schwartz began to calm down a bit. Yet he and his wife were racked with consternation, as if a man's deliverance were for them a public and private calamity, an enormous offense against heavenly justice. The other jailers, the soldiers passing to and fro exchanged with them words filled with the same despair, the same terror. In their eyes an attempted escape was obviously the blackest of crimes. Good God! how dreadful I found them, these mercenaries devoted to the barbarous occupation of depriving their fellow creatures of the sacred right of liberty! Yet suddenly it seemed that supreme equity had resolved to inflict exemplary punishment on my two jailers. Frau Schwartz who had gone into her den for a moment came back out screaming. "Gottlieb! Gottlieb!" she choked. "Stop! Don't shoot, don't kill my son, it's him, it's him for sure!"

Amid their frenzy I understood from Frau and Herr Schwartz's tangle of words that Gottlieb was not in his bed nor anywhere else in their lodgings, that he had probably, without anyone's noticing, resumed his old habit of running around up on the roof in his sleep. Gottlieb was a sleepwalker!

As soon as this news had spread throughout the citadel, things began to calm down. Each jailer had had time to make his rounds and to see that no prisoner had disappeared. People resumed their duties without a worry. The officers were delighted by the way things had turned out; the soldiers laughed at their alarm; Frau Schwartz, who was beside herself, was tearing all over the place, and her husband was mournfully inspecting the moat, fearing that the uproar of the cannon and guns had startled poor Gottlieb out of his sleep and made him fall in the course of his perilous chase. I followed along behind Herr Schwartz. Perhaps it would have been a good time for me to attempt an escape since people seemed distracted and doors were standing open. Yet I did not dwell on the thought, focused on finding the poor invalid who had shown me such affection.

Yet when Herr Schwartz, who never totally loses his head, saw that it was dawn, he begged me to return to my room since it was entirely against his orders to let me wander around at all hours. He took me back to lock me in. Yet the first thing that struck my eye as I crossed the threshold was Gottlieb, peacefully asleep in my armchair. Fortunately he had taken refuge there before the alarm had reached every corner of the fortress, or else he had been sleeping so soundly and running so nimbly that he had escaped every danger. I advised his father not to wake him abruptly and promised to watch over him until Frau Schwartz was told the good news.

When I was alone with Gottlieb, I gently laid my hand on his shoulder. Speaking very softly, I tried questioning him, for I had heard that sleepwalkers can connect with friendly souls and give them lucid replies. My experiment worked wonderfully well.

"Gottlieb," I asked, "so where have you been tonight?"

"Tonight? It's already night? I thought I saw the morning sun up on the roof."

"So you've been on the roof?"

"For sure. The robin, that good little angel, came calling at my window; I flew off with him, and up we went up, up and away into the sky, right near the stars, and almost to where the angels dwell. As we were leaving, we saw Beelzebub running over the roofs and the parapets trying to catch us. But he can't fly because God has condemned him to a long penance, and he watches angels and birds fly without being able to get them."

"And yet, after running around in the clouds, you came back down here?"

"The robin said to me, 'Let's go see my sister who is ill,' and I came back with him to come see you in your cell."

"You were able to enter my cell, Gottlieb?"

"For sure, several times I've come to watch over you since you've been ill. The robin steals the keys from under my mother's pillow, and try as he might, Beelzebub can't wake her up once the angel has put her to sleep by flitting invisibly around her head."

"So who taught you to know angels and demons so well?"

"My master," replied the sleepwalker with a childish smile full of naïve enthusiasm.

"And who is your master?" I asked.

"First, God, and then . . . the sublime shoemaker."

"And what's the name of this sublime shoemaker?"

"Oh, it's a great name! But one mustn't say it, you understand? It's a name my mother doesn't know. She doesn't know that I've got two books in the hole in the fireplace. One that I don't read, and another that I've been devouring for four years, that is my heavenly bread, my spiritual life, the book of truth, the salvation and light of the soul."

"And who wrote this book?"

"He did, the shoemaker of Gorlitz, Jacob Boehme!"

Then we were interrupted by the arrival of Frau Schwartz. It wasn't easy to prevent her from rushing up and throwing her arms around her son! The woman adores her offspring: may her sins be forgiven! She tried to talk to him, but Gottlieb didn't hear her. I alone was able to get him to return to his bed where he went on peacefully sleeping, I was assured this morning. He hadn't noticed a single thing, even though today his strange malady and last night's alarm are all the talk of Spandau.

So here I am back in my cell after a few hours of half liberty that were very painful, very agitated. I have no desire to go out again at such a price. Yet perhaps

I could have escaped! . . . Now that I feel myself under the thumb of a scoundrel and threatened by dangers worse than death, worse than eternal suffering, this will be my only focus. From now on I'm going to give it serious thought, and who knows? Maybe I'll succeed! It is said that a persevering will triumphs over every obstacle. O my God, protect me!

May 5th.—Since these last events my life has been fairly quiet. I have come to count my days of rest as days of happiness and to give thanks to God as in prosperous times one gives him thanks for years that go by without calamity. It's clear that one must know hardship to leave behind the apathetic ingratitude where people usually live their lives. Today I reproach myself for having let so many lovely days of my carefree youth slip away without sensing how precious they were, without blessing Providence for them. Back then I didn't tell myself often enough that I didn't deserve them, and that's no doubt why I somewhat deserve the troubles that overwhelm me now.

I haven't seen that odious recruiter again. He frightens me more than he did on the banks of the Moldau, when I took him quite simply for an ogre, a child-eater. Now I see in him an even more abominable and dangerous persecutor. When I consider the wretched man's revolting pretensions, the authority he wields around me, the ease with which he could slip into my cell at night, with the Schwartzes, greedy, servile beasts that they are, perhaps unwilling to lift a finger in my defense, I could die of shame and despair. . . . I see the pitiless bars that would prevent me from jumping out the window. I can't get my hands on any poison, I don't even have a weapon to open my chest. . . . Yet I've got a few reasons for hope and confidence that I relish calling to mind, for I don't want to let fear debilitate me. First of all, Schwartz doesn't like the adjutant who, from what I've been able to understand, gets first crack at exploiting the wants and needs of the prisoners by selling them a breath of air, a ray of sun, a morsel of bread above and beyond the ration, and other bounties of the prison regime, all to the great detriment of Schwartz, who'd like to have a monopoly on that trade. Then, the Schwartzes, especially the wife, are getting friendly because of Gottlieb's feelings for me and the salutary influence they say I have on his mind. If I were threatened, they might not come to my rescue, but as soon as things became serious, I could have them take my complaints to the fortress commander, who seemed gentle and humane the one time I saw him. . . . Besides, Gottlieb will do me this favor right away and, without explaining anything, I've made arrangements with him. He's all prepared to deliver a letter that is already written. But I'm hesitant to call for help before there's real trouble; for my enemy, if he were to stop tormenting me, could brush off as a joke a declaration that I would have been a ridiculous prude to take seriously. At any rate, I'm sleeping with one eye open and training my muscles for a fist fight, if need be. I'm lifting my furniture, stiffening my arms against the iron bars of my window and toughening up my hands by beating on the walls. Anyone watching these exercises of mine would think me crazy or desperate. Yet I'm doing all this in the most somber, cold-blooded manner, and I've discovered that I'm much stronger physically than I had thought. In the security of ordinary life we don't test our ability to defend ourselves, we don't know what we're capable of. Knowing how strong I am, I feel myself gaining courage, and my confidence in God grows with my efforts to help him protect me. I often remember the lovely verses that Porpora said he had read on the walls of a dungeon of the Inquisition in Venice:

Di che mi fido, mi guarda Iddio;
Di che non mi fido, me guarderò io.[2]

More fortunate than the hapless being who wrote out that grim invocation, I at least can trust unreservedly in the purity and devotion of this poor fanatic Gottlieb. He hasn't had any more sleepwalking episodes; besides, his mother is keeping a close eye on him. During the day he comes to my room to talk. I haven't wanted to go down on the esplanade since I ran into Mayer there.

Gottlieb has explained me his religious beliefs. I found them to be very beautiful, though often strange, and I wanted to read that theology of his by Boehme, since he is clearly a disciple, in order to see what notions of his own devising he has added to the inspired dreams of the illustrious shoemaker. He lent me the precious volume, and I plunged in at my own risk. Now I understand how the book has unhinged this simple mind; Gottlieb takes literally the symbols of a mystic who was himself a bit crazy. I don't pride myself on fully understanding and explaining them, but I think I see there a ray of lofty religious intuition and the fount of generous poetry. What struck me the most was his theory about the devil: "In the battle with Lucifer, God did not destroy him. O man, in your blindness, you do not see the reason why. It is because God was contending with God. It was the struggle of one part of God against the other." I remember Albert explaining nearly the same way the transitory reign of the principle of evil over the earth, with the chaplain at Riesenburg listening in horror to this tenet and calling it *Manichaeism*. Albert maintained that our Christianity was a Manichaeism more complete, more superstitious than his own, since it consecrated the principle of evil as something eternal, whereas his system acknowledged the rehabilitation of evil, in other words, its conversion and reconciliation. Evil, according to Albert, was merely error, and one day the light of God would dispel error and put an end to evil. I confess, my friends, even at

2. God preserves me from those I trust; Myself I'll preserve from those I mistrust.

the risk of appearing very heretical in your eyes, that Satan's being doomed for all eternity to stirring up evil, loving evil, and closing his eyes to the truth looked like impiety to me as well, and that's still the case.

In short, I take Jacob Boehme for a millenarian, in other words, a believer in the resurrection of the righteous and their life with Jesus Christ upon a new earth, born of the dissolution of the present one, for a thousand years of unmitigated bliss and consummate wisdom; after which will come the full reunion of these souls with God, plus the rewards of eternity, even more perfect than the millennium. Count Albert explained this symbol, I clearly remember, while telling me the stormy history of his old Bohemia and dear Taborites, imbued with these beliefs that they had revived from early Christianity. Albert took all this less literally and without making any pronouncements about how long the resurrection would last or when it would take place. Yet he had a prophetic sense and vision that society would soon fall apart, having to make way for an era of sublime renovation; and Albert had no doubt that his soul, emerging from the fleeting grasp of death to embark upon a new series of lives here below, would be called to contemplate this providential reward and the days, by turns terrifying and magnificent, that were promised to humanity's endeavors. This magnanimous faith that seemed monstrous to the upholders of orthodoxy at Riesenburg, that became my own after having first struck me as so new and so strange, is one that belongs to every age and nation. Moreover, despite the efforts of the Roman church to smother it or Rome's inability to clarify these beliefs and purify them of their literal and superstitious meaning, it's clear to me that this faith has filled many fervently religious souls with enthusiasm. It is even said that great saints have had this faith. So I've become a believer without remorse or fear, certain that an idea espoused by Albert can only be grand. Besides, it appeals to me, diffusing heavenly poetry over my notion of death and the sufferings that will no doubt hasten for me the appointed hour. I like this Jacob Boehme. This disciple who is down in the Schwartzes' filthy kitchen, engrossed in his sublime dreams and heavenly visions, while his parents concoct their schemes, make their deals and degrade themselves, seems to me so pure and so touching, with his book that he knows by heart without understanding it well, and the shoe that he is making so as to model his life on his master's, but without being able to finish the job. Disabled in body and mind, but simple, sincere, and living like an angel! Poor Gottlieb, you're no doubt doomed to break your bones by falling off a high rampart in your imaginary flight through the heavens or to sink under the weight of precocious infirmities! You will have passed over the earth like an unrecognized saint, an angel in exile, without having understood evil, without having known happiness, without even having felt the warmth of the sun that lights the world, since you've been so absorbed in contemplating the mystical sun that shines in your mind! No one will have known you, no one will have given you the pity and admiration you deserve! And I, the only one to have found out your secret meditations, I who understand ideal beauty as well and would have had the strength to seek it out and give it reality in the course of my life, I'll die like you in the flower of my youth, without having done anything, without having lived. In the cracks of the walls sheltering and devouring us, there are miserable little plants that the wind beats down, that the sun never suffuses with color. They wither away without flower or fruit. Yet they seem to come up again and again, but that's because the wind blows seeds from far away to the same old places, and they try to grow and live off the remains of the previous ones. That's how captives live their dormant lives, how prisons replenish their populations.

Yet isn't it strange that I find myself here with another person given to ecstasies? While Gottlieb's are of a lesser order than Albert's, he too is attached to a secret religion, to beliefs that are jeered at, persecuted, or despised. Gottlieb says that Boehme has many other disciples here in this land, that several shoemakers openly profess his doctrine, that its basic principles have been forever implanted in the humble souls of many unknown philosophers and prophets who fanaticized Bohemia long ago and who now keep a sacred fire smoldering beneath the ashes all over Germany. In fact, I remember the fervent Hussite shoemakers that Albert told me about, their bold sermons and terrifying exploits back in the days of Jan Zizka. The very name of Jacob Boehme bears witness to that glorious beginning. I don't know much about what is going on in the contemplative minds of patient Germania. My busy, dissipated life kept me away from such an investigation. But even if Gottlieb and Zdenko were the last disciples of the mysterious religion that Albert preserved like a precious talisman, I still feel that this is my religion, since it proclaims the future equality of one and all as well as the coming revelation of God's justice and goodness on this earth. Oh yes, I have to believe in this kingdom of God that Christ announced to mankind! I have to trust that these iniquitous monarchies and corrupt societies will be overthrown so as not to doubt Providence, seeing where I am!

. . . .

No news from prisoner no. 2. If it's not an impudent lie that Mayer relayed to me, Amalia of Prussia is accusing me of having betrayed her. May God forgive her for doubting me. Even though I've heard the same accusations on her account, I've never doubted her. I won't do anything more to try and see her. By trying to justify myself, I could further compromise her, having already done so unwittingly.

. . . .

My robin is a faithful companion. Seeing Gottlieb in my cell without his cat, the robin has warmed up to him, and poor Gottlieb has gone completely crazy with pride and joy. He calls him *lord* and doesn't allow himself to be familiar with him. He offers him food with the deepest respect and a kind of religious quiver. It's no use trying to convince him that this is just a bird like the others; no matter what I say, he won't give up the idea that a heavenly spirit has taken this form. I'm trying to distract him by teaching him a little something about music, and he truly has a fine mind for it. His parents are delighted by my care and attention, and they've offered to put a spinet in one of their rooms where I could give him lessons and do some work myself. A few days ago I would have been overjoyed by this proposal, but now I don't dare accept it. I no longer even dare sing in my cell since I'm so afraid of drawing over here that crude music lover, that ex-teacher of trumpet, may God confound him!

May 10th.—For a long time I was wondering what had become of the anonymous friends, the marvelous protectors whose intervention in my affairs the Count de Saint-Germain announced to me and whose meddling apparently only hastened the disasters that the king's benevolence hastened to rain down on me. If those were the conspirators whose punishment I'm sharing, they were all scattered and destroyed at the time of my arrest, I was thinking, or else they turned their backs on me when I refused to escape from Herr Buddenbrock's clutches the day of my transfer from Berlin to Spandau. Well, here they are again, and they've made Gottlieb their emissary. How reckless they are! Let's hope they won't bring down upon that innocent's head the same evils they've brought down upon mine!

This morning Gottlieb secretly brought me a note worded as follows:

"We are working toward your deliverance; the time is near. But a new danger, one that would delay the success of our endeavor, threatens you. Beware of anyone urging you to escape before we have given you sure directives and precise details. A trap is being laid for you. Stay on your guard and persevere in your strength.

Your brothers: *The Invisibles*"

This note fell at Gottlieb's feet this morning as he was crossing a prison courtyard. He, for one, firmly believes that it came down from heaven and that the robin had something to do with it. While encouraging him to talk, without much trying to counter his fantastic ideas, I nonetheless learned some strange things which may contain an element of truth. I asked him if he knew what the *Invisibles* were.

"Nobody knows," he replied, "even though everybody pretends to know."

"How's that, Gottlieb? So you've heard talk about these people?"

"While I was an apprentice to the master cobbler in the city, I heard lots of things on the subject."

"So there's talk? Do working folks know about them?"

"This is how it came to my ears, and of everything I've heard said, these are some of the few words worth listening to and remembering. One poor fellow in our workshop hurt his hand so grievously that there was talk of cutting it off. He was the sole breadwinner for a big family that he'd been looking after with lots of love and courage. He came to see us with his hand in a bandage and said sadly while watching us work, 'How lucky you are to have your hands unfettered! I'll soon have to go off to the poorhouse, I guess, and my mother will be left begging so that my little brothers and sisters don't starve to death.' Somebody suggested that we draw up a collection, but we were all so poor, and even though my parents are rich, I had so little money handy that we couldn't pull together enough to be any decent help for our poor comrade. We emptied our pockets, then racked our brains to find a way to get Franz out of this fix. But nobody came up with anything because Franz had knocked at every door, only to be rebuffed by one and all. It is said that the king is very rich, that his father left him a huge treasure. But it's also said that he spends it outfitting soldiers, and as there was a war on, with the king away and everybody afraid of shortages, the poor working folks were having a hard time, and Franz couldn't get enough help from kindhearted souls. As for the hard-hearted ones, they've never got a penny in their pockets. All of a sudden a young man from the workshop said to Franz, 'If I were in your shoes, I know just what I'd do! But maybe you won't have the guts.' 'It's not guts I'm short of. What should I do?' asked Franz. 'Go ask the *Invisibles*.' Franz seemed to understand, since he shook his head reluctantly and didn't say a word. When a few young men like me didn't know what that meant and asked for an explanation, the reply from every quarter was, 'You don't know the *Invisibles*? What children you are, that's plain to see! The *Invisibles* are people you don't see, but they do things, all sorts of good, all sorts of evil as well. It's not known if they live in some particular place, but they're everywhere, in all four corners of the earth, or so people say. They assassinate a good many travelers and defend others from bandits; it all depends whether these are found worthy of punishment or protection. They're behind every revolution, reaching into every court, conducting every kind of business, deciding whether there'll be war or peace, ransoming prisoners, comforting those in distress, punishing scoundrels, making kings tremble on their thrones; in short, they're the cause of everything good or bad that happens in the world. Perhaps they've been wrong more than once, but it's said that they mean well. And besides, who can say if today's sorrow won't be the cause of a great joy tomorrow?'

"We were listening with great wonder and awe," Gottlieb continued, "and little by little I understood enough to be able to tell you what workingmen and poor ignorant folks make of the *Invisibles.* Some say they're wicked people, worshipers of the devil, who imparts to them his power, the knack for knowing secret things, the ability to tempt men by the lure of the riches and honors at their disposal, the skill of divining the future, making gold, curing the sick, rejuvenating the old, raising the dead, preventing the living from dying, for they've discovered the philosopher's stone and the elixir of life. Others think they are religious, benevolent men who have pooled their resources to assist those in distress and work together to right wrongs and reward virtue. In our workshop everyone had something or another to say. 'They're the old Order of the Knights Templar,' said one. 'Now they're called Freemasons,' another added. 'No,' a third chimed in, 'they're Zinzendorf's *Herrnhuters,* in other words, the Moravian Brethren, formerly the United Brethren, the Orphans of Mount Tabor; in short, old Bohemia still alive and well and secretly threatening all the dominions of Europe because it wants to turn the whole universe into a republic.'

"Still others claimed they were just a handful of sorcerers, students and disciples of Paracelsus, Boehme, Swedenborg, and *now Schröpfer the lemonade-seller* (what a fine addition to the group), all eager to rule the world and overthrow empires with magic tricks and demonic rites. Most agreed that they were the old secret tribunals of free-judges, which had never disbanded in Germany; now, after having worked underground for several centuries, they were beginning to rear their heads with pride and make felt their arms of iron, swords of fire, and diamond scales of justice.

"As for Franz, he was hesitant to appeal to them, for he said that once you had accepted their favors, you were bound to them for this life and the next, which put your salvation in great jeopardy and your family in grave danger. Yet necessity won out over fear. A fellow worker, the one who had given him that piece of advice and who was greatly suspected of being a member of the Invisibles, even though he vigorously denied it, secretly let him know how to make what he called the signal of distress. We never learned what it was. Some said that Franz drew a cabalistic sign on his door in his own blood; others, that he went at midnight to a knoll where four roads met at the foot of a cross and there a horseman in black appeared before him; and still others simply said that he deposited a letter in the hollow of an old weeping willow at the gate of the cemetery. What is certain is that he got help; his family did not have to beg while waiting for him to heal, and he managed to get treatment from a skillful surgeon who fixed him all up. About the *Invisibles*, he never said a single word, except that he would bless them his whole life long. And that, sister, is how I first heard about these terrifying and benevolent creatures."

"But you who've got more learning than the young men in your workshop, what do you think of the *Invisibles*?" I asked Gottlieb. "Are they cultists, charlatans, or conspirators?"

Up to that moment Gottlieb had been making a lot of sense, but then he slipped back into his usual ramblings, and I couldn't make out a thing except that they were truly invisible, impalpable beings, that like God and the angels they could only be apprehended by our senses when they had assumed certain forms in order to communicate with humans.

"It's very clear," he said, "that the end of the world is near. Unmistakable signs have burst forth. The Antichrist is already born. Some say that he's in Prussia and is called Voltaire, but I don't know this Voltaire, and it may be somebody else, all the more because *V* is not *W*, and the name that the Antichrist will bear among men will begin by that letter, and it will be a German name.[3] While awaiting the great wonders that are going to burst forth in this century, God who doesn't take part in anything ostensibly, who is *eternal silence*,[4] is raising up among us beings with natures superiorly endowed for good and for evil, occult forces, angels and demons, the latter for testing the righteous, the former for ensuring their triumph. And then, the great battle between the two principles has already begun. The king of evil, the father of error and ignorance is defending himself in vain. The archangels have drawn the bow of knowledge and truth, and their arrows have pierced Satan's armor. Satan is still roaring and writhing, but soon he'll renounce falsehood, lose all his venom, and rather than the impure blood of reptiles, he'll feel the dew of pardon running through his veins. This is the clear and certain explanation for the incomprehensible, frightening things happening in the world. Good and evil are wrestling in a higher realm far removed from human endeavor. Victory and defeat hover over us, and no one can subject them to his will. Frederick of Prussia attributes to his mighty weapons triumphs that destiny alone has granted him before he is crushed or raised up according to its secret designs. Yes, I tell you, it's very plain that nobody

3. Perhaps Weishaupt, who was born in 1748. [Translator's addition: A professor at Ingolstadt, Adam Weishaupt founded in 1776 a philosophical society called the Illuminati. It had close affinities with the Freemasons and was organized along Masonic lines.]

4. Jacob Boehme's expression.

understands what's going on in the world any longer. They see impiety taking up the arms of faith and vice versa. They suffer oppression, poverty, and all the scourges of discord without their prayers being heard, without the miracles of the old religion interceding. They no longer agree about anything, they quarrel without knowing why.

They're marching blindfolded toward an abyss. The *Invisibles* urge them on, but who knows if the wonders signaling their mission are the work of God or the devil. In the same way, in the early years of Christianity, many people considered Simon Magus just as powerful, just as divine as Christ. Now I say that every wonder comes from God since Satan can't perform any wonders without God's consent, and that among those who are called the *Invisibles*, some act by the direct light of the Holy Spirit whereas others receive the power through a cloud and are destined to do good, believing all the while that they're doing evil."

"That explanation is quite abstract, my dear Gottlieb. Is it Jacob Boehme's or your own?"

"It's his, if one wants to understand it that way; it's mine, if his inspiration didn't suggest it to me."

"Fine, Gottlieb! I'm no further along than before, since I still don't know if these *Invisibles* are my good or bad angels."

May 12th.—The wonders have indeed begun, and my destiny is churning in the hands of the Invisibles. Like Gottlieb I'll ask, "Are they from God or the devil?" Today Gottlieb was called over by the sentry who guards the esplanade and is assigned to the little bastion at the end of it. This sentry, according to Gottlieb, is none other than an Invisible, a spirit. The proof of this is that he knows all the sentries and gladly chats with them when they fool around and order shoes from him, but he's never seen this one before; plus, this sentry seemed to be of superhuman stature, and the expression on his face defied definition. "Gottlieb," he said in a very low voice, "Porporina must be delivered three nights from now. It depends on you, you can get the keys for her room from under your mother's pillow, take her through the kitchen, and bring her here, to the end of the esplanade. I'll take care of the rest. Warn her so that she'll keep herself ready; and remember, if you're not sufficiently careful and zealous, we're done for, all three of us."

That's where things stand now. This news has made me sick with emotion. All night long I ran a fever; all night long I heard the fantastic violin. Escaping! Getting out of this dreary prison! Above all, getting away from the terror this Mayer stirs up in me! Oh, if that means risking my life alone, I'm ready, but what will be the consequences for Gottlieb, for this sentry, a stranger to me, who is sacrificing himself so unselfishly, and finally for these unknown accomplices who are about to assume a new burden? I tremble, I hesitate, I'm wavering. Here I am writing to you again without giving a thought to preparing my escape. No, I won't run away unless I'm reassured about the fate of my friends and protectors. There is nothing that daunts Gottlieb's resolve. When I ask if he's not afraid of anything, he tells me that he'd gladly give his life for me; and when I add that he may miss seeing me, he replies that this is his business, that I have no idea what he intends to do. Besides, all this seems to him a divine injunction, and he unthinkingly obeys the unknown power that drives him on. I, on the other hand, I read over and over the note I received a few days ago from the *Invisibles*, and I fear that the sentry's words may in fact be the trap that I've been warned about. I've still got forty-eight hours. If Mayer shows up again, I'll risk everything; if he keeps on ignoring me, and if I have no better guarantee than a stranger's tip, I'll stay.

May 13th.—Yes indeed, I trust in destiny, in Providence that has sent me help out of the blue. I'm leaving, I'm leaning on the strong arm that shields me! . . . While walking on the esplanade this morning, where I had ventured in hopes of receiving some new revelation from the spirits all around me, I cast an eye at the bastion where the sentry stands. There were two of them, one keeping watch, shouldering his gun; the other marching to and fro, as if he were looking for something. The second one attracted my attention because he was so tall; I had the feeling that he wasn't a stranger to me. But I could only throw him furtive glances, and at each lap around the esplanade I had to turn my back to him. Finally, once when I was advancing toward him, he was also coming toward us, as if by chance; and even though he was on a level much higher up, I recognized him perfectly. I had to stifle a cry. It was Karl the Bohemian, the deserter I rescued from Mayer's clutches in the Bohemian Forest; Karl whom I saw next at Roswald, in Moravia, at Count Hoditz's estate, and who gave up for my sake a dreadful design for revenge. . . . This man is devoted to me, body and soul, and today, with his ferocious face, flat nose, red beard, and porcelain-blue eyes, to me he looked as beautiful as the angel Gabriel.

"That's him!" Gottlieb whispered to me, "the *Invisibles*' emissary. He's an *Invisible* himself, I'm sure of it! At least, he would be if he wanted to. He's your liberator, he's the one who's going to get you out of here tomorrow night."

My heart was pounding so hard that I could barely stand; tears of joy were streaming from my eyes. To hide my emotion from the other sentry, I moved away from the bastion toward the parapet and pretended to contemplate the weeds in the moat. Even so I managed to spy Karl and Gottlieb who, without much trying to cover it up, exchanged a few words that didn't reach my ears. A few seconds later Gottlieb returned and hurriedly said, "*He*'s going to come down here, *he*'s going to come to our place and drink a bottle of wine. Pretend not to pay him any attention. My father is out. While my mother is fetching the wine from the canteen, return to the kitchen as if you were going back to your room, and you'll have a chance to speak to *him* for a second."

Indeed, after Karl had chatted for a few minutes with Frau Schwartz, who doesn't sniff at the chance to make some money by providing refreshment to the citadel's veterans, I saw Gottlieb appear at the door. I understood that this was the signal. I went in and found myself alone with Karl. Gottlieb had followed his mother to the canteen. Poor child! It seems that friendship has suddenly revealed to him the cunning and presence of mind necessary in real life. He deliberately blundered around, dropping the candle, exasperating his mother, and keeping her out long enough so that I could reach an understanding with my savior.

"Signora," he said, "here I am! And here you are at long last! The recruiters nabbed me again, it was my fate. But the king recognized me and took mercy on me, maybe because of you. Then he let me go, even promising me money, which by the way I never saw. I was on my way home when I learned that you were here. I went to see a famous sorcerer to find out how to go about helping you. The sorcerer sent me to Prince Heinrich, and Prince Heinrich sent me back to Spandau. We're surrounded by powerful people that I don't know, but they're working for you, not sparing money or effort, to be sure. Everything is finally ready. Tomorrow night the doors will open in front of us all by themselves. Every possible obstacle has been overcome. The Schwartzes are the only ones who aren't with us. But tomorrow they'll be sleeping heavier than usual, and by the time they wake up, you'll be long gone. We're taking Gottlieb, who has asked to follow you. I'm clearing out with you, we're not taking any risks, everything has been taken care of. Be ready, Signora, and now get back to the esplanade so that the old woman doesn't find you here."

Expressing my gratitude to Karl with tears alone, I hurried away to hide them from Frau Schwartz's inquisitorial eye.

O my friends, so I'll see you once again, and I'll hold you in my arms! Once again I'll get away from this dreadful Mayer! I'll see again the full sweep of the firmament, lovely countrysides, Venice, Italy; I'll sing again, once again I'll find hearts and minds in sympathy with mine! Oh, this prison has renewed my life and revived my heart which was languishing in dull indifference. How I'm going to live, love, be pious and good!

And yet, the human heart is such an enigma! I feel terrified and almost sad at the idea of leaving this cell where I've spent three months perpetually striving to be brave and resigned, this esplanade where I've gone round and round with so many melancholy reveries, these old walls that look so high, so cold, so serene by moonlight! And this great moat whose dismal waters have been such a beautiful shade of green, and the thousands of woebegone flowers that spring sowed on its banks! And most of all, my robin! Gottlieb claims that he will follow us, but at that hour he'll be asleep in the ivy and won't notice our leaving. O dear little creature! May you be the companion and consolation of the one who takes my place in this cell, and may she look after you and respect you as I have!

Now, let's try and get some sleep so that I'll be strong and calm tomorrow. I'm sealing this manuscript that I want to take with me. Gottlieb helped me get a fresh supply of paper, pencils, and candles, which I want to leave in my hiding place, so that these priceless treasures for prisoners will make somebody else happy after me. . . .

. . . .

Here ends Consuelo's diary. We'll resume a faithful narration of her adventures.

The reader needs to be informed that Karl was not telling a lie when he boasted about being aided and employed by powerful individuals. The invisible knights working toward our heroine's deliverance had distributed huge amounts of gold. Several members of the prison staff, eight or ten veterans and even an officer, had promised to keep quiet, to see nothing, and, if there were an alarm, to go after the fugitives purely as a matter of form. On the evening appointed for the escape Karl had supper with the Schwartzes. Pretending to be drunk, he invited them to drink with him. Frau Schwartz had a parched throat like most women given to the culinary art. Her husband had no aversion to schnapps from his own canteen when he drank it at somebody else's expense. A narcotic drug that Karl secretly put in the flask enhanced the effects of the strong drink. Herr and Frau Schwartz had a hard time getting to bed and snored so loudly that Gottlieb, who attributed everything to supernatural influences, thought that somebody had cast a spell over them when he came to steal the keys; Karl had gone back to the bastion to keep watch. Consuelo had no trouble getting there with Gottlieb and intrepidly climbed up the rope ladder that the deserter tossed down to her. But poor Gottlieb, who stubbornly insisted on escaping with her despite all her objections, became a great problem at this point. During his bouts of somnambulism he could run like a cat over roofs and gutters, but awake he was not able to take three nimble steps over the most even ground. Convinced that he was following a heavenly messenger, he had no fear and would not have hesitated to jump down off the ramparts if Karl had advised him to do so. Yet his reckless confidence added to the dangers of his awkwardness. He climbed without method or forethought, refusing to see or calculate anything. After having made Consuelo shudder twenty times, certain each time that he was doomed, he finally reached the platform of the bastion. From there our three fugitives made their way through the corridors of that part of the citadel where the functionaries who were in on their plot had their quarters. Things were going along fine when all of a sudden they found themselves face to face with Adjutant Nanteuil, in other words, the ex-recruiter Mayer. Consuelo thought she was doomed, but Karl stopped her from running away by saying, "Never fear, Signora, the adjutant is on your side."

"Stop right here," Nanteuil said to them hurriedly. "There's a snag. Wouldn't you know, Adjutant Weber took it into his head to come have supper in our quarters with that old fool of a lieutenant. They're in the hall that you've got to go through, and we've got to get them out of there. Karl, hurry back to your post, somebody might see too soon that you're gone. I'll come fetch you when it's time. Madame will step into my room, and Gottlieb will come along with me. I'll say that he's sleepwalking; my two boobies will tear off to go have a look, and when they've vacated the premises, I'll take the key so that they can't come back."

Gottlieb, unaware that he walked in his sleep, looked at him reproachfully, but when Karl motioned that he should obey, he submitted blindly. Consuelo felt insurmountable revulsion at the idea of entering Mayer's room.

"Why are you afraid of the man?" whispered Karl. "He stands to earn too much money to think of betraying you. His advice is good, and I'm going back to the bastion. Too much haste could be our ruin."

"Too much composure and caution could also be our ruin," Consuelo thought to herself. Yet she gave in. She was carrying a weapon. On her way through the Schwartzes' kitchen she had grabbed a little knife whose company reassured her a bit. She had turned over to Karl her money and her papers, keeping only her crucifix, nearly an amulet in her mind.

Mayer locked her in his room for greater safety and went off with Gottlieb. Ten minutes later, which felt like a hundred years to Consuelo, Nanteuil returned, and she noted with terror that he locked the door behind him and put the key in his pocket.

"Signora," he said to her in Italian, "you must be patient for half an hour still. The rascals are drunk and won't raise the siege till the clock strikes one. Then the guard who looks after these quarters will put them out."

"And what have you done with Gottlieb, Signore?"

"Your friend Gottlieb is safe behind a pile of firewood where he can get some sleep. Maybe that will make him lighter on his feet, all the better to follow you."

"Karl will be alerted, won't he?"

"Unless I wish to have him hanged," said the adjutant with a look that struck Consuelo as diabolical, "I'll take good care not to leave him there. Are you pleased with me, Signora?"

"I am not in a position to demonstrate my gratitude just now, Signore," replied Consuelo in a chilly voice, vainly trying to conceal her disdain, "but I hope that I'll soon be able to give you proper thanks."

"Good lord, you can thank me right now (Consuelo shuddered with horror) by showing me a little affection," added Mayer, his wheedling tone heavy and coarse. "Now, look here, if I weren't such a passionate lover of music . . . and if you weren't so pretty, it would be very wrong of me to fail in my duty by letting you escape. Do you think I'm doing it for the money? Basta! I'm rich enough to get along without you folks, and Prince Heinrich doesn't have enough clout to save me from hanging or spending the rest of my life in prison if I'm found out. In any case, as a result of my negligence I'll be disgraced and transferred to a fortress that's not so nice, not so near the capital. . . . All this requires some consolation. Come on, don't be so proud. You know I'm in love with you. I've got a tender heart, I do! That's no reason to take advantage of my weakness. Hell, you're no nun, no prissy little saint! You're a charming theater girl, and I'll just bet that you didn't get your leading roles without bestowing a few tender favors on your directors. By God, if you've sung for Maria Theresa, as they say, you've been through Prince von Kaunitz's boudoir. Now here you are in less splendid digs, but your freedom is in my hands, and freedom is even more precious than an empress's blessing."

"Is that a threat, Signore?" replied Consuelo livid with indignation and disgust.

"No, it's a plea, lovely Signora."

"It's no condition, I hope?"

"By no means! How shabby! Never! That would be an outrage!" said Mayer with impudent irony, approaching Consuelo with open arms.

Horrified, Consuelo ran to the far side of the room. Mayer followed. She was doomed, it was clear to her, unless she were to sacrifice humanity to honor. Suddenly inspired by the formidable pride of Spanish women, she received the scoundrel's embrace and stuck the point of the blade into his chest. Mayer was very plump, and the wound was not dangerous. Yet, when he saw his own blood, since he was as much a coward as a voluptuary, he thought he was dead and fainted, belly down on his bed, muttering, "I am murdered! I am doomed!"

Consuelo thought that she had killed him and nearly fainted herself. Yet after a few seconds of silent terror she dared approach him. Seeing that he was not moving, she ventured to pick up the key that had dropped at his feet. It was scarcely in her hand when she felt her courage reborn. Without a moment's hesitation she left the room and ran haphazardly through the halls. All of the doors in front of her were standing open, and she went down a flight of stairs without knowing where they might lead. Yet her legs buckled when she heard the alarm bell, then the drum and the cannon that had given her such a turn the night that Gottlieb's sleepwalking had set off an alert. She fell to her knees on the last steps, joined her hands, and prayed for poor Gottlieb and generous Karl. Separated from them after having let them risk death for her sake, she had no more strength, no desire for deliverance. Heavy, hurried footsteps rang in her ears, bright torches flashed before her frightened eyes, and she no longer knew whether they were real or the product of her delirium. She let herself sink into a corner and completely blacked out.

Chapter XX

When Consuelo regained consciousness, she felt an incomparable sensation of well-being without being able to tell where she was nor how she had gotten there. She was lying down out in the open, and without feeling the slightest chill from the cold night air, she could look all around at the stars shining in the vast, cloudless sky. This enchanting sight was soon followed by the sensation of rather swift, but smooth and pleasant motion. From the sound of an oar dipping into water at short intervals she understood that she was in a boat crossing the lake. A gentle warmth suffused her limbs, and in the calm of the still waters where the breeze ruffled the various reeds and rushes there was something suave that reminded her of the lagoons of Venice on lovely spring nights. Consuelo lifted her languid head, glanced around and saw two oarsmen, one in the bow and the other in the stern, rowing with all their might. She looked for the citadel and saw it already far away, dark as a mountain of stone amid the transparency of air and water. She told herself that she was saved, but just then she thought of her friends and anxiously uttered Karl's name. "I'm right here! Not a word, Signora. Complete silence!" said Karl, pulling on the oars in front of her. Consuelo thought that the other oarsman was Gottlieb, and too weak to worry any longer, she let herself sink back into her initial state of mind. A hand drew back around her the soft, warm cloak in which she had been wrapped, but she gently pushed it aside from her face so as to contemplate the boundless expanse of star-spangled blue that fanned out over her head.

While feeling her strength and flexibility return after a violent, paralyzing attack of nerves, she gathered her thoughts; and the recollection of Mayer rose up horrible and bloody in front of her. She again tried to sit up and noticed that her head was lying on someone's knees, her body supported by his arm. She had not yet seen this third passenger, or to be more exact, she had taken him for some kind of bundle, since he was stretched out behind her, all covered up, hidden and motionless, at the bottom of the boat.

Consuelo was seized with terror when she recalled the reckless confidence that Karl had shown Mayer and wondered if the person beside her might not be that wretched man. Her suspicions were aggravated by the apparent care he took to remain concealed. It mortified her to think that she had reclined against his breast, and she almost reproached Providence for having let her enjoy a few moments of salutary oblivion and ineffable well-being under his care.

Fortunately the boat reached land at that moment, and Consuelo jumped up to take Karl's hand and leap onto shore, but there was such a jolt upon landing that she staggered and fell back into the arms of the mysterious man. She saw him standing just then, and by the faint light of the stars she was able to discern a black mask over his face. But he was a full head taller than Mayer, and despite the long cloak enveloping him, his elegant bearing suggested a sleek, supple body. This completely reassured the fugitive. She accepted the arm he offered her in silence and walked with him some fifty paces on the shore. Following behind were Karl and the other person, both of whom had gestured to her once again that she was not to say a single word. The countryside was silent and desolate; things seemed to have quieted down at the citadel. Behind a thicket they found a carriage hitched up with four horses. The stranger climbed in with Consuelo. Karl took the driver's seat. The third person vanished without Consuelo's taking notice. She yielded to the silent, solemn haste of her liberators, and soon the carriage, excellent and exquisitely smooth, took off into the night with lightning speed. The noise of the wheels and the galloping horses hardly encouraged conversation. Alone with the stranger, Consuelo felt very intimidated and even a bit frightened. Yet, seeing that it was no longer dangerous to break the silence, she felt duty-bound to tell him her gratitude and joy, but there was no reply. He had taken a seat across from her, as a sign of respect; he took her hand and pressed it between his own, without saying a single word; then he sank back into a corner of the carriage; and Consuelo, who had hoped to start up a conversation, dared not insist in the face of this tacit refusal. She was very eager to know to what generous, devoted friend she owed her deliverance, but she felt for him, without knowing him, an instinctive feeling of respect mingled with fear, and her imagination lent this strange traveling companion all the romantic qualities appropriate to the circumstances. Finally it occurred to her that he was a minor agent of the *Invisibles*, perhaps a faithful servant who feared that he might breach the duties of his rank by having a conversation alone with her at night.

They sped along for two hours, then stopped in the middle of a dark wood. The relay that they were to find there had not yet arrived. The stranger wandered off a short way to see if it was coming or to conceal his impatience and worry. Consuelo stepped down as well and strolled on a sandy path nearby with Karl, for whom she had a thousand questions.

"Thank God, Signora, here you are alive," said the faithful squire.

"And you yourself, dear Karl?"

"I couldn't be better, now that you're safe."

"And Gottlieb, how is he doing?"

"I suppose that he's just fine in his bed at Spandau."

"Good heavens! You mean Gottlieb stayed back? Does that mean he's going to pay for us?"

"He won't be paying for himself, for anybody else either. When somebody raised the alarm, I don't know who, I ran over to be with you, just in case, seeing that it was time for the big gamble. I crossed paths with Adjutant Nanteuil, that is Mayer the recruiter, who was looking terribly pale. . . ."

"You crossed paths with him, Karl? He was up and around?"

"Why not?"

"He wasn't hurt?"

"Ah! Indeed, he was. He said he'd fallen over a stack of guns in the dark and bunged himself up a bit. But I didn't pay much attention to that and asked him right away where you were. He didn't have a clue, he'd lost his head. It even looked to me that he meant to betray us, since the alarm bell I had heard, whose sound I recognized, is the one from his room, for his quarters. But he seemed to have changed his mind, for the rascal knew that he'd earn a bundle for getting you out. So he helped me divert the storm by telling everyone we met that Gottlieb the sleepwalker had once again set off a false alarm. As a matter of fact, as if Gottlieb had wanted to prove him right, we found him asleep in a corner, in that strange sleep that often comes over him right in the middle of the day, wherever he may be, even on the parapet of the esplanade. The idea of taking off apparently put him in such a tizzy that he was asleep on his feet, which I find really amazing, unless at supper he accidentally drank a few drops of the potion I poured out so generously to his dear parents. This I know, we locked him up in the first room we found so that he wouldn't go wandering around on the fortifications, and I thought it best to leave him there until further notice. Nobody will be able to accuse him of anything, and my escape will explain yours well enough. As for the Schwartzes, they were too sound asleep to hear the bell, and nobody will have gone to see if your room was open or locked. So there won't be a serious alert until tomorrow. Nanteuil helped me calm things down, and I went looking for you, pretending to be on my way back to my barracks. I had the good luck to find you three steps away from the gate we had to use for our getaway. The jailers in that area were all on our side. At first I was really scared to find you almost dead. But dead or alive, I didn't want to leave you there. I had no trouble carrying you to the boat waiting for us along the side of the moat.

And then . . . I had a rather nasty little adventure that I'll tell you about some other time, Signora. . . . You've had enough excitement today as it is, and what I've got to say might give you a bit of a start."

"No, no, Karl! Tell me everything, I can take it."

"Oh, I know you, Signora! You'll put the blame on me. You've got your way of seeing things. I remember Roswald, where you stopped me from. . . ."

"Karl, your refusal to talk is cruel torture. Tell me, I beg you, I insist."

"Well, Signora, it's a little problem, after all, and if sin there be, it concerns me and me alone. As I was ferrying you under a low arch, very slowly so that I wouldn't make too much noise with my oars in that spot where every sound is magnified, all of a sudden, at the end of a little pier that half blocks the passage, there were three men who grabbed me by the neck and jumped into the boat. I've got to tell you that your fellow passenger in the carriage, who was already one of ours," Karl added, lowering his voice, "had been so reckless as to give Nanteuil two thirds of the appointed sum at the last postern. Nanteuil, thinking he could make do with that amount and get the remainder by betraying us, was lying in wait along with two scoundrels of his own kind to recapture you. First he was hoping to get rid of your protector and me so that nobody could say a thing about the money he'd got. That's no doubt why these rascals were ready to murder us. Yet your traveling companion, Signora, however peaceable he may look, is a lion in combat. That I'll remember for a long time to come, I swear. In short order the first scoundrel hit the water; the second one, cowed, jumped back onto the path alongside and kept his distance to see how my struggle with the adjutant would wind up. My word, Signora, I didn't settle things as gracefully as his excellent lordship. . . . I don't know what his name is. It took half a minute, to be sure, which does me no honor, since Nanteuil, who is usually strong as a bull, seemed soft and unstrung, as if he'd had a scare or the wound that he'd mentioned were worrying him. Finally, when I felt him losing hold, I picked him up and dipped his feet in the water. Then *his lordship* said, "Don't kill him, there's no point." But I knew exactly who he was; I knew how well he swims, how tenacious and cruel he is, how he stops at nothing; at another time and place I had known the power of his fists, and I had old scores to settle with him. So I couldn't help giving him a good knock on the head with my clenched fist . . . a knock that will preserve him from ever giving or getting another one, Signora! May God rest his soul and forgive mine! He went down straight as a post, leaving a big ring in the water, and never coming back up, as if he were made of marble. His pal, after being knocked out of the boat by his lordship, had taken a dive and was already at the edge of the pier where the last one, the most cautious of the three, was helping him get back on his feet. This was no easy task; the pier is so narrow right there that the one dragged down the other, and they both fell back in. While they were flailing about, swearing at each other, and having a little swimming party, I pulled on the oars with all my might, and soon I reached the spot where a second oarsman, a good man who fishes for a living, had promised to come help me row across the water. By the way, Signora, it's a good thing I'd learned something about being a sailor on the ponds at Roswald. I had no idea when you saw me taking part in such a fine rehearsal that one day I'd be fighting a naval battle, a bit less magnificent, but a bit more serious, for your sake. That memory crossed my mind when I found myself far out on the water, and I started laughing like mad . . . but what awful laughter it was! I didn't make the slightest sound; at least I didn't hear a thing. But my teeth were chattering in my mouth: I felt as though a hand of steel were at my throat, and sweat, icy cold sweat, was running down my forehead! Oh, it's clear that one doesn't kill a man as easily as a fly. Still he's not the first one, for I've seen combat, but that was war! Yet like that, in a corner at night behind a wall, without saying a word to each other, that's like premeditated murder. And yet it was a case of legitimate defense! Even though it wasn't the first assassination I'd premeditated! You remember, Signora? Had it not been for you, I would have done it! But I don't know if I wouldn't have felt bad about it later. Yet this much is certain: it was a nasty laugh I had out there on the water . . . And even now I can't help it. . . . He was so funny, plummeting into the moat! like a reed slipping down into the muck! And when there was nothing more to be seen but the tip of his head sinking fast, his head flattened by my fist. . . . Mercy, he was so ugly! And I was so scared! I can still see him!"

Consuelo, fearing the effects of this dreadful emotion on poor Karl, tried to master her own feelings in order to calm him down and distract his mind. Karl was born gentle and patient like a true Bohemian serf. He was not made for the tragic life into which fate had thrown him, and his acts of energy and revenge cost him the horror of remorse and the terrors of religious fervor. Consuelo diverted him from his gloomy thoughts, perhaps to give her own the slip. She too had armed herself for murder that same night. She too had struck a blow and drawn a few drops of blood from the impure victim. An upright, pious soul cannot approach the thought of homicide and form that resolve without cursing and bewailing the circumstances that turn a dagger into the defender of honor and life. Consuelo was deeply distressed and appalled, and she no longer dared tell herself that her freedom was worth the price of blood, even the blood of a scoundrel.

"My poor Karl," she said, "we've both acted as executioners tonight, and that's dreadful! Console yourself with the thought that we neither planned nor anticipated what necessity drove us to do. Now tell me about this nobleman who worked so unselfishly to help deliver me. You don't know who he is?"

"Not a clue, Signora. Tonight is the first time I've ever seen him, and I don't know his name."

"But where's he taking us, Karl?"

"I don't know, Signora. I've been forbidden to ask. Plus, I've even been told to tell you this: If you were to make the slightest effort to find out where you are and where you're going, they would have no choice but to abandon you along the way. It's clear that they only mean to do us good. So, as far as I'm concerned, I've made up my mind to let them lead me like a child."

"Have you seen this nobleman's face?"

"I caught a glimpse by lamplight while depositing you in the boat. He's got a handsome face, Signora, I've never seen handsomer. He looks like a king."

"Merely that, Karl? Is he young?"

"Around thirty."

"What language does he speak to you?"

"Plain Bohemian, the true language of Christians! He only said four or five words to me. But what a pleasure it would have been to hear them in my language . . . had it not been such an ugly moment! '*Don't kill him, there's no point.*' Oh, he was wrong, it was truly necessary, right, Signora?"

"So what did he say when you arrived at this terrifying decision?"

"I think, God forgive me, he didn't notice. He'd thrown himself down in the boat where you were looking dead. Fearing that you'd been hit, he used his body as a bulwark to protect you. And when we were far out on the water and safe, he raised you up in his arms, wrapped you in a warm cloak that he must have brought along for that purpose and held you against his heart, like a mother holding her child. Oh, you're obviously very dear to him, Signora! It can't be that you don't know him."

"Perhaps I do, but since I haven't managed to catch sight of his face!"

"How strange that he keeps himself hidden from you! Nothing, however, ought to surprise anyone about these folks."

"What folks? Tell me."

"The ones known as the *chevaliers*, the *black masks*, the *Invisibles*. I don't know anything more about them than you do, Signora, even though for the last two months they've been holding me by the traces and guiding me step by step to help and rescue you."

The dull thud of horses galloping over grass reached their ears. In two minutes the horses had been changed, also the postilion who was not part of the king's service. The latter stepped aside for a few quick words with the stranger, who then came and offered his hand to Consuelo, and she climbed back into the carriage with him. He sat in the back, as far away from her as possible, and he interrupted the solemn silence of the night only to have his watch strike two. Dawn was still far off even though one could hear quail singing in the heather and farm dogs barking in the distance. The night was magnificent, the constellation of the Great Bear spread out as it dipped down over the horizon. The rumbling of the carriage smothered the harmonious chorus of the countryside, and they turned their backs to the great stars of the northern skies. Consuelo understood that she was going south. Karl, up in the driver's seat, did his best to repel Mayer's ghost that seemed to come floating before his eyes at every intersection in the forest, at the foot of every cross, or beneath the towering groves of firs. Thus he scarcely gave a thought to seeing in what direction his good or his evil star was leading him.

Chapter XXI

Porporina, judging that her companion had resolved not to exchange one single word with her, decided that she could do nothing better than to respect the strange vow he apparently meant to observe, like knights-errant of old. To escape the gloomy images and dismal reflections that Karl's tale called to mind, she tried to focus on nothing but the unknown future opening up before her. Little by little she fell into a charming reverie. Only a few privileged constitutions have the gift of keeping their thoughts under control when they find themselves in a state of contemplative idleness. Consuelo had often had, and mainly during her three months of isolation at Spandau, the opportunity to exercise that faculty, which is granted less to the fortunate of this world than to those who spend their lives vying with toil, persecution, and danger. For one must recognize the providential mystery of *graces of state*, those special graces granted to people in particularly trying circumstances, without which the strength and serenity of certain hapless beings would seem impossible to those who have had only a passing acquaintance with adversity.

Besides, the circumstances in which our fugitive found herself were strange enough to give rise to many a castle in Spain. This mystery that enveloped her like a cloud, this fate that was drawing her into a fantastic world, this sort of paternal love that surrounded her with miracles was quite enough to enchant a young imagination richly endowed with poetry. She remembered these words of Scripture that she had set to music during her days in captivity:

I shall send thee one of my angels who will hold thee in his arms lest thou dash thy foot against a stone.

. . . .

I walk through the shadows, and I walk without fear, for the Lord is with me.

These words took on a clearer, more divine meaning for her. In a time when people no longer believe in God's direct revelation and tangible manifestation, heavenly protection and help are translated as aid, affection, and dedication on the part of our fellow creatures. It is so sweet to turn over the conduct of our own destiny to those who love us and to feel ourselves being carried, so to speak, by others. It is such great happiness that it would soon corrupt us unless we ourselves struggled not to abuse it. It is the happiness of a child whose golden dreams upon his mother's breast are untroubled by any real worries.

These thoughts, which came like a dream to Consuelo at the sudden, unexpected end of such a cruel existence, lulled her into a state of saintly pleasure; then sleep came washing over them, mixing them all together in that state of rest for soul and body that could be called a sense of nothingness known and relished. She had totally forgotten the presence of her silent traveling companion when she woke up right beside him, her head on his shoulder. At first it did not occur to her to move; she had just been dreaming about riding in a cart with her mother, and it seemed to her that the arm around her was the Zingara's. When she was more awake, she felt embarrassed by her inadvertence, but the stranger's arm seemed to have become a magic chain. In vain she made furtive attempts to free herself. Apparently asleep himself, the stranger had automatically taken his companion into his arms when fatigue and the moving carriage had caused her to slip toward him. He had joined his two hands around Consuelo's waist, as if to keep her from sinking down to his feet while he was nodding off. Yet sleep had not relaxed the strength of his grip, and it would have been necessary to wake him up altogether to loosen his fingers. Consuelo did not dare. She hoped that he would unwittingly free her all by himself and that she would be able to return to her place without seeming to have taken positive notice of all the delicate circumstances of their tête-à-tête.

Yet, while waiting for the stranger to fall into a deeper sleep, Consuelo, reassured by his calm respiration and motionless repose, overcome as well by the exhaustion that follows great turmoil, fell back asleep herself. The next time she woke up, her companion's head was bent down over hers, his mask had come off, their cheeks were touching, their breath commingled. She jerked away, without thinking to take a look at the stranger's face. Besides, it would have been rather difficult to see anything, given how dark it was outside and especially so inside the carriage. The stranger drew Consuelo to his breast, whose heat inflamed her own by some magnetic force, depriving her of the strength and desire to pull back. Still there was nothing violent or brutal about the man's sweet, burning embrace. Her chastity felt neither alarmed nor sullied by his caresses; and Consuelo, as if a spell had been cast over her, forgetting the control, one could even say the virginal coldness that she had never been tempted to abandon, even in the arms of impetuous Anzoleto, returned the enthusiastic, penetrating kiss that the stranger was seeking on her lips.

As everything was strange and unusual about this mysterious being, he seemed neither surprised, emboldened, nor intoxicated by Consuelo's involuntary transport. Once more he slowly pressed her to his heart, and even though his embrace was extraordinarily strong, it did not give her the pain that violent pressure always causes a delicate being. Nor did she feel the horror and shame that such a remarkable lapse from her customary reserve should have brought on after a moment's reflection. No thought came to trouble the ineffable serenity of that moment of love known and shared as if by miracle. This was the first such moment in her life. It was for her a matter of instinct, rather a revelation, and its charm was so complete, so deep, so divine that it seemed that nothing could ever change it. The stranger was to her a being apart, some kind of angel by whose love she was sanctified. He brushed Consuelo's eyelids with his fingertips, softer than the petals of a flower, and she instantly fell back asleep as if by enchantment. He stayed awake this time, but with an air of composure, as though he were invincible, as though no arrows of temptation could have penetrated his armor. He kept watch while carrying Consuelo off to unknown places, like an archangel bearing under his wing a young seraph utterly dazed and consumed by God's radiant beams.

Dawn and the morning chill finally roused Consuelo out of this sort of lethargy. Finding herself alone in the carriage, she wondered if she had loved in a dream. She tried to lower one of the blinds, but they were all fastened with an outside bolt or a spring she did not how to work. She was able to get air and watch the white or green shoulders of the road running by as broken, confused lines, but could not make out anything about the countryside nor for that reason make any observation, any discovery about where she was headed. There was something absolute and despotic about the protection encompassing her. This looked like an abduction, and she began to feel worried and frightened.

With the stranger gone, the poor sinner finally felt all the anguish of shame, all the stupor of amazement wash over her. Perhaps there were not many *Opera girls* (as female dancers and singers were then called) who would have tortured themselves for responding to the kiss of a very discreet stranger in the dark, especially since Karl had assured Porporina that he was a young man with admirable presence and looks. Yet that act of folly was so far outside the ways and ideas of virtuous, wise Consuelo that she felt deeply humiliated. Begging Albert's ghost for forgiveness, she blushed down to the bottom of her soul for having been unfaithful in her heart to him so precipitously, with so little reflection and dignity. "The evening's tragic events and the joy of my deliverance must have made me delirious," she thought to herself. "How else could I have imagined feeling love for a man who didn't say a single word to me, whose name I don't know, and whose face I haven't even seen! That's like the most shameful adventures at masked balls, those ridiculous attacks of desire that Corilla confessed to me, that I considered impossible for any woman aside from her. What contempt that man must have felt for me! He must not have taken advantage of my folly because of his sense of honor, or because he's no doubt bound by oath to higher duties, or else because he was right to scorn me. How I hope he understood or divined that I was just suffering a bout of fever, a moment of delirium!"

It was in vain that Consuelo heaped upon herself all these reproaches, for she could not defend herself against a bitter regret still greater than all the jeers of her conscience—she had lost her traveling companion, and she felt that she had no right nor any strength to accuse or curse him. Deep down she considered him a superior being with powers that were magical, perhaps diabolical, but certainly irresistible. She was afraid of him, and yet she wished not to have been so abruptly cut off from him and for all eternity.

The carriage slowed to a walk, and Karl opened a blind. "If you wish to walk a bit, Signora, the chevalier urges you to do so," he said. "It's a steep climb for the horses, and we're in the middle of the woods. There's apparently no danger."

Consuelo leaned on Karl's shoulder and hopped down to the ground without giving him time to lower the steps. She hoped to catch sight of her traveling companion, her impromptu lover. Indeed she saw him, but thirty paces ahead, which meant that his back was turned, and he was still draped in that huge grey cloak that he seemed determined to wear day and night. His bearing and the little she could see of his hair and boots revealed great distinction as well as the elegance of a man who strove to enhance by *gallant* attire, as one was wont to say, *the advantages of his person*. The hilt of his sword caught the rays of the rising sun and shone like a star on his flank while the powder that fashionable people of the time chose with the greatest of care let trail behind him in the morning air the sweet-smelling trace of a *proper gentleman*.

"Alas, my God," Consuelo thought to herself, "maybe he's some fop, a phony little lord or proud aristocrat. Whoever he is, he's turned his back on me this morning, and he's certainly right."

"Why do you call him *the chevalier*?" she asked Karl, continuing her thoughts aloud.

"Because that's what I hear the postilions call him."

"The chevalier of what?"

"Just the chevalier, nothing more. But why do you ask, Signora? Since he doesn't want you to know who he is, it seems to me that he's rendering you such great services at the risk of his own life that you ought to leave well enough alone. As for me, I'd travel around with him for ten years without asking where he was taking me. He's so handsome, so brave, so good, so lighthearted!"

"So lighthearted? That man is lighthearted?"

"For sure. He is so happy to have saved you that he can't keep quiet about it. He asks me a thousand questions about Spandau, about you, about Gottlieb, yours truly, and the King of Prussia. I tell him everything I know, everything that has happened to me, even the adventure at Roswald! It feels so good to talk Bohemian and have the ear of a quick-witted man who understands, instead of all these Prussian asses who only understand their own lousy language."

"So he's Bohemian?"

"I took the liberty of asking, and he just said no. He was even a bit gruff. I was wrong to question him when he only wanted to hear my answers."

"Does he always wear a mask?"

"Only around you, Signora. Oh, the man's a joker; he's no doubt teasing you."

Karl's cheerful banter and confidence did not entirely reassure Consuelo. She could see that he was very brave and determined, but also so straightforward and simple-hearted that he might be easily deceived. Hadn't he counted on Mayer's sincerity? Hadn't he pushed her into the wretched man's room? And now he was blindly obeying a stranger to carry her off, perhaps exposing her to seductions more refined and more dangerous! She recalled the note from the *Invisibles*: "A trap is being laid for you, a new danger threatens you. Beware of anyone urging you to escape before we have given you sure directives. Persevere in your strength, etc." No other note had come to confirm this one, and Consuelo, giving herself up to the joy of seeing Karl again, had believed this worthy servant sufficiently sanctioned to serve her. Was the stranger not a traitor? Where was he taking her with such mystery? Consuelo did not know of anyone among her friends who had anything like the chevalier's splendid bearing except for Frederick von Trenck. Yet Karl knew him perfectly well, so it was not he. The Count de Saint-Germain was older, Cagliostro less tall. After studying the stranger from a distance to try and discern an old friend in him, Consuelo came to the conclusion that she had never seen anyone walk with such ease and grace. Albert alone could have had such majesty; but his slow gait and habitual prostration had nothing of the stranger's air of strength, his chivalrous mien.

The woods were thinning out, and the horses began trotting to join up with the travelers who had gone on ahead. Without turning around, the chevalier stretched out his arms and shook his handkerchief whiter than snow. Karl understood the signal and had Consuelo get back into the carriage, saying, "By the way, Signora, under the seats you'll find big trunks with linens, clothes, and everything you may need for lunch and dinner, if necessary, books as well. In short, this seems to be a hotel on wheels, and you may not be leaving it for a while."

"Karl," said Consuelo, "please ask the chevalier if I'll be free, once we're over the border, to thank him and go my own way."

"Oh, Signora, I'd never dare say anything so unpleasant to such a gracious man."

"Never mind, I insist. Give me his answer at the next stop, since he doesn't wish to talk to me."

The stranger replied that the traveler was perfectly free, that her every wish was a command; yet her safety, the life of her guide and Karl's as well depended on not interfering with the plans for her itinerary and place of refuge. Karl added, with an ingenuous air of reproach, that this lack of trust seemed to have pained the chevalier considerably, that he had become sad and gloomy. This made her feel sorry, and she told Karl to tell him that she was putting her fate in the hands of the *Invisibles.*

The whole day was uneventful. Shut up and hidden away in the carriage like a prisoner of state, Consuelo could not begin to guess where she was headed. She was extremely happy to change her clothes, for she had noticed by daylight a few drops of Mayer's black blood on her dress and was horrified. She tried to read, but her mind was too preoccupied. She decided to sleep as much as possible, hoping to forget more and more the mortification of her last adventure. But when it was night, and the stranger remained up in the driver's seat, she felt even more embarrassed. He, obviously, had not forgotten a single thing, and his respectful delicacy made Consuelo even more ridiculous and guilty in her own eyes. At the same time, she suffered for the discomfort and fatigue he was enduring up on that seat which was tight for two people sitting side by side, he who seemed to be of such studied elegance with a soldier who was indeed very neatly disguised as a servant, but whose trusting, long-winded conversation could eventually become hard to bear; lastly, because he was exposed to the night's chill and deprived of sleep. So much courage might also look like presumptuousness. Did he consider himself irresistible? Did he think that Consuelo, now recovered from falling victim to her imagination for the first time, would not defend herself from his overly paternal familiarity? The poor child kept telling herself all this to console her downcast pride, but most certain of all, she wanted to see him again and feared above all else that his disdain or the triumph of too much virtue would make them forever strangers to each another.

Toward the middle of the night they came to a halt in a ravine. The weather was gloomy. The wind in the leaves sounded like running water. "Signora," said Karl opening the door, "here we are at the most difficult point in our travels: we've got to cross the border. With daring and money one gets out of every fix, people say. Yet it wouldn't be wise for you to make a try on the main road and under the eye of the police. There's no risk for a nobody like me. I'm going to walk the carriage, with just one horse, as if I were bringing this new acquisition to my masters at a nearby country estate. You, on the other hand, you take the shortcut with the chevalier, and some of the paths may be a bit challenging. Do you feel strong enough to do a couple of miles on foot over poor trails?"

Having replied in the affirmative, Consuelo found the chevalier's arm ready to accept hers. Karl added, "If you get to our meeting place before I do, you'll wait for me without fear, won't you, Signora?" "I fear nothing," Consuelo replied with a mixture of tenderness and pride towards the stranger, "since I'm under the gentleman's protection. But, my poor Karl, is there no danger for you?"

Karl shrugged his shoulders and kissed Consuelo's hand. Then he ran to see about the horse, and Consuelo immediately set out across country with her taciturn protector.

Chapter XXII

The sky became darker and darker, the wind kept rising, and our two fugitives had been struggling along for half an hour, sometimes over rocky paths, sometimes through brambles and tall grass, when all of a sudden rain began pelting down with extraordinary force. Consuelo still had not spoken a word to her companion, but seeing that he was worried about her and looking around for shelter, she finally said, "Have no fear for me, sir; I am strong, and I'm only sorry to see you exposed to such exertion and worry for a person who means nothing to you, who knows not how to thank you."

The stranger made a joyful gesture when he caught sight of an abandoned hovel in a corner of which he managed to shield his companion from the torrential downpour. The ruin no longer had a roof, and the protection afforded by an angle of the walls was so slight that the stranger had to stay out in the rain unless he stood right next to Consuelo. Yet he respected her situation and kept his distance so that she would have no reason to be afraid. But Consuelo soon found such self-sacrifice intolerable. She called him over, and seeing that he refused to budge, she left her shelter, trying to sound a playful note and saying, "Each one in turn, sir; I can certainly get a bit wet. You're going to take my place, since you refuse to take your portion." The chevalier attempted to lead Consuelo back to the spot which had become the prize in a contest of generosity, but she resisted. "No, I won't yield. It's clear that I offended you today when I said I wanted to part company with you at the border. I must atone for my wrongs. I wish it would cost me a good cold!"

The chevalier yielded and took shelter. Consuelo, reckoning that she owed him great amends, came and stood next to him, even though she felt humiliated that it might seem as if she were making advances to him. Yet she preferred to look shameless rather than ungrateful in his eyes, and to this she tried to resign herself to atone for the wrong she had done him. The stranger understood her so well that he stayed as far away from her as possible in a space two or three feet square. Leaning against the remains of a plaster wall, he made a show of turning his head so as to avoid embarrassing her and giving the impression that he might be emboldened by the care she was showing him. Consuelo admired that a man condemned to silence, who condemned her to the same to some extent, divined her feelings so well and made his intentions so clear. Every passing moment raised her esteem for him, and that singular feeling made her heart pound so furiously that she could hardly breathe the air that the respiration of this incomprehensibly sympathetic man had turned to fire.

A quarter of an hour later, the downpour had sufficiently abated so that the two travelers could continue on their way, but the rain-soaked paths had become nearly impassable for a woman. For a few instants the chevalier, apparently impassive, let Consuelo slip, slide, and hang onto him in order not to fall at every step. But suddenly, tired of seeing her wear herself out, he took her in his arms and carried her off like a child, even though she scolded him for it, but her reprimands did not go as far as resistance. Consuelo felt fascinated and overcome. She traversed the wind and storm in the arms of this somber chevalier who resembled the spirit of night, whisking his burden over ravines and bogs with such a fleet, sure foot as though he were an immaterial being. Thus they arrived at a ford in a stream. The stranger leaped in, lifting Consuelo higher and higher in his arms as the water got deeper and deeper.

Unfortunately the heavy, sudden downpour had swelled the creek, now a fast, murky, foam-covered torrent with a deep, sinister gurgle. Already waist deep in the stream, the chevalier was trying so hard to keep Consuelo up out of the water that he risked slipping on the mucky bottom. Consuelo grew afraid for him and said, "Let go of me, I know how to swim. In the name of heaven, let go! The water's getting higher and higher, you're going to drown!"

Just then a furious blast of wind knocked down one of the trees on the far bank, dragging into the water a huge mass of dirt and rocks which for an instant seemed to form a natural dam against the violent current. Fortunately the tree had fallen upstream, and the stranger began to catch his breath when the water, forcing its way through the jam, surged with such strength that it became nearly impossible for him to carry on. He stopped, and Consuelo tried to free herself from his arms.

"Let me go," she said, "I don't want to be the cause of your death. You're not the only one who's strong and brave! Let me struggle along with you."

But the chevalier pressed her against his heart with renewed energy. One would have said that he meant to die there with her. She was afraid of this black mask, this silent man who, like the water sprites in old German ballads, seemed to want to drag her down into the abyss. She dared not resist any longer. For more than a quarter of an hour the stranger fought, with truly frightening sangfroid and obstinacy, the furious water and wind, still holding Consuelo up out of the water, and moving forward about a foot every four or five minutes. He calmly assessed his situation. It was no easier for him to retreat than to advance; he had got past the deepest spot, and he felt that if he tried to turn around, the water might lift him up and make him lose his footing. At last he reached the bank and kept on going without letting Consuelo put a foot down, without pausing to catch his breath until he heard the whistle of Karl, who had been anxiously awaiting him. Then he placed his precious burden in the deserter's arms and fell exhausted to the ground. His exhalations were nothing but deep groans; his chest sounded as though it were about to burst.

"Oh my God, Karl, he's going to die!" said Consuelo, throwing herself on the chevalier. "Listen to that rattle! That's the sound of death. Let's get the mask off. It's smothering him."

Karl was about to obey; but the stranger, struggling to lift his icy hand, blocked his move.

"He's right!" said Karl. "I took an oath, Signora. I swore to him that even if he were dying before your eyes, I wouldn't touch his mask. Run to the carriage, Signora, and fetch me my flask of schnapps on the driver's seat; a few drops will revive him."

Consuelo tried to get up, but the chevalier held her back. If he was going to die, he meant to breathe his last at her feet.

"Once again he's right," said Karl, who, despite his rough exterior, understood the mysteries of love (he had loved!). "You'll take better care of him. I'll go get the flask. Look here, Signora," he added in a low voice, "I really think that if you had some feelings for him and were kind enough to tell him, he wouldn't let himself die. Without that, I won't vouch for a thing."

Karl went away with a smile. He did not altogether share Consuelo's alarm; it was clear to him that the chevalier's gasps and wheezes were already less labored. But Consuelo was terrified. Thinking that she was witnessing the generous man's last moments, she wrapped her arms around him and brushed kisses all over the top of his broad forehead, the only part of his face that the mask left exposed.

"Oh my God," she said, "take it off; I won't look at you, I'll go away; at least you'll be able to breathe."

The stranger took Consuelo's hands and placed them on his heaving chest, as much to feel their gentle warmth as to rid her of the desire to help him by uncovering his face. At that moment her entire soul was in that chaste embrace. She remembered what Karl had said to her, half joking, half deeply moved.

"Don't die," she said to the stranger. "Oh, don't let yourself die. Don't you feel that I love you?"

No sooner had she said these words than she thought that they had been uttered in a dream. But they had escaped her lips, as though against her will. The chevalier had heard them. He struggled up, got to his knees, and embraced those of Consuelo, who burst into tears without knowing why.

Karl returned with his flask. The chevalier rejected the deserter's favorite remedy. Leaning on Karl, he made his way to the carriage where Consuelo sat down beside him. She was very worried about his catching a chill from his wet clothing.

"Have no fear, Signora," said Karl. "The chevalier hasn't had time to get cold. I'm going to put my cloak around him. I stowed it in the carriage when I saw the rain coming on, for I suspected that one of you would get wet. If you put dry, thick wraps over wet clothes, you can keep warm for quite a while. It's like being in a lukewarm bath, and it's doesn't do one any harm."

"But Karl, do the same thing," said Consuelo. "Take my mantelet, for you got wet to protect us."

"Oh well, I've got thicker skin than the two of you. Put the mantelet around the chevalier, too. Bundle him up well, and even if it means finishing off this poor horse, I'll get you to the next relay without going numb with cold."

For an hour Consuelo kept her arms wrapped around the stranger; and her head, which he had drawn down to his breast, restored his vital heat better than all of Karl's prescriptions and recipes. Sometimes she felt his forehead and warmed it with her breath so that the perspiration gathered there would not grow cold. When the carriage came to a halt, he pressed her against his heart with a strength that let her know that he was to the fullest measure alive and happy. Then he dashed out of the carriage and disappeared.

Consuelo found herself in some sort of shed, face to face with an elderly servant who was more or less a peasant. Holding a dark lantern, he led her over a hedge-lined path alongside a modest-looking house to a lodge. He stayed outside while showing her in, then shut the door behind her. Seeing another door standing open, she entered a little two-room apartment, very clean and simple: a well-heated bedroom with a good bed all made-up, and another room lit with candles where a cozy supper was laid out. She was disappointed to see only one place setting; and when Karl arrived with her parcels and offered to serve her at table, she dared not say that her protector's company at supper was her only wish.

"Go eat and sleep yourself, my good Karl," she said. "I don't need a thing. You've got to be more worn out than I am."

"No more than if I'd just said my prayers beside the fire with my poor wife, God rest her soul! Oh, this time when I saw that I was once again out of Prussia I kissed the earth, even though I truly don't know if we're in Saxony, Bohemia, Poland, or *in China*, as we used to say back at Count Hoditz's estate in Roswald."

"And how can it be, Karl, that up in the driver's seat you didn't recognize a single place we passed through today?"

"Apparently I've never taken this route, Signora. And then, I don't know how to read what is written on the walls and signposts. Plus, we didn't stop in any town or village. All our relays have been in the woods or the courtyard of some private house. Finally, reason number four, I gave the chevalier my word of honor not to tell you, Signora."

"That's where you should have started, Karl; I wouldn't have made any objections. But tell me, does the chevalier seem ill to you?"

"Not at all, Signora. He comes and goes in the house, where he really does not seem to have much important business, for the only other person I see is an old gardener who doesn't talk much."

"So go offer him your services, Karl. Run along and let me be."

"What am I to do? He refused them, ordering me to look after you alone."

"Well then, look after yourself, my friend, and have pleasant dreams about your freedom."

Consuelo went to bed at the first light of dawn, and when she was up and dressed, her watch said two. The day looked clear and sunny. She tried to open the shutters, but in both rooms she found that they were fastened with a secret lock, like those in the post chaise in which she had been traveling. She tried to go out; the doors were bolted shut from the outside. She returned to the window and made out a modest orchard in the foreground. Nothing suggested a town or highway nearby. There was total silence inside the house, and outside it was broken only by buzzing insects, pigeons cooing on the roof, and every now and then the plaintive creaking of a wheelbarrow in paths that her eyes could not see. She listened mechanically to these sounds that were sweet to her ear, so long deprived of the echoes of country life. Consuelo was still a prisoner, and all the care taken to keep that from her made her rather worried. But for a while she would resign herself to a captivity that hardly seemed cruel, and the chevalier's love did not cause her the same horror as Mayer's.

Although faithful Karl had told her to ring as soon as she was up, she did not want to bother him, considering that he needed his rest more than she. She especially feared waking up her other traveling companion, whose fatigue had to be extreme. She went into the other room, and on the table where supper had been served the evening before and cleared away without her noticing she found heaps of books and writing paraphernalia.

The books did not tempt her much. She was too restless to read. Since in the midst of her perplexities she took irresistible pleasure in retracing the events of the previous night, she made no effort to take her mind off them. Little by little, given that she was still being kept in solitary confinement, it came to her to continue her diary, and as a preamble she wrote this page on a loose sheet of paper.

"Dear Beppo, it's for you alone that I'll go on with the tale of my strange adventures. Since I'm used to talking to you with the expansiveness inspired by the closeness of our ages and the kinship of our ideas, I can share with you emotions that my other friends wouldn't understand, that they would no doubt judge more harshly than you. You can guess from this beginning that I don't feel that I've done nothing wrong; in my own eyes I have done something wrong, even though I still have no idea what the significance and consequences of that may be.

"Joseph, before I tell you how I escaped from Spandau (which, in truth, seems to me almost nothing in comparison with what is on my mind just now), I have to tell you . . . how to tell you? . . . I myself don't know. Was it a dream? Yet I feel my head burning and my heart tossing as though it wanted to leap out of me and lose itself in another soul. . . . Well, I'll tell you very simply, because everything is in this word, my dear friend, my good chum: I'm in love!

"I love a man whom I don't know, whose face I haven't seen, whose voice I haven't heard. You're going to say that this is madness, and you're quite right: Isn't love serious madness? Listen, Joseph, and don't doubt my happiness which surpasses all the illusions of my first love in Venice, a happiness so intoxicating that I can't feel shame about having accepted it so hastily, so madly, nor can I fear that I may have misplaced my affection, or even that my love won't be requited. . . . Oh! I am loved, I feel it so clearly! . . . You can be sure that I'm not wrong, that this time I'm truly in love, dare I say passionately? Why not? Love comes to us from God. It's not up to us to light it in our hearts as we would light a candle on the altar. All the efforts I made to love Albert (whose name I can't write anymore without trembling!) didn't manage to kindle that ardent, sacred flame; since I've lost him, I've loved the memory of him more than I ever loved the person. Who knows how I might love him if he were given back to me? . . ."

No sooner had Consuelo written these last words than she rubbed them out, perhaps not well enough to prevent someone from still being able to read them, but well enough to elude the fear of having thought them. She was all aflutter, and her innermost depths betrayed, despite herself, the truth of her amorous inspiration. In vain she strove to go on writing so as better to explain to herself the mystery of her own heart. To render its subtle nuance she found nothing but these terrifying words, "Who knows how I might love Albert if he were given back to me?"

Consuelo did not know how to lie; she had thought herself in love with the memory of a dead man; but she felt her bosom brimming with life, and a real passion annihilating an imaginary one.

To get herself out of this inner turmoil she tried to reread everything that she had written and found precisely nothing but turmoil. Having lost all hope of being able to enjoy enough composure to sum up her thoughts, feeling that this effort was bringing on a fever, she crumpled up the sheet and threw it on the table until there came an opportunity to burn it. Trembling like a soul wracked with guilt, her face on fire, she paced around wildly, not understanding anything any longer except that she was in love and that it was not up to her to doubt it.

There was a knock on her bedroom door, and she went to let Karl in. His face was flushed, his eyes bleary, and his jowls a bit slack. She thought he was sick with exhaustion, but soon she understood from his replies that he had indulged a bit too much in the wine or beer of welcome the morning of their arrival. This was poor Karl's only failing. A certain dose made him overly confident; a stronger one could make him terrifying. Fortunately, he had limited himself to the dose of expansiveness and good will, and he was still feeling a few of the effects, even after having slept all day. He was crazy about the chevalier and could speak of nothing else. The chevalier was so kind, so humane, hardly proud with humble folks! He had sat Karl down facing him rather than letting Karl serve him at table; he had forced Karl to share his meal and poured him the best wine, clinking glasses at every refill, and keeping up with him like a true Slav.

"What a pity he's only Italian!" said Karl. "He deserves to be Bohemian; he holds his wine as well as I do."

"That may not be saying much," replied Consuelo, none too pleased about the chevalier's great aptitude for drinking with footmen.

But she immediately upbraided herself for having been capable of considering Karl, after all he done for her, inferior to her or her friends. Besides, the chevalier had no doubt sought out the company of this devoted servant to hear someone talk about her.

"Oh, Signora," he naively added, "this worthy young man is madly in love with you. For you he'd commit crimes, even despicable deeds!"

"I'd certainly spare him that," said Consuelo, who disliked this language, even though Karl no doubt failed to measure its impact. "Could you explain to me," she asked, to change the subject, "why I am kept so carefully under lock and key here?"

"Oh! Signora, if I knew that, they'd have to cut out my tongue before I'd say so. I gave the chevalier my word of honor not to answer any of your questions."

"Many thanks, Karl! So you love the chevalier much more than you do me?"

"Oh, never! That's not what I'm saying. But since he's proven to me that it's for your own good, I must serve you despite yourself."

"How did he do that?"

"I've got no idea; but I'm sure of it. He ordered me as well, Signora, to keep you shut away, under surveillance, in short, a prisoner in solitary confinement until we arrive."

"So we're not staying here?"

"We're leaving again as soon as it's dark. We won't be traveling by day any longer, to spare you fatigue, and for other reasons that I don't know."

"And you're going to be my jailer the whole time?"

"As you say, Signora. I swore it on the Gospel."

"Come on now! The chevalier is playing a joke. I'll make the best of it, Karl. I'd rather deal with you than Herr Schwartz."

"And I'll keep you a bit better," replied Karl, with a jolly laugh. "For starters, I'm going to fix your dinner, Signora."

"I'm not hungry, Karl."

"Oh, that's impossible. You've got to have dinner, and a good dinner, Signora. Those are my orders, as Master Schwartz used to say."

"If you do exactly as he did, you won't force me to eat. He was delighted to charge me again the next day for the meal that he'd conscientiously put back in the larder."

"That was good for his business. With me it's different. The chevalier takes care of the business end of things. He's not stingy, that one; he's spending money hand over fist. He must be awfully rich, or his inheritance won't last long."

Consuelo had him bring her a candle, then went into the next room to burn what she had written. But she looked for it in vain; the sheet was nowhere to be found.

Chapter XXIII

A few seconds later Karl came back with a letter written in a hand that was unfamiliar to Consuelo. This is more or less what it said:

"I'm leaving, perhaps never to see you again. I'm giving up three days that I still could have spent with you, three days that I may never see again my whole life long! I do so willingly. I must. One day you'll appreciate the saintliness of my sacrifice.

"Yes, I love you, I too love you *passionately*! Yet I know you scarcely more than you know me. You don't owe me any thanks for what I've done for you. I was obeying the highest orders, fulfilling the duties of my charge. Hold me to account merely for the love that I have for you, that I can prove to you only by going away. This love is as violent as it is respectful. It will be as lasting as it was sudden and impulsive. I've hardly seen your face, I know nothing of your life, but I felt that my soul belonged to you, that I could never take it back. Were your past as sullied as your brow is pure, I would hold you no less worthy of respect and no less dear. I leave, my heart brimming with pride, joy, and bitterness. You love me! How shall I bear the idea of losing you if the dreadful will that disposes of your life and mine condemns me to that? . . . I do not know. Just now I cannot be unhappy, despite my terror. I'm too drunk on love, yours and mine, to feel any pain. Were I to spend my whole life searching in vain for you, I shall not lament having met you, having tasted in your kiss a happiness that will leave me eternal regrets. Nor shall I lose hope of finding you again one day; were it only for a second, were I never to know any other expression of your love than this saintly kiss given and returned, I'll still find myself a hundred times happier than I had been before knowing you.

"And now, saintly girl, poor troubled soul, you too must remember without shame or fear those brief, divine moments in which you felt my love entering your heart. As you said, love comes to us from God, and it is not up to us to smother love or kindle it despite itself. Were I unworthy of you, that sudden inspiration that made you respond to my embrace would be no less celestial. But the Providence that is watching over you would not have the treasure of your love fall into the mire of a cold, egotistical heart. Were I ungrateful, there would merely be on your part a noble instinct gone astray, a saintly inspiration spent and lost. I adore you, and whatever else I may be, it was no delusion when you thought yourself loved. You have not been profaned by the beating of my heart, the press of my arm, the breath from my lips. Our mutual confidence, blind faith, and irresistible impulse raised us up in a second to the sublime abandon sanctified by long passion. Why regret it? I realize that there's something frightening in this destiny that has thrust us together. But it's the hand of God, don't you see? That we cannot fail to recognize. I'm carrying this awful secret away with me. You keep it too; don't entrust it to anyone. *Beppo* might not understand. Whoever that friend may be, I'm the only one who can respect you in your madness and revere you in your weakness, since that madness and that weakness are mine. Adieu! Perhaps forever. Yet I am free in the eyes of the world; it seems to me that you are, too. I can love no one but you, and it's clear to me that you love no one else. . . . But our fate is no longer in our hands. I am bound by eternal vows, as you too will no doubt soon be. At least, the Invisibles have you in their power, and that power is without appeal. Therefore adieu. . . . my breast is being rent asunder, but God will give me the strength to accomplish this sacrifice, and even more exacting ones if there be. Adieu. . . . Adieu! O great God, have pity on me!"

The unsigned letter was written in a labored or disguised hand.

"Karl!" exclaimed Consuelo, pale and trembling. "Wasn't it the chevalier who gave you this?"

"Yes, Signora."

"And he wrote it himself?"

"Yes, Signora, which wasn't easy. He's got a wound on his right hand."

"A wound, Karl? A bad one?"

"Maybe. It's deep, even though he hardly seems to give it a thought."

"But where did he get it?"

"Last night, while we were changing horses before reaching the border, the wheel horse tried to bolt before the postilion had mounted the lead. You were alone in the carriage; the postilion and I were four or five steps away. The chevalier held the horse with the strength of a demon and the courage of a lion, for it was a terrifying animal!"

"Oh yes, I felt some violent jerks. But you told me it was nothing."

"I hadn't seen that the chevalier had split open the back of his hand on a harness buckle."

"Always for me! Tell me, Karl, has the chevalier left?"

"Not yet, Signora, but his horse is being saddled, and I've just packed his bag. You've got nothing to fear now, he says, and the person who is to take his place with you has already arrived. I hope that we'll see him again soon; I'd be awfully sad otherwise. Yet he won't be pinned down, and to all my questions he always says, *Perhaps*!"

"Karl, where is the chevalier?"

"I've got no idea, Signora. His room is over here. Do you want me to tell him for you that . . . ?"

"No, don't say a thing, I'll write something. No . . . tell him I want to thank him . . . see him for an instant, just to press his hand. . . . Go on, hurry up, I'm afraid he may be already gone."

Karl left, and Consuelo immediately regretted having entrusted him with this message. She told herself that if the chevalier had never remained in her proximity during this journey except when absolutely necessary, it was probably not without having promised as much to the strange, dreadful Invisibles. She made up her mind to write to him, but scarcely had she traced a few words and rubbed them out when a slight noise made her look up. There in front of her eyes was sliding open a woodwork panel that formed a secret communicating door between the little room where she had already done some writing and a nearby room, no doubt the chevalier's. Yet the panel only opened wide enough to let through a gloved hand that seemed to beckon for Consuelo's. She sprang up and seized that hand, saying "The other hand, the wounded one!"

The stranger remained out of sight behind the panel and stretched forth his right hand. Consuelo took it, hurriedly undid the bandage and saw the wound which was indeed deep. She kissed it with her lips and wrapped it in her handkerchief, then drew from her breast the little filigree cross that she superstitiously cherished and put it in the beautiful hand that looked all the whiter against the crimson blood.

"Here," she said, "this is the most precious thing I have in the world, my mother's legacy, my good-luck charm from which I've never been separated. Never have I loved anyone so much that I'd trust him with this treasure. Keep it until I find you once again."

The stranger drew Consuelo's hand back behind the woodwork that kept him hidden and covered it with kisses and tears. Then, hearing Karl coming with her message, he pushed it away and hurriedly shut the panel. Consuelo heard a bolt slip. She listened in vain, hoping to catch the sound of the stranger's voice. He was talking very quietly, or he had gone away.

Karl returned a few seconds later.

"He's left, Signora," he said gloomily. "He left without wanting to bid you farewell, and he filled my pockets with I don't know how many ducats, for any unexpected needs you may have on the way, or so he said, given that the ordinary expenses are covered by the . . . covered by God or the devil, no matter! Now there's a little man in black who only unclenches his teeth to give orders in a high, crisp voice. I don't cotton to him at all. He's the one replacing the chevalier, and I'll have the honor of his company up on the driver's seat, which won't make for much lively conversation. The poor chevalier! I pray that he'll be returned to us!"

"But do we have to follow this little man in black?"

"Indeed we do, Signora. The chevalier made me swear that I'd obey this one as I do him. Well, Signora, here's your dinner. Don't turn up your nose; it looks good. We'll leave when it gets dark, only stopping where it may please . . . God or the devil, as I just said."

Consuelo, sad and bewildered, stopped listening to Karl's chatter. She was not the least bit worried about her travels or her new guide. Nothing mattered, now that the dear stranger had abandoned her. Sunk in misery, she made perfunctory attempts to please Karl by nibbling here and there. Yet, as she felt more like crying than eating, she asked for a cup of coffee to give herself at least a little strength and bodily courage. It was brought to her.

"Well, Signora," said Karl, "the little gentleman insisted on making the coffee himself so that it would be really good. I've got the feeling he used to be a manservant or a butler and, after all, he's not as devilish as he looks. He's basically good-natured, I think, though he doesn't like to gab. He gave me some schnapps aged at least a hundred years, the best I've ever drunk. If you wanted a little taste, it might do you more good than this coffee, no matter how delicious. . . ."

"Karl, my good man, go drink whatever you wish, and leave me alone," said Consuelo, gulping down her coffee, hardly giving a thought to its quality.

She had no sooner got up from the table than she felt overcome by an extraordinary sluggishness of mind. When Karl came to tell her the carriage was waiting, he found her dozing in her chair.

"Give me your arm," she said. "I can't hold myself up. I must have a fever."

She was so knocked out that the carriage, her new guide, and the concierge of the house, who wouldn't accept any reimbursement from Karl on her behalf, swam before her eyes. As soon as they got moving, she went sound asleep. The carriage had been arranged and decorated with cushions like a bed. From that moment on Consuelo was conscious of nothing. She did not know how long they traveled; she did not even notice whether it was day or night, whether they stopped or went on without a break. Once or twice she caught sight of Karl at the door and understood neither what he was asking her nor why he was alarmed. It seemed to her that the little man was taking her pulse and making her drink a refreshing potion while saying, "It's nothing. Madame is just fine."

Yet she felt a vague malaise, an insurmountable weariness. Her eyelids were so heavy that she could not see beyond them, and her mind was not clear enough for her to understand what objects were meeting her gaze. The more she slept, the more she wanted to sleep. It did not even occur to her to wonder if she was ill, and she could only repeat to Karl the last words she had said to him, "Leave me alone, good Karl."

Finally, she felt a bit freer in body and mind. Taking a look around, she understood that she was lying in an excellent bed, between four huge white satin curtains with gold fringe. The little man in charge of the voyage, who wore a black mask like the chevalier's, was making her sniff from a phial that seemed to clear her mind and take her out of her fog into the light of day.

"Are you a physician, sir?" she finally asked, with a bit of effort.

"Yes, Countess, I am," he replied in a voice that did not seem altogether unfamiliar to her.

"Have I been ill?"

"Just a bit under the weather. You must be feeling much better?"

"I'm feeling fine, and I thank you for your care."

"Please accept my respects. Your Ladyship will not be seeing me again unless I am summoned for reasons of illness."

"Have I arrived at the end of my journey?"

"Yes, Madame."

"Am I free or a prisoner?"

"You are free, Countess, everywhere within the bounds of your abode."

"I see, I'm in a big, beautiful prison," said Consuelo looking at her large, bright room, the walls upholstered with white silk half-damask with a gold leaf motif and trimmed with magnificently sculpted, gilded woodwork. "Shall I be able to see Karl?"

"I don't know, Madame, I am not the master here. I am going now; you no longer need my services; and I have been forbidden to indulge in the pleasure of conversing with you."

The man in black left, and Consuelo, still weak and listless, tried to get up. The only garment at hand was a long gown of white wool, of a wonderfully soft texture, that looked rather like the tunic of a Roman lady. She picked it up, and out fell a note in gold lettering, "Behold the spotless robe of the neophytes. If thy soul is impure, this noble adornment of innocence will be for thee the blazing tunic of Deïanira."

Consuelo, accustomed to enjoying a peaceful conscience (perhaps even too peaceful), smiled and put on the beautiful gown with naïve pleasure. She picked up the note to read it again and found it childishly emphatic. Then she went up to a sumptuous white marble dressing table with a huge mirror framed with exquisitely tasteful gilded scrollwork. But her eye was caught by an inscription placed in the ornament over this mirror, "If thy soul is as pure as my crystal, thou wilt see thyself eternally young and beautiful; yet if vice hath tarnished thy heart, thou shouldst fear finding in me a grim reflection of thy inner ugliness."

"Neither beauty nor blame have been my lot," Consuelo thought to herself. "So this mirror lies in any case."

She gazed into the mirror without fear and did not find herself ugly. The beautiful flowing gown and her long, streaming black hair made her look like a priestess of antiquity, but she was struck by her extreme pallor. Her eyes were less clear and sparkling than usual. "Have I become ugly," she immediately thought, "or is the mirror accusing me of something?"

She opened a drawer of the dressing table and found, among countless tokens of studied elegance and luxury, various items with mottos and maxims that were both naïve and pedantic: a jar of rouge with these words engraved on the cover, "Fashion and falsehood! Paint doth not restore to cheeks the freshness of innocence nor erase the ravages of debauchery"; exquisite perfume, with this motto on the phial, "A faithless soul, indiscreet lips are like open phials whose precious essence hath spilled out or been corrupted"; and finally some white silk ribbons bearing these words woven in gold, "Sacred bands for a spotless brow; the cord, the torture of slaves, for a head laden with infamy."

Consuelo lifted her hair and complaisantly tied it up, in antique fashion, with these ribbons. Then she studied with curiosity the strange enchanted palace to which her romantic destiny had led her. She walked through the various rooms of her sumptuous, huge apartment. A library, a music room full of perfect instruments, numerous scores, and precious manuscripts, a delightful boudoir, a little gallery adorned with superb paintings and charming statues. It was worthy of a queen for its riches, of an artist for its taste, of a nun for its chastity. Dazzled by this lavish and refined hospitality, Consuelo decided that she would wait until her mind was better rested to study in detail all the symbols hidden in the choice of books, objets d'art, and paintings in this sanctuary. The desire to know where on earth this marvelous residence was located made her turn her attention to the outside. She approached a window, but before raising the taffeta blind, she found another maxim, "If the thought of evil is in thy heart, thou art not worthy to contemplate nature's divine spectacle. If virtue dwelleth in thy soul, behold and bless the God who openeth the door of earthly paradise before thee." She quickly opened the window to see if the landscape matched these proud promises. It was indeed an earthly paradise, and Consuelo thought she was dreaming. The garden, laid out in English fashion, a very rare thing at the time, yet with studied German elegance in its details, offered pleasant vistas, magnificent patches of shade, fresh lawns, the wild abandon of nature and, at the same time, the exquisite tidiness, the many sweet flowers, the fine sand, the crystal waters of a garden maintained with intelligence and love. Over these beautiful trees rose the high walls of a narrow valley sown or rather carpeted with flowers and crisscrossed with clear, lovely streams, a sublime horizon of blue mountains of various heights and imposing peaks. The landscape was unfamiliar to Consuelo. As far as her eyes could reach, she found nothing indicating any particular place in Germany, where there are so many beautiful sites and noble mountains. Only the more advanced flowering and the warmer climate than in Prussia attested that she had come a bit south. "O my good canon, where are you?" Consuelo thought to herself, contemplating the clumps of white lilacs, the hedges of roses, and the earth strewn with narcissus, hyacinths, and violets. "O Frederick of Prussia, bless you for having taught me through long privations and cruel trials how to savor as I ought the delights of such a refuge! And you, almighty invisible, keep me forever in this sweet captivity; I consent with all my soul . . . especially if the chevalier. . . ." Consuelo did not finish putting words to her desire. Since having emerged from her lethargy, she still had not thought about the stranger. This burning memory rose up and made her reflect on the meaning of the threatening words inscribed on all the walls and furniture of the magic palace, even on the adornments that she had ingenuously donned.

Chapter XXIV

Consuelo felt above all a desire and need for freedom, quite natural after so many days of slavery. So she took extreme pleasure rushing out into a vast space that looked much vaster still through the labors of art and ingenious layout of the shrubs and paths. Yet, after a two-hour walk she felt saddened by the solitude and silence that reigned over this beautiful place. She had already gone around the garden several times without seeing even the trace of a human foot on the fine, freshly raked sand. Rather high walls masked with dense vegetation prevented her from wandering off on unfamiliar paths. She already knew by heart all the ones that wove back and forth under her feet. In a few spots the wall gave way to broad moats brimming with water, and the eye could play over lovely lawns sloping up into woods or the starting points of the mysterious, charming paths that meandered off into the brush and disappeared. From her window Consuelo had the whole of nature before her eyes. Down on the ground she found herself boxed in and blocked wherever she turned, and all the exquisite things within could not overcome her feeling of being held captive. She looked around for the enchanted palace where she had awakened. It was a tiny Italianate building, luxuriously decorated inside, elegantly done outside, sitting at the foot of a steep cliff. While its effect was picturesque, the cliff formed a better natural enclosure for that whole end of the garden and a more impenetrable obstacle for the eyes than the highest walls and the thickest fortifications at Spandau. "My fortress is beautiful," Consuelo said to herself, "but that only makes it more secure, as I can see."

She went to take a rest on the house terrace which was decorated with vases of flowers and a little fountain. It was a delightful spot. From there one could see nothing but the interior of a garden, with a few glimpses of the grounds of some fine estate and high mountains whose blue crests loomed over the trees, which only made the view all the more fresh and charming. Yet Consuelo, instinctively frightened by the care being taken to get her settled, perhaps for a long time, in a yet another prison, would have given all the blooming catalpas and brilliantly colored flower beds for a bit of real countryside with a little thatch-roofed cottage, bumpy roads, and the free and open look of land that one could get to know and explore. From the terrace she could not see anything in the middle ground between the high green walls that rose up all around her and the vague jagged lines of the horizon already obscured in the haze of the setting sun. The song of the nightingales was admirable, but there was no sound of a human voice announcing any neighbors. Consuelo could see that her little abode on the edge of some grand grounds and what might be a huge forest was simply a lodge belonging to a much larger estate. What she could see of the grounds only made her want to see more. Herds of elk and roe deer were ambling about, grazing on the hillsides with such confidence as though a mortal's approach would have been an unknown experience to them. These were the sole creatures that met her eye. Finally, the evening breeze parted a curtain of poplars on one side of the garden, and in the twilight Consuelo caught a glimpse of the white turrets and pointed roofs of a rather imposing castle half concealed behind a wooded hillock about a quarter of a league away. In spite of her great desire not to dwell on the chevalier any longer, Consuelo convinced herself that he had to be there, and her eyes fastened eagerly on the castle, perhaps imaginary, whose approach seemed to her forbidden. Little by little the veils of night came over the castle, and it disappeared in the distance.

When it was altogether dark, Consuelo saw the reflection of the lights from the lower floor of her lodge on the shrubs nearby, and she raced down, hoping to see at last a human face in her house. This pleasure was not afforded her. The servant whom she found busy lighting candles and serving supper was, like the doctor, wearing a black mask, which seemed to be the uniform of the Invisibles. He was old, with a wig as smooth and stiff as brass, and properly attired in a livery the color of a love apple.

"I humbly beg Madame's pardon," he said in a cracked voice, "to appear before her with such a face. I'm following orders, and it is not my place to understand why this is necessary. I hope that Madame will have the grace to get used to it and not be afraid of me. I am at Madame's service. My name is Matteus. I'm at one and the same time the keeper of this lodge, the director of the garden, the butler, and the valet. I've been told that Madame, having traveled a good deal, was somewhat used to looking after herself; that, for example, she might not require the services of a maid. It would be difficult for me to find a maid for Madame, seeing that I don't have a wife and this lodge being off-limits to all the maids at the castle. Even so, a maid will come in here every morning to help me clean, and from time to time a garden boy will come water the flowers and attend to the paths. In this regard I have a most humble observation for Madame: any servant, except for me, to whom Madame is even suspected of saying a word or making a sign will be dismissed on the spot, which would be most unfortunate for that person, since this is a good household and obedience is well compensated. Madame is too generous and fair-minded, no doubt, to wish to expose these poor folks. . . ."

"Put your mind at rest, Monsieur Matteus," replied Consuelo. "I wouldn't be rich enough to compensate their loss, and I'm not the kind of person to make anyone stray from his duty."

"Besides, I'll never take my eyes off them," Matteus went on, as though he were talking to himself.

"You need not worry about that. I am much too beholden to those who brought me here, also to those, I think, who are my hosts in this place, to attempt anything that might displease them."

"Oh! Madame is here of her own free will?" asked Matteus. It seemed that curiosity was less strictly forbidden to him than expansiveness.

"Please consider me a willing captive, and on my honor."

"Oh, that's just the way I see it. I've never kept anyone otherwise, even though quite often I've seen such prisoners of mine weep and worry as though they regretted having given their word. And yet God knows they were well treated here! But in those cases they were released from their oath when they insisted on it; nobody is ever detained here by force. Madame's supper is served."

The penultimate sentence of the tomato-colored butler restored his new mistress's appetite on the spot. She found supper so good that she gave fine compliments to its maker, who seemed greatly flattered by such appreciation, and it was clear to Consuelo that she had earned his respect. Yet he was neither more trusting nor less wary. He was an excellent man, at once simple and crafty. Consuelo quickly sized him up, seeing how he, with a mixture of good-heartedness and cunning, anticipated all the questions she might ask him so as not to get tripped up and to devise replies to his liking. Thus she was told everything that she had not asked to know, yet without learning a single thing. His masters were very rich, very powerful, very generous, but very severe, especially in the matter of discretion. The lodge was part of a beautiful residence, sometimes inhabited by the masters of the house, sometimes entrusted to the care of the very faithful servants, very well paid and very discreet. The land was rich, fertile, and well governed. The people living there were not in the habit of complaining about their lords. Besides, they wouldn't have had an easy time doing that around Master Matteus, who respected people and the law and could not abide indiscreet remarks. Consuelo found his clever insinuations and officious information so tedious that as soon as supper was over, she smiled and said, "I would fear being indiscreet myself, sir, if I were to enjoy your conversation any longer. I don't need anything more today, and I wish you good evening."

"Madame will do me the honor of ringing whenever she wishes anything," he replied. "I live behind the house, at the foot of the cliff, in a pretty hermitage where I grow magnificent watermelons. I would be delighted if Madame could give them an encouraging glance, but I've been particularly forbidden ever to open that door to Madame."

"I understand, Master Matteus, I must never go out except in the garden, and I mustn't blame your whim, but the will of my hosts. I'll obey the rule."

"All the more because Madame would find it very hard to open the door. It is so heavy. . . . And then there's a secret spring in the lock that could grievously wound Madame's hands if she weren't forewarned."

"My word is even stronger than all your locks and bolts, Monsieur Matteus. Sleep in peace, as I too mean to do."

Several days went by without Consuelo receiving any word from her hosts, without setting eyes on any face aside from Matteus's black mask, more pleasant perhaps than his actual features. This worthy attendant served her with a zeal and punctuality for which she could not thank him enough. Yet she was prodigiously bored by his conversation, which she felt obligated to endure, for he always stoically refused her presents, and she had no way to show her gratitude other than letting him prattle on. He was passionately fond of talking, and this was all the more remarkable because he never strayed from the strange reserve required of him and had a knack for broaching many topics without ever touching on the reserved sins entrusted to his discretion. Consuelo was told precisely how many carrots and stalks of asparagus the castle produced every year; how many fawns were born on the grounds, the history of every swan in the pond, every chick in the pheasantry and every pineapple in the greenhouse. Yet she could not guess for an instant in what country she was, whether the master or masters of the castle were absent or present, whether she was to communicate with them one day or remain alone indefinitely in the lodge.

In short, nothing that truly interested her escaped Matteus's prudent, yet lively lips. She feared that it would be altogether uncouth even to go within earshot of the gardener and the maidservant who came moreover very early in the morning and disappeared almost as soon as she was up. She did nothing more than glance into the grounds from time to time without ever seeing anyone go by, unless at too great a distance for any real observation, and contemplate the top of the castle that glimmered with a few lights every evening, always extinguished at an early hour.

It was not long before she fell into deep melancholy, and boredom, over which she had triumphed at Spandau, assailed and overwhelmed her in this opulent dwelling, among all the comforts of life. Are there earthly treasures that one can enjoy utterly alone? Prolonged solitude casts a pall over the loveliest things and robs them of their charm; it strikes terror into the most stalwart soul. Soon Consuelo found the hospitality of the Invisibles even more cruel than strange, and a mortal disgust took hold of all her faculties. The sound of her magnificent harpsichord seemed to her too bright in these empty, resonant rooms, and she was spooked by her own voice. When she ventured to sing, if the first shadows of night took her by surprise in the midst of this pursuit, she thought she could hear angry echoes coming back at her and see restless shadows skulking along the silk-lined walls and over the noiseless carpets. When she tried to get a good look at them, they sank back, slinking off behind the furniture to whisper, mock, and mimic her. Yet it was only the evening breeze playing in the leaves around her windows or the vibrations of her voice in the surrounding air. But her imagination, weary of questioning all these silent witnesses to her ennui, the statues, the paintings, the Japanese vases full of flowers, the huge mirrors clear and deep, was beginning to fall prey to a vague fear, of the kind that results from anticipating some unknown event. She remembered the strange powers that the common folk ascribed to the Invisibles, the weird illusions with which Cagliostro had surrounded her, the apparition of the woman in white at the palace in Berlin, the Count de Saint-Germain's marvelous promises regarding Count Albert's resurrection. She told herself that all these unexplained things probably emanated from the secret work of the Invisibles in society and in her own particular destiny. She did not believe in their supernatural power, but it was clear to her that they were intent on conquering people's minds by every means, appealing either to the heart or the imagination, using threats or promises, terror or temptation. So she was in the grip of some fearsome revelation or cruel hoax and, like cowardly children, she could have said that she was *afraid of being afraid.*

At Spandau she had steeled her will against extreme danger and real suffering; she had triumphed valiantly over everything; resignation, moreover, had seemed natural to her at Spandau. A fortress's sinister look is in harmony with solitude's gloomy meditations, whereas in her new prison everything seemed set up for a life of poetic effusion or peaceful intimacy; and this eternal silence, this lack of all human sympathy destroyed the harmony of the place like a monstrous misconception. One would have thought it the charming retreat of two happy lovers or an elegant family, a pleasant home suddenly hated and abandoned because of some painful breakup or sudden catastrophe. The numerous inscriptions that decorated every flourish no longer made her smile like so many emphatic bits of childish drivel. Words of encouragement were combined with threats, conditional praise was corrected with humiliating accusations. She could no longer lift her eyes without discovering some new maxim that had escaped her notice, that seemed to forbid her from breathing easily in this sanctuary of wary, watchful justice. Her soul had collapsed in on itself after the crises of the escape and her impromptu love for the *stranger*. Her lethargic state, no doubt deliberately induced to prevent her from seeing where her refuge was located, had left her with a secret languor, along with a resulting nervous irritability. For that reason she soon felt both restless and nonchalant, by turns alarmed by a trifle, then indifferent to everything.

One evening she thought she could just barely hear an orchestra far off in the distance. She went up to the terrace and saw the castle shimmering with light through the leaves. The strains of a symphony, proud and vibrant, came to her clearly. The contrast between a festive gathering and her solitude moved her more than she wanted to admit. It had been so long since she had exchanged a word with intelligent or rational beings! For the first time in her life she fancied a marvelous night at a concert or a ball and, like Cinderella, she wished that some good fairy would whisk her up and away into the enchanted palace through a window, if only to remain there sight unseen, relishing the view of human beings enjoying themselves together.

The moon was not yet up. Although the sky was clear, there were such deep shadows under the trees that Consuelo could easily slip over there without anyone noticing, even if she had been surrounded by invisible guards. A fierce temptation came over her, and all the specious reasons that curiosity calls up when it intends to mount an assault on our conscience thronged into her mind. Had they shown her any trust, delivering her sound asleep and half dead to this gilded, yet implacable prison? Had they the right to exact blind submission from her when they did not even deign to ask her for it? Besides, didn't they mean to tempt her and lure her on with these sham festivities? Who knows? Everything that the Invisibles did was bizarre. Perhaps, in trying to find a way out of the compound, she might just happen upon an open gate, a gondola on the stream flowing from the grounds into her garden through an arch in the wall. She paused on this last supposition, the most gratuitous of all, and went down to the garden determined to try her luck. Yet she had not taken fifty steps when she heard overhead something that sounded rather like a huge bird taking flight at a fantastic rate of speed. At the same moment she found herself in a great wash of bluish-white light that lasted only a few seconds, then flared back up almost immediately with a loud bang. At that point, Consuelo understood that it was neither lightning nor a meteor, but the start of fireworks at the castle. Her hosts' entertainment promised to give her a lovely show up on the terrace and, like a child trying to shake off the boredom of a long penance, she raced back to the lodge.

Yet in the glare that these long streaks of artificial lightning, sometimes red, sometimes blue, cast over the garden, twice she saw a tall man in black standing motionless at her side. She had not had the time to get a good look at him before the glowing ball fell back to earth in a rain of fire and fizzled out, leaving everything in even greater darkness for eyes that had been momentarily dazzled. At that point, Consuelo was frightened and dashed away from where she had seen the specter. Yet at the second sinister flash she found herself two steps away from him. By the third flash she had reached the steps of the lodge; he was in front of her, blocking her way. Seized with insuperable terror, she uttered a piercing cry, lost her balance, and would have fallen backward down the stairs if the mysterious visitor had not grabbed her in his arms. No sooner had he brushed his lips over her brow than she felt and recognized the chevalier, the *stranger*, the man she loved, the man she knew loved her.

Chapter XXV

Finding him once more, like an angel of consolation, in that intolerable solitude filled her with a joy that silenced all the scruples and fears still in her mind only a second before, when she had been musing about him without any immediate hope of seeing him again. She responded to his embrace with passion; and as he was already trying to break loose from her arms to pick up his black mask which had fallen off, she clung to him, crying, "Don't leave me, don't abandon me!" Her voice was supplicating, her caresses irresistible. The stranger sank down to her feet and hid his face in the folds of her dress, covering it with kisses. There he remained a few seconds as though torn between delight and despair. Then he grabbed his mask, slipped a letter into Consuelo's hand, and dashed into the lodge, disappearing before she could catch a glimpse of his face.

She followed him, and by the light of a little alabaster lamp that Matteus lit every evening at the foot of the steps, she hoped to find him again, but before she had gone up a few stairs, he seemed to have vanished into thin air. In vain she searched every nook and cranny in the lodge; there was not a trace of him to be found; were it not for the letter in her trembling hand, she could have thought that she had been dreaming.

At last she decided to go back to her boudoir to read the letter. This time the handwriting struck her as deliberately disguised rather than deformed by pain. The letter said more or less this:

"I can neither see you nor talk to you; but I've not been forbidden to write to you. Will you allow me this? Will you dare reply to the *stranger*? Were I to be so fortunate, I could, while you were sleeping, go fetch your letters and place my own in a book that you would leave in the evening on the garden bench at the water's edge. My love for you is passionate, idolatrous, mad. I am vanquished, my strength is broken; my activity, my zeal, my enthusiasm for the work to which I've devoted my life, everything, even the sense of duty, is annihilated in me if you don't love me. Bound to strange and terrible duties by my vows, by the surrender and renunciation of my will, I am floating between thoughts of infamy and suicide, for I can't convince myself that you truly love me and that distrust and fear haven't already blotted out your involuntary love for me. Could it be otherwise? For you I'm nothing but a shadow, a night's dream, a fleeting illusion. Well, in order to make you love me, I feel ready, twenty times a day, to sacrifice my honor, to betray my word, to defile my conscience by breaking a vow. If you managed to escape from this prison, I'd follow you to the ends of the earth, even if that meant having to expiate by a life of shame and remorse the intoxication of seeing you, if only for a day, and hearing you say once again, 'I love you.' And yet, if you refuse to join in the work of the Invisibles, if you find frightening and repugnant the vows that no doubt will soon be required of you, I'll be forbidden ever to see you again! . . . But I won't obey, I won't be able to. No! I've suffered enough, toiled enough and served enough the cause of humanity; if you are not the reward for my labors, I'll quit and lose myself by going back to the world, to its laws and customs. I'm not in my right mind, as you can see. Pity, oh, pity me! Don't say you don't love me anymore. I couldn't take it, I wouldn't want to believe it, or were I to believe it, I'd have to die."

Consuelo read this note amid the din of the fireworks, rockets, and bombs bursting overhead, without hearing them. Totally absorbed in her reading, she nonetheless felt, albeit unwittingly, the electric commotion generated, especially in impressionable organisms, by exploding gunpowder and violent noise as a whole. It particularly affects the imagination when it does not physically act upon a weak, sickly body by causing painful shudders. On the contrary, it excites the mind and senses of brave, well-constituted people. In some women it even arouses fearless instincts, ideas of combat and something like vague regrets not to be a man. In short, if a certain pronounced accent makes us find almost musical pleasure in the voice of a rushing torrent, the roar of a breaking wave, the rumble of thunder, this accent of rage, threat, pride, this mighty voice, so to speak, is found in the booming cannon, the whistling volleys, and the air being rent asunder by which fireworks mimic the clash of battle. Perhaps Consuelo felt that effect while reading the first real love letter, the first *billet-doux* she had ever received. She felt courageous, brave, and almost reckless. A kind of drunken elation made her find this declaration of love warmer and more persuasive than all of Albert's words, just as she had found the stranger's kiss sweeter and more impassioned than all of Anzoleto's. So she began writing without hesitation, and while detonations were rattling the grounds, with the odor of saltpeter overwhelming the perfume of the flowers and Bengal lights flashing over the facade of the lodge, Consuelo took no notice and replied,

"Yes, I love you, I've said it, I've confessed it to you, and even if I had to repent and blush for it a thousand times over, I can never erase from the strange, incomprehensible book of my destiny the page that I myself have written there and which is in your hands! It was the expression of a reprehensible impulse, perhaps mad, but profoundly true and ardently felt. Were you the vilest of men, I would still have placed in you my ideal! Even if you were to demean me by contemptuous and cruel behavior, I would still have felt at the touch of your heart an intoxication that I had never known, that seemed to me as holy as the angels are pure. You see, I'm repeating back to you what you wrote to me about the things I confided in *Beppo*. All we're doing is repeating back and forth to each other something we both earnestly feel, I think, and truly believe. Why and how could we be wrong? We don't know each other; perhaps we never will. Strange fate! Yet we love each other, and we can no more explain the primary causes of this love than we can foresee its mysterious ends. Well, I am abandoning myself to your word, to your honor; I'm not fighting the feelings you inspire in me. Don't let me fool myself. There's only one thing in the world I ask of you: Don't pretend to love me, don't ever see me again if you don't love me; leave me to my lot, whatever that may be, without fear that I'll accuse you or curse you for the fleeting illusion of happiness you've given me. It seems to me that what I'm asking here is so easy! There are moments, I confess, when I am frightened by the blind confidence thrusting me toward you. But from the moment that you appear, that my hand is in yours or that I see something you've written (even if your handwriting is misshapen and tortured, as though you did not want me to know the slightest external and visible sign of you); finally, I just hear your step, and all my fears vanish, and I can't help believing that you are my best friend on earth. But why do you conceal yourself as you do? What terrifying secret lies behind your mask and your silence? Have I seen you somewhere else? Must I be afraid of you? Will I have to drive you away the day I learn your name, see your face? If you are utterly unknown to me as you have said in a letter, why do you so blindly obey the strange law of the Invisibles, all the while writing to me today that you are ready to break free of them in order to follow me to the ends of the earth? And if I were to make it a condition of running away with you that you wouldn't keep any more secrets from me, would you take off your mask? Would you speak to me? In order to get to know you, I must, you say, commit myself . . . to what? that I bind myself by vows to the Invisibles? . . . But for what purpose? What? With my eyes closed, my conscience silent, and my mind in the dark, I must *surrender* and *renounce* my will, as you yourself did, knowing at least what you were doing and why? And to induce me to carry out these extraordinary acts of blind devotion, you won't commit the slightest infraction of the rules of your order! For it is clear to me that you belong to one of those mysterious orders called *secret societies* here and said to be legion in Germany.

Unless it's quite simply a political conspiracy against . . . as I was told in Berlin. Well, whatever the case may be, if they leave me free to refuse once I know what is required of me, I'll bind myself by the most terrible vows never to reveal a thing. Can I do anything more without being unworthy of the love of a man who is so scrupulous, so faithful to his vows that he does not want to let me hear the words that I myself uttered, flying in the face of the prudence and modesty imposed upon my sex: *I love you*!"

Consuelo put the letter in a book that she deposited in the garden at the appointed spot. Then she slowly walked away and hid for a long while in the foliage, hoping to catch a glimpse of the chevalier and trembling to have left there the confession of her innermost feelings, which could fall into the wrong hands. Yet, seeing the hours go by without anyone appearing and remembering these words from the stranger's letter, "I'll fetch your reply while you're sleeping," she decided that she ought to comply with his instructions in every respect and withdrew into her apartment. There, after a thousand restless musings, painful and delectable by turns, she finally fell asleep to the faint reverberation of the dance music starting up again, the fanfares sounding over supper and the faraway rumble of carriages announcing at dawn the departure of the many guests from the manor.

At precisely nine o'clock the recluse entered the room where she took her meals, always served with painstaking punctuality and an elegance worthy of the premises. Matteus, in keeping with the respectfully phlegmatic mien that was his custom, stood behind her chair. Consuelo had just gone down to the garden. The chevalier had come for her letter, for it was no longer in the book. Yet Consuelo had been hoping to find a new letter from him, and she was already accusing him of going lukewarm on their correspondence. She felt anxious, excited, and a bit exasperated by the immobility of the life that they seemed bent on forcing upon her. So she decided to stir things up a bit to see if she could speed up the course of the events slowly being prepared around her. It so happened that this very day, for the first time, Matteus was gloomy and tight-lipped.

"Master Matteus," she said with forced gaiety, "I can see through your mask that you've got circles under your eyes and a tired complexion; you hardly slept a wink last night."

"Madame does me too much honor to wish to taunt me," replied Matteus a bit sourly. "Yet since Madame has the pleasure of living without a mask, it is easier for me to see that she is ascribing to me the fatigue and insomnia she herself suffered last night."

"Your talking mirrors have already informed me of that, Monsieur Matteus. I know it's made me awfully ugly, and things are bound to get even worse if boredom keeps eating away at me."

"Madame is bored?" replied Matteus in the same tone he would have used to ask, "Madame rang?"

"Yes, Matteus, tremendously bored, and I'm starting to find it intolerable being shut away like this. As I've received neither a letter nor a visit, I presume they've forgotten about me here; and since you're the only one kind enough not to do the same, I think I'm entitled to tell you that I'm beginning to find my situation perplexing and bizarre."

"I cannot permit myself to judge Madame's situation," Matteus replied. "Yet it seemed to me that not long ago Madame received a visit and a letter?"

"Who told you such a thing, Master Matteus?" exclaimed Consuelo, blushing.

"That I would say," he replied in an ironically unctuous tone, "were I not afraid of offending Madame and boring her with my chatter."

"Were you my servant, Master Matteus, I don't know what grand airs I could put on with you, but as I've scarcely had any servant aside from myself up till now, and as you moreover seem to be my jailer here more so than my butler, I beg you to chat, if you are so inclined, as much as you have on other days. You're too witty this morning to bore me."

"That's because Madame is too bored to be prickly just now. So I'll tell Madame that there was a grand gala last night at the castle."

"I know. I heard the fireworks and the music."

"Well then, a person who has been kept under close watch here since Madame's arrival thought he could take advantage of the bustle and noise to slip into the restricted area of the grounds, defying the strictest prohibitions against trespassing. That led to an unfortunate event. . . . But I fear distressing Madame by telling her about it."

"I think now that distress is preferable to boredom and anxiety. Be quick about it, Monsieur Matteus."

"Well, Madame, this morning I saw being led off to prison the most amiable and youthful, the most handsome, courageous, generous, and witty, the greatest of all my masters, Chevalier Liverani."

"Liverani? Who is Liverani?" exclaimed Consuelo, gripped with emotion. "He's in prison, the chevalier? Tell me! Oh, my God, who is this chevalier, who is this Liverani?"

"I've told Madame quite enough about him. I don't know if she knows him a little or a lot, but this much is certain, he's been taken to the great tower for speaking and writing to Madame as well as refusing to divulge to His Highness Madame's reply to him."

"The great tower. . . . His Highness. . . . Do you mean everything you're saying, Matteus? Am I here under the domination of a sovereign prince who is holding me as a prisoner of state, who punishes his subjects for showing me the slightest interest or pity? Or am I being tricked by some rich lord with bizarre ideas, who is trying to give me a scare to test my gratitude for services rendered?"

"It's not forbidden for me to tell Madame that her host is a very wealthy prince, a man of intelligence, and a great philosopher. . . ."

"As well as the supreme head of the Council of the Invisibles?"

"I don't know what Madame means by that," replied Matteus with utter indifference. "In the list of His Highness's titles and offices I've never seen any such mention."

"But won't I be allowed to see this prince, to throw myself at his feet, to request that he release this Chevalier Liverani, who is, I can swear to it, innocent of any indiscretion?"

"I have no idea, and I think it will at least be very difficult. Yet every evening, for a few seconds, I see His Highness to give an account of Madame's health and activities. If Madame were to write a note, perhaps I could manage to have it read without it going through the secretaries."

"Dear Monsieur Matteus, you are the soul of kindness, and I'm sure that you must enjoy the prince's trust. Yes, of course, I'll write, since you're generous enough to take an interest in the chevalier."

"It is true that I take a greater interest in him than in anyone else. He risked his own life to rescue me from a fire. He took care of me, healed my burns, and replaced the possessions I lost. He spent nights watching over me, as if he were my servant and I his master. He wrested one of my nieces from a life of vice and, with his good words and generous help, made an honest woman out of her. What good things he has done in this entire land and all over Europe, from what I hear! He is the finest young man in the world, and His Highness loves him like a father."

"Yet His Highness puts him in prison for a slight misdeed?"

"Oh! Madame does not know that no misdeed is slight in the eyes of His Highness when it's a matter of indiscretion."

"So the prince is quite absolute?"

"Admirably just, but terribly severe."

"But how can I play a part in the prince's concerns and his council's decisions?"

"That I do not know, as Madame can well imagine. There is always a flurry of secrets in this castle, especially when the prince comes to stay for a few weeks, which doesn't happen often. A poor servant such as myself who would permit himself to delve into such matters would not be tolerated long here; and as I'm the oldest member of the staff, Madame must understand that I am neither curious nor talkative, otherwise. . . ."

"I understand, Monsieur Matteus. But would it be indiscreet of me to ask if the chevalier is being subjected to a harsh regime in prison?"

"That must be the case, Madame. Although I know nothing about what goes on in the tower or the dungeons, I've seen more people go in than come out. I don't know if there are exits into the forest. As far as I know, there isn't one into the grounds."

"You're making me shudder, Matteus. Could it be that I've brought serious trouble down on the head of this worthy young man? Tell me, does the prince have a cold or violent disposition? Are his decrees dictated by fits of pique or long, reasoned displeasure?"

"It is not seemly for me to enter into such details," was Matteus's chilly reply.

"Well then, tell me about the chevalier, at least. Is he the sort of man that asks for mercy and gets it, or the sort that withdraws into a haughty silence?"

"He is tender and mild, full of respect and submission for His Highness. But if Madame has confided some secret in him, she has nothing to fear. He would undergo torture rather than betray another's secret, even to the ear of a confessor."

"Well then, I myself shall reveal to His Highness this secret that he deems important enough to kindle his anger against a hapless creature. Oh, my good Matteus, can't you take my letter right away?"

"That's impossible before night, Madame."

"All the same, I'm going to write it now. An unexpected occasion may arise."

Consuelo went into her study and wrote to ask the nameless prince for an interview in which she pledged to answer frankly all the questions he might deign to ask her.

At midnight Matteus brought her back this sealed reply:

"If it is to the prince that you wish to speak, your request is insane. Never will you see him, meet him, or learn his name.—If you wish to appear before the Council of the Invisibles, you will be heard, but carefully consider the consequences of your resolution; it will determine the course of your life as well as that of another."

Chapter XXVI

It was necessary to wait another twenty-four hours after receiving that letter. Matteus declared that he would rather cut off one of his hands than ask to see the prince after midnight. At breakfast the next morning he appeared even a bit more expansive than the day before, and it seemed to Consuelo that the chevalier's imprisonment had soured him on the prince to such a point that for the first time in his life he had quite an itch to be indiscreet. Yet, after having let him prattle on for over an hour, she saw that she was no further along than before. Whether he had feigned simplicity in order to study Consuelo's thoughts and feelings, or whether he knew nothing about the Invisibles and his master's role in their activities, Consuelo was left floating in a strange muddle of contradictory notions. With regard to the prince's position in society, Matteus had entrenched himself behind the impossibility of breaking the strict silence imposed upon him. He shrugged his shoulders, it is true, at the mention of that bizarre injunction. He confessed not to understand why it was necessary to wear a mask in order to communicate with the individuals who arrived one after the other at various intervals and for retreats of various length in the lodge. He *could not help saying* that his master had inexplicable whims and devoted himself to incomprehensible labors, but all curiosity as well as all indiscretion were paralyzed in him by the fear of terrible punishment, the nature of which he did not explain. In short, Consuelo learned nothing, except that there were strange goings-on at the castle, that people there hardly slept at night, that all the servants had seen ghosts, that Matteus himself, who maintained that he was fearless and free-thinking, had often encountered on the grounds in winter, when the prince was away and the castle deserted, shapes that made him shudder, that had got in there he knew not how and left the same way. All this did not shed much light on Consuelo's situation. She had to resign herself to waiting till evening to send this new petition: "Whatever may be the consequences for me, I earnestly and humbly ask to appear before the Tribunal of the Invisibles."

The day seemed mortally long to her. She did her best to overcome her impatience and anxiety by singing everything that she had composed in prison about the pain and tedium of solitude. As night was falling, she ended with Almirena's sublime aria in Handel's *Rinaldo*:

Lascia ch'io piango
La dura sorte,
E ch'io sospiri
La libertà.

She had scarcely finished when a violin of extraordinary resonance repeated from outside the admirable phrase she had just sung, its expression just as sorrowful and deep as her own. Consuelo ran to the window, but saw no one, and the phrase died away in the distance. The instrument as well as the way it was played were remarkable, and it seemed to her that they could only belong to Count Albert; but she soon chased away that thought, considering it another one of those painful, dangerous illusions from which she had already suffered so much. She had never heard Albert play a single phrase of modern music, and only a crackpot would persist in evoking a ghost every time a violin was heard. Yet this feeling troubled Consuelo and threw her into such deep, dismal reveries that it was nine in the evening before she noticed that Matteus had brought her no lunch or supper and that she had had nothing to eat since morning. This made her fear that Matteus, like the chevalier, had become a victim of the interest he had shown her. No doubt the walls had eyes and ears. Perhaps Matteus had said too much; he had grumbled a bit about Liverani's disappearance; that was probably enough for them to make him share the same fate.

These new anxieties prevented Consuelo from feeling how hungry she was. Yet it was getting later and later, and still there was no sign of Matteus; she ventured to ring for him. Nobody came. She was feeling very weak and, above all, very bewildered. Leaning on the window sill, her head in her hands, she was reviewing in her mind, already a bit addled by pangs of hunger, the strange events of her life, and wondering if she was remembering something real or a long dream. Just then a hand cold as marble bore down on her head, and a low, deep voice uttered these words, "Your request has been granted, follow me."

Being able to discern things clearly in the twilight up to that moment, Consuelo had not yet thought to light any candles, and she tried to get a look at the person who had spoken these words to her. All of a sudden she was in thick darkness as if the air had become solid and the starry sky a leaden vault. She lifted a hand to her smothered brow and recognized a hood as light and impenetrable as the one that Cagliostro had once thrown over her head without her feeling it. An invisible hand swept her down the stairs of the lodge, but she soon realized that there were more steps than in the lodge, and they led down into subterranean passages where she marched for nearly half an hour. Fatigue, hunger, inner commotion, and oppressive heat made her go slower and slower. Ready to faint at every moment, she was tempted to beg for mercy. Yet a certain pride made her cringe at the idea of apparently going back on her resolve, so she bravely struggled on. At last she reached the end of her journey and was given a chair. At that moment she heard a lugubrious tone, like that of a gong, slowly tolling the midnight hour, and at the twelfth stroke the hood was lifted from her brow bathed in sweat.

Initially, she was dazzled by the brilliant lights. Clustered opposite her, they formed a thick cross blazing on the wall. When her eyes had adjusted, she saw that she was in a great hall in Gothic style whose vaulted ceiling, divided into flattened arches, resembled that of a deep dungeon or underground chapel. At the far end of the chamber, truly sinister in its aspect and lighting, she made out seven figures in red cloaks with ghastly white masks that made them look like corpses. They were seated behind a long black marble table. In front of the table, down a level, there also sat an eighth specter dressed in black with a white mask. Against the walls on both sides there stood in total silence some twenty-odd men in black cloaks and masks. Consuelo turned around and saw more black ghosts behind her. Two more were standing at each door, with broad, gleaming swords in their hands.

In other circumstances, Consuelo might have told herself that this lugubrious ceremonial was only a game, one of those Masonic ordeals she had heard about in Berlin. But aside from the fact that Freemasons did not appoint themselves as judges and assume the right to summon non-initiates to appear before their secret assemblies, she was inclined, because of everything leading up to this, to consider it serious, even frightening. She saw that she was visibly trembling, and had the assembly not kept utterly silent for five minutes, she would have lacked the strength to pull herself together and prepare to answer.

Finally, the eighth judge rose and gestured to the two ushers standing with drawn swords on either side of Consuelo to bring her up to the foot of the tribunal, where she remained standing in a somewhat affected posture of calm and courage.

"Who are you, and what do you want?" asked the man in black without getting up.

For a few seconds Consuelo was speechless. She finally took courage and answered, "I am Consuelo, a singer by profession, also known as Zingarella and Porporina."

"Don't you have another name?" asked the questioner.

Consuelo hesitated, then said, "I could lay claim to another one, but I've given my word never to do so."

"So you're hoping to hide something from this tribunal? Do you think you are standing before ordinary judges, elected to adjudicate ordinary concerns, in the name of a crude and blind set of laws? Why have you come here if you intend to delude us with vain pretexts? State your name, make yourself known for what you are, or withdraw."

"You know who I am, you no doubt know as well that my silence is a duty, and you will encourage me to persevere in it."

One of the red cloaks leaned over, gestured to a black cloak and instantly all the black cloaks left the hall except for the examiner, who remained in place and went on in these words.

"Countess von Rudolstadt, now that the investigation is being conducted in secret and that you are alone in the presence of your judges, will you deny that you are lawfully married to Count Albert Podiebrad, known as Rudolstadt according to his family's claims."

"Before I answer that question," said Consuelo firmly, "I want to know what authority disposes of me here, and what law obligates me to recognize it."

"What law would you invoke? Human or divine? By the law of society you are still under the absolute domination of Frederick II, King of Prussia, Elector of Brandenburg, from whose territory we had you removed to free you from indefinite imprisonment and yet more dreadful dangers, as you know."

"I know," said Consuelo with a curtsey, "that I am bound to you by eternal gratitude. I would therefore invoke divine law alone, and I beg you to define for me that rule of gratitude. Does it command that I bless you and devote myself to you wholeheartedly? That I accept. But if it prescribes that I go against my conscience to oblige you, mustn't I object? Judge for yourselves."

"May your thoughts and deeds in the world succeed in matching your words! But the circumstances that put you here under our authority defy all common sense. We are above all human law, as you've been able to see from our power. We are also beyond all human considerations: biases based on fortune, rank, and birth, scruples and niceties of position, fear of opinion, respect even for commitments to ideas and individuals in society. None of that has any meaning for us or value in our eyes while we, gathered far from the eyes of men and armed with the sword of divine justice, weigh in the palm of our hands the trifles of your frivolous, fearful lives. Give us, we who are the support, the family, and the living law of every free being, a straightforward account of yourself. There will be no hearing until we know in what capacity you are coming before us. Who is appealing to us, Consuelo the Zingarella or Countess von Rudolstadt?"

"Countess von Rudolstadt, having given up all her rights in society, has none to claim here. Consuelo the Zingarella. . . ."

"Stop and weigh the words you've just said. If your husband were alive, would you have the right to rescind your vows, to renounce his name, to repudiate his fortune, in short, to become once again Consuelo the Zingarella to spare the childish, insane pride of his family and his caste?"

"Certainly not."

"So you think that death has severed your bonds forever? Do you not owe Albert's memory respect, love, and fidelity?"

Consuelo got red and flustered, then paled again. The idea that they, like Cagliostro and the Count de Saint-Germain, were going to speak to her about Albert's possible resurrection and even show her his ghost filled her with such fear that she could not say a word.

"Wife of Albert Podiebrad," the examiner continued, "your silence indicts you. Albert is entirely dead for you, and in your eyes your marriage is nothing more than an incident in your life of adventure, without any consequences, without any obligations for the future. Zingara, you can go now. It was only because of your ties to the most excellent of men that we took an interest in your fate. You were not worthy of our love because you were not worthy of his. We don't regret having liberated you; every reparation of the evils of despotism is for us a duty and a pleasure. But our protection will go no further. Tomorrow you shall leave this refuge which we had given you in the hope that you would depart from it being made pure and holy; you shall go back to the world: the chimera of glory, the intoxication of mad passions. May God have pity on you! We are forsaking you forever."

This verdict left Consuelo momentarily stunned. A few days before she would not have accepted it without lodging an appeal, but the words *mad passions* that had just been uttered brought back before her eyes, then and there, the insane love that she had conceived for the *stranger*, whom she had welcomed into her heart almost without reflection or struggle.

She was humiliated in her own eyes and found herself deserving of the Invisibles' verdict up to a certain point. Their austere language inspired respect and terror in her, and she no longer thought of rebelling against the right that they assumed to judge and condemn her as a person under their jurisdiction. Whatever our natural pride or the irreproachability of our lives, we seldom manage to block the force of a solemn accusation that catches us off guard; instead of questioning it, we search our souls to see if above all else we do not deserve the blame. Consuelo did not consider herself entirely above reproach, and the formalities of the setting made her position singularly painful. Yet she promptly remembered that she had not asked to appear before this tribunal without having prepared for their severity and resigned herself to it. She had come resolved to accept reproof, punishment if necessary, provided that the chevalier be exonerated or pardoned. So putting aside all pride, she took their rebuke without bitterness and briefly meditated the terms of her reply.

"It may be that I deserve that strong curse," she said at last. "I am far from being satisfied with myself. Yet I came here imbued with a certain idea of the Invisibles that I want to share with you. The little that I've heard rumored about you as well as the liberty you've given me have led me to think that you are men as perfect in virtue as you are powerful in society. If you are such as I wish to believe, why are you rejecting me so abruptly, without showing me how to correct the error of my ways and become worthy of your protection? I know that it was on account of Albert von Rudolstadt, the most excellent of men, as you have rightly called him, that his widow deserved some measure of interest, but were I not Albert's wife, or had I always been unworthy of him, Consuelo the Zingara, the girl without a name, without a family, without a country, wouldn't I still be entitled to your paternal care? Supposing I'm a great sinner, are you not like the kingdom of heaven where one reprobate's repentance brings more joy than the perseverance of a hundred righteous souls? Finally, if the law that draws you together and inspires you is divine, you are wrong to drive me away. You had undertaken, you say, to make me pure and holy. Strive to lift my soul up to the level of yours. I am ignorant, not rebellious. Prove to me that you are saints by showing me patience and mercy, and I'll accept you as my masters and models."

There was a moment of silence. The examiner turned toward the judges, and they seemed to be deliberating. At last one of them spoke up and said, "Consuelo, you approached us with pride; why do you not wish to leave the same way? We were entitled to rebuke you since you came here to question us. We have no right to put your conscience in chains and take hold of your life if you don't freely and voluntarily surrender them to us. Can we ask this sacrifice of you? You don't know us. This tribunal whose saintliness you invoke may be the most perverse or at the least the most daring ever to have labored in the shadows against the principles that rule the world. What do you know about this? And if we were to reveal to you the deep science of an utterly new morality, would you have the courage to devote yourself to very long and arduous study before knowing its goal? Could we ourselves have confidence in the persevering faith of a neophyte as poorly prepared as you? We might have important secrets to entrust to you, and we would seek no guarantee outside of your generous instincts. We know them well enough to believe in your discretion, but it is not discreet confidants that we need. We have enough of those. We need, to further the law of God, fervent disciples, free of all prejudice and egotism, of all frivolous passions and worldly habits. Look deep into yourself. Can you make all these sacrifices for us? Can you model your actions and conform your life to the instincts that you feel as well as to the principles that we would instill in you to develop them? Woman, artist, child, would you dare reply that you can join with solemn men to help carry out the work of the centuries?"

"Indeed, everything you say is very weighty," Consuelo replied, "and I scarcely understand it. Will you give me time to think? Don't chase me from your midst without having examined my heart. I don't know if it is worthy of the enlightenment you can diffuse there. But what sincere soul is unworthy of the truth? How can I be of service to you? I cringe at my powerlessness. Woman and artist, which means child! Yet, to protect me as you have, you must have sensed something in me. . . . And something tells me that I must not leave you without having tried to prove to you my gratitude. So don't banish me; try teaching me."

"We'll give you another week to think about it," said the red-gowned judge who had already spoken. "But first you must give your word of honor not to make the slightest effort to learn where you are and who the people are that you see here. You must also pledge not to leave the enclosure reserved for your walks, even if you were to see the gates standing open and the ghosts of your dearest friends beckoning to you. You must not ask a single question of your servants nor of any person who might secretly gain entrance to your quarters."

"That will never happen," Consuelo briskly replied. "I give my word, if you wish, never to receive any visit without your authorization, and in return I humbly request the favor. . . ."

"There will be no favors requested, no conditions proposed. All your needs, soul and body, have been foreseen for the duration of your stay here. If you are missing any relative, friend, or servant, you are free to go. Solitude or the companionship we see fit to give you will be your lot here with us."

"I ask nothing for myself, but I've been told that one of your friends, disciples, or servants (for I do not know his rank among you) was being severely punished because of me. I stand ready to take upon myself the wrongs being imputed to him, and that is why I asked to appear before you."

"Are you offering us a sincere and detailed confession?"

"If that is necessary for his absolution . . . even though, for a woman, it is strange moral torture to confess aloud before eight men."

"Spare yourself that humiliation. We would not have any guarantee of your sincerity, and besides even a short while ago we still had no rights over you. What you said, what you thought an hour ago is, for us, part of your past. But bear in mind that we are henceforth entitled to probe the most secret recesses of your soul. It is your responsibility to keep that soul sufficiently pure so that you may always be ready to unveil it without suffering or shame."

"Your generosity is delicate and fatherly. But this doesn't involve me alone. Someone else is atoning for my wrongs. Mustn't I justify him?"

"That is not your concern. If there is a guilty party among us, he will exonerate himself, not by vain pretexts and reckless allegations, but by acts of courage, devotion, and virtue. If his soul has faltered, we will raise it up again and help him become master of himself. You speak of severe punishment; the only kind of punishment we inflict is moral. That man, whoever he is, is our peer, our brother; there are no masters, servants, subjects, nor princes among us. You've no doubt been deceived by false reports. Go in peace and refrain from sin."

At this last word the examiner rang a little bell. The two masked men clad in black and bearing swords returned, replaced the hood over Consuelo's head, and took her back to the lodge by the same circuitous underground route by which she had come.

Chapter XXVII

According to the kindly, paternal language of the Invisibles, Porporina no longer had reason to be seriously concerned about the chevalier. Considering as well that Matteus had not been very clear-sighted in this matter, she felt greatly relieved leaving the mysterious conclave. Everything that had just been said to her was floating in her imagination like rays of light behind a cloud. No longer sustained by anxiety or the exercise of will, she was soon overcome with fatigue on the way back. Suffering cruel pangs of hunger and smothering under the gummy hood, she stopped several times; to keep on going she had to take the arms of her guides; reaching her room, she fell down in a faint. A few seconds later she felt herself being revived by a phial that was presented to her and the good air circulating through the apartment. Then she noticed that the men who had brought her back were hurriedly leaving while Matteus was busy putting a most appetizing supper on the table and the little masked doctor who had drugged her into a state of lethargy to bring her to this estate was taking her pulse and lavishing her with care. She easily recognized him because of his wig, also because of his voice that she had heard somewhere before, though in what circumstances she could not say.

"Dear Doctor," she said with a smile, "I think the best prescription will be to give me supper right away. The only thing wrong with me is hunger, but this time I beg you to spare me the coffee you make so well. I think I wouldn't be strong enough to take it."

"My coffee," replied the doctor, "is an excellent sedative. But have no worry, Countess, my prescription is for nothing of the sort. Will you entrust yourself to me today and let me sup with you? It is His Highness's wish that I not leave your side until you are altogether well again, and I think that within half an hour the refection will have entirely driven away this weakness."

"If such is His Highness's pleasure as well as your own, Doctor, it will be mine as well," said Consuelo, letting Matteus roll her chair up to the table.

"I won't be useless to you," the doctor went on, starting to demolish a superb pheasant pasty and slicing into the birds with the dexterity of a consummate practitioner. "Without me here you might yield to the insuperable voraciousness that comes after a long fast and suffer the consequences. Having no such fears for myself, I'll take care to count your morsels while putting the double on my plate."

Despite herself, Consuelo was preoccupied by the voice of this gastronomic physician. But great was her surprise when he deftly unfastened his mask and put it down on the table saying, "To hell with this childish nonsense that prevents me from breathing and tasting what I eat!"

Consuelo was startled to recognize in this rake of a doctor the one she had seen at her husband's deathbed, Supperville, first physician to the Margravine von Bayreuth. Since then she had caught sight of him from afar in Berlin without having had the courage to look him in the eye or speak to him. Just now the contrast between his gluttonous appetite and her drained emotional state reminded her of his matter-of-fact thoughts and remarks amid the dismay and grief of the Rudolstadt family, and she had a hard time hiding the unpleasant impression he caused her. But Supperville, engrossed by the pheasant's aroma, seemed utterly unaware that she was ill at ease.

With an ingenuous exclamation, Matteus put the finishing touch on the ridiculous situation that the doctor had created for himself. The wary servant had been serving the doctor for five minutes without seeing that his face was bare, and only after Matteus had mistaken the mask as the pasty's cover and methodically placed it over the open gash in its side did he shriek with terror, "Mercy, Doctor, you've dropped your *face* on the table!"

"To hell with it, I say! I'll never get used to eating with the thing. Put it aside, and give it back to me when I leave."

"As you wish, Doctor," said Matteus in a dismayed tone of voice. "I wash my hands of it. But Your Lordship knows that every evening I have to give a detailed account of everything that has been said and done here. I'll say in vain that your *face* came off inadvertently; I won't be able to deny that Madame has seen what is underneath."

"Fine, my good man. You make your report," said the doctor unperturbed.

"And you'll observe, Monsieur Matteus," noted Consuelo, "that I in no way incited this disobedience on the doctor's part nor is it my fault if I recognized him."

"You need not worry, Countess," Supperville went on with his mouth full. "The prince is not as bad as he is made out to be, and I'm hardly afraid of him. I'll tell him that having allowed me to sup with you, by the same token he gave me leave to rid myself of any impediment to mastication and deglutition. Besides, I was too well known to you not to have been already betrayed by the sound of my voice. So it's an idle formality I'm casting aside, and the prince will be the first to make light of it."

"All the same, Doctor," said Matteus scandalized, "I'm glad it was you and not I to have made that joke."

The doctor shrugged his shoulders, scoffed at fainthearted Matteus, ate an enormous amount, and drank commensurately, after which, Matteus having left to bring in another course, he pulled up his chair, lowered his voice, and said to Consuelo, "Dear Signora, I am not the glutton I appear to be (Supperville, having satisfactorily gorged himself, felt very comfortable saying this), and my object in coming to sup with you was to apprise you of important matters of very particular interest to you."

"On whose behalf and in what name do you wish to reveal these matters to me, Monsieur?" asked Consuelo, remembering the promise she had just made to the Invisibles.

"I do so in my own right and of my own free will," replied Supperville. "So have no worry. I'm not an informer, I'm being frank with you and don't much care if my words are repeated."

For a second Consuelo thought it her duty to shut the doctor absolutely up so as not to become an accessory to his treason, but she also thought to herself that a man so devoted to the Invisibles that he would undertake to half-poison people to bring them, without their knowledge, to this castle could not be acting as he was without having been secretly authorized to do so. "This is a trap they're setting for me," she said to herself, "the first in a series of tests. Well then, let's observe the attack."

"So I must tell you, Madame," said the doctor, "where you are and in whose house."

"There we are," Consuelo said to herself, then hastened to reply, "Thank you very much, Doctor, I didn't ask for that information, and I don't wish to know."

"Tut, tut, tut!" Supperville retorted. "You've fallen straight into the romantic vein into which the prince likes to drag all his friends. But don't take this nonsense seriously. At the least you'd go mad and swell his retinue of madmen and visionaries. For my part, I don't intend to break my promise to him not to tell you either his name or the name of this place. Besides, that's the last thing you should be thinking about, for it would only satisfy your curiosity, and that's not the malady I mean to treat in you, which is, on the contrary, excessive confidence. So you can learn, without disobeying him and risking his displeasure (I am interested in not betraying you), that your host is the best and most absurd of old men. A man of intellect, a philosopher, a soul courageous and tender to the point of heroism, of insanity. A dreamer who treats the ideal as though it were something real, life as though it were a novel. A scholar who, by poring over the writings of wise men and seeking the quintessence of ideas, has come, like Don Quixote after reading all his books about chivalry, to take inns for castles, convicts for innocent victims, and windmills for monsters. In short, a saint, if one considers only the beauty of his intentions, a madman if one weighs the results. He has imagined, among other things, a network of permanent and universal conspiracy to entrap and paralyze the action of evildoers throughout the world: 1st to combat and thwart the tyranny of those who govern; 2nd to reform the immorality or barbarism of the laws that rule society; 3rd to pour enthusiasm for his propaganda and zeal for his doctrine into the hearts of all men of courage and dedication. Just that and nothing more? And he thinks he'll manage! If only he were assisted by a few sincere, reasonable men, the bit of good he succeeds in doing could bear some fruit! But unfortunately he is surrounded by a gang of schemers and bold impostors who pretend to share his faith and serve his projects, who use his credit to corner good positions in every court in Europe, not without getting their hands on the better part of the money destined to his good works. That's the man and his entourage. It's for you to judge in what hands you find yourself, and whether this generous protection that fortunately snatched you out of the clutches of little Fritz doesn't risk making you fall into something worse, all for wishing to lift you up into clouds. Now you've been warned. Beware of the fine promises and beautiful speeches, the tragic scenes and sleights of hand of men like Cagliostro, Saint-Germain, and associates."

"Are those last two here right now?" asked Consuelo, a bit unsettled. She was also floating between the danger of being tricked by the doctor and the plausibility of his assertions.

"I have no idea," he replied. "Everything that goes on here is mysterious. There are two castles: one plain to the eyes and palpable, where one sees the arrival of fine ladies and gentlemen who suspect nothing at all, where there are festivities and all the trappings of a princely existence, frivolous, and inoffensive. This castle covers and conceals the other one, which is a little subterranean world rather cleverly disguised. It's in the invisible castle that all the pipe dreams of His Highness are lucubrated. Innovators, reformers, inventors, sorcerers, prophets, alchemists, all architects of a new society ever ready, so they say, to swallow up the old one tomorrow or the day after. They are the mysterious guests that are welcomed, put up, and consulted without anybody knowing a thing about it at ground level, or at least without any one of the profane being able to explain the noises coming from down below, aside from there being goblins and pesky ghosts in the foundations. Now, draw your conclusion. The aforesaid charlatans may be a hundred leagues away from here, for they are by nature great travelers, or a hundred feet from us, in good rooms with secret doors and false floors. It is said that this old castle used to be a meeting place for Free-Judges, and that since then, because of certain hereditary traditions, the ancestors of our prince have always amused themselves by hatching dreadful plots which, to my knowledge, have never amounted to anything. It's an old custom around here, and even the finest minds go in for it quite a lot. As for me, I haven't been initiated into the wonders of the invisible castle. Every now and then I spend a few days here when my sovereign, Princess Sophie of Prussia, Margravine of Bayreuth, lets me go for a breath of air outside of her realm. Now, given that I'm tremendously bored at the delightful court of Bayreuth, that at bottom I'm fond of the prince of whom we speak, that I'm not sorry to play a little trick every now and then on the Great Frederick whom I detest, I render the aforesaid prince a few disinterested services, which amuse me first and foremost. As I take orders only from him, these services are always very innocent. I found nothing loathsome about the orders to help get you out of Spandau and bring you here like a poor sleeping dove. I knew that you would be well treated, and I thought that you would have a chance to have some fun. But if, on the contrary, you're being tormented, if the quack counselors of His Highness are trying to get their grips on you and make you an instrument of their social schemes. . . ."

"I fear nothing of the sort," replied Consuelo, more and more amazed by the doctor's explanations. "I'll manage to protect myself from their suggestions if they offend my principles and revolt my conscience."

"Are you so sure, Countess?" asked Supperville. "Beware, and don't pride yourself on anything. Very reasonable and honest people have come out of here half-cracked and all ready for mischief. The schemers exploiting the prince won't stop at anything, and the dear prince is so easy to dazzle that he himself has had a hand in the destruction of a few good souls he thought he was saving. I'm telling you, these schemers are very clever, they've got secret ways to frighten and persuade, to excite the emotions, intoxicate the senses and impress the imagination. First, steady pestering and a multitude of incomprehensible little ploys, followed by formulas, methods, and weird tricks at their disposal. They'll send you ghosts, make you undergo fasts to addle your wits, beleaguer you with lovely or terrifying phantasmagoria. In a word, they'll make you superstitious, perhaps they'll make you go mad, as I had the honor of telling you, and then. . . ."

"And then? What can they expect to get out of me? What am I in the world that they would feel a need to snare me?"

"Indeed! The Countess von Rudolstadt has no idea?"

"None at all, sir."

"Yet you must remember that Cagliostro showed you the late Count Albert, your husband, alive and busy."

"How do you know that, if you are not initiated into the mysteries of the subterranean world you've just mentioned?"

"You said as much to Amalia of Prussia, who is something of a gossip, like all curious people. Are you not aware, moreover, that she is very thick with Count von Rudolstadt's ghost?"

"A certain Trismegistus, from what I've heard!"

"Precisely. I've seen this Trismegistus, and it's true that he bears a surprising resemblance to the count at first glance. It can be made even stronger by coiffing and dressing him as the count used to do, giving him a deathly pale face, and making him study the bearing and manner of the deceased. Now do you understand?"

"Less than ever. What would be the point in making this man pass for Count Albert?"

"How simple and honest you are! Count Albert died, leaving a great fortune which, without any male heirs, is going to pass from the hands of Canoness Wenceslawa into those of little Baroness Amalia, Count Albert's cousin, unless you assert your rights to a dower or to the use and enjoyment of the estate for as long as you shall live. First, they'll try to make you decide to do that. . . ."

"That's true," exclaimed Consuelo. "You're enlightening me as to the meaning of certain words."

"This is nothing so far. This life-time usufruct, very contestable, at least in part, won't satisfy the appetite of the crooks who want you in their clutches. You are childless; you need a husband. Well then, Count Albert is not dead; he had fallen into a state of catalepsy and was buried alive; the devil got him out of there; Cagliostro gave him a potion; Saint-Germain took him away. In short, after a year or two he shows back up, recounts his adventures, throws himself at your feet, consummates his marriage to you, heads off to the Castle of the Giants, has himself recognized by the old canoness and a few elderly servants who don't see too well, brings about an enquiry if there are objections and pays off the witnesses. He even travels to Vienna with his faithful wife to reclaim his rights at the court of the empress. A little bit of scandal doesn't hurt this kind of business. All the fine ladies are interested in a handsome man, the victim of a sinister adventure, of a silly, ignorant doctor as well. Prince von Kaunitz, who doesn't dislike female singers, takes you under his wing; your cause prevails; you make a triumphant return to Riesenburg and show your cousin Amalia the door; you are rich and powerful; you join together with the prince *here* and his charlatans to reform society and change the face of the world. That's all very nice, and it only costs you a bit of self-deception to replace an illustrious husband with a smart, handsome adventurer who is a great fortune-teller to boot. Now do you understand? Think it over. It was my duty as a doctor, as a friend of the Rudolstadt family, and a man of honor to tell you all this. They had counted on me to ascertain, if need be, that Trismegistus was Count Albert. But I who saw him die, not with the eyes of imagination, but with those of science, I who have very clearly observed certain differences between the two, and who know that in Berlin people have long been familiar with this adventurer, I will not lend myself to such a hoax. No thank you! I know that you wouldn't either, but they'll do everything to convince you that Count Albert has grown two inches taller and become fresh and pink in his coffin. I hear Matteus; he's a good old dolt and doesn't suspect a thing. As for me, I'll go now, I've said my piece. I'm leaving the castle in an hour, as I've got nothing more to do here."

After having gone on this way with remarkable volubility, the doctor replaced his mask, made a deep bow to Consuelo and left, letting her finish her supper all alone if she so desired. She was hardly so inclined. Upset and overwhelmed by everything that she had just heard, she withdrew to her bedroom and found a bit of rest only after suffering at length through the most painful perplexity and the most indeterminate anguish of doubt and disquiet.

Chapter XXVIII

The next day Consuelo felt shattered in mind and body. Supperville's cynical revelations following fast upon the Invisibles' fatherly encouragement was like being plunged into icy waters after basking in warmth. For a moment she had soared toward the heavens, then plummeted back to earth. She almost bore a grudge against the doctor for having disabused her, for in her dreams she had already taken to endowing with dazzling majesty this august tribunal that was reaching out to her like an adoptive family, a refuge from the dangers of the world and the errors of youth.

Yet the doctor seemed deserving of gratitude, and Consuelo acknowledged this without being able to entertain any such feeling for him. Wasn't his behavior that of a sincere, courageous, and disinterested man? But Consuelo found him too skeptical, too much of a materialist, too inclined to despise good intentions and jeer at beautiful souls. Despite what he had said about the imprudent and dangerous credulity of the nameless prince, she still had an exalted idea of this noble old man who desired the good with the ardor of youth and enjoyed a child's simple faith in human perfectibility. The words that they had spoken to her in that subterranean hall ran through her head again, and she found them full of serene authority and austere wisdom. Charity and goodness peered out from behind the threats and silences of a sham severity, ready to be cast aside at the slightest appeal from Consuelo's heart. Would shifty, grasping charlatans have talked to her and treated her that way? Their valiant undertaking to reform the world, so ridiculous in the eyes of irreverent Supperville, responded to the eternal desire, the romantic hopes, the enthusiastic faith that Albert had inspired in his wife, that she had rediscovered with kindly sympathy in Gottlieb's sick but generous mind. Wasn't this Supperville odious to want to dissuade her from this, to take away her faith in God and at the same time her trust in the Invisibles?

Consuelo, much more inclined to the poetry of the soul than to the hardboiled assessment of the sad realities of the here and now, wrestled with Supperville's judgments and did her utmost to repudiate them. He who confessed not to have been initiated into the *subterranean world* and appeared ignorant of the very name and existence of the Council of the Invisibles, hadn't he indulged in gratuitous assumptions? It was possible that Trismegistus was a crook, even though Princess Amalia asserted the contrary; plus, his friendship with Count Golowkin, the best and the wisest of the great men that Consuelo had met in Berlin, spoke in his favor. It was also conceivable that Cagliostro and Saint-Germain were frauds as well, even though they too could have been fooled by an extraordinary resemblance. But even if these three adventurers could be tarred with the same brush, it did not necessarily follow that they were members of the Council of the Invisibles, nor that this group of virtuous men would fail to reject their suggestions as soon as Consuelo herself had stated that Trismegistus was not Albert. Wouldn't there still be time after this decisive test to take back her trust if they persisted in wanting to practice such gross deception on her? Until then Consuelo wanted to tempt fate and get to know better these Invisibles to whom she owed her freedom, whose paternal reproaches had touched her heart. She decided on the latter course, and while waiting to see how things turned out, she resolved to treat everything that Supperville had said as a test that he had been authorized to give her, or as a need to vent his spleen against rivals that enjoyed more respect and better treatment at the hands of the prince.

One last hypothesis tormented Consuelo more than all the others. Was it absolutely impossible that Albert was alive? Supperville had not observed the phenomena that over the course of two years had preceded his last illness. He had even refused to believe them, stubbornly holding to the view that the young count's frequent retreats underground were for trysts with Consuelo. She alone, along with Zdenko, knew about his attacks of catalepsy. For reasons of pride, the doctor was unable to admit that he could have been wrong to certify Albert's death. Now that Consuelo was aware of the existence and material strength of the Council of the Invisibles, she ventured to speculate in various and sundry ways about how they might have been able to wrest Albert from the horrors of premature burial and secretly give him refuge among them for unknown purposes. Everything that Supperville had told her about the castle's mysteries and the prince's eccentricities helped confirm this supposition. That an adventurer named Trismegistus bore such a resemblance to Albert might add a fantastic twist to the feat, but without destroying its possibility. This thought took such a hold on poor Consuelo that she fell into deep melancholy. If Albert were alive, she wouldn't hesitate to go to him as soon as she could and devote herself to him for all eternity. Yet more than ever she felt that she was bound to suffer from a devotion in which love had no part. The chevalier arose in her imagination as a cause for bitter regret, in her conscience as a source of future remorse. If she had to give him up, newborn love would take the usual course of thwarted inclination and turn into passion. Consuelo did not ask herself with hypocritical resignation why dear Albert wanted to leave his cozy tomb. She told herself that she was fated to sacrifice herself to him, perhaps even beyond the grave, and she wanted to fulfill that destiny right to the end. Yet she was suffering uncommonly and grieving over the stranger, her most involuntary, her most ardent love.

She was distracted from her meditations by a slight noise and the flick of a little wing on her shoulder. She gasped with surprise and joy seeing a pretty little robin fluttering around her room and approaching her without fear. After a moment of shyness he deigned to eat a fly out of her hand.

"Is it you, my poor friend, my faithful companion?" Consuelo asked with tears of childlike joy. "Could it be that you went searching and found me here? No, that's not possible. You pretty, confident creature, you look like my friend, and you're not him. You belong to some gardener, and you've escaped from the greenhouse where you spent the cold days among flowers that never lose their beauty. Come to me, you consoler of prisoners. Since the instinct of your kind draws you to solitary souls and captives, I want you to have all the affection I felt for your brother."

Consuelo had been earnestly playing with the bird for a quarter of an hour when she heard a faint whistle outside that seemed to give the lovely, intelligent creature a start. He dropped the dainty little morsels that his new friend had been lavishing on him, hesitated a moment, flashed his big black eyes and suddenly decided to fly to the window, having no choice but to answer a second summons of irrecusable authority. Consuelo watched him disappear into the leaves. Yet while trying to see where he had gone, she noticed at the far end of her garden, on the other side of the stream marking its boundary, in a spot where the foliage thinned out a bit, someone easily recognized despite the distance. It was Gottlieb hauling himself along the water's edge in a rather jolly way, singing and trying to skip. Consuelo, momentarily forgetting the Invisibles' prohibition, did her best to attract his attention by waving her handkerchief out the window. But he was engrossed in calling back his robin. His head was angled up toward the trees while he whistled, and he went on without having seen Consuelo.

"Thank God, and the Invisibles too, despite Supperville!" she said to herself. "The poor boy looks happy and healthier; his guardian angel the robin is with him. I think this foretells a happy fate for me as well. Now then, let's not have any more doubts about my protectors. Suspicion shrivels the heart."

After wondering how she could fruitfully spend her time in preparation for the new moral education that had been announced to her, she decided to read, for the first time since her arrival at ***. She went into the library over which she had cast only an absent-minded glance so far and resolved to give serious study to the choice of books at her disposal. They were few in number, but extremely curious and probably very rare, if not unique for the most part. It was a collection of the writings of the most remarkable philosophers of all time and every nation, but abridged and reduced to the essence of their doctrines and translated into the various languages that Consuelo understood. Several, never having been published in translation, were handwritten, especially those of the heretics and famous innovators of the Middle Ages, precious relics from the past of which the important fragments and even a few complete copies had escaped the Inquisition's searches and the Jesuits' last violations in the old heretical castles of Germany during the Thirty Years' War. Consuelo was unable to appreciate the value of these philosophical treasures collected by some fervent bibliophile or brave disciple. The originals would have interested her because of the lettering and vignettes, but she saw only translations, carefully prepared and elegantly calligraphied by some modern scribe. Yet she preferred to hunt around for faithful renderings of John Wyclif, Jan Hus, and other Christian philosophers and reformers who, as precursors, contemporaries, or successors, were associated with these fathers of the new age of religion. Although she had not read them, they were familiar enough to her because of her long conversations with Albert. Leafing through their works, she scarcely read them now, and yet she knew them better and better. Consuelo's soul was essentially religious, without her mind being philosophical. Had she not lived in the critical, clear-eyed world of her times, she would easily have turned to superstition and fanaticism. Yet such as she was, she understood Gottlieb's frenzied speeches better than the writings of Voltaire, even though all the fine ladies of the day were reading him fervently. This girl, intelligent and simple, courageous and tender-hearted, did not have a head for the subtleties of argument. Her heart always enlightened her before her brain. Seizing upon all the revelations of feeling and quickly assimilating them, she could learn philosophy; and she had been remarkably taught for her age, sex, and position by Albert, with his friendly, eloquent, and warm words. By the nature of their constitutions artists learn more from the emotions of a lecture or sermon than from the patient, often cold study of books. Such was Consuelo. She could not read a whole page with concentration, but if a great thought, felicitously rendered and summed up in a colorful way, happened to strike her, her soul would cling to it; she would repeat it over and over again like a musical phrase; the meaning, however deep it might be, would penetrate her being like a ray of divine light. She would live on this idea, applying it to all her feelings, drawing from it real strength, remembering it her whole life long. And it was not for her an empty saying; it was a rule of life, armor for battle. What need had she to analyze and abstract the book where she had found it? The whole book was written in her heart as soon as the inspiration from which it had sprung took hold of her. Her fate did not order her to go any further. She was not aspiring to set up a scholarly philosophical system. She felt the warmth of secret revelations that are granted to poetic souls when their nature is loving. Thus she read for several days without reading a thing. She could not have given an account of anything, but more than one page where she had seen only a line were damp with her tears, and often she ran to the harpsichord to improvise airs whose tenderness and grandeur were the fervent, spontaneous expression of her generous feeling.

A whole week went by in which her solitude was no longer troubled by Matteus's tales. She had promised herself not to ask him the slightest question anymore, and perhaps he had been scolded for his indiscretions, since he was now as taciturn as he had been garrulous during the first days. The robin came back to see Consuelo every morning, but without being accompanied by Gottlieb from afar. It seemed that the little creature (Consuelo was not far from believing that he was bewitched) had a schedule for coming by to cheer her up and returning promptly around noon to his other friend. In point of fact, there was nothing supernatural about this. Animals in liberty have habits and organize their days with even more intelligence and foresight than their domestic counterparts. One day, however, Consuelo noticed that he was not flying as gracefully as usual. He seemed hampered and out of sorts. Instead of coming to peck at her fingers, he was only interested in using his claws and beak to get rid of some pesky bind. Consuelo came closer and saw a black thread hanging from a wing. Had the poor little thing been caught in a snare, and had he escaped only by dint of courage and skill, with a piece of his noose? She had no trouble removing that thread, but it was a bit of a challenge to free him from a strand of silk that went neatly over his back and fastened under his left wing a tiny sachet made of very sheer brown material. In the sachet there was a note written in almost invisible letters on such flimsy paper that she feared her breath might make it disintegrate. From the first words she saw that it was a short message from her dear stranger, as follows.

"They entrusted me with a generous deed, hoping that the pleasure of doing good would calm my restless passion. But nothing, not even the practice of charity, can distract a soul over which you reign. I accomplished my task sooner than they thought possible. Now I'm back, and I love you more than ever. Yet the sky is looking brighter. I don't know what transpired between you and *them*, but they seem more favorable, and my love is no longer treated like a crime, but a misfortune for me alone. A misfortune! Oh, they do not love! They don't know that I cannot be unfortunate if you love me, and you do love me, don't you? Tell that to the robin from Spandau. It is he. I carried him in my bosom. Oh, let him repay me for my care by bringing me a word from you! Gottlieb will faithfully deliver it to me without taking a look."

Mysteries and romantic circumstances fuel love's fire. Consuelo felt the most violent temptation to reply, and her fear of displeasing the Invisibles and scruple about breaking her promises held her back only slightly, it must be confessed. Yet the thought that she could be found out and cause the chevalier to be exiled once again gave her the courage to refrain. She set the robin free without a single word of reply, all the while shedding bitter tears over the pain and disappointment that this harsh treatment would elicit in her lover.

She tried to resume her studies, but neither reading nor singing could distract her from the ferment seething in her breast now that she knew the chevalier to be nearby. She could not help hoping that he would disobey for both of them, that come evening she would see him slip into the flowering shrubs of her garden. Yet she did not want to encourage him by showing herself. She spent the evening shut away, peeping through her venetian blind, her heart pounding, brimming with fear and desire, yet resolved not to reply to his call. Not seeing him appear, she felt hurt and amazed as though she had been counting on a daring deed even though it would have excited her blame and terror. In a matter of hours all of the mysterious little dramas of young, ardent love were played out in her bosom. This was a new phase in her life, with emotions she had never known before. In the evening she had often waited for Anzoleto on the quays of Venice or terraces of the Corte Minelli; meanwhile, she would go over her morning's lesson or say the rosary, without impatience or fear, palpitations or anguish. That childhood love was still so close to friendship that it bore no resemblance to what she was now feeling for Liverani. The next day she waited anxiously for the robin, who did not come. Had he been snatched in midflight by some ferocious Argus? Had his exasperation with the silken girdle and the sachet, for him a heavy burden, stopped him from going out? But he was so intelligent, he would have remembered that Consuelo had freed him the day before and come to beg her to do him another favor.

Consuelo spent the day weeping. She whose eyes remained dry in great disasters, she who had not shed a single tear over her misfortune at Spandau, she felt shattered and consumed by the sufferings of love and sought in vain the strength with which she had confronted all the other hardships in her life.

In the evening she was doing her best to read a score at the harpsichord when two figures in black suddenly appeared at the entrance to the music room without her having heard them come up the stairs. A cry of fear escaped her lips at the sight of these ghosts, but one of them said to her in a gentler voice than the first time, "Follow us."

And she rose in silence to obey them. She was given a silken sash and told, "Cover your eyes yourself, and swear that you will do so conscientiously. Swear too that if the sash happens to fall off or slip down, you'll keep your eyes closed until we've told you to open them."

"I swear," said Consuelo.

"Your vow has been accepted as valid," replied the guide.

And Consuelo walked through the subterranean passages as she had the first time, but when she was told to stop, an unfamiliar voice added, "Take off the sash yourself. From now on no one will ever lay a hand on you again. Your only guard will be the word you've given."

Consuelo found herself in a vaulted chamber lit by only one small sepulchral lamp hanging from the keystone in the center. A single judge, in a red robe with a ghastly white mask, was sitting in an antique chair at a table. He was bent over with age; a few silver locks escaped from beneath his cap. His voice was broken and quavering. At the sight of old age the fear that Consuelo could not help feeling in front of an Invisible changed to respectful deference.

"Heed me well," he said, gesturing to her to sit down on a stool at some remove. "You are here before your confessor. I am the oldest member of the council, and the serenity of my entire life has made my mind as chaste as the most chaste of Catholic priests. I do not lie. Do you, however, wish to refuse me? You are free to do so."

"I accept you," replied Consuelo, "but on the condition that my confession does not implicate that of another person."

"A vain scruple!" said the old man. "A boy at school doesn't tell the teacher when his classmate misbehaves, but a son quickly alerts his father to his brother's wrongdoing because he knows that a father curbs and corrects without punishing. That at least ought to be the law of the family. You are here in the bosom of a family that seeks to put that ideal into practice. Do you have faith in that?"

This question, rather arbitrary in the mouth of a stranger, was asked so gently, in a voice resonant with such sympathy, that Consuelo, suddenly carried away with emotion, replied without hesitation, "Yes, totally."

"Heed this too," said the old man. "When you first appeared before us, you said a few words that we took in and weighed: 'it is strange moral torture for a woman to confess aloud before eight men.' We've taken your sense of modesty into consideration. You will make your confession to me alone, and I won't betray your secrets. I have been fully empowered, even though I am superior to none in the council, to guide you in a particular matter of a delicate sort, one that is related only indirectly to your initiation. Will you answer me without embarrassment? Will you bare your heart to me?"

"I will."

"I'll ask you nothing about your past. As you were told, your past does not belong to us, but you were warned to purify your soul from the instant that marked the beginning of your adoption. You must have reflected on the difficulties and consequences of this adoption; it is not to me alone that you owe that account; there's a different matter between the two of us. So give me your answer."

"I am ready."

"One of our children has conceived feelings of love for you. In the last week have you been responding to that love or rejecting it?"

"I have rejected it in all my actions."

"That I know. Your slightest actions are known to us. I'm asking you the secret of your heart, not of your conduct."

Consuelo felt her cheeks burn and kept silent.

"You find my question very cruel. Yet you must answer. I do not wish to guess anything. I must know and record."

"Well then, I love!" said Consuelo, carried away by the need to be true.

But no sooner had she uttered these bold words than she burst into tears. She had just surrendered the virginity of her soul.

"Why are you weeping?" asked the confessor gently. "Is it out of shame or repentance?"

"I don't know. I don't think it's out of repentance; I love too much for that."

"Whom do you love?"

"You know that, but I don't."

"But what if that weren't so? What is his name?"

"Liverani."

"That's no one's name. It is common to all the disciples among us who wish to go by that name and make use of it; a nom de guerre, like those that nearly all of us employ in our travels."

"I don't know him by any other name, and it's not from him that I learned it."

"How old is he?"

"I haven't asked him."

"What does he look like?"

"I haven't seen his face."

"How would you recognize him?"

"By touching his hand, I think."

"And if your fate were to hang on this test and you happened to be wrong?"

"That would be horrible."

"So tremble for your recklessness, poor child! Your love is insane."

"I know it well."

"And you don't fight it in your heart?"

"I don't have the strength for that."

"Do you have the desire to fight it?"

"Not even."

"So your heart is free of any other affection?"

"Entirely."

"But you are a widow."

"I believe so."

"And if you weren't?"

"I would struggle against my love and do my duty."

"With regret? With pain?"

"With despair perhaps. But I would do it."

"So you didn't love the man who was your husband?"

"I loved him like a brother; I did everything I could to love him like a lover."

"And you weren't able to?"

"Now that I know what it is to love, I can say that I wasn't able."

"Don't feel any remorse about that; love is not subject to command. You think you love this Liverani? Seriously, religiously, ardently?"

"That's what I feel in my heart, unless he is unworthy!"

"He is worthy."

"Oh, father!" Consuelo exclaimed, transported with gratitude and ready to kneel down before the old man.

"He is as worthy of an immense love as Albert himself! But you must give him up."

"So I'm the unworthy one?" Consuelo asked mournfully.

"You would be worthy, but you are not free. Albert von Rudolstadt is alive."

"My God, forgive me!" Consuelo murmured, falling to her knees and hiding her face in her hands.

The confessor and the penitent kept a pained silence. But soon Consuelo, remembering Supperville's accusations, was flooded with horror. Was this old man, whose presence imbued her with awe, lending himself to an infernal plot? Was he exploiting poor Consuelo's virtue and sensitivity to throw her into the arms of a despicable impostor? She raised her head and, pale with terror, her eyes dry and lips trembling, she tried to pierce with her eyes the impassive mask that was perhaps hiding the ashen face of a culprit or the diabolical laugh of a scoundrel.

"Albert is alive?" she asked. "Are you quite sure of it, sir? Are you aware that there is a man who resembles him, that I myself thought I was looking at Albert when I set eyes on him?"

"I know the whole absurd story," replied the old man unperturbed. "I know all the preposterous things that Supperville has invented to exonerate himself from the crime that he committed against science by having a sleeping man buried alive. Two words will bring down that ridiculous house of cards. In the first place, Supperville was judged incapable of going beyond the lowest degrees of the secret societies of which we are the supreme directors, and his wounded vanity, plus his morbid and indiscreet curiosity, could not bear the outrage. Second, Count Albert has never dreamed of reclaiming his inheritance. He gave it up it of his own accord, and he would never agree to reassume his name and rank in the world. He couldn't do it now without giving rise to scandalous disputes about his identity, which his pride would find intolerable. He may have misunderstood his true duties when he, so to speak, renounced himself. He could have made better use of his fortune than his heirs. He deprived himself of one of the means of practicing charity that Providence had placed in his hands, but he still has enough other ones. Besides, in this matter his love spoke louder than his conscience. He reminded himself that you had not loved him precisely because he was rich and noble. He wanted to forswear his name and fortune without any possibility of retrieving them. He did so, with our permission. Now you don't love him, you love someone else. He will never ask you to recognize him as your husband, a title that he, in the throes of death, owed only to your compassion. He will have the courage to give you up. Our only power over you and the man you call Liverani is that of persuasion. If you want to run away together, we cannot prevent it. We have neither dungeons nor constraints nor corporal punishments at our service, no matter what a credulous, fearful servant may have told you in that respect; we hate the ways of tyranny. Your fate is in your hands. Go think things over once again, poor Consuelo, and may God inspire you!"

Consuelo was utterly stupefied listening to this speech. When the old man had finished, she got up and briskly said, "I don't need to think things over, my mind is made up. Is Albert here? Take me to him."

"Albert is not here. He could not be a witness to this struggle. He does not even know about the crisis you're undergoing just now."

"Oh my dear Albert!" exclaimed Consuelo, lifting her arms to the heavens, "I'll come out of this triumphant." Then she knelt down in front of the old man and said, "Father, forgive me and help me never to see this Liverani again; I don't want to love him any longer, I won't love him any longer."

The old man spread his trembling hands over Consuelo's head, but when he withdrew them, she was unable to get up. She had forced her tears back into her breast, and broken by a battle beyond her strength, she was forced to lean on the confessor's arm to make her way out of the chapel.

Chapter XXIX

The next day at noon the robin came pecking and scratching at Consuelo's window. As she was about to open up and let him in, she noticed the black thread across his red breast, and her hand involuntarily leaped to the window latch. But she immediately pulled it back. "Go away, you bringer of trouble," she said. "Go away, poor innocent with your burden of guilty letters and criminal words. I might not have the courage not to reply to a last farewell. I must not even let it be known that I am suffering and having regrets."

She fled into the music room to escape the winged tempter who, used to a better welcome, fluttered about and flew against the glass in a sort of rage. She sat down at the harpsichord to avoid hearing the screeching and scolding of her darling who had followed her to the window of this room, all the while feeling something like the anguish of a mother who closes her ears to the cries and entreaties of her child being chastised. Yet it was not to the robin's outrage and grief that poor Consuelo was most sensitive just then. The note that he was carrying under his wing had a voice that she found much more heartrending. This was the voice, or so it seemed to our romantic recluse, weeping and wailing to be heard.

She nevertheless resisted. Yet it is the nature of love to resent obstacles and renew the attack, ever more imperious and triumphant after each one of our victories. It could be said, quite literally, that resisting love only furnishes it with new weapons. Around three, Matteus came in with the flowers he brought his prisoner every day (for at bottom he loved her for her gentle, kind disposition), and, as usual, she undid the bunch so as to arrange the blooms herself in the beautiful vases on the console. This was one of the pleasures of her captivity, but this time she was rather indifferent to it and merely going through the motions, as though to kill a few seconds of the long hours that were eating away at her. But when she untied the clump of narcissus at the center of the sweet-smelling spray, out fell a letter, carefully sealed but without any address. In vain she tried to convince herself that it could be from the tribunal of the Invisibles. Would Matteus have brought it to her otherwise? Unfortunately, Matteus was no longer there to explain anything. She had to ring for him. He generally showed up in five minutes; this time he happened to take at least ten. Consuelo had shown too much courage with the robin to have any left for the bouquet. By the time Matteus was there, the letter had been read, and Consuelo had just arrived at the following postscript: "Don't ask Matteus anything; he is not aware of the infraction I am making him commit." Matteus was simply asked to wind up the clock that had stopped.

The chevalier's letter was more impassioned, more impetuous than all the others; it was even imperious in its delirium. We shall not transcribe it. Love letters convey no emotion except to the heart that inspires them and burns with the flame that has dictated them. One is just like all the others, but lovers always find in the letters written to them an irresistible power, an incomparable novelty. No one else can be loved so much nor in the same way; each lover is the most loved, the only beloved in the whole world. Without this ingenuous blindness, this proud fascination, there is no passion, and passion had at last invaded Consuelo's peaceful, noble heart.

The stranger's note threw her into a dither. He was begging to see her. More than that, he announced that it was going to happen and excused himself ahead of time for having to make the most of these final moments. He feigned to believe that Consuelo had loved Albert and could love him again. He also feigned to want to submit to her decree, meanwhile demanding a word of pity, a tear of regret, a last farewell; always this last farewell that is like the announcement of a great artist's last appearance, fortunately followed by many others.

Sad Consuelo (sad and yet consumed with a secret, involuntary, and burning joy at the prospect of seeing him) felt by her flushed brow and pounding heart that she had an adulterous soul despite herself. She felt that neither her resolutions nor her willpower were saving her from being carried away by an unthinkable impulse, and if the chevalier were to decide to break his vow by speaking to her and showing her his face, as he sounded determined to do, she would not have the strength to prevent that violation of the Invisibles' rules. Her only refuge was to beg for help from this very tribunal. But would she have to accuse and betray Liverani? The venerable old man who the night before had revealed to her that Albert was alive and lent her a fatherly ear would hear this secret as well under the seal of confession. He would take pity on the chevalier's delirium, condemning him only in the depths of his heart. Consuelo wrote to him that she wanted to see him at nine o'clock that very evening, that her honor, her repose, perhaps her life were at stake. This was the hour at which the stranger had said he would come, but to whom and by whom could the letter be sent? Matteus refused to set foot outside the compound before midnight;

those were his orders, nothing could shake his resolve. He had been sharply reprimanded for not fully living up to all his duties toward the prisoner; he was henceforth inflexible.

The hour was drawing near, and Consuelo, all the while seeking a way around the fateful ordeal, had not given a moment's thought to the means of withstanding it. O virtue imposed on women, you will never be more than just a name as long as men do not take on half the task! All your defense strategies amount to mere subterfuge; all your sacrifices of personal happiness come to nothing before the fear of driving the beloved to despair. Consuelo fastened on a last resort, a suggestion of the heroism and weakness dividing her mind. She began searching for the mysterious entrance to the subterranean passages, somewhere in the lodge itself, for she was determined to run down and take her chances on an unwarned appearance before the Invisibles. For no particular reason she assumed that their chambers would be accessible once she had got down inside and that they gathered every evening in the same place. What she did not know was that they were all absent that day and that Liverani had returned alone after having pretended to follow them on a mysterious outing.

But all her efforts to find the secret entrance or trapdoor to the subterranean passages were fruitless. She no longer had, as at Spandau, the composure, perseverance, and faith necessary to discover the tiniest crack in a wall, the slightest protrusion of a stone. Her hands were shaking as she examined the woodwork and wainscoting; her eyes were bleary as well; at every instant she thought she heard the chevalier's steps on the sand in the garden or the marble of the peristyle.

All of a sudden she thought she heard steps coming from down below, as though he were climbing the stairs hidden beneath her feet, nearing an invisible door or, in the manner of familiar spirits, were about to come right through the wall before her eyes. She dropped her candle and fled to the far end of the garden. The lovely stream running through it broke her stride. She listened and heard or thought she heard steps behind her. Then she lost her head somewhat and leaped into the little boat the gardener used to bring sand and sod in from outside. Consuelo thought that by untying the boat she would run aground on the opposite bank, but the stream was running fast on its way out of the compound through a low, narrow arch closed with a grate. Swept along by the current, the boat was soon going to crash into the grate. Consuelo preserved herself from too severe a shock by jumping into the bow and spreading out her hands. It was impossible for a child of Venice (and a child of the people) to have much trouble performing such a move. But, by a bizarre stroke of fortune, the grate gave way at the touch of her hand, thrown open by the sheer force of the current carrying the boat. "Alas," Consuelo thought to herself, "perhaps they never close this passage, for I'm a prisoner of my word, and yet I'm fleeing and breaking my vow! But I'm only doing so to seek shelter and refuge among my hosts, not to abandon and betray them."

She jumped out onto the bank where her little boat had beached in a bend of the stream and plunged into thick brush. Consuelo could not run very fast under the dense cover. The path wound back and forth, getting narrower and narrower. The fugitive was crashing into trees at every instant and several times she fell to the grass. Yet she felt hope returning to her soul; she found the darkness reassuring; it seemed impossible that Liverani could find her here.

After having walked haphazardly a long while, she found herself at the foot of a rock-strewn hill dimly silhouetted against a grey, cloudy sky. A rather chilly storm wind had come up, and it was beginning to rain. Consuelo dared not turn back for fear that Liverani had picked up her trail and was searching for her along the stream. So she took a gamble on the rather steep path going up the hill, figuring that once having reached the top she would be able to see the lights of the castle, wherever it might be. But when she got there in the dark, the lightning that was starting to streak through the sky revealed in front of her the ruins of a huge edifice, an imposing and melancholy wreck from another age.

The rain forced Consuelo to seek shelter there, but finding it was no easy task. The towers had collapsed in upon themselves, and flocks of gerfalcons and tiercels stirred up at her approach, uttering that wild, piercing call that seems the voice of sinister spirits living among the ruins.

Amid the rocks and brambles Consuelo picked her way through the roofless chapel, the skeletal forms of its dilapidated arches standing out in the bluish glare of the lightning, and she reached the courtyard whose level surface was covered with short, even grass; she sidestepped a deep well flush with the ground that was betrayed only by luxuriant maidenhair ferns and a superb wild rose, the tranquil proprietor of its inner wall. The heap of ruins around this abandoned courtyard were the most fantastic sight and, with each flash of lightning, the eye struggled to make out these thin, wasted specters, all these incoherent shapes of destruction: huge hoods of fireplaces, their undersides still black with smoke from hearths forever extinguished, flaring out from bare walls at a terrifying height; broken staircases launching their spirals into nothingness, as though they were leading witches to their aerial dance; whole trees that had taken root and grown in apartments still decorated with vestiges of frescoes; stone benches in deep window recesses, and always nothingness inside and out of these mysterious retreats, refuge for lovers in times of peace, hideaways for sentries in hours of danger; finally, loopholes festooned with dainty garlands, lonely gables rising into the air like obelisks, and doorways piled high with debris right up to the tympanum. It was a frightening and poetic place; Consuelo was filled with a sort of superstitious terror, as if her presence had profaned a close reserved for funereal conversations or the voiceless reveries of the dead. On a clear night and in calmer circumstances she could have admired the austere beauty of the monument; perhaps she would not have made the classical lament about the rigors of time and fate, pitilessly destroying palaces and fortresses and depositing their rubble in the grass next to those of cottages. The sadness inspired by the ruins of these daunting dwellings is not the same in the artist's imagination and the patrician's heart. But in this moment of commotion and fear, and on this stormy night, Consuelo, not being sustained by the enthusiasm that had moved her to more serious undertakings, felt herself reverting to her humble childhood, trembling at the prospect of seeing the ghosts of the night and especially fearing those of the old feudal lords, ferocious oppressors while they lived and desolate, threatening specters once they had died. The thunder was raising its voice, the wind was tearing bricks and mortar out of the crumbling walls, long shoots of brambles and ivy writhed like snakes from the battlements of the towers. Consuelo, still looking for shelter from the rain and falling debris, made her way under the arch of a staircase that looked better preserved than the others; it was that of the great feudal tower, the oldest and most solid structure in the entire edifice. Twenty stairs up, she found a great octagonal hall that occupied the whole inside of the tower, the spiral staircase having been built, as in all constructions of this sort, within the walls which were between eighteen and twenty feet thick. The arched ceiling of the hall was shaped like the inside of a beehive. All the doors and windows were gone, but these openings were so narrow and deep that they kept the wind out. Consuelo decided to wait there for the weather to subside, and drawing near a window, she spent over an hour contemplating the imposing spectacle of lightning streaking through the sky and listening to the terrifying roar of the storm.

At last the wind fell, the clouds scattered, and Consuelo thought of leaving, but turning around, she was surprised to see inside the hall a light steadier than flashes of lightning. This glimmer, after some hesitation, so to speak, grew and filled the whole arch while little crackling sounds came from the fireplace. Consuelo looked over that way and saw beneath the half-moon of that ancient hearth, a huge maw gaping wide at her, some branches that seemed to have just burst into flames all by themselves. She drew nearer and saw some half-consumed logs and all the debris of a fire tended until a little while ago, then rather carelessly abandoned.

Frightened to find this sign that someone was living there, even though she could not see any trace of furniture, Consuelo briskly turned back to the stairs and was about to start down when she heard voices coming from below and feet crunching over the chunks of plaster that littered the steps. Then her fantastic fears became real alarm. This damp, devastated tower could only be inhabited by some gamekeeper, perhaps as wild as his dwelling place, perhaps drunk and brutal, and most likely less civilized and respectful than courteous Matteus. The steps were drawing near rather fast. Consuelo dashed up the stairs to avoid running into these problematic comers, and after having climbed another twenty steps, she found herself on the third floor. They were not likely to follow her up there, for the roof was gone, which made the place uninhabitable. Fortunately for Consuelo the rain had stopped; she even saw a few stars shining through the stray vegetation that had invaded the top of the tower, about twenty yards above her head. Soon she noticed a ray of light on the somber walls. It was coming from beneath her feet, and Consuelo, carefully inching forward, saw through a wide crevice what was happening on the floor below. There were two men in the hall, one walking around and stamping his feet as if to get warm, the other bent over under the huge hood of the chimney and stirring the fire which was starting to burn well. At first she could only see attire that announced their brilliant rank and caps that kept their faces hidden, but when the fire burned brighter and the one who was poking it with the tip of his sword stood up to hang his cap on a stone protruding from the wall, Consuelo saw black locks of hair that gave her a start and the upper part of a face that nearly wrung from her a shriek of terror and tenderness at one and the same time. He raised his voice, and Consuelo's doubts were gone, it was Albert von Rudolstadt.

"Come over here, my friend," he said to his companion, "and warm yourself at the only fireplace still standing in this huge manor. These are dismal quarters, Trenck, but you've had worse in your arduous travels."

"And often I've even had none at all," replied Princess Amalia's lover. "Truly, this is more comfortable than it looks, and more than once I'd have been happy to make do with it. So, my dear Count, you occasionally come here to mediate on these ruins and make a knightly vigil in this infernal tower?"

"Indeed, I come here often, but for more conceivable reasons than that. I can't tell you now, but later on you'll learn why."

"Anyway, I can guess. From the top of this tower you can see into a certain enclosure and command a view of a certain lodge."

"Not so, Trenck. That place is hidden behind the woods on the hill, and I don't see it from here."

"But you can easily get there in a few moments, then take refuge here from troublesome guards. Come on, admit that a little while ago, when I met you in the woods. . . ."

"I can admit to nothing, Trenck my friend, and you gave me your word not to question me."

"True. I should only be rejoicing that I ran into you on the grounds of this immense estate, rather in this forest. I'd got so lost that without you I'd have fallen into some picturesque ravine or drowned in some limpid mountain stream. Are we far from the castle?"

"More than a quarter of a league away. So dry your clothes while the wind dries out the trails through the grounds, and then we'll get going."

"This old castle pleases me less than the new one, I confess, and I can certainly understand why it's been abandoned to the ospreys. Yet I'm glad to find myself here alone with you at this hour and on this gloomy evening. It reminds me of our first meeting in the ruins of an ancient abbey in Silesia, my initiation, the vows I made before you, my judge, examiner, and master back then, my brother and friend today! Dear Albert! What strange and sinister vicissitudes we've been through since then! Both of us dead to our families, our countries, perhaps our loves! What will become of us, and what will be our lives henceforth among men?"

"Yours may still be full of glory and pleasure, my dear Trenck! On the soil of Europe there are limits, thank God, to the power of the tyrant who hates you."

"But my mistress, Albert, is it possible that she'll remain eternally and fruitlessly faithful to me?"

"You ought not wish that, friend, but it's only too certain that her passion will be as lasting as her sorrows."

"So tell me about her, Albert! You're luckier than I; you can see her, hear her voice!"

"Not any longer, dear Trenck; don't fool yourself on that score. The fantastic name and bizarre character of Trismegistus that was rigged up for me, that shielded me for several years in my brief and mysterious relations with the palace in Berlin have lost their charm; my friends will be discreet, and my dupes (since, for the sake of our cause and your love, I was most innocently forced to make a few dupes) wouldn't be anymore clear-sighted than in the past; but Frederick has smelled a plot, and I can't go back to Prussia. My efforts would be stymied by his suspicions, and the doors of Spandau wouldn't spring open a second time for my escape."

"Poor Albert! You must have suffered in that prison as much as I did in mine, perhaps more!"

"No, I was close to *her*. I could hear her voice, I was working for her deliverance. I don't regret enduring the horrors of the dungeon or trembling for her life. If I suffered for myself, I took no notice; if I suffered for her, I've forgotten about it now. She is saved, and she'll be happy."

"Through you, Albert? Tell me that she'll only be happy through you and with you, or else I have no respect for her, I take back my admiration and friendship."

"Don't say such things, Trenck. That's an outrage against nature, love, and heaven. Our wives have the same freedom as our lovers, and wanting to put them in chains in the name of a duty which benefits us alone would be a crime and a sacrilege."

"I know, and without raising myself to that level of virtue, I certainly feel that if Amalia, instead of confirming her pledge to me, had withdrawn it, I wouldn't have stopped loving her and blessing the days of happiness she has given me, but surely I'm allowed to love you more than myself and to hate anyone who doesn't love you? You're smiling, Albert, you don't understand my friendship, and I don't understand your courage. Ah, if it's true that the woman who received your troth has fallen in love (while still in mourning, what madness!) with one of our *brothers*, even if he were the most deserving among us, and the most seductive man on earth, I'll never be able to forgive her. Forgive her yourself, if you can!"

"Trenck, Trenck, you don't know what you're saying, you don't understand, and I can't explain myself. Don't pass judgment on her yet; later on, you'll get to know this admirable woman."

"And who is stopping you from justifying her in my eyes? Say something! Why this mystery? We're alone here. She can't be compromised by what you have to say, and as far as I know, you aren't bound by any oath to hide from me what we all suspect from the way you're behaving. She doesn't love you anymore? What's her excuse?"

"Had she ever loved me?"

"That's her crime. She never understood you."

"She couldn't, and I couldn't reveal myself to her. Besides, I was ill, I was mad. Nobody loves a madman; they are pitied and feared."

"You were never mad, Albert; I've never seen you in that condition. On the contrary, I've always been dazzled by your wisdom and intelligence."

"You've seen me steady and self-possessed in action; you've never seen me in the throes of idleness, the torments of discouragement."

"So you know discouragement, you? I never would have thought so."

"That's because you don't see all the dangers, obstacles, and vices of our endeavors. You've never gone down into the depths of the abyss where I've sunk my whole soul, cast my whole life; you've envisaged only the chivalrous, high-minded side of things, embraced only the easy tasks and pleasant prospects."

"That's because I'm less great, less enthusiastic and, since it must be said, less fanatic than you, noble count! You wanted to drain the cup of zeal, and when you choked on the bitter dregs, you doubted heaven and humankind."

"Yes, I had doubts, and I was most cruelly punished for them."

"And you still have doubts now? Are you still suffering?"

"Now I hope, believe, and act. I feel strong and happy. Don't you see my face radiant with delight? and don't you feel my heart brimming with joy?"

"And yet you've been betrayed by your mistress! What am I saying, by your wife!"

"She was never either one or the other. She owed me nothing, nor does she owe me anything now; she is not betraying me. God has sent her love, the most celestial of the graces from on high, as a reward for having shown me a moment of pity on my deathbed. And I, to thank her for having closed my eyes, grieved over me and given me her blessing on the eternal threshold I thought I was crossing, I should invoke a promise wrested from her generous compassion, her sublime charity? I should say to her, 'Woman, I am your master, you are mine by law, through your own recklessness and error. You shall submit to my embrace because on a day of parting you deposited a farewell kiss on my icy brow! You shall put your hand in mine forever, follow in my footsteps, bear my yoke, destroy a newborn love in your heart, repress unconquerable desires, and waste away with regret in my profane arms, on my selfish, cowardly heart!' Oh, Trenck, do you think I could be happy this way? Wouldn't my life be even more bitter torment than hers? Isn't the slave's suffering the master's curse? Great God! Who is so vile, so brutish as to take pride and pleasure in love which is not shared, in fidelity against which the victim's heart is rebelling? Thank heaven, I am not, nor shall I ever be, someone of that sort. This evening I was going to see Consuelo, to say all these things to her and set her free. I didn't run across her in the garden where she usually takes a stroll; then the storm came and removed any hope of seeing her down into the garden. I didn't want to go to her rooms. I would have gone in with a husband's rights, but just seeing her start with horror, her face pale with despair, would have pained me in a way that I couldn't bring myself to face."

"And in the darkness didn't you meet up with Liverani's black mask?"

"Who is this Liverani?"

"You don't know your rival's name?"

"Liverani is a false name. Do you know this man, this happy rival?"

"No, but you've got a strange look asking me that. Albert, I think I'm understanding you. You forgive your unfortunate wife, you are abandoning her, you must do so, but you'll punish, I hope, the coward that seduced her."

"Are you sure he's a coward?"

"What! The man entrusted with rescuing and looking after her during a long and dangerous trip! The man who was to protect and respect her, not to speak a single word to her nor show her his face! A man invested with the powers and blind trust of the Invisibles! Your brother in arms, your brother by oath, just as I am, no doubt! Ah, had your wife been entrusted to me, Albert, I wouldn't even have dreamed of such criminal treachery, of making her fall in love with me!"

"Trenck, once again, you don't know what you're saying! Just three men among us know this Liverani and his crime. In a few days you'll stop blaming and cursing the happy mortal to whom God in his goodness, perhaps in his justice, has given Consuelo's love."

"What a strange, sublime man you are! You don't hate him?"

"I cannot."

"You won't disturb his happiness?"

"On the contrary, I'm fervently working to ensure it, and in that I am neither sublime nor strange. You'll soon be smiling at the praise you're giving me."

"What! You aren't even suffering?"

"I am the happiest of men."

"In that case, you don't love much, or you don't love any longer. Such heroism is not human; it's almost monstrous; and I cannot admire what I don't understand. Just a minute, Count; you're making fun of me, and I'm a simpleton. Now I've got it. You're in love with another woman, and you're blessing Providence which is freeing you from your obligations to Consuelo by making her unfaithful."

"So I'll have to bare my heart to you, Baron; you don't leave me any choice. Listen, it's a long and complicated story, a whole novel, but it's cold here, and this little fire can't take the chill out of these old walls. Besides, I'm afraid they'll wind up giving you an unhappy reminder of Glatz. The sky has cleared, we can start back to the castle, and since you're leaving at dawn, I don't want to keep you up too late. On the way I'll tell you a strange tale."

The two friends shook the rain off their caps and put them back on their heads. After scattering the embers with a few kicks to extinguish the fire, they left the tower arm in arm. Their voices grew fainter and fainter in the distance, and soon the old manor ceased resonating with the echo of their footsteps over the wet grass of the courtyard.

Chapter XXX

Consuelo remained sunk in a strange stupor. What astonished her the most, what she found hard to believe despite the evidence of her eyes and ears was not Albert's magnanimous conduct nor his heroic sentiments, but the miraculous ease with which he himself was unraveling the terrible problem of her destiny, a problem of his making. Was it so easy then for Consuelo to be happy? Was Liverani's love so right? She thought that what she had just heard was a dream. Already she could give way to her impetuous feelings for the stranger. The austere Invisibles considered him Albert's equal in greatness of soul, courage, and virtue. Albert himself justified Consuelo and defended her against Trenck's blame. In short, Albert and the Invisibles, far from condemning their mutual passion, were abandoning them to their own free choice, their invincible sympathy, and all that without struggle or effort, without cause for regret or remorse, without anyone having to shed a tear! Consuelo, trembling more from emotion than cold, went back down to the vaulted hall and revived the fire that Albert and Trenck had just scattered in the hearth. She looked at their damp footprints on the dusty flagstones, which testified that they had indeed been there. Consuelo needed to examine this evidence to believe it. Crouching under the hood of the fireplace, like dreamy Cinderella over whom the elves of the hearth kept watch, she fell into a deep meditation. Such an easy triumph over destiny did not seem made for her, she felt. Yet no fear could prevail over Albert's marvelous peace of mind. That was precisely the thing that Consuelo could doubt the least. Albert was not suffering; his love was not in revolt against his sense of justice. With a kind of enthusiastic joy he was making the greatest sacrifice that man can offer God. The strange virtue of this unique man amazed and horrified Consuelo. She asked herself if such total detachment from human weaknesses could be reconciled with human affections. Wasn't Albert's apparent insensibility the sign of a new phase of delirium? After the exacerbated disorders that come from living in the past and having just one focus for his emotions, wasn't Albert undergoing some kind of paralysis of the heart and memory? Could he be cured of his love so quickly, and was this love such a trifling thing that a simple act of will, a single rational decision could wipe out even its slightest trace? All the while admiring this triumph of philosophy, Consuelo could not help feeling a bit humiliated to see this long passion, of which she had been rightly proud, destroyed with one breath. She reconsidered every last thing he had just said and could still see the look on his face while he was saying it. She had never seen him with that look before. Albert was as different outside as he was inside. He was truly a new man, and had the sound of his voice, the lines of his face, and the reality of his words not confirmed the truth, Consuelo could have thought that she had seen not Albert but his so-called double, this imaginary Trismegistus, that the doctor stubbornly wanted to put in his place. The changes that this state of calm and good health had wrought in Albert's outward appearance and manners seemed to confirm Supperville's error. No longer was he frightfully thin, and he looked taller now that a youthful, erect posture had replaced his languid slouch. His bearing was different; his movements were more supple, his step firmer, his clothing was as elegant and natty as it had once been neglected and, as it were, an object of scorn. Even his slightest preoccupations astonished Consuelo. In the past he would not have thought to make a fire; he would have felt sorry that his friend Trenck was wet, and it would not have crossed his mind, exterior objects and material cares having become so foreign to him, to gather the scattered embers under his feet; he would not have shaken off his cap before putting it back on; he would have let the rain stream down his long hair without feeling it. Finally, he was carrying a sword, and never in the past would he have agreed to handle, even in sport, this ceremonial weapon, this symbol of hatred and murder. Now it did not get in his way; he could see the blade shining before the flames without its reminding him of the blood spilled by his ancestors. The expiation inflicted on Jan Zizka, on his person, was a painful dream that salutary sleep had at last completely erased. Perhaps he had lost that memory along with the other memories of his life and his love, which seemed to have been for him, though no longer, life itself.

Something uncertain and inexplicable took place in Consuelo, something resembling sorrow, regret, wounded pride. She repeated to herself Trenck's final conjectures about Albert's new love, which seemed plausible to her. This new love was the only thing that make him so tolerant and merciful. The parting words to his friend promising a *tale*, a *novel*, did they not confirm this suspicion, were they not the confession and explanation of the deep, discreet joy with which he seemed to be brimming? "Yes, his eyes had a shine I've never seen before," Consuelo thought to herself. "His smile was an expression of triumph, of heady pleasure, and he was smiling, almost laughing, even though laughter seemed unknown to him in the past; there was even something like irony in his voice when he said to the baron, 'Soon you too will be smiling at the praise you're giving me.' There's no doubt now, he's in love, and it's not with me any longer. He's not holding back, nor is he thinking of fighting it; he's blessing my infidelity, urging me on and rejoicing in it; he's not blushing for me, but abandoning me to a weakness that will make me alone blush, and all the shame will be on my head! Oh heavens! I was not the only guilty party, and Albert was even more so! Alas, why did I overhear the secret of a generosity that I would have so admired, that I never would have wanted to accept? I know now that there's something sacred about sworn faith; God alone who changes our hearts can release us from it. Then maybe those who have been joined by a vow can give and receive in turn the sacrifice of their rights. But when mutual infidelity alone presides over a divorce, there is something dreadful, like a partnership in parricide, the two killing in cold blood the love in their hearts that had made them one."

After spending the whole night in the tower, absorbed in a thousand sad, somber thoughts, Consuelo returned to the woods at dawn's first light. She found the path back to her lodgings without any problem, even though she had come this way in the dark and her hasty flight had made it seem less long than on the return. She went down the hill and followed the stream back to the grate which she deftly maneuvered by stepping on the crosspiece joining the vertical bars at the level of the water. She was no longer fearful or agitated. Determined to come right out and tell her confessor everything, she did not care if anyone caught sight of her. Besides, she was so engrossed in her past feelings that present concerns were now only of secondary interest. Liverani scarcely existed for her. Such is the human heart: new love requires dangers and difficulties; old love is revived when it is no longer up to us to rekindle it in another's heart.

This time the Invisibles keeping watch over Consuelo seemed to have fallen asleep, and her nocturnal outing had apparently gone unnoticed. She found a new letter from the stranger in her harpsichord, and it was as tenderly respectful as the previous one had been bold and passionate. He complained that she was afraid of him, he reproached her for having retrenched herself in her rooms as though she mistrusted his timid veneration. He humbly begged her just to let him catch a glimpse of her in the garden at dusk; he promised not to say a word to her nor to show himself if she so required. "For reasons of detachment or conscience," he added, "Albert is giving you up, and he seems calm, even cold-blooded about it. Duty speaks louder than love in his heart. In a few days the Invisibles will let you know his resolution and pronounce your freedom. Then you can stay here to be initiated into their mysteries if you persist in that generous intention, and up to that time I'll respect my vow to them not to appear before your eyes. But if you made that promise only out of compassion for me, if you wish to be released from it, just say the word, and I'll break all my commitments and run away with you. I, for one, am not Albert; I have more love than virtue. Choose!"

"Yes, indeed," said Consuelo, dropping the stranger's letter on the keys of her harpsichord. "This man loves me, and Albert does not. Perhaps he never loved me, and my image was only a figment of his delirium. Yet to me that love seemed sublime, and would to heaven that it were still so enough to conquer mine by a painful and sublime sacrifice! That would be better for the two of us than the calm separation of two adulterous souls. Better too for Liverani that I abandon him at the price of struggle and suffering rather than accepting him as a necessity in my solitude, on a day of indignation, shame, and grievous intoxication!"

She made this brief reply to Liverani: "I am too proud and too sincere to deceive you. I know what Albert thinks, what he has resolved to do. I overheard him confiding in a mutual friend. He is abandoning me without regrets, and it is not virtue alone that has triumphed over his love. I will not follow his example. I have loved you, and I'm giving you up without loving another. I owe this sacrifice to my dignity and my conscience. I hope that you won't come near my lodge any longer. If you were to yield to a blind passion and wring some new confession out of me, you would regret it. You might owe my trust to a broken heart's rightful anger, a forsaken soul's feelings of terror. It would be my torment and yours. If you persist, Liverani, the love in you is not the love of my dreams."

Yet Liverani persisted; he wrote another letter and was eloquent, persuasive, and sincere in his humility. "You appeal to my pride," he said, "and I have no pride with you. If you were to regret someone else while I held you in my arms, I would suffer without taking offense. I would beg you, prostrate and bathing your feet with my tears, to forget him, to trust in me alone. However you love me, and however little, for that I shall be grateful as for an immense happiness." This was the substance of a series of letters, ardent and timid, submissive and persevering. Consuelo felt her pride dissolving before the penetrating charm of true love. By imperceptible degrees she got used to the idea that she had not yet ever been truly loved previously, not even by Count von Rudolstadt. Then she rebuffed the involuntary spite that this outrage against the holiness of her memories aroused in her, for she was afraid, were she to let it show, of standing in the way of the happiness that Albert could hope to find in a new love. So she resolved to accept in silence the decree of separation that he apparently wanted the tribunal of the Invisibles to issue, and she abstained from writing his name in her replies to the stranger, ordering him to respect the same reserve.

These replies, moreover, were full of caution and tact. While separating herself from Albert and opening her soul to the thought of another affection, Consuelo did not want to yield to blind intoxication. She forbade the stranger to appear before her and to break his vow of silence until the Invisibles had released him from it. She told him that she freely and voluntarily wanted to join the mysterious association that inspired her with both respect and confidence, that she was determined to undertake the necessary studies to learn their doctrine and to refrain from all personal concerns until she had earned, by a little virtue, the right to think of her own happiness. She did not find the strength to say that she did not love him, but she mustered up enough to tell him that she did not want to love him rashly.

Liverani appeared to submit, and Consuelo carefully studied several tomes that Matteus had brought her one morning from the *prince*, along with the report that *His Highness* and *his court* had left the *residence*, but that she would soon have *news*. She simply listened to the message, asked no questions of Matteus, and read the history of the mysteries of antiquity, Christianity, and the various sects and secret societies that have grown out of them, a very learned compilation handwritten in the library of the Order of the *Invisibles* by some patient, conscientious disciple. This heavy reading, laborious at the beginning, gradually took hold of her mind, even her imagination. The depiction of the ordeals in the ancient temples of Egypt gave her many terrifying, poetic dreams. The account of the persecution suffered by the sects of the Middle Ages and the Renaissance moved her heart more than ever, and that history of enthusiasm inclined her soul to the religious fanaticism of an imminent initiation.

For two weeks she had no word from outside and lived in retreat, surrounded by the chevalier's mysterious attentions, but firm in her resolution not to see him or give him too much hope.

The summer heat was coming on, and Consuelo, absorbed in her studies, could rest and breathe easily only during the cool of the evening. Little by little she resumed her slow, dreamy walks through the cloistered garden. She thought she was alone there, and yet every now and then some vague feeling made her fancy that the stranger was nearby. The lovely nights, the beautiful shade trees, the solitude, the languid murmur of running water amid the flowers, the perfume of the plants, the passionate voice of the nightingale followed by even more voluptuous silences; the moon casting its broad, oblique beams under the transparent shadows of the fragrant bowers, the evening star setting behind the pink clouds on the horizon, and who knows what else! All the classic feelings of youth and love, but eternally new and powerful, plunged Consuelo's soul into dangerous reveries; her own slender shadow on the silvery sand of the paths, the flight of a bird roused by her approach, a leaf stirring in the breeze were enough to make her jump and quicken her pace; yet no sooner had these slight fears been dissipated than they were replaced by an undefinable regret, and the thrill of anticipation was stronger than any prompting of the will.

Once she was flustered more than usual by the rustling leaves and obscure sounds of the night. She had the feeling that someone was walking close by, fleeing at her approach and coming near when she was sitting down. Her restlessness heightened her sense of alarm. She felt unable to defend herself against an encounter in this beautiful spot, under this magnificent sky. Puffs of hot wind blew over her brow. She fled to the lodge and shut herself away in her room. The candles had not been lit. She hid behind a blind and ardently desired to see the one by whom she did not want to be seen. Indeed, she saw a man appear and stroll under her windows without calling her name, without making a gesture, submissive and apparently content to gaze at the place where she lived. It had to be the stranger; at least, Consuelo felt at first that it had to be because of the emotion that washed over her, and she thought she recognized his height and bearing. But soon her mind was seized by strange doubts and distressing fears. The man walking in silence reminded her of Albert at least as much as Liverani. They were the same size; and now that Albert, transformed by his return to health, moved with ease and no longer kept his head bent over or cupped in his hand in a sick or sorry way, Consuelo scarcely knew any better what he looked like than she did the chevalier. Once in full daylight she had caught a brief glimpse of the chevalier walking far ahead of her and enveloped in the folds of a cloak. For a few seconds in the deserted tower she had also seen Albert, now so different from the man she had known; and here she was seeing one or the other not at all distinctly by starlight, and each time that she was about to settle her doubts, he slipped into the shade under the trees and disappeared as though he were a shade himself. He finally vanished altogether, and Consuelo was left torn between joy and fear, upbraiding herself for not having had the courage to call Albert by name to see what would happen and have it out with him fairly and frankly.

As he withdrew farther and farther away from her, this regret grew ever stronger, along with the conviction that it was indeed Albert whom she had just seen. Carried along by the habitual devotion that had always stood in the place of love for him, she told herself that if he came roaming around her like this, it was in the timid hope of speaking to her. This was not the first time; he had said as much to Trenck on an evening when he may have crossed paths with Liverani in the dark. They needed to talk, and Consuelo resolved to make it happen. Her conscience required that she clear up her doubts about her husband's real frame of mind, generous or fickle. She went back down to the garden and ran after him, trembling and yet courageous, but she had lost track of him, and she went back and forth through the whole enclosure without encountering him.

All of a sudden, as she was emerging from a thicket, she saw a man standing at the water's edge. Was this the one she had been seeking? She called out Albert's name; he shuddered, passed his hands over his face, and when he turned around, the black mask already covered his features.

"Albert, is that you?" cried Consuelo. "It's you, you alone that I've been seeking."

A stifled exclamation betrayed some emotion in the stranger, either joy or pain. He seemed to want to flee. Thinking that she had recognized Albert's voice, Consuelo leaped forward and held on to his cloak. But she stopped, for the cloak had pulled open and there on the man's chest was a rather large silver cross that Consuelo knew only too well: her mother's, the very one that she had entrusted to the chevalier during their travels together, as a token of gratitude and sympathy.

"Liverani!" she exclaimed. "It's always you! Since that's the case, good bye! Why have you disobeyed me?"

He threw himself at her feet, wrapped his arms around her, and lavished fervent, respectful embraces on her that Consuelo no longer had the strength to fend off.

"If you love me and want me to love you, leave me," she said. "It's before the Invisibles that I want to see and hear you. Your mask frightens me, your silence makes my heart go cold."

Liverani raised his hand to his mask, he was going to rip it off and speak. Consuelo, like curious Psyche, no longer had the courage to close her eyes . . . but suddenly the black veil of the secret tribunal's messengers slipped down over her head. The stranger's hand that had hastily grabbed hers was loosed in silence. Consuelo felt herself being led away without violence or apparent wrath, but swiftly. She was swept up off the ground, she felt the bottom of a boat give beneath her feet. She glided downstream a long while without anyone saying a word to her, and when light was restored to her, she found herself in the subterranean hall where she had made her first appearance before the tribunal of the Invisibles.

Chapter XXXI

There they were, all seven of them, just like the first time, masked, silent, impenetrable as ghosts. The eighth figure, who had spoken to Consuelo on that occasion and was apparently the mouthpiece for the council and the initiator of the disciples, addressed her in these terms.

"Consuelo, you have already undergone trials from which you have emerged to your glory and our satisfaction. You have our confidence, and we're going to prove it to you."

"Wait," said Consuelo. "You believe me without reproach, and that's not so. I've disobeyed you; I left the retreat that you assigned me."

"Out of curiosity?"

"No."

"Can you say what you learned?"

"What I learned is very personal to me; I have among you a confessor to whom I can and will reveal it."

The old man that Consuelo was invoking stood up and said, "I know everything. The child's fault is minor. She knows nothing of the matters about which you want her to know nothing. She'll confide in me once the two of us are alone together. Meanwhile, put this time to good use and reveal to her without delay what she needs to know. I vouch for her in all things."

The initiator continued after having turned to the tribunal and received a sign of agreement.

"Listen carefully," he said to her, "I'm speaking to you in the name of those whom you see gathered here. It is their spirit, their breath, so to speak, that inspires me. It is their doctrine that I'm going to explain to you.

"The distinctive feature of the religions of antiquity is that they had two faces, one outward and public, one inward and secret; one being the spirit; the other, the form or the letter. Behind the crude and material symbol, the deep meaning, the sublime idea. Egypt and India, great examples of ancient religions and mothers of pure doctrine, exhibit to the highest degree that dual aspect, the inevitable and fatal sign of societies in their infancy and of the suffering that goes along with humanity's developing genius. You recently learned what the great mysteries of Memphis and Eleusis were all about, and now you know why the knowledge of God, politics, and society, which was all in the hands of the chief priests with their three-fold powers, religious, military and industrial, did not pass down to the lower classes in these ancient societies. The idea of Christianity, enveloped in purer, more transparent symbols in the words of the revealer, was born to bring the knowledge of truth and the light of faith down into the souls of the people. But theocracy, an inevitable abuse of religions constituted amid turmoil and danger, soon did its best to put the dogma under a veil once again, and it was corrupted in the process. Idolatry and mysteries reappeared, and in Christianity's painful development one saw the chief priests of apostolic Rome lose, by divine punishment, the divine light and sink back into the darkness into which they wanted to plunge all humanity. From that point on human intelligence developed in ways completely different from those of the past. The temple was no longer, as in antiquity, the sanctuary of truth. Superstition and ignorance, the crude symbol, the dead letter, held sway on the altars and thrones. The spirit descended at last into the classes that had been demeaned too long. Poor monks, obscure doctors, humble penitents, all virtuous apostles of primitive Christianity, turned the secret, persecuted religion into the asylum of unknown truth. They did all they could to initiate the people into the religion of equality; and in the name of Saint John they preached a new gospel, that is to say, a freer, bolder, purer interpretation of the Christian revelation. You know the history of their labors, struggles, and martyrdom; you know how the peoples have suffered, their ardent inspirations, terrifying bursts of energy, grievous downfalls and stormy reawakenings; and through so many exertions, by turns dreadful and sublime, their heroic perseverance in fleeing the darkness and finding the ways of God. The time is near when the veil of the temple will be forever rent asunder, when the mob will storm the sanctuaries of the holy ark. Then symbols will vanish, and access to truth will no longer be guarded by the dragons of religious and monarchical despotism. Every man will be able to walk in the way of light and approach God with all the strength of his soul. No one will say to his brother any longer, 'Your lot is ignorance and humility. Close your eyes and take the yoke.' On the contrary, every man will be able to ask his peers to use their eyes, hearts, and arms to help him fathom the secrets of sacred knowledge. But that time is not yet here, and today we can only hail the glimmer of dawn on the horizon. This is still the age of secret religion, mystery's task is not yet accomplished. We are still shut in the temple, busy forging the weapons to ward off the enemies who come between us and the peoples and forced as yet to keep our doors closed and words secret so that no one can come wrest out of our hands the holy ark, rescued with such difficulty and reserved for the community of mankind.

"So now you're being welcomed in the new temple, but it's still a fortress that has been upholding the cause of liberty for centuries without having won it. War is all around us. We want to be liberators, we're still only combatants. You're here to receive the fraternal communion, the banner of salvation, the emblem of liberty and perhaps to die in the breach among us. This is the destiny you've accepted; perhaps you'll succumb without having seen the standard of victory waving over your head. It is still in the name of Saint John that we call men to the crusade. It is still a symbol that we invoke; we are heirs to the Johannites of long ago, the unknown, mysterious, and steadfast successors to Wyclif, Jan Hus, and Luther; we want, as they did, to emancipate the human race, but, like them, we ourselves are not free, and like them, we may be marching to the stake.

"Yet the battle is being fought on new ground, and the weapons are of a different sort. We still defy the law in its irascible severity and face proscription, poverty, imprisonment, death, for the means of tyranny are always the same, whereas ours are no longer incitements to material revolt and bloody sermons about the cross and the sword. Our war is wholly intellectual, as is our mission. We appeal to the mind and spirit, and we act by the same. It's not with weapons that we can overthrow governments, organized and sustained with all the resources of brute force nowadays. We're waging a slower, stealthier, and deeper war by going after their hearts. We're unsettling their foundations by demolishing the blind faith and idolatrous respect they seek to inspire. We're making what no one dares any longer call the poison of philosophy penetrate everywhere, into the courts, even into the restless, fascinated minds of princes and kings; we're destroying all the illusions, and from the top of our fortress we're launching a bitter attack on the altar and the throne with fervent truth and implacable reason. Victory will be ours, have no doubt. In how many years, how many days? That we don't know. But our endeavor has such a long history, it has been conducted with such faith, smothered with so little success, resumed with such ardor, pursued with such passion that it cannot fail; it has become immortal in nature like the immortal goods it has resolved to conquer. This work was begun by our ancestors, and every generation has dreamed of completing the task. Were we ourselves not animated by some of the same hope, perhaps our zeal would be less fervent, less effective, but if the spirit of doubt and irony now ruling the world were to prove to us, by its cool calculations and overwhelming arguments, that we are chasing a dream that can only be realized several centuries from now, our firm belief in our saintly cause would be unshaken; despite the extra toil and pain, we wouldn't work any less hard for the men of the future. That's because there is uniting us to the men of the past and the generations of the future a religious bond so tight and so strong that we've almost smothered in ourselves the selfish and personal side of human individuality. This is what the common man cannot understand, and yet there is in aristocratic pride something like our hereditary religious enthusiasm. Great lords sacrifice much to glory to be worthy of their ancestors and bequeath many honors to posterity, whereas we, architects of the temple of truth, sacrifice much to virtue to carry on the work of the masters and train hardworking apprentices. By the mind, spirit, and heart we live in the past, present, and future at one and the same time. Those who have gone before and those who will come after are as much *us* as we ourselves. We believe in the transmission of life, feelings, and generous instincts in souls just as patricians believe in the transmission of racial excellence through their blood. We go even further: we believe in the transmission of life, individuality, the soul and the human person. We feel ourselves fatally, providentially called to carry on the work that we have already dreamed, always pursued and promoted from century to century. Among us there are even a few who have pushed the contemplation of the past and future to the point of almost losing the notion of the present; that's the sublime fever, the ecstasy of our believers and saints; for we have our saints, our prophets, perhaps also our fanatics and visionaries; but however frenzied or sublime their transports, we respect their inspiration, and in our midst Albert the ecstatic and *seer* has only found brothers full of sympathy for his pain, of admiration for his enthusiasm.

"We also have faith in the convictions of the Count de Saint-Germain, whom the world considers an impostor or a madman. Even though his reminiscences of a past inaccessible to human memory are calmer, more precise, and even more inconceivable than Albert's ecstasies, they are likewise endowed with a sincere, lucid quality which it is impossible for us to mock. We have among us many other fanatics, mystics, poets, men of the people, philosophers, artists, ardent members of sects gathered under the banners of various leaders: Boehmists, theosophists, Moravians, Herrnhuters, Quakers, even pantheists, Pythagoreans, Xerophagists, illuminati, Johannites, Knights Templar, millenarians, Joachimites, etc. All these ancient sects, even though less widespread now than when they first sprang up, are still in existence, and they haven't even changed much. It is the nature of this age to reproduce at one and the same time every form of religious and philosophical thought that the genius of innovation or reform created one after the other in the past. So we recruit our disciples in these various groups without requiring that their precepts be absolutely identical, which would be impossible these days. All that we need to see in them is an ardor for destruction, and they are summoned into our ranks. The whole of our organizing skill consists in choosing *constructors* only from among those minds that are above factional bickering, whose passion for truth, thirst for justice, and instinct for moral beauty are stronger than family habits and sectarian rivalry. Moreover, it's not as difficult as one thinks to make very different elements work together; these differences are more apparent than real. At bottom, all heretics (I use this word with respect) agree on the main point, which is to destroy intellectual and material tyranny or at least to protest it. The antagonisms that have thus far delayed the fusion of all this generous and useful resistance come from pride and jealousy, which are inherent vices in the human condition, the fatal and inescapable counterweight to all human progress. By dealing deftly with this touchiness and allowing each communion to keep its leaders, institutions, and rituals, one can constitute, if not a society, at least an army, and, as I've told you, we are still only an army marching toward the conquest of a promised land, an ideal society. Human nature has only come so far, and there are so many shades of character in people, so many different degrees in the conception of truth, such varied aspects, all ingenious manifestations of the rich nature that created human genius, that it is absolutely necessary to leave to each the conditions of his inner life and the elements of his force of action.

"Our work is great, our task immense. It is not merely a universal empire that we want to found on a new order and equitable foundation; we want to reconstitute a religion. We feel certain, moreover, that one is impossible without the other. For that reason we have two modes of action. One is wholly material, undermining and bringing down the old world by criticism, analysis, even derision, Voltairianism and everything that goes along with it. The formidable alliance of all those with bold resolve and strong passions speeds us on in that direction. Our other mode of action is entirely spiritual; it's a matter of building the religion of the future. The very finest models of intellect and virtue are assisting us in this unceasing labor of thought. The Invisibles function as a council that cannot meet publicly because of its persecution by the official powers, but it deliberates without pause and works with one inspiration all over the civilized world. Mysterious communications bring the grain to the threshing-floor as it ripens and sow it in the field of humanity after we've stripped it from the stalk. It is in this underground work that you can join. Once you've accepted this mission, we'll tell you how."

"I accept," said Consuelo in a firm voice, stretching forth her arm to signify her vow.

"No hasty promises, woman of generous instincts and enterprising soul. You may not have all the virtues such a mission would require. You have traveled through the world and there you've already learned prudence, what is called savoir-vivre, discretion, decorum."

"I don't flatter myself in that regard," replied Consuelo smiling with modest pride.

"Well then, you've learned at least to doubt, to argue, to scoff, to question."

"To doubt, perhaps. Rid me of doubt which was not part of my nature, which has made me suffer, and I shall bless you. Rid me, above all, of self-doubt, which would sap all my strength."

"We'll rid you of doubt only by explaining our principles to you. As for giving you material assurances of our good faith and power, we won't do anything more than we have done thus far. Let the services already rendered you suffice; we'll always assist you when need be, but we'll make you privy to the mysteries of our thoughts and actions only insofar as we've assigned you a role in them. You won't know who we are. You'll never see our faces. You'll never know our names unless some great interest of the cause forces us to break the rule of anonymity and invisibility that we maintain with our disciples. Can you obey and blindly trust men who will never be anything more to you than abstract beings, living ideas, mysterious supporters, and advisers?"

"Only vain curiosity could make me want to know you otherwise. I hope never to feel that childish impulse."

"It is not a matter of curiosity, but of mistrust. Yours would be justified according to the world's logic and prudence. A man is responsible for his actions; his name acts as a guarantee or a warning; his reputation supports or undermines his deeds or designs. Have you considered that you'll never be able to compare the conduct of anyone of us in particular with the precepts of the order? You'll have to believe in us as though we were saints, not knowing if we're not hypocrites. You may even have to witness injustice, perfidy, and apparent cruelty stemming from our decisions. You won't be able to examine our methods anymore than our intentions. Will you have faith enough to walk on the edge of an abyss with your eyes closed?"

"That was the way I practiced Catholicism as a child," replied Consuelo after a moment's reflection. "I opened my heart and surrendered my conscience to a priest whose face remained hidden behind the veil of the confessional, whose name and life remained unknown to me. In him I saw nothing but the mediator with God; the man was nothing to me. I was obeying Christ and didn't bother about the minister. Do you find that so difficult?"

"Now then raise your hand if you mean to carry on."

"Wait," said Consuelo. "Your answer may decide the rest of my life, but will you allow me one question, for the first and last time?"

"You see! Already you're hesitating and seeking assurances beyond your spontaneous inspiration and the impetus of your heart toward the idea that we represent. Speak even so. The question you are eager to ask will enlighten us as to your frame of mind."

"Here it is. Has Albert been initiated into all your secrets?"

"Yes."

"In all respects?"

"In all respects."

"And he's with you?"

"Say rather that we're with him. He is one of our council's luminaries, the purest, perhaps the most divine."

"Why didn't you tell me that in the first place? I wouldn't have hesitated for an instant. Lead me where you wish, dispose of my life. I am yours, and so I swear."

"You're stretching out your hand! But on what do you swear?"

"On Christ whose image I see here."

"Who is Christ?"

"The mind of God, revealed to humanity."

"Is the whole mind of God in the letter of the Gospels?"

"I don't believe so, but I do believe it is all there in the spirit of the Gospels."

"We are satisfied with your answers and accept the vow you've just made. Now we're going to instruct you in your duties to God and to us. First, learn the three words that are the whole secret of our mysteries, words that we reveal to many members only very slowly and cautiously. You don't need a long apprenticeship, and yet you'll have to do some thinking to understand their full significance. *Liberty, fraternity, equality*: this is the mysterious, deep formula of the work of the Invisibles."

"Is that really the whole mystery?"

"It seems like no mystery to you, but look at the state of society, and you'll see that, for men used to being ruled by despotism, inequality, antagonism, it takes a whole education, conversion, revelation to arrive at a clear understanding of the human possibility, social necessity, and moral obligation of this triple precept: *liberty, equality, fraternity*. The few right minds and pure hearts that naturally protest against tyranny's injustice and disorder grasp the secret doctrine right away. They make rapid progress, for it's only a matter of teaching them the methods of application that we've discovered. But for the great majority, prominent people, courtiers, and those with power, imagine all the care and address it requires to let them ponder the immortal work's sacred formula. One has to use all kinds of symbols and circumlocutions and convince them that it is nothing more than an illusory liberty confined to the exercise of individual thought, a relative equality extended only to members of the association and to be enjoyed only in its secret, voluntary meetings; finally, a romantic fraternity agreed upon by a certain number of persons and limited to little favors, a few good works and mutual assistance. For these slaves to custom and prejudice, our mysteries are merely the statutes of heroic orders revived from ancient chivalry, doing no harm to the powers that be nor offering any remedy to the suffering of the peoples. For such individuals, there are only insignificant ranks, degrees of trivial knowledge, or banal antiquity, a series of initiations whose bizarre rites amuse their curiosity without enlightening their minds. They think they know everything and know nothing."

"What use are they?" asked Consuelo, who was listening carefully.

"They shield the ones who understand and know so that these can freely carry out their work," replied the initiator. "This will be explained to you. First, hear what we expect of you.

"Europe (Germany and France mainly) is teeming with secret societies, underground laboratories where a great revolution, whose crater will be Germany and France, is being prepared. We have the key to all these associations, which is not known to the majority of their members, nor is it known from one association to the other, and we are striving to put them under our control. Even though our goal has not yet been achieved, we have managed to gain a foothold everywhere. The most prominent members are now ours, and they are giving us a hand. You'll enter all these sacred sanctuaries, all these profane temples, for corruption and frivolity have also raised up their cities, and in some, vice and virtue share in the same work of destruction without evil understanding how it is collaborating with the good. Such is the rule of conspiracies. You'll learn the secret of the Freemasons, a great brotherhood that, with the most sundry forms and diverse conceptions, works to organize the practice of equality and spread the notion. You'll receive the degrees of all the rites, even though women are only admitted by virtue of adoption and not made privy to all the secrets of the doctrine. We'll treat you like a man, giving you all the insignia, titles, and formulas necessary for the relations that we'll have you set up with the *lodges* and the negotiations that you'll be instructed to conduct with them. Your profession, itinerant life, and talents, the charm of your sex, youth, and beauty, your virtues and courage, integrity and discretion make you fit for this role and give us the necessary guarantees. Your past life, which we know down to the minutest detail, is for us sufficient assurance. You've voluntarily undergone more trials than Masonic mysteries could ever invent, and you've emerged from them stronger and more victorious than their disciples from the vain illusions designed to test their constancy. Moreover, the wife and student of Albert von Rudolstadt is our daughter, sister, and equal. Like Albert, we profess the divine equality of men and women. Yet we are forced to recognize that the education of women, their social situation, and habits have had unfortunate results for your sex, to wit, a dangerous flightiness and whimsical instincts, and for this reason we cannot fully put the precept of equality into practice. There are only a few women that we can trust, and some secrets we will impart to you alone.

"The talisman of our investiture will also open to you the other secret societies of Europe so that, no matter where you are, you'll find the opportunity to help us out and serve our cause. If necessary, you'll even penetrate the impure Order of the Mops and the other mysterious dens of promiscuity and unbelief of this day and age, bringing in reforms and the notion of a purer, more extended fraternity. In the course of your mission you won't be anymore sullied by the spectacle of the debauchery of the great than you were by the licentious displays in the wings of the theater. You'll be a sister of charity to sick souls; we'll also give you the means to destroy the associations that you may not be able to set right. You'll work mainly on women; your genius and celebrity open palace doors; Trenck's love and our protection have already given you the heart and secrets of an illustrious princess. You'll be even closer to more powerful heads, and you'll make them our auxiliaries. The ways of achieving that will be the object of special communications and training that you'll receive here. In all the courts and cities of Europe where you may wish to go, we'll find you friends, associates, brothers to assist you, mighty protectors to preserve you from the dangers of your undertaking. You'll be entrusted with considerable sums of money to remedy the ills of our brothers and all the unfortunates who, wherever you are, appeal for our help with their *signals of distress*. Among the women you'll set up new secret societies, founded by us on the principles of our own but appropriate, in their forms and composition, to the ways and customs of various countries and classes. As far as you are able, you'll bring about the cordial and sincere reconciliation of the great lady and the bourgeoise, the affluent woman and the humble wage earner, the virtuous matron and the adventuresome artist. *Tolerance and good works*, this will be the version, toned down for society, of our true and austere formula: *equality, fraternity*. At first sight, as you can see, your mission will gladden your heart and bring honor to your life, yet it is not without danger. We are powerful, but betrayal can destroy our endeavors and enfold you in our disaster. It may well be that Spandau will not be the last of your prisons, nor the tantrums of Frederick II the only king's wrath that you may ever encounter. You must be prepared for anything and already determined to suffer the martyrdom of persecution."

"I am," replied Consuelo.

"We are sure of it, and any fears that we may have for you do not concern weakness of character but despair. At this point we must warn you about the most loathsome aspect of your mission. The lowest ranks in secret societies, particularly in Freemasonry, are almost meaningless in our eyes, and we consider them useful only as tests of the postulants' instincts and character. Most never get beyond these first degrees where, as I've already said, vain ceremonies amuse their frivolous curiosity. To the next ranks only promising candidates are admitted, and yet they are still kept at a distance from the goal while we examine and test them, fathom their souls, and prepare them for a fuller initiation or abandon them at an interpretation beyond which they cannot go without danger for the cause and for themselves. This is still only a nursery out of which we choose the strong seedlings destined for transplantation in the sacred forest. The important revelations are only for the highest ranks, and that is where you are starting out with us. But the role of *master* carries many duties, and there the charm of curiosity, the intoxication of mystery, the illusion of hope come to an end. It's no longer a matter of learning, amid enthusiasm and emotion, the rule that turns a neophyte into an apostle, a novice into a priestess, but rather practicing it while teaching others and seeking to recruit, among the poor in heart and weak in spirit, Levites for the sanctuary. Then, poor Consuelo, you'll come to know the bitterness of dashed illusions and the hard work of perseverance when you see, among all the many eager, curious braggarts pursuing the truth, how few serious, steady, and sincere minds there are, how few souls worthy of receiving the truth and capable of understanding it. Among hundreds of children all puffed up about using the formulas of equality and pretending to live by them, you'll be hard put to find one man imbued with their significance and courageously interpreting them. You'll have to speak in riddles to them and make a sorry game of deceiving them about the substance of the doctrine. This is the case of most of the princes enrolled under our banner. Adorned with vain Masonic titles which amuse their foolish pride, they only serve to ensure our freedom of movement and the tolerance of the police. Yet some of them are or were sincere. Frederick who is called the Great and could certainly make himself worthy of the name became a Freemason before he was king, and at that time liberty appealed to his heart and equality to his mind. Even so, during his initiation we had him surrounded by clever, prudent men who did not let him in on the secrets of the doctrine. Had that not been so, how we would have come to regret it! Now Frederick mistrusts, spies on, and persecutes another Masonic rite that has been established in Berlin in competition with the lodge over which he presides; he does the same with other secret societies of which his brother Prince

Heinrich has eagerly taken charge. And yet Prince Heinrich, just like his sister the Abbess of Quedlinburg, has only been initiated to the second degree and will never go any higher. We know princes, Consuelo, and we know that one must never entirely rely on them or their courtiers. Frederick's brother and sister suffer from his tyranny and curse it. They would gladly conspire against him, but to their own advantage. Despite their fine qualities we'll never place the reins of our enterprise in their hands. They are in fact conspiring, but they don't know to what dreadful designs they are lending their names, fortunes, and reputations. They imagine that they're only working to curtail their master's authority and paralyze the invasions of his ambition. In Princess Amalia's zeal there is even a sort of republican enthusiasm, and in these times hers is not the only crowned head stirred by a certain dream of ancient grandeur and philosophical revolution. As children, all the little sovereigns of Germany learned Fénelon's *Telemachus* by heart, and now they are living and breathing Montesquieu, Voltaire, and Helvetius; but they scarcely go beyond a certain ideal of aristocratic government, wisely balanced, in which they would be entitled to the highest positions. You can judge the logic and good faith of them all by the strange discrepancy that you saw in Frederick between rule and practice, words and deeds. They are all just copies, more or less understated, more or less overdrawn, of this model of the tyrant philosopher. But since they don't have absolute power, their conduct is less shocking and may create illusions about how they would use such power. We won't let ourselves be fooled; we let these jaded masters, these dangerous friends sit on the thrones of our symbolic temples. They believe they are the pontiffs; they imagine they hold the key to the sacred mysteries, just as in the past the head of the Holy Empire, speciously elected the secret tribunal's grand master, convinced himself that he had at his command the terrifying army of Free-Judges, who were the masters of his power, his designs and his life. But while they think they are our generals, they act as our lieutenants, and until the fateful day marked in the book of destiny for their fall they will never know that they are helping us work against themselves.

"Such is the bleak and bitter side of our work. Certain rules of a peaceful conscience have to be compromised when opening one's soul to our holy fanaticism. Will you have this courage, young priestess of pure heart and candid tongue?"

"After everything I have just heard from you, there can be no going back," replied Consuelo after a moment's silence. "An initial scruple might drag me into a series of reservations and fears that would turn me into a coward. I've received your austere secrets; I feel that I no longer belong to myself. Alas! yes, I must say that I'll often suffer in the role you've ordained for me, for I've already bitterly suffered from having to lie to King Frederick to save friends in peril. Let me blush one last time as a soul free of all guile and shed a tear for the candor of my ignorant, peaceable youth. I can't help feeling these regrets, but I'll know how to avoid pusillanimous remorse later on. I must no longer be the innocuous, useless child that I was just a while ago, which I've already ceased to be, since here I am forced to choose between conspiring against humanity's oppressors or betraying their liberators. I've eaten of the tree of knowledge; its fruit is bitter, but I won't cast it far from me. Knowledge is pain, but it's a crime to refuse to act when one knows what must be done."

"Your replies have been wise and brave," said the initiator. "We are pleased with you. Tomorrow night will be your initiation. Take the whole day to prepare for a new baptism, a tremendous commitment, by meditation and prayer, even by confession if your soul is not free of all personal concerns."

Chapter XXXII

Consuelo was awakened at the break of day by sounding horns and barking dogs. When Matteus brought her breakfast, she was told that a great hunt of stags and wild boars was taking place in the forest. Over a hundred guests, he said, had gathered at the castle for this lordly recreation. Consuelo understood that a great number of Invisibles had ostensibly convened for the hunt here at the castle where they generally held their most important conclaves. She felt a bit intimidated by the thought that all these men might witness her initiation and wondered if the order really considered it interesting enough to bring together so many of its members. To comply with the prescriptions of the *initiator* she did her best to read and meditate, but she was even more distracted by inner commotion and vague fears than by the fanfares, galloping horses, and howling bloodhounds echoing through the surrounding woods all day long. Was this a real hunt or not? Had Albert undergone such a conversion to all the habits of ordinary life that he would take part in this and fearlessly shed the blood of innocent beasts? Wasn't Liverani going to take advantage of the confusion to steal away from the festivities and come disturb the neophyte in the privacy of her retreat?

Consuelo saw no part of what was going on outside, and Liverani did not come. Matteus, too busy no doubt at the castle to give a thought to her, did not bring her dinner. Was this, as Supperville maintained, a fast deliberately imposed to weaken the disciple's strength of mind? She resigned herself to it.

Toward nightfall, returning to the library that she had left an hour before to get some air, she recoiled in fear at the sight of a masked man all in red sitting in her armchair, but she immediately felt reassured, having recognized the frail old man who served, so to speak, as her spiritual father.

"Child," he said getting up and coming toward her, "have you nothing to tell me? Do I still have your trust?"

"You do, sir," replied Consuelo, making him sit back down in the armchair and taking a campstool next to him in the recess of the window. "I've been very eager to talk to you, and for a long time."

Then she gave him a faithful account of everything that had transpired between herself, Albert, and the stranger since her last confession and without hiding any of her involuntary feelings.

Once she had finished, the old man was silent for such a long time that Consuelo became troubled and embarrassed. After she urged him to render his judgment, he finally said, "Your behavior is excusable, almost irreproachable, but what can I say about your feelings? This sudden, overwhelming, and violent affection called love springs from the good or bad instincts that God had placed in souls or let enter them for their refinement or punishment in this life. Bad human laws that thwart the will of nature and the designs of Providence in nearly everything often make a crime of the very things that God had inspired and curse the feelings he had blessed, all the while sanctioning vile unions and sordid instincts. It is up to us, extraordinary legislators, secret architects of a new society, to discern as far as possible right and true love from that which is wrong and hollow so that we can decide, in the name of a law more pure, generous, and just than the world's, the fate you deserve. Do you wish to submit to our decision? Will you give us the right to bind or unbind you?"

"You inspire absolute trust in me, I've already said so, and now I'm saying it again."

"Well then, Consuelo, we shall weigh this question of life and death for your soul and Albert's."

"Won't I have the right to make the cry of my conscience heard?"

"Yes, in order to enlighten us; I have heard it, and I'll be your advocate. You must waive the secrecy of your confession to me."

"What! You'll no longer be the sole confidant of my innermost feelings, my trials and tribulations?"

"If you were to sue for divorce in court, wouldn't you have to lodge a public complaint? That grief will be spared you. You won't have to bring an action against anyone. Isn't confessing love sweeter than declaring hatred?"

"So simply experiencing a new love gives one the right to forswear the previous one?"

"You didn't love Albert."

"It seems to me that I didn't; yet I wouldn't swear to it."

"Had you loved him, you wouldn't have any doubts. Besides, your question is in itself an answer. Each new love perforce excludes the previous one."

"Don't be too hasty in your judgment, father," said Consuelo with a sad smile. "I may love Albert differently from the *other one*, but I don't love him any less than I used to. Who knows if I don't love him more? For his sake I feel prepared to sacrifice this stranger, the thought of whom robs me of sleep and makes my heart pound even now as I'm speaking to you."

"Is it not pride in duty, eagerness for sacrifice more than affection that exhort you to this sort of preference for Albert?"

"I don't believe so."

"Are you quite sure? Bear in mind that here you are far from the world, safe from its judgments, outside all its laws. If we give you a new formula and new notions of duty, will you persist in preferring the happiness of the man you don't love to that of the man you do?"

"Have I ever said that I didn't love Albert?" Consuelo burst out.

"I can only answer your questions with other questions, daughter. Can one heart hold two loves at one and the same time?"

"Yes, two different loves. One loves at one and the same time a brother and a husband."

"But not a husband and a lover. The rights of a husband and a brother are indeed different. Those of a husband and a lover would be the same unless the husband were to agree to become a brother again. Then the law of marriage would be broken in its most mysterious, intimate, and sacred essence. That would be a divorce, minus the publicity. Tell me this, Consuelo. I am an old man on the edge of the grave, and you a child. I am here as your father, your confessor. I cannot alarm your sense of modesty with this delicate question, and I hope that you'll give me a courageous answer. In your enthusiastic affection for Albert, wasn't there always a secret, overwhelming terror at the idea of his caress?"

"That is true," said Consuelo blushing. "That idea wasn't ordinarily associated with that of his love, it seemed foreign to it, but when it cropped up, the chill of death would run through my veins."

"And the man you know as Liverani, hasn't his breath given you the fire of life?"

"That too is true. But mustn't we smother such instincts with our willpower?"

"For what reason? Did God instill them in you for nothing? Did he authorize you to forswear your sex, to pronounce in marriage the vow of virginity or the still more hideous and degrading vow of servitude? Slavery's passivity has something of the coldness, the brutishness of prostitution. Is it part of God's design that a being such as you should be so degraded? Woe to the children born of such unions! God inflicts on them some disgrace, a deficient, delirious, or stupid constitution. They bear the seal of disobedience; they aren't fully human, for they weren't conceived according to humanity's law of mutual desire, of shared aspirations between man and woman. Where there is no such reciprocity, there is no equality, and where equality is broken, there is no real union. So rest assured that God, far from imposing such sacrifices on your sex, rejects them and denies you the right to undertake them. Committing suicide in this way is as guilty and even more cowardly than giving up life. The vow of virginity is antihuman and antisocial, but sacrificing yourself without love is something similarly monstrous. Think it over, Consuelo, and if you persist in annihilating yourself to this point, consider the role that you would be reserving for your husband if he were to accept your submission without understanding it. Unless he were deceived, he would never accept it, that I need not tell you, but deluded by your spirit of sacrifice, intoxicated by your generosity, wouldn't he soon seem to you strangely egotistical or crass in his error? Wouldn't you be degrading him in his own eyes, degrading him in fact before God, by setting this trap for his simplicity, by giving him this nearly irresistible opportunity to fall into it? Where would be his grandeur, his sensitivity, if he failed to notice your pale lips and teary eyes? Do you really think that, despite yourself, hatred wouldn't enter your heart, along with shame and grief at not having been understood or divined? No, woman! You have no right to betray the love in your heart, you would instead have that of quashing it. No matter what cynical philosophers may have said about the passive condition of females in the natural order, what will always distinguish man's companion from that of an animal is discernment in love and the right to choose. Vanity and greed turn most marriages into *sworn prostitution*, as the ancient Lollards used to say. Self-sacrifice and generosity can lead a simple soul to the same result. I've had to instruct you, a virgin, in these delicate matters that your pure life and thoughts have prevented you from anticipating or analyzing. When a mother marries off her daughter, she half reveals to her, with more or less wisdom and decorum, the mysteries that she has kept hidden until then. You had no mother when you vowed, with an enthusiasm more fanatic than human, to belong to a man you didn't love completely. Today you've been given a mother to help and enlighten you in your new resolutions at the hour of divorce or the definitive sanction of this strange marriage. I am that mother, Consuelo, and I'm no man but a woman."

"You, a woman?" said Consuelo looking in surprise at the skinny, bluish hand, yet delicate and truly feminine that had taken hers during this speech.

"This little old man, gaunt and decrepit," said the problematic confessor, "this overburdened, suffering creature whose feeble voice no longer has a sex is a woman broken by pain, illness, and worry more than age. I am no more than sixty, Consuelo, even though in this habit, which I only wear for my functions as an *Invisible*, I look like a doddering octogenarian. For that matter, whether in woman's dress or this habit, I am nothing but a wreck underneath, yet I was once a tall, strong, beautiful woman of commanding presence. But by the age of thirty I was already bent over and trembling as you see me now. And do you know, child, the cause of that precocious collapse? This is the misfortune from which I want to save you. It was incomplete affection, an unhappy union, a horrifying labor of courage and resignation that kept me bound for ten years to a man I esteemed and respected without managing to love him. A man wouldn't have been able to tell you a woman's sacred rights and true duties in the domain of love. Men have made their laws and formed their ideas without consulting us, yet I have often enlightened the consciences of my fellow Invisibles in that respect, and they have had the courage and fair-mindedness to hear me out. But, believe me, I was sure that unless they put me in direct contact with you, they wouldn't find the key to your heart and might condemn you to eternal suffering, total degradation, all the while believing that they were assuring your happiness in the comfort of virtue. So open your whole soul to me now, tell me if this Liverani. . . ."

"Alas, this Liverani, I love him; it's only too true," said Consuelo lifting the mysterious sibyl's hand to her lips. "His presence alarms me even more than Albert's, but how different the alarm, and how mingled with strange delights! His arms draw me like a magnet, and with a kiss to my brow he takes me to another world where I live and breathe in some new way."

"Well then, Consuelo, you must love this man and forget the other one. I am pronouncing your divorce here and now, which is my duty and my right."

"Despite what you say, I cannot accept this verdict before I've seen Albert, before he's told me himself that he's giving me up without regret and releasing me from my vow without contempt."

"You don't know Albert yet, or you're afraid of him. I, however, know him. I have even more rights over than him than over you, and I can speak in his name. We are alone, Consuelo, and I've not been forbidden to open myself fully to you even though I'm part of the supreme council, whose members are never known to their closest disciples. Yet my situation and yours are exceptional, so take a good look at my withered face and tell me if it seems unknown to you."

With these words the sibyl whipped off her mask, beard, cap, and wig, and Consuelo saw the head of a woman who was indeed old and sick, but the lines of her face were incomparably beautiful and her expression sublimely kind, sad, and strong. These three habits of the soul, so different and so rarely conjoined in the same person, were apparent in the broad forehead, maternal smile, and deep gaze of the unfamiliar woman. The shape of her head and jaw demonstrated an innately strong constitution, but the ravages of pain were only too visible, and this beautiful head reminiscent of Niobe dying, or rather Mary collapsing at the foot of the cross, was nodding with a sort of nervous tremor. Gray hair, fine and smooth as virgin silk, parted over her broad forehead and neatly looped back at the temples, completed the noble peculiarity of these striking features. In those years all women wore their hair powdered, teased up, and drawn back, leaving exposed a bare, bold forehead. The sibyl had tied hers back to accommodate her disguise, never suspecting that this coiffure was the most harmonious with the form and expression of her face. Consuelo contemplated her for a long while with respect and admiration; then all of a sudden, struck with amazement, she grabbed the old woman's hands and exclaimed, "Oh! My God, how much you look like him!"

"Yes, I look like Albert, or rather Albert looks prodigiously like me," she replied. "But haven't you ever seen a portrait of me?" And seeing that Consuelo was trying to remember, she helped her out by adding, "A portrait that resembled me as much as art can resemble nature, of which I am nothing more than a shadow today; a grand portrait of a young, fresh, radiant woman with a gold brocade bodice laden with jeweled flowers, a crimson cloak, and locks of black hair escaping from knots of rubies and pearls and curling down over her shoulders. That's what I was wearing more than forty years ago, the day after my wedding. I was beautiful, but not for long; in my soul I was already dead."

"That portrait," said Consuelo turning pale, "is at the Castle of the Giants in Albert's old room. . . . It's the portrait of his mother whom he scarcely knew and yet adored . . . and he believed that he could see and hear her in his transports of ecstasy. So would you be a close relative of the noble Wanda z Prachalitz, and therefore. . . ."

"I am Wanda z Prachalitz herself," replied the sibyl, regaining some firmness of voice and bearing. "I am the mother of Albert and the widow of Christian von Rudolstadt; I am the descendant of Jan Zizka of the Chalice and the mother-in-law of Consuelo, but now I only wish to be her friend and adoptive mother because Consuelo doesn't love Albert and Albert's happiness mustn't come at the price of his companion's."

"His mother! You, his mother!" exclaimed Consuelo trembling and falling to Wanda's knees. "Are you a ghost then? Wasn't your death mourned at the Castle of the Giants?"

"Twenty-seven years ago," replied the sibyl, "Wanda z Prachalitz, Countess von Rudolstadt, was buried at the Castle of the Giants, in the same chapel and under the same slab where Albert von Rudolstadt, who suffered from the same malady and was subject to the same attacks of catalepsy, was buried last year, a victim of the same error. The son never would have risen from that horrible tomb if the mother, attentive to the danger looming over him, hadn't kept an invisible vigil by his deathbed and anxiously watched over his interment. It's his mother who saved a being still full of strength and life from the worms of the sepulcher to which he had been already abandoned; his mother who wrested him from the yoke of the world where he had lived only too long, where he couldn't live any longer, to transport him into this mysterious realm, this impenetrable asylum where she herself had recovered, if not the health of the body, at least the life of the soul. It's a strange story, Consuelo, and you have to know it to understand Albert's story, his sad life, so-called death, and miraculous resurrection. The Invisibles won't start your initiation until midnight. So lend me your ears, and may the emotions of this bizarre tale brace you for those yet to come."

Chapter XXXIII

"Rich, beautiful, and of illustrious birth, I was married at the age of twenty to Count Christian, who was already over forty. He could have been my father, and I felt affection and respect for him, but no love. I had been reared in ignorance of the place that love might have in a woman's life. My parents, stern Lutherans but forced to practice their religion as discreetly as possible, were in their habits and ideas excessively rigid and resolute. Their hatred of foreigners, their inner revolt against the religious and political yoke of Austria, their fanatical attachment to the old freedoms of the fatherland were passed on to me, and these passions were sufficient to my proud youth. I had no idea there could be others, and my mother, who had never known anything but duty, would have thought it a crime to let me have any inkling of such things. For a long time Emperor Charles, Maria Theresa's father, persecuted my family for heresy and put a price on our wealth, our liberty, and nearly our lives. I could redeem my parents by marrying a Catholic aristocrat devoted to the empire, and I offered myself up with a sort of enthusiastic pride. Among those who were pointed out to me, I chose Count Christian because his character, sweet, conciliatory, and even weak in appearance, gave me hope of secretly converting him to my family's politics. My parents accepted and blessed my sacrifice. I thought that virtue would make me happy, but unhappiness, its measure fathomed, its injustice known and felt, is not a milieu where the soul can easily flourish. I soon recognized that under his calm, wise, and kindly demeanor Christian was hiding invincible obstinacy, opinionated attachment to the customs of his caste and prejudices of his entourage, a sort of pitiful hatred and pained contempt for any notion of opposition or resistance to the established order. His sister Wenceslawa, tender, vigilant, and generous, but even more riveted to the niceties of piety and the pride of rank, was bittersweet company for me: tender yet overwhelming tyranny, devoted affection that was extremely exasperating. I suffered mortally from having no emotional and intellectual sympathies with these people, despite my feelings for them; living in their midst was killing me; breathing their air was slowly withering me away. You know the story of Albert's youth, his bridled enthusiasms, his misunderstood religion, his evangelical notions taxed as heresy and madness. My life was a prelude to his, and in the Rudolstadt family you must have heard occasional gasps of horror and pain about the ominous resemblance between mother and son, inside and out.

"I suffered most from the absence of love, and from there sprang all my other afflictions. I was very fond of Christian, but nothing in him could inspire any enthusiasm in me, and I would have required enthusiastic feeling to compress the deep divide between our ways of thinking. My stern religious upbringing did not allow me to separate reason from love. I was eating myself alive. My health began to deteriorate; an extraordinary excitement took hold of my nervous system, I had hallucinations, spells of ecstasy that they called madness and carefully concealed instead of trying to cure them. Yet they tried to keep me entertained and take me out in society, as if balls, performances, and galas could have taken the place of sympathy, love, and trust in my life. I became so ill in Vienna that they brought me back to the Castle of the Giants. I still preferred this dismal place, the chaplain's exorcisms, and the canoness's cruel affection to the court of our tyrants.

"My five children dying one after the other were the final blows. It seemed to me that God had cursed my marriage; I energetically desired death. I hoped for nothing more in life. I did my best not to love Albert, my last born, convinced that he was doomed like the others and that I could do nothing to save him.

"One last misfortune brought my exasperation to a climax. I loved, I was loved, and the austerity of my principles forced me not even to acknowledge within my own heart this tremendous emotion. The doctor who treated me during my frequent and painful crises looked less young and handsome than Christian. So it was not the charms of his person that moved me, but the deep sympathy of our souls, the correspondence of our ideas or at least our religious and philosophical instincts, an incredible affinity between our temperaments. Marcus, I can refer to him only by this name, had the same energy, active mind, and patriotic feeling as I did. The words that Shakespeare put into Brutus' mouth fit him as well as me: "I am not one to bear injustice with a serene countenance." The misery and degradation of the poor, serfdom, despotic laws, and their monstrous abuses, all the ungodly rights of conquest made him rage with indignation. Oh, what torrents of tears we both shed over the wretched plight of our homeland, of the whole human race, everywhere enslaved or deceived! Here besotted by ignorance, there decimated by rapacity and greed, elsewhere raped and demeaned by the ravages of war, debased and hapless all over the face of the earth. Yet Marcus, more educated than I, was concocting a remedy to so many ills and often told me about strange and mysterious projects for organizing a universal conspiracy against despotism and intolerance. I listened to his plans as though to romantic dreams. I had no more hope; I was too sick and broken to believe in the future. He loved me ardently; I saw it, I felt it, I shared his passion, and yet, during five years of apparent friendship and chaste intimacy, we never revealed to each other the fateful secret that united us. He didn't ordinarily live in the Bohemian Forest; at least he was often away, ostensibly to treat distant patients and actually to coordinate the conspiracy he was always talking about without convincing me of its results. Each time I saw him again, I felt myself more inflamed by his genius, courage, and perseverance. Each time he returned, he found me weaker, more consumed by an inner fire, more devastated by physical suffering.

"During one of his trips I had horrible convulsions that the ignorant and vain Doctor Wetzelius, whom you know, who treated me in his absence, called *malignant fever*. Afterward I fell into a total prostration that they took for death. I had no pulse; my breathing was imperceptible. Yet I was fully conscious; I heard the chaplain praying and my family weeping. I heard the heartrending cries of my only child, my poor Albert, and I couldn't make a single movement; I couldn't even see him. They had closed my eyes, and it was impossible for me to open them again. I wondered if this was death and if the soul, no longer able to animate the dead body, still experienced the pain of living and the horror of the grave. I heard terrible things being said around my deathbed; the chaplain, trying to calm the canoness's keen and sincere sorrow, told her that we should thank God for all things and that it was a great blessing for my husband to be delivered from the anguish of my long suffering and the storms of my reprobate soul. Though his words were not so harsh, they amounted to the same thing, and the canoness listened to him and little by little came around to his point of view. Then I even heard him trying to console Christian with the same arguments, expressed in still milder fashion, yet just as cruel for me. I was hearing clearly and understanding in exquisite pain. It was, they thought, God's will that I not rear my son and that he at his tender age be protected from the poison of heresy with which I was infected. That's what they said to my husband when he pressed Albert to his breast and exclaimed, "Poor child, what will become of you without your mother?" The chaplain replied, "You'll raise him up in the ways of God."

"Finally, after three days of motionless, mute despair I was buried without having recovered the ability to move, without having lost for one instant the certainty of the horrible death they were going to inflict on me! They covered me in diamonds, dressed me in the magnificent array I wore for my engagement in the portrait you saw. They placed a crown of flowers on my head, a gold crucifix on my breast and laid me in a long hollow of white marble cut into the crypt of the chapel. I felt neither the cold nor the lack of air; I was alive in mind only.

"Marcus arrived an hour later, so distraught at first that he couldn't think. He lay down over my tomb like an automaton; they tore him off; he came back in the night, this time with a hammer and crowbar. A sinister thought had crossed his mind. He knew my attacks of catalepsy; he had never seen them so long, so total; still, from having observed that bizarre condition for a few instants, he concluded that there might have been a dreadful error. He had no trust in Wetzelius as a doctor. I heard his steps overhead and recognized them. The sound of the iron bar raising the slab made me shudder, but I couldn't utter a cry, a moan. When he lifted the veil over my face, I was so exhausted from all the exertions I had just made to call out to him that I seemed deader than ever. He hesitated a long while; a thousand times he checked my arrested breathing, my heart, my icy hands. I was stiff as a cadaver. I heard his heartrending murmur, "So it's all over! There's no more hope! Dead, she's dead! Oh, Wanda!" He let the veil fall back but didn't replace the slab. There was once again a horrifying silence. Had he fainted? Was he too abandoning me, so horrified by the view of the woman he had once loved that he had forgotten to close my sepulcher?

"Marcus, sunk in somber meditation, was devising a plan as lugubrious as his grief, as strange as his nature. He wanted to steal my body from the ravages of destruction, secretly make off with it, embalm it, seal it in a metal casket, and keep it always at his side. He was wondering if he had the courage when all of a sudden, in a sort of frenzy, he told himself that he would indeed. He took me in his arms and, without knowing if he had the strength to carry a cadaver all the way home, more than a league away, he put me down on the stone floor and replaced the slab with the dreadful composure that one often has in acts of delirium. Then he wrapped me up in his cloak so that I was completely hidden and left the castle, which wasn't locked up with the same care as nowadays, given that gangs of malefactors, driven to despair by war, hadn't yet appeared in those parts. I had become so thin that I truly wasn't much of a burden. Marcus went through the woods, taking the most desolate trails. Several times he laid me down on the rocks, overcome with grief and terror even more than weariness. He has since told me that more than once he felt horrified to have stolen a dead body and was tempted to return me to my tomb. At last he arrived home, crept silently into the garden and, without anybody seeing, carried me to an isolated lodge he had turned into a study. Only there did the joy of my rescue, the first impulse of joy I had felt in ten years, loose my tongue and let me utter a faint cry.

"A violent paroxysm followed this prostration. Suddenly I was endowed with tremendous strength; I screamed and roared. Marcus's housekeeper and gardener came running, thinking he was being murdered. He had the presence of mind to head them off, saying that a lady had come to deliver a baby in secret and that he would kill whoever tried to see her and fire anybody who dared say a word. The ploy succeeded. I was dangerously ill in the lodge for three days. Marcus, shut away with me, ministered to me with a zeal and intelligence worthy of his willpower. When I was out of danger and could collect my thoughts, I threw myself into his arms, terrified at the thought that we would have to part.

"'Oh Marcus!' I cried, 'why didn't you let me die here, in your arms! If you love me, kill me; going back to my family is for me worse than death.'"

"'Madame,' was his firm reply, "you'll never go back there, that's a vow I've made to God and to myself. Now you're mine alone. You won't leave my side ever again, or you'll only get out of here over my dead body.'"

"This dreadful resolution horrified and charmed me all at once. I was too confused and weak to appreciate what it involved. I listened to him with the timid, trusting submission of a child and let myself be nursed back to health. Little by little I grew used to the idea of never returning to Riesenburg, never dispelling the notion that I had died. Marcus deployed impassioned rhetoric to convince me. He told me that I couldn't survive in that marriage and that I had no right to go back to a certain death. He swore that he could keep me out of the public eye for a long time and make me invisible my whole life long to those who knew me. He promised to look after my son and arrange for me to see him in secret. He even gave me sure guarantees of these strange possibilities, and I let myself be persuaded. I agreed to leave with him and never to go back to being Countess von Rudolstadt.

"But just as we were about to depart, in the middle of the night, Marcus was summoned to attend Albert, who was said to be dangerously ill. A mother's tender love, which hardship seemed to have smothered, reawakened in my breast. I wanted to go with Marcus to Riesenburg; no human power, not even his, could have deterred me. I climbed into his carriage and, enveloped in a long veil, waited anxiously at some remove from the castle for him to see my son and bring me news of him. Indeed he soon returned, assured me that the child was not in danger, and wanted to take me back to his place so that he could spend the night with Albert. I couldn't make up my mind to do it. I wanted to go on waiting, hidden behind the castle's dark walls, quivering with anxiety, while he went back to tend to my son. The moment I found myself alone, a thousand worries set upon my heart. I imagined that Marcus was hiding from me the truth about Albert, that he was perhaps at death's door, that he was going to die without my last kiss. Overcome by this fateful notion, I dashed under the portico of the castle; a footman that I encountered in the courtyard dropped his torch and fled, making the sign of the cross. My face was veiled, but any woman appearing in the middle of the night was enough to arouse the superstitions of these credulous servants. There was no doubt that I was the ghost of the unhappy, ungodly Countess Wanda. By an unexpected stroke of luck I found my way to my son's room without running into anyone else and arrived just when the canoness had stepped out to fetch some medicine prescribed by Marcus. My husband, as usual, was off praying in his private chapel rather than doing anything to help matters. I ran to my son and pressed him to my bosom. He wasn't at all afraid of me and hugged me in return; he hadn't understood that I had died. Just then the chaplain appeared at the door. Marcus thought that all was lost. Yet, with a rare presence of mind, he didn't move and made as if I weren't there beside him. Before the chaplain dared take a step in my direction, he choked out a few words of exorcism and fell down in a faint. At that point I resigned myself to escaping by another door and made my way in the dark back to where Marcus had left me. I was reassured, I had seen that Albert was better, his little hands were warm, and his cheeks were no longer flushed with fever. The chaplain's faint and fright were attributed to a vision. He claimed that he had seen me next to Marcus, holding my son in my arms. Marcus claimed that he hadn't seen a single thing. Albert had fallen asleep. But the next day he asked for me again, and the following nights, convinced that I hadn't gone to sleep forever as they tried to tell him, he dreamed of me, thought he saw me again and called out for me several times. From then on the child was kept under close watch, and the superstitious souls of Riesenburg prayed and prayed to ward off the baleful attentions of my ghost around his cradle.

"Marcus took me back to his place before dawn. We postponed our departure by another week, and when my son was fully recovered, we left Bohemia. Since then I've led an itinerant, mysterious life. Always hidden away in my lodgings, always veiled while traveling, using an assumed name and for a long time having no other confidant in the world but Marcus, I spent several years abroad with him. He maintained a close correspondence with a friend who kept him up on everything at Riesenburg, including ample details about the health, character, and upbringing of my son. My deplorable state of health allowed me to lead a most secluded life and see no one at all. I passed for Marcus's sister and lived for several years down in Italy, in an isolated villa, while Marcus, for a part of each year, went on traveling and pursuing his vast projects.

"I was not Marcus's mistress; I had remained under the sway of my religious scruples, and it took me more than ten years of meditation to understand that human beings have the right to throw off the yoke of society's merciless, mindless laws. Given that I was thought dead and had no wish to jeopardize the liberty I had conquered at such a cost, I couldn't invoke any religious or civil authority to end my marriage to Christian, nor would I have wanted to reopen old wounds for him. He didn't know how miserable I'd been with him; he thought that I had gone down to the repose of the grave for my own happiness, his family's peace and my son's salvation. In such circumstances I saw myself eternally condemned to remain faithful to him. Later on, when the disciples of a new faith had come together and secretly constituted themselves as a religious authority through the good offices of Marcus, when I had changed my ideas enough to accept this new council and join the new Church that could have pronounced my divorce and sanctified our union, it was too late. Marcus, weary of my being so stubborn, had felt the need to find love elsewhere, and I had heroically urged him on. He was married; I was his wife's friend; yet he wasn't happy. Her mind and heart weren't big enough to satisfy the mind and heart of a man of his sort. His projects were beyond her; he took care not to let her in on his accomplishments. She died a few years later without having divined that Marcus still loved me. I took care of her while she was dying and closed her eyes without having to reproach myself for a single thing in her regard, without rejoicing at the disappearance of this obstacle to my long, cruel passion. Youth had fled; I was broken; my life had been too serious and too austere for me to do things differently now that my hair was turning gray. I entered at last into the calm of old age and deeply felt all that is august and sacred in that phase of our lives as women. Yes, there is something more serious about our old age than that of men, about our whole lives as well, when we have a good understanding of them. Men can beguile the march of time; they can still make love and have children later than we can. For us women, nature instead marks a term after which there is something monstrous and ungodly about wanting to reawaken love and encroach with ridiculous delirium upon the splendid privileges of the next generation that has already come forth and cast a shadow over us. Plus, the lessons and examples they expect from us in this solemn moment require a quiet life of contemplation that would be fruitlessly troubled by the commotion of love. Youth can be inspired by its own fervor and find lofty revelations there. Ripe old age only relates to God in the august serenity that comes as a final blessing. God himself offers gentle help and by an imperceptible transformation starts us down that path. He takes care to soothe our passions and turn them into peaceable affections; he rids us of the charms of beauty, thereby removing dangerous temptations. So there is nothing easier than growing old, no matter what is said and thought by all the insane women who bustle about the world, having fallen prey to a sort of stubborn rage to hide from others as well as themselves the decay of their charms and the end of their mission as women. What! Age unsexes us, releases us from the awful labors of maternity, and we would fail to see that this is the moment to raise ourselves up to a sort of angelic state? But, dear daughter, you are so far away from this term, frightening and yet desirable like a port after a storm, that all my reflections on this subject are untimely. Therefore, may they merely help you understand my story. I remained what I had always been, a sister to Marcus, and these bridled emotions, these vanquished desires that had tortured our youth gave to our mature friendship at least qualities of strength and enthusiastic trust not found in ordinary friendships.

"I've still said nothing about the mental labors and serious undertakings that for the first fifteen years prevented us from being engrossed by our sufferings and since then from regretting them. You know the nature of our work, its purposes and results; you were initiated into this last night; you'll be more fully so this evening by the Invisibles. I can only tell you that Marcus sits among them and that he himself set up their secret council and organized their entire society with the help of a virtuous prince who has devoted the sum total of his fortune to this mysterious and grandiose enterprise. It has been my whole life as well for the last fifteen years. After twelve years away I was, on the one hand, too much forgotten and, on the other, too much changed not to be able to reappear in Germany. Besides, the strange life that befits certain functions of our order favored my incognito. Charged not with active propaganda, which is the reserve of your glamorous life, but with secret missions that my prudence could carry out, I made a few trips I'll tell you about a while later. And since then I've lived here altogether hidden away, ostensibly fulfilling the lowly functions of a governess in the prince's household, but in fact seriously engaged only with the secret work, keeping up a vast correspondence in the name of the council with all the important members, serving as their host here and often presiding over their conferences alone with Marcus when the prince and the other supreme heads were away, finally exercising at every moment a rather marked influence on those decisions of theirs that seemed to call for the subtle views and particular discernment of a woman's mind. Aside from the philosophical questions debated and weighed here, and from which the maturity of my intellect has earned me the right not to be excluded, there are often matters of feeling to be argued and adjudicated. You can well imagine that in our work outside we are often helped or hampered by individual passions, love, hatred, jealousy. By the intermediary of my son and even in person, presenting myself as a sorceress or soothsayer, both disguises being very fashionable among the ladies at court, I've frequently been in touch with Princess Amalia of Prussia, with the interesting and unfortunate Princess von Kulmbach, finally with the young Margravine von Bayreuth, Frederick's sister. We had to conquer their hearts even more than their minds. I labored nobly, I dare say, to win them over, and I've succeeded. But that's not the facet of my life I want to share with you. In your future undertakings you'll find my tracks and carry on what I began. I want to talk to you about Albert and tell you a whole side of his life that you know nothing about. We still have the time. Listen a bit longer. You'll understand how I finally came to know, in this dreadful and bizarre life I've made for myself, tender feelings and maternal joys."

Chapter XXXIV

"Thoroughly informed by Marcus about everything going on at the Castle of the Giants, I had no sooner learned of their resolution to send Albert on a journey and the direction in which he was to go than I hastened to place myself along his way. At the time I myself was traveling, often with Marcus, as I mentioned a short while ago. The tutor and servants assigned to Albert had not known me, so I had no fear of their seeing me. I was so impatient to set eyes on my son that it was hard to make myself stay a few hours behind him on the road to Venice, which was his first destination. Yet I had resolved to reveal myself to him only with some sort of mysterious solemnity, for it was not merely a mother's ardent instinct pushing me into his arms; I had a more serious design, an even more motherly duty to fulfill; I wanted to extricate Albert from the narrow-minded superstitions in which they had tried to snare him. I would have to take hold of his imagination, his trust, his mind, and his entire soul. I believed him to be an ardent Catholic, and on the face of things he then was. He regularly observed all the public rites of the Roman church. The people who had given Marcus these details didn't know what Albert thought and felt deep down, and his father and aunt scarcely knew any better. They found nothing to reproach him aside from a fierce rigorism, a way of interpreting the Gospels that was too naïve and too fervent. They didn't understand that in his rigid logic and candid simplicity my noble child, with his stubborn determination to practice true Christianity, was already a passionate, incorrigible heretic. I was a bit alarmed by the Jesuit tutor attached to him; I feared not being able to get near him without being seen and thwarted by a fanatical Argus. But I soon learned that the unworthy Abbé *** didn't even look after my son's health and that Albert, neglected as well by his servants to whom he loathed giving orders, lived quite a solitary life and was left to his own devices in all the cities he visited. I anxiously observed all his movements. Staying at the same hotel in Venice, I ran across him alone at last, musing in the stairs and loggias, on the quais. Oh, you can just guess how my heart pounded at the sight of him, what a stir there was deep inside me, and what torrents of tears flowed from my bewildered, delighted eyes! Here was the sole object on the face of the earth I was allowed to love, and he looked so handsome, so noble and, alas, so sad! I followed him cautiously. Night was falling. He went into the Chiesa dei SS Giovanni e Paolo, an austere basilica full of tombs that you no doubt know well. Albert knelt down in a corner; I slipped in with him and hid behind a tomb. The church was deserted; it was getting darker and darker with every passing second. Albert was still as a statue. Yet he seemed absorbed in reverie rather than prayer. The sanctuary lamp threw a faint light on his face. He was so pale that it frightened me! His fixed gaze and half-open lips, something desperate in his posture and physiognomy broke my heart; I was trembling like the flickering light of the lamp. If I were to reveal myself to him just then, I felt he would faint dead away. I recalled everything that Marcus had told me about his nervous susceptibility and how dangerous sudden emotions were for such an impressionable nature. So as not to surrender to my impetuous love, I left and went to wait for him under the portico. Over my dress which was in any case very simple and dark I had thrown a brown cloak with a hood that hid my face and made me look like a humble Venetian woman. When he came out, I involuntarily took a step toward him; he stopped and, thinking me a beggar, randomly took a gold coin from his pocket and offered it to me. Oh, with what pride and gratitude I received these alms! Look, Consuelo, a Venetian sequin; I had a hole bored through it for a chain, and I always wear it over my heart like a precious jewel, a relic. Since that day I've never taken it off, this token sanctified by the hand of my child. I lost control of my feelings, seized that beloved hand, and drew it to my lips. With a sort of terror he pulled it back, bathed with my tears.

"'What are you doing, woman?' he asked in a voice whose pure and resonant timbre reverberated down into my bones. 'Why are you giving me such a blessing for so meager a gift? You must be in great misery, and I've given you too little. What do you need to put an end to your suffering? Speak. I want to console you, and I hope that I am able.'

"And he gathered all his gold in his hands, without giving it so much as a glance.

"'You've given me enough, kind lad,' I replied. 'I'm content.'

"'But why the tears?' he asked, struck by the sobs choking me. 'Do you have some sorrow that my riches cannot remedy?'

"'No, I'm weeping tears of tenderness and joy.'

"'Joy! So there are tears of joy? And all for a piece of gold? Oh, wretched mankind! Take all the rest, woman, I beg you, but don't weep for joy. Give a thought to all your brothers in poverty, so many, so demeaned, so miserable, and why can't I help them all?"

"He went away with a sigh. I dared not follow for fear of betraying myself. He had left his gold on the pavement, having offered it to me with a sort of haste to be rid of it. I gathered it up and put it into the alms box to satisfy my son's noble charity. The next day I once more kept an eye out for him and saw him go into San Marco; I had resolved to be stronger and more controlled, and I was. We were alone again, in the semidarkness of the church. As before, he mused a long while, then all of a sudden I heard him get up and mutter in a deep voice, "O Christ, they crucify you every day of their lives!"

"'Yes!' I replied, half reading his thoughts, 'the Pharisees and the Doctors of the Law!'

"He shuddered, was silent for a moment, then said in a low voice without turning around, without trying to see who was talking to him like this, 'My mother's voice again!'

"Consuelo, I nearly fainted when I heard Albert invoking my memory, keeping alive in his heart the instinct of this filial divination. Yet the fear of unsettling his mind, already at such a feverish pitch, stopped me again; I once more waited for him under the portico, and when he went by, I didn't approach, satisfied to have seen him. But he caught sight of me and drew back in horror.

"'Signora,' he said after a moment's hesitation, 'why are you begging today? Is it indeed a profession, as say the merciless rich? Don't you have any family? Can't you make yourself useful to someone, instead of wandering around churches at night like some kind of ghost? Wasn't what I gave you yesterday enough to keep you out of want today? Do you mean to hoard your brothers' share?'

"'I'm not begging," I replied. 'I put your gold into the alms box except for a sequin I intend to keep out of love of you.'

"'So who are you?' he exclaimed, seizing my arm. 'Your voice stirs me to the very depths of my soul. I have a feeling I know you. Show me your face! . . . No, don't! I don't want to see it, you frighten me.'

"'Oh, Albert!' I was beside myself. Throwing caution to the winds, I blurted out, 'So you too, you're afraid of me!'

"He shuddered from head to toe and murmured again with a look of terror and religious awe, 'Yes, that's her voice, my mother's voice!'

"'I don't know who your mother is,' I said, alarmed by my recklessness. 'I only know your name because it's already known among the poor. Why are you afraid of me? Is your mother dead?'

"'That's what they say,' he replied, 'but my mother's not dead for me.'

"'So where does she live?'

"'In my heart, in my thoughts, ceaselessly, eternally. I've dreamed of her voice, her face a hundred, a thousand times.'

"I was as much frightened as charmed by that imperious expansiveness that was drawing him to me. But I noted that he was showing signs of frenzy and subdued my emotions to calm him down.

"'Albert,' I said, 'I knew your mother; I was her friend. She charged me to talk to you about her one day when you were old enough to understand what I've got to say. I am not what I seem. I followed you yesterday and today only to have a word with you. So listen to me quietly and don't let idle superstitions upset you. Will you come talk with me under the arcades of the Procuratie, deserted at this hour? Do you feel calm and collected enough to do this?'

"'You, my mother's friend!' he exclaimed. 'She charged you to talk to me about her? Oh, yes, talk, talk indeed; you see, I wasn't wrong, I was hearing an inner voice! I had a feeling there was something of her in you. No, I'm not superstitious, not mad; only my heart is more alive and open than many others to certain things that other people don't understand and feel. You'll understand that if you understood my mother. So tell me about her; talk to me again with her voice, her spirit.'

"Having managed, though imperfectly, to rechannel his emotion, I led him under the arcades and began asking about his childhood, his memories, the principles he had been taught, his notion of his mother's principles and ideas. My questions made it clear that I knew his family's secrets and could understand those of his heart. Oh, my daughter, what enthusiastic pride I felt seeing Albert's ardent love for me, his faith in my piety and virtue, his horror of the superstitious aversion that my memory evoked in the Catholics of Riesenburg; the purity of his soul, the grandeur of his religious and patriotic feeling, finally, all these sublime instincts that a Catholic upbringing had not been able to smother in him! Yet, at the same time, what deep sorrow when I saw the precocious, incurable sadness of this young soul and the battles that were already breaking it, just as they had done their best to break mine! Albert still thought he was a Catholic. He dared not openly revolt against the decrees of the Church. He needed to believe in an established religion. Already educated and meditative beyond his years (he was scarcely twenty), he had thought a great deal about the long, gloomy history of heresy and could not bring himself to condemn certain doctrines of ours. Forced nonetheless to believe that the innovators were wrong, their errors so exaggerated and envenomed by the church historians, he was floating in a sea of uncertainties, sometimes condemning revolt, sometimes cursing tyranny and unable to come to any conclusion, aside from thinking that men of virtue had gone astray in their attempts at reform and that men of blood had defiled the sanctuary meaning to defend it.

"So it was necessary to illuminate his mind, to make allowances for the faults and excesses of both camps, to teach him to defend courageously the cause of the innovators while deploring their inevitable rages, to exhort him to turn his back on the party of cunning, violence, and subjection while acknowledging the excellence of a certain mission in a more distant past. I had no trouble enlightening him. He had already foreseen, already divined, already concluded before I had finished proving. His admirable instincts responded to my inspiration, but when he had understood it all, pain more overwhelming than uncertainty took hold of his despondent soul. Nowhere on earth was truth recognized! In no sanctuary was the law of God alive any longer! No people, no caste, no school was practicing Christian virtue or striving to clarify and develop it! Catholics and Protestants had abandoned the ways of God! Everywhere might prevailed over right, everywhere the weak were chained and demeaned; every day Christ was crucified on all the altars raised by men! This bitter, searching conversation went on the whole night long. The clocks slowly tolled the hours without Albert giving them a thought. I was frightened by the intensity of his intellect, which let me sense in him such a taste for struggle and such a capacity for pain. I admired the male pride and heartbreaking expression of my noble, unhappy child; I altogether recognized myself in him; I felt that I was reading my past life and starting all over again with him the story of the long torments of my heart and brain; by the light of the moon I contemplated on his broad brow the idle physical and moral beauty of my lonely, misunderstood youth; I wept for both of us at one and the same time, and these complaints were long and heartrending. I dared not reveal to him the secrets of our conspiracy; I was afraid he might not understand them right away and, in his pain, reject them as futile, dangerous efforts. Worried that he had been up walking and talking for such a long time, I pledged to give him a glimpse of a safe haven if he would only wait and prepare himself for some austere secrets; I gently stirred his imagination in anticipation of a new revelation and brought him back to the hotel where we were both staying, promising another conversation several days later so as not to overstimulate his faculties.

"Only when we were about to go our separate ways did he think to ask who I was.

"'That I cannot tell you,' I said. 'I am using an assumed name; I have reasons for hiding; don't say a word about me to anyone.'

"He didn't ever ask me any other questions and seemed content with my reply, but his delicate reserve was accompanied by another sentiment as strange as his nature and somber as his usual frame of mind. Long afterwards he told me that from then on he always took me for his mother's soul, appearing to him in the flesh and in circumstances explicable for ordinary people, but in fact supernatural. Thus, despite me, my dear Albert doggedly went on identifying me as his mother. He preferred inventing a realm of fantasy rather than doubting my presence, and try as I might, I couldn't deceive his heart's victorious instinct. All my efforts to keep his excitement in check only served to maintain him in a sort of calm, contained delirium that had neither naysayer nor confidant, not even I who was its object. He religiously submitted to the will of the ghost who forbade him to identify or name her, but he stubbornly believed himself in a ghost's power.

"From that terrifying equanimity that Albert subsequently carried over into the aberrations of his imagination and the somber, stoic courage that always made him face without blanching the phantoms generated by his brain, there ensued a long and fateful error on my part. I was unaware of his bizarre way of accounting for my reappearance on earth. I thought he took me for a mysterious friend of his dead mother and childhood self. True, I was amazed by his slight curiosity about me and the small wonder that my constant attentions caused him, but this blind respect and delicate submission, this absence of worry regarding all of life's realities seemed so consonant with his absorbed, dreamy, and contemplative nature that I didn't try hard enough to understand them and fathom their secret causes. So by working to fortify his reason against his excessive enthusiasm, I unwittingly helped develop in him that sort of madness, both sublime and deplorable, of which he has been so long the toy and the victim.

"Little by little, in a series of conversations without confidants or witnesses, I expounded the doctrines of which our order has made itself the repository and secret propagator. I initiated him into our project for universal regeneration. In Rome, in the subterranean chambers set aside for our mysteries, Marcus introduced Albert and had him received into the first degrees of Freemasonry, while reserving the right to reveal to him ahead of time the symbols hidden in the vague, bizarre forms whose many interpretations lend themselves so well to the measure of the disciples' intelligence and courage. For seven years I followed my son on all his travels, always departing and arriving one day later. I always made a point to find lodgings at a certain distance from his and never to be seen by his tutor or attendants. As I recommended, he took care to change his servants often and to remain aloof from them. Every now and then I asked if he wasn't surprised to see me everywhere.

"'Not at all!' he replied. 'I know you'll follow me wherever I go.'"

"And when I asked him to explain why he felt so sure about that, he said, 'My mother charged you to give me life, and you know I'd die if you were to abandon me now.'

"His words were always fervent, as though inspired. I grew used to seeing him like that and unknowingly became so myself while talking with him. Marcus often reproached me, as I myself did, for feeding in this way the inner flame that was devouring Albert. Marcus would have wanted to enlighten him by more positive lessons and cooler reasoning. Yet at other moments I reassured myself thinking that, without the sustenance I was giving him, that flame would have consumed him more quickly and cruelly. My other children had shown a similar inclination to enthusiasm. People had compressed their souls, trying to extinguish them like torches deemed to be burning too bright, and they had succumbed before they had the strength to resist. Without my breath constantly reviving the sacred spark in free, pure air, Albert's soul might have gone to join those of his brothers, just as without Marcus's breath I would have died before I had lived. I also strove to give his mind frequent diversions from his eternal aspiration to the realm of ideas. I advised him, I required him to study the real world; he was sweet and conscientious about obeying me. He studied the natural sciences, the languages of the various countries where he was traveling; he read enormously; he even cultivated the arts and took up music on his own. All this was just a game, a pastime for his great, lively intellect. A stranger to all the intoxications of youth, a born enemy of the world and its vanities, he lived everywhere in deep retreat, and stubbornly resisting his tutor's advice, he refused to set foot in any salon, to be introduced at any court. He scarcely saw, in two or three capitals, his father's oldest and most serious friends. In their presence he put on a solemn, reserved face that gave them no opportunity to criticize him, and he was open and expansive only with a few disciples of our order to whom Marcus particularly recommended him. He begged us, moreover, not to require him to do any proselytizing until he felt that he had developed a gift for persuasion, and he often frankly told me that he didn't have it because he still didn't have enough faith in the excellence of our methods. He let himself be promoted to higher and higher degrees like a docile student, but examining everything with severe logic and scrupulous honesty, he always reserved the right, he said, to suggest reforms and improvements when he felt sufficiently enlightened to dare give rein to his personal inspiration. Until then he wanted to remain humble, patient, and obedient to the prescribed forms of our secret society. Immersed in study and meditation, he held his tutor in check with his serious nature and chilly demeanor. Thus, the abbé came to consider him a dreary pedant and kept his distance as much as possible, busying himself exclusively with the intrigues of his order. Albert even had rather long stays in France and England without the abbé, who was often a hundred leagues away and only met with Albert when he felt like a change of scenery; even then they often did not travel together. Then I was entirely free to see my son, and his exclusive affection repaid me a hundred times over for the care I gave him. My health had improved. It sometimes happens that seriously impaired constitutions grow used to their afflictions and stop suffering, which was the case with me; I almost didn't notice mine any longer. Fatigue, late nights, long talks, and arduous journeys, instead of finishing me off, kept me in a chronic low fever that became and has remained my normal state. Frail and quaky as you see, I can endure any toil or exhaustion better than you, a lovely spring flower. Ferment has become my element, and there I take my rest, forever on the move like those career couriers who have learned to sleep at a gallop.

"This experiment in what an energetic soul can endure and accomplish in a sickly body has made more confident in Albert's strength. I've grown used to seeing him like me sometimes flagging and broken, lively and feverish at other moments. We've often suffered together the same bodily pains resulting from the same keen emotions; and perhaps our closeness has never been sweeter and more tender than in those times of trial with the same fever burning in our veins and the same prostration making our feeble sighs indistinguishable. How many times did it seem to us that we were the same being! How many times did we break the silence into which the same reverie had sunk us only to say the same words to each other! How many times, finally, one of us ebullient and the other one broken, have we exchanged by a squeeze of the hand that languor and that energy! What good things and bad we've experienced together! O my son! My only passion! Flesh of my flesh, bone of my bone! What storms we've traversed, protected by the same heavenly shield! How much devastation we've withstood, holding each other tight and uttering the same words of salvation: love, truth, justice!

"We were in Poland on the border with Turkey, and Albert, having gone through all the subsequent Masonic initiations and superior ranks that are the last link between that preparatory society and our own, was headed for that part of Germany where we are now in order to be admitted to the sacred banquet of the Invisibles. Just then Count Christian von Rudolstadt called him back home. I was thunderstruck. As for Albert, despite all my care to keep him from forgetting his family, he no longer loved them except as a tender memory out of the past; he no longer understood how he could live with them. Yet it did not occur to us to resist that command formulated with the cold dignity and confident paternal authority of the Catholic, patrician families in our country. Albert prepared to leave me, not knowing for how long we would be separated, but trusting that he would soon see me again and pull together with Marcus the association that needed him. Albert had little notion of time and even less the ability to appreciate the material contingencies of life.

"'Are we parting?' he asked, seeing me weep despite myself. 'That cannot be. Every time I've called out to you from the depths of my heart, you've appeared. I'll call out to you once again.'

"'Albert, Albert!' I replied, 'I can't follow you to where you're going this time.'

"He turned pale and clung to me like a frightened child. The moment had come to reveal my secret.

"'I am not your mother's soul,' I said after a bit of a preamble. 'I am your mother herself.'

"'Why are you telling me this?' he said with a strange smile. 'Didn't I know it? Don't we look alike? Haven't I seen your portrait at Riesenburg? Besides, had I forgotten you? Hadn't I always seen you, always known you?'

"'And you weren't surprised to see me alive, I who am supposed to be buried in the chapel at the Castle of the Giants?'

"'No, I wasn't surprised; I was too overjoyed for that. God can work miracles, and it is not for man to wonder at them.'

"The strange child had a harder time understanding the frightening realities of my story than the marvelous illusion he had cherished. He had believed in my resurrection as in Christ's; he had taken my doctrines about the transmission of life literally; he believed in them to excess, in other words, he was not astonished to see me keep the memory and certainty of my individuality after having cast off one body for another. I don't even know if I managed to convince him that my swoon hadn't meant the end of my life and that my mortal shell hadn't remained in the sepulcher. He listened to me with a vacant yet ardent look on his face, as though he were hearing other words than those I was saying. Something inexplicable was going on inside him just then. A terrific bond was still holding Albert's soul on the edge of the abyss. He would remain alienated from reality until he himself had undergone that final crisis out of which I had miraculously emerged, that apparent death that would be in him the ultimate struggle between the notions of time and eternity. It broke my heart to leave him; I had a vague, painful premonition that he was about to enter that climacteric phase, so to speak, which had so violently shaken my existence, that the hour was near when Albert would be utterly destroyed or renewed. I had noticed that he was prone to catalepsy. Before my eyes he had fallen into sleep so long, so heavy, so frightening; his breathing was then so feeble, his pulse so nearly imperceptible that I kept saying or writing to Marcus, 'We must never let anybody bury Albert, or we mustn't fear breaking open his tomb.' Unfortunately for us, Marcus could no longer show his face at the Castle of the Giants, nor could he set foot in the Empire. He'd been seriously compromised in an insurrection in Prague in which he had in fact had an influence. Only flight had saved him from the rigors of Austrian law. Devoured with worry, I came back here. Albert had promised to write me every day, and I had promised myself that as soon as a letter failed to arrive, I'd leave for Bohemia and show up at Riesenburg, no matter what the consequences might be.

"The pain of our separation was at first less cruel for him than for me. He didn't understand what was happening; he seemed not to believe it. But once he was back under that sinister roof where the air is like poison for the ardent hearts of Zizka's descendants, he suffered a terrible shock in every part of his being; he ran and locked himself up in my old room; he called out to me, and not seeing me appear, became convinced that I had died a second death and wouldn't be restored to him in the course of his present life. That at least is how he has since explained to me what was going on in that fateful hour that unsettled his mind and faith for years on end. He gazed at my portrait for a long time. A portrait is never anything more than an imperfect likeness, and an artist's particular impression of us always falls so short of the notions of those who love us passionately that no likeness can ever satisfy them; it can even hurt and sometimes offend them. Albert, looking at that representation of my past youth and beauty, didn't find his dear old mother, with her gray hair that he found more dignified and the withered pallor that spoke to his heart. He shrank back in terror from the portrait and reappeared before his relatives, somber, tight-lipped, and distraught. He went to visit my tomb where he was seized with vertigo and horror. The idea of death struck him as monstrous, and yet, to console him, his father told him that I was there in the tomb, that he should kneel down and pray for the repose of my soul.

"'Repose!' exclaimed Albert, beside himself, 'the repose of the soul! No, my mother's soul is not meant for such nothingness, no more than mine. Neither my mother nor I want repose in a tomb. Never, never! I am horrified by this Catholic crypt, these sealed sepulchers, this forsaking of life, this divorce between heaven and earth, between body and soul!'

"With such talk Albert began to instill fear in his father's simple, timid soul. His words were relayed to the chaplain so that he might try and explain them. That narrow-minded man took them as nothing more than a cry wrung from Albert's soul by the feeling that I was damned for all eternity. The superstitious terror that began to spread around Albert, plus his family's attempts to lead him back to Catholic submission soon became torture for him, and his excitability altogether assumed the morbid quality you saw in him. He became confused. Repeatedly seeing and touching the proof of my death, he forgot that he had known me alive, and I seemed to him nothing more than a fleeting ghost always ready to forsake him. His imagination conjured up this ghost, lending it only incoherent ravings, mournful cries, and sinister threats. When he calmed down, his mind remained under a cloud. He couldn't remember recent events; he convinced himself that he had only dreamed spending eight years with me; rather, these eight years of happiness, activity, and strength seemed to him an hour's dream.

"Not having had any letter from him, I was going to rush off to Riesenburg. Marcus held me back, maintaining that our letters were being intercepted by the postal service, or else that the Rudolstadt family was doing away with them. He was still getting news of Riesenburg from his faithful correspondent; my son was said to be calm, healthy, and happy with his family. You know what care they took to conceal his condition, and at first they succeeded.

"In his travels Albert had met young Trenck and struck up a warm friendship with him. Trenck, who was loved by the Princess of Prussia and persecuted by King Frederick, wrote to my son about his joys and sorrows and begged that he come to Dresden to give him help and advice. Albert set out in that direction, and no sooner had he left gloomy Riesenburg than his memory, zeal, and reason came back to him. Trenck had met my son in the militia of neophyte Invisibles. There they had made a pact and sworn a knightly bond of brotherhood. When Marcus told me about their projected meeting, I rushed to Dresden, saw Albert again, and followed him to Prussia, where he slipped into the royal palace in disguise to help out Trenck in his love affair and deliver a message for the Invisibles. Marcus thought that these activities and the knowledge that he was doing something useful and generous would rescue Albert from his dangerous melancholy. He was right; Albert was coming back to life among us; when he returned, Marcus wanted to bring him here and have him stay a while with the most revered leaders of the order; he was convinced that breathing the true and vital atmosphere of his excellent soul would make Albert recover his lucid genius. But an unfortunate event suddenly shook my son's confidence. He had crossed paths with the impostor Cagliostro, whom the Rosicrucians in their imprudence had initiated into some of their mysteries. Albert, a long-standing Rosicrucian, had risen in rank and become the grand master of one of their assemblies. Then he saw at close range what he had thus far only sensed. He touched all these sundry elements that make up the Masonic network; he recognized the error and faddishness, the vanity and deception, even the fraud that was creeping into these sanctuaries already invaded by the insanity and vices of the age. Cagliostro, with his vigilant monitoring of society's little secrets that he presented as the revelations of a familiar spirit, with his specious eloquence that parodied great revolutionary inspirations, with his art of illusion that conjured up so-called ghosts; Cagliostro, scheming and greedy, horrified the noble disciple. The credulousness of polite society, the petty superstition of a great number of Masons, the shameful cupidity excited by the promises of the philosopher's stone, and so many other miseries of the times in which we live, shed sinister light in his soul. Living a secluded, studious life, he hadn't sufficiently fathomed the human race and wasn't prepared to do battle with so many vile instincts. Unable to endure such wretchedness, he wanted the charlatans and the sorcerers unmasked and ignominiously driven off and away from the confines of our temples. He couldn't tolerate that we should put up with the degrading assistance of Cagliostro because it was too late to get rid of him, because the man, once irritated, could be the ruin of many respectable men, whereas, flattered by their protection and ostensible trust, he could render many services to the cause without really knowing what it was all about. Albert waxed indignant and pronounced on our work the anathema of a steadfast, ardent soul; he predicted that we would fail for letting the alloy penetrate too far into the chain of gold. He left saying he was going to think about what we were striving to make him understand about the dreadful necessities of conspiratorial work and would return asking for baptism once his piercing doubts were dispelled. We didn't know, alas, what gloomy thoughts were his when he was alone at Riesenburg. He told us nothing about them; perhaps he didn't remember them once their bitterness had dissipated.

"He spent another year there swinging back and forth between calm and great excitement, exuberant strength and painful prostration. He occasionally wrote to us without any mention of his suffering and the decline of his health. He put up a bitter fight against our political moves. He wanted us henceforth to stop working in the shadows and beguiling people to make them drink of the cup of regeneration.

"'Off with your black masks, out of your caves,' he said. 'Erase the word *mystery* from the pediment of your temple; you stole it from the Roman church, and it doesn't suit the men of the future. Don't you see that you're behaving like Jesuits? No, I can't work with you; that's like looking for life among cadavers. Come at last into the light of day. Don't waste precious time organizing your army. Count a bit more on its spirit, on the sympathy of the people and the spontaneity of generous instincts. Besides, an army goes corrupt in inactivity, and all their crafty maneuvers to lie in ambush sap the strength and vitality they need to fight.'

"Albert was right in principle, but the time had not yet come for him to be right in practice. That time still may be far off!

"You finally arrived at Riesenburg and surprised him in the midst of his soul's greatest distress. You know, or rather you don't, what an effect you had on him, to the point of making him forget everything that was not you, of giving him new life, of giving him death.

"When he thought it was all over between the two of you, he lost all his strength and let himself waste away. Until then I was ignorant of the real nature and gravity of his illness. Marcus's correspondent told him that the Castle of the Giants was more and more closed to profane eyes, that Albert never left the premises any longer, that society considered him a monomaniac, but that the poor loved him and always blessed his name, and that a few people of uncommon sense who had seen him, first taken aback by his bizarre manner, paid tribute upon leaving to his eloquence, great wisdom, and grand ideas. But when I finally heard that Supperville had been summoned, I tore off to Riesenburg, despite Marcus who, seeing that I would stop at nothing, risked everything to follow me. We arrived at the walls of the castle disguised as beggars. No one recognized us, as I hadn't been seen around there for twenty-seven years and Marcus for ten. We were given alms and sent away. But we found a friend, an unexpected savior in the person of poor Zdenko. He treated us like brother and sister and took a liking to us because he understood how much we cared about Albert; we knew how to speak to his enthusiasm and make him reveal every secret about his friend's mortal pain. Zdenko was no longer the raging madman who had threatened your life. Beaten down and broken, he went like us humbly begging news of Albert at the castle gate, and like us he was put off with vague answers, which we in our anguish found terrifying. By a strange coincidence with Albert's visions, Zdenko claimed that he knew me. I had appeared in his dreams, in his ecstasies, and with childlike abandon he unwittingly surrendered his will to me.

"'Woman,' he often said to me, 'I don't know your name, but you're my *Podiebrad*'s good angel. Many a time in his good hours, when the heavens opened and there before his eyes he saw clustered around his bed those who are no longer, or so people say, he sketched your face and described your voice, your gaze, and your gait.'

"Far from giving Zdenko's effusions a cold shoulder, I encouraged them. I flattered his illusion and managed to get him to take Marcus and me down into the Schreckenstein cave. When I saw that subterranean abode and learned that my son had spent weeks, almost entire months there unbeknownst to all, I understood why his thoughts were so gloomy. There I saw a tomb that Zdenko seemed to worship, and it took some trouble to learn whose grave it was. This was Albert's and Zdenko's deepest, darkest secret.

"'Alas!' the madman told me, 'that's where we buried Wanda z Prachalitz, mother to my Albert. She didn't want to stay in that chapel where they had sealed her in stone. Her bones did nothing but toss and turn, and those who are here,' he added pointing to the Taborite ossuary at the edge of the spring, 'were always getting after us for not bringing her to them. We went to fetch those sacred remains and reburied them here, and every day we'd bring down flowers and kisses.'

"Horrified by this situation, which might bring about the discovery of my secret, Marcus questioned Zdenko and learned that he had brought my coffin there without opening it. Albert was therefore so ill and deranged that he no longer remembered that I was alive and persisted in believing that I was dead. But wasn't all this one of Zdenko's dreams? I couldn't believe my ears. 'Oh my friend,' I said in despair to Marcus, 'if the light of his reason is so extinguished, if he is to remain in this state forever, may God have mercy and let him die!'

"Finally in possession of all of Zdenko's secrets, we learned that we could get into the Castle of the Giants through subterranean corridors and secret passages; we followed him there one night and waited at the entrance to the cistern while he slipped into the house. He came back laughing and singing and told us that Albert was cured, that he was asleep, and they had dressed him in new clothes and put a crown on his head. I dropped as though I'd been struck by lightning; I understood that Albert had died. I don't know what happened after that; I woke up several times in a fever; I was lying on bearskins and dry leaves, in Albert's subterranean room under Schreckenstein. Zdenko and Marcus took turns watching over me. One kept telling me with an air of triumphant joy that his Podiebrad was cured, that he would soon be coming to see me; the other, pale and pensive, would say, 'All is not lost, perhaps; let's not give up hoping for the miracle that made you rise out of the grave.' I didn't understand a thing, I was delirious; I wanted to get up, run, scream; I couldn't, and poor Marcus seeing me in such a state had neither the strength nor the leisure to look after me in earnest. His whole mind, his every thought were absorbed by an even more terrible anxiety. Finally one night, I think it was the third of my crisis, I was calm and feeling stronger. I tried to collect my thoughts, I managed to get up; I was alone in that horrible cave scarcely lit by a sepulchral lamp; I wanted to get out, I was locked in; where were Marcus, Zdenko . . . and, above all, Albert? . . . My memory came back, I screamed, and the icy vault replied with such a lugubrious echo that sweat ran down my forehead, cold as the damp of the grave; I thought I was once again buried alive. What had happened? What was going on even now? I fell to my knees, wrung my hands in a desperate prayer and screamed furiously for Albert. Finally, I heard heavy, uneven steps drawing near, like those of people with a heavy burden. A dog barked and moaned, and faster than the others, he scratched at the door several times. The door was flung open, and I saw Marcus and Zdenko bringing me Albert, stiff, wan, by all appearances dead. His dog Cinnabar was jumping up and licking his hanging hands. Zdenko was improvising a song in a sweet, serious voice, 'Come sleep on your mother's breast, poor friend so long deprived of rest; come sleep until it's day, we'll wake you for the dawn.'

"I rushed over to my son. 'He's not dead?' I exclaimed. 'Oh, Marcus, you've saved him, haven't you? He's going to wake up?'

"'Don't delude yourself, Madame,' Marcus replied, horrifyingly firm. 'I know nothing, I can believe nothing; be brave, no matter what. Give me a hand, forget yourself.'

"I don't need to tell you everything we tried to revive Albert. Thank heaven, there was a stove in the cave. We managed to warm his limbs. 'You see,' I said to Marcus, 'his hands are a bit warm!'

"'Marble can be warmed up,' he replied in a sinister tone, 'which doesn't give it life. This heart is still as stone!'

"Dreadful hours dragged on in expectation, terror, discouragement. Marcus, down on his knees, his ear glued to my son's chest, his face glum, watched in vain for a faint sign of life. Fainting, exhausted, I dared not say another word nor ask any questions. I studied Marcus's ghastly brow. A moment came when I didn't even dare look at him any longer; it seemed to me that I had read the supreme sentence.

"Zdenko, sitting in a corner, was playing with Cinnabar like a child and still singing. Sometimes he would stop and say that we were tormenting Albert and should let him sleep, that he, Zdenko, had seen him like that for weeks on end, that he would wake up all by himself. Marcus suffered cruelly from the madman's confidence and couldn't share it, but I stubbornly wanted to have faith in it and felt quite inspired. The madman was possessed with heavenly divination, the angelic certainty of the truth. Finally, I thought I saw an imperceptible change in Marcus's stony brow, that it was less tightly knit. I saw his hand quiver, only to stiffen in a fresh attempt at courage; then he heaved a deep sigh, lifted his ear from the chest where my son's heart had perhaps taken a beat, tried to say something, contained himself, frightened by the joy, perhaps illusory, he was about to give me, leaned back down, listened again, shuddered, suddenly straightened up and threw his arms back, then sagged and dropped as though as if he were about to die. 'Is there no more hope?' I exclaimed, tearing at my hair.

"'Wanda!' he choked, 'your son's alive!'

"And broken by the strain of his attention, courage, and concern, my stoical, tender friend, absolutely spent, dropped to the floor near Zdenko."

Chapter XXXV

Countess Wanda, shaken by the force of the memory, was silent for a few minutes, then went on with her tale.

"We spent several days in the cave, with my son regaining his strength and health amazingly fast. Marcus, surprised to find that Albert hadn't suffered any organic lesion or basic harm to his vital functions, was nonetheless frightened by his obdurate silence and indifference, apparent or real, to our effusions of joy and his strange situation. Albert's memory was completely gone. Sunk in a somber meditation, he made secret, futile efforts to understand what was going on around him. As for me, knowing that heartache was the sole reason for his illness and the resulting catastrophe, I was not as impatient as Marcus to see him recover the poignant memories of his love. Marcus himself acknowledged that this mental blotting out of the past could alone explain why his physical strength was returning so fast. His body was reviving at the expense of his mind as quickly as it had broken under the strain of his thoughts.

"'He's alive, and he'll surely survive,' he said to me, 'but will he ever recover his wits?'

"'Let's get him out of this tomb as soon as possible. Air, sun, and movement will no doubt rouse him out of this slumber of the soul,' I replied.

"'Above all, let's get him out of this false, impossible life that killed him,' Marcus went on, 'away from this family and world that thwart all his instincts. Let's take him to those sympathetic souls in whose fellowship his own soul will regain its strength and lucidity.'

"Could I hesitate? Cautiously wandering around Schreckenstein at dusk, where I pretended to beg from the rare travelers on those roads, I learned that Count Christian had fallen into a sort of second childhood. He would not have understood his son's return, and the spectacle of that death before its time, if Albert in turn had understood his father's condition, would have utterly overwhelmed him. Were we therefore to render him, to abandon him to the inept care of the old aunt, the benighted chaplain, and the idiotic uncle who had all made him live such a wretched life and die such a dismal death? 'Ah, let's run away with him!' I said to Marcus at last. 'I don't want him to witness his father's last gasps and the horrifying display of Catholic idolatry at a deathbed. My husband didn't understand me, but I always revered his pure and simple virtues and respected him as religiously after I left him as I had while we were together; and now it breaks my heart to think that he's going to leave this earth without it being possible for us to forgive each other. Yet, since that's the way it must be, since my apparition as well as my son's could only cause him indifference or death, let's leave and not give Albert back to the tomb of Riesenburg. We've reconquered him from death, and life, at least I hope so, is opening a sublime path before him. Ah, let's follow the first impulse that led us here! Let's free Albert from captivity, from the false duties created by rank and fortune. These duties will always be crimes in his eyes, and if he persists in fulfilling them for the sake of old and moribund relatives, he'll only die trying and be the first to go. I know what I suffered in that slavery of the mind, that fatal, unending contradiction between the life of the soul and day to day living, between principles and instincts, on the one hand, and forced habits, on the other. It's clear to me that he's gone the same way and absorbed the same poisons. So let's save him, and later on, if he wants to go back on our decision, won't he be free to do so? If his father goes on living, and if his own mental health permits, won't there still be time for him to return here and console Christian's last days with his presence and love?'

"'Not easily!' Marcus replied. 'I foresee terrible obstacles if Albert wants to go back on his divorce from established society, the world, and the family. But why would he want to do that? This family may die out before he recovers his memory. As for those things to be conquered in the world, name, honor, and fortune, I have no doubt what his opinion of them will be once he's himself again, and I pray that this day may come! Our most important and pressing task is to put him in an environment where he can heal.'

"So one night, as soon as Albert could hold himself up, we left the cave. At a short distance from Schreckenstein, we put him on a horse and made our way to the border, which is very near in those parts, as you know, and there we found easier, faster transportation. The relations that our order maintains with the multitude of Freemasons assure us, inside the whole of Germany, smooth traveling incognito and free of police checks. Bohemia was the only perilous place for us because of the recent agitation in Prague and the vigilant eye of the Austrian authorities.'

"And what about Zdenko?" asked the young Countess von Rudolstadt.

"Zdenko was nearly our ruin with his stubborn attempts to stop us, or at least Albert, from leaving. He didn't want to be separated from him, nor did he want to follow him anywhere. He doggedly believed that Albert would die away from fateful, gloomy Schreckenstein. 'Only here is my Podiebrad at peace; everywhere else people torture him, stop him from sleeping, make him forswear our fathers of Mount Tabor and lead a life of shame and perjury that exasperates him. Leave him here with me; I'll take good care of him as I've done so often. I won't trouble his meditations; when he wants to keep quiet, I won't make any noise walking around, and I'll hold Cinnabar's muzzle for hours lest the dog lick his hand and give him a start; when he wants to make merry, I'll sing him the songs he likes and compose some new ones that he'll like as well, for he liked all my songs and he alone understood them. Leave me my Podiebrad, I tell you. I know better than you what's good for him, and when you want to see him again, he'll be playing the violin or placing beautiful branches of cypress that I'll cut for him in the forest over the tomb of his beloved mother. I'll feed him well, I will! I know all the huts where folks never refuse good old Zdenko bread, milk, and fruit, and for a long time now the poor peasants of the Bohemian Forest, though they don't know it, have been feeding their noble master, rich Podiebrad. Albert doesn't like fancy meals where people eat the flesh of animals; he prefers the innocent, simple life. He has no need to see the sun; better a moonbeam through the trees. And when he wants company, I take him to the wilderness clearings where our good friends the zingari, these children of the Lord, who know neither law nor money, make their camps at night.' "

"I listened carefully to Zdenko because his innocent babble revealed the life that Albert had led with him during his frequent retreats to Schreckenstein. 'Have no fear,' he added, 'that I'll ever let his enemies know about his secret place. They are so crazy and such liars that now they're saying, "Our child, our friend, our master is dead." They wouldn't be able to believe that he's alive even if they saw him with their own eyes. Besides, didn't I use to answer when they'd ask if I'd seen Count Albert, "He's no doubt dead?" And as I'd laugh saying that, they'd said I was crazy. But I was talking about death to make fun of them because they believe or pretend to believe in death. And when the people in the castle made as if to follow me, didn't I have a thousand tricks to throw them off? Oh, I know all the wiles of the hare and the partridge. Like them, I know how to take cover in a thicket, disappear into the heather, go the wrong way, spring up, cross a roaring stream, stop and hide so that they pass me by, and, like the will-o'-the-wisp, make them get lost and risk their necks in swamps and bogs. They call Zdenko *the simpleton*. The simpleton is cleverer than all of them. There's never been but one girl, a saintly girl, who could outfox canny Zdenko. She knew magic words to chain his fury; she had charms to overcome every trap or danger; her name was Consuelo.'

"Whenever Zdenko said your name, Albert would quiver slightly and turn his head away, but then let it drop back down toward his chest a second later, without his memory coming awake.

"In vain I tried to work out a compromise with this keeper so devoted and so blind, promising to bring Albert back to Schreckenstein on condition that Zdenko first accompany him to a place where Albert wanted to go. That didn't work, and when at last we had made him, like it or not, agree to let my son leave the cave, he trailed along behind us, crying, muttering, and singing in a pitiful voice until beyond the mines of Kuttenburg. When we reached a famous spot where Zizka had one of his great victories over Sigismund long ago, Zdenko recognized the high crags that mark the border, for no one else knows better from his wanderings all the trails in the area. There he came to a halt, stamped his foot on the ground, and said, 'Never again will Zdenko leave the land where the bones of his fathers lie! Not long ago, when I was exiled and banished by my Podiebrad for having misunderstood and threatened the saintly girl he loves, I spent weeks and months on foreign land. I thought I'd go mad. I returned to my beloved forests a little while ago to watch Albert sleep because a voice sang to me in a dream that he wasn't angry any longer. Now that he's no longer cursing me, you're stealing him away from me. If you're taking him to his Consuelo, so be it. But leaving my country all over again, talking the language of our enemies, giving them my hand, leaving Schreckenstein empty and abandoned, I won't do it again. It's beyond my strength, and besides, the voices in my sleep have forbidden me to do it. Zdenko must live and die in the land of the Slavs; he must live and die singing in the tongue of his fathers the glory of the Slavs and their sufferings. Farewell and be gone! If Albert hadn't forbidden me to shed human blood, you wouldn't be carrying him off like this, but he would curse me again if I raised a hand against you, and not seeing him again is better than seeing him angry with me. You hear me, oh my Podiebrad!' he exclaimed, kissing the hands of my son who was looking at him and hearing without understanding. 'I'm obeying you and going away. When you come back, you'll find your stove lit, your books in place, your bed of leaves freshly made, and your mother's tomb strewn with palms always green. If it's the right season, there'll be flowers over her and the bones of our martyrs at edge of the spring. . . . Farewell, Cinnabar!' Having tearfully choked out these words, poor Zdenko leaped onto the rocky incline sloping toward Bohemia and vanished as quickly as a deer at dawn's first light.

"I won't tell you, dear Consuelo, how anxiously we waited during our first weeks here with Albert. Hidden away in the lodge where you are now, he gradually recovered the inner life that we were striving to reawaken in him, albeit slowly and carefully. The first word that crossed his lips after two months of absolute silence was in response to music. Marcus had understood that Albert's life was tied to his love for you, and he had resolved to invoke that memory only insofar as he knew you to be worthy of that love and free to respond to it one day. He made the most thorough inquiries about you, and before long he knew everything about your character and your life, past and present. Thanks to the clever organization of our order, our relations with every other secret society, and a multitude of neophytes and disciples whose work it is to probe with the most scrupulous care the things and people that interest us, nothing can escape our investigations. The world holds no secrets for us. We know how to penetrate the deepest mysteries of politics, of court intrigues as well. So your spotless life and straightforward character weren't difficult for us to know and judge. Baron von Trenck, upon learning that the man who had loved you, whose name you had kept quiet, was his friend Albert, talked to us about you with such feeling. The Count de Saint-Germain, very absentminded in appearance, but in fact one of the most clairvoyant of men, this strange visionary, this superior spirit who seems to live only in the past and doesn't miss a thing in the present, quickly gave us the most complete information about you, and it was of such a nature that from then on I felt tenderly attached to you and thought of you as my own daughter.

"Once we knew enough to act with certainty, we had skilled musicians come play under the window where we're now sitting. Albert was there where you are, leaning against this curtain and contemplating the sunset; Marcus was holding one of his hands and I the other. Right in the middle of a symphony that we had had expressly composed for four instruments, with various themes from the Bohemian tunes that Albert plays with such soul and religious feeling, up rose the hymn to the Virgin with which you had charmed him in the past, 'O Consuelo de mi alma. . . .'

"Just then Albert, who had shown a little emotion hearing these old Bohemian melodies, threw himself into my arms and dissolved into tears, crying 'Mother, oh mother!'

"Marcus stopped the music, content with the emotion it had aroused and not wanting to overdo it the first time. Albert had spoken. He had recognized me and refound the strength to love. It took several more days before his mind had regained all its liberty. Yet he had no spells of delirium. When he seemed worn out from using his faculties, he would lapse back into dismal silence, but by imperceptible degrees his physiognomy looked less glum, and bit by bit we gently and gingerly made headway against that taciturn tendency. We were glad at last to see his need for rest from intellectual labor disappear, and thereafter the only interruption in the workings of his mind was during hours of sleep that was regular, peaceful, and quite like that of other men. Albert recognized himself again, with his love for you and for me, his charity and enthusiasm for his fellow men and for virtue, his faith and his need to make it triumph. He went on cherishing you without bitterness, mistrust, or regret for all that he had suffered for you. Yet, despite all his care to reassure us and demonstrate his courage and selflessness, we could see that his passion had lost none of its intensity. He had merely become stronger, in mind and body, to bear up under it; we made no attempt to fight it. On the contrary, Marcus and I joined forces to give him hope and resolved to let you know that this husband for whom you were mourning religiously, not in your dress but in your soul, was alive. But Albert, with generous resignation and a good sense of his situation with regard to you, stopped us from rushing forward. 'She wasn't in love with me,' he said. 'She took pity on a dying man; it must have been with terror and perhaps despair that she promised to spend her life with me. Now she would come back to me out of duty. It would make me so unhappy to rob her of her freedom, the thrills of her art, and perhaps the joys of a new love! It's quite enough to have had her compassion; don't reduce me to being the object of her pained devotion. Let her live; let her know the pleasures of independence, the heady delights of glory, and even greater joys if need be! It's not for me that I love her, and while it's only too true that she is necessary to my happiness, I can certainly give that up as long as my sacrifice is to her benefit! Besides, was I born for happiness? Am I entitled to happiness while the whole world suffers and groans? Don't I have other duties aside from the pursuit of my own gratification? While performing these duties won't I find the strength to forget myself and not to desire anything more for me alone? I want to try at least; and if I fall by the wayside, you'll take pity on me and urge me on; better that than coddling me with fond hopes and endlessly reminding me that my heart is sick and consumed with the selfish desire for happiness. Love me, friends! Bless me, mother, and don't talk to me about the things that sap my strength and virtue when despite myself I feel the goad of my torments! I know full well that the greatest pain I suffered at Riesenburg was the pain I inflicted on others! I would go mad again, perhaps die with blasphemy on my lips if I were to see Consuelo suffer the anguish I failed to spare the other objects of my affection.'

"He seemed altogether well again, and my tender love wasn't the only thing helping him battle his unhappy passion. Marcus and a few superiors of the order gave him a fervent initiation into the mysteries of our endeavors. He took serious and melancholy joy in these vast projects and bold hopes, above all in the long philosophical discussions. Even though he wasn't always of one mind with his noble friends, he at least felt his soul in touch with theirs in all matters relating to deep, ardent feeling, the love of the good, the desire for justice and truth. His aspiration toward the ideal, for a long time cramped and beaten down by the narrow-minded terrors of his family, found at last room to grow, and this, seconded by noble sympathies, even stimulated by frank, friendly contradictions, was the vital atmosphere in which he could breathe and act, despite the secret pain devouring him. Albert is essentially metaphysical. He has never taken pleasure in the frivolous life on which egotism feeds. He was born to contemplate the highest truths and practice the most austere virtues; yet, at the same time, thanks to a perfection of inner beauty very rare among mankind, he is endowed with an essentially tender and loving soul. Charity is not enough for him, he needs affection. His love reaches out to everyone, and yet he needs to focus it more particularly on a few. He has a fanatic sense of dedication, but there is nothing fierce in his virtue. Love intoxicates him, friendship rules him, and his life is a rich, inexhaustible give-and-take between the abstract being he passionately reveres under the name of humanity and the particular beings he delights in cherishing. In short, his excellent heart is a hearth of love; all the noble passions find a home there and dwell in peace. If God could be represented in the form of a finite, mortal being, I would dare say that my son's soul is the image of the universal soul we call God.

"That is why he, a feeble human creature with infinite aspirations and limited means, couldn't live with his family. Had it not been for his fervent love for them, he could have made a life apart in their midst, with a calm, robust faith different from theirs and indulgence for their innocuous blindness, but such strength would have required a certain coldness that was as impossible for him as it was for me. He couldn't live isolated in mind, spirit, and heart; with anguish he implored their adhesion, with despair he appealed for the communion of ideas between him and those he held dear. That is why, shut up alone inside the brass walls of their Catholic obstinacy, social prejudices, and hatred for the religion of equality, he fell broken and moaning against their bosom, he withered like a plant deprived of dew and invoking the rain that would have let him live with those he loved. Weary of suffering alone, of loving alone, of believing and praying alone, he thought he had found life again in you, and when you accepted and shared his ideas, he regained composure and reason, but you didn't share his feelings, and your separation would throw him back into a deeper and more intolerable solitude.

"His faith, repudiated and relentlessly attacked, became torture beyond human strength. His mind reeled. Unable to refresh the most sublime essence of his life by steeping it in souls like his own, he had to let himself die.

"As soon as he found these hearts made to understand and help him, we were amazed by his mild-mannered way of discussing things, his tolerance, confidence, and modesty. We had feared, because of his past, something too fierce, opinions too personal, a harsh tongue worthy of respect in an earnest, enthusiastic mind but dangerous to his progress and harmful to an association of our sort. We were amazed by his openness, simplicity, and charming companionship. His words and lessons made us better and stronger, but he was convinced that we were giving him everything he was giving us. He was soon the object of boundless veneration here, and you ought not be surprised that so many people were involved in bringing you back to him when you realize that his happiness had become a collective effort, a need felt by everyone who had drawn near him, if only for an instant."

Chapter XXXVI

"But the cruel destiny of our race was not yet fulfilled. Albert had still to suffer, his heart had to bleed eternally for this family, innocent of all its woes, but condemned by a bizarre fatality to break him while crumbling at his feet. We told him, as soon as he was strong enough to hear the news, that his worthy father had died shortly after his own death, for I have to use that strange expression for such a strange event. Albert mourned his father with a tender, uplifted heart, with the certainty that he had not left this life for the Catholic nothingness of paradise or hell, with the kind of solemn joy that inspired in him the hope of a better, more abundant life here below for that pure, deserving man. He was therefore much more distressed by the bereavement of Baron Frederick and Canoness Wenceslawa, his other relatives, than by his father's departure. Reproaching himself for enjoying far from them consolations that they didn't share, he resolved to go spend some time with them, to let them in on the secret of his healing and miraculous resurrection and to make their lives as happy as possible. He knew nothing about his cousin Amalia's disappearance. That had happened while he was ill at Riesenburg, and they had carefully concealed it from him to spare him further pain. We hadn't thought it advisable to tell him about it; we had failed to preserve my wretched niece from a deplorable error, and when we were about to get our hands on the man who had seduced her, the Saxon branch of the Rudolstadt family, with their less indulgent pride, had got there first. They had Amalia secretly arrested in Prussia where she had thought to find refuge and turned her over to the harsh treatment of King Frederick, who gave the family a gracious token of his protection by locking a hapless young girl up in the fortress of Spandau. There she spent nearly a year in dreadful captivity, in total isolation, and having to count herself lucky that her disgrace was a tightly guarded secret, thanks to the generous protection of the jailer king."

"Oh, Madame," Consuelo burst in, "is she still at Spandau?"

"We've just got her out of there. Albert and Liverani couldn't spirit her away at the same time as you because she was kept on a much closer watch, her revolts, reckless attempts at escape, impatience and tantrums having aggravated the rigors of her confinement. But we have other means aside from those to which you owe your rescue. Our disciples are everywhere, and a few cultivate credit at court to help further our designs. We managed to get Amalia under the wing of the young Margravine von Bayreuth, the Prussian king's sister, who asked for and obtained her release, promising to take responsibility for her and answer for her future conduct. In a few days the young baroness will be with Princess Sophia Wilhelmina, who is as good-hearted as she is sharp-tongued, who will treat her with the same indulgence and generosity as she did the Princess von Kulmbach, another unfortunate who, like Amalia, is tarnished in the eyes of the world and has also been a victim of the penitentiary regime of the royal fortresses.

"So Albert was unaware of his cousin's plight when he resolved to go see his uncle and aunt at the Castle of the Giants. He wouldn't have been able to understand the inertia of Baron Frederick who had the animal energy to live, hunt, and drink in the wake of so many disasters nor the devout impassibility of the canoness who feared that taking measures to find Amalia would make her scandalous adventures even more notorious. We were horrified and fought Albert's project, but he persisted in it unbeknownst to us. One night he set out, leaving a letter promising us that he'd soon return. Indeed, he was away only a short while, but what grief he brought back with him!

"After entering Bohemia in disguise, he made a surprise visit to his solitary friend Zdenko at the Schreckenstein cave. From there he wanted to write to his family to tell them the truth and prepare them for the shock of his return. He knew Amalia as the most courageous as well as the most frivolous, and it was to her that he planned to have Zdenko deliver his first missive. Just when he was about to start on it, Zdenko was out on the mountain, it was near dawn, and he heard a shot, then a heartrending cry. He dashed outside, and the first thing that struck his eye was Zdenko carrying Cinnabar covered in blood. Albert's first impulse was to run to his poor old dog without giving a thought to covering his face, but while bringing the faithful animal, fatally wounded, back to the place called *Monk's Cave*, he saw racing toward him, as fast as age and obesity would allow, a hunter eager to retrieve his prey. It was Baron Frederick. Out stalking at dawn's first light, he had mistaken Cinnabar's tawny coat for that of a wild animal and aimed through the branches. Alas, he still had a good eye and a sure hand; he had hit him twice in the side. All of a sudden he spotted Albert. Thinking he was seeing a ghost, he stopped short, frozen in terror. No longer conscious of any real danger, he stepped back to the edge of the steep trail he was following, rolled off a cliff, and smashed down on the rocks below. He died instantly, on the fateful spot where for centuries there had stood the accursed tree, the famous oak of Schreckenstein called the *Hussite*, a witness and accessory to the most horrible catastrophes long ago.

"Albert saw his uncle fall and left Zdenko to run to the edge of the cliff. Then he saw the baron's servants anxiously trying to get him up, all the while filling the air with their moans, for he showed no signs of life. Albert heard these words from down below, 'Dead, our poor master's dead! Alas, what will the canoness say?' Albert no longer gave any thought to himself; he shouted and called out to them. As soon as they set eyes on him, these credulous servants were seized with panic. They were already abandoning the body of their master and running away when old Hanz, the most superstitious but also the most courageous of the lot, stopped them and said, making the sign of the cross, 'Children, that's not our master Albert. It's the spirit of Schreckenstein, who has taken his form to make us all die here if we don't show some courage. I saw him myself, he's the one who made the baron fall. He wants to make off with the body and devour it, he's a vampire! Come on, children, let's have some courage. They say the devil is a coward. I'll draw a bead on him while you recite the chaplain's prayer of exorcism.'

"With these words Hanz, having crossed himself several more times, raised his gun and fired at Albert while the other servants huddled round the baron's body. Fortunately Hanz was too upset and terrified to aim well; he was in a sort of delirium. Yet the bullet nearly grazed Albert's head, for Hanz was the best shot around, and had he been cool and collected, he surely would have killed my son. Albert stopped and hesitated.

"'Courage, children, courage!' shouted Hanz reloading his gun. 'Fire away, he's scared! You won't kill him, bullets can't touch him, but you'll make him back off, and that will give us time to rescue our poor master's body.'

"Albert, seeing all these guns pointing at him, ducked into the brush and, without anybody noticing, ran down the mountain and soon confirmed the horrible truth with his own eyes. The broken body of his wretched uncle was lying on the bloody rocks, his skull split open, and old Hanz mournfully shouting these dreadful words, 'The brains, get the brains off the rocks, every last speck! Otherwise, the vampire's dog will come lick them up.'

"'Yes, yes, there was a dog,' replied a second servant. 'At first I thought it was Cinnabar.'

"'But Cinnabar disappeared when Count Albert died,' said yet another. 'Nobody's seen him around anywhere since. He must have gone and died in some corner, and the Cinnabar we saw up there is a ghost, just like the vampire that looks like Count Albert. What an abominable sight! It'll always be there in front of my eyes. Lord God, have mercy on us, and mercy on the soul of the baron who's died without the sacraments because of the spirit's malice.'

"'Alas, I kept telling him he'd come to a bad end,' said Hanz in a piteous tone, picking up shreds of the baron's clothing with hands stained with his blood. 'He always wanted to hunt in this thrice accursed place! He'd taken it into his head that every critter in the forest took cover here because there was never anybody in these parts, but God knows, the only game that's ever been on this infernal mountain was the gallows bird still hanging from that oak when I was a boy. Accursed Hussite! Tree of perdition! Devoured by heaven's fire, but as long as there's a single root left in the earth, those evil Hussites will come back here for revenge on the Catholics. Come on, come on, hurry up with the stretcher and let's get moving! It's not safe here. Ah, the canoness, poor mistress, what's to become of her? Who'll dare be the first to go to her and say as on other days, "Here's the baron back from the hunt." She'll say, "Serve lunch at once." Ah, yes, lunch! It'll be a long time before anyone in the castle has any appetite. Too many bad things happen in this family, and I know where that's coming from, I do."

"While the body was being placed on the stretcher, Hanz, pressed with questions, replied, shaking his head, 'In that family everybody was a devout believer and died a Christian death until the day when Countess Wanda, God have mercy on her soul, died without confession. Since then they've all had to go the same way. Count Albert didn't die in a state of grace, no matter what was said to him, and his worthy father was punished for it; he gave up the ghost without knowing what he was doing, so that's another one who went without the sacraments, and I bet the canoness too will go without having had the time to think of it. Fortunately for her, that saintly woman is always in a state of grace!'

"Albert didn't miss a single one of these distressing words, a crude expression of real grief and a terrifying reflection of the fanatical horror that people felt for both of us at Riesenburg. In a long daze he watched from afar as the lugubrious cortege wended its way over the trails through the ravine and dared not follow, even though he felt that in the natural order of things he should have been the first to bring his elderly aunt this sad news and comfort her in her mortal sorrow. But there's no doubt that had he suddenly appeared before her eyes, she would have dropped dead or gone mad. This he understood, and he withdrew in despair to his cave where Zdenko, who had seen nothing of the worst accident of that fateful morning, was busy washing Cinnabar's wound; but it was too late. Cinnabar, seeing his master's return, moaned in distress; despite a broken back, he crawled to Albert and died at his feet, with his last caress. Four days later Albert returned from Riesenburg, pale and overwhelmed by these new blows. For several days he didn't speak a word or shed a tear. At last he wept on my bosom.

"'I am cursed among men,' he told me, 'and it seems as though God wants to shut me out of this world where I shouldn't have loved a single soul. I can't ever reappear there without causing terror, death, or madness. It's all over; I mustn't see ever again the people who looked after me as a child. Their ideas about the eternal separation of the soul and body are so absolute, so horrifying that they'd rather believe me forever chained in the grave than be exposed to seeing my sinister face again. What a strange and dreadful notion of life! The dead become objects of hatred for those who cherished them the most, and if their ghost appears, they think it's been belched out of hell rather than sent down from heaven. Oh, poor uncle! and noble father! You were heretics in my eyes as I was in yours; and yet, if you appeared to me, if I were so fortunate as to see once again your images destroyed by death, I'd get down on my knees and reach out my arms to them; I'd believe they had come away from the bosom of God where souls go to be refreshed and forms recast. I wouldn't say to you your abominable formulas of rejection and malediction, ungodly exorcisms born of fear and abandonment; on the contrary, I'd call out to you; I'd want to contemplate you lovingly and keep you around as salutary influences. Oh, mother, it's all over; I've got to be dead for them! Let them die by me or without me!'

"Albert didn't leave his native land until he was sure that the canoness had withstood this last blow. That old woman, as ill and tough as I am myself, also knows how to live out of a sense of duty. Respectable in her convictions and her adversity, she counts with resignation the bitter days that God wills her to endure. Yet in her pain she maintains a certain stiff pride that outlives feeling. She recently said to a person who relayed her words to us, 'If not for reasons of duty, we'd still have to put up with life out of respect for decorum.' That remark is a portrait of the canoness, inside and out.

"From then on Albert no longer gave any thought to leaving us, and his courage seemed to grow with his trials. He even seemed to have conquered his love for you, and throwing himself into a life given wholly to philosophy, he was apparently concerned with nothing but religion, ethics, and revolutionary action. He devoted himself to the most serious tasks, and his vast intelligence took a turn as serene and magnificent as his grieving heart had grown excessive and feverish far away from us. This bizarre man whose delirium had dismayed the souls of Catholics became a torch of wisdom for minds of a higher order. He was initiated into the Invisibles' most intimate secrets and took rank among the leaders and fathers of the new church, who received with love and gratitude all the enlightenment he gave them. The reforms that he proposed were agreed upon, and in the exercise of a militant faith he regained hope as well as the equanimity that makes heroes and martyrs.

"He so carefully concealed from us his struggles and suffering that we assumed that he had overcome his love for you. But one day the letters from the disciples, which could no longer be kept hidden from him, brought into our sanctuary a cruel, albeit uncertain report. A few people in Berlin took you for the mistress of the Prussian king, and appearances did nothing to dispel the notion; Albert said nothing and went pale.

"'My beloved friend,' he said to me after a few moments of silence, 'this time you'll let me go without fear; a duty of love is calling me to Berlin, and my place is near the woman I love, who accepted my protection. I'm not assuming any rights over her. If she is drunk on the dismal happiness being ascribed to her, I won't use any authority to make her give it up, but if, as I am sure, she is beset with snares and dangers, I'll know how to save her from them.'

"'Stop, Albert,' I said. 'You ought to fear the power of this fatal passion that has already done you so much harm. The suffering that it will cause you is the sole suffering beyond your strength. I can see that you are living only for virtue and love. If that love dies in your heart, will virtue be enough for you?'

"'And why should my love die?' asked Albert excitedly. 'You think she may have already ceased to be worthy of it?'

"'And what if that were the case, Albert?'

"He smiled, with those colorless lips and shining eyes that he has when in the grip of strong and painful enthusiasm.

"'If that were the case,' he replied, 'I would go on loving her; for the past is not a fading dream in me, and you know that I've often confused it with the present to the point of not being able to tell one from the other. Well, I'd do the same thing again; I'd love in the past the angelic figure, the poetic soul that suddenly lit up my gloomy life and set it afire. And I wouldn't see that the past is behind me, I'd keep its burning trace in my bosom; the one gone astray, the fallen angel would still inspire in me such tenderness and solicitude that I'd devote my life to consoling her for her fall and preserving her from the scorn of cruel men.'

"Albert left for Berlin with several of our friends, ostensibly to talk to his protectress, Princess Amalia, about Trenck, then in prison at Glatz, as well as some Masonic business in which she has been initiated. You saw him presiding over a lodge of Rosicrucians, and at that time he was unaware that Cagliostro, having learned his secrets in spite of us, had used that occasion to unsettle your mind by arranging for you to see Albert on the sly as though he were a ghost. Merely for having let *profane* eyes catch a glimpse of Masonic mysteries, scheming Cagliostro would have deserved to be forever excluded from them. But we didn't know about this for some time, and you must remember how terrified he was leading you to the *Temple*. Treachery of this sort is severely punished by the disciples, and by exploiting the mysteries of his order for the so-called wonders of his wizardry the magician was perhaps risking his life, at least his great reputation as a necromancer, for we would have unmasked him and immediately cast him out.

"During that short and mysterious stay in Berlin, Albert was able to fathom your thoughts and deeds well enough to feel reassured about your situation. He kept a close eye on you without your knowing it and came back apparently calm but more ardently in love with you than ever. For several months he traveled abroad, actively serving our cause. But having been alerted that a few schemers, perhaps spies for the Prussian king, were in Berlin trying to foment a particular conspiracy that would put the existence of Freemasonry in danger and probably prove fatal to Prince Heinrich and his sister the Abbess of Quedlinburg, Albert dashed to Berlin to warn them about the absurdity of such an undertaking and the trap he thought it concealed. That's when you saw him, and despite your horror at his apparition, you were so brave afterwards and expressed to his friends such devotion and respect for his memory that he regained hope that you loved him. He was then determined to have you learn by a series of mysterious revelations that he was truly alive. He was very often near you, and even hidden in your rooms, during your stormy exchanges with the king, without your knowing it. Meanwhile, the conspirators were bristling at the obstacles that Albert and his friends were putting in the way of their culpable or senseless designs. When the *sweeper* appeared, the ghost that all conspirators parade through palace hallways to create disorder and fear, Frederick II became suspicious. A new Masonic lodge was formed, with Prince Heinrich at its head, and from the very beginning it took issue with the doctrines of the lodge over which the king himself presided. This struck Frederick as a significant act of revolt. Perhaps this new lodge was in fact a clumsy mask for certain conspirators or an attempt to compromise some prominent people. Fortunately, they protected themselves against that, and the king, ostensibly furious to find only lowly culprits, but secretly satisfied not to have to scourge members of his own family, at least wanted to make an example. My son, the most innocent of all, was arrested and moved to Spandau, almost at the same time as you, whose innocence was no less established, but you were both guilty of refusing to save yourselves at anyone else's expense, and you paid for all the others. You spent several months in prison not far from Albert's cell, and you must have heard the passionate accents of his violin, the same way he heard those of your voice. Prompt and reliable means of escape were at his disposal, but he refused to make use of them before having ensured your own escape. The golden key is stronger than all the bolts of the royal prisons, and Prussian jailers, disgruntled soldiers, or disgraced officers for the most part, are eminently corruptible. Albert escaped at the same time as you, but you didn't see him, and for reasons that you'll learn later on, Liverani was charged with bringing you here. Now you know the rest. Albert loves you more than ever, but he loves you more than himself, and seeing you happy with another man will make him a thousand times less unhappy than it would to have you with him if you couldn't fully share his happiness. The moral and philosophical laws, the religious authority under which both of you now find yourselves allow his sacrifice and render your choice free and respectable. So choose, daughter, but remember that Albert's mother begs you on bended knee not to do any harm to her son's sublime simplicity; don't make for his sake a sacrifice that will embitter his life. He'll suffer if you leave him, but it will kill him to have your pity without your love. The time has come for a decision. I mustn't know what it is. Go to your room; there you'll find two very different kinds of attire. The one you choose will decide my son's fate."

"And which one will mean my divorce from him?" asked Consuelo, trembling from head to toe.

"I was told to tell you that, but I won't. I want to know if you'll guess."

With these words Countess Wanda replaced her mask, pressed Consuelo to her heart, and quickly left.

Chapter XXXVII

The two outfits that the neophyte found laid out in her room were a splendid wedding gown and a mourning dress with all the distinctive signs of widowhood. For a few seconds she hesitated. As to the choice of husband, her mind was made up, but which of these two costumes would bear witness to her intention? After brief reflection she donned the bride's white gown, veil, flowers, and pearls. Its design was chaste and extremely elegant. Consuelo was soon ready, but when she looked at herself in the mirror framed with threatening maxims, she no longer felt like smiling as she had the first time. Her face was deathly pale, and there was fear in her heart. No matter what she decided, she felt that there would be reason for regret or remorse, that a soul would be crushed by her desertion, and her own was frightfully torn ahead of time. Seeing her cheeks and lips as white as her veil and bouquet of orange blossoms, she feared equally for Albert and Liverani the sight of such violent emotion and was tempted to put on some rouge, but she immediately discarded the notion. "While my face may be telling a lie," she thought to herself, "will my heart be able to do the same?"

She knelt down against her bed. Hiding her face in the draperies around it, she remained absorbed in pained meditation until the clock tolled midnight. She immediately got up and saw an Invisible with a black mask standing behind her. Some vague instinct made her think it was Marcus. She was not wrong, yet he did not make himself known to her and simply said in a sad, gentle voice, "Madame, everything is ready. Please take this cloak and follow me."

Consuelo followed the Invisible to the far end of the garden where the stream disappeared under the leafy arches of the grounds. There was an open gondola, entirely black, just like those in Venice, and she recognized the gigantic rower in the prow as Karl. Catching sight of her, he made the sign of the cross, which was his way of expressing the greatest possible joy.

"May I speak to him?" Consuelo asked her guide.

"You may say a few words to him aloud," he replied.

"Well, dear Karl, my liberator and friend," said Consuelo, moved to see a familiar face after having been shut away for so long among mysterious beings, "can I hope that nothing is troubling your pleasure in seeing me again?"

"Nothing, Signora!" Karl replied in a steady voice. "Nothing, except for the memory of *her*, who is no longer of this world, whom I always think I'm seeing right next to you. Take heart and be of good cheer, kind mistress and good sister! Here we are as we were the night of our escape from Spandau!"

"This too is a day of deliverance, brother!" said Marcus. "Let's go; ply the oar with your skill and might, now matched by the prudence of your tongue and the strength of your soul. This does indeed resemble an escape, Madame," he added, turning to Consuelo, "but the chief liberator is not the same. . . ."

With these words Marcus gave her his hand to help her sit down on the cushioned seat. He felt her quiver at the thought of Liverani and asked her to cover her face for just a few seconds. Consuelo obeyed, and the gondola, propelled by the deserter's robust arm, glided swiftly over the dark, still waters.

At the end of a journey whose length could scarcely be gauged by pensive Consuelo, she heard voices and instruments in the distance; the boat slowed down and rocked a bit as it ran aground without coming to a full stop. The hood slowly slipped off, and at the sight of the enchanting spectacle that lay before her eyes the neophyte felt that she was passing from one dream to another. The boat was skimming alongside a smooth bank bordered with flowers and fresh grasses. The rushing stream had become the broad, still waters of a vast basin that seemed all aflame, reflecting columns of light writhing like blazing serpents or bursting into showers of sparks as the gondola moved along at a slow, even pace. Wonderful music filled the resonant air and gave the impression of floating over the shrubs of roses and sweet-smelling jasmine. Once Consuelo's eyes had grown used to the sudden brightness, she trained them on the illuminated façade of the palace that rose up nearby and plunged into the reflecting pool with magical splendor. The elegant edifice silhouetted against the starry sky, the harmonious voices, the concert of fine instruments, the open windows with their crimson curtains blazing with light and in front of them, richly attired men and women strolling about, glittering with embroidery, diamonds, gold and pearls, their powdered heads casting an effect of whiteness, something effeminate and fantastic, over social gatherings in that period—this whole princely gala, plus the beauty of a warm, clear night that sent whiffs of sweet-smelling, fresh air into the splendid rooms, thrilled Consuelo and made her feel rather drunk. A child of the people, yet the queen of patrician festivities, she could not witness a spectacle of this sort, after so many days of captivity, solitude, and somber musings, without feeling a burst of energy, a need to sing, a singular shiver at the approach of an audience. So she stood up in the gondola which was drawing nearer and nearer to the castle, and suddenly uplifted by Handel's chorus.

See, the conqu'ring hero comes!
Sound the trumpets, beat the drums.
Sports prepare, the laurel bring,
Songs of triumph to him sing,

she forgot everything to lend her voice to this hymn of grandiose enthusiasm.

But the boat, gliding along the bank and occasionally running into a branch or a tuft of grass, rocked again and made her lose her balance. Only when she was forced to hang onto the first hand that offered her support did she notice a fourth person in the boat, a masked Invisible who had certainly not been there when she had stepped in.

A huge dark gray cloak with long folds, a broad-brimmed hat worn in a certain way, something about the features of the mask through which the human physiognomy seemed to speak, but, more than all the rest, the pressure of the trembling hand that would not release its grip on hers made Consuelo recognize the man she loved, Chevalier Liverani, as he had first revealed himself to her on the lake at Spandau. At that point the music, the lights, the enchanted palace, the intoxicating festivities, even the approach of the solemn moment that would determine her fate, everything that was not this immediate emotion vanished from Consuelo's memory. Flustered and as if overcome by a superhuman force, she fell back quivering on the cushions near Liverani. The other stranger, Marcus, was standing at the prow with his back to them. The fast, Countess Wanda's tale, the anticipation of some dreadful denouement, the unexpected festivities glimpsed along the way had broken all of Consuelo's strength. She felt nothing more than Liverani's hand clasping hers, his arm delicately around her waist, ready to prevent her from pulling away, and the divine commotion that the beloved's presence communicates even to the air that one breathes. Consuelo remained in this state for a few minutes, seeing the sparkling palace no more than if it had been subsumed in darkness, hearing nothing more than the burning respiration of her lover at her side and the beating of her own heart.

"Madame," said Marcus turning around all of a sudden, "don't you know the aria being sung just now, and wouldn't you like to stop and hear this magnificent tenor?"

"Whatever the aria and the voice," replied Consuelo, preoccupied, "let's stop or go on; do as you will."

The boat was nearly at the foot of the castle. One could make out the figures at the windows, even those moving deep inside the rooms. They were not ghosts floating in a dream any longer, but real people, lords, great ladies, learned men, and artists of which many were known to Consuelo. But she made no effort to remember their names, nor the theaters or palaces where she had seen them. All of a sudden for her the world had once again become a magic lantern without meaning or interest. The only living being in all the universe seemed to be the one whose hand was stealthily burning hers under the folds of the cloaks.

"Don't you know this beautiful voice singing a Venetian melody?" asked Marcus once again, surprised by Consuelo's stillness and apparent indifference.

And as she seemed to hear neither the voice speaking to her nor the one singing, he came a bit closer and took the seat facing her to ask the question again.

"A thousand pardons, sir," replied Consuelo, having made an effort to listen. "I wasn't paying attention. Indeed I know this voice, and that's a melody I composed a long, long time ago. It's very bad and very poorly sung."

"So what's the name of the singer for whom you seem to me too severe? As for me, he's admirable!"

"Ah, you didn't lose it?" Consuelo said under her breath to Liverani. He had just pressed into the hollow of her hand the little filigree cross that she had taken off for the first time in her life and entrusted to him on the trip from Spandau.

"You don't remember this singer's name?" Marcus stubbornly went on, scrutinizing Consuelo.

"Pardon, sir!" she replied a bit impatiently. "His name is Anzoleto. Ah! what a bad D. He missed that note."

"Don't you want to see his face? Perhaps you're wrong. From here you could see him perfectly, for I've got a good view of him. He's a very handsome young man."

"What's the use of looking at him?" asked Consuelo, somewhat peeved. "I'm sure he's still the same."

Marcus gently took Consuelo's hand, and Liverani also helped her up so that she could peer into the wide open window. Consuelo who might have resisted the one, surrendered to the other and glanced at the singer, this handsome Venetian on whom over a hundred women were fastening their gaze, protective, ardent, and lascivious.

"He's put on a lot of weight!" said Consuelo, sitting back down and furtively resisting Liverani's fingers. He was trying to get the little cross back from her and in fact succeeded,

"That's the only way you remember an old friend?" asked Marcus, still watching her like a lynx through his mask.

"He's just a colleague," replied Consuelo, "and in our circles colleagues aren't always friends."

"But wouldn't you enjoy talking to him? What if we went into this palace and you were asked to sing with him?"

"If this is a *test*," said a bit mischievously Consuelo, who was beginning to see how insistent Marcus was, "I'll gladly do so, since I must obey your every command. But if this is a matter of my pleasure, I'd rather not."

"Am I to stop here, brother?" asked Karl, making a military gesture with the oar.

"Go on, brother, and head out to the open water!" replied Marcus.

Karl obeyed, and a few seconds later the boat had crossed the basin and plunged into a thick overhang of vines. It became very dark. There was only the bluish glimmer of the gondola's little lantern on the surrounding foliage. Every now and then through the somber leaves one could still catch a faint flicker of the palace lights off in the distance. The sound of the orchestra slowly faded away. The boat skimmed along the bank, stripping branches covered with flowers, and Consuelo's black cloak was strewn with their fragrant petals. She was starting to come back to herself, to struggle against the undefinable voluptuousness of love and night. She had withdrawn her hand from Liverani's, and her heart was breaking as the veil of intoxication was being dispelled by glimmers of reason and will.

"Listen!" said Marcus. "Can't you hear the audience applauding? Yes, indeed! Clapping and cheering. They're delighted by what they've just heard. That Anzoleto has scored a great success at the palace."

"They are no experts!" said Consuelo brusquely, seizing a magnolia that Liverani had just plucked and furtively thrown onto her knees.

She convulsively gripped the flower in her hands and hid it in her bosom, like the last relic of an untamed love that the fateful ordeal would sanctify or break off forever.

Chapter XXXVIII

The boat made its final landing at the edge of the gardens and the woods, in a picturesque spot where the stream plunged down among ancient rock formations and ceased to be navigable. Consuelo had little time to contemplate the austere, moonlit landscape. It was still within the vast enclosure of the estate, but here art had been applied only to preserve nature's primeval beauty: the old trees randomly seeded in the dark lawns, the felicitous rise and fall of the land, the rugged hills and waterfalls, the herds of bounding, timorous deer.

Another person had drawn Consuelo's attention: Gottlieb, lounging on the pole of a sedan chair, looking as though he were calmly, dreamily waiting for something. He gave a start when he recognized his friend from prison, but Marcus made a gesture, and he said not a word to her.

"So you won't let the poor child come shake my hand?" Consuelo whispered to her guide.

"After your initiation you'll be free to do as you please here," he whispered back. "Be satisfied for now to see how Gottlieb's health has improved, how he's recovered his strength."

"Can't you at least tell me if he suffered any persecution on my account after I escaped from Spandau?" asked the neophyte. "Pardon my impatience. This thought went on torturing me until the day I saw him walking along the wall by the lodge."

"He suffered indeed," Marcus replied, "but briefly. As soon as he knew that you'd been rescued, he boasted with naïve enthusiasm about having had a hand in it, and the involuntary revelations he made in his sleep were nearly fatal to a few of us. They wanted to put him in a madhouse as much to punish him as to prevent him from helping other prisoners. At that point he ran away, and as we were keeping an eye on him, we had him brought here where his body and soul have been lavished with care. We'll send him back to his family and country once we've instilled in him the necessary strength and prudence to be useful to our mission, which has become his own, for he's one of our purest and most fervent disciples. But the chair is ready, Madame; please get in. I'm not leaving you, even though I shall entrust you to the sure and faithful arms of Karl and Gottlieb."

Consuelo climbed docilely into the sedan chair, enclosed on all sides and receiving air only from a few slits in the roof. So she saw nothing more of the things going on around her. Sometimes she saw twinkling stars and concluded that she was still outside; at other times they disappeared without her knowing if that was due to buildings or the thick shade of trees. The porters walked fast and in utter silence; for a while she tried to make out from the occasional crunch of feet over the ground if she had four or only three escorts. Several times she thought she could hear Liverani's footsteps to her right, but that was perhaps an illusion, and besides she felt it her duty not to think about that.

When the chair stopped and was opened, Consuelo could not help feeling terrified when she found herself under the portcullis, still gloomily standing, of an old feudal manor. The moon was shining brightly over the courtyard surrounded by ruins and filled with figures in white coming and going, some singly and others in groups, like capricious ghosts. The massive black arch over the entrance made everything in the background look more blue, transparent, and fantastic. The wandering shades, silent or speaking in whispers, their noiseless movements through the high grasses of the courtyard, the sight of the ruins that Consuelo recognized as those she had once visited, where she had seen Albert, so affected her that she felt a spasm of superstitious fright. Instinctively she looked around for Liverani. He was in fact there with Marcus, but it was so dark under the arch that she could not distinguish which of the two gave her his hand; and this time her heart, chilled by a sudden sadness and an undefinable fear, told her nothing.

They fixed her cloak and hood in such a way that she could see everything without anyone recognizing her. Someone whispered to her not to let a single word, a single exclamation escape her lips, no matter what she might see, and she was led to the far end of the courtyard, where a strange spectacle indeed met her eyes.

Just then a faint, lugubrious bell summoned the shades to the ruined chapel where not so long ago by lightning's glare Consuelo had sought refuge from the storm. Now the chapel was lit by candles systematically arranged. The altar seemed to have been raised recently; it was covered with a shroud and decorated with strange emblems, where Christian and Jewish symbols mixed with Egyptian hieroglyphs and cabalistic signs. In the middle of the choir, whose perimeter had been marked off anew with balustrades and symbolic columns, there was a coffin surrounded by candles, its lid covered with crossbones and surmounted by a skull in which a blood-red flame was burning. A young man was led to the cenotaph. Consuelo could not see his face, half concealed by a broad blindfold. He was a new initiate who looked broken by fatigue or emotion. An arm and a leg were bare, his hands bound behind his back, and his white robe was stained with blood. A band around his arm suggested that he had just been bled. Two shades brandished torches of burning resin around him, showering his face and chest with clouds of smoke and flurries of sparks. Then, between the young man and those presiding over the ceremony and decked out with the distinctive insignia of their various ranks, there began a bizarre exchange that reminded Consuelo of the dialogue between Albert and nameless others to which Cagliostro had made her privy in Berlin. Next, some shades armed with swords, whom she heard called the *Dreadful Brothers*, lay the initiate down on the stone floor and bore down on his heart with the points of their weapons while several others engaged in a fierce battle, their blades clicking and clanking, one faction intending to prevent the admission of the new brother, calling him perverse, unworthy, and treacherous, while the other claimed to fight for him in the name of truth and a right that he had earned. This strange scene affected Consuelo like a painful dream. The struggle, the threats, the magic rites, the adolescents sobbing around the coffin were so well simulated that any spectator who had not been initiated ahead of time would have been truly horrified. After the new initiate's *godfathers* had won the battle of words and swords, he was raised up, given a dagger, ordered to march forward and strike anyone who might try and stop him from entering the temple.

That is all Consuelo saw. Just when the new initiate, his arm held high and in a sort of delirium, was heading for a low door toward which he was being pushed, the two guides who had not let go of Consuelo's arms swept her off as though to save her from a grisly sight. Pulling the hood down over her face, they led her in a roundabout way, and among piles of rubble on which she stumbled more than once, to a place of utter silence. There light was restored to her eyes, and she found herself in the great octagonal hall where she had overheard Albert's conversation with Trenck. This time all the openings were closed up tight and carefully veiled; the walls and ceiling were hung with black; candles were burning here, too, but in a different arrangement from those in the chapel. The huge hearth was masked by an altar in the shape of Calvary with three crosses on top. In the middle of the room there was a tomb on which were laid out a hammer, nails, a spear, and a crown of thorns. Masked figures in black were kneeling or sitting around it on carpets seeded with silver tears; they neither wept nor moaned; they held themselves as though in austere meditation or mute, profound sorrow.

Consuelo's guides led her to the coffin. After the men standing guard had risen and lined up at the far end of it, one of them said to her, "Consuelo, you've just witnessed a Masonic initiation ceremony. There as well as here you've seen unknown rites, mysterious signs, funereal images, initiating pontiffs, and a coffin. What is your understanding of this simulation, these terrifying ordeals for the initiate, the words said to him, the displays of respect, love, and grief around an illustrious tomb?"

"I don't know if I've understood well," Consuelo replied. "I found the scene upsetting and the ceremony barbarous. I felt sorry for the initiate whose courage and virtue were submitted to entirely material ordeals, as if physical courage sufficed to initiate one into the endeavors of moral courage. I object to what I saw, and I deplore these cruel games of somber fanaticism or these childish experiments in a wholly outward and idolatrous faith. I heard him being asked obscure riddles, and the initiate's explanation of them seemed to me dictated by a suspicious or crude catechism. Yet the bloody tomb, the immolated victim, the ancient myth of Hiram, the divine architect assassinated by jealous and greedy workers, the sacred word lost for centuries and promised to the initiate as the magic key that will open the doors of the temple to him, I don't take this as a symbol without grandeur or interest, but why is the fable so poorly spun or so speciously interpreted?"

"What do you mean by that? Did you listen well to the tale you're calling a fable?"

"Here's what I understood and what I had learned beforehand in the books I was told to meditate during my retreat. Hiram, who was in charge of building Solomon's temple, had divided the workers into categories with different salaries, unequal rights. Three ambitious workers from the lowest category resolved to share in the salary reserved for the rival class and pry out of Hiram the watchword, his secret formula for distinguishing the journeymen from the masters at the solemn hour of reckoning. They lay in wait for him in the temple where he had stayed alone after the ceremony, and posting themselves at each of the three exits from the holy place, they prevented him from leaving, threatened him, cruelly beat and assassinated him without managing to get his secret out of him, the fateful word that was to make them equal to him and his privileged ones. Then they carried off his body and buried it under piles of rubble, and to this day the faithful disciples of the temple, Hiram's friends are still mourning his sinister fate, searching for his sacred word and rendering almost divine honors to his memory."

"And now, how do you explain this myth?"

"I pondered it before coming here, and here's how I understand it. Hiram is the cold reason and clever governance of ancient societies, based on inequality, on a caste system. The Egyptian fable suited the hierophants' mysterious despotism. The three ambitious workers are indignation, revolt, and vengeance; perhaps the three castes inferior to the priestly caste, and they try to take their rights by violent means. Hiram assassinated is despotism having lost its prestige and might and gone to the grave with the secret of dominating men by blindness and superstition."

"Is this truly the way you'd interpret the myth?"

"I read in your books that it was brought from the East by the Knights Templar and that they used it in their initiations. So they must have interpreted it more or less this way, but by baptizing theocracy as *Hiram* and the *assassins* as impiety, anarchy, and ferocity, the Knights Templar, who wanted to subject society to a sort of monastic despotism, were lamenting their impotence personified by Hiram's annihilation. The key word of their empire, which was lost, then rediscovered, was association or ruse, something like the ancient city or the Temple of Osiris. That's why I'm astonished to see this fable still being used for your initiations into the work of universal deliverance. I'd like to think that it's proposed to your disciples only as a test of their intelligence and courage."

"Well, we who did not invent these forms of Masonry and indeed use them only as spiritual tests, we who are more than journeymen and masters in this symbolic knowledge, since, after having gone through all the Masonic degrees, we're no longer Masons as the term is understood in the common ranks of the order, we beseech you to explain to us your understanding of the myth of Hiram so that we may pronounce upon your zeal, intelligence, and faith a judgment that will either stop you here at the door of the true temple or give you access to the sanctuary."

"You're asking me for Hiram's shibboleth, *the lost word*. That's not the one that will open the doors of the temple to me, for this word is tyranny or falsehood. But I know the true words, the names of the three doors of the sanctuary through which those who destroyed Hiram came to force this chief to bury himself under the ruins of his work; they are liberty, fraternity, equality."

"Consuelo, your interpretation, whether it be exact or not, reveals to us the depths of your heart. You need never kneel on Hiram's tomb. Neither will you ever go for the degree where the neophyte prostrates himself over the simulacrum of the ashes of Jacques Molay, the grand master and great victim of the Temple, of the monk-soldiers and the prelate-knights of the Middle Ages. You would emerge victorious from the second test as from the first, discerning the insidious traces of a fanatic barbarism still necessary today as formulaic guarantees for minds imbued with the principle of inequality. Remember that for the most part Freemasons of the first degrees only aspire to raising a profane temple, a mysterious refuge for an association elevated to the status of a caste. You understand things otherwise, and you are going to march straight to the universal temple that is to receive all humanity united in one form of worship, in one love. Yet you must make one last station here and prostrate yourself before this tomb. You must adore Christ and recognize in him the one true God."

"You're saying this to me as yet another test," replied Consuelo in a firm voice. "But you have deigned to open my eyes to lofty truths by teaching me to read in your secret books. Christ is a divine man whom we revere as antiquity's greatest philosopher and saint. We adore him as much as it is permitted to adore the best and the greatest of masters and martyrs. We can indeed call him the savior of mankind in the sense that he taught the people of his time truths that they had only glimpsed, which were to make humanity enter into a new phase of light and holiness. We can indeed kneel before his ashes to thank God for having given us such a prophet, such an example, such a friend, but we adore God in him and refrain from the crime of idolatry. We distinguish the divine nature of the revelation from that of the revealer. So I willingly render to these emblems of a martyrdom forever illustrious and sublime the homage of pious gratitude and filial enthusiasm, but I do not believe that the last word of the revelation was understood and proclaimed by mankind at the time of Jesus, for it hasn't yet officially come to earth. Out of the wisdom and faith of his disciples, out of the continuation of his work over the course of seventeen centuries, I am awaiting a more practical truth, a more complete application of the holy word and brotherly doctrine. I am awaiting the development of the Gospel, I am awaiting something more than equality before God. It is this that I await, that I invoke among mankind."

"Your words are bold and your doctrines rife with danger. Have you thought that through in your solitude? Have you foreseen the trouble that your new faith was already gathering around your head? Do you know the world and your own strength? Do you know that we are one against a hundred thousand in the most civilized countries on the globe? Do you know that in these times, between those who worship the sublime revealer Jesus in a crude, abusive way and those, now nearly as many, who deny his mission and even his existence, between the idolaters and the atheists, the only place for us is amidst mankind's persecutions, jibes, hatred, and scorn? Do you know that in France right now Rousseau and Voltaire, the religious philosopher and the unbelieving philosopher, are proscribed almost equally? Do you know this, which is even more frightening and incredible, that from the depths of their exile they proscribe each other? Do you know that you are going to return to a world where everything will conspire to shake your faith and corrupt your mind? Last, do you know you'll have to work as an apostle amid danger, doubt, disappointment, and suffering?"

"I am so resolved," replied Consuelo lowering her eyes and placing her hand over her heart, "God help me!"

"Well then, daughter," said Marcus, still holding Consuelo's hand, "we are going to subject you to some mental suffering, not to test your faith, about which we can now have no doubt, but to strengthen it. It is not in quiet repose nor in worldly pleasures that faith grows and intensifies, but in tears and tribulation. Do you feel the courage to confront painful emotions, perhaps violent fears as well?"

"If it is necessary, and if it will benefit my soul, I submit to your will," replied Consuelo, feeling a bit breathless.

The Invisibles immediately began removing the carpets and candles from around the coffin. It was rolled off into one of the deep window recesses, and several disciples, having armed themselves with iron bars, hastened to raise a round paving stone in the middle of the floor. Then Consuelo saw a circular opening big enough to let one person through. Its granite rim, blackened and timeworn, was without doubt as ancient as the other architectural details of the tower. A long ladder was brought forth and sunk into the shadowy void of the orifice. Then Marcus, leading Consuelo to the entrance, asked her three times in a solemn tone if she felt the strength to descend alone into the dungeons of the great feudal tower.

"Listen, my fathers or my brothers, for I don't know what to call you . . . ," said Consuelo.

"Call them your brothers," said Marcus. "You are here among the Invisibles, your equals in rank if you persevere one hour more. You are going to say farewell to them here and meet up with them again an hour later along with the council of the supreme leaders, whose voices are never heard, whose faces are never seen. These you will call your fathers. They are the sovereign pontiffs, the spiritual and temporal heads of our temple. We shall appear before them and you as well without our masks if you are firmly resolved to come join us at the door of the sanctuary by means of the dark and terrifying path starting here beneath your feet, where you must walk alone, shielded by nothing more than your courage and perseverance."

"I'll do so if I must," replied the trembling neophyte. "But this ordeal, which you declare so grim, is there no way around it? Oh my brothers, you surely don't want to trifle with the mind of a woman without affectation or false pride. It's already been put to the test quite enough. Today you've condemned me to a long fast, and even though emotion has kept hunger at bay for several hours, I feel physically weak; I don't know if I won't succumb to the labors you're imposing on me. I don't much care, and so I swear, if my body suffers or grows weak, but won't you take as moral cowardice what is only a physical failing? Tell me that you'll forgive me for having a woman's nerves as long as, once I'm myself again, I still have a man's heart."

"Poor child," replied Marcus, "I prefer to hear you acknowledge your weakness rather than to try and dazzle us with foolish audacity. If you wish, we'll let you have a guide, only one, to help and comfort you, if need be, on your pilgrimage. Brother," he said to Chevalier Liverani, who had stood near the door throughout this entire dialogue, his eyes fixed on Consuelo, "take your sister's hand and lead her through the subterranean passages to the place where we'll all meet again."

"And you, brother," said Consuelo distraught, "don't you also want to accompany me?"

"That I cannot do. You're allowed only one guide, and the one I've assigned you is the only one I can give you."

"I'll be brave," said Consuelo, wrapping herself in her cloak. "I'll go alone."

"You're refusing the arm of a brother and a friend?"

"I refuse neither his sympathy nor his interest, but I'll go alone."

"Then go, noble girl, and have no fear. She who descended alone into the *cistern of tears*, at Riesenburg, she who faced so many dangers to find the secret cave of Schreckenstein, will easily find her way through the bowels of our pyramid. Go then, like the young heroes of antiquity, seeking initiation through the ordeals of the sacred mysteries. Brothers, give her the cup, the precious relic that one of Zizka's descendants brought us, in which we consecrate the solemn sacrament of fraternal communion."

Liverani went to the altar and took a crudely carved wooden chalice, filled it, and gave it to Consuelo with some bread.

"Sister," said Marcus, "this is not merely sweet, generous wine and pure wheat bread that we're offering you to restore your physical strength; this is the body and blood of the divine man, as he himself understood it, in other words, the symbol, at one and the same time heavenly and earthly, of fraternal equality. Our fathers, the martyrs of the Taborite church, believed that the ungodly and sacrilegious priests were less worthy, for the consecration of the solemn sacrament, than the pure hands of a woman or child. Take communion with us here while waiting to take your place at the temple banquet, where the great mystery of the last supper will be more clearly revealed to you. Take this cup and drink first. If you do this with faith, a few drops will be a sovereign tonic for your body, and your fervent soul will carry off your whole being on wings of fire."

Consuelo, having taken the first drink, handed the cup back to Liverani, and once he had drunk in turn, he passed it to all the brothers. After Marcus had drunk the last drops, he blessed Consuelo and beseeched the assembly to turn their thoughts inward and pray for her; then he gave the neophyte a little silver lamp and helped her place her feet on the first rungs of the ladder.

"I need not tell you," he added, "that your days are not threatened; but fear for your soul; fear never to reach the door of the temple if you are so unfortunate as to glance back a single time during your march. You'll have several stations along the way; you must then examine everything that meets your eye, but as soon as a door opens in front of you, pass through it and don't turn around. That, as you know, is the rigid prescription of the ancient initiations. You must also, according to the ancient rites, take care to keep the flame of your lamp burning, as the emblem of your faith and zeal. Go, daughter, and may this thought give you superhuman courage: What you are doomed to suffer now is necessary for your heart and spirit to grow in virtue and true faith."

Consuelo cautiously climbed down the ladder, and as soon as she reached the last rung, they pulled it up, and she heard the heavy paving stone fall back into place with a great thud, sealing off the entrance to the dungeons overhead.

Chapter XXXIX

At first Consuelo, going from a hall blazing with a hundred candles to a place lit only by the flicker of her little lamp, discerned nothing around her except for a luminous haze that her gaze could not penetrate. But little by little her eyes adjusted to the darkness, and seeing nothing terrifying between her and the walls of a room whose size and octagonal shape were identical to the one where she had just been, she felt reassured enough to go have a close look at the strange writing on the walls. It was one long inscription that went round and round the room, uninterrupted by any doors or windows. While taking note of this, Consuelo did not wonder how she would get out of this dungeon, but what could have been the use of such a construction. Sinister thoughts that she at first dismissed came to mind, but these were soon confirmed by the inscription that she read by slowly walking and moving her lamp along at the height of the letters.

"Contemplate the beauty of these walls that rise up out of bedrock, four and twenty feet thick, that have stood for a thousand years, impervious to the assaults of war, the wear of time or the laborer's toil! This masterpiece of architectural masonry was erected by the hands of slaves, no doubt to bury the treasures of a magnificent master. Yes! to bury in the rocky bowels, in the depths of the earth, treasures of hatred and vengeance. Here have perished, here have suffered, here have wept, roared and blasphemed twenty generations of men, innocent for the most part, some of them heroes, all of them victims or martyrs: prisoners of war, serfs having risen up in revolt or too overburdened with taxes to pay new ones, religious innovators, sublime heretics, hapless wretches, vanquished creatures, fanatics, saints, as well as scoundrels, men hardened to the ferocity of army life, to the law of murder and pillage, subjected in their turn to horrible reprisals. These are the catacombs of feudalism, of military or religious despotism. These are the dwellings that powerful men had built by slaves to stifle the screams and conceal the corpses of their conquered brothers in chains. Here, no air to breathe, no ray of light, not a single stone on which to lay one's head; nothing but iron rings embedded in the wall to fasten the prisoners' chains and prevent them from choosing a spot to rest on the damp, icy ground.

Here, air, light, and food when it so pleased the guards on duty in the room above to crack the vault open a second and toss down a morsel of bread to hundreds of unfortunates heaped one on top of the other, the day after a battle, maimed or battered for the most part and, occasionally, something even more ghastly, one lone man, the last survivor, suffering and dying in despair amid the rotting corpses of his comrades, sometimes eaten by those same worms even before he was altogether dead and rotting away himself before the sensation of life and the horror of thought were annihilated in his brain. This, oh neophyte, is the source of the human grandeur you may have contemplated with admiration and envy among the mighty of this world! Skulls without flesh; human bones, dry and broken; tears and bloodstains; this is the meaning of the emblems on your coats of arms if your forefathers bequeathed to you the taint of patricians; this is what should be represented on the blazons of the princes you have served, or that you aspire to serve if you are from the plebs. Yes, this is the basis of aristocratic titles, this is the source of the glories and hereditary fortunes of this world; this is how a caste that the other castes still fear, flatter, and caress has raised itself up and prevailed. This, this is what men, from father to son, have invented to exalt themselves over other men."

After having deciphered this inscription by going three times round the dungeon, Consuelo, overwhelmed with grief and horror, put down her lamp and dropped to her knees for a rest. Deep silence reigned over this gloomy place, and terrifying thoughts were crowding into her mind. Consuelo's vivid imagination conjured up somber visions around her. She thought she was seeing ghastly shades covered with hideous wounds fluttering along the walls or crawling over the ground at her side. She thought she was hearing their pitiful moans, their dying gasps, their feeble sighs, the grating of their chains. She resurrected in her mind how people must have lived back in the Middle Ages and even not so long ago during the Wars of Religion. She thought she was hearing, in the guardroom overhead, the heavy, ominous tread of these iron-shod men, their pikes echoing on the paving stones, their crude laughter, their songs of orgy, their threats and curses when the victims' complaints reached their ears from down below, interrupting their dreadful sleep, for these jailors had slept, they had had to sleep, they had been able to sleep above this dungeon, this filthy abyss venting the miasmas of the grave and the roars of hell. Pale with horror, her gaze vacant, her hair standing on end, Consuelo could no longer see or hear anything. When she came back to herself and stood up to escape the chill creeping over her, she noticed that a flagstone had been uprooted and thrown down below during her painful trance, opening a new way before her. She went closer and saw a steep, narrow staircase that was hard to descend. It took her to another underground chamber, narrower and squatter than the first. When she felt the soft, almost velvety ground underfoot, Consuelo lowered her lamp to see if she was not sinking into mud. She saw only gray powder, finer than the finest silt, with a pebble-like bump every now and then that turned out to be a broken rib, the neck of a thighbone, the remains of a skull, a jawbone still sporting white, solid teeth, evidence of youth and strength suddenly shattered by violent death. A few nearly complete skeletons had been plucked out of this dust and propped up against the walls. One was perfectly preserved, standing with a chain fastened around his middle, as if he had been condemned to die there without being able to lie down. His body, instead of slumping over forward, bent and out of joint, had gone stiff and rigid, arched back in a posture of superb pride and implacable disdain. The ligaments of his frame and limbs had turned to bone. With his head thrown back and his teeth clenched in an ultimate contraction of the jaws, he seemed to be gazing up at the vaulted ceiling and laughing in some terrifying burst of hilarity or sublime fanaticism. On the wall overhead his name and history were spelled out in big red letters. He was an obscure martyr of religious persecution and the last of the victims immolated in this place. At his feet there knelt a skeleton whose head, detached from the vertebrae, was lying on the ground, but whose stiff arms still embraced the martyr's knees. This was his wife. Among various other details, the inscription said, "N*** perished here along with his wife, his three brothers and his two children for refusing to abjure the Lutheran faith and persisting, even under torture, in his denials of papal infallibility. He died on his feet and desiccated, petrified as it were, and without being able to see his family dying at his feet on the ashes of his friends and forefathers."

Opposite this inscription was another one that read, "Neophyte, this friable ground on which you tread is twenty feet thick. It is neither sand nor earth, but human dust. This was the castle's boneyard. This is where the bodies of those who had died in the dungeon overhead were thrown when there was no more room for newcomers. These are the ashes of twenty generations of victims. Happy and few are the patricians who can count among their ancestors twenty generations of assassins and executioners."

Consuelo was less horrified by the sight of these funereal objects than she had been by the suggestions of her own mind in the dungeon. There is something too serious, too solemn about the sight of death itself to let debilitating fear or heartrending pity cast a pall over the enthusiasm or equanimity of strong, faithful souls. In the presence of these relics the noble disciple of Albert's religion felt more respect and charity than terror or dismay. She knelt down before the martyr's remains and, feeling her inner strength returning, kissed the fleshless hand and cried, "Oh! it is not the august spectacle of glorious destruction that calls forth horror or pity, but rather the idea of life in the throes of death. It's thinking what must have transpired in these desolate souls that fills the minds of the living with bitterness and terror! But you, hapless victim, who died on your feet, with your head turned to the heavens, you are not to be pitied, for you did not surrender, and you breathed out your soul in a transport of fervor that fills me with awe."

Consuelo slowly got up and rather calmly detached her bridal veil which had snagged on the bones of the woman kneeling at her side. A low, narrow door had just opened in front of her. Picking up her lamp and taking care not to turn back around, she entered a dark, narrow passage that made a steep descent. To her right and left she saw entrances to cells smothered under the weight of truly sepulchral architecture. These dungeons were too low for one to stand up and hardly long enough for one to lie down. They seemed to be the work of Cyclopes, so sturdily built and skillfully contrived in the solid mass of masonry, like pens for ferocious, dangerous animals. Yet Consuelo could make no mistake. She had seen the amphitheater at Verona and knew that the tigers and bears set aside for circus entertainments and gladiator contests long ago were housed a thousand times better. Besides, she read on the iron doors that these inexpugnable dungeons had been reserved for conquered princes, valiant captains, prisoners whose rank, intelligence, or energy made them the most important and the most feared. That such formidable precautions had been taken against their escape testified to the love and respect they had inspired in their followers. This is where the roar of these lions that had made the world quake fell silent. Their might and will were broken against an angle of a wall; their Herculean breasts had gone dry seeking a breath of air from an imperceptible flue slanting through twenty feet of quarry stone. Their eagle eyes had grown dim watching for a faint glimmer in eternal darkness. This is where the men whom one did not dare kill by light of day were buried alive. There illustrious minds and magnanimous hearts had expiated the use and no doubt as well the abuse of the rights of force.

After having wandered a while through these dark, dank passages that sank deep into the rock, Consuelo heard a gurgling sound that reminded her of the fearsome underground torrent at Riesenburg, but she was too preoccupied by humanity's troubles and crimes to give much thought to herself. She was forced to pause a moment to circumvent a torch-lit sinkhole flush with the ground. On a signpost under the torch she read these few words, which had no need of commentary, "Here's where they were drowned!"

Consuelo bent over to take a look inside. Here the stream of water on which she had navigated so peacefully not an hour before dashed down into terrifying depths, whirling and roaring as though it were eager to seize and drag off a victim. The ruddy glow of the resin torch gave these sinister waters the color of blood.

At last Consuelo arrived at a massive door that she tried in vain to move. She wondered if, as in initiations in the pyramids of Egypt, she was going to be swept into the air by means of invisible chains while an abyss opened at her feet and a sudden violent gust of wind blew out her lamp. Something else gave her more serious alarm. Since entering the passage she had become aware that she was not alone; someone was walking close behind her with such a light step that she could not detect the slightest sound; yet she thought she had felt a garment brush against her own, and when she had gone past the well, the light of the torch behind her had cast on the wall two flickering shadows instead of one. So who was this fearsome companion at whom she was forbidden to look on pain of forfeiting the fruit of all her labors and never crossing the threshold of the temple? Was it some terrifying shade so ugly that he would have chilled her courage and addled her wits? She no longer saw his shadow, but she imagined that she could hear him breathing right beside her, and that fateful door would not budge! The two or three minutes that went by as she waited there seemed to her a hundred years long. This mute acolyte frightened her; she feared that he wanted to put her to the test by speaking to her, forcing her by some trick to look at him. Her heart was pounding; finally she noticed an inscription above the door that she had yet to read.

"Here awaits your last ordeal, and it is the most cruel. If you've exhausted your courage, knock twice on the left side of this door; otherwise, knock three times on the right. Bear in mind that the glory of your initiation will be commensurate to your efforts."

Without hesitating Consuelo knocked three times on the right side of the door. It seemed to open all by itself, and she entered a vast, torch-lit hall. There was no one there, and at first she understood nothing about the bizarre objects symmetrically arranged in rows around her. There were contraptions of wood, iron, and bronze for what use she knew not; strange weapons laid out on tables or hanging on the walls. For a second she thought she was in an artillery museum; for there were indeed muskets, cannons, culverins, and a whole set of instruments of war in front of yet others. Someone had taken pleasure in collecting all the means of destruction that men had invented for their mutual immolation. But when the neophyte had advanced a few steps through this arsenal, she saw other objects of a more refined barbarity: racks, wheels, saws, cast-iron tanks, pulleys, hooks, an entire museum of instruments of torture; and on a large signboard standing in their midst, on top of a trophy of sledgehammers, pincers, scissors, files, axes with sawtooth blades, and all the torturer's abominable tools, it was written, "These are all most precious, all authentic; *they have all been used*."

Then Consuelo felt her whole being faint away. A cold sweat drenched her braids. Her heart stopped beating. Unable to pull herself away from the terrifying spectacle and bloody visions besetting her from every side, she examined the objects in front of her with that stupid, baleful curiosity that takes us in its grip when we are overwhelmed with horror. Instead of closing her eyes, she contemplated some kind of bronze bell with a monstrous head and a round helmet set on a great, formless body without legs and cut off at the knees. It looked like a colossal statue of crude workmanship meant to decorate a tomb. Little by little Consuelo, emerging from her stupor, understood, involuntarily intuited that the torture victim was made to squat under the bell. It was so dreadfully heavy that there was no human way for him to lift it, and it was such a snug fit that he could not move a muscle. Yet he was not put there to be smothered, for the visor of the helmet that came down over the face as well as the part that went all around the head were pierced with little holes in a few of which were still planted slender probes. By means of these cruel perforations the victim was tortured to wring out of him a confession of his crime, real or imaginary, a denunciation of his relatives or friends, an avowal of his political or religious faith.[1] On the top of the helmet one could read, in letters cut into the metal, these words in Spanish, "Long live the Holy Inquisition!" And below that, a prayer that seemed dictated by some fierce compassion, but which may have come from the heart and hand of the poor workman condemned to make this vile contraption, "Holy Mother of God, pray for the poor sinner!"

Beneath the prayer there was still a clump of hair ripped out in the course of torture and no doubt glued with blood, like frightening and indelible stigmata. The hairs were protruding from one of the holes that had been stretched wider by the probe, and they were white!

All of a sudden Consuelo saw nothing more, and her suffering ceased. Without any warning sensation of physical pain, for her soul and body no longer existed except in the raped and mutilated body and soul of humanity, Consuelo fell flat on her face to the stone floor, like a statue breaking off from its pedestal, but just as her head was about to hit the bronze of the infernal contraption she was gathered into the arms of a man whom she did not see. It was Liverani.

1. Everyone can see an instrument of this kind along with a hundred others no less ingenious at the Venice Arsenal. Consuelo had not seen it there. These horrible instruments of torture as well as the interior of the dungeons of the Holy Office and the Prison of Lead at the Doges' Palace were opened to the public only after the French entered Venice during the Wars of the Republic.

Chapter XL

Coming back to her senses, Consuelo saw that she was sitting on crimson carpets over the white marble steps of an elegant Corinthian peristyle. Two masked men whom she recognized from the color of their cloaks as Liverani and Marcus, as she had been right to think the second one had to be, were holding her in their arms and endeavoring to revive her. Some forty others with cloaks and masks, the same ones that she had seen around the simulacrum of Jesus's coffin, made two rows across the steps, and they were singing in chorus a solemn hymn in an unknown tongue while waving crowns of roses, palm branches and sprays of flowers. The columns were festooned with garlands like an arch of triumph over the closed door of the temple and above Consuelo's head. The moon, resplendent at its zenith, illuminated the white façade all by itself; and all around the sanctuary ancient yews, cypresses, and pines formed an impenetrable grove, like a sacred wood, while mysterious waters with silver reflections murmured at their feet.

"Sister," said Marcus, helping Consuelo up, "you've emerged victorious from your ordeals. Don't blush for having suffered and physically flagged under the burden of pain. Your noble heart broke with indignation and pity at the palpable evidence of humanity's crimes and afflictions. Had you got here on your feet and unassisted, we would have less respect for you than we do carrying you, moribund and sorely distressed. You have seen the crypts of a seigneurial castle, not of any one place more famous than all the others for the crimes committed there, but like all those whose ruins cover a great deal of Europe, frightening remains of the vast network by means of which feudal power enveloped the civilized world for so many centuries and oppressed mankind with the crime of its fierce domination and the horrors of civil war. These hideous dwellings, these desolate fortresses necessarily served as dens of all the heinous crimes that humanity had to see accomplished before arriving at the notion of truth, by means of the wars of religion, the work of emancipating sects, and the martyrdom of the best of men. Just travel through Germany, France, Italy, England, Spain, and the Slavic countries. You won't find a valley or climb a mountain without seeing up above the forbidding ruins of some grim manor, or at least without discovering at your feet, in the grass, some vestige of fortifications. These are the bloody traces of the right of conquest exercised by the patrician caste over the castes they enslaved. And if you explore all these ruins, if you excavate the earth that has swallowed them up and is relentlessly working to make them disappear, in every single one you'll find vestiges of what you've just seen here: dungeons, vaults for the surfeit of dead bodies, cramped, stinking cells for important prisoners, a corner for silent assassinations, and, at the top of some old tower or somewhere deep underground, a rack for recalcitrant serfs and rebellious soldiers, a gallows for deserters, and cauldrons for heretics. How many have died boiled in pitch, drowned, or buried alive in the mines? Oh, if castle walls, lakes, rivers, and rocky caves could talk and recount all the iniquities that they have witnessed and concealed! So many that history cannot render detailed accounts!

"But it is not just the feudal lords, not the patrician race alone who have reddened the earth with so much innocent blood! Kings and priests, thrones and the church, these are the great sources of iniquity, the vital forces of destruction. In one of the rooms of our ancient manor, austere diligence, a gloomy but great notion has gathered a collection of some of the instruments of torture invented by the hatred of the strong for the weak. A description of them would not be credible; the eye can scarcely comprehend them, the mind refuses to acknowledge them. And yet they were used for centuries, these hideous devices, in the castles of kings as well as in the citadels of minor princes, but above all in the dungeons of the Holy Office; what I am saying? There they are still being used, but less frequently. The Inquisition is still going on, still torturing; and in France, the most civilized of all countries, there are still provincial parliaments that burn alleged sorcerers at the stake.

"Besides, has tyranny really been overthrown? Do kings and princes no longer lay waste to the earth? Does war not bring desolation to opulent cities and poor cottages at the slightest whim of the most trifling sovereign? Is bondage not still in force in half of Europe? Aren't soldiers nearly everywhere still subjected to whipping and flogging? The bravest and most handsome soldiers in the world, the soldiers of Prussia, aren't they trained like animals with rod and cane? Aren't Russian serfs ruled with the knout? Aren't blacks in America treated worse than dogs and horses? While the fortresses of the old barons have been dismantled and turned into harmless dwellings, aren't those of the kings still standing? Aren't they used more often as prisons for the innocents than for the guilty? And you, sister, you the sweetest and most noble of women, weren't you held captive at Spandau?

"We knew your generosity, we were counting on your sense of justice and charity, but seeing that you were destined, like some of those here, to return to the world, to be part of court society, to approach kings and queens, to be, you in particular, the object of their seductions, it was our duty to put you on your guard against the intoxications of that glamorous, dangerous life, it was our duty not to spare you any lessons, even the most horrifying. We have spoken to your mind by the solitude to which we sentenced you and the books that we made available to you, to your heart by fatherly words and exhortations alternately stern and tender, to your eyes by ordeals more painful and more meaningful than those of the ancient mysteries. Now, if you persist in receiving the initiation, you can go without fear before those incorruptible, yet fatherly judges whom you already know, who are awaiting you here, either to give you a crown or to set you free to leave us forever."

With these words Marcus raised his arm and pointed out to Consuelo the door of the temple above which the three sacramental words, *Liberty, Equality, Fraternity*, had just blazed up in letters of fire.

Consuelo, weak and broken in her body, was now living by the spirit alone. She had not been able to listen to Marcus's speech on her feet. Forced to sit down on the foot of a column, she leaned on Liverani, but without seeing him or giving him a thought. Yet she had not missed a single word spoken by the initiator. Pale as a ghost, her eyes intent and her voice extinguished, she did not have the bewildered look that follows nervous crises. Concentrated excitement filled her breast, and her breathing was so shallow that Liverani could no longer detect it. Her dark eyes, somewhat sunken into their orbits by exhaustion and suffering, burned with a somber flame. A slight furrow in her forehead betrayed unshakable resolve, the first in her life. Her beauty at that moment frightened those present who had known her elsewhere as invariably sweet and kind. Liverani began to tremble like the jasmine leaf that the night breeze was ruffling on his beloved's brow. She got to her feet with more energy than he would have expected, but her knees immediately buckled, and she let him almost carry her up the steps, without the clasp of these arms which had so thrilled her, without the nearness of this heart which had set hers afire distracting her for one instant from her inner meditation. He put between his hand and hers the silver cross, the talisman that had given him rights over her, that he had used to make himself known to her once again. Consuelo seemed to recognize neither the token nor the hand presenting it. Hers was contracted in pain, its grip automatic, as when one hangs onto a branch to stop from going over the edge of a cliff, but no blood from the heart could reach that icy hand.

"Marcus!" Liverani whispered as Marcus drew near on his way up to knock on the door of the temple, "don't leave us. The ordeal was too much. I'm afraid!"

"She loves you," replied Marcus.

"Yes, but she may die!" said Liverani with a shudder.

Marcus knocked three times on the door, which opened and closed again as soon as he was inside with Consuelo and Liverani. The other brethren remained on the peristyle, waiting to be ushered in for the ceremony; for between the initiation and the last ordeals there was always a secret conversation among the leaders of the Invisibles and the person being received.

The interior of the temple-shaped summerhouse used for these initiations at the castle of *** was magnificently adorned, with statues of the greatest friends to humanity standing between the columns. That of Jesus Christ was placed at the center of the amphitheater, between Pythagoras and Plato. Apollonius of Tyana was next to Saint John, Abelard beside Saint Bernard, Jan Hus and Jerome of Prague beside Saint Catherine and Joan of Arc. But Consuelo did not stop to consider exterior objects. Deep in meditation, without surprise or emotion, she set eyes once again on these same judges who had probed her heart to such depths. She no longer felt at all abashed in the presence of these men, whoever they were, and she awaited their verdict with apparent great calm.

"Brother presenter," said to Marcus the eighth person, who was seated below the seven judges and invariably served as their spokesman, "whom are you bringing before us? What is her name?"

"Consuelo Porporina," Marcus replied.

"That is not what they are asking you, brother," said Consuelo. "Don't you see that I've come here in a wedding gown and not mourning weeds? Announce the Countess Albert von Rudolstadt."

"Daughter," said the brother orator, "I'm speaking to you in the name of the council. You no longer bear the name you invoke. Your marriage to Count von Rudolstadt is dissolved."

"By what right, and by virtue of what authority?" asked Consuelo in a short, strong voice, as though in a fever. "I don't recognize any theocratic power. You yourselves have taught me to recognize that the only rights you have over me are those that I've freely given you and to submit only to a fatherly authority. Your authority would not be fatherly if it were to dissolve my marriage without my husband's assent as well as my own. Neither he nor I have given you this right."

"You're wrong, daughter. Albert gave us the right to dispose of his fate and yours, and you yourself did the same when you opened your heart to us and confessed your love for another man."

"I confessed nothing to you," replied Consuelo, "and I deny the consent that you are trying to wring out of me."

"Bring in the sibyl," said the orator to Marcus.

A tall woman, all draped in white, her face hidden beneath a veil, came in and sat down in the center of the semicircle formed by the judges. Consuelo easily recognized Wanda because of her nervous tremor.

"Speak, priestess of the truth," said the orator. "Speak, interpreter and revealer of the most intimate secrets, the most subtle stirrings of the heart. Is this woman the wife of Albert von Rudolstadt?"

"She is his faithful, worthy wife," replied Wanda, "but you must forthwith pronounce her divorce. You see who brings her here; you see that the one among our children whose hand she is holding is the man she loves and to whom she must belong, in virtue of the inalienable right of love in marriage."

Consuelo turned in surprise toward Liverani and looked at her hand, numb and seemingly dead in his. She looked as though she were in the power of some dream and struggling to wake up. At last she briskly loosed herself from that grasp, and looking at the hollow of her hand, she saw the imprint of her mother's cross.

"So this is the man I've loved!" she said, with the melancholy smile of holy ingenuousness. "That is indeed so. I've loved him tenderly, madly, but it was a dream! I thought Albert was no more, and you told me that this man was worthy of my respect and confidence. Then I saw Albert again. I thought I understood from what he said that he no longer wished to be my husband, and I couldn't help loving this stranger whose missives and attentions intoxicated me with a mad desire. But I was told that Albert still loved me, that he was giving me up out of virtue and generosity. And why then was Albert convinced that my sense of devotion would be less than his? What crime have I committed thus far to be thought capable of shattering his soul by accepting a selfish happiness? No, I'll never sully myself with such a crime. If Albert deems me unworthy of him for having loved someone else in my heart; if he has a scruple about destroying that love and doesn't want to inspire a greater love in me, I'll submit to his decree; I'll accept this sentence of divorce against which my heart and conscience rebel, but I'll be neither wife nor lover to another man. Farewell, Liverani, or whoever you may be, to whom I entrusted my mother's cross in a day of abandon that leaves me neither shame nor remorse. Give me back this token so that there is nothing more between us than a memory of mutual respect and the sense of a duty fulfilled without bitterness or effort."

"We don't recognize such morals, you know," said the sibyl. "We don't accept such sacrifices. We want to inaugurate and sanctify love, lost and profaned in the world, the free choice of the heart, the holy and voluntary union of two beings equally in love. Over our children we have the right to mend consciences, forgive faults, match up affinities, break the shackles of the old society. You therefore don't have the right to sacrifice yourself, you cannot stifle the love in your breast and deny the truth of your confession without our having authorized you to do so."

"Why are you talking to me about liberty, about love and happiness?" exclaimed Consuelo, taking a step toward the judges in an explosion of enthusiasm, her physiognomy radiantly sublime. "Haven't you just made me undergo ordeals that must leave the brow eternally wan and the soul invincibly austere? What kind of callous, cowardly person do you take me for if you think I'm still capable of dreaming of personal pleasures and pursuing them after what I've seen, after what I've understood, after what I now know about people's lives and my duties in this world? No, no! No more love, no more marriage, no more liberty, no more happiness, glory, or art, nothing more for me if I have to make the least of my peers suffer! And hasn't it been proven that every joy in today's world is bought at the price of some one else's? Isn't there something better to do than to seek one's own gratification? Isn't that the way Albert thinks, and don't I have the right to think as he does? Doesn't he hope to find, even in the sacrifice of himself, the strength to work for humanity with more ardor and intelligence than ever? Let me be as great as Albert. Let me flee the lying, criminal illusion of happiness. Give me work, weariness, pain, and enthusiasm! I no longer understand joy except in suffering; I yearn for martyrdom ever since you've imprudently shown me the trophies of torture. Oh, shame on those who have understood their duty and still worry about enjoying their share of happiness and repose on earth! I'm talking about us, about me! Oh, Liverani, if you're in love with me after having undergone the ordeals that bring me here, you're mad, you're nothing but a child unworthy of being called a man, surely unworthy that I should sacrifice to you Albert's heroic affection. And you, Albert, if you're here, if you can hear me, you ought not refuse at least to call me your sister, to offer me your hand and help me walk the arduous path that leads you to God."

Consuelo's enthusiasm was at its peak; words no longer sufficed to express it. A sort of vertigo came over her and, like the priestesses of Apollo who in the paroxysm of their divine crises would abandon themselves to cries and strange frenzies, she was swept away to the point of manifesting her overwhelming emotion in the way most natural to her. She began to sing in a resounding voice, enraptured at least as much as she had been singing this same aria in Venice, in public for the first time in her life, and in the presence of Marcello and Porpora:

I cieli immensi narrano
Del grande Iddio la gloria!

This hymn came to her lips because it may be the most naïve and striking expression that music has ever given to religious enthusiasm. But Consuelo was not composed enough to contain and control her voice. After these two verses her intonation became a sob in her throat, she dissolved in tears and fell to her knees.

The Invisibles, galvanized by her fervor, had stood up all at once as though to hear on their feet, in the posture of respect, the song of the inspired one. But seeing her succumb to her emotion, they all came down from their box and gathered round while Wanda seized Consuelo, threw her into Liverani's arms and exclaimed, "Now then! Take a look at him, and know that God has granted you to reconcile love and virtue, happiness and duty."

Consuelo, deaf for an instant, and as though carried off to another world, finally looked at Liverani, whose mask has just been ripped off by Marcus. She uttered a piercing cry and nearly expired on his breast as she recognized Albert. Albert and Liverani were the same man.

Chapter XLI

At that moment the doors of the temple swung open with a metallic click, and the Invisibles marched in two by two. The magical voice of the glass harmonica, this instrument of recent invention,[1] whose penetrating vibration was a marvel unknown to Consuelo's senses, issued forth, apparently wafting down from the cupola whose windows stood ajar to moonbeams and the night's refreshing breezes. Flower petals gently rained down on the happy couple at the center of this solemn procession. Standing beside a golden tripod, Wanda was making bright flames and clouds of incense billow forth with her right hand, and in her left she held the two ends of a chain of symbolic flowers and leaves that she had thrown around the lovers. The leaders of the Invisibles, their faces draped with their long red veils and their brows wreathed with the same leaves of oak and acacia hallowed by their rites, were on their feet, their arms stretched out as though to welcome the brethren who bowed as they passed by. These leaders had the majesty of ancient Druids, but their hands which had never known the stain of blood were open only to bestow blessings, and in the hearts of the disciples religious respect took the place of the fanatic terror of past religions. As the initiates stepped up to the venerable tribunal, they removed their masks to greet barefaced these august characters whose identities remained

1. Everyone knows that the glass harmonica created such a sensation when it first appeared in Germany that poetic imaginations wanted to think that they were hearing the supernatural voices evoked by the consecrators of certain mysteries. There was a time when German disciples of theosophy exalted this instrument, hailed as magical before it became fashionable, to the same divine honors as the lyre in Antiquity as well as several other musical instruments used by the primitive Himalayans. They turned it into a hieroglyph, representing a fantastic chimera, in their mysterious iconography. Hearing it for the first time after the terrors and emotions of their arduous ordeals, the neophytes of secret societies were so awed that several fell into trances of ecstasy. They believed that they were hearing the music of invisible forces, for the performer and the instrument were very carefully concealed from their sight. There are extremely curious details about the extraordinary role of the glass harmonica in the Illuminati's initiation ceremonies. [Translator's note: This instrument invented in the eighteenth century was made up of a set of glass strips struck by a little hammer or crystal glasses filled with water and made to vibrate with the tips of one's fingers.]

secret, never having made themselves known to the initiates except through acts of merciful justice, fatherly love, and great wisdom. Faithful to the religion of their oaths, without regret or mistrust, the disciples did not attempt to read beneath these impenetrable veils with a curious glance. No doubt these high priests of a new religion were known to their disciples without the latter realizing it. They mingled with them in society and in the very midst of their assemblies; they were the best friends, the most intimate confidants of most of them, perhaps of each one in particular. Yet when they came together in worship, the person of the priest was always veiled, like the oracle in Antiquity.

Oh happy childhood of naïve belief, oh quasi fabulous dawn of sacred conspiracies, that the night of mystery has always enveloped in poetic uncertainties! Even though scarcely a hundred years separate us from these Invisibles, they pose a problem for the historian, but thirty years later Illuminism revived these forms unknown to the crowd and, drawing on the inventive genius of its leaders as well as the tradition of secret societies in mystical Germany, it terrified the world with the most tremendous, the most clever of political and religious conspiracies. For an instant it shook all the dynasties on their thrones, then succumbed in its turn, while passing on to the French Revolution something like an electric current of sublime enthusiasm, ardent faith, and terrible fanaticism. Half a century before these fateful days, and while the gallant monarchy of Louis XV, the philosophical despotism of Frederick II, the skeptical, mocking sovereignty of Voltaire, the ambitious diplomacy of Maria Theresa and the heretical tolerance of Ganganelli seemed to announce that for a long time to come the world would know nothing but decrepitude, antagonism, chaos, and dissolution, the French Revolution was brewing in the dark and germinating underground. It was looming in the minds of fanatic believers as a dream of universal revolution; and while debauchery, hypocrisy, or unbelief officially reigned over the world, a sublime faith, a magnificent revelation of things to come, plans for organization as profound and perhaps more sophisticated than our present-day Fourierism and Saint-Simonism, were already bringing forth in a few groups of exceptional men the ideal conception of a future society, diametrically opposed to the one that covers and still conceals their action in history.

This contrast is one of the most striking features of the eighteenth century, brimming over with so many ideas and intellectual labor of all sorts that the philosophical historians of our times have not yet been able to produce any clear and useful synthesis of it. There is such a mass of contradictory documents and misunderstood facts, at first impossible to grasp, springs roiled up by the turbulent times and requiring patient filtering in order to find the solid bottom. Many energetic laborers have remained obscure, carrying their secret missions to the grave. So many dazzling glories absorbed their contemporaries' attention, and still today so many brilliant works monopolize the critics' look back in time! But bit by bit light will emerge from this chaos; and if our century manages to sum itself up, it will also sum up the life of its father, the eighteenth century, this enormous logogriph, this brilliant nebula, where so much cowardliness contrasts with such grandeur, so much knowledge with such ignorance, so much barbarism with such civilization, so much enlightenment with such errors, so much seriousness with such intoxication, so much unbelief with such faith, so much learned pedantry with such frivolous mockery, so much superstition with such proud reason; this century, which saw the reigns of Madame de Maintenon and Madame de Pompadour, Peter the Great, Catherine II, Maria Theresa and that Dubarry woman, Voltaire and Swedenborg, Kant and Mesmer, Jean-Jacques Rousseau and Cardinal Dubois, Schroepfer and Diderot, Fénelon and Law, Zinzendorf and Leibniz, Frederick II and Robespierre, Louis XIV and Philippe-Egalité, Marie-Antoinette and Charlotte Corday, Weishaupt, Babeuf and Napoleon. . . . A terrifying laboratory where so many heterogeneous forms were thrown into the crucible that their monstrous ebullition belched forth a torrent of smoke through which we are still marching, enveloped in darkness and confusion.

Consuelo no more than Albert, the leaders of the Invisibles no more than their disciples cast a very lucid gaze on this century into which they yearned to throw themselves in the enthusiastic hope of regenerating it at one fell swoop. They believed themselves on the eve of an evangelical republic, like the disciples of Jesus eagerly awaiting the kingdom of God on earth, like the Bohemian Taborites, who thought paradise close at hand, like the French Convention that years later felt it would soon win over the entire planet. Yet, without such mad confidence, where would the great sacrifices be; without great madness, where the great achievements? Without the utopia of the divine dreamer Jesus, where would the notion of human brotherhood be? Without the contagious visions of the ecstatic Joan of Arc, would we still be French? Without the noble chimeras of the eighteenth century, would we have conquered the rudiments of equality? This mysterious revolution—every sect in times past having dreamed that it would happen in their day, and the mystical conspirators of the last century having vaguely predicted that it would occur fifty years earlier, as a time of political and religious renovation—neither Voltaire nor the calm philosophical minds of his time nor Frederick II himself, relying on cold, logical force to realize his ambitions, foresaw its sudden storms, its abrupt miscarriage. The most ardent as well as the most sage were far from reading clearly in the future. Jean-Jacques Rousseau would have repudiated his works, had the Mountain, with the guillotine looming over it, appeared to him in a dream. Albert von Rudolstadt would all of a sudden have reverted to the cataleptic madman of Schreckenstein, had these bloody glories, followed by Napoleon's despotism, the restoration of the Old Regime, and then the reign of the most vile material interests been revealed to him, he who believed that he was laboring to overturn, now and forever, scaffolds and prisons, barracks and convents, brokerage houses and citadels!

So they dreamed, these noble children, and they acted on their dreams with all the strength of their souls. They were neither more nor less of their century than the clever politicians and sage philosophers, their contemporaries. They saw neither more nor less than these the absolute truth of the future, that great Unknown that we all invest with the attributes of our own power, who deceives every one of us, at the same time validates us when she appears to our sons, clad in her imperial gown of many colors of which we have each prepared a piece. Fortunately, every new century sees her as more majestic, given that each one produces more people laboring for her triumph. As for those who wish to shred her royal purple and dress her in eternal mourning, they can do nothing against her, they do not understand her. Slaves to present-day reality, they do not know that the Immortal One has no age and that those who do not dream of her as she may be tomorrow do not see her at all as she must be today.

Albert, in that moment of supreme happiness when Consuelo's eyes, full of delight, at long last fastened on his; Albert, rejuvenated by the benefits of health and handsome in the intoxication of bliss, felt imbued with that almighty faith that would move mountains if in such moments there were other mountains to move than the weight of our minds reeling with joy. Consuelo was finally before him, like Galatea, that creation of the artist beloved by the gods, waking at one and the same time to love and life. Wordless and rapt in meditation, her physiognomy haloed with celestial light, she was totally, incontestably beautiful for the first time in her life, because she was indeed totally and truly alive for the first time. A sublime serenity shone on her brow, and her large eyes were brimming with that deep pleasure of the soul of which sensual delight is but a feeble reflection. She was so beautiful only because she had no idea what was going on in her heart and on her face. Albert alone existed for her; rather, she now existed only in him, and to her he alone seemed worthy of immense respect and boundless admiration. Albert too was transformed, as if he were invested with supernatural radiance as he contemplated her. Deep in his eyes she could see all the solemn grandeur of the noble pains he had endured, but this past bitterness had left no trace of physical suffering on his features. He had the placid brow of a resurrected martyr who sees the earth red with his blood falling away beneath his feet and the heaven of infinite rewards opening overhead. Never had an inspired artist created a nobler face of a hero or saint in the finest days of ancient or Christian art.

All of the Invisibles, awestruck in their turn, gathered round, then stopped and for a few instants surrendered to the noble pleasure of contemplating this beautiful couple, so pure in the presence of God, so chastely happy in the presence of man. Then twenty generous male voices sang in chorus to a broad rhythm of ancient simplicity, "*Hymen o Hymenaee!*" The music was by Porpora, to whom the words had been sent along with the request that he compose an epithalamium for an illustrious wedding, and he had been worthily compensated without ever knowing by whom. Just as Mozart, on the eve of his death, was one day to find his most sublime inspiration for a mysteriously commissioned *Requiem*, old Porpora had rediscovered all the genius of his youth to write a wedding song whose poetic mystery had reawakened his imagination. From the first measures Consuelo recognized the style of her beloved teacher and, struggling to pull away from her lover's gaze, she turned toward the coryphaei to find her adoptive father, but he was there only in spirit. Among those who had become the worthy interpreters of his piece Consuelo recognized several friends, Frederick von Trenck, Porporino, Benda the Younger, Count Golowkin, Schubart, the Chevalier d'Eon, whom she had met in Berlin and whose true sex remained unknown to her as well as to all of Europe; the Count de Saint-Germain, Chancellor Coccei̇̈, Barberini's husband, Nicolaï the bookseller, Gottlieb, whose beautiful voice dominated all the others, and finally Marcus, whom Wanda vigorously pointed out. An instinctual affinity had already led Consuelo to recognize him as the guide who had introduced her and acted as her godfather or putative father. All of the Invisibles had parted their long, gloomy black robes and thrown them over their shoulders. Simple, elegant suits of white and crimson with gold chains bearing the order's insignia gave the group a festive look. Their masks were wrapped around their wrists, all ready to be slipped back on at the slightest signal from the watchman posted as a sentry on the dome.

The *orator*, who acted as the intermediary between the leaders of the Invisibles and the disciples, removed his mask as well and congratulated the happy spouses. It was the Duke of ***, the rich prince who had devoted his fortune, mind, and enthusiastic zeal to the Invisibles. He was their host, and for a long while his residence had welcomed Wanda and Albert, hidden from profane eyes. It was also the headquarters for the order's tribunal, even though it had several other venues, and rather numerous gatherings took place there only once a year, for a few days of summer, except in extraordinary cases. Initiated into all the leaders' secrets, the duke acted for and with them, although he never betrayed their incognito. Taking upon himself alone all the dangers of the enterprise, he was their interpreter and visible means of contact with the members of the association.

After the bride and groom had exchanged sweet expressions of joy and affection with their brothers, they all went back to their places, and the duke, acting as the orator once again, said these words to the couple crowned with flowers and kneeling at the altar, "My dear, beloved children, in the name of the true God, all power, love, and intelligence; and after him, in the name of the three virtues that are God's reflection in the human soul: action, charity, and justice, which in practice are translated by our formula: *liberty, fraternity, equality*; finally, in the name of the Tribunal of the Invisibles that has devoted itself to the triple duty of zeal, faith, and study, in other words, to the triple pursuit of political, moral, and divine truths: Albert Podiebrad, Consuelo Porporina, I pronounce the ratification and confirmation of the marriage that you previously contracted before God and family, and even before a priest of the Christian religion, at the Castle of the Giants, on *** of the year 175*. This marriage, valid in the eyes of men, was not valid in the eyes of God. Three things were lacking: 1st the absolute commitment of the wife to live with a husband who seemed on the point of death; 2nd the sanction of a moral and religious authority recognized and accepted by the husband; 3rd the consent of a person here present, whose name I am not permitted to say, but who is a close blood relation to one of the spouses. If these three conditions are now fulfilled, and if neither one of you has any complaints or objections, join hands and stand to take heaven as your witness to the liberty of your act and the holiness of your love."

Wanda, retaining her incognito in front of the brothers of the order, took the hands of her two children. The three of them stood up, all moved by the same impulse of love and enthusiasm, as though they were one.

The wedding formulas were spoken, and the simple, touching rites of the new religion were fulfilled in a meditative, fervent spirit. This pledging of mutual love was not an isolated act amid indifferent spectators, strangers to the spiritual bond being contracted. They were all called to sanction this religious consecration of two beings bound to them by a common faith. They raised their arms over the bride and groom to bless them, then all joined hands to form a vibrant circle, a chain of fraternal love and religious fellowship around them, while promising to help and protect them, to defend their honor and their lives, to sustain their needs if need be, to do everything to redeem them if they ever faltered along virtue's arduous path, to preserve them as much as possible from persecution and the world's seductions, in every occasion and at every juncture; finally, to give them a love so holy, cordial, and earnest as though they were all joined by name and blood. Handsome Trenck uttered this formula for all the others simply and eloquently, then turned to the groom and added, "Albert, it is the profane and criminal custom of the old world, from which we secretly withdraw so to bring it round to us one day, for the husband to impose fidelity on his wife in the name of a humiliating, despotic authority. If she succumbs, he must kill his rival; he even has the right to kill his wife, which is called washing in blood the stain on one's honor. Also, in the old world, in its blindness and corruption, every man is the natural enemy of this happiness and honor, so ferociously guarded. Friends, even brothers, assume the right to rob a friend and brother of his companion's love; or at least they give themselves the cruel and cowardly pleasure of stirring up his jealousy, rendering his surveillance ridiculous and sowing mistrust and mischief between him and the object of his love. Here, as you know, we have a better understanding of friendship, honor and family pride. We are brothers before God, and he among us who would cast a bold, disloyal glance at his brother's wife has, in our eyes, already committed the crime of incest in his heart."

All the brothers, carried away by emotion, drew their swords and swore to turn these arms against themselves rather than to break the vow that they had just uttered in the words of Trenck.

But the sibyl, in the throes of one of those inspired transports that gave her such a hold on their imagination and often modified the opinions and judgments of the leaders themselves, broke the circle and sprang into the center. Her words, always brisk and fiery, enthralled their assemblies; her great stature, the ample gowns floating over her gaunt body, her majestic though unsteady bearing, the convulsive tremor of her head with its ever present veil, and yet a sort of grace that revealed her past beauty, this charm so powerful in a woman that it lingers on even once it has disappeared and still moves the soul even though it can no longer arouse the senses; finally, even her feeble voice that suddenly, with the intensity of her feeling, burst forth in strange, strident tones; all this contributed to her mystery, almost frightening at first, and soon invested with persuasive power and irresistible fascination.

Everyone fell silent to hear the inspired one speak. Consuelo was as moved as they were, and perhaps more so, knowing as she did the secret of that strange life. She wondered, with an involuntary shudder of horror, if this specter who had escaped the tomb was really part of this world and if, after having issued her oracle, she would not vanish into thin air with the flame of the tripod that gave her a bluish, transparent cast.

"Hide from me the glint of these swords!" exclaimed Wanda all aquiver. "These are unholy oaths, sworn on instruments of hatred and murder. I know well that the old world was wont to gird the flank of every man reputed to be free, as a mark of independence and pride; I know well that, among the old world ideas that you've preserved despite yourselves, the sword is the symbol of honor, that you believe you're undertaking sacred commitments when you swear by the sword like the citizens of ancient Rome. But here that is to profane an august oath. Swear instead by this tripod's flame, the symbol of life, light, and divine love. But do you still need emblems and visible signs? Are you still idolaters? And the figures adorning this temple, do they represent for you something other than ideas? Ah, swear instead by your own feelings, by your better instincts, by your own hearts; and if you dare not swear by the living God, by the true, eternal, and sacred religion, swear by holy Humanity, by the glorious impulses of your courage, by this young woman's chastity and her husband's love. Swear by Consuelo's genius and beauty that your desires and even your thoughts will never profane this sacred ark of marriage, this invisible, mystical altar on which the hands of the angels are engraving and recording the oath of love. . . .

"Do you really know what love is?" added the sibyl, after having drawn into herself an instant. With every passing moment her voice was clearer and more penetrating. "If you knew, oh you venerable leaders of our order and ministers of our worship, you would never have anyone utter before you this formula of eternal commitment that God alone can ratify, which, consecrated by man, is a sort of profanation of the most divine of all mysteries. What strength can you impart to a commitment that by itself is a miracle? Yes, it is a miracle when two wills abandon themselves to each other and become one, for every soul is eternally free by divine right. And yet, when two souls give and bind themselves by love one to the other, their mutual possession becomes as sacred, as much a matter of divine right as individual liberty. You can see that it's a miracle, and one that God keeps forever a mystery, like life and death. You're going to ask this man and this woman if they want to belong to each other exclusively in this life, and their fervor is such that they'll reply, "Not just in this life, but for all eternity." God, by the miracle of love, inspires them with far more faith, strength, and virtue than you could or would dare ask of them. Away then with sacrilegious oaths and crude laws! Leave them their ideal, and don't fasten them down to reality with the chains of law. Let God take care of making the miracle last. Prepare souls for this miracle to happen in them, mold them to the ideal of love; exhort, instruct, praise, and demonstrate the glory of fidelity, without which there is no inner strength or sublime love. But don't interfere, like Catholic priests, like judges back in the old world, in the oath's fulfillment. For, I'm telling you once again, man can neither guarantee nor ensure that a miracle will last forever. What do you know about the Eternal One's secrets? Have we already entered that temple of the future, that celestial realm where man, we are told, will converse with God in the sacred grove as a friend with his friend? Has the law of indissoluble marriage issued forth from the mouth of the Lord? Have his designs in this regard been proclaimed on earth? And you yourselves, oh children of man, have you promulgated this law with one accord? Have the pontiffs of Rome, who claim to be infallible, never dissolved a marriage? On the pretext that certain commitments were null and void, these pontiffs have consecrated veritable divorces whose scandal has gone down in history. Plus, following the example of the teachings of Moses and all the ancient religions, some Christian societies and reformed sects, the Greek church as well, have frankly inaugurated the law of divorce in our modern world. So what happens to the sanctity and efficacy of an oath made to God when it is a matter of record that man will be able to release us from it one day? Ah, don't touch love by profaning marriage! You would only succeed in extinguishing love in pure hearts! Consecrate marriage by exhortations, prayers, public displays that give it respect, by poignant ceremonies; you must do so if you are our priests, which is to say, our friends, guides, counselors, consolers, and beacons. Prepare souls for the sanctity of a sacrament; and just as the father seeks to establish his children in conditions of comfort, dignity, and security, so should you, our spiritual fathers, work hard to establish your sons and daughters in conditions that favor the development of true love, virtue, and sublime fidelity. And when you have put them through religious ordeals to see that in their pursuit of each other there is neither cupidity nor vanity, frivolous intoxication nor sensual blindness devoid of idealism; when you are sure that they understand the grandeur of their feelings, the sanctity of their duties and the freedom of their choice, then let them give themselves to each other and alienate one to the other their inalienable liberty. Let their families, friends, and the great family of the faithful intervene with you to ratify this union that the solemnity of the sacrament must make worthy of respect. But heed my words: Let the sacrament be a religious permission, a paternal and social authorization, an encouragement and exhortation to the commitment's perpetuity, and never a commandment, an obligation, a law with threats and punishments, imposed slavery, with scandal, prison, and chains in the case of infractions. Otherwise you'll never see the miracle happen wholly and lastingly on earth. Providence, eternally fruitful, God, tireless giver of grace, will always bring before you young couples, fervent and naïve, ready to make sincere commitments in time and eternity. But your antireligious laws and antihuman sacraments will always destroy in them the work of grace. The inequality of conjugal rights according to one's sex, an impiety consecrated by the laws of society, the difference between their duties in public opinion, the false distinctions of conjugal honor, and all the absurd notions born of prejudice in the wake of wicked institutions will always snuff out faith and chill the couple's enthusiasm; and the most sincere, the most inclined to fidelity will be the first to lose heart, to have qualms about the length of their commitment and grow disenchanted with each other. Indeed, it goes against the will of nature and the cry of conscience to renounce one's liberty whenever man gets involved, for he brings in the yoke of ignorance and brutality; it is in accord with the wish of noble hearts and necessary to the religious instincts of strong wills when it is God giving us the means to struggle against all the pitfalls that man has set up around marriage, so as to make it the tomb of love, happiness, and virtue, to turn it into *sworn prostitution*, as our forefathers the Lollards used to say, whom you know well and often invoke! Render unto God what is God's, and take from Caesar that which is not Caesar's!

"And you, my sons," she said returning to the center of the group, "you who have just sworn to do no harm to the marriage bond, you may not have understood that this oath means. You've obeyed a generous impulse and enthusiastically responded to the appeal to honor. That is worthy of you, disciples of a triumphant faith. But now I must tell you that in so doing you've gone beyond individual virtue and consecrated a principle without which there can never be any possibility of conjugal chastity or fidelity. So enter into the spirit of the oath and recognize that there will never be any true individual virtue until everyone stands together in this regard.

"Oh love, oh flame sublime! so mighty and so frail, so sudden and so fleeting! A bolt out of the heavens, it seems that you have to flash through our lives and burn out in us before we ourselves die, for fear of consuming and destroying us! We all feel that you are the vital fire emanating from God himself and that he among us who could keep you burning bright and whole in his breast up to the hour of death would be the happiest and greatest of men. That is why disciples of the ideal will always seek to make you pleasing sanctuaries in their souls so that you won't hasten to abandon them for home. But alas! you of whom we've made a virtue, one of the foundations of our human societies, so as to honor you as we would desire, you've nonetheless refused to let yourself be chained as our institutions would have it, and you've remained free as a bird in the sky, capricious as a flame on the altar. You seem to laugh at our oaths, our contracts, even our willpower. You fly from us, despite everything we've invented to fix you in our ways and habits. You dwell neither in the harem over which vigilant sentries keep watch nor in the Christian family amidst the priest's threats, the judge's verdicts and opinion's yoke. Why are you so fickle, so ungrateful, oh mysterious charm, oh love cruelly symbolized as a god both infant and blind? What tenderness and scorn do these human souls inspire in you by turns? First you set them all ablaze with your fire, then you forsake nearly every one, leaving them to perish in the throes of regret, repentance or disgust, even more dreadful. Why do people all over the face of our globe invoke you on their knees, exalt and defy you? Why do divine poets sing of you as the world's soul, and barbarians make human sacrifices to you by throwing widows onto their husbands' funeral pyres? Why do young hearts call out to you in their sweetest dreams, and old people curse life when you abandon them to the horrors of solitude? Why this cult by turns sublime or fanatic that has been rendered you since the golden days of Humanity's youth up though our age of iron, if you're nothing but a chimera, a drunken moment's dream, the delusion of an imagination excited by sensual delirium?—Oh, that is so because you're not a vulgar instinct, a simple animal need! No, you're not the blind infant of paganism, you are the son of the true God and the very element of Divinity! But thus far you've revealed yourself to us only through the clouds of our errors, and you've refused to dwell among us because you won't be profaned. You'll return, as in the mythic age of Astraea and the poets' visions, and make your home in our earthly paradise when by sublime virtues we've made ourselves worthy of a guest such as you. Oh, then life on this earth will be sweet, and it will be good to be born here! Then we'll all be sisters and brothers, and marriages will be freely consented and freely maintained just through the strength we draw from you. Then, instead of the dreadful, impossible struggle that conjugal fidelity now has to conduct against the ungodly endeavors of debauchery, hypocritical seduction, unbridled violence, treacherous friendship, and sophisticated depravity, every husband will find himself surrounded by nothing but chaste sisters, jealous and discerning guardians of the happiness of a sister they've given him to be his companion, while every wife will find in other men her husband's brothers, happy and proud of his happiness, born protectors of his repose and dignity! Then the faithful wife will no longer be the lonely flower hiding herself away to preserve her honor's fragile treasure, the often forsaken victim pining away alone with her tears, unable to revive in her beloved's heart the flame that she has kept pure in her own. Then the brother will no longer be forced to avenge his sister and kill the man she loves, for whom she yearns, in order to give her back a semblance of false honor; then the mother will no longer tremble for her daughter, and the daughter will no longer be ashamed of her mother; then, above all, the husband will no longer be suspicious or despotic; and the wife will renounce the victim's bitterness or the slave's rancor. Atrocious suffering, abominable injustice will no longer blight the pleasant, peaceful sanctuary of the home. It will be possible for love to endure, and then who knows! perhaps one day priests and judges, rightly counting on the permanent miracle of love, will be able to consecrate indissoluble unions in the name of God himself with as much wisdom and justice as they unwittingly do today with impiety and madness.

"But these days of reward have not yet to come to pass. Here, in this mysterious temple where we are gathered, according to the words of the Gospel, three or four together in the name of the Lord, we can only dream and experiment virtue among ourselves. We cannot invoke as a sanction of our promises, as a guarantee of our institutions, the outside world that would condemn us to exile, prison, or death if it were to penetrate our secrets. Rather than imitating its ignorance and tyranny, let us consecrate the conjugal love of these two children who have come to ask for the blessing of paternal and fraternal love, in the name of the living God, the giver of all love. Let us authorize them to promise each other eternal fidelity, but without inscribing their vows in a book of death, to remind them of it later through terror and constraint. Let God be the guardian of their vows. Let them pray to God every day of their lives that he keep burning in their hearts the sacred fire that he has sent down to them."

"That's what I was waiting to hear from you, oh inspired sibyl!" exclaimed Albert, reaching out for his mother, exhausted from having spoken so long with such conviction. "I was waiting for you to acknowledge my right to promise everything to the woman I love. You recognize that this is my dearest and most sacred right. Therefore I promise her, I swear to her that I will faithfully love her and her alone my whole life long, with God as my witness. Tell me, oh prophetess of love, that this is not blasphemy."

"You are under the power of the miracle," replied Wanda. "God is blessing your vow since he's the one inspiring you with the faith to utter these words. *Always* is the most passionate word on the lips of lovers, in the ecstasy of their most divine joys. It is then an oracle escaping from their breasts. Eternity is the ideal of love, as it is of faith. Never does the human soul come any closer to reaching the height of its power and lucidity than when inspired by a great love. The *always* of lovers is an inner revelation, a divine manifestation that will shed its sovereign radiance and salutary warmth over every instant of their union. Woe to him that profanes these sacred words! He falls from grace into sin, extinguishing his heart's faith, light, strength, and life."

"And I," said Consuelo, "I receive your vow, oh Albert! And I beseech you to receive mine. I too am under the power of the miracle, and this *always* of our short lives seems nothing to me in comparison with eternity, and it's for eternity that I want to promise to be yours."

"Woman of sublime daring!" said Wanda, with a smile of enthusiasm that seemed to shine through her veil, "ask God for eternity with the man you love as a reward for being faithful to him in this brief life."

"Oh, yes!" exclaimed Albert, lifting to the heavens his wife's hand clasped in his. "That's the goal, the hope, and the reward! To love each other greatly and ardently in this phase of life so as to be together once again in the others! Oh, I know in my heart that this is not the first day of our union, that we've already loved, already possessed each other in an earlier life. Such happiness is no mere accident. It's the hand of God bringing us back together like the two halves of one being inseparable in eternity."

After the celebration of the wedding, and even though it was very late, they proceeded with the ceremonies for Consuelo's definitive initiation into the Order of the Invisibles; thereafter, the members of the tribunal having disappeared, they strolled through the sacred wood, soon to gather round a banquet of fraternal communion. Presiding over the banquet was the prince (*brother orator*), who undertook to explain to Consuelo its deep and moving symbols. The meal was served by faithful attendants who had attained a certain degree in the order. Karl introduced Matteus to Consuelo, and she finally saw his honest, gentle face without a mask, but she noted with admiration that these worthy valets were not treated as inferiors by their brothers who occupied other degrees. There was no distinction between them and the eminent members of the order, whatever their rank in the world. The *ministering brothers*, as they were called, were willing and eager to fulfill their duties as cupbearers and servers; they attended to the order of the courses as aids skilled in the art of preparing a feast, which they moreover considered a religious ceremony, a eucharistic meal. So they were no more demeaned by this function than temple Levites presiding over the details of the sacrifices. Whenever they finished serving a table, they sat down themselves, not at places set apart and isolated from the others, but laid for them among the other guests. Everyone called out to them, vying for the pleasure and duty of filling their cups and plates. As in Masonic banquets a cup was never lifted to the lips without a noble idea, a generous sentiment, or some august patronage being invoked. But the rhythmic outbursts of noise, the childish gestures of the Freemasons, the mallet, the jargon of the toasts, and the vocabulary of tools were excluded from this expansive yet solemn feast. The ministering brothers maintained a bearing that was respectful without servility, modest without constraint. Karl sat between Albert and Consuelo during one course. She was moved to see not only his sobriety and good behavior, but also the extraordinary progress that had taken place in this worthy peasant's mind. Capable of learning through the heart, he had been initiated into healthy notions of religion and morality through a rapid and admirable education of feeling.

"Oh my friend," she said to her husband, when the deserter had changed places and Albert returned, "that was the slave beaten by the Prussian militia, the wild woodcutter from the Bohemian Forest, the would-be assassin of Frederick the Great! Enlightened, charitable lessons have in such a short time turned him into a sensible, pious, and just man, instead of a bandit that the ferocious justice of nations would have driven to murder and punished with the whip and the gallows."

"Noble heart," said the prince who had taken his place to the right of Consuelo, "at Roswald you gave great lessons of religion and mercy to this heart bewildered by despair, yet endowed with the noblest instincts. After that his education was quick and easy, and every time we had a good lesson for him, he would immediately take us at our word and exclaim, 'That's what the *signora* used to say!' You may be sure that it would be easier than one thinks to enlighten and edify the coarsest of men if one were really willing to do so. Improving their situation and instilling them with self-respect by starting to value and love them requires nothing more than sincere charity and respect for human dignity. But you see that these good men have so far been initiated only into the lowest degrees, for we test the capacity of their minds and their progress in virtue to admit them more or less into our mysteries. Old Matteus is two degrees beyond Karl, and if he doesn't advance, it will be because his mind and heart won't have been able to go any further. We won't ever be stopped by low extraction or humble station; and here you see Gottlieb the shoemaker, the jailer's son at Spandau, admitted to a degree equal to yours, even though he fulfills, by taste and habit, lowly functions in my house. His vivid imagination, passion for study, enthusiasm for virtue, in a word, the incomparable beauty of the soul dwelling in that ugly body made him very quickly worthy of being treated like an equal and brother inside the temple. There was almost nothing in the realm of ideas or virtues to be transmitted to this noble child. On the contrary, he had too many of them. We had to calm the excesses of his feeling and treat the maladies of his body and mind that would have driven him mad. The immorality of his entourage and the perversity of official life would have exasperated him without corrupting him, but we alone, armed with the spirit of Jacob Boehme and the true explanation of his profound symbols, we could convince him without disenchanting him and correct the aberrations of his mystic poetry without chilling his zeal and faith. You must have noticed that curing the soul has had effects on the body. He was restored to health as though by magic, and his bizarre appearance has already been transformed."

After the meal they again took their cloaks and strolled on the far and gentler side of the hill shaded by the sacred wood. The ruins of the old castle reserved for the ordeals dominated this beautiful site, and little by little Consuelo recognized the trails over which she had raced during a stormy night a short time before. The abundant spring once consecrated to superstitious devotions came pouring out of a grotto rustically carved into the rock and babbled through the heather to the far end of the valley where it became the beautiful brook so well known to the captive in the lodge. Crossing back and forth under the lovely shade trees, paths naturally covered with fine-grained sand had a silvery sheen in the moonlight, and there groups of wanderers met and mingled in sweet conversation. The enclosure with the vast, sumptuous summerhouse that passed as a study, the prince's favorite retreat, was surrounded by a high lattice-work fence, forbidden to the idle and indiscreet. The ministering brothers strolled about as well, in groups, but along the fence, keeping watch in order to warn the *brothers* if anyone profane were to approach. This danger was not the object of much fear. The duke seemed to busy himself only with Masonic mysteries, as he in fact did secondarily, but Freemasonry at that time was tolerated by the law and protected by the princes who had been initiated or thought they had been. No one suspected the importance of the superior degrees that led step by step up to the Tribunal of the Invisibles.

Besides, at that moment the highly visible festivities illuminating the façade of the ducal palace in the distance were absorbing the prince's numerous guests so completely that no one thought to leave the glittering rooms and new gardens for the rocks and ruins of the old grounds. The young Margravine von Bayreuth, the duke's close friend, was doing the honors for him at the gala. He had feigned a malaise so that he might disappear, and immediately after the Invisibles' banquet he went back to preside over his illustrious guests' supper at the palace. As Consuelo, leaning on her husband's arm, saw these lights shimmering from afar, she again remembered Anzoleto and candidly accused herself, in front of Albert who was taking her to task for it, of having been momentarily cruel and ironic toward the cherished companion of her childhood.

"Yes, it was wrong of me," she told him, "but I was so unhappy just then. There I was determined to sacrifice myself to Count Albert, and the mischievous, cruel Invisibles were again throwing me into the arms of dangerous Liverani. I was sick at heart. It delighted me to find him once more, it drove me to despair having to part with him, and all the while Marcus was trying to distract me from my pain by making me admire handsome Anzoleto! Ah, never would I have dreamed of seeing him again with such indifference! But I thought I was doomed to the ordeal of singing with him, and I was ready to hate him for stealing my last moment, my last dream of happiness. Right now, my friend, I could set eyes on him again without bitterness and treat him with indulgence. Happiness makes one so kind and merciful! Let me one day render Anzoleto service and inspire him with a serious love of art, if not a taste for virtue!"

"Why despair of it?" said Albert. "Let's wait for a day when he's down on his luck and alone. Now, in the midst of his triumphs, he'd be deaf to sage advice. But let him lose his voice and his looks, and we may take hold of his soul."

"That's a conversion for you to undertake, Albert."

"Not without you, my Consuelo."

"So you have no fear of old memories?"

"No, I'm presumptuous to the point of fearing nothing. I'm under the power of the miracle."

"I am too, Albert, I feel so sure of myself! Oh, how right you are to be so tranquil!"

Day was breaking, and a thousand charming fragrances were stirring in the pure morning air. It was the loveliest time of summer. Nightingales were singing in trees, calling back and forth from one hill to the next. The groups that formed at every moment around the couple, far from annoying them, added to their pure delight the sweetness of fraternal affection or, at the very least, the most exquisite sympathies. All of the Invisibles present at these festivities were introduced to Consuelo as members of her new family. They were the best of the order's talents, minds, and virtues, some being illustrious in the outside world and others quite obscure, but renowned within the temple for their labors and lights. Plebeians and patricians mingled in tender intimacy. Consuelo had to learn their real names as well as the more poetic ones they bore in the secrecy of their fraternal relations: Vesper, Ellops, Peon, Hylas, Euryalus, Bellerophon, and the like. Never had she found herself surrounded by so numerous a choice of noble souls and interesting personalities. The tales they told about their proselytizing, the dangers they had faced, and the results they had achieved charmed her like poems whose reality she would not have believed compatible with the ways of the insolent, corrupt world she had traversed. These tokens of affection and esteem, even to the point of tender effusions, without the slightest taint of trite gallantry or insinuation of dangerous familiarity, this elevated language, this charming commerce where equality and fraternity were realized in their most sublime forms, the lovely golden light that was dawning on life and in the heavens at the same moment, it was all like a divine dream in the lives of Consuelo and Albert. Arm in arm, they gave no thought to leaving their beloved brothers. An inner joy, sweet and suave as the morning air, filled their breasts and souls, and their hearts were so brimming with love that nothing could make them shudder. Trenck recounted his sufferings in prison at Glatz and his dangerous escape. Like Consuelo and Haydn in the Bohemian Forest, he had made his way across Poland, but in bitterly cold weather and covered in rags, with a wounded companion, the *amiable Shelles*, that Trenck's memoirs have since portrayed as the most gracious of friends. He had fiddled for peasants in exchange for bread, like Consuelo on the banks of the Danube. Then he lowered his voice to talk about Princess Amalia, his love and his hopes. Poor Trenck! He did not foresee the dreadful storm gathering over his head any more than the happy couple destined to go forth from this beautiful summer night's dream into a life of struggle, disappointment, and suffering.

Under the cypresses, Porporino sang an admirable hymn that Albert had composed to the memory of the martyrs of their cause. Young Benda accompanied him on his violin, and Albert himself took the instrument and delighted the listeners with a few notes. Consuelo could not sing, for she was weeping tears of joy and enthusiasm. The Count de Saint-Germain related the conversations of Jan Hus and Jerome of Prague with such fervor, eloquence, and verisimilitude that it was impossible while listening not to believe that he had been there. In such hours of deep emotion and delight, gloomy reason is defenseless against the magic of poetry. With sharp, subtle strokes and enchanting taste the Chevalier d'Eon painted the wretchedness and folly of the most illustrious tyrants of Europe, the vices of the courts, and the weakness of this social structure that enthusiasm deemed so pliable in its blazing flight. Count Golowkin drew a charming portrait of his friend Jean-Jacques Rousseau's great soul and artless foibles. This philosophic nobleman (these days he would be called an eccentric) had a very beautiful daughter whom he was rearing as he saw fit; and she was both Emile and Sophie, sometimes the most handsome boy, sometimes the most appealing girl. He was to introduce her at the initiation and put Consuelo in charge of her education. The illustrious Zinzendorf explained how his colony of Moravian Herrnhutters was organized and their evangelical way of life. With deference he consulted Albert about several difficulties, and wisdom seemed to issue forth from Albert's lips. This was so because he was inspired by Consuelo's presence and gentle gaze. For her he was a god. He enjoyed every sort of prestige in her eyes: a philosopher and artist, a martyr who had been put to the test, a triumphant hero; solemn as an ancient Greek stoic, beautiful as an angel, playful on occasion and naïve as a child, as a blissful lover; perfect, in short, as is the man one loves! Consuelo had thought she would die of exhaustion and emotion knocking at the door of the temple. Now she felt strong and spirited as in the days when she used to play on the shores of the Adriatic with all the vim of adolescence, under a burning sun tempered by the breeze from the sea. It seemed that life in all its power, happiness in all its intensity had seized her by every one of her fibers and that she was sucking them in through all her pores. She was not counting the hours; she would have wanted this enchanted night never to end. Why can't one keep the sun below the horizon on certain nights when one feels all the fullness of being, when every dream of enthusiasm seems to have come true or to be within the realm of possibility!

Finally the sky turned purple and gold, and a silver bell warned the Invisibles that night was taking back its protective veils. They sang a last hymn to the rising sun, an emblem of the new day that they were dreaming and preparing for the world. Then they bid each other fond farewells and arranged various meetings, some in Paris or London, others in Madrid, Vienna, Petersburg, Warsaw, Dresden, and Berlin. They all promised to come together the following year, on the same day, at the door of this blessed temple, with new neophytes or old brothers now absent. Then they wrapped themselves in their cloaks to hide their elegant attire and silently scattered over the shady trails of the grounds.

Albert and Consuelo, guided by Marcus, went down the ravine to the stream. Karl welcomed them into his closed gondola and conveyed them to the lodge. On the threshold they paused a second to contemplate the majesty of the rising sun. Up until that moment Consuelo, replying to Albert's passionate words, had always given him his true name, but when he tore her away from the meditation in which she seemed rapt, she could only say to him, leaning her burning brow on his shoulder, "*Oh Liverani.*"

Epilogue

If, with regard to the lives of Albert and Consuelo after their wedding, we had been able to obtain the faithful, detailed documents that have guided us thus far, we could no doubt go on recounting their travels and adventures a good while longer.

But, oh persevering reader, we cannot satisfy you; and you, weary reader, we ask just a moment more of your patience. For this we deserve from you neither reproach nor commendation. The truth is that the materials that have allowed us to coordinate the events in this history up to the present moment disappear in large part for us after the romantic night when the union of our two heroes was blessed and consecrated at the Invisibles' gathering. Whether the commitments they made in the Temple prevented them from confiding in friends in their letters, whether their friends, themselves members of secret societies, thought it prudent to destroy their correspondence in times of persecution, we no longer see them except through a cloud, under the Temple's veil or the disciples' masks. If we were to rely uncritically upon the rare traces of their lives in our manuscripts, we would often go astray in their pursuit; for contradictory evidence shows the two of them in different spots simultaneously or headed in different directions at one and the same time. But we can easily guess that they willfully gave rise to these errors, now engaged in some secret enterprise directed by the Invisibles, now forced to elude, amid a thousand perils, the governments' inquisitorial police. This much we can affirm regarding the existence of this soul in two persons bearing the names Consuelo and Albert: their love kept its promises, while destiny cruelly belied those that it had seemed to make them in those delightful hours they called their *midsummer's night's dream*. Yet they were not ungrateful to Providence that had given them this fleeting happiness in all its plenitude and which, amid their setbacks, kept alive in them the miracle of the love that Wanda had proclaimed. In poverty, suffering, and persecution they always harkened back to this sweet memory that stood out in their lives like a celestial vision, a covenant with God that they would enjoy a better life after a phase of toil, trial, and sacrifice.

Everything, moreover, becomes so mysterious for us in this history that we have not even been able to discover in what part of Germany the enchanted estate was located. It was there that, cloaked by the commotion of hunts and galas, a prince who remains anonymous in our documents acted as the rallying point and principal mover in the Invisibles' social and philosophical conspiracy. They had given this prince a symbolic name which, after much painstaking work to divine the code used by the disciples, we presume to be Christopher, *Christ-bearer*, or perhaps Chrysostom, *mouth of gold*. They poetically referred to the temple where Consuelo was married and initiated as the *Holy Grail* and the leaders of the Tribunal as the *Guardians of the Temple*, romantic emblems revived from ancient legends about the golden age of chivalry. Everyone knows that, according to these lovely fictions, the Holy Grail was hidden in a mysterious sanctuary deep in a cave unknown to mortals. It was there that the Guardians of the Temple, those illustrious saints of early Christianity who already in this world were devoted to immortality, kept the precious cup that Jesus had used to consecrate the miracle of the Eucharist while eating the Passover with his disciples. That cup no doubt contained heavenly grace, represented now by the blood, now by the tears of Christ, a divine potion, in short, a eucharistic substance whose mystical nature was not explained, yet the mere sight of it was enough for one to be transformed inside and out, to be forever safe from death and sin. These pious paladins, after dreadful vows, terrible mortifications, and earthshaking feats, took up ascetic lives as *knights-errant*, and it was their ideal to find the Holy Grail at the end of their peregrinations. They searched for it in the icy North, on the shores of Brittany, deep in the forests of Germany. In order to carry out this sublime conquest they had to face dangers comparable to those of the garden of the Hesperides, to overcome monsters, the elements, barbarian peoples, hunger, thirst, even death. It is said that a few of these Christian Argonauts discovered the sanctuary and were regenerated by the divine cup, but they never betrayed this awful secret. Their triumph was known by the strength of their arms, the holiness of their lives, their invincible weapons, and the transfiguration of their whole beings; but they did not long survive, among us, such a glorious initiation; they disappeared from our midst, like Jesus after his resurrection, and left earth for heaven without undergoing the bitter transition of death.

Such was the magic symbol that in fact adapted quite well to the Invisibles' work. For several years the New Guardians of the Temple preserved the hope of making the Holy Grail accessible to all mankind. Albert undoubtedly worked hard and well to spread the doctrine's main ideas. He attained the order's highest degrees, for we have somewhere the list of his titles, which would be evidence that he had time to win them. Now, as everyone knows, it took eighty-one months just to rise up through the thirty-three degrees of Freemasonry, and we are sure that much more was then required to complete the limitless number of the Holy Grail's mysterious degrees. The names of the Masonic degrees are no longer a mystery to anyone, but perhaps one wouldn't mind if we were to recall a few of them here, for they are a rather good illustration of the inspired genius and felicitous imagination that presided over their creation one after the other:

"Apprentice, Fellow of the Craft and Master Mason, Secret Master and Perfect Master, Secretary, Provost and Judge, English Master and Irish Master, Master in Israel, Master Elect of the Nine and Fifteen, Elect of the Unknown, Sublime Chevalier Elect, Grand Master Architect, Royal-Arch, Great Scot of the Sacred Lodge or Sublime Mason, Chevalier of the Sword, Chevalier of the Orient, Prince of Jerusalem, Chevalier of the Orient and Occident, Rose Croix of France, Heredom and Kilwinning, Grand Pontiff or Sublime Scot, Architect of the Sacred Arch, Pontiff of the Celestial Jerusalem, Sovereign Prince of Masonry or Master *ad vitam*, Noachite, Prince of Lebanon, Head of the Tabernacle, Chevalier of the Bronze Serpent, Trinitary Scot or Prince of Mercy, Grand Commander of the Temple, Chevalier of the Sun, Patriarch of the Crusades, Grand Master of the Light, Chevalier Kadosh, Chevalier of the White and Black Eagles, Chevalier of the Phoenix, Chevalier of the Iris, Chevalier of the Argonauts, Chevalier of the Golden Fleece, Grand Inspector-Inquisitor-Commander, Sublime Prince of the Royal Secret, Sublime Master of the Ring of Light, etc."[1]

Next to these or at least most of them, we find lesser known titles joined to the name of Albert Podiebrad, written in a code less legible than that of the Freemasons, such as Chevalier of Saint John, Sublime Joannite, Master of the New Apocalypse, Doctor of the Eternal Gospel, Elect of the Holy Spirit, Guardian of the Temple, Areopagite, Magus, Man-People, Man-Pontiff, Man-King, New-Man, etc. We were surprised to see here some titles that would seem to be advance borrowings from Weishaupt's Illuminism, but that particularity was later explained to us and will not require comment for our readers by the end of this history.

Working through the labyrinth of obscure but significant facts regarding the Invisibles' labors and accomplishments, dispersion and apparent extinction, we find it quite difficult to follow from afar the adventurous star of our young couple. Still, with a prudent commentary making up for the missing pieces, here is

1. Several of these degrees are from various creations and rites. A few of them may be from a later time than the period of which we speak, and for rectification we refer to the learned tilemakers [Translator's note: brothers whose duty is to guard the entrance of the lodge]. There were, I believe, more than a hundred degrees in certain rites.

more or less a brief history of the main events in their lives. The reader's imagination will help fill things in; for our part, we have no doubt that the best endings are those that the reader is willing to undertake himself, in the narrator's stead.[2]

It was probably after leaving the *Holy Grail* that Consuelo went to the little court of Bayreuth where Frederick's sister the margravine had palaces, gardens, summerhouses, and waterfalls in the style of Count Hoditz's at Roswald, although less sumptuous and expensive, for this clever princess had been married without a dowry to a very poor prince, and only for a short while had she been enjoying dresses with reasonable trains and pages without threadbare doublets. Her gardens, rather her garden, to speak plainly, was set in an admirable landscape, and there, in an ancient temple, she indulged in the pleasure of an Italian opera house of somewhat Pompadour style. The margravine was very philosophical, meaning Voltairean. The young hereditary margrave, her husband, was the zealous leader of a Masonic lodge. I don't know whether Albert was in communication with the margrave, with his incognito under the protection of the brothers' secrecy, or whether he stayed away from that court and rejoined his wife a bit later. Consuelo no doubt had some secret mission there. It may be as well that she did not openly live with her husband at first so as to avoid drawing him into the limelight that was everywhere fixed on her. At that point their love undoubtedly had all the attraction of mystery, and if the public celebration of their union, consecrated by the fraternal sanction of the Guardians of the Temple, had seemed to them sweet and exhilarating, the secrecy with which they surrounded themselves in a hypocritical, licentious world was in the beginning a necessary shield for them, a sort of silent protest from which they drew their inspiration and strength.

Several Italian singers were then the delight of the little court at Bayreuth. Corilla and Anzoleto appeared there, and the inconsequent prima donna again burned with passion for the traitor whom she had consigned to all the furies of hell a short while before. But Anzoleto, while cajoling the tigress, cautiously strove, and with a mysterious reserve, to find favor with Consuelo, whose talent, expanded by so many secret and profound revelations, eclipsed all rivalry. Ambition had become the young tenor's dominant passion, love having been smothered under spite, even pleasure under surfeit. So he loved neither chaste

2. That is why the story about Johann Kreissler strikes us as Hoffmann's most wonderful novel. Death having taken the author by surprise before the end of his work, the poem has a thousand different imagined endings, each one more fantastic than the others. This is how a beautiful river branches off near its mouth and vanishes into the shore's golden sands in a thousand whimsical rivulets. [Translator's note: The novel to which Sand refers is *Lebenansichten des Katers Murr* by E. T. A. Hoffmann (1776–1822), a German Romantic writer and composer.]

Consuelo nor impetuous Corilla, but he tactfully managed the two of them, all prepared to hook up ostensibly with whichever one would help him along to fame. Consuelo showed him tranquil friendship and spared him neither the good advice nor the conscientious lessons that could make his talent soar. But she no longer felt any stirrings of emotion around him, and being able to forgive him with such mansuetude made her realize how absolute was her detachment from him. Anzoleto made no mistake about it. After having benefited from the artist's lessons and feigned heartfelt attention to the friend's advice, he lost patience at the same time as he lost hope, and his deep resentment and bitter disappointment permeated his words and bearing despite himself.

In the meantime it seems that the young Baroness Amalia von Rudolstadt arrived at the court of Bayreuth with the Princess von Kulmbach, Countess Hoditz's daughter. If several indiscreet or exaggerating witnesses are to be believed, some rather strange little dramas took place among these four individuals, Consuelo, Amalia, Corilla, and Anzoleto. Seeing the handsome tenor unexpectedly appear on the stage of the Bayreuth opera house, the young baroness fell into a faint. No one thought to note the coincidence, but Corilla, sharp-eyed as a lynx, had caught a particular glow of smug self-satisfaction on the tenor's brow. He had botched the passage meant to create an *effect*; the court, distracted by the swooning baroness, had not encouraged the singer; and instead of cursing between his teeth as he always did in such cases, an unequivocal smile of triumph played on his lips.

"Well!" Corilla whispered to Consuelo back in the wings, "it's not you or me that he loves, but that little fool who just made a scene for him. Do you know her? Who is she?"

"I don't know," replied Consuelo, who had not seen a thing, "but I can assure you that it's neither she nor you nor I who matters to him."

"Who then?"

"Himself, *al solito*!" said Consuelo with a smile.

The chronicle adds that the next morning Consuelo was summoned to a grove at some distance from the residence for a conversation with Baroness Amalia that went more or less as follows.

"I know everything!" said the latter testily before Consuelo could even open her mouth. "You're the one he loves! You wretched woman, scourge of my life, you've robbed me of Albert's heart as well as *his*."

"His, Madame? I don't know. . . ."

"Don't pretend with me, Anzoleto loves you, you're his mistress, you already were in Venice and you still are. . . ."

"That's a vile calumny or a conjecture unworthy of you, Madame."

"It's the truth, I tell you. He told me so last night."

"Last night! Oh, Madame, what are you telling me?" Consuelo exclaimed, blushing with shame and chagrin.

Amalia dissolved in tears, and when Consuelo had succeeded in calming her jealousy, she learned despite herself the secrets of this unhappy passion. Having seen Anzoleto sing on stage in Prague, Amalia became intoxicated with his handsome looks and success. Knowing nothing about music, she did not hesitate to take him for the best singer in the world, all the more so that in Prague he was quite the vogue. She had him come give her singing lessons, and while her poor father, old Baron Frederick, paralyzed by idleness, snoozed in his armchair and dreamed of furious packs of hounds and boars at bay, she succumbed to seduction. Boredom and vanity drove her to her ruin. Anzoleto, flattered by this illustrious conquest, and wanting to make himself all the rage by means of scandal, persuaded her that she had the stuff to become the greatest singer of the century, that the life of the artist was paradise on earth and that she had nothing better to do than run away with him and make her debut at Hay Market in Handel's operas. At first Amalia rejected with horror the idea of abandoning her elderly father but just when Anzoleto was about to leave Prague, feigning a despair he did not feel, she surrendered to a sort of vertigo and went off with him.

Her intoxication was brief; Anzoleto's insolence and crude ways once he had ceased to play the seducer made her come to her senses. So it was with a sort of joy that three months later she was arrested in Hamburg, brought back to Prussia, and mysteriously incarcerated at Spandau at the request of the Saxon Rudolstadts, but her punishment was too long and too severe. Amalia grew weary of repentance as quickly as she had tired of passion; she yearned for liberty, comfort, and respect for her rank, of which she had been so suddenly and cruelly deprived. Amidst her own suffering she scarcely felt the pain of losing her father. Upon learning that she had been freed, she finally realized all the troubles that had befallen her family, but not daring to go back to the canoness and fearing the galling tedium of a life of reprimands and sermonizing, she begged the Margravine von Bayreuth's protection; and the Princess von Kulmbach, who was then at Dresden, undertook to bring Amalia to her relative. In this philosophizing, frivolous court Amalia discovered the amiable *tolerance* that the fashionable vices made the future's only virtue. But when she again set eyes on Anzoleto, she had already fallen victim to the diabolical sway that he knew how to exercise over women, against which chaste Consuelo herself had waged such a struggle. At first her heart was stricken with terror and chagrin, but after her swooning fit she went out alone at night for a breath of air in the gardens and happened to run into him. He felt emboldened by her emotion, and his imagination chafed against the obstacles that had cropped up between them. Now she was in love with him again, she was red with embarrassment and frightened, and she confessed her faults to Consuelo, her former singing teacher, with a mixture of feminine modesty and philosophical cynicism.

It seems certain that Consuelo was able to find the way to Amalia's heart with ardent exhortations, convincing her to return to the Castle of the Giants to extinguish her dangerous passion there in solitude and to look after her elderly aunt.

After this adventure Consuelo could no longer bear to stay in Bayreuth. She was singularly weary of the stormy jealousy of Corilla who, still foolish as ever and still basically good-hearted, would heap gross accusations on Consuelo, then throw herself at her feet an instant later. Anzoleto, for his part, who had figured that he could take revenge on Consuelo for her disdain by affecting passion for Amalia, was not about to forgive her for having rescued the young baroness from danger. He played a thousand nasty tricks on her, such as making her miss all of her stage entrances as well as taking her part in the middle of a duet so as to throw her off and, by his own aplomb, make the ignorant public think that she was in the wrong. If she had stage business with him, he would go right instead of left, try to trip her, or get her tangled up with the extras. These mean pranks fell flat in front of Consuelo's composure and presence of mind, but she was less stoical finding that he was spreading the most shameful calumnies about her and that the idle great lords, in whose eyes a virtuous actress was a phenomenon impossible to admit or at least tiresome to acknowledge, were lending him an ear. She saw libertines of every age and rank make bold with her and, refusing to believe that her resistance was sincere, they joined forces with Anzoleto to malign and disgrace her in a spirit of cowardly vengeance and ferocious spite.

These cruel, miserable persecutions were the beginning of a long martyrdom that the unfortunate prima donna suffered heroically throughout her career in the theater. Whenever she ran into Anzoleto, he caused her a thousand troubles, and it is sad to say that she ran into more than one Anzoleto in the course of her life. Other Corillas tormented her with their envy and ill will, more or less treacherous or brutal, and of all these rivals the first was still the least nasty and the most capable of a good impulse. But whatever may be said about the spitefulness and jealous vanity of women in the theater, Consuelo felt that when these vices entered a man's heart, he was even more degraded by them and became more unworthy of his role in humanity. The haughty, debauched lords, the theater directors and the gazetteers, depraved as well by contact with so much filth; the fine ladies, curious and whimsical protectresses, quick to impose, but soon peeved to find a girl *of that sort* with more virtue than they had or wished to have; lastly, the audiences often ignorant, almost always ungrateful or biased, these were the enemies against which Liverani's austere wife had to struggle with incessant bitterness. Persevering and faithful, in art as in love, she never lost heart and carried on, ever more adept in music and virtue, often failing in the thorny pursuit of success, often lifting herself up as well through deserved triumphs, remaining despite everything the priestess of her art, better than Porpora himself understood it, and always drawing new strength from her religious faith, immense consolation from her husband's ardent, devoted love.

The husband's life, albeit parallel to hers, for he accompanied her on all her travels, lies under a thicker cloud. The presumption is that he did not make himself a slave to his wife's riches and devote all his energy to keeping track of her income and expenses. Besides, Consuelo had rather small gains from her profession. Audiences did not remunerate artists back then with the prodigious bounty that distinguishes our times. Artists got rich mainly through gifts from princes and prominent people, and women who knew how to *make the most of things* were already acquiring great wealth, but chastity and disinterestedness are the worst enemies of prosperity for a woman in the theater. Consuelo earned high levels of respect, sometimes enthusiasm, for her singing when by chance the perversity of her entourage did not come too much between her and the real audience, but she had no success as a coquette, and infamy did not crown her with diamonds and millions. Her laurels remained immaculate, and they were not tossed up on stage to her by self-serving hands. After working and traveling ten years long she was no richer than at the start; she had not known how to speculate and, what is more, she had not wanted to; and in such conditions wealth does not come seeking workers of any class against their will. Plus, she had not saved the often contested fruit of her labors, but constantly used it for good works, and in a life secretly devoted to active proselytizing, her resources alone had not always been enough; sometimes the Invisibles' central authority had provided additional funds.

What was the real success of Albert's and Consuelo's ardent, tireless pilgrimage through France, Spain, England, and Italy? None was obvious to the world, and I believe that one must look ahead twenty years to discover, by induction, what was wrought by secret societies in the history of the eighteenth century. Did these societies have more effect in France than in the womb of Germany which gave birth to them? The French Revolution energetically replies in the affirmative. Yet the Illuminist conspiracy all over Europe and Weishaupt's gigantic notions also show that the divine dream of the Holy Grail had kept on stirring German imaginations for thirty years, despite the first disciples' dispersion or defection.

We read in old gazettes that Porporina made a great splash in Paris in Pergolesi's operas, in London in Handel's oratorios and operas, in Madrid where she appeared with Farinelli, in Dresden with Faustina and Mingotti, and in

Venice, Rome, and Naples in the operas and sacred music of Porpora and other great masters.

We know nothing about Albert's moves. A few notes from Consuelo to Trenck or Wanda show us this mysterious character full of faith, confidence, activity and enjoying lucid thoughts more so than any other man up until a time when we utterly lack reliable documents. Here is what was said among a certain group of people, now nearly all dead, about Consuelo's last appearance on stage.

It was in Vienna around 1760. The singer could have been about thirty; she was, people said, more beautiful than in her early youth. A pure life, habits of inner calm, and physical sobriety had preserved her in all the power of her grace and talent. She was accompanied by beautiful children, yet her husband was nowhere to be seen, though she was said to have one and to be irrevocably faithful to him. Porpora, after several trips to Italy, had returned to Vienna and was putting on a new opera at the imperial theater. So little is known about the last twenty years of this great composer's life that we have been unable to find the name of this last work in any of his biographies. We only know that Porporina took the leading role with undeniable success and drew tears from the entire court. The empress deigned to be satisfied. But in the night following this triumph some invisible messenger brought Porporina some news that horrified and dismayed her. At seven in the morning, that is to say at the moment when the empress was alerted by the faithful servant known as Her Majesty's Polisher (given that his functions in actual fact consisted in opening the shutters, making the fire, and polishing the room, while Her Majesty gradually awoke), Porporina, having won over all the guardians of the sacred avenues with gold and eloquence, appeared at the very door of the august bedroom.

"My friend," she said to the polisher, "I must throw myself at the empress's feet. A good man's life is in danger, and a family's honor in jeopardy. A great crime may be consummated a few days from now if I don't see Her Majesty this very instant. I know that you are incorruptible, but I know as well that you are a generous and magnanimous man. Everyone says so; you have obtained many graces that the haughtiest courtiers would not have dared solicit."

"Good heavens! Is it you again, at long last, oh my dear mistress!" exclaimed the polisher, joining his hands and dropping his feather duster.

"Karl!" she exclaimed in turn, "oh, thank you, God, I'm saved! Albert has a good angel even in this palace."

"Albert? Albert!" said Karl, "my God, is he the one in danger? Then hurry up and come right in, Signora, even if it gets me sacked. . . . And God knows I'd miss this position, for here I'm doing some good and serving our holy cause better than I've been able to do anywhere else so far. But Albert! Look, the empress is a kind woman when she's not ruling," he added in a low voice. "Go on in, the valets will think you were here before I was. Let the blame fall on these rascals that don't deserve to serve a queen, for they tell her nothing but lies."

Consuelo went in, and when the empress opened her eyes heavy with sleep, she saw Consuelo on her knees, prostrate as it were, at the foot of the bed.

"What's this?" exclaimed Maria Theresa, draping her coverlet over her shoulders with a majestic bearing that was not at all affected and sitting up, as superb and daunting in bed with her night-cap as she would have been on her throne, with a crown on her head and a sword at her side.

"Madame," replied Consuelo, "a humble subject, an unfortunate mother, a desperate wife is begging you on bended knee for her husband's life and liberty."

Just then Karl came in, feigning great surprise.

"Wretched woman!" he thundered, with a show of horror and rage, "who let you in here?"

"Bravo, Karl, for your vigilance and fidelity!" said the empress. "Never in my whole life has such a thing happened to me, to be awakened with a start and face such insolence!"

"A word from Your Majesty," said Karl boldly, "and I'll kill this woman before her very eyes."

Karl knew the empress very well; he knew that she liked to perform acts of mercy in front of witnesses, that she knew how to be a great queen and great woman, even in front of her valets de chambre.

"That is too much zeal!" she replied with a smile that was both majestic and maternal. "Go away, and let this poor weeping woman have her say. I'm not in danger with any of my subjects. What do you want, Madame? Well, well, it's you, my lovely Porporina! You're going to ruin your voice sobbing like that."

"Madame," said Consuelo, "I've been married in the Catholic church for ten years now. I don't have a single offence against honor on my conscience. My children are legitimate, and I'm bringing them up in virtue. So I dare. . . . "

"In virtue, I know," said the empress, "but not in religion. You're well- behaved, that I've been told, but you never go to church. Still, have your say. What misfortune has befallen you?"

"My husband, whose side I've never left," the supplicant went on, "is currently in Prague and, through what vile machination I know not, has just been arrested, thrown into a dungeon, accused of wanting to take a name and title that are not his and to despoil an inheritance, of being, in short, a schemer, an impostor, and a spy, accused therefore of high treason, and condemned to life in prison, perhaps to death at this very moment."

"In Prague? an impostor?" said the empress calmly. "There's a similar story in my secret-police reports. Now, by what name does your husband go, since you people don't take your husbands' names."

"Liverani is his name."

"That's the one. Well, my child, it saddens me to know that you're married to such a wretched man. This Liverani is indeed a crook or a madman who, thanks to a perfect resemblance, is trying to pass himself off as a Count von Rudolstadt who died over ten years ago, which is an established fact. He weaseled his way in with an elderly Canoness von Rudolstadt, making so bold as to claim to be her nephew, and he would surely have usurped her estate if, just as she was drawing up her will in his favor, good people devoted to the family hadn't freed the poor lady, now in her dotage, from her obsession. He was arrested, of which I heartily approve. I understand your chagrin, but that I cannot remedy. The case is under investigation. If it is recognized that the man, as I wish to believe, is insane, he'll be placed in an asylum, where you'll be able to see and look after him. But if he's merely an underhanded thief, as I fear, he'll have to be detained on somewhat harsher terms to prevent him from making trouble for the true Rudolstadt heir, a Baroness Amalia, I believe, who after a few youthful indiscretions, is about to marry one of my officers. I prefer to think, *mademoiselle*, that you are unaware of your husband's conduct and that you're deluding yourself about his character; otherwise, I would find your entreaties most unseemly. But I feel too much pity for you to want to mortify you. . . . You may go."

Consuelo saw that she had nothing to hope for, that any attempt to prove that Liverani and Albert von Rudolstadt were one and the same person would only put her cause in greater and greater jeopardy. She stood up and walked toward the door, pale and ready to faint. Following her with a searching eye, Maria Theresa felt sorry for Consuelo and called her back.

"You are much to be pitied," she said less curtly. "All this is not your fault, I'm sure. Calm down, and take care of yourself. The matter will be conscientiously examined, and if your husband doesn't wish to consummate his own ruin, I'll arrange for him to be considered insane. If you can communicate with him, make him understand that. That's my advice to you."

"I'll follow that advice, blessing Your Majesty. But without Your Majesty's protection I won't be able to do a single thing. My husband is locked up in Prague, and I'm under contract at the imperial theater here in Vienna. If Your Majesty deigns not grant me leave and deliver me orders allowing me to communicate with my husband who is being held in solitary confinement. . . . "

"You're asking a great deal! I don't know if Herr von Kaunitz will wish to grant you this leave nor if it will be possible to replace you at the theater. We'll see about that in a few days."

"In a few days!" exclaimed Consuelo, recovering her courage. "But in a few days time will have run out! I have to leave this very instant!"

"That's enough," said the empress. "Your insistence will do you harm if you bring it before judges less calm and indulgent than I. Go, Mademoiselle."

Consuelo ran to the home of Canon *** and entrusted her children to him, announcing that she was leaving, not knowing for how long.

"If you're away a long time, too bad for us!" replied the kind old man. "As for the children, I won't complain. They're perfectly well-behaved, and they'll be company for Angela, who gets a bit bored with me."

"Listen!" Consuelo went on, unable to keep back her tears after having gone to hug her children one last time, "don't tell them that I'll be away a long time, but I'll have you know that it could be forever. I may be about to undergo suffering from which I won't recover unless God works me a miracle; pray for me, and have my children do the same."

The good canon did not attempt to pry her secret out of her; yet, as his peaceful, nonchalant soul did not easily admit the idea of misfortune without remedy, he did his best to console her. Seeing that he was not succeeding in giving her hope, he at least wanted to reassure her about her children.

"*My dear Bertoni*," he said in a heartfelt tone, striving for a playful note through his tears, "if you don't return, just remember that your children are mine! I'll see to their education. I'll marry off your daughter, which will reduce Angela's dowry a bit and make her more industrious. As for the boys, I'm warning you that I'll make musicians out of them!"

"Joseph Haydn will share the burden," said Consuelo, kissing the canon's hands, "and old Porpora will surely give them a few more lessons. My poor children are docile and show signs of intelligence; I'm not worried about their material existence. One day they'll be able to earn an honest living. But my love and advice. . . . You alone can stand in for me there."

"And that's my promise to you," exclaimed the canon. "I certainly hope to live long enough to see them all settled. I'm not too fat yet, I've still got good legs. I'm only sixty, even though that wicked Brigitte once tried to make me older so that I'd have to draw up my last will and testament. There now, daughter! Courage and health to you! Go now and come back to us! The good Lord is on the side of decent folks."

Consuelo, without bothering about her leave, had post-horses hitched up to her carriage. Yet, just as she was climbing in, Porpora, who was alarmed to see her departing, held her up. Foreseeing the storm, she had wanted to avoid him. He was afraid, despite the stiff, preoccupied promises she gave him, that she would not be back for the opera the next day.

"Who the devil dreams of a trip to the country in the dead of winter?" he said with a nervous tremor, half from old age, half from anger and apprehension. "If you catch cold, my success is jeopardized, and things were going so well! I don't understand you. A triumph yesterday, and today you're off on some trip!"

This quarrel delayed Consuelo a quarter of an hour and gave the theater management, already on the alert, time to warn the authorities. A squad of uhlans arrived and unhitched the carriage. Consuelo was begged to return home, and her house put under guard to prevent her from fleeing. She was taken with fever, of which she took no notice, pacing back and forth in her rooms, prey to a sort of frenzy, and making no reply, aside from somber stares, to Porpora's irritating questions and those of the director. She did not go to bed and spent the night in prayer. Come morning she seemed calm and went to rehearsal *on orders*. Her voice had never been lovelier, but she had bouts of absentmindedness that terrified Porpora. "Oh blasted marriage! Oh infernal folly of love!" he muttered in the orchestra, pounding on his harpsichord hard enough to break it. Old Porpora was still the same; gladly would he have said, "Better that all the lovers, all the husbands on this earth perish rather than my opera!"

In the evening Consuelo dressed as usual and went on stage. She assumed her pose, and her lips formed a word . . . but no sound came from her throat; she had lost her voice.

The dumbfounded audience rose to its feet. The courtiers, who had begun to hear something or another about her attempted flight, declared that this was an intolerable caprice. There was shouting, booing, clapping each time the singer tried again. She attempted to say something and could not utter a single word. Yet she remained upright and dejected, not thinking about her lost voice, not feeling humiliated by her tyrants' indignation, but resigned and proud like an innocent condemned to iniquitous torture, and thanking God for sending her this sudden infirmity that would let her leave the theater and go to Albert.

It was suggested to the empress that she put the recalcitrant artist in prison to make her recover her voice and good will. Her Majesty had been briefly angry, and people thought that they were paying her court by heaping reproach on the accused. But Maria Theresa, who sometimes allowed crimes from which she drew advantage, was not fond of making others suffer unnecessarily.

"Kaunitz," she said to her prime minister, "have a passport delivered to that poor creature, and I don't want to hear anything more about it. While losing her voice may be a stratagem of war, it's at least an act of virtue. Few actresses would sacrifice an hour of success to a life of conjugal love."

Consuelo, provided with all the necessary papers, finally departed, still ill, but oblivious to it. Here we once again lose the thread of the events. Albert's trial could have been a cause célèbre, but it was handled as a secret matter. It was probably a trial similar in substance to the one that Frederick von Trenck at about the same time began, endured and lost after many years of struggle. Who today in France would know the details of that iniquitous affair if Trenck himself had not taken the trouble to publish them and reiterate his heated complaints during thirty years of his life? But Albert did not leave behind any documents. For that reason we are forced to refer to Baron von Trenck's story since he is one of our heroes as well, and perhaps his troubles will shed some light on those of Albert and Consuelo.

Scarcely a month after the reunion of the Holy Grail, about which Trenck kept the deepest secret in his Memoirs, he had been recaptured and locked up at Magdeburg, where he wasted the ten best years of his youth in a dreadful dungeon, sitting on a stone already bearing his epitaph, *Here lies Trenck*, and laden with eighty pounds of irons. Everyone is familiar with this notorious calamity and the odious circumstances that went along with it, such as being made to suffer pangs of hunger for eighteen months and having his prison built at his sister's expense to punish her with financial ruin for having given him asylum; his miraculous attempts to escape, the incredible energy that, never abandoning him, was foiled by his acts of chivalrous imprudence; the artwork that he accomplished in prison, the marvelous engravings that he managed to do with the point of a nail on pewter goblets, whose allegorical subjects and versified mottoes are so profound and so poignant;[3] finally, his secret contacts, in spite of everything, with Princess Amalia of Prussia; the despair that consumed her, the pains that she took to make herself ugly with a corrosive liquid that nearly blinded her, the deplorable state of health to which she deliberately reduced herself in order to elude the obligation to marry, the dreadful revolution in her disposition; finally, the ten years of tribulation that made Trenck a martyr and his illustrious lover, an old, ugly, and nasty woman, instead of the angel of sweetness and beauty that she had once been, that she could have continued to be in a happy state.[4] This is all a matter of history, but people have not borne this sufficiently in mind when drawing the portrait of Frederick the Great. This crime, accompanied by acts of gratuitous and refined cruelty, is an indelible blot on the philosopher-tyrant's memory.

Trenck was ultimately freed, as everybody knows, thanks to Maria Theresa,

3. There are still some in a few private museums in Germany.

4. See in Thiébault [Dieudonné Thiébault (1733–1807), *Mes souvenirs de vingt ans de séjour à Berlin* (Paris: Buisson, 1805)] the portrait of the Abbess of Quedlinburg, and the curious revelations in that regard.

who claimed him as her subject; and he finally acquired that belated protection through the efforts of *Her Majesty's Bedchamber Polisher*, none other than our Karl. There are, on the subject of this magnanimous plebeian's ingenious schemes with regard to his sovereign, some very curious and very touching pages in the memoirs of the time.

During the first years of Trenck's captivity, his cousin, the notorious Pandur, the victim of accusations more deserved but no less hateful and cruel, died of poisoning at Spielberg. Trenck the Prussian had scarcely been freed from prison when he arrived in Vienna to lay claim to Trenck the Austrian's immense estate. But Maria Theresa was of no mind to turn it over to him. She had benefited from the pandur's exploits, she had punished his acts of violence, she meant to profit from his plundering, and indeed she did. Like Frederick II, like all crowned heads with great minds, while the powers of her role were dazzling the masses, she did not deny herself those secret iniquities for which God and man will require reckoning on the day of judgment, which will weigh as heavily on one side of the scales as official virtues on the other. Conquerors and sovereigns, in vain you use your treasures to raise up temples: this doesn't make you any less wicked when a single piece of that gold comes at the cost of blood and suffering. In vain you subject whole races by the splendor of your arms: the men most blinded by the prestige of glory will reproach you a single man, a single blade of grass broken in cold blood. The muse of history, still blind and uncertain, all but concedes that the past holds great crimes that were necessary and justifiable, but humanity's inviolable conscience protests against its own error, reproving at least the crimes that contributed nothing to the success of great causes.

The empress's greedy designs were marvelously seconded by her deputies, the ignoble agents that she had appointed as administrators of the pandur's estate, and the dishonest judges who adjudicated the heir's rights. Each one had his share of the spoils. Maria Theresa thought to take the lion's share for herself, but it was in vain that a few years later she sent off to prison and the galleys the unfaithful accomplices in that great misappropriation: She was not able to recover all the profits. Trenck was ruined and never obtained justice. Nothing has taught us more about Maria Theresa's character than the part of Trenck's memoirs where he gives an account of his discussions with her on this subject. Without departing from respect for royalty, which was then an official religion for patricians, he makes us feel the great woman's coldness, hypocrisy, and greed, a reunion of contrasts, a character sublime and petty, naïve and deceitful, like every beautiful soul doing battle with the corruption of absolute power, this antihuman cause of all evil, this inevitable reef against which all the noble instincts are fatally drawn to their destruction. Determined to send the plaintiff away empty-handed, the sovereign often deigned to console him, give him back hope, promise him her protection against the vile judges who were fleecing him; and when it was all over, pretending that she had failed in the pursuit of truth and no longer understood a thing about the mazelike intricacies of this interminable trial, she offered him, in compensation, a meager grade of adjutant and the hand of an old maid, ugly, churchy, and coquettish. Upon Trenck's refusal, the *matrimoniomaniacal* empress told him that he was mad, presumptuous, that she knew of no way to satisfy his ambition, then turned her back on him and had nothing more to do with the man. The reasons put forward for confiscating the pandur's estate had varied according to the persons and circumstances. One tribunal had found that the pandur, who died condemned of a crime that stripped him of his civil rights, had not been entitled to make a will; another one, that while the will was valid, the rights of the heir, in his quality as a Prussian subject, were not; yet another, finally, that the debts of the deceased absorbed the entire estate and more, etc. Points of law were raised one after the other; justice was sold to the plaintiff several times, and he was never done justice.[5]

There was no need of all these artifices to despoil and proscribe Albert, and the spoliation no doubt took place with less ado. It was enough to consider him dead and forbid him the right to come back to life in untimely fashion. Albert had most certainly not laid claim to anything. We only know that at the time of his arrest Canoness Wenceslawa had just died in Prague, where she had gone to receive treatment for her acute ophthalmia. When Albert heard that she was near death, he could not resist the voice of his heart crying for him to go shut the eyes of his dear aunt. He left Consuelo at the Austrian border and rushed to

5. Here we shall remind the reader, once and for all, about the rest of Trenck's story. He grew old in poverty, occupied his energy with the publication of dissident newspapers that took very advanced views for his time; he married a woman of his choice and fathered several children; persecuted for his opinions, his writings, and no doubt as well for his membership in secret societies, he sought refuge in France at an advanced age. There he was welcomed with the enthusiasm and confidence that characterized the beginnings of the Revolution. Yet, destined to be the victim of the most sinister mistakes, he was arrested as a foreign agent during the Terror and led to the scaffold, to which he marched with great firmness. Just a short while before he had seen himself praised and depicted on stage in a melodrama retracing his captivity and deliverance. He had hailed liberty in France with transports of joy. On the fateful tumbrel he smiled and said, "This too is a comedy."

He had seen Princess Amalia again just once in more than sixty years. When he learned that Frederick the Great had died, he rushed to Berlin. The two lovers, who were at first frightened at the sight of one other, dissolved in tears and exchanged vows of a new affection. The abbess ordered him to bring his wife to Berlin, took charge of their welfare, and wanted to take one of his daughters on as her reader or governess, but she was unable to keep her promises. A week later she was dead!–Trenck's memoirs, written with a youth's passion and an old man's prolixity, are nevertheless one of the most noble and endearing monuments to the history of the last century.

Prague. This was his first time back in Germany since the year of his wedding. He wanted to think that ten years away and certain precautions of dress would prevent him from being recognized, and he approached his aunt without much mystery. He wanted to receive her blessing and to repair, in a last effusion of love and pain, the neglect in which he had been forced to leave her. The canoness, nearly blind, was struck only by the sound of his voice. She did not fully understand what she was feeling, but she abandoned herself to the tender instincts that had survived memory and reasoning; she pressed him in her feeble arms, calling him her beloved Albert, her son forever blessed. Old Hanz had died, but Baroness Amalia and a woman from the Bohemian Forest who was in service to the canoness and had once been Albert's sick-nurse were amazed and frightened by this alleged doctor's resemblance to the young count. It does not seem, however, that Amalia had positively recognized him; we do not want to believe that she was an accomplice to the persecutions that hounded him. We do not know what alerted the swarm of agents, half-magistrate half-stool pigeon, thanks to which the Viennese court ruled the subjugated nations. This much is certain: No sooner had the canoness breathed her last in her nephew's arms than he was arrested and interrogated about his station in life and the intentions that had led him to the dying woman's bedside. They wanted to see his doctor's diploma; he had a proper one; but they challenged the name Liverani that he bore, and certain individuals remembered having met him elsewhere under the name of Trismegistus. They accused him of being a quack and a magician. It was impossible to prove that he had ever taken any money for his treatments. They brought him before Baroness Amalia, and this was his ruination. Irritated and pushed to the limit by the investigations which he was having to undergo, weary of secrecy and disguise, he abruptly confessed to his cousin, in a private conversation that was being observed, that he was Albert von Rudolstadt. Amalia no doubt recognized him at that moment, but she fainted, terrified by such a bizarre event. From that point on things took another turn.

They wanted to consider Albert an impostor; yet, in order to raise one of those interminable disputes that are the ruin of both parties, some functionaries, of the ilk that had despoiled Trenck, worked furiously to compromise the accused by getting him to say and maintain that he was Albert von Rudolstadt. A long investigation ensued. They invoked the testimony of Supperville, who, no doubt in good faith, refused to doubt that he had witnessed his death at Riesenburg. They ordered that his cadaver be exhumed. In his tomb they found a skeleton that it had not been difficult to put there the day before. They convinced his cousin that it was her duty to put up a fight against an adventurer determined to despoil her. No doubt they did not allow them to see each other again. They smothered the captive's complaints and his wife's fervent protests under the bolts and tortures of prison. Perhaps the two of them fell ill and nearly died in separate dungeons. Once things had got underway, Albert could no longer clamor for his honor and liberty except by proclaiming the truth. To no avail he protested that he had renounced his inheritance, that he now wanted to make a will in his cousin's favor, they wanted to draw out the suit and confuse matters, which they had no trouble doing, because the empress had either been deceived or made to understand that confiscating this fortune was no more to be disdained than confiscating the pandur's. In order to do so, they tried to pick a quarrel with Amalia herself, they stealthily harked back to the scandal of her old escapade, they noted her lack of devotion and secretly threatened to have her shut away in a convent if she refused to abandon her rights to a disputed estate. She had to give in and content herself with her father's estate, which was significantly diminished by the enormous fees that she had to pay for a lawsuit that they had forced her to pursue. Finally the castle and domain of Riesenburg were confiscated by the state after the lawyers, managers, judges, and court reporters had placed liens on these spoils amounting to two thirds of their value.

Such is our commentary on the mysterious lawsuit that lasted five or six years and after which Albert was expelled from Austria as a dangerous madman, by the empress's special grace. From that point on, it is almost certain that an obscure and ever more impoverished life was the couple's lot. They took their youngest children with them. Haydn and the canon tenderly refused to give them back the oldest children, who were being educated under the watch of these faithful friends and at their expense. Consuelo had irrevocably lost her voice. It seems all too certain that captivity, idleness, and the pain of his companion's sufferings had once again unsettled Albert's mind. It does not however appear that their love became less tender, their souls less proud, and their conduct less pure. The Invisibles had disappeared under persecution. Their work had been ruined, especially by the charlatans that had speculated on enthusiasm for new ideas and the love of things supernatural. Persecuted once again as a Freemason in intolerant, despotic lands, Albert had to take refuge in France or England. Perhaps he continued his proselytizing there, but it must have been among the people, and his labors, if they bore fruit, went unnoticed.

There is a great lacuna here for which we cannot compensate by imagination. Yet one last authentic and very detailed document shows us, around the year 1774, the couple wandering through the Bohemian Forest. We shall transcribe this document as it came to us. This will be our last word on Albert and Consuelo; for after that, regarding their life and their death, we know absolutely nothing.

Letter from Philon[1] *to Ignatius Joseph Martinowicz Professor of physics at the University of Lemberg*

Swept along in his swirling wake like the satellites of a royal planet, we followed *Spartacus*[2] over the steep trails and through the most silent shady recesses of the Bohemian Forest. O friend! why weren't you there? You would have forgotten to gather pebbles in the silvery bed of the mountain streams, to study now the veins, now the bones of our mysterious foremother, *terra parens*. The master's ardent words gave us wings; we traversed ravines and peaks without counting our steps, without gazing down at the abysses over which we reigned, without seeking on the horizon the faraway shelter where we were to take our evening rest. Never had *Spartacus* seemed to us greater, more imbued with almighty truth. The beauties of nature act upon his imagination like those of a great poem; and despite his flashes of enthusiasm, his spirit of learned analysis and ingenious combination never wholly abandons him. He explains the stars and the planets, the earth and the seas, with the same clarity, the same order that rule over his essays on law and the arid things of this world. Yet how his soul expands when, alone and free with his chosen disciples, under the azure of the starry firmament or with his face turned to the first blush of dawn, he traverses time and space to embrace the human race at a glance, as a whole and in its parts, to fathom the fragile destiny of empires and the imposing future of peoples! You've heard him speaking from his chair, this young man of lucid words; why haven't you seen and heard him on the mountain, this man whose wisdom flies ahead of the years, who seems to have lived among men since the infancy of the world!

1. Probably the famous Baron von Knigge, known as Philon in the Order of the Illuminati.

2. It is known that this was Adam Weishaupt's nom de guerre. Is this really the person in question here? Everything points in that direction. [Translator's note: Spartacus was the slave who incited an insurrection of his fellow slaves against their masters in first-century Rome.]

Having arrived at the border we hailed the land that saw the exploits of the great Zizka, and we bowed even more deeply before the pits that served as tombs for the martyrs to the nation's ancient liberty. There we resolved to go our separate ways so to direct our research and investigations on all points at once. *Cato*[3] went northeast, *Celsus*[4] southeast, *Ajax*[5] went due east, and we would all meet up again in Pilsen.

Spartacus kept me with him and resolved to proceed at random, counting, he said, on chance, on a certain secret inspiration to show us the way. I was somewhat amazed to see him abandon calculation and reasoning; this seemed to me contrary to his methodical habits.

"Philon," he said, when we were alone, "I do believe that men like us are the ministers of Providence here below, but do you think I believe her to be inert and disdainful, this motherly Providence through which we feel, will, and act! I've noticed that you enjoy her favors more than I; your designs nearly always meet with success. So, forge on ahead, and I'll follow, having faith in your second sight, that mysterious light that our Illuminist ancestors naïvely invoked, those pious fanatics of the past!"

This truly seems to have been a prophecy on the master's part. Before the end of the second day we had found what we had come looking for, and this is how I became the tool of destiny.

We had reached the edge of the woods, and there was a fork in the road ahead. One road plunged down and away into the lowlands, the other ran along the gentle flanks of the mountain.

"Which way shall we go?" asked *Spartacus*, sitting down on a rock. "Here I see tilled fields, meadows, wretched huts. We were told that *he* is poor; *he* must live among the poor. Let's go ask the humble shepherds in the valley about him."

"No, master," I replied, pointing out to him the road halfway up the slope. "On my right I see steep hillocks and the crumbling walls of an ancient manor. We were told that he was a poet; he must love ruins and solitude."

"Besides," said *Spartacus* with a smile, "I see Vesper rising white as a pearl in the still rosy sky above the ruins of the old estate. We are the shepherds searching for a prophet, and the miraculous star leads the way."

We soon reached the ruins. It was an imposing edifice, with parts dating from various periods, but vestiges of the era of Emperor Charles lay next to those of feudal times. It was not the centuries, but the hands of men that had re-

3. No doubt Xavier Zwack, who was a court councilor and suffered exile for having been one of the principal leaders of the Illuminati.

4. Baader, the Dowager Electress's physician and a member of the Illuminati.

5. Massenhausen, a councilor in Munich and a member of the Illuminati.

cently presided over that destruction. It was still full daylight when we clambered up the side of a dry moat and slipped in under the rusted, motionless portcullis. The first thing that we encountered, sitting on the rubble at the entrance to the courtyard, was an old man covered in bizarre rags, and more like a man out of the past rather than the present. His beard, the color of yellowed ivory, hung down over his chest, and his bald head was shining like a lake in the sun's last rays. *Spartacus* shuddered, hurried up to him and asked the name of the castle. The old man seemed not to hear us; he stared at us with glassy eyes that seemed not to see. We asked him his name; he made no reply; his physiognomy expressed only a dreamy indifference. Yet his Socratic features were not those of a mindless idiot; his ugliness had a certain beauty that comes from a pure, serene soul. *Spartacus* put a piece of silver in his hand; he brought it very close to his eyes and let it drop without seeming to understand its use.

"Is it possible," I asked the master, "for an old man totally deprived of his senses and reason to be abandoned like this far away from any dwelling, in the middle of the mountains, without a guide, without a dog to lead him around and beg in his place?"

"Let's take him along to some shelter," replied *Spartacus*.

But as we were preparing to lift him up to see if he could stand on his legs, he motioned to us not to bother him by placing a finger on his lips and pointing to the far end of the courtyard with his other hand. We looked over that way and didn't see anyone, but just then our ears were struck by the sound of a violin being played with extraordinary strength and accuracy. Never have I heard any musician give his bow such a broad, penetrating vibration and create such an intimate rapport between the strings of the soul and those of the instrument. The melody was simple and sublime, unlike anything I've heard in our concerts and theaters. It filled the heart with an emotion that was both pious and warlike. We felt a sort of rapture, the master and I, and we told each other with our eyes that this was something great and mysterious. A sort of vague brilliance, like that of ecstasy, had once again come over the old man's eyes. A smile of beatitude parted his withered lips, a good sign that he was neither deaf nor insensible.

Everything fell silent again after a short, adorable melody, and then we saw a man of mature years, whose aspect filled us with emotion and respect, emerge from a chapel opposite us. The beauty of his austere face and the noble proportions of his stature contrasted with the deformed limbs and wild features of the old man that *Spartacus* compared to a *converted, baptized faun*. The violin player walked straight up to us, his instrument under his arm, and his bow slipped through his leather belt. Loose-fitting trousers of rough material, sandals that looked like ancient buskins, and a sheepskin tunic of the sort worn by our

Danube peasants gave him the appearance of a shepherd or ploughman. But his fine white hands were not those of a man who spent his life working the land. They were the hands of an artist. Likewise, the cleanliness of his garments and the pride in his eyes seemed to protest his wretched poverty and refuse to accept its hideous, degrading consequences. The master was struck by the man's aspect. He squeezed my hand, and I could feel that his was trembling.

"That's him!" he said. "I didn't know he was a musician, but I recognize his face for having seen it in my dreams."

The violin player came toward us without demonstrating any embarrassment or surprise. With kindly dignity he returned our greeting, and drawing near the old man, he said, "Come on, Zdenko, I'm on my way, lean on your friend."

The old man made an effort, the musician lifted him up, and bending over beneath him as though to act as his staff, he guided the old man's tottering steps and slowed down his own pace accordingly. There was in this filial care, in the patience of a noble, handsome man still limber and strong, crawling along under the weight of an old man in rags, something more touching, if that's possible, than the solicitude of a young mother adjusting her gait to her child's first halting steps. I saw the master's eyes fill with tears, and I too was moved, contemplating now our Spartacus, this man of genius and the future, now this stranger in whom I sensed the same grandeur buried in the shades of the past.

Determined to follow and question him, but not wishing to distract him from his pious task, we trailed behind at a short distance. He was headed for the chapel out of which he had come, and once inside, he stopped and seemed to contemplate some broken tombstones invaded by brambles and moss. The old man had knelt down, and when he got back up, his friend kissed one of the tombstones, and they started off together.

It was only then that he noticed us nearby, and he seemed a bit taken aback, but there was no mistrust in his gaze, bright-eyed and placid like that of a child. Yet he appeared to be over fifty, and the thick gray locks billowing around his manly face played up the flash of his large dark eyes. His mouth had an indefinable expression of strength and simplicity. One would have said that he had two souls, one all enthusiasm for things celestial, the other all benevolence for mankind here below.

We were searching for a pretext to say a few words to him when all of a sudden he connected with our thoughts, by a naïve stroke of extraordinary expansiveness, and said, "You've seen me kiss this piece of marble, and the old man has prostrated himself on these tombs. Don't take this as acts of idolatry. One kisses the clothes of a saint as one wears a token of love and friendship over the heart. Mortal remains are merely used clothing. We don't trample on them with indifference; we keep them with respect and leave them with regret. Oh my father, oh my beloved family! I know full well that you aren't here, and these inscriptions lie when they say: *Here repose the Rudolstadts*! The Rudolstadts are all on their feet, all living and acting in the world according to God's will. Under these pieces of marble there are just bones, forms that came to life, that life abandoned to take on other forms. Blessed be the ashes of ancestors! Blessed be the grass and ivy crowning them! Blessed be the earth and rock defending them! But blessed, above all, be the living God who says to the dead, 'Rise up and return to my fertile soul! where nothing dies, where everything is renewed and purified!' "

"Liverani or Zizka Trismegistus, is this you I see once again on the tomb of your ancestors?" exclaimed *Spartacus* enlightened by a celestial certainty.

"Neither Liverani, nor Trismegistus, nor even Jan Zizka," replied the stranger. "Specters besieged my ignorant youth, but they've been absorbed by divine light, and the ancestors' names have faded from my memory. My name is *man* and I am nothing more than other men."

"Those are profound words, but also wary," said the master. "You can trust this sign; don't you recognize it?"

And thereupon *Spartacus* made him Masonic signs of the upper degrees.

"I've forgotten that language," replied the stranger. "I don't despise it, but it's become useless to me. Brother, don't insult me by supposing that I don't trust you. Your name, yours too, is it not *man*? Men have never done me harm, or if they have, I'm not aware of it any longer. It was therefore very limited harm, compared with the infinite good they can do each other, for which I must be grateful to them ahead of time."

"Is it possible, oh good man," exclaimed *Spartacus*, "that time counts for nothing in your notion and feeling of life?"

"There is no such thing as time, and if men meditated more on the divine essence, they wouldn't count centuries and years any more than I do. What does it matter to one who partakes of God to the point of being eternal, to one who has always lived and will never cease to live, that there is a bit more or a bit less sand at the bottom of the clepsydra? The hand turning the hourglass can speed up or slow down; the hand providing the sand knows no cease."

"You mean to say that man can forget about counting and measuring time, that life always flows rich and abundant from the bosom of God? Is that your thought?"

"You've understood me, young man. But I have a more beautiful demonstration of the great mysteries."

"The mysteries? Yes, I've come from far away to ask you questions and learn from you."

"So listen!" said the stranger, making the old man, who obeyed him with the trust of a little child, sit down on a tombstone. "This place particularly inspires me, and it's here in the last rays of the sun and the first pale glimmer of the moon that I want to lift up your soul to knowledge of the most sublime truths."

We were quivering with joy at the idea of having found at last, after two years of seeking and searching, this wise man of our religion, this philosopher, both metaphysician and organizer, who was to entrust us with Ariadne's thread and guide us out of the labyrinth of the ideas and things of the past. But the stranger seized his violin and began playing with verve. His vigorous bow made the leaves rustle like the evening breeze and the ruins echo like the human voice. His melody had a particular quality of religious enthusiasm, ancient simplicity, and stirring warmth. The motifs had a majestic fullness in their energetic brevity. There was nothing languorous or dreamy in these unfamiliar melodies. They were like songs of war, and they made triumphant armies bearing the banners, palms, and mysterious symbols of a new religion pass before our eyes. I saw the peoples in their immensity having come together under one flag; no turmoil in the ranks, a fever without delirium, an impetuous élan without anger, human activity in all its splendor, victory in all its mercy, and faith in all its sublime expansion.

"Magnificent!" I exclaimed after he had given a fiery performance of five or six of these admirable melodies. "That's the *Te Deum* of Humanity rejuvenated and reconciled, thanking the God of all religions, the light of all men."

"You've understood me, child!" said the musician, wiping the sweat and tears streaming down his face, "and you see that time has just one voice for proclaiming the truth. Look at this old man, he's understood as well as you have, and now he's thirty years younger."

We turned our eyes to the old man whom we had already forgotten. He was on his feet, walking about with ease and tapping his foot to the rhythm, as though he wanted to spring up and leap like a youth. The music had worked a miracle in him; he went down the hill with us without wanting to lean on any of us. When his pace slackened, the musician asked, "Zdenko, do you want me to play you again the march of *Procopius the Great* or the benediction of the Horebites' flag?"

But the old man signaled that he still had strength, as though he were afraid of squandering a celestial remedy and using up his friend's inspiration.

We were heading for the hamlet that had been on our right at the far end of the valley when we had taken the road to the ruins. On the way *Spartacus* questioned the stranger.

"You've played incomparable melodies for us," he said, "and with this brilliant prelude I understand that you meant to incline our senses to the enthusiasm that brims over in you, you wanted to lift yourself up, like a pythoness or prophet, so that you could utter your oracles, armed with all the power of inspiration, and totally filled with the spirit of the Lord. So now speak. The wind is still and the path easy, the moon is lighting our way. All nature seems deep in meditation to hear you, and our hearts are calling for your revelations. Our vain science, our proud reason, will grow humble under your fervent words. Speak, the moment has come."

But the stranger refused to explain himself.

"What would I say that I haven't just said in a more beautiful language? Is it my fault if you failed to understand me? You think I wanted to speak to your senses, and it was my soul speaking to you! What am I saying? It was the soul of all Humanity speaking to you through mine. Then I was truly inspired, and now I'm not. I need to rest. You'd feel the same way if you had taken in everything that I was trying to impart."

It was impossible for *Spartacus* to get anything more out of him that evening. When we reached the first cottages, the stranger said to us, "Friends, don't follow me any further, and come back to see me tomorrow. Just knock on the first door you come to. You'll be welcomed everywhere here if you know the language of the land."

There was no need to flash the small amount of money we had. The Bohemian peasant's hospitality is worthy of ancient times. We were welcomed in a calm, obliging way, which soon turned affectionately cordial when they heard us speak the Slavic language fluently; the people here are still wary of anyone who approaches them in German.

We soon learned that we were at the foot of the mountain and castle *of the Giants*, and, on the basis of the name, we could have thought ourselves magically transported to the great northern chain of the Carpathians. But we were told that one of the Podiebrad ancestors had baptized his estate with this name to commemorate a vow he had made in the *Riesengebürge*. They also told us how the Podiebrad descendants had changed their own name, after the disasters of the Thirty Years' War, and taken that of Rudolstadt; the persecution at that time went so far as to Germanize the names of cities, estates, families, and individuals. All of these traditions are still alive in the hearts of the Bohemian peasants. So the mysterious Trismegistus for whom we were searching is very truly the same Albert Podiebrad who was buried alive twenty-five years ago, wrested from his tomb by what miracle it has never been known, who then disappeared for a long time, only to be persecuted and locked up some ten or fifteen years later for being a falsifier, an impostor and, above all, a Freemason and Rosicrucian; this famous Count von Rudolstadt whose strange trial was carefully hushed up, whose identity could never be ascertained. So trust the master's inspirations, friend; you trembled to see us, on the basis of vague and incomplete revelations, racing off in search of a man who could be, like so many other Illuminati of the previous generation, a careless crook or a ridiculous adventurer. The master had guessed right. From a few scattered traits, a few mysterious writings by this strange character, he had sensed a man of intelligence and truth, a precious guardian of the sacred fire and holy traditions of earlier Illuminism, a disciple of the ancient secret, a doctor of the new interpretation. We've found him, and today we know more about the history of Freemasonry, about the famous Invisibles whose work and even existence we once threw into doubt, about ancient and modern mysteries than we had learned seeking to decipher lost hieroglyphs or consulting former disciples worn down by persecution and debased by fear. We've found, in short, a man, and we're returning to you with this sacred fire that once turned a clay statue into an intelligent being, a new god, a rival to the old gods, fierce and stupid. Our master is Prometheus. Trismegistus had the flame in his heart, and we've stolen enough of it from him to initiate you all into new life.

Our fine hosts' tales kept us awake around the rustic hearth quite a while. They hadn't paid any heed to the judgments and legal attestations declaring that Albert von Rudolstadt had forfeited, by reason of an attack of catalepsy, his name and rights. Their love of his memory, their hatred of the foreigners, these Austrian despoilers who, after having forcibly procured the rightful heir's conviction, came and divided up his land and castle among themselves; the shameless squandering of the great fortune that Albert would have put to such noble use, and above all the wrecking hammer doggedly knocking down the ancient seigneurial manor so that the materials could be sold off cheaply, as if certain beasts destructive and sacrilegious by nature had needed to pollute and spoil the prey that they could not manage to carry off. All this was quite enough to make the peasants of the Bohemian Forest prefer a poetically miraculous truth to the conquerors' reasonably odious assertions. It was twenty-five years ago that Albert Podiebrad disappeared, and nobody here has wanted to believe him dead, even though all the German gazettes said so as confirmation of an iniquitous judgment, even though the whole Viennese court laughed with scorn and pity listening to the story of a maniac who sincerely took himself for a dead man come back to life. And for a week now Albert von Rudolstadt has been here in these mountains, praying and singing every evening on the ruins of his forefathers' castle. And for a week now as well all the men old enough to have seen him in his youth have been recognizing him with his grey hair and bowing down before him as their true master and old friend. There is something admirable about this memory, about the love of these people for him; nothing, in our corrupt world, can give an idea of the pure morals and noble sentiments we've encountered here. This fills *Spartacus* with awe, and he's all the more impressed because a minor episode of persecution that we endured at the hands of these peasants confirmed to us how faithful they are to misfortune and gratitude.

Here's what happened. When, at the break of day, we wanted to leave the cottage to go ask about the violin player, we found a picket of improvised foot-soldiers guarding all the exits.

"We beg your pardon," stated the head of the family calmly, "for having called all our friends and relatives, with their flails and scythes, to keep you here against your will. You'll be free to go this evening." And given our astonishment at this violence, our host continued with a grave look, "If you are good men, if you understand friendship and devotion, you won't be angry with us. If, on the other hand, you're traitors and spies sent here to persecute and kidnap our Podiebrad, we won't tolerate it, and we'll keep you here until he's far away, out of your reach."

We understood that these good men, at first so expansive with us, had grown suspicious during the night, and we could only admire their solicitude. But the master was desperate about losing sight of this precious hierophant that we had come seeking with such trouble and so few chances of success. He decided to write to Trismegistus in Masonic code, telling him his name and position, giving him some inkling of his designs and invoking his allegiance to shield us from the peasants' suspicions. A few seconds after that letter had been taken to the next cottage, there arrived a woman before whom the peasants respectfully opened their phalanx bristling with rustic weapons. We heard them murmuring, "*The Zingara! the Zingara of consolation!*" And soon this woman came into the cottage where we were, and closing the doors behind her, she began interrogating us, with scrupulous severity, by means of the signs and formulas of the Scottish rite. We were most surprised to see a woman initiated into these mysteries that, as far as I know, no other woman has ever possessed, and her commanding presence and searching gaze inspired in us a certain respect, despite the quite obviously zingaro costume that she wore with the ease that comes of habit. Her striped skirt, the big cloak of tawny homespun thrown over her shoulder like an ancient toga, her hair black as night, parted on the forehead and fastened by a band of blue wool, her large eyes full of fire, her ivory-white teeth, her weather-beaten but smooth complexion, her little feet and slender hands, and, as the finishing touch of her portrait, a rather beautiful guitar hitched up crosswise under her cloak, everything about her person and costume announced straight off a Zingara's looks and trade. As she was very clean and her manner calm and dignified, we thought her the queen of her camp. But when she told us that she was Trismegistus' wife, we gazed at her with greater interest and attention. She is no longer young, and yet one would be hard put to say if she is a person of forty withered with fatigue or a remarkably well-preserved fifty-year-old. She is still beautiful, and her elegant, lithe carriage is so noble, so chastely graceful that seeing her walking one would take her for a young maiden. When the initial severity of her features had softened, we were gradually penetrated by her charm. Her gaze is angelic, and the sound of her voice stirs your heart like a celestial melody. Whoever this woman may be, the philosopher's legitimate wife or a generous adventuress trailing after him because of an ardent passion, it is impossible to think while gazing at her and listening to her voice that any vice, any degrading instinct could have sullied someone so calm, so frank, and so good. We had been alarmed, at first, to find our sage demeaned by carnal bonds. It didn't take us long to discover that, in the ranks of true nobility, that of the heart and mind, he had met a poetic lover, a sister soul, to accompany him through the storms of life.

"Pardon me my fears and suspicion," she said to us once we had satisfied her questions. "We've been persecuted, we've suffered a great deal. Thank heaven, misfortune has made my friend lose his memory; nothing can worry him or make him suffer any longer. But I whom God has placed near him for his safekeeping, I have to worry in his stead and watch over him. Your physiognomies and the tone of your voices reassure me even more than the signs and words we've just exchanged; for people have made strange misuse of the mysteries, and there have been as many false brothers as quack doctors. Human prudence should give us leave not to believe in anything or anyone from now on, but God preserve us from ever reaching that degree of egotism and impiety! True, the family of the faithful is scattered; there is no longer any temple in which to commune in spirit and in truth. The disciples have lost the sense of the mysteries; the letter has killed the spirit. Divine art is misconceived and profaned among men, but what does it matter if faith persists in a few? What does it matter if the word of life remains in trust in some sanctuary? It will emerge once again, go forth into the world once again, and perhaps the temple will be rebuilt by the Canaanite's faith and the widow's penny."

"That word of life is precisely what we've come to find," replied the master. "It is uttered in every sanctuary, and it's true that no one understands it any more. We've made fervent explications of it, we've persevered in bearing it within our hearts and minds and, after years of work and meditation, we believe that we've found the true interpretation. That's why we've come to ask your husband to sanction our faith or correct our error. Let us speak with him. Have him hear us out and tell us what he thinks."

"That's not up to me," replied the Zingara, "and even less to him. Trismegistus isn't always inspired, even though he's now living under the spell of poetic illusions. Music is his usual manifestation. Rarely are his metaphysical ideas lucid enough to be abstracted from emotions of an exalted sort. Just now he won't be able to tell you anything satisfying. His words are always clear to me, but that wouldn't be the case for you who don't know him. I have to warn you; according to men blinded by their cold reason, Trismegistus is mad; and while the people, poets each and every one, humbly offer gifts of hospitality to the sublime virtuoso who moved and delighted them, the vulgar throw alms of pity at the vagabond rhapsodist who wanders through the cities with his inspiration. But I've taught our children that they mustn't gather up these alms, or only for the crippled beggar whom we see along the way, to whom the heavens have denied the genius for moving and persuading mankind. We, on the other hand, we have no need of the rich man's money, we're not begging; alms demean the receiver and harden the giver. Everything that is not exchange must disappear in future society. In the meantime, God allows my husband and me to practice that life of exchange and thereby to partake of the ideal. We bring art and enthusiasm to souls capable of feeling the one and aspiring to the other. We receive the religious hospitality of the poor, we share their meager shelter, their frugal meals, and when we need a crude garment, we earn it by staying for a few weeks and giving the family music lessons. When we pass by a lord's proud manor, since he is our brother as well as the shepherd, the laborer, and the craftsman, we sing under his window and move on without waiting for wages; we consider him an unfortunate who is unable to exchange anything with us, so it is we who give him alms. In short, we've fulfilled the life of the artist as we've come to understand it; for God made us artists, and we had to make use of his gifts. We have friends and brothers everywhere in the bottom ranks of this society that would find it demeaning to ask us our secret for being honest and free. Every day we make new disciples of art, and when we've exhausted our strength, when we can no longer feed and carry our children, they'll carry us in turn, and we'll be fed and consoled by them. If our children were to leave us, swept far away by different vocations, we would do like old Zdenko whom you saw yesterday, and who, after having charmed forty years long all the peasants of the land with his legends and songs, is taken in and looked after in his last years as a friend and venerable teacher. With simple tastes and frugal habits, the love of the road, the health given by a life in accord with nature's will, with the enthusiasm of poetry, the absence of evil passions and above all faith in the future of the world, do you believe it mad to live as we do? Yet Trismegistus may seem to you deranged by enthusiasm, as he once seemed to me deranged by pain. But if you follow him a while, perhaps you'll see that it's the insanity of men and the error of institutions that make men of genius and invention seem mad. Look, come along for the day with us, if that's what it takes. Perhaps there'll come an hour when Trismegistus will be talking about something other than music. You mustn't ask that of him, it will just happen all by itself at a given moment. Something random can reawaken his old ideas. We're leaving in an hour, our being here can bring down new dangers on my husband's head. Anywhere else we don't run the risk of being recognized after so many years of exile. We are going to Vienna, by way of the mountains through the Bohemian Forest and the course of the Danube. I traveled that route in the past, and I'll do it again with pleasure. We're on our way to visit two of our children, the older ones that well-off friends wanted to keep to see about their education; for not everyone is born to be an artist, and we all have to walk the path in life that Providence has drawn for us."

Such were the explanations that the strange woman, pressed by our questions and often interrupted by our objections, gave about the way of life that she had taken up according to her husband's tastes and ideas. We joyfully accepted her invitation to follow along behind, and when we stepped out of the cottage with her, the civilian guard formed for the purpose of detaining us had opened its ranks to let us go.

"Come on, children," the Zingara cried to them in her full, harmonious voice, "your friend awaits you under the linden trees. It's the loveliest moment of the day, and we'll have morning prayer in music. You can trust these two friends," she added, waving her hand toward us in her beautiful, naturally theatrical way. "Their cause is ours, and they only wish us well."

The peasants, shouting and singing, dashed after us. On the way the Zingara told us that she and her family were leaving the hamlet this very morning.

"You mustn't say so," she added. "That would cause too many tears, for we have many friends here. But we aren't safe in these parts. Some old enemy can come along and recognize Albert von Rudolstadt in Bohemian dress."

We arrived at the hamlet's green, a grassy clearing surrounded by superb linden trees that through their enormous flanks gave one a glimpse of humble little houses and whimsical paths drawn and beaten down by herds of animals. This seemed to us an enchanted place, with the emerald carpet of the meadows glistening in the first oblique rays of sun and silvery morning mists folding over the flanks of the surrounding mountains. The shady areas seemed to have kept something of the night's bluish luminosity while the treetops were turning gold and crimson. Everything was pure and clear, everything seemed to us fresh and young, even the ancient linden trees, the moss-eaten roofs and the white-bearded old men coming out of their cottages with a smile. In the middle of the clearing where crystalline water trickled forth in two streams crisscrossing back and forth under one's feet, we saw Trismegistus surrounded by his children, two charming little girls and a boy of fifteen, beautiful as the Endymion of sculptors and poets.

"This is Wanda," said the Zingara introducing the elder girl, "and the younger one is Wenceslawa. As for our son, who was given the cherished name of his father's best friend, he is called Zdenko. Old Zdenko has a marked preference for him. You see that he's holding Wenceslawa between his knees, and the other one on his lap. But his mind is not on them. He's got his eyes fastened on my son, as if he couldn't get enough of looking at him."

We turned our eyes to the old man. Tears were streaming down his cheeks, and his bony face, furrowed with lines, had an expression of beatitude and ecstasy while he was contemplating the young man, the last scion of the Rudolstadts, who bore his slave name with joy, standing next to him, holding his hand. I would have liked to paint this group, and Trismegistus beside them, contemplating them in turn with a tender look while tuning his violin and trying his bow.

"It's you, friends?" he cordially replied to our respectful greeting. "So my wife went to fetch you? Good for her. I've got fine things to say today, and I'd be happy to have you hear them."

Then he played the violin with even greater exuberance and majesty than the day before. This at least was our impression, which became stronger and more delectable through contact with that rustic assembly that quivered with pleasure and enthusiasm hearing the old ballads of the fatherland and the sacred hymns of ancient liberty. Their emotion was translated in various ways on these manly faces. Some, carried away like Zdenko into a vision of the past, were holding their breath and seemed imbued with that poetry, like a parched plant meditatively imbibing drops of salutary rain. Others, transported with holy furor at the thought of the present troubles, clenched their fists, threatened invisible enemies and seemed to take heaven as witness to their dashed dignity, their outraged virtue. There were sobs and roars, frenetic applause, and delirious shouts.

"Friends," Albert said to us at the end, "see these simple men! They've understood perfectly what I wanted to tell them; they don't ask me, as you were doing yesterday, what my prophecies mean."

"Yet you spoke to them only of the past," said *Spartacus*, hanging on his words.

"Past, future, present! What vain niceties!" said Trismegistus with a smile.

"Doesn't man carry all three in his heart, and doesn't his whole existence partake of this triple medium? But since you absolutely require words to depict your ideas, listen to my son. He's going to sing you a hymn, his mother having written the music, and I the words."

The beautiful adolescent came forward with a calm, modest bearing to the center of the circle. It was clear that his mother, without believing that she was flattering a weakness, had told herself that, by right, perhaps also by duty, one had to respect and groom the artist's beauty. She dresses him with a certain studied elegance; his superb locks are carefully combed, and the materials of his rustic costume are of a brighter hue and finer texture than those of the rest of the family. He removed his cap, greeted his listeners by blowing them all a kiss from the tips of his fingers, to which a hundred of the same were the effusive reply; and after his mother had played a guitar prelude with a particular meridional flair, he began to sing, with her accompaniment, the following words that I'm translating for you from the Slavic language, and whose admirable melody they kindly let me take down:

The Gentle Goddess of Poverty
Ballad

"Sandy paths of gold, verdant moors, ravines cherished by the mountain goat, great mountains crowned with stars, vagabond torrents, impenetrable forests, make way, make way for the gentle goddess, the goddess of poverty!

"Since the beginning of the world, since mankind was made, she has been rambling over the earth, she lives in our midst, she roams as she sings, or she sings as she works, the goddess, the gentle goddess of poverty!

"A few men joined together to curse her. They found her too beautiful and blithe, too nimble and strong. Let's tear off her wings, they said; let's put her in chains and give her a good thrashing; let her suffer and die, the goddess of poverty!

"They chained the gentle goddess, they beat and persecuted her; but they could not demean her; she took refuge in the souls of poets and peasants, of artists and martyrs and saints, the gentle goddess, the goddess of poverty!

"She has wandered more than the Wandering Jew; she has traveled more than the swallow; she is older than the cathedral of Prague and younger than the wren's egg; she has sprung up all over the earth more than wild strawberries in the Bohemian Forest, the goddess, the gentle goddess of poverty!

"She has had many children, and she has taught them the secret of God; she has spoken to the heart of Jesus on the mountain; to the eyes of Queen Libussa falling in love with a ploughman; to the spirits of Jan and Jerome on the pyre at Constance. She knows more than all the doctors of the church and all the bishops, the gentle goddess of poverty!

"She always does the greatest and most beautiful things seen on this earth; she tills the fields and prunes the trees; she leads the flocks while singing the most beautiful melodies; she sees the dawning of the day and gathers the sun's first smile, the gentle goddess of poverty!

"It is she who frames the woodcutter's hut out of green branches, who gives the poacher his eagle eye; it is she who raises the most beautiful marmots and makes the plough and the spade light in the hands of old men, the gentle goddess of poverty!

"It is she who inspires the poet and makes the violin, guitar, and flute eloquent under the fingers of the vagabond artist; it is she who carries him on her light wings from the headwaters of the Moldau to those of the Danube; it is she who crowns his locks with pearls of dew; for him she makes the stars shine brighter and clearer, the goddess, the gentle goddess of poverty!

"It is she who schools the clever craftsman and teaches him how to cut stone, carve marble, work gold and silver, copper and iron; it is she who makes the hands of the elderly mother and young maid spin linen supple and fine as a thread of hair, the gentle goddess of poverty!

"It is she who holds up the cottage shuddering in the storm; it is she who husbands the resin for the torch and the oil for the lamp; it is she who kneads the family's bread and weaves their summer and winter garments; it is she who nurtures and feeds the world, the gentle goddess of poverty!

"It is she who raised up the great castles and ancient cathedrals; it is she who bears the saber and the gun; it is she who makes war and conquest; it is she who gathers up the dead, cares for the wounded, and hides the vanquished warrior, the gentle goddess of poverty!

"You are all mildness and patience, all strength and mercy, oh gentle goddess! It is you who gather together all your children in holy love, who give charity, faith, hope, oh goddess of poverty!

"One day your children will cease carrying the world on their shoulders; they'll be rewarded for their pain and labor. The time is coming when there'll no longer be either rich men or poor, when one and all will eat of the fruits of the earth and enjoy equal shares of God's bounty; but you'll not be forgotten in their hymns, oh gentle goddess of poverty!

"They'll remember that you were their fertile mother, their robust nurse and militant church. They'll pour balm on your wounds and make the earth, once again young and fragrant, into a bed where you'll at last be able to take your rest, oh gentle goddess of poverty!

"While awaiting the day of the Lord, torrents and forests, mountains and valleys, moors teeming with little flowers and birds, sandy paths of gold that have no masters, make way, make way for the gentle goddess, the goddess of poverty!"

Just imagine this ballad rendered in beautiful verse in a sweet, naïve language that seems made for adolescent lips, set to a melody that stirs the heart and brings forth the purest tears, a seraphic voice that sings with exquisite purity, an incomparable musical accent; and all this in the mouth of Trismegistus' son, the Zingara's student, the most beautiful, the most candid and gifted among the children of the earth! If you can picture this among a vast number of men's faces, ingenuous and picturesque, amidst one of Ruysdael's landscapes, and the mountain stream that, though out of sight, was wafting from the depths of the ravine a refreshing harmony mingled with the distant bells of the goats on the mountain, you'll understand our emotion and the ineffable poetic delight in which we were long immersed.

"Now, my children," said Albert Podiebrad to the villagers, "we have prayed; there is work to be done. Off to the fields with you. As for me, I'm off to the forest, along with my family, in search of inspiration and life."

"You'll be back come evening?" shouted all the peasants.

The Zingara made an affectionate gesture that they took as a promise. The two little girls, understanding nothing about the course of time or the vicissitudes of travel, shouted "Yes! Yes!" with infantile joy, and the peasants went their ways. Old Zdenko sat down on the cottage doorsill after having made sure in a fatherly way that the family's lunch was tucked away in his godson's game-bag. Then the Zingara motioned that we should follow, and we left the village on the heels of our itinerant musicians. We had to go up the far side of the ravine. The master and I each took one of the little girls into our arms, which gave us a chance to approach Trismegistus who hadn't yet seemed to notice that we were there.

"You see that I'm musing a bit," he told me. "It pains me to deceive the friends that we're leaving, also the old man whom I love. Tomorrow he'll go searching for us over every path in the forest. But Consuelo wanted it this way," he added, pointing to his wife. "She thinks it dangerous for us to stay here any longer. For my part, I can't believe that we arouse anyone's fear or envy at this point. Who would understand our happiness? But she says that we bring the same dangers down on the heads of our friends, and even though I don't see how, I yield to that consideration. Besides, her will has always been my will, just as mine has always been hers. We won't return to the hamlet this evening. If you are our friends as you seem to be, you'll go back there after dark, once you've had a long enough walk, and you'll explain this to them. We didn't bid them farewell so as not to grieve them, but you'll tell them that we'll be back. As for Zdenko, you need only say *tomorrow*, he doesn't see any further ahead than that. Every day, the whole span of life, that's his *tomorrow*. He's stripped away the error of human notions. His eyes are open to eternity, and he's ready to let himself be absorbed into its mystery so as to partake of life's youth there. Zdenko is a wise man, the wisest I've ever known."

Trismegistus' ramblings had a noteworthy effect on his wife and children. Far from feeling embarrassed in front of us, far from suffering for themselves, they heeded every word with respect, and it seemed that they found in his oracles the strength to rise above this present life and themselves. I believe that this noble adolescent eagerly poring over each one of his father's thoughts would have been astonished and incensed if he'd been told that these were the thoughts of a madman. Trismegistus rarely spoke, and we noticed as well that neither his wife nor his children ever prompted him to do so unless absolutely necessary. They had a religious respect for the mystery of his reverie, and even though the Zingara kept her eyes on him at every moment, she certainly seemed rather more worried about his being importuned than about the dreary isolation in which he found himself. She had studied his bizarrerie, and I use this word so as no longer to pronounce the word "madness" that I find even more repugnant with regard to such a man, a state of soul so respectable and moving. Seeing this Trismegistus, I understood the veneration that the peasants, great theologians, and great metaphysicians without their knowing it, and the peoples of the East feel for men deprived of what is called the torch of reason. They know that when one does not trouble this abstraction of the mind by vain exertion and cruel mockery, it can become an exceptional faculty of the most poetically divine sort, instead of turning to furor or stupidity. I don't know what would happen to Trismegistus if his family didn't act like a rampart of love and fidelity between him and the world. But if he were in this case to succumb to his delirium, that would be yet more proof of what respect and solicitude are due to invalids of his sort, and to all invalids, whoever they may be.

This family walked with an easy, nimble gait that had soon exhausted our strength. If the little children hadn't been carried to prevent them from getting tired, they would have devoured space. They feel born to walk, so it seems, as do fish to swim. The Zingara doesn't want her son picking up the little girls, even though he would certainly like to, until he is fully grown and his voice has gone through that crisis that singers call the molt. She hoists up onto her robust shoulders these lithe, confident creatures and carries them as lightly as her guitar. Physical strength is one of the benefits of this nomadic life that becomes a passion for impoverished artists, for beggars and naturalists as well.

We were worn out by the time we had trudged over the most rugged trails to a wild, romantic place called Schreckenstein. As we were drawing near, we noticed Consuelo looking at her husband more attentively and walking closer beside him as though she were fearing some danger or painful emotion. Yet nothing troubled the artist's placidity. He sat down on a great rock dominating an arid slope. There is something frightening about the spot. There are heaps of boulders all over the place, and they are continually shattering trees as they come crashing down. The trees that have endured all have exposed roots, and by these knotty limbs they seem to hang on to the rock that they threaten to drag off. A deathly silence reigns over this chaos. Shepherds and woodcutters keep away out of terror, and wild boars plough up the earth. Tracks of wolves and mountain goats litter the ground as though wild animals were sure of finding shelter from men there. Albert dreamed a long while on that rock, then he looked back at his children playing at his feet and his wife standing in front of him, trying to read what was going on inside his head. All of a sudden he stood up, knelt down before her, and beckoning to his children, uttered with profound feeling, "Bow down before your mother, for she is the consolation that heaven sends to those in distress; she is the peace of the Lord promised to men of good will!"

The children knelt down around the Zingara and wept, covering her with caresses. She too wept, clasping them to her breast, then making them turn back around, she had them render the same homage to their father. *Spartacus* and I bowed down along with them.

After the Zingara had spoken, the master transferred his homage to Trismegistus and seized the moment to exhort him with eloquence, to ask him for enlightenment while telling him everything that he had studied, everything that he had meditated and suffered in preparation for it. I, on the other hand, remained as though enchanted at the Zingara's feet. I don't know if I dare tell you what was happening inside me. This woman could no doubt be my mother; well, there is still some undefinable charm emanating from her. Despite my respect for her husband, despite the terror that washed over me at the mere idea of forgetting that respect, I felt my entire soul spring impulsively toward her with an enthusiasm that neither the radiance of youth nor the prestige of luxury have ever inspired in me. Oh, let me meet a woman just like this Zingara and devote my life to her! But I do not cherish the hope, and now that I won't ever see her again, there is deep in my heart a sort of despair, as though it had been revealed to me that there is no other woman for me to love on this earth.

The Zingara did not even see me. She was listening to *Spartacus*, she was struck by his ardent, sincere language. Trismegistus too was moved by it. He clasped his hand and made *Spartacus* sit down next to him on the rock of Schreckenstein.

"Young man," he said to him, "you've just reawakened in me all the memories of my life. I thought I was hearing myself talking at the age you are now, when I was ardently asking men ripe with years and experience to teach me virtue. I had decided not to say anything to you. I was wary, not of your intelligence or honesty, but of your heart's naïveté and fire. I didn't feel capable, moreover, of transcribing back into the language that I once spoke the thoughts that I've since grown used to manifesting through the poetry of art, through feeling. Your faith has won, it has worked a miracle, and I feel I must speak to you. Yes," he added after studying him in silence for a moment that seemed to us a century, for we were trembling at the sight of this inspiration escaping from him, "Yes, now I recognize you! I remember you, I've seen you, loved you, and toiled with you in some other phase of my earlier life. Your name was great among men, but I don't remember it; I just remember your gaze, your words, and that soul from which mine parted only with effort. Now I read the future better than the past, and the coming centuries often appear to me as glistening with light as the days that I have yet to live in today's form. Well, I'm telling you this, you'll be great once again in this century, and you'll do great things. You'll be rebuked, accused, slandered, hated, condemned, persecuted, exiled. . . . But your idea will survive you in other forms, and you'll stir things up here and now with a formidable plan, immense notions that the world won't forget and which may smite the last blows to social and religious despotism. Yes, you're right to seek to act in society. You're obeying your destiny, that is to say your inspiration. This is enlightening me. What I felt listening to you, what you were able to communicate to me about your hopes is great proof of the reality of your mission. So go forth, act and work. Heaven has made you an organizer of destruction. Destroy and dissolve, that is your mission. It takes faith to bring down as it does to raise up. As for me, I had chosen to stand back from the paths down which you are rushing, as I had judged them to be evil. They were no doubt only accidentally so. If true servants of the cause feel called to give them another try, that means that they've become practicable once again. I thought that there was nothing more to be hoped for from official society and that one couldn't reform it while remaining part of it. I made myself an outsider, and despairing of ever seeing salvation descending to the people from the heights of that corruption, I've been devoting the last years of my strength to direct action on the people. I've turned to the poor, the weak, the oppressed, and I've preached to them through art and poetry, which they understand because of their love for them. It may be that I was too wary of the good instincts that still vibrate in men of knowledge and power. I haven't had any dealings with them since I got fed up with their skepticism as well as their even more unholy superstition and went off in disgust to seek out the simplehearted. They've probably had to change, to amend their ways and learn. What am I saying? Certainly this world has marched on, refined itself and grown in the last fifteen years; for every human thing ceaselessly gravitates to the light, and everything joins together, good and evil, to spring toward the divine ideal. You want to speak to the world of scholars, patricians, and rich men; you want to level things by persuasion; you want to seduce, even kings, princes, and prelates, with the charms of truth. You feel seething in you that confidence and strength that surmount all obstacles and rejuvenate everything old and worn. Obey, obey the breath of the spirit! carry on and expand our work; gather up our weapons scattered over the battlefield where we met defeat."

Then there began between *Spartacus* and the divine old man a conversation that I'll never forget my whole life long, for there happened a marvelous thing. This Rudolstadt, who at first had wanted to speak to us only through music, like Orpheus in ancient times, this artist who was telling us that he had long ago abandoned logic and pure reason for pure feeling, this man whom vile judges have called insane and who has accepted passing as such, this man, making a sublime effort out of charity and divine love, all of a sudden became the most reasonable of philosophers, to the point of guiding us along the path of the true method and of certainty. *Spartacus*, for his part, revealed all the ardor of his soul. One was the complete man, in whom all the faculties were in unison; the other was like a neophyte full of enthusiasm. I was reminded of the Gospel, where it is said that Jesus spoke on the mountain with Moses and the Prophets.

"Yes," said *Spartacus*, "I feel that I have a mission. I've approached those who rule the earth, and I was struck by their stupidity, ignorance, and hardness of heart. Oh, how beautiful Life is, and Nature, and Humanity! But what do they care about Life, Nature, and Humanity? . . . And I wept a long while seeing that I as well as all mankind, who are my brothers, and the whole of God's creation, we are all slaves to such wretched men! . . . And when I had moaned a long while like a feeble woman, I said to myself, 'Who is stopping me from tearing off their chains and living free?' . . . But after a phase of solitary stoicism I saw that being free alone is not being free. Man cannot live alone. Man is man's object; he cannot live without his necessary object. And I said to myself, 'I'm still a slave, let's deliver my brothers. . . ." And I found noble hearts that joined together with me . . . and my friends call me *Spartacus*."

"I had indeed told you that you would do nothing but destroy!" replied the old man. "Spartacus was a rebellious slave. But once again, never mind. Organize in order to destroy. May your voice call forth a secret society to destroy the current form of the great iniquity. But if you want it strong, efficient, powerful, put all the living, eternal principles that you can into that society destined to destroy so that it may first destroy (because in order to destroy, it must live and be, all life is positive) and then, out of the work of destruction, allow the rebirth of those things that must be reborn."

"I hear you; you're putting considerable limits on my mission. Never mind. Small or great, I'll take it."

"All that is according to God's counsel is great. Know one thing which must be the rule of your soul. *Nothing is ever lost.* Even if your name and the form of your works were to disappear, even if you were to work *namelessly* as I do, your work would not be lost. The divine scales are mathematics itself, and in the crucible of the divine chemist, every atom is reckoned according to its exact value."

"Since you approve of my designs, teach me, open the way to me. What is to be done? How is one to act upon men? Is imagination the main way to reach them? Is it necessary to take advantage of their weakness and penchant for the supernatural? You yourself have seen that one can do good with the supernatural!"

"Yes, but I've also seen all the evil that can be done. If you knew the doctrine well, you'd know in which age of humanity we're living and you'd choose your means of action accordingly."

"So teach me the doctrine, teach me the method of action, teach me certainty."

"You're asking an artist for method and certainty, a man who's been accused of insanity and persecuted on this pretext! It seems that you're talking to the wrong person; go ask that of philosophers and scholars."

"You're the one I'm talking to. As for them, I know what their knowledge is worth."

"Well then, since you insist, I'll tell you that the method is identical to the doctrine itself, because it is identical to the supreme truth revealed in the doctrine. And, when you give it some thought, you'll understand that it cannot be otherwise. So everything comes down to knowledge of the doctrine."

Spartacus reflected, and after a moment of silence he said, "I'd like to hear out of your mouth the supreme formula of the doctrine."

"You'll hear it, not out of my mouth but out of that of Pythagoras, who is himself the echo of all wisdom: O DIVINE TETRAD! This is the formula. This is the formula that, through all sorts of images, symbols, and emblems, Humanity has proclaimed by the voice of the great religions when it hasn't succeeded in grasping it in a purely spiritual way, without incarnation, without idolatry, such as it has been given to the revealers to reveal to themselves."

"Speak, speak. And in order to make yourself understood, remind me of a few of those emblems. Afterward you'll take the austere language of the absolute."

"I can't separate, as you would wish, these two things, religion in itself, in its essence, and manifested religion. It is part of human nature, in these times, to see the two together. We judge the past, and, without living in it, we find there the confirmation of our ideas. But I'm going to explain what I mean. Now then, let's first speak of God. Does the formula apply to God, to the infinite essence? It would be a crime were it not to apply to the one from whom it proceeds. Have you thought about the nature of God? No doubt; for I feel that you carry Heaven, the true Heaven, in your heart. Well, what is God?"

"God is the Being, the Absolute Being. *Sum qui sum*, says the great book, the Bible."

"Yes, but don't we know anything more about his nature? Hasn't God revealed something more to Humanity?"

"The Christians say that God is three persons in one, the Father, the Son, the Spirit."

"And the traditions of the ancient secret societies that you've consulted, what do they say?"

"They say the same thing."

"Haven't you been struck by that correspondence? The official, triumphant religion as well as the secret, proscribed religion agree on the nature of God. I could talk to you about the cults that preceded Christianity, and you'd find, hidden in their theology, the same truth. India, Egypt, Greece knew the one God in three persons; but we'll return to this point. What I now want to make you understand is the formula in its whole extension, in all its aspects, in order to arrive at what interests you, the method, the organization, the politics. I'll continue. From God, let's go on to man. What is man?"

"After one difficult question, you ask me another that is scarcely less difficult. The oracle at Delphi declared that all knowledge consisted in the answer to this question: *Man, know thyself.*"

"And the oracle was right. A good understanding of human nature is the source of all wisdom, all ethics, all organization, all true politics as well. So let me repeat my question to you. What is man?"

"Man is an emanation of God. . . ."

"No doubt, like all living beings, since God alone is the Being, the Absolute Being. But you aren't, I hope, like the philosophers that I saw in England, France, and Germany as well, at the court of Frederick. You aren't like this

Locke, the subject of so much talk these days on account of Voltaire, his popularizer; you aren't like Helvetius, with whom I often conversed, nor La Mettrie whose materialist audacity so delighted the court in Berlin. You don't say, as they do, that there is nothing particular that distinguishes man from animals, trees, and rocks. God, no doubt, gives life to all nature, as he gives life to man, but there is order in his theodicy. There are distinctions in his thought, and consequently in his works, which are his thoughts fulfilled. Read the great book called *Genesis*, this book that the common man rightfully considers sacred without understanding it; you'll see there that it is through divine light establishing distinctions among beings that there is eternal creation: *fiat lux, et facta est lux*. There you'll also see that each being having a name in the mind of God is a species: *creavit cuncta juxta genus suum et secundem speciem suam*. So what is the particular formula of man?"

"I hear you. You want me to give you a formula of man analogous to that of God. The divine Trinity must be rediscovered in all the works of God; each one of God's works must reflect God's nature, but in a special way; each one, in short, according to its species."

"Most certainly. The formula of man, here it is. It will still be a long time before the philosophers, now divided in their ways of seeing, come together to understand it. Yet there is one who came to understand it already quite some time ago. This one is greater than the others, even though he is infinitely less well known to the common man. While the school of Descartes is lost in pure reason, making man a machine of reasoning and syllogisms, an instrument of logic; while Locke and his school are lost in sensation, making man a sensitive plant; while others, like some that I could cite in Germany, are absorbed in feeling, making man a double-personed egotism if it's question of love, a three- or four-personed egotism or more if it's question of the family; he, the greatest of all, began to understand that man was all that in one, all that indivisibly. This philosopher is Leibniz. He's the one who understood the main things; he didn't share the absurd scorn that our ignorant century feels for antiquity and Christianity. He dared to say that there were pearls in the dung of the Middle Ages. Pearls! Yes, indeed! Truth is eternal, and all the prophets have received it. So I say to you with him, and with an affirmation stronger than his, that man is a trinity, like God. And this trinity is called, in human language: sensation, feeling, knowledge. And the unity of these three things constitutes the human Tetrad, corresponding to the divine Tetrad. From there proceeds all history, from there proceeds all politics, and it's from this source that you must draw, as from an ever living spring."

"You're leaping over abysses, and my wits, less nimble than yours, can't keep up," said *Spartacus*. "How do a sure method and a rule of certainty follow from the psychological definition you've just given me? That's my first question to you."

"The method follows from it easily," Rudolstadt replied. "Human nature being known, it's a matter of cultivating it in accord with its essence. If you understood the unrivaled book from which the Gospel itself is derived, if you understood *Genesis*, attributed to Moses, and which, if it really comes from this prophet, was carried off by him from the temples at Memphis, you would know that human *dissolution*, or what *Genesis* calls the *flood*, has no cause other than the separation of these three faculties of human nature, no longer unified, and thereby isolated from the divine unity, where intelligence, love, and action remain eternally associated. You would then understand how each and every organizer must imitate Noah, the *regenerator*, what Scripture calls the generations of Noah as well as the order in which it arranges them, and the harmony that it establishes among them would act as your guide. Thus you would at the same time find in metaphysical truth a sure method for cultivating human nature in a dignified manner in each and every person and a beacon to enlighten you about true social organization. Yet I'll tell you again, I don't believe that the present time is made for organizing. There is too much to destroy. So it's above all as a method that I recommend that you adhere to the doctrine. The time of dissolution is drawing hear, or rather it's already here. Yes, the time has come when the three faculties of human nature will once again break apart, when their separation will be the death of the social, religious, and political body. What will happen? Sensation will bring forth its false prophets, and they will champion sensation. Feeling will bring forth its false prophets, and they will champion feeling. Knowledge will bring forth its false prophets, and they will champion knowledge. The last ones will be arrogant sorts resembling Satan. The second ones will be fanatics as ready to fall into evil as to march toward the good, without any *criterion* of certainty or rules. The others will be what Homer said became of Odysseus's companions under Circe's wand. Do not follow any one of these three paths which, taken separately, will lead to an abyss; the first to materialism, the second to mysticism, the third to atheism. There is but one sure path to the truth, the one that responds to human nature in its wholeness, to human nature developed in all its aspects. Do not leave this path; meditate, therefore, without cease the doctrine and its sublime formula."

"There you are teaching me things that I had already glimpsed. But tomorrow I won't have you any longer. Who'll guide me to the theoretical knowledge of the truth, and thereby to its practice?"

"You'll have other reliable guides. Above all, read *Genesis*, and strive to grasp its meaning. Don't take it for a history book, a monument of chronology.

There is nothing so insane as that opinion, which is nonetheless generally accepted, by scholars and pupils, and in all the Christian communions. Read the *Gospel* in parallel with *Genesis* and understand it through *Genesis*, after having tasted it with your heart. How strange that the *Gospel*, like *Genesis*, is adored and misunderstood! These are the main things. But there are still others. Meditate piously what we still have of Pythagoras. Read as well the writings conserved under the name of the divine theosophist whose name I bore in the Temple. Don't think, my friends, that I would have dared to take the revered name of Trismegistus on my own authority. It was the Invisibles who ordered me to do so. These writings of Hermes, nowadays disdained by pedants, who foolishly believe them to be an invention of some Christian of the second or third century, hold the ancient knowledge of Egypt. The day will come when they, explicated and brought to light, will appear to be what they are, monuments more precious than those of Plato, for it is from there that Plato drew his knowledge, and one must add that he strangely misunderstood and distorted the truth in his *Republic*. So read Trismegistus and Plato, and those who in their wake meditated on the great mystery. Among this number I recommend to you the noble monk Campanella, who suffered dreadful torture for having dreamed what you are dreaming, human organization founded on truth and knowledge."

We were listening in silence.

"When I speak to you about books," Trismegistus continued, "don't think that, like Catholics, I incarnate life in tombs in idolatrous fashion. I'll say about books what I said to you yesterday about other monuments of the past. Books and monuments are remains of life on which life can and must feed. But life is always present, and the eternal Trinity is better inscribed in us and on the brows of the stars than in the books of Plato and Hermes."

Without meaning to do so, I gave the conversation a bit of a random turn.

"Master," I said, "you've just said, 'The Trinity is better inscribed on the brows of the stars. . . .' What do you mean by that? I certainly see, as the Bible says, the glory of God shining in the bright stars, but I don't see them as proof of the general law of life that you call the Trinity."

"That's because," he replied, "the physical sciences are still insufficiently developed, or rather because you haven't kept up with their advances. Have you heard about the discoveries in the domain of electricity? No doubt, for they have occupied the attention of all educated men. Well, haven't you noticed that the scholars who were so incredulous, so mocking with regard to the divine Trinity have come to recognize the Trinity in these phenomena? For they themselves say that there is no electricity without heat and without light, and vice versa; in a word, there they see *three in one*, which they don't want to acknowledge in God!"

He then began to talk to us about nature and the necessity of relating all these phenomena to a general law.

"Life," he said, "is one; there is but one act of life. It's just a matter of understanding how all particular beings live by the grace and intervention of the Universal Being without however being absorbed in him."

For my part, I would have been delighted to hear him develop this grand topic. But for some time *Spartacus* had seemed less attentive to his words, not because he didn't take interest in them, but the old man's concentration wouldn't last forever, and he wanted to take advantage of that by bringing him back to his favorite subject.

Rudolstadt noticed a sort of impatience.

"You're not following me any longer," he said to him. "Does it seem to you impossible to gain knowledge of nature according to my way of thinking? If that's the case, you're wrong. I appreciate as much as you the current work of scientists, turned to nothing but experimentation. Yet, by continuing in that vein, one won't be creating knowledge, but only nomenclatures. Moreover, I'm not the only one to hold that belief. In France, I met a philosopher of whom I was very fond, Diderot, who often exclaimed about the heaps of scientific material lacking any general idea, 'This, at the very most, is the work of a stonecutter, but I don't see either a building or an architect in it.' Just know that sooner or later the doctrine will deal with the natural sciences; one will have to build with these stones. And then, do you think that physicists today can really comprehend nature? Having stripped nature of the living God that fills it, can they feel it, can they know it? They take light, for example, for matter, sound for matter, when it's light and sound. . . ."

"Ah!" *Spartacus* exclaimed, interrupting him, "don't think I reject your intuitions about nature. No, I feel that there will only be true science through knowledge of divine unity and the perfect similitude of all phenomena. But you're opening all the paths to us, and I shudder to think that you'll soon stop talking. I'd like you to walk me a few steps down one of these paths."

"Which one?"

"It's humanity's future that concerns me."

"I see. You'd like me to tell you my utopia," said the old man, with a smile.

"That's what I came here to ask of you," said *Spartacus*, "your utopia, the new society that you're carrying in your brain and your guts. We know that the Society of the Invisibles sought and dreamed its foundations. All this work has ripened in you. Let us profit from it. Give us your republic. We'll try it out, insofar as it seems to us feasible, and the sparks from your fire will begin stirring up the world."

"Children, you're asking me for my dreams?" replied the philosopher. "Yes, I'll try and lift the corners of the veil that so often conceals the future from my very own eyes! This may be for the last time, but I must try again today; for I've got faith that with you all will not be lost in the golden dreams of my poetry!"

Then Trismegistus went into a sort of divine transport; his eyes shone like stars, and his voice bowed us over like a hurricane. For more than four hours he spoke, and his words were pure and beautiful as a hymn. He composed, out of the religious, political, and artistic work of all the centuries, the most magnificent poem that can ever be conceived. He interpreted all the religions of the past, all the mysteries of the temples, poems, and laws; all the efforts, all the tendencies, all the labors of humanity in earlier times. In the things that had always seemed to us dead or doomed, he rediscovered elements of life, and even out of the obscure tales of Greek gods and heroes he brought forth flashes of truth. He explained the myths of antiquity; he set forth, in his lucid and ingenious demonstration, all the connections, all the points of contact among the various religions. He showed us the true needs of humanity more or less understood by the legislators, more or less fulfilled by the peoples. He reconstituted before our eyes the unity of life in humanity and the unity of dogma in religion, and out of all the materials scattered throughout the ancient world and the new, he formed the basis of his future world. In short, he made the discontinuities that had held us up so long in our studies disappear. He filled up the abysses of history that we had found so terrifying. In a single infinite spiral he unwound the thousands of sacred bandages from around the mummy of science. And when we had understood quick as lightning what he was teaching us at lightning speed; when we had grasped the whole of his vision, and the past, the father of the present, rose up before us like the luminous man of the Apocalypse, he stopped and said to us with a smile,

"Now you understand the past and the present; need I show you the future? Is the Holy Spirit not shining before your eyes? Do you not see that everything sublime that man has dreamed and desired is possible and certain in the future, for the simple reason that the truth is eternal and absolute, despite the weakness of our organs to conceive and possess it? And yet we all possess it by hope and desire. It lives in us, it has forever existed in humanity as a seed awaiting the supreme fecundation. Verily I say unto you, we are gravitating toward the ideal, and this gravitation is infinite as is the ideal itself."

He went on speaking, and his poem about the future was as magnificent as the one about the past. I won't try to translate it here for you. I'd spoil it, and one must be oneself fired by inspiration to impart what inspiration has uttered. I may need two or three years of meditation before I'll be able to write a worthy account of what Trismegistus told us in two or three hours. Writing the life of Socrates was Plato's lifework, and writing the life of Jesus has been the work of seventeen centuries. You can see that I, unworthy wretch that I am, must be shuddering at the idea of my task. Yet I'm not giving up. The master isn't troubled by the transcription such as I have in mind to do. He's a man of action, and he's already drawn up a code that in his view summarizes Trismegistus's entire doctrine as clearly and precisely as though he had spent his whole life doing an in-depth commentary on it. He assimilated, as though by electrical contact, the philosopher's whole mind and soul. It is his, he has mastered it; he'll make use of it as a man of politics. He'll be the living and immediate translation, instead of the belated, dead letter that I'm meditating. And before I've produced my work, he will have transmitted the doctrine to his school. Yes, perhaps within two years, the strange and mysterious words that have just risen up in this wilderness will have thrown roots among numerous disciples; and we'll see this vast underground world of secret societies that is today stirring in the shadows unite under one doctrine, receive new laws, and rediscover their means of action by initiating themselves into the word of life. We are bringing it to you, this much desired monument, that confirms the predictions made by *Spartacus*, that sanctions the truths that he has already conquered and expands his horizon with all the power of inspired faith. While Trismegistus was speaking and I was listening, avid and trembling that I might miss a single sound of these words that were to me like sacred music, *Spartacus*, who remained in control of himself in his intense excitement, his eyes on fire, but his hand firm and his mind even more open than his ears, was quickly tracing signs and figures on his tablets, as though the metaphysical conception of this doctrine had come to him in the form of geometry. When, that same evening, he consulted these bizarre notes which made no sense to me, I was surprised to see him use them to write out and organize, with incredible precision, the deductions of the philosopher's poetic logic. Everything had been simplified and summarized as though by magic in this mysterious alembic which is our master's practical intelligence.[6]

Yet he still wasn't satisfied. Inspiration seemed to be abandoning Trismegistus. His eyes were dimming, his body seemed to be collapsing, and the Zingara gestured to us not to ask him any more questions. But, ardent in his pursuit of the truth, Spartacus would no longer listen to her and pressed him with imperious questions.

6. It is well known that Weishaupt, who was an eminent organizer, used material signs to summarize his system and that he sent to his faraway disciples his entire theory represented by circles and lines on a little square of paper.

"You've painted for me the kingdom of God on earth," he said, shaking the old man's chilly hand, "but Jesus said, 'My kingdom is not *yet of this time*,' and for seventeen centuries humanity has been waiting in vain for his promises to be fulfilled. I haven't lifted myself up as high as you have in the contemplation of eternity. Time shows you, as it does to God himself, the spectacle or the idea of permanent activity, whose every phase responds at every moment to your lofty sentiment. As for me, I live closer to earth. I count the centuries and the years. I want to read my own life. Tell me, prophet, what I am to do in this phase where you see me, tell me what your words have brought forth in me, and what they will bring forth through me in the century rising up before us. I don't want to have passed through it in vain."

"What does it matter to you what I may know about that?" replied the poet. "Nothing lives in vain; nothing is lost. None of us is useless. Let me turn my eyes from this detail, which saddens the heart and withers the spirit. Giving it a moment's thought has utterly worn me out."

"Revealer, you have no right to give into that exhaustion," *Spartacus* said with energy, striving to communicate the fire of his gaze to the vague, already dreamy gaze of the poet. "If you turn your eyes away from the spectacle of human misery, you are not the true man, the complete man of whom an ancient said, "*Homo sum et nihil humani a me alienum puto*." No, you don't love men, you aren't their brother if you don't take an interest in the troubles they suffer throughout every hour of eternity, if you don't hasten to seek the remedy to these in the application of your ideal. Oh wretched the artist who doesn't feel a devouring fever consuming him in that terrifying and delicious quest!"

"So what are you asking of me?" replied the poet, moved and almost irritated in his turn. "Are you so proud as to think yourself the sole laborer, and do you think I grant myself the honor of being the sole giver of inspiration? I'm no seer; I scorn false prophets; I struggled against them quite long enough. My predictions, on the other hand, are reasonings; my visions are perceptions elevated to their highest power. The poet is not the same as a sorcerer. He does indeed dream, while the other one randomly devises. I believe in your action because I feel the contact of your power; I believe in the sublimity of my dreams because I feel myself capable of bringing them forth and because humanity is grand enough and generous enough to accomplish a hundred times over and as one body what one of its members managed to conceive alone."

"Well," said *Spartacus*, "I'm asking you for this humanity's destiny, in the name of this humanity that is stirring in my loins as well, which I'm bearing inside with greater anxiety and perhaps greater love than you yourself do. An enchanting dream veils their suffering from your eyes, while I'm touching them and shuddering with every passing hour. I yearn to give them peace, and like a doctor at the bedside of a dying friend, I'd rather kill them through imprudence than let them die without assistance. You see, I'm a dangerous man, a monster perhaps, if you don't turn me into a saint. Tremble for the dying patient if you don't give the enthusiast the remedy! Humanity is dreaming, singing, and praying in you. In me it is suffering, clamoring, wailing. You've opened your future to me, but your future is far away, whatever you may say, and it'll take a lot of my sweat to distill a few drops of your balm on bleeding wounds. Generations are languishing and passing away without light or action. I, the body of suffering Humanity; I, the cry of distress and the will to salvation, I want to know if my action will do harm or good. You haven't so thoroughly averted your eyes from evil that you don't recognize its existence. Where to run first? What to do tomorrow? Is clemency, is violence the means to be used against the enemies of the good? Remember your dear Taborites; they saw an ocean of blood and tears between them and the gates of paradise. I don't take you for a seer, but I see in you a powerful logic, a magnificent radiance shining through your symbols; if you can surely predict the most distant future, you can even more surely penetrate the veiled horizon limiting the scope of my vision."

It looked as though the poet were racked with suffering. His forehead was dripping with sweat, he gazed at *Spartacus* now with dread, now with enthusiasm; he was oppressed by a terrific struggle. His wife, horrified, kept her arms wrapped around him and shot our master looks of mute reproach where there was nonetheless a respectful fear. Never have I felt Spartacus's power more than in that instant when with all his fanatic will to righteousness and truth he was dominating the tortures of this prophet wrestling with inspiration, the pain of this supplicant woman, the terror of their children, and the reproaches of his own heart. I myself was trembling, I found him cruel. I feared seeing the poet's beautiful soul broken in an ultimate exertion, and the tears that shone on Consuelo's dark lashes fell bitter and burning to my heart. All of a sudden Trismegistus stood up. Pushing away both *Spartacus* and the Zingara, gesturing to the children to stand back, he looked to us transfigured. His eyes seemed to be reading in an invisible book, vast as the world, written in luminous strokes on the canopy of the heavens.

He exclaimed, "Am I not *man*? . . . Why wouldn't I say what human nature is calling for, what it will consequently carry out? Yes, I am *man*, so I can say what *man* wants, and the things that *man* will bring to pass. He who sees the gathering clouds can predict the lightning and the hurricane. I, I know what I have in my soul and what will issue forth from it. I am *man*, and I'm in touch with *humanity* in my time. I've seen Europe, and I know the storms rumbling in its breast. . . . Friends, our dreams are not dreams, I swear to this on human nature! These dreams are dreams only with regard to the present form of the world. But which one has the initiative, spirit or matter? The Gospel says, "The spirit blows where it will." The spirit will blow and change the face of the world. It is said in *Genesis* that the Spirit blew on the waters when everything was chaos and darkness. Now, creation is eternal. So let us create; in other words, let us obey the breath of the Spirit. I see the darkness and the chaos! Why should we remain darkness? *Veni, creator Spiritus!*"

He broke off, then continued in this fashion, "Is it Louis XV who can struggle against you, *Spartacus*? Frederick, Voltaire's disciple, is less powerful than his master. . . . And if I compared Maria Theresa to my Consuelo. . . . But what blasphemy!"

He broke off, "Come on, Zdenko! You, my son, you who descend from the Podiebrads and bear the name of a slave, prepare to sustain our cause. You are the new man. Which side will you take? Will you be with your father and mother, or with the tyrants of the world? In you is strength, new generation. Will you confirm slavery or liberty? Son of Consuelo, son of the Bohemian woman, godson of the slave, I hope that you'll be with the Bohemian woman and the slave. Otherwise, I, born of kings, I renounce you."

He added, "He who would dare say that the divine essence, which is beauty, goodness, and power, will not come to be on earth, he is Satan."

He added yet more, "He who would dare say that the human essence created, as the Bible says, in the image of God, and which is sensation, feeling, and knowledge, will not come to be on earth, he is Cain."

He was silent a while, then went on in this fashion, "Your strong will, *Spartacus*, has acted like a conspiracy. . . . How weak are these kings on their thrones! They think themselves powerful because everything bends before them. . . . They don't see the danger. . . . Ah, you've overthrown the nobles and their armies, the bishops and their clergy; and you think that you're so mighty! but it was your strength that you've overthrown; it's not your mistresses, your courtiers, or your abbots that will defend you, poor monarchs, vain phantoms. . . . Off to France with you, *Spartacus*! France will soon destroy. . . . She needs you. . . . Off to France, I tell you, hurry up, if you want to take part in the work. . . . France is predestined among the nations. Join with the elders of the human race, my son. . . . I hear the voice of Isaiah echoing over France, 'Arise, shine; for your light has come, and the glory of the Eternal One has descended upon you; and the nations will march toward your light.' The Taborites once sang this about Tabor; now Tabor is France!"

He was silent a while. An expression of happiness had come over his physiognomy.

"I am happy," he exclaimed. "Glory to God! Glory to God in the highest, as the Gospel says, and peace on earth to men of good will! This is what the angels sing; and I feel like the angels, and I would sing with them. So what's going on? I'm still among you, my friends, I'm still with you, oh my Eve, oh my Consuelo! Here are my children, the souls of my soul. But we aren't in the mountains of Bohemia any longer, on the rubble of my forefathers' castle. I feel that I'm breathing light, enjoying eternity. . . . So who among you was saying just a moment ago, 'Oh, how beautiful life is, and nature, and humanity!'" But he added, "The tyrants have spoiled all that. . . . Tyrants! There are no more tyrants. Men are equal. Human nature is understood, recognized, sanctified. Men are free, equal, and brothers. There is no other definition of man. No more masters, no more slaves. . . . Do you hear the cry: *Long live the republic.* Do you hear the countless throng proclaiming *liberty, fraternity, equality.* . . . Ah, that was the formula that was whispered in our mysteries, that only disciples of the highest degrees exchanged with each other. There's no reason for secrecy any longer. The sacraments are for one and all. The chalice for one and all! as our Hussite fathers used to say."

But alas! all of a sudden he began weeping hot tears. "I knew that the doctrine wasn't sufficiently developed! Not enough men bore it in their hearts or understood it in their minds!"

"How horrible!" he went on. "War everywhere! And what war!"

He wept a long while. We didn't know what visions were pressing before his eyes. It seemed to us that he was seeing the war of the Hussites all over again. All his faculties seemed perturbed; his soul was like Christ's on Calvary.

I suffered a great deal, seeing him suffer so much. *Spartacus* was firm like a man consulting the oracles.

"Lord! Lord!" cried the prophet after having wept and wailed a long while, "have pity on us. We are in your hands; do with us as you will."

While uttering these last words, Trismegistus reached out for the hands of his wife and his son, as though he had been suddenly deprived of sight.

The little girls, all alarmed, ran to his bosom, and they remained clutched together in utter silence. There was an expression of terror on the Zingara's face, and young Zdenko studied his mother's eyes fearfully. *Spartacus* didn't see them. Was the poet's vision still before his eyes? Finally he approached the group, and the Zingara motioned to him not to wake her husband. His eyes were open and staring into space, and he was either asleep like a sleepwalker, or he was seeing the dreams that had stirred him slowly fading on the horizon. After a quarter of an hour he took a deep breath, his eyes lit up, and he drew his wife and son to his breast and held them in a long embrace.

Then he stood up and motioned that he wanted to get back on the road.

"The sun is very warm for you just now," Consuelo said to him. "Wouldn't you rather have a nap under these trees?"

"This sun is fine," he replied with an ingenuous smile, "and if you don't fear it more than usual, it'll do me a great deal of good."

They each picked up their burden, the father the packsack, the young man the musical instruments, and the mother the hands of her two daughters.

"You've made me suffer," she said to *Spartacus*, "but I know that one has to suffer for the truth."

"Don't you fear that this crisis will have untoward effects?" I asked her with emotion. "Let me follow you a while longer, I can be of service."

"Bless you for your charity," she said, "but don't follow us. The only thing I fear for him is a bit of melancholy, lasting a few hours. But in this spot there was a danger, a dreadful memory, from which you preserved him by occupying him with other thoughts. He had wanted to come here, and thanks to you, he didn't even recognize the place. So I bless you in any case and wish you the opportunity and means to serve God with all your will and all your power."

I kept the children back to stroke them and prolong the fleeting instants, but their mother took them away from me, and I felt as though I were abandoned by all when she bade me farewell for the last time.

Trismegistus did not bid us farewell. He seemed to have forgotten us. His wife begged us not to distract him. He descended the hill with a firm gait. His face was calm, and he was helping, with a sort of lighthearted glee, his elder daughter leap over bushes and rocks.

Handsome Zdenko was walking behind him with his mother and youngest sister. We followed them for a long while with our eyes on the *sandy path of gold*, the forest path *that has no master*. They finally disappeared behind the firs; and just when she was about the last one to slip from view, we saw the Zingara grab her little Wenceslawa and put her on her robust shoulder. Then she quickened her pace to join back up with her dear caravan, as alert as a true Bohemian girl, as poetic as the gentle goddess of poverty.

. . . .

And we too, we are on the road, we are marching on! Life is a voyage that has life as its goal, and not death, as one says in a crude, material sense. We consoled the hamlet's inhabitants as best we could, and we left old Zdenko awaiting *his tomorrow.* We met up again with our brothers in Pilsen, where I've written out this tale for you, and we're about to leave again on other quests. And you, too, friend! Keep yourself prepared for relentless travel, for unflinching action. We're on our way to victory or martyrdom![7]

7. Martinowicz, to whom this letter was addressed, a distinguished scholar and enthusiastic illuminist, was decapitated in Buda in 1795, along with several Hungarian noblemen, his accomplices in the conspiracy.

Notes

Introduction

1. The three main translations, with the earliest American dates and places of publication that I've been able to discover, are the ones by Francis George Shaw (Boston: William D. Ticknor and Co., 1847), by Fayette Robinson (Philadelphia: T.B. Peterson, 1851), and finally by Frank Hunter Potter (New York: Dodd, Mead & Co., 1891). It is interesting to note that Walt Whitman had in his personal library a copy of the second edition of the Shaw translation (New York: William H. Graham, 1848), now in the Library of Congress.

This brief introduction is intended for general readers who have little or no knowledge of French. Readers at ease in French would be well advised to turn to the introductions that have accompanied the re-editions of *Consuelo* and *La Comtesse de Rudolstadt* in France over the last fifty years, to wit, the 1959 Classiques Garnier edition by Léon Cellier and Léon Guichard (now reissued in Folio Classique), with its extensive discussions of Sand's literary sources, of music, the supernatural, and secret societies in the work; the 1983 edition by Simone Vierne and René Bourgeois (Éditions de l'Aurore), with its full appendix of the music and the musicians mentioned in the work; as well as the 1999 edition by Robert Sctrick (Phébus) and the 2004 edition by Nicole Savy and Damien Zanone (Éditions Robert Laffont). This flurry of re-editions testifies to the enduring importance and appeal of George Sand's works and of this work in particular.

2. George Sand and Pauline Viardot, *Lettres inédites de George Sand et de Pauline Viardot (1839–1849)*, ed. Thérèse Marix-Spir (Paris: Nouvelles éditions latines, 1959), 44; my translation.

3. As defined by Lucienne Frappier-Mazur, "The novel of initiation develops metaphysical, usually religious concerns and a sense of the mystical and supernatural. It must, at least metaphorically, stage a descent into hell which leads to a second birth, and even its most profane versions end with the hero's access to a higher plane of being, if not with some form of renunciation of terrestrial happiness." In "Desire, Writing, and Identity in the Romantic Mystical Novel: Notes for a Definition of the Feminine," *Style* 18, 3 (Summer 1984): 333. See also Chapter 8, "*Consuelo* and *La Comtesse de Rudolstadt*: From Gothic Novel to Novel of Initiation," in Isabelle Hoog Naginski's *George Sand: Writing for Her Life* (New Brunswick, N.J.: Rutgers University Press, 1991), 190–220.

4. See her letter to Pierre Leroux of 15 June 1843 in George Sand, *Lettres d'une vie*, ed. Thierry Bodin (Paris: Folio Classique, 2004), 421–22; my translations throughout.

5. George Sand, *Jean Ziska: épisode de la guerre des hussites (Jan Zizka: An Episode in the War of the Hussites)* (Brussels: Société belge de librairie, 1843), 38–40.

6. Nineteenth-century reform societies advocating better social and industrial conditions for the working class.

7. Letter of 26 February 1843 to Charles Poncy, *Lettres*, 407–8.

8. With regard to Leroux in the context of Romantic socialism, see Naomi J. An-

drews, "'La Mère Humanité': Femininity in the Romantic Socialism of Pierre Leroux and the Abbé A. L. Constant," *Journal of the History of Ideas* 63, 4 (October 2002): 697–716, and by the same author, "Utopian Androgyny: Romantic Socialists Confront Individualism in July Monarchy France," *French Historical Studies* 26, 3 (Summer 2003): 437–57.

9. Andrews, "La Mère Humanité," 710.

10. With regard to the status of women in secret societies, it should be noted that in the late eighteenth century women could be initiated into some lodges of Freemasonry in France, but only in so-called lodges of adoption especially for women. That possibility of sexually segregated access disappeared early in the nineteenth century and was reinstated only after George Sand's death. For a detailed discussion of this matter along with an extensive bibliography, see James Smith Allen, "Sister of Another Sort: Freemason Women in Modern France, 1725–1940," *Journal of Modern History* 75 (December 2003): 783–835.

11. See her letter of 7 June 1841, *Lettres*, 346.

12. See her letter of 28 August 1842, *Lettres*, 390.

13. See her letter of 13 August 1843, *Lettres*, 425.

14. Sand, *Ziska*, 30–31.

15. See her letter to Henriette de la Bigottière, dated "end of December 1842," *Lettres*, 399.

16. Frappier-Mazur, "Desire, Writing, and Identity," 328; see her illuminating and wide-ranging discussion of the male-centered novel of initiation that Sand inherited from tradition and her subversion of this model.

Chapter I

1 Frederick the Great: Frederick II of Prussia (1712–86, r. 1740–86). The action of the novel begins in 1751.

1 Voltaire: French author and philosopher of the Enlightenment (1694–1778).

1 Big Willy: Frederick William I of Prussia (1688–1740, r. 1713–40).

2 *Phaëton*: Composed by K. Heinrich Graun (1704–59).

2 dear readers: Here and frequently elsewhere Sand uses the exclusively feminine form "lectrices" to refer to her readers.

2 Consuelo's last adventures: *The Countess von Rudolstadt* is the last part of Sand's monumental novel titled *Consuelo*.

2 d'Argens and La Mettrie: Jean-Baptiste de Boyer, Marquis d'Argens (1704–71), who taught at the Academy in Berlin. Julien Offray de La Mettrie (1709–51), French physician, philosopher of atheistic materialism, and hedonist who lived in Berlin under the protection of Frederick the Great.

2 Metastasio and Hasse: Pietro Metastasio (1698–1792), Italian poet whose opera librettos were set to music by many composers. Johann Adolph Hasse (1699–1783), German composer known chiefly for his many operas written in the Italian style.

2 Zingarella: Italian word meaning "little Gypsy girl."

5 Mlle Cochois: A French actress who had secretly become the Marquis d'Argens's wife.

6 such a great scholar: Pierre-Louis Moreau de Maupertius (1699–1783), French naturalist and president of the Berlin Academy.

Chapter II

8 Dr. von Hoffmann: A German doctor famous for his drops made of ether and alcohol.

9 General Quintus Icilius: This eminent specialist of Latin was born with the name Charles Théophile Guichard. When Frederick proposed that he become the commander of a regiment because he knew the work of Julius Caesar so well, Guichard took the name of the famous Roman general Quintus Icilius.

10 Dionysius of Syracuse: Tyrant of Syracuse (368–344 B.C.). His uncle Dion of Syracuse, along with Plato, had unsuccessfully tried to make him into a model philosopher-king.

10 Marcus Aurelius: Roman emperor and Stoic philosopher (121–180) often considered a model of the philosopher-emperor.

15 Panurge: Panurge, as well as Pantagruel and Gargantua, who are soon to be mentioned, are all larger-than-life characters created by Rabelais, the Renaissance humorist and satirist (1483–1553).

17 *"C'est toi qui l'as nommée!"*: from Racine's *Phèdre.*

Chapter III

18 Trajan's: The Roman emperor (53–117) also known as Germanicus.

22 Cytherea: Another name for Venus or Aphrodite, the goddess of love.

23 Richelieu: The Duke de Richelieu (1696–1788), a libertine aristocrat and one of Voltaire's patrons; Lauzun: the Duke de Lauzun (1633–1723), notorious for his love affair with Mlle de Montpensier at the court of Louis XIV.

Chapter IV

32 fortress of Glatz: In 1743 Princess Anna Amalia of Prussia (1723–87) secretly married Baron Friedrich von der Trenck. When her brother Frederick II discovered this, he had the marriage annulled, sent her off to the Abbey of Quedlinburg, and imprisoned Trenck for ten years at the Silesian prison of Glatz. The princess corresponded with Trenck until her death.

Chapter V

39 fable suits you: The fable about the Lion and the Gnat was told by Aesop and retold by Jean de La Fontaine (1621–95).

Chapter VI

41 Trenck the Pandur will perish in Spielberg: Franz Freiherr von der Trenck

(1711–49), an Austrian soldier, died in the fortress of Spielberg after having been brought before a court-martial for multiple infractions while serving Maria Theresa.

43 *Jan Zizka of the Chalice*: Jan Zizka (1374?–1424), Bohemian military leader and head of the Hussite forces during the crusades that the Holy Roman Emperor Sigismund (1368–1437) led against them.

44 Trismegistus: This name recalls that of Hermes Trismegistus, the legendary author of treatises on magic and alchemy.

Chapter VII

50 Zingarella: The term "zingaro" means Gypsy. "Zingara" is the feminine form, and "zingarella" a feminine diminutive.

50 *scuola dei mendicanti*: Literally, the beggars' school.

51 Hus: Jan Hus (1369?–1415), Czech religious reformer influenced by John Wyclif and generally considered a forerunner of the Protestant Reformation; finally tried for heresy, he was burned at the stake.

53 Taborite: The Taborites were a splinter group of Hussites who took their name from Tabor, their religious and military stronghold and once a center of retreat for Jan Hus. This group found many adherents among the peasants and expressed messianic hopes of abolishing the feudal system and establishing a classless society. Their influence in Bohemia nearly vanished after their military defeat in 1534.

53 King George Podiebrad: Hussite king of Bohemia (1420–71), who ruled from 1458 until his death.

54 Waldensians: Protestant religious group that originated in Lyons, France, in the late twelfth century and spread into the Alpine regions of France and Italy as well as parts of Switzerland. They preached apostolic poverty and simplicity; Anabaptists of Munster: Anabaptists, who were prominent in Europe in the sixteenth century, rejected infant baptism, thereby incurring the condemnation of Catholics and Protestants alike. In 1534, a group of Anabaptists took up arms in Munster, Germany and set up a short-lived theocracy during which polygamy was legalized and property communized; Picards: Another group of heretics that appeared in Bohemia in the early fifteenth century.

57 Prison of Lead: A famous Venetian prison located in the attic of the Doges' Palace. As the roof was covered in sheets of lead, the cells were often extremely hot or extremely cold.

Chapter VIII

61 Haydn . . . fifteen: Franz Joseph Haydn (1732–1809), a prolific Austrian composer.

64 *Virtuosi ridicoli*: Perhaps the 1749 light Italian opera by Matteo Buini, *La Virtuosa corteggiata da trei cisisbei ridicoli*, according to the suggestion made in the Cellier & Guichard edition.

Chapter IX

70 Herr Graun: Karl Heinrich Graun (1701–59), singer, composer and conductor of the royal orchestra at the court of Frederick II; Benda: Franz Benda (1709–1786), composer and violinist; Herr Quantz: Johann Joachim Quantz (1697–1773), flutist, flutemaker, and composer known for his treatise on flute technique.

70 basilisk: A legendary monster, part bird and part reptile, that reputedly killed by means of its breath and glance.

Chapter X

79 Georg Benda (1722–95), clavier player, oboist, and pioneer of the musical melodrama, such as his *Ariadne auf Naxos.*

84 Mlle Clairon: A French actress (1732–1802) renowned for her performance in plays by Voltaire.

Chapter XI

93 Polyhymnia: the ancient Greek muse of sacred song.

93 *Ariadne Abandoned*: Perhaps Georg Benda's *Ariadne auf Naxos*. Several eighteenth-century operas bear this title.

Chapter XII

99 *redoute*: In German this word of French origin generally means "ballroom."

103 Sigismund: As king of Germany (1410–37), Sigismund (1368–1437) betrayed Jan Hus and was largely responsible for his death at the stake at the conclusion of the Council of Constance (1417). The burning of Hus encouraged the Reformation in Bohemia and earned Sigismund the enmity of the Czechs. As king of Bohemia (1419–37), he called for a crusade against the Hussites who, under the command of Jan Zizka and others, won several victories against him.

Chapter XIII

111 reign of a petticoat: Frederick feared what he called "French ladies" and referred to Mme de Pompadour (1721–64), the mistress of Louis XV of France, as "Her Majesty Petticoat III."

113 *ab irato*: "*Out of anger*." Original in Latin.

114 your father's inquisition: At the age of eighteen, Frederick was publicly beaten by his father. Afterward he and his friend Hans Hermann von Katte tried to escape from Prus-

sia but were caught. Because both were officers in the Prussian army, they were charged with treason and threatened with the death penalty. Although the king decided to spare his son's life, Frederick was forced to watch the decapitation of his friend von Katte in 1730.

Chapter XIV

120 Schwartz: "Schwartz" in German means "black."

Chapter XV

125 reserved sins: Grave sins, the absolution of which requires the intervention of a pope, bishop, or delegated priest.

125 *groschen*: "Pennies." In German in the original.

125 Egeria of his greedy inspirations: According to Roman myth, Egeria was a fountain nymph who acted as an advisor to Numa, the second king of Rome. In more general usage, it refers to a woman who is a secret and well-respected counselor.

125 claims on their behalf: Prussian law forbade lending any sum of money to actors and declared null and void the debts that they might contract.

127 with him in its middle: Throughout her novels and personal correspondence Sand often refers to herself in the masculine

Chapter XVI

130 *planetary*: Meaning here "astrologer," according to one of the definitions of "planetarius" in Low Latin. While this is a rare meaning of the French term "planétaire," it is recorded in the 1752 edition of the Latin-French *Dictionnaire de Trévoux.*

130 Philip the Fair: Philip IV of France (1268–1314), who prosecuted the Knights Templar.

131 Cardinal Fleury: Cardinal André Hercule de Fleury (1653–1743) became Louis XV's chief minister in 1726. Although he strove for peace abroad, he was drawn into wars involving the Polish and Austrian successions.

131 Charles Edward back on the throne: After his defeat at Culloden in 1745, Charles Edward Stuart, called the Young Pretender, had been forced to renounce the English throne.

132 Monsieur Jourdain's Nicole: An allusion to Molière's *Le Bourgeois Gentilhomme*, Act III, scene 2, where Monsieur Jourdain is threatening his servant Nicole.

132 hanging only by a thread: These are allusions to the complex situation leading up to the Seven Years' War (1756–63).

Chapter XVII

139 Phèdre or Chimène: The female leads in Racine's tragedy by the same name and Corneille's tragicomedy *Le Cid.*

139 Electra or Semiramis: Mlle Clairon interpreted these roles in Voltaire's *Oreste* and *Sémiramis*.

Chapter XVIII

141 Gottlieb: In German, "love of God."

142 Saint Crispin's trade: Saint Crispin was, according to legend, a third-century Christian. Born to a noble family in Rome, he fled to Soissons during Diocletian's persecution of the Christians. There he set himself up as a shoemaker. For his services he would only take money that was freely offered him. After his martyrdom he became known as the patron saint of shoemakers, cobblers, and other leatherworkers.

143 all their peers: See La Fontaine's fable, "The Eagle and the Owl."

144 Cerberus: In Greek mythology, a three-headed dog who guards the entrance to Hades.

144 old Fate: The Fates, usually three in number, are the elderly divinities who determine the course of human life in Greek mythology.

145 gold Frederick: A gold coin bearing the likeness of Frederick II of Prussia.

Chapter XIX

151 My Lindor: Lindor is a character type in Spanish literature, a lovesick, serenading suitor.

151 hidalgo: In Spanish in the original, but the French usage of the term designates someone of no social importance, far less than a member of the lower nobility of Spain, which is the signification of the term in English.

152 *the laces of his shoes*: Words attributed to John the Baptist; see Matthew 3: 11, Mark 1: 6, and Luke 3: 16. Note that the French possessive adjective here can be translated as *his* or *hers*, whereas English allows no such ambiguity.

155 Apollonius of Tyana: A Neo-Pythagorean philosopher of the first century A.D. who supposedly understood the language of birds.

155 another species: George Sand, granddaughter of a birdseller, was herself capable of taming birds.

157 *Corte Minelli*: A location in central Venice.

157 *il firmamento lucido*: In Italian in the original.

169 Jacob Boehme: German religious mystic (1575–1624), author of *De signatura rerum* and *Mysterium magnum*.

172 *millennium*: Period lasting a thousand years during which Christ will reign over the earth, according to the millenarians; see Revelation 20.

176 *Herrnhuters*: An evangelical Christian group that originated in Bohemia with the disciples of Jan Hus. In 1722, Count von Zinzendorf welcomed them to his Saxon estate, and their colony became known as Herrnhut (the Sheepfold of the Lord).

176 Paracelsus: Swiss physician and alchemist (1493?–1541).

176 Swedenborg: Emanuel Swedenborg, Swedish scientist and religious mystic

(1688–1772), whose religious system is sometimes known as Swedenborgianism. After his death his disciples organized the Church of the New Jerusalem.

176 *Schröpfer the lemonade-seller*: Café owner in Liepzig who in 1768 founded a Masonic lodge known for communicating with souls of the dead.

176 free-judges: In fourteenth and fifteenth century Germany the Free-Judges constituted a secret tribunal that worked to put down abuses on the part of aristocrats.

178 Simon Magus: A powerful sorcerer practicing in Samaria at the time of the disciples; see Acts 8:9–24.

Chapter XXI

192 the Lord is with me: These seem to be adaptations of Psalms 91: 11–12 and 23: 4.

Chapter XXIII

211 Deïanira: Deïanira, the wife of Heracles, gave her unfaithful husband a poisoned robe that consumed him in horrible suffering.

Chapter XXIV

217 reserved sins: Grave sins that can be absolved only by a pope, a bishop or a specially delegated priest.

Chapter XXVI

229 La libertà: "Let me weep over my cruel fate and yearn for liberty." From Act II, scene 4 of the 1711 opera.

Chapter XXVII

240 Free-Judges: In fourteenth- and fifteenth-century Germany the Free-Judges constituted a secret tribunal that worked to put down abuses on the part of aristocrats.

Chapter XXVIII

246 Thirty Years' War: The Thirty Years' War (1618–48) was in good part a struggle between Protestant princes of Germany against the Holy Roman Empire allied with the Catholic princes of Germany.

246 John Wyclif: English theologian (1330–84) condemned as a heretic and considered a forerunner of the Protestant Reformation. Wyclif attacked the doctrine of transubstantiation, championed the cause of the people against the clergy, argued that the church should give up its property, and initiated the first translation of the Bible into English. Jan Hus: Bohemian religious reformer (1372?–1415) influenced by Wyclif. After being excommunicated and tried for heresy, Hus was burned at the stake.

Chapter XXX

270 Psyche: In the *Metamorphoses* of Apuleius, Psyche is loved by Cupid, who visits her only at night, unseen and unrecognized. Curious to know her lover, she lights a lamp and inadvertently spills a drop of hot oil on his face. Cupid awakes and disappears. She is reunited with her lover only after having completed several purifying ordeals.

Chapter XXXI

272 Memphis: City of ancient Egypt and capital of the Old Kingdom, during which the pyramids were built; Eleusis: City of ancient Greece that was the seat of the mystery cult of Demeter and Persephone.

272 Christian revelation: Here Sand is alluding to the Johannites. In *Jean Ziska: Épisode de la guerre des hussites* (1843) she affirms that "the interpretation and application of the fraternal and egalitarian Gospel of Saint John" is the ferment of many heresies and sects, such as the Hussites, Taborites, and Lollards, that she considers to be one (46).

274 the soul and the human person: In *Jean Ziska*, Sand notes that the Taborites came to believe that the transmission of life meant the return of the dead to this earth in new bodies; they believed, for example, that Zizka was Hus come back to life.

274 Moravian Herrnhuters: an evangelical Christian group that originated in Bohemia with the disciples of Jan Hus, who broke with Rome in 1467. In 1722 Count von Zinzendorf welcomed them to his Saxon estate at Herrnhut. Xerophagists: After a papal bull of 1738 forbade the practice of Freemasonry, many Italian Freemasons continued to meet under the name of Xerophagists. Joachimites: Followers of the Cistercian abbot and mystic Joachim of Flora (circa 1132–1202).

278 by virtue of adoption: Lodges for women, known as lodges of adoption, were created in the eighteenth century, disappeared early in the nineteenth century, and were reconstituted some twenty years after the death of George Sand.

279 Order of the Mops: A secret society that existed briefly in mid-eighteenth-century Germany. Open to both men and women, it had a reputation for a certain gallant lasciviousness.

279 *signals of distress*: A triangle formed by the shoulders with uplifted arms and clasped hands, accompanied by the words: "To me, the Children of the Widow."

280 Levites for the sanctuary: To be taken figuratively here. In its literal sense, the term designates a priestly Hebrew tribe whose members were assigned to lesser ceremonial offices in the temple.

281 Fénelon's *Telemachus*: François de Salignac de la Mothe-Fénelon, French priest and writer (1651–1715). His novel *Telemachus* (1699), written for the young crown prince he was tutoring, was inspired with the principles of tolerance and moderation.

281 Montesquieu, Voltaire, and Helvetius: Montesquieu (1689–1755), French writer, lawyer, and political philosopher who criticized despotism and absolute monarchy; Voltaire (1694–1778), French writer and philosopher of the Enlightenment; Helvetius (1715–1771), French philosopher, proponent of sensationalism and utilitarianism.

Chapter XXXII

286 as the ancient Lollards used to say: Disciples of John Wyclif in fourteenth- and fifteenth-century England and Scotland who exercised a significant influence on the Hussites in Bohemia; also, followers of the Franciscan Walter Lolhard, who converted to the Waldensian faith and was burned at Cologne in 1322.

287 Niobe dying or rather Mary collapsing: Niobe of Greek mythology and Mary of Christianity were both mothers who lost their children and typify maternal pain.

288 Wanda z Prachalitz: Here and elsewhere in the novel, Wanda's name is rendered as "Prachalitz." The 1959 French edition of *La Comtesse de Rudulstadt* by Léon Cellier and Léon Guichard conserves this spelling in the text of the novel, but the appendix of variants lists "Prachalitz" as a typo for "Prachatitz" and adds that this error occurred in the original serial publication of the novel, finally to be corrected in the 1857 edition by Michel-Lévy frères. The "Prachalitz" spelling has been maintained in recent French re-editions of *La Comtesse de Rudolstadt*. "Prachalitz" is not a Czech toponym, whereas "Prachatitz" is in the immediate vicinity of the birthplace of Jan Hus, so important in the novel. In Czech "z" is the genitive marker, the equivalent of "of" or "from." Given the hostility of Wanda's family toward Austria and their strong allegiance to the Czech homeland for political and religious reasons, I thought it important to render her name in a Czech manner.

Chapter XXXIII

291 serene countenance: Here Sand seems to be paraphrasing rather than quoting from *Julius Caesar*, perhaps because she was using a French translation of the original.

Chapter XXXIV

299 Argus: A monster in Greek mythology with one hundred eyes, some of which were always awake.

300 Venetian sequin: A gold coin formerly in circulation in Italy and Turkey.

306 Poland on the border with Turkey: In other words, the Ottoman Empire, which ranged far beyond the borders of present-day Turkey. Poland likewise occupied much more area in the mid-eighteenth century than the nation now known under that name.

309 grand master of one of their assemblies: The esoteric society of the Rosicrucians

was founded in Germany in the early seventeenth century. Rapidly finding adherents in Austria, Holland, France, and England, it amalgamated teachings drawn from various domains such as alchemy, astrology, the Kabbalah, and Campanella's utopia.

311 *Podiebrad's good angel*: In Chapter VII Albert is identified as a matrilineal descendant of George Podiebrad, the Hussite king who ruled Bohemia from 1458 until his death in 1471.

Chapter XXXV

316 Mount Tabor: The city of Tábor, now in the Czech Republic, was built in 1420 around the castle of Kotnov by disciples of Jan Hus. It was named after Mount Tabor, where the transfiguration of Jesus was supposed to have taken place.

317 Kuttenburg: Otherwise known as Kutna Hora, this was the site of Jan Zizka's 1421 victory against the Emperor Sigismund. Kuttenburg occupied a strategic location in eastern Bohemia and was important for its silver mines.

318 O Consuelo de mi alma: "O Consolation of my soul . . ."

Chapter XXXVII

332 Handel's chorus: Sand is drawing on a French adaptation of Handel's *Judas Maccabaeus* (1746). The two lines she quotes, "Chantons la Gloire / Du Juda vainqueur!" are a conflation of the first and fourth lines of the chorus sung by the youths and the Israelites in the third act. I am quoting the four lines in their entirety to preserve the rhyme.

Chapter XXXVIII

339 Jacques Molay . . . the prelate-knights of the Middle Ages: Jacques Molay (1243?–1314) was the last grand master of the Knights Templar. In 1307 he and the other Knights Templar in France were arrested, brought before the Inquisition, charged with heresy, and tortured. In 1314 Molay was burned at the stake.

Chapter XXXIX

349 *they have all been used*: This chapter is based in part on a visit Sand made to the Palace of the Inquisition in Barcelona.

Chapter XL

355 I cieli immensi narrano / Del grande Iddio la gloria! "The immense skies tell the glory of the greatness of God!"; Psalm 19: 1 (18 in the Catholic versions).

Chapter XLI

357 leaves of oak and acacia: In Masonic symbolism a branch of acacia marked the site of Hiram's tomb. Oak is not a part of the Masonic system, but the subsequent allusion to Druids explains its presence here.

358 hundred years separate us from these Invisibles: *Consuelo, La Comtesse de Rudolstadt* was first published in installments in 1843–44, whereas the action of the novel begins in the early 1750s.

358 Illuminism: In 1776 Adam Weishaupt (1748–1830) founded the Order of the Illuminati at Ingolstadt, Germany.

358 Ganganelli: The surname of Clement XIV, who reigned as pope from 1769 to 1774 and abolished the Order of the Jesuits.

358 Fourierism and Saint-Simonism: Two utopian socialist groups inspired by the writings of Charles Fourier (1772–1837) and Claude-Henri de Saint-Simon (1760–1825). Their thought was very influential among reformists in France in the 1830s and 1840s.

359 Madame de Maintenon: Writer and governess of the sons of Louis XIV of France (1635–1719); eventually she became the king's wife and exercised a powerful influence over him, especially in the area of religion; Madame de Pompadour: Mistress of Louis XV of France as well as a friend and supporter of many Enlightenment philosophers (1721–64); Peter the Great: Peter I, Czar of Russia (1682–1725); Catherine II: Also known as Catherine the Great, Czarina of Russia (1729–96); Maria Theresa: Archduchess of Austria, Queen of Bohemia and Hungary (1717–80); also, the mother of Marie-Antoinette of France; that Dubarry woman: Marie-Jeanne Dubarry, a favorite of Louis XV during the last decade of his reign; guillotined during the French Revolution for dissipation of public funds (1743–93); Voltaire: French philosopher of the Enlightenment, fierce critic of Catholicism and absolutism (1694–1778); Swedenborg: Swedish scientist, religious teacher, and mystic (1688–1772); Kant: German philosopher who attempted to determine the nature and limits of knowledge (1724–1804); Mesmer: Austrian physician known for his experiments with "animal magnetism" and hypnosis (1734–1815); Jean-Jacques Rousseau: Swiss-French novelist and philosopher of the Enlightenment (1712–78); Cardinal Dubois: French statesman and cardinal of the Catholic church during the Regency of Philip II d'Orléans (1656–1723); Schroepfer: Café owner in Leipzig who in 1768 founded a Masonic lodge known for communicating with souls of the dead; Diderot: French Encyclopedist and philosopher of the Enlightenment (1713–84); Fénelon: French theologian and author of educational treatises, including *Télémachus* (1651–1715); Law: Scottish financier whose attempts to regenerate the French economy precipitated widespread ruin (1671–1729); Zinzendorf: German churchman who offered refuge to the Hussite Bohemian Brethren on his estate in Saxony and fostered the Moravian movement (1700–1760); Leibniz: German philosopher and mathematician (1646–1716); Frederick II: King of Prussia, also known as Frederick the Great (1712–86); Robespierre: French revolutionary often identified with the Terror (1758–94); Louis XIV: French king who consolidated absolute monarchy (1638–1715); Philippe-Egalité: Louis-Philippe-Joseph, Duc d'Orléans, a long-time enemy of absolute monarchy who sided with the Jacobins during the French Revolution and voted for the death of Louis XVI (1747–93); Marie-Antoinette: Wife of Louis XVI at the time of the French Revolution, guillotined ten months after her husband had met the same end (1753–93); daughter of

Maria Theresa of Austria; Charlotte Corday: Assassin of the French revolutionary Jean-Paul Marat (1768–93); Weishaupt: Founder in Ingolstadt, Germany, in 1776 of the Order of the Illuminati (1748–1830); Babeuf: French revolutionary who called for economic equality in addition to political equality (1760–97); Napoleon: Ruler and emperor of France from 1799 until 1814 (1769–1821).

359 French Convention: The radical phase of the French revolution that in September 1792 abolished the monarchy and set up a republican form of government.

359 the Mountain: The Jacobins and revolutionary groups on the extreme left.

360 restoration of the Old Regime: Here Sand is summarizing French history from the advent of the French Revolution to the period in which she wrote this novel: the wars of the Revolution and the Terror, the Napoleonic Empire, the Restoration, and the July Monarchy.

360 like Galatea: After Pygmalion sculpted the statue of beautiful Galatea, Aphrodite granted his wish that the stone come alive.

361 *Hymen o Hymenaee!*: Standard refrain for a wedding song, as in Catullus LVI and LXII.

361 whom Wanda vigorously pointed out: Here among the Invisibles who have not been previously mentioned in the novel figure the German poet and musician Schubart (1739–91), the Chevalier d'Eon (1728–1810) who cultivated the belief that he was a woman throughout much of the century and Nicolaï (1733–1811), the Berlin bookseller and proponent of the Enlightenment.

367 Astraea: In Greek mythology, the goddess of justice and daughter of Zeus and Themis. At the end of the Golden Age she left the Earth to mark her refusal of the wickedness of man and became the constellation Virgo.

368 words of the Gospel: See Matthew 18: 20.

373 dreadful storm gathering over his head: Trenck would later be kidnapped by Frederick II's soldiers and spend ten years imprisoned in a dungeon deep underground.

373 Emile and Sophie: Rousseau published in 1762 his influential treatise on education *Emile, ou de l'éducation*, in which he prescribed educational regimes leading to distinct and unequal social roles for boys, represented by Emile, and for girls, represented by Sophie.

Epilogue

376 garden of the Hesperides: The mythical garden in which a fierce dragon guarded the tree that produced golden apples. One of the labors of Heracles involved killing the dragon and taking the apples.

379 *al solito*: "As usual," in Italian.

386 *My dear Bertoni:* The name Consuelo gave herself when disguised as an itinerant *zingaro* musician in Chapter VIII.

Letter from Philon to Ignatius Joseph Martinowicz

393 Ignatius Joseph Martinowicz: Hungarian arrested in 1794 for having fomented an insurrection in Vienna, beheaded in Buda in 1795.

394 Pilsen: These details are borrowed from Augustin Barruel's *Memoirs Illustrating the History of Jacobinism (Mémoires pour servir à l'histoire du jacobinisme)*, first published in 1797. Barruel, a Jesuit priest, argued that the French Revolution was the result of a conspiracy of secret societies, especially the Illuminati of Bavaria, to destroy monarchies and the Church.

394 Vesper: The evening star (Venus).

394 Emperor Charles: Probably Charles VI of the Holy Roman Empire (1685–1740) and the father of Maria Theresa.

398 Ariadne's thread: In Greek mythology Ariadne gave Theseus a thread so that he could find his way out of the labyrinth.

398 *Procopius the Great:* A former Catholic priest and military leader (d. 1434) who succeeded Jan Zizka as head of the Taborites after the latter's death. After winning several victories for the Taborites, Procopius died on the battlefield in 1434.

398 Horebites: A Hussite faction founded by Jan Zizka in 1423 when he split from the more radical Taborites.

399 *Riesengebürge:* Mountains of the Giants, in German in the original.

400 Prometheus: In Greek myth Prometheus is credited from at least the fifth century B.C. with creating man from earth and water as well as stealing fire from the gods, but that he stole fire in order to give life to mankind is not found until later Roman sources. It is noteworthy that Pierre Leroux, among others, helped disseminate this view of Prometheus in nineteenth-century France.

401 hierophant: Literally, the chief priest of the Eleusinian mysteries in ancient Greece.

402 Canaanite's faith and the widow's penny: For the Canannite, see Matthew 15: 21–28 and Mark 7: 24–30; for the widow's penny, Mark 12: 41–44 and Luke 21: 1–4. This remark foreshadows the ballad of the final chapter, *The Gentle Goddess of Poverty*.

405 Endymion of sculptors and poets: In Greek mythology Endymion, a king or shepherd of rare beauty, was loved by Selene, goddess of the moon. Endymion was a highly favored motif in classical and neoclassical art.

406 Queen Libussa falling in love with a ploughman: Libussa was a legendary Czech princess of the eighth century who married a ploughman, prophesied the construction of Prague, and led her people to the place where the castle and city would be founded.

406–7 Jan and Jerome on the pyre at Constance: Jan Hus was burned at the stake in Constance in 1415, and Jerome of Prague in 1416.

408 Ruysdael's landscapes: Either Jacob van Ruysdael (1628?–1682) or his uncle Salomon (1602?–1670), who were both Dutch landscape painters.

409 crisis that singers call the molt: This term, which derives from the French *mue*, is still in current usage for the change of voice in adolescent males as well as the periodic shedding of feathers, skin, antlers, etc. in various animals.

412 Orpheus: Poet and musician in Greek mythology who could charm the gods, mankind and the animals with his lyre.

412 Moses and the Prophets: Episode in the Gospels known as the Transfiguration;

see Matthew 17: 1–8; Mark 9: 2–9; Luke 9: 28–36. In the Gospels, however, just two prophets appear, Moses and Elijah.

413 O DIVINE TETRAD: In other words, a group made up of four elements. A major Pythagorean teaching is that numbers constitute the true nature of things, and in this philosophy the number four is the symbol of justice.

414 *Sum qui sum:* I am who I am. See Exodus 3: 14.

415 Locke: English philosopher and founder of empiricism (1632–1704).

415 *fiat lux, et facta est lux:* "Let there be light, and there was light." Genesis 1: 3.

415 *creavit cuncta juxta genus suum et secundem speciem suam:* "He created every being after its kind and according to its species." Genesis 1: 20ff.

415 Descartes: René Descartes (1596–1650), French philosopher, mathematician and scientist whose methodology was crucial for the transition from medieval to modern thought.

416 Odysseus's companions under Circe's wand: In other words, swine.

417 knowledge of Egypt: The writings known as the *Books of Hermes* and attributed to the mythical Hermes Trismegistus are a compendium of the knowledge of the ancient Egyptians.

417 Campanella: Tomasso Campanella (1568–1639), Italian Renaissance writer and philosopher. His *City of the Sun* sets forth a utopian society modeled on Plato's *Republic.*

419 Apocalypse: See Revelation 1: 12–16.

421 'My kingdom is not *yet of this time*': Perhaps an adaptation of part of John 18: 36, but with a significant change, for it reads, "My kingdom is not of this world."

421 *"Homo sum et nihil humani a me alienum puto":* Terence, from his *Heautontimoroumenos:* "I am a man, and I consider nothing human to be alien to me."

423 "The spirit blows where it will": John 3: 8.

423 *Veni, creator Spiritus!:* "Come, Creator Spirit!" the opening of a hymn often used in the Catholic church at Pentecost.

423 march toward your light: An adaptation of Isaiah 60: 1, 3.

Acknowledgments

Many people have contributed to the making of this book, and it is a delight to express my gratitude to them here.

I thank Lucienne Frappier-Mazur and Frank Paul Bowman with whom I had the great good fortune to study at the University of Pennsylvania. At a time when George Sand was just being rediscovered in American universities, I had the pleasure and privilege of reading *La Comtesse de Rudolstadt* with Lucienne. To Frank I owe an appreciation of the complexities of Romantic socialism. They both taught me the joy and challenge of trying to read works in their fullest possible context.

I thank the friends and colleagues who painstakingly read parts of this manuscript and offered me their sage advice: Jane Ambrose, Therese Dolan, Nane Doll-Peyron, Elizabeth Ferguson, David Powell, and Janet Whatley. I owe a special debt of gratitude to Marie Gendrot Tapia, who eagerly pored over every line of *La Comtesse de Rudolstadt*, the original French side by side with my English translation.

I thank the University of Vermont and the Department of Romance Languages, especially Gayle Nunley and Joyce Boyer, for the generous support and understanding afforded me from the very start of this long undertaking. Without the sabbatical leave I enjoyed in 2004–5 this translation would not have seen the light of day.

I thank the University of Pennsylvania Press, especially Jerry Singerman, for the enthusiasm with which they embarked upon this immense task of publication.

I thank my husband, Z. Philip Ambrose, for the encouragement he unfailingly gives me, for his rigorous analysis and passionate questions. He is the finest and most stimulating companion in philological exercise.

www.ingramcontent.com/pod-product-compliance
Lightning Source LLC
Chambersburg PA
CBHW032111110726
47902CB00003B/548

* 9 7 8 0 8 1 2 2 2 0 1 4 8 *